WHO'S THE MURDERER?

WHO'S THE MURDERER?

OR THE

MYSTERY OF THE FOREST.

𝔄 𝔫𝔬𝔳𝔢𝔩

BY

ELEANOR SLEATH.

Nought is there under heaven's wide hollownesse
That moves more deare compassion of the mind,
Than beautie brought t'unworthie wretchednesse
Thro' envie's snares or fortune's freaks unkind.

SPENCER.

EDITED WITH A NEW INTRODUCTION BY
J. S. MACKLEY

VALANCOURT BOOKS

First published London: Lane and Newman, 1802
First Valancourt Books edition 2017

This edition © 2017 by Valancourt Books
Introduction © 2017 by J. S. Mackley

Published by Valancourt Books, Richmond, Virginia
http://www.valancourtbooks.com

All Valancourt Books publications are printed on acid free paper that meets all ANSI standards for archival quality paper.

ISBN 978-1-943910-72-4 (hardcover)
ISBN 978-1-943910-73-1 (trade paperback)
Also available as an electronic book.

Set in Dante MT

CONTENTS

CONTENTS

INTRODUCTION

Eleanor Sleath

Without a doubt, modern interest in Eleanor Sleath's work is because of her inclusion in Jane Austen's Gothic parody, *Northanger Abbey*. Here, Austen's thrill-seeking socialite, Isabella Thorpe, discusses with Catherine Morland a list of novels that they must read after finishing Ann Radcliffe's *The Mysteries of Udolpho* and *The Italian*. These titles are: *Castle of Wolfenbach* and *The Mysterious Warning* by Eliza Parsons; *Clermont* by Regina Maria Roche, *The Midnight Bell* by Francis Lathom; *The Necromancer (or, The Tale of the Black Forest)*, by Peter Teuthold; *Horrid Mysteries*, written by Carl Grosse, and translated by Teuthold under the pseudonym of Peter Will; and finally *The Orphan of the Rhine* by Eleanor Sleath. At the end of the list, Catherine demands "are you sure they are all horrid?"

For a long time, it was considered that these seven "horrid" novels were a product of Austen's imagination until they were discovered in the 1920s by Austen's biographer Michael Sadleir. In fact, Austen is referring to titles that were, at the time that she was writing, recent publications by the Minerva Press that she herself had read and enjoyed. In a letter to her sister Cassandra dated 24 October 1798, Austen explains "My father is now reading the 'Midnight Bell,' which he has got from the library, and mother sitting by the fire".[1] Indeed the majority of books published by the Minerva Press were too expensive for private individuals and were obtained instead through the Circulating Library: the publication over multiple volumes meant that the book could be read simultaneously by more people; they were also read until they were worn out. Blakey observes that "the Minerva novel … was never intended for re-reading and study, but as a means of passive recreation. Such *'time killing'* drugs may be worth the

---

1 Deirdre Le Faye (ed.), *Jane Austen's Letters*, 4th ed. (Oxford: Oxford University Press, 2011), p. 15.

charge made by a circulating library; they are not worth more."[1] Although there was a tendency to scorn gothic literature, and particularly women gothic writers who were not held in the same esteem as their male counterparts, by the time that Ann Radcliffe was writing it was "the earliest popular literature, appealing to all classes of readers rather than just to an élite literary culture".[2]

The small list in *Northanger Abbey* presents a useful overview of how Gothic literature was progressing in the last decade of the eighteenth century. Considering Sleath's *The Orphan of the Rhine*, Devendra Varma describes her as "one of a number of minor 'gothic' writers whose works were animated by the last flicker of enthusiasm for gothic fiction".[3]

Until recently, Eleanor Sleath has been a somewhat enigmatic figure: most of what has been said with any certainty about her has been a list of titles and dates of her publications:

The Orphan of the Rhine (4 vols., 1798)
Who's the Murderer?; or, The Mystery of the Forest (4 vols., 1802)
The Bristol Heiress; or, The Errors of Education (5 vols., 1809)
The Nocturnal Minstrel; or, The Spirit of the Wood (2 vols., 1810)
Pyrenean Banditti (3 vols., 1811)
Glenowen; or, The Fairy Palace (1815)

Devendra Varma oversaw the republication of two of these novels: *The Orphan of the Rhine* (Folio Press, 1968), and *The Nocturnal Minstrel* (Arno Press, 1972). In his introduction to *The Orphan of the Rhine*, Varma follows Michael Sadleir's speculation that Sleath was a Catholic based on the "wise and spiritual disposition" of her ecclesiastical figures.[4] However, Varma did correctly ascertain that Sleath was born in Leicestershire, and came

1 Dorothy Blakey, *The Minerva Press, 1790-1820* (Oxford: Oxford University Press, 1939), pp. III, 115.

2 Rictor Norton, *Gothic Readings: The First Wave, 1764-1840* (London: Leicester University Press, 2000), p. vii.

3 Devendra P. Varma, *The Gothic Flame* (Metuchen, NJ and London: Scarecrow Press, 1987), p. 173.

4 Michael Sadleir, *The Northanger Novels: A Footnote to Jane Austen*, The English Association, Pamphlet No. 68 (Oxford: The English Association, 1927), p. 22.

tantalisingly close to identifying Eleanor Sleath by recognising "the death of a military doctor of the name of Sleath". The surgeon's widow was dismissed because there was "no supporting evidence" and the other speculations on the identity of Eleanor Sleath were implausible.[1]

Since Varma's conjecture concerning Sleath's identity, a study has been undertaken by Rebecca Czlapinski and Eric C. Wheeler.[2] Based on their researches through the Leicestershire archives, they reveal that Mrs Sleath was born Eleanor Carter, the youngest of five children of Thomas and Elizabeth Carter; she was baptised in Loughborough Parish Church on 15 October 1770. Her father died when she was very young, but the family had sufficient wealth to ensure that the children received a good education. Eleanor married Dr John Barnabas Sleath of Calverton, Buckinghamshire on 14 September 1792: John established himself as a surgeon and apothecary in Nuneaton, Warwickshire, some 50 miles from Calverton, and 30 miles from Loughborough. Shortly afterwards, Eleanor's son, Joseph Barnabas Sleath was born, but he died in September 1794, and her husband died the following month. Eleanor's mother, brother, and brother-in-law dealt with the debts that remained after Joseph's death.

In 1798, Sleath published her first novel, *The Orphan of the Rhine*. In particular, this was influenced by the *Sturm-und-Drang* literature—usually translated as "Storm and Stress", which allowed authors to explore the extremes of emotion. Michael Sadler describes this novel as "a genuine product of the influence of Mrs Radcliffe. It contains sensibility with sensation, being more terrific than [Regina Maria Roche's] *Clermont* but more melodious and picturesque than the horror-novel pure and simple."[3]

In 1801, Eleanor's brother, John, moved the whole family to Scraptoft Hall, a short distance from Leicester. She was living here in 1802 when she published *Who's the Murderer?* Amongst others in their social circle, Eleanor and her family associated

1 Devendra P. Varma, "Introduction" in *The Orphan of the Rhine* by Eleanor Sleath (London: Folio Press, 1968), p. vii.

2 Rebecca Czlapinski and Eric C. Wheeler, 'The Real Eleanor Sleath', *Studies in Gothic Fiction*, Vol. 2.1 (2011): 5-12.

3 Michael Sadleir, *Things Past* (London: Constable, 1944), p. 180.

with the Rev. John Dudley, vicar of Humberstone, although a sarcastic comment from Eleanor's sister-in-law gave rise to a speculation concerning an affair between Eleanor and John Dudley, aggravating Ann Dudley's jealousy. Ann eventually resorted to spreading slanderous gossip about Eleanor, which led to John separating from his wife in 1808. Shortly after this time, Eleanor published three novels, *The Bristol Heiress*, *The Nocturnal Minstrel* and *Pyrenean Banditti*.

In 1813, when Eleanor's brother died, his estate was divided between his wife and sisters; Eleanor moved back to Loughborough, only a short distance from Sileby where John Dudley was then vicar. Around this time, she published *Glenowen, or, The Fairy Palace* (1815). Less than two months after the death of Ann Dudley in 1823, John Dudley and Eleanor were married on 1st April in the same Parish Church of Loughborough where Eleanor had been baptised. After her marriage to John, she assumed the role of the vicar's wife until she died on 5th May 1847, aged 77.

Who's the Murderer?

Who's the Murderer?; or, The Mystery of the Forest was published in four volumes in 1802 when Sleath was about 32. Each volume cost 4/6d. This was Sleath's second novel: the first, *The Orphan of the Rhine* did not receive positive reviews. Indeed, while *The Critical Review* praised the "creative genius and the descriptive powers" of Ann Radcliffe, the reviewer notes "If, however, we have sinned in suffering ourselves to be seduced by the blandishments of elegant fiction, we endure a penance adequately severe in the review of such vapid and servile imitations as 'The Orphan of the Rhine'."[1]

By contrast, *Who's the Murderer?* received a positive review in *The Monthly Magazine* in 1803, even though the reviewer is generally derisive of volumes published by the Minerva Press. The discussion for *Who's the Murderer?* is also more detailed, compared to other reviews on the same page which receive only a four-word notice:

1 *The Critical Review, or Annals of Literature*, vol. 27 (London: S. Hamilton, November 1799), p. 356.

We shall conclude our notice of novels and romances with acknowledging the amusement we have derived from a perusal of MISS SLEATH's *"Who's the Murderer?"* a novel which evinces in the authoress considerable talents.

Miss Sleath is conversant in Italian scenery, which she sketches with a warm and animated pencil; her characters are well supported, and are sufficiently uncommon to excite interest. After the pains which are taken to prevent Varano from being introduced to the lovely Cecilia by the vigilant De Sevignac, it is not a little singular and inconsistent in the latter to propose a journey, in which the lovers are to be in the perpetual presence of each other? Miss Sleath has a richness of language which does not often issue from the Minerva press.[1]

In 1809, Sleath received a page and a half review praising *The Bristol Heiress, or The Errors of Education* (although it is erroneously attributed to "Mrs Heath") in *The Critical Review*: the critic concludes that "upon the whole we are inclined to give much praise to this work, and to say, that if people will read modern novels, let them read the Bristol Heiress".[2]

Prior to the publication of this present edition, *Who's the Murderer?* has been a very rare book: undoubtedly, there are copies held in private libraries, but there are only around a dozen references on WorldCat, in the United States, in Germany and in Switzerland—and most of these copies are microfiche or digital copies. Where a physical copy does exist, it may be just a single volume of this four-volume novel. In addition, there are places where the photographs on the microfiche are defective. Consequently, scans for some pages of this volume have been provided by the Houghton Library at Harvard University.

The plot

The novel is set around 1763-65. The infant Cecilia is placed in

1 *The Monthly Magazine; or, British Register*, vol. 15 (London: Richard Phillips, July 1803), p. 639. Despite this praise, Eleanor Sleath does not feature in Dorothy Blakey's *The Minerva Press*, except in the lists that form the appendices.

2 *The Critical Review, or Annals of Literature*, 3rd Series, vol. 19 (London: J. Mawman, January 1810): 97-98, p. 98.

the care of a young widow, and later with the elderly aristocrats Madame de Villeneuve and her brother Monsieur de Sevignac; thus her parentage is concealed. When Cecilia is 19, she becomes the focus of interest of a young noble, Lorenzo di Varàno. De Sevignac warns, however, that Varàno is not free to marry where he chooses.

Shortly afterwards Madame de Villeneuve dies. De Sevignac's health also begins to fail and he is advised to travel and to seek the restorative air of Italy. On this journey, bad weather forces the travellers to seek shelter in an isolated building, which they discover is the hideout of a party of banditti, and where Varàno discovers the body of "a newly murdered man" before he flees.

De Sevignac leaves Cecilia in the dubious care of his aristocratic relatives in Genoa while he and Varàno proceed to Pisa. Cecilia is often scorned for apparently assuming a place in polite society. When De Sevignac dies, Cecilia discovers that she has not been included in his will, so Boraccio—husband of De Sevignac's niece, Viola—becomes her legal guardian. Cecilia comes to the attention of Count Morsino, whose attempts to petition her become increasingly aggressive and intimidating. Boraccio sows seeds of suspicion concerning Cecilia's relationship with Varàno and informs Cecilia that she must marry. Cecilia steadfastly refuses Morsino's entreaties and thus she agrees to be removed to a convent. On this journey, she is kidnapped and immured in a chateau in the forest.

This incarceration is a further attempt by Morsino to persuade Cecilia to marry him; however, falling ill, Cecilia is able to escape with the assistance of a surprise ally. He begins to understand something of her background and this knowledge brings a surprising connection to another character; Varàno suspects that he has a rival for Cecilia's affections. His jealousy gives rise to misunderstandings and leaves Cecilia in an impossible position and vulnerable to Morsino's plans.

Narrative style

This summary cannot do justice to a highly complex, character-driven plot. What is presented here is intended merely to give the reader an overview without revealing the intricacies and revelations of the plot as well as the relationships between the characters. The narrative style (third person omniscient) reports the events as they unfold around Cecilia. The dialogue appears as though it has been replicated from actual discussions, consequently, it is often verbose and individual speeches are excessively lengthy; the conversation continues long after the necessary information has been conveyed to the reader, and many of the speech tags are hyperbolical, for example: "cried", "rejoined", "resumed", "interrupted" and "exclaimed". There are also moments of narratorial intrusion as the narrator speaks directly to the reader. On some occasions, this serves to pull the reader away from the bigger story and to focus on a particularly judgmental statement about a character: "the sentimental Novel-readers of the present period who have imbibed the accommodating maxim ... will condemn her as fastidious ... The nice observer ... may object to the character we have but attempted to delineate". On other occasions, the narrator intervenes to elicit sympathy with Cecilia. This is most clearly seen when discussing the contents of De Sevignac's will, which should have "surprised the reader as much as Cecilia, that her name was nowhere inserted in it". And, as with novels by Ann Radcliffe, the final intrusion comes in the form of a moral at the end of the tale.

The title of the novel, *Who's the Murderer?*, is rather misleading and gives the impression of an Agatha Christie novel where a dozen suspects, each with a motive, are investigated. In fact, for the majority of the novel, the murder is barely alluded to at all. There are a couple of subtle references, as well as some scenes that suggest a murder—a body is discovered when the main characters are delayed whilst on their way to Genoa and have to shelter from a storm in a dwelling occupied by banditti. Later, when Cecilia is confined in a castle in a forest (hence the subtitle *The Mystery of the Forest*), she finds blood-stained clothes presumably from decades before. However, the majority of the story takes place in chateaux and palaces and society functions of Genoa, Pisa and Venice, and not in the forest at all. It is not until the final volume that we discover which character has been murdered—and fate ties the murderer to his victim as well as to

Cecilia herself. It is the subsequent trial and twists that bring the strands of the story together. Only in the final chapters is everything explained, leading to an ironic ending. So while the title is dramatic and the subtitle is vague, they do not really give an adequate description of what will occur in the text.

Eleanor Sleath and Ann Radcliffe

Who's the Murderer? sits securely in a category of Romantic fiction, although there are Gothic elements throughout. The influence of Ann Radcliffe—most notably *The Mysteries of Udolpho*—is particularly apparent. The novel also shares plot strands with Sleath's earlier novel, *The Orphan of the Rhine*, including a child who is fostered under mysterious circumstances, a vulnerable female character, a forced marriage, a lost bracelet which later reveals the identity of its owner and a character's apparent return from the dead. J.M.S. Tompkins lists a number of themes used by Ann Radcliffe that are borrowed by other authors.[1] In fact, many of these themes also appear in *Who's the Murderer?* including: the pastoral family home at St Foix equating to Emily's home at La Vallée; the mystery surrounding Cecilia's birth; the return of a character who is previously assumed to be dead (a device also used in *The Nocturnal Minstrel*); Cecilia reads a manuscript which contains details of a torture and execution ordered by the Inquisition; her protagonists shelter in a partially-ruined building which is home to numerous banditti. In addition one may see similarities in the details such as the laments, when seeing the portrait of a mysterious woman, of both St Aubert in *The Mysteries of Udolpho* and De Sevignac in *Who's the Murderer?* Likewise, the heroine is informed of mysterious papers from the father figure on his deathbed, although Emily in *The Mysteries of Udolpho* is ordered to burn them unread, while Cecilia may read hers when they are delivered to her after a suitable interval; even then, the suspense is drawn out as Cecilia delays reading the content as

---

1 J.M.S. Tompkins, *Ann Radcliffe and her Influence on Later Writers* (New York: Arno Press, 1980), p. 117-118. Tompkins only mentions Sleath in relation to the theme of "mysterious music" that appears in her novel *The Nocturnal Minstrel*.

she does not wish the occasion to be tainted with melancholy. The bracelet that gives a clue to Cecilia's identity replaces the miniatures that help identify the heroines in both *The Mysteries of Udolpho* and *The Italian*.

Ellen Moers notes that for male authors of the Gothic, the heroine "was quintessentially a defenseless victim, a weakling, a whimpering, trembling, cowering little piece of property whose sufferings are the source of her erotic fascination".[1] For the character of Cecilia in *Who's the Murderer?*, Sleath follows the model of the Radcliffian heroine, a woman who is able to maintain her dignity and integrity at times of extreme adversity. Unlike Emily, however, Cecilia faces most of her trials without fainting.

The lengthy journeys from Provence to Nice, and on to Genoa, Pisa and Venice (with lofty sublime descriptions that would greatly appeal to readers of Ann Radcliffe's novels) further serve to distance the heroine from her home. Ellen Moers notes that "the gothic novel was a device to send maidens on distant and exciting journeys without offending the proprieties."[2] Faced with the machinations of the villains, the heroine finds an inner strength to evade their manipulation. The journey is both physical and psychological: Cecilia is distanced from her home and isolated both in terms of society and class, as well as from any protection from those who do not have her best interests at heart, as she remains with her foster-family in Genoa. Naturally, the loss of both parent figures leaves the heroine vulnerable; the benevolent father figure is replaced by the oppressive and autocratic stepfather, and the heroine is then oppressed by the machinations of the Italian Count. Where, in *The Mysteries of Udolpho*, Emily flees Montoni only to learn of Valancourt's supposed betrayal, so Cecilia flees Morsino, only to have Varàno accuse her of betrayal himself and thus he becomes the representative of both father figures, both beloved and oppressor at the same time.

Who's the Murderer? is not set in the ancient past which is unlike the traditional framing of a Gothic novel; instead, the events are set just a few years before Sleath herself was born. However, they are set abroad and the descriptions of the landscape—which

1 Ellen Moers, *Literary Women* (London: Women's Press Lit, 1978), p. 137.
2 Moers, *Literary Women*, p. 126.

Sleath is unlikely to have seen for herself—are likely to have been influenced by James Edward Smith's *A Sketch of a Tour on the Continent in the years 1786 and 1787* and Smollett's *Travels through France and Italy*. Michael Sadleir recognises the "affinity to the Radcliffean school of sensational landscape-fiction staged abroad".[1]

Unlike Ann Radcliffe, Sleath does not engage with the supernatural. Everything has a rational explanation. As Tompkins observes, "more exquisite sensations can be extrapolated from the suggestion of terror than from any definite event".[2] The lavish descriptions on the journey serve to show how far Cecilia is from her home and how isolated—as well as providing an armchair journey for Sleath's readers. Jane Spencer discusses how "the focus of the Gothic novel is on the heroine's mind: it is not only what happens to her but how she reacts to it. Her travels and her adventures can be seen as journeys into the self … The mysterious castles that imprison her and the sublime landscapes on which she gazes can be interpreted as projections of herself".[3] However, once she has reached Genoa, she no longer has the protection of her stepfather. Consequently, as one would expect from a "female gothic" novel, the evil that men do is worse than any horror that the supernatural could generate. The text relies on terror throughout, particularly in the conditions that Cecilia must endure, rather than overt horror. Certain plot devices rely on an uncanny coincidence, and chance encounters with characters who play a significant part later in the story.

That said, there are some truly horrific moments, and Sleath cleverly uses a variety of devices to convey seemingly supernatural moments without losing the credibility of the plot. There are suggestions of supernatural tales that are told by the domestics, although Cecilia quietly mocks their "superstitious credibility". There is a horrific scene of Varàno discovering the body of "a newly murdered man"; a scene where Cecilia goes to find the body of her stepfather at midnight during a thunderstorm. Other devices include the Signora di Rosalvo reading from a book about

1 Michael Sadleir, *The Northanger Novels*, p. 22.
2 Tompkins, p. 20.
3 Jane Spencer, *The Rise of the Woman Novelist* (London: Blackwell, 1986), p. 193.

auto-da-fé, a truly unsettling scene which stirs a latent memory for Cecilia. Likewise Cecilia experiences hallucinations following cruel treatment at the hands of the Count and a violent dream sequence, the tone of which is comparable with many contemporary gothic terror novels:

> At length the wind dropped, the sounds were hushed into repose, and the jarring of a distant door, which moved slowly on its grating hinges, alone disturbed the almost deathlike stillness that prevailed. [...] Cecilia stepped back—her blood was chilled, and she turned to regain the door; but before she could seize it, it shut to with a thundering clap, and she was left alone among the dead. As she advanced again from the door, she thought the figures on the coffins began to move, their marble features became fleshy—the lights they held waxed pale—a strong sulphureous vapour rose from the tombs—and a loud crash of thunder, like the noise of a thousand pieces of artillery, reverberated, and shook the inmost bowels of the earth. Horror again overwhelmed her, and again she made an effort to depart; but her feet, when she would have moved, sunk imperceptibly into the ground—a hot boiling fluid seemed to be gathering around them—and in a moment she was involved in a sea of blood!

Although *Who's the Murderer?* has no representation of the supernatural, this is not the case in some of Sleath's other works. Set at the end of the fifteenth century and focusing on the story of the recently widowed Baroness Gertrude Fitzwalter, *The Nocturnal Minstrel; or, The Spirit of the Wood* is scattered with apparently supernatural incidents, including the otherworldly music played at night (as seen in *The Mysteries of Udolpho*) and the ghost of the baron which appears in full armour to admonish the baroness (as seen in *The Castle of Otranto*). Likewise, in Sleath's final novel, *Glenowen, or, The Fairy Palace*, the two orphaned children are supported by their ghostly benefactress, Peribanou, on account of their moral upstanding.

There is a satisfying, if somewhat implausible, explanation to both of these stories. In *The Nocturnal Minstrel*, the ghost had been one of the heroine's suitors, and the "dead baron" is actually alive and observing how Gertrude was behaving as a widow before revealing himself, and the baron and baroness are then reunited. In *Glenowen*, the fairy is revealed to be a woman who had formerly been engaged to the children's father, and who pretended to be a fairy so that she could aid the children anonymously. These plots, in particular, show how Sleath was developing as a writer of gothic motifs, even though she was still clearly influenced by Radcliffe's dependency on the "explained supernatural".

Loss of Protector

It is a traditional gothic motif that the heroine becomes vulnerable when she loses her male protector, either her father or husband: we see this in Ann Radcliffe's novels, for example in *The Mysteries of Udolpho* with the death of St Aubert, and in *A Sicilian Romance* where Julia flees her manipulative father and ultimately finds her imprisoned mother. It is noteworthy that this motif of loss of male protector carries through all of Sleath's novels, perhaps reflecting her own experiences of the father she barely knew, as he died when she was barely three years old. In both *Who's the Murderer?* and *The Orphan of the Rhine* the protagonist is adopted as a baby, although the mystery of her parentage is resolved at the end of the novels. Likewise, in *Pyrenean Banditti*, Adelaide has to live with her aunt and uncle—her uncle makes her a virtual prisoner within his castle (just as Cecilia must live with Boraccio following the death of De Sevignac and she too is confined while he tries to force her to adhere to his wishes). Also, Charles and Rosa live with Nurse Morgan following the death of their mother in *Glenowen*. *The Nocturnal Minstrel* begins by establishing Baroness Fitzwalter as a widow, while at the beginning of *The Bristol Heiress*, Caroline Percival is sent to school in London while her father, recently a widower himself, remains in Bristol. Sleath uses these as a means of overcoming (particularly male) oppression. Once the female protagonists are separated from their protectors, they are able to demonstrate courage in the face of terror and determination when being manipulated. That said, the moral examples of Charles and Rosa Evelynn when forced into poverty following the death of their mother in *Glenowen* are related to Christian didacticism as the children are rewarded for their virtue in the face of such adversity.

Confinement and freedom

David Punter describes how Emily in *The Mysteries of Udolpho* "spends the whole of her time imprisoned: occasionally in 'vile' and 'noisome' dungeons, more often in the castles of her oppressors, always inside her own restricted psychic outlook".[1] The same can be said of Cecilia. While at the beginning of the novel, she seems open and carefree whilst living with De Sevignac, she is still restricted, both by her familial duty to him, as well as the uncertainty of her own parentage and her status when receiving the affection of Varàno. While Varàno pledges his love for Cecilia, she observes that his father will not let him marry beneath his status and that his "obligations to [his] family precede every other".

This restriction owing to a lack of status is particularly seen when Cecilia is introduced to the aristocratic society; here social standing is paramount. As Cecilia has been adopted by De Sevignac, she has no blood lineage to aristocracy. Without De Sevignac's protection, she is described as a "mere nobody ... born to herd with the canaille" (or underclasses), as she is "no more than the rank of a servant", who has been "educated beyond her status". Lady Viola argues that Cecilia has "pretensions" to beauty beyond her status, concluding that "one can only be beautiful if one is a person of manners". Conversely, Lady Olivia adds that someone who is rich and powerful is not necessarily virtuous: "This is the first time ... that I ever heard riches and power confounded with mental excellence." In *Who's the Murderer*, feminine malice is not delivered through the cruelties that Madame Montoni inflicts on Emily, as in the *Mysteries of Udolpho*, instead, they are delivered through the subtleties of society. The discussion of whether one is moral if one is educated for society

1 David Punter, *Gothic Pathologies* (Basingstoke: Macmillan, 1998), pp. 30-31.

is also seen in Sleath's 1809 novel, *The Bristol Heiress, or The Errors of Education*. When this was discussed in *The Critical Review*, the critic noted the didactic message of the texts and that one may "be betrayed into instruction and pass the hour with at least the possibility of receiving some benefit … that happiness does not consist in splendid pleasures, but rather in the rational exercise of the benevolent affections".[1]

In *Who's the Murderer?* the family note the affection between Varàno and Cecilia and are concerned that Varàno, as the last of his line, should form an attachment with a noble house, rather than "to allow his reason to be seduced by the blandishments of an obscure and … insidious girl". Varàno's father, the Marchese, opposes his son's interest in Cecilia, demanding that he marry according to rank, rather than for affection. The Marchesa at least understands the attraction between Cecilia and Varàno. She says of Cecilia, "I know no one, Olivia excepted, that I should prefer to her for my son; but he is the last of his line, and he must not unite himself with a beggar." Her empathy comes from the fact that she too once loved a man of inferior rank to her own, but acquiesced to her father's demand that she marry the candidate of his choice. The Marchese concludes with the moral of her tale:

A short time discovered to me the precipice from which I had escaped: my former lover, of whom I received occasionally some accidental information, evinced himself incapable of a serious attachment; he proved gay, thoughtless, and dissipated; and I had soon reason to congratulate myself on our separation.

Likewise, Cecilia is ensnared by her pragmatism concerning the likelihood of a unity with Varàno. "Whilst he is here … I am unhappy because I know him to be the cause of unhappiness to others". The moral of these restrictions appears to be that one may be at liberty to marry, but remain unhappy, or to accept the restrictions and find contentment.

It is the second volume which serves to highlight Cecilia's position as Gothic heroine—friendless, in a situation above her station, and without means of escaping, she is left at the mercy of men with dishonourable intentions. Yet, although she is isolated, she is able to maintain her composure and avoid agreeing to a

1 *The Critical Review*, (January 1810), p. 97.

union against her wishes. This leads to her *physical* confinement: the irony is that it is only when Cecilia is immured in the chateau in the forest, and imprisoned by her own illness, that she begins to become liberated as she begins to understand something of her heritage. She also maintains her inner strength, resolving not to submit "to the will of this detested tyrant". Yet, with this emotional, psychological and ultimately physical, release, it is ironic that rather than being free to discover happiness, she instead finds herself further away from Varàno and trapped in a moral dilemma.

Who's the Murderer? is not a "horrid" novel in comparison with some of its contemporary publications. Eleanor Sleath creates terror by isolating Cecilia from her protectors and leaving her vulnerable to the prejudices of society and the conspiracies of those who plot against her. But it is easy to see how Sleath's novels would have appealed to Catherine and Isabella when they listed *The Orphan of the Rhine* amongst their "horrid novels". As with those named by Austen, *The Mysteries of Udolpho*, *Castle of Wolfenbach*, *The Mysterious Warning* and *Clermont*, Eleanor Sleath's novels have many gothic conventions and lengthy descriptions of exotic European landscapes, as well as exciting and convoluted plots. Most particularly, however, there is a female protagonist with whom the thrill-seeking young women readers could identify.

J.S. Mackley
University of Northampton
August 2014

J. S. Mackley is Programme Leader for English at the University of Northampton, and Assistant Adjunct Professor of Fantasy Literature at Richmond University, the American International University in London. He received his MA in Late Medieval Studies and a PhD which focused on the Latin and Anglo-Norman versions of the Legend of St Brendan, both from the University of York. A monograph based on his thesis was published by Brill in 2008. He is a Fellow of the Higher Education Academy and has presented and published articles on folklore and medieval literature, as well as Gothic literature (particularly the late Victorian Penny Dreadful series) and contemporary fantasy literature.

A note on the text

This edition follows the text of the only edition of Sleath's text, published in London at the Minerva Press on Leadenhall Street for Lane and Newman in 1802. The novel was originally published in four volumes; the beginning and end of each volume is signalled in this edition.

For the Valancourt Books edition, spelling and punctuation have been retained nearly unchanged from the 1802 edition to capture the flavour of the original text. Sleath's apostrophes have been retained with pronouns to indicate the possessive "your's", "her's", "our's" and "their's". Spellings such as "chuse", "shew", "gulph", "alledge", "corse", "recal", "controul", "unburthen", "appretiate" and "subtile" are unlikely to cause the reader any difficulty. Sleath adds her own footnotes for some French and Italian terminology.

The only place where the spelling could potentially cause confusion is in place names: "Bourdeaux", "Thoulouse" and "Nismes" (Nîmes) retain eighteenth century spellings. However, there are errors in the locations when travelling through France towards Italy: Sleath refers to Vannes and Anbibes, when she actually means Cannes and Antibes. Whether this is a mistake in her source, in typesetting or whether Sleath has misremembered the name is uncertain. There are some places where Sleath has quoted from a text, either as part of the narrative or as an epigraph: these, likewise, have been left as Sleath presented them.

Bibliography

The Critical Review, or Annals of Literature. Vol. 27. London: S. Hamilton, November 1799.

The Critical Review, or Annals of Literature. 3rd series. vol. 19. London: J. Mawman, January 1810.

The Monthly Magazine; or, British Register. Vol. 15. London: Richard Phillips, July 1803.

Austen, Jane. *Northanger Abbey*. Oxford: Oxford University Press, 2008.

Blakey, Dorothy. *The Minerva Press, 1790-1820*. Oxford: Oxford University Press, 1939.

Czlapinski, Rebecca and Wheeler Eric C. "The Real Eleanor Sleath", *Studies in Gothic Fiction*, Spring 2012: 5-12.

Le Faye, Deirdre, ed., *Jane Austen's Letters*. 4th ed. Oxford: Oxford University Press, 2011.

Moers, Ellen. *Literary Women*. London: Women's Press Lit, 1978.

Norton, Rictor. *Gothic Readings: The First Wave, 1764-1840*. London: Leicester University Press, 2000.

Punter, David. *Gothic Pathologies*. Basingstoke: Macmillan, 1998.

Sadleir, Michael. *Things Past*. London: Constable, 1944.

Sadleir, Michael. *The Northanger Novels: A Footnote to Jane Austen*. English Association, Pamphlet No. 68, 1922.

Sleath, Eleanor. *The Orphan of the Rhine: A Romance*. London: Folio Press, 1968.

Sleath, Eleanor. *The Bristol Heiress; or, The Errors of Education*. 5 vols. London: Lane & Newman, 1809.

Sleath, Eleanor. *The Nocturnal Minstrel; or, The Spirit of the Wood*. Edited by Devendra P. Varma. 2 vols. New York: Arno Press, 1972.

Sleath, Eleanor. *Pyrenean Banditti*. Edited by Rebecca Czlapinski and Eric C. Wheeler. Kansas City: Valancourt Books, 2010.

Sleath, Eleanor. *Glenowen; or, The Fairy Palace*. Edited by Rebecca Czlapinski. NP: Lulu.com, 2011.

Smith, James Edward. *A Sketch of a Tour on the Continent in the Years 1786 and 1787*. 3 vols. London: J. Davis, 1793.

Smollett, Tobias. *Travels through France and Italy*. Oxford: Oxford World Classics, 1999.

Spencer, Jane. *The Rise of the Woman Novelist*. London: Blackwell, 1986.

Tompkins, J.M.S. *Ann Radcliffe and her Influence on Later Writers*. New York: Arno Press, 1980.

Varma, Devendra P. *The Gothic Flame*. Metuchen, NJ and London: Scarecrow Press, 1987.

Varma, Devendra P. 'Introduction' in *The Orphan of the Rhine by Eleanor Sleath*. London: The Folio Press, 1968.

WHO'S THE MURDERER?

OR THE

MYSTERY OF THE FOREST.

A Novel.

IN FOUR VOLUMES.

BY

ELEANOR SLEATH,

AUTHOR OF

THE ORPHAN OF THE RHINE, &c.

" Nought is there under heaven's wide hollownesse
" That moves more deare compassion of the mind,
" Than beautie brought t'unworthie wretchednesse
" Thro' envie's snares or fortune's freaks unkind."

SPENCER.

VOL. I.

LONDON:

PRINTED AT THE

Minerva-Press,

FOR LANE AND NEWMAN,

LEADENHALL-STREET.

1802.

Title page of the first edition (1802).

WHO'S THE MURDERER?

CHAPTER I

> Alas! poor wretch! why dost thou rave and weep?
> Why, with that up-turn'd eye, which would win Heav'n
> To sheathe its sword of justice, claimest thou thus
> Compassion's sigh!—Hence to the forest's gloom,
> And tell the hungry wolf, who nightly prowls,
> Baying the list'ning moon, that thou art wretched!
> Or stop the fierce hyena in his chore,
> Savage and wild as his own native haunts,
> And while his jaws yet reek with human gore
> Tell him to list thy tale of misery!——

"HAVE pity—for the love of Heaven, have pity upon me!—think what it is to be poor—a wanderer in an unknown province—ill, and abandoned to the heaviest of misfortunes!—Oh, do not turn me hence!——One night—a few hours only: as you hope—as you expect that mercy I would demand from you, at the hour when you shall most need it."

"*Morbleu! q'uelle pauvre diable!*" returned a rough uncourteous voice, "so you would advise me to turn my house, one of the best accustomed inns in all Gascony, into a hospital for mendicants—for female adventurers, forsooth! who, without a single sous in their pockets, are to have the liberty of entering my doors, walking through my apartments, and chusing their own accommodations!—No, no, my little Princess, it is not by admitting passengers *gratis* that I have gained a fortune of fourteen hundred Louis-d'ors;—so out—tramp—we have no room for vagabonds!"

The above sarcasm, which contained a strange mixture of Spanish gravity and French buffoonery, was directed by the land-

lord of a small *auberge* at St. Bertrand, in Gascony, to an unfortunate female, called Blanche de Coucy, who, overcome with grief,
and the fatigue of a very long journey, which she had performed
chiefly on foot, had stopped there on her way toward Provence.

The reply, inhuman as it was, struck like a dagger to the heart
of the mourner. She arose, and, bursting into tears, suddenly
withdrew.

Passing through the door, she stopped to make way for a new
traveller; who, seeing a young woman decently attired, and of
a very interesting figure—her cheek pale, and her eyes suffused
with tears, which seemed to be the ebullitions of no common
sorrow, paused to survey her.

Blanche was proceeding without appearing to notice him;
when the traveller, placing himself between her and the door,
demanded the cause of her uneasiness.—Blanche started; and,
looking up, her eyes encountered those of the stranger, who
seemed to be regarding her with looks of peculiar earnestness.
He was a tall, well-made man, apparently about thirty; he wore
the dress of an Izard hunter; and the bold outline of his figure,
the agility of his movements, and the deep tan of his complexion,
seemed to mark him for the profession he had chosen.

Blanche did not evade the enquiry. She told him she was
the widow of a Gascon soldier, whom she had followed to
Bourdeaux, where, she was informed, he had died of a wound,
inflicted by a musket-shot. To add to her misfortunes, she had
been robbed, she said, of the little property she had about her by
two men, belonging to those straggling parties of banditti which
infest the Pyrenees; one of them, more compassionate than
his companion, had thrown after her a few *maravedies*, which,
though still in her possession, were coin not current in France.

A fresh burst of grief accompanied every sentence of this
speech. The traveller seemed to sympathize in the recital: his
countenance often varied, and he more than once interrupted it
with some attempt at consolation. The reappearance of the host
threw the poor narrator into new disorder, who, without waiting for a repetition of his unfeeling orders, quitted the *auberge*,
resolving, though exhausted by fatigue, to seek her way to the
next village.

She was on her road thither, when, accidentally turning back, she perceived, at some distance, the stranger whom she had encountered at the *auberge*. His countenance and address had at first impressed her in his favour; but the circumstance of his following her excited suspicions as to his intentions, and she redoubled her speed, eager to obtain the village ere her pursuer could overtake her. The man, as if aware of her design, called aloud to her to stop. Blanche deliberated, but obeyed. They were already at some distance from the town, the spot was lonely, and no person or habitation was to be seen.

"Fear not," said the hunter, "I have no intention of harming you.—You are poor, and have been unfortunate;—consent to accompany me to a place only a few miles from hence, and you shall be relieved from your distresses. A competence will be provided for you on your acquiescence with my terms; and you shall be conducted in safety to your own province. All I require is, that you will preserve a strict silence as to every thing that may happen to you; and that you will forbear from every possible attempt to investigate the motives for my conduct, however mysterious it may appear."

When he had proceeded thus far, he paused, and looked full at Blanche.

"Let your resolution be speedy," said he; "the time allotted for my expedition is already expired. Are you satisfied?—If not, be quick, that I may seek elsewhere."

Blanche trembled; and, regardless of what the stranger had just said, tremulously demanded whither he would take her; and why so much secrecy was requisite?

"This is no answer," rejoined the hunter, angrily; "nor have I leisure for persuasion. Are you inclined to consent?—If so, be resolute, and follow me; if not, I have no other means of assisting you."

Blanche hesitated; and for a moment both were silent.

"Alas! what have I to apprehend," thought she; "poor and destitute as I am, what have I to lose but my existence?—and why am I thus anxious to preserve a life, at once wretched and unprofitable?"

"Are you determined?" repeated he.

Blanche replied that she was. The hunter gave a nod of approbation; and they returned together to St. Bertrand. A mule was
instantly procured: the hunter mounted it first; and Blanche, with
more firmness in her manner than she had hitherto assumed,
seated herself behind him.

They pursued their way in silence till they had reached the
foot of the Pyrenees: Blanche musing, as she went, on this
very extraordinary adventure, and secretly wondering in what
manner it would terminate; whilst the stranger, immersed in his
own solitary ruminations, seemed wholly regardless of his timid
companion, whose frequent tears and heavy sighs would have
penetrated any heart, unshielded by apathy, or, like his, absorbed
in some nearer subject of interest.

They had ascended one of the highest ridges of that immense
chain of mountains, which overtops the wide province of Gascony, and were descending on the contrary side, when a vast
forest, spreading itself in the misty moonlight, caught the attention of our travellers.

The hunter, pointing to it, told her that in that forest their journey was to conclude. Blanche shuddered, and again terror and
mistrust rushed, unresistedly, to her mind. For what was she to
be conveyed to a forest so dreary?—a place seemingly containing
no human habitation, and which appeared destined for the commission of the most daring crimes!—"Who knows," thought she,
trembling still more, "but it may be his intention to murder me!"

Those evils which, whilst distant or uncertain, we imagine we
can encounter with an heroic firmness, appear tremendous and
awful as they approach; and the mind, however solicitous, while
under the dominion of this acquired energy, to reduce the object
of its alarm to a reasonable dimension, fails not to give a Colossal
form to dangers when they seem to advance. Lightly as she had
before treated the idea of death—an idea which misery and misfortune had rendered familiar, and even pleasant—the thoughts
of meeting with it under so dreadful a shape, almost overpowered
her reason;—she caught the arm of the stranger, and, in accents of
piercing distress, conjured him to be merciful. The hunter made
no reply; but clapping spurs to his mule, pursued rapidly his way.

The path still winding round the ridge, they saw arise before them the dim towers and winding walls of an ancient fortress, overlooking one of the grand passes of the Pyrenees. The hunter, dismounting, led the terrified Blanche through the shattered gateways, from whence they issued to the forest.

They followed the track through a number of labyrinths, which gradually descended, till they entered upon a rough glen, overshadowed with dark and lofty trees. Blanche's heart sunk at every step; trembling, yet not daring to enquire into conduct so inexplicable, she suffered herself to be led along: often starting at the roar of waters dashing beneath her feet, their white surges gleaming faintly in the moonlight, or at the loud scream of the vulture wheeling high among the rocks:———she thought too she heard the howling of wolves!

As they pierced still deeper into the shades, Blanche perceived a light, which, as she observed it more attentively, evidently issued from some low building, whose humble roof was almost lost amid the luxuriant vegetation of this wild and almost deserted tract of land. She continued to survey it, with a mixture of hope and apprehension, till she plainly discerned, at some distance, a kind of low cabin, built entirely of wood, at the door of which the traveller at length stopped.

"It is the abode of a shepherd," thought Blanche; "or of some hunter, who lives unmolested among these dreary wilds."

She had scarcely time for surmise, when the door was opened, and a venerable figure (bearing in one hand a taper, and in the other a crucifix, so formed as to supply the double office of a staff and religious memento) stood before them. He wore the habit of a Carmelite; but his white locks, contrary to the custom of his Order, shaded his temples, and fell upon his shoulders. His countenance was mild, melancholy, and expressive of the sincerest devotion.

"Come along," said he, "my children; you are welcome."

The hunter entered, and commanded his companion to follow. A scream of joy and surprise caught the ear of Blanche ere she had passed the threshold; and her astonishment may be easily conceived when she saw a young and very beautiful woman, dressed in the Spanish costume, who threw herself into the arms of the stranger, and instantly fainted.

"Save you, my daughter!" cried the Father; "these are indeed trials; but look up, my child—my forlorn one, and be comforted. A few years—a few fleeting years, and all will be forgotten!"

He stopped; and a tear, he would have checked, rolled down his aged cheek.

The lady revived before he had finished speaking; but she revived only to a sense of the deepest anguish. She raised her hands towards heaven in an attitude of supplication, and sinking upon her knees, with a look expressive at once of sorrow and contrition, Blanche, for the first time, beheld a lovely little girl, seemingly about three years of age, whose resemblance to the lady indicated her to be her daughter. The child smiled; the lady clasped her to her breast—tears streamed in torrents from her eyes. The stranger was scarcely less affected: he drew his hand thrice across his forehead, and then withdrew; making a signal, as he went out, for Blanche to follow him.

When alone with her, he disclosed the reason of his conducting her thither, which was to place the child she had seen under her care. Blanche, now delivered from her fears, accepted, joyfully, the trust; and the hunter, putting a purse of gold into her hand, with a promise of conveying the same sum to her annually, engaged to conduct her safe to St. Bertrand. The little Cecilia was accordingly committed to the care of Blanche.

Morning had dawned some time before the lady, who had taken little rest throughout the night, could exert fortitude enough to tear herself from her unfortunate offspring, who, shrinking from the embraces of a stranger, clung to her mother; and, with all the fascination of infant eloquence, besought her not to part with her. The look of soft distress which accompanied these artless supplications, was so touching to the heart of the lady, that she was in danger of relapsing into her former state of insensibility. The hunter, dreading the indulgence of this tenderness, forced the child from her arms, and, regardless of their cries, placed it upon the mule. Blanche having seated herself as before, they hastened from the door, and plunging into the depths of the forest, soon lost sight of the cabin and its mysterious inhabitants.

On their arrival at St. Bertrand, the travellers were placed by the stranger, whom we now introduce by the name of Verezio, under the care of a *voiturier*, who had orders to convey them to Perpignan; from which place they were to take advantage of a vessel bound for the coast of Provence. Here Verezio repeated his severe injunction to Blanche to conceal the manner in which she had received the child, and then took his leave of her.

A short time brought Blanche and her little companion to the destined port; from whence they performed an easy and pleasant voyage to Marseilles.—The village of St. Foix, the late residence of Blanche, was only at a few miles' distance from this city.

CHAPTER II

There is in innocence a wondrous charm!
A magic sweet, which steals upon the soul:
And while it touches all the secret springs
Of heav'nly sympathy, doth more persuade,
Than the full pow'rs of manly eloquence.

WHEN Blanche was again settled in her former abode, she began to think seriously on the past. The air of mystery which seemed to involve every thing relative to the child, awakened a sentiment of curiosity, as little adapted to her feelings, as to the promise she had now to perform. The rapidity with which the late succeeding events had passed before her eyes, had opposed all her efforts to account for them; and now that she had leisure for reflection, they appeared to her so strange, so wild, so incomprehensible, that every endeavour to ascribe them to any probable cause, served only to involve them in deeper obscurity. The whole had the air of fiction rather than of truth; and as she strove to recollect the train of providential circumstances, which had led to her present good fortune, they reminded her of the wild, improbable incidents delineated in a Romance, rather than the occurrences of real life.

Her first care was, in what manner she must conduct herself under her present engagement, and how she should most effectually prevent the enquiries of her neighbours, who would, doubtless, propose some questions respecting her new charge, who, in a village like St. Foix, would soon become an object of attention and curiosity.

She was called Cecilia; but the name of her father, her mother, and every other particular, incident to her situation, had been scrupulously concealed. As it was necessary, however, to give some little account of her, she resolved, St. Bertrand being the place where she first met with Verezio, to call her Cecilia de St. Bertrand; and to introduce her to her acquaintance as the daughter of a friend, lately deceased, who, hearing that she was in Gascony, had resigned her to her care in her last moments.

The news of Blanche's return, and that of the death of Harald, her husband, which had already reached St. Foix, drew a number of peasants of all descriptions to her cottage: some to afford consolation under the sorrows of widowhood; and others to inform themselves to whom the child, now her only companion, belonged. All were anxious to behold the new-comer, whose reputation for infant beauty and engaging manners soon spread around the country.

Amongst a variety of other visitors, was a lady of the name of Villeneuve, a widow, who resided with M. de Sevignac, her brother, in a chateau, situated at about half a league's distance from St. Foix.

Madame de Villeneuve had known Blanche previous to her late journey to Bourdeaux; but as the life of this lady, since the demise of her husband, had been passed at the chateau in a state of almost constant retirement, the news of the little stranger's arrival at the village of St. Foix, had not yet reached her; she was consequently much surprised, on entering the cottage, to see a beautiful little girl, dressed in a plain camblet frock with short slashed sleeves, sitting against the door; her lap covered with flowers, and her whole attention directed toward a dog, she called Fan-fan, who was feeding from her hand.

To Madame's enquiries concerning the child, Blanche returned the same answer which she had done to others; and then calling Cecilia from the door, she desired her, in an indulgent tone, to speak to the lady, who was very good, and would love her.

Cecilia flew instantly to her nurse; but, disconcerted at the appearance of a stranger, hid her face in her apron, and remained silent and abashed. Blanche kissed her cheek.

"Alas! poor babe," said she, "you have no friend but me!"

Madame, affected by these words, took the child upon her knee, and, wiping away a tear, said, smiling sweetly—

"And what is your name, my love?"

"Cecilia," replied the child.

"Cecilia!" repeated she, "and what beside Cecilia?"

"Alas! she knows no other name," said Blanche, piteously.

"Is it not St. Bertrand?" asked Madame de Villeneuve.

"No," cried the child, hesitating, "it is Cecilia."

"She will be nothing but Cecilia," rejoined Blanche, colouring.

"And where do you come from, my dear?" demanded Madame.

The child looked earnestly in her face, but made no answer.

"Poor innocent! She knows nothing about that neither," continued Blanche. "You come from a great way off, don't you, my dear?"

"Yes," said the child.

"But you are very happy here?" cried Madame.

"Yes."

"And who do you love?"

"Blanche, and you, and poor Fan-fan," returned Cecilia.

The simplicity with which these words were delivered, and the innocent action that accompanied them, were so affecting both to Madame de Villeneuve and Blanche, that neither of them had power to utter a syllable. The former, at length breaking silence, demanded of Blanche a further account of her late unfortunate expedition.

The poor woman gave a brief relation of her misfortunes till the time of her arrival at St. Bertrand, which she concluded with many tears shed to the memory of the ill-fated Harald, who had fallen, as she had been informed, on the frontiers of Spain, after a long and obstinate engagement. On her mentioning her loss, and the brutal reception she had met with at the *auberge* in Gascony, Madame presented her with some Louis-d'ors, desiring her to apply to her again when these should be expended.

The extraordinary beauty and sweet manners of the child

impressed the heart of Madame de Villeneuve, which was keenly
susceptible of fine, humane sensations, and she soon became an
almost constant visitor at the cottage.

The tenderness lavished upon her little favourite, was repaid
with the most lively effusions of infant gratitude. Cecilia's walks
were never so delightful as when Madame was her companion.
She loved to sit upon her knee—to gather flowers for her bosom;
and, when she condescended to instruct her, discovered a facility
of comprehension, and a retention of memory, which excited
equally her curiosity and admiration. On Madame's return to the
chateau, her conversation with her brother usually turned upon
Cecilia, whose lively remarks and judicious replies were recited
and enlarged upon with a partiality almost maternal.

Several months passed on, during which Blanche was in continual expectation of seeing Verezio. The time appointed for this
meeting was already expired, when she was suddenly attacked
by a disorder, attended with symptoms of alarming danger.—
Madame de Villeneuve's time was now occupied between Blanche
and Cecilia; and she proposed to her brother that, during the sickness of the former, Cecilia should be removed to the chateau. De
Sevignac objected not to this plan.

"I wonder," said he, "Louisette, you never thought of it before.
The child may be a source of amusement to you now; and, if
educated according to your own system, an useful companion to
you hereafter. If the woman has no objection to parting with it,
and there is no reason why she should not give up her charge, the
chateau will afford her a much more comfortable asylum than an
obscure cottage. It is our duty to befriend the unfortunate; and
we cannot better discharge this duty, than by taking the infant
under our immediate and entire protection."

This was a proposal extremely pleasing to Madame. On her
return to St. Foix, she found Blanche, now confined to her room,
in earnest conversation with a stranger, who was Verezio. He
withdrew on her entrance, leaving her to impart, with more
animation than was usual to her, the conversation just passed
between her and De Sevignac. Blanche, aware of her approaching
end, received the proposal with rapture; and informed Verezio, in
private, to whom she had committed her charge.

Soon after Verezio's departure, Blanche expired in the arms of Madame—closing an innocent, but unfortunate life by a happy death. A few moments before she died, she recommended Cecilia, in a solemn manner, to the friendship of her beloved benefactress. Cecilia was with pleasure received into the chateau.

The Chateau de St. Foix was an ancient, and had once been a magnificent mansion: the front, which opened to the north, presented a view of the river and the plains beyond, interspersed with dark woods, vineyards, and plantations of olive; on the south, a range of hills, bold, lofty, and varied with masses of grotesque rock, formed a vast and magnificent background, from whose heights might be dimly and imperfectly seen, as the curling vapour rolled along, the majestic summits of the Hyeres, which, after stretching themselves into the Mediterranean, rise proudly from its shores, and rearing their tremendous heads into the clouds, veil them in an awful obscurity.

With a mind exquisitely susceptible of the beauties of nature, cultivated by taste, and adorned by science, M. de Sevignac was enabled to command all those resources which may be termed the requisites of retirement, and which bestow, when the heart is sufficiently at ease to become sensible of their influence, delights beyond what the most refined arts of the voluptuary can ever reach.

In his youth he had seen life under its most alluring forms: his pursuits were various and enterprising, and he entered upon them with all that sanguineness usually attached to that flattering period; till a disappointment of a tender nature put an end to his exertions, and hurried him into retirement.

M. de Sevignac had had two sisters. Madame de Villeneuve was the elder, who, having been unfortunate in her marriage, had retired with him to the chateau. The younger had been united to the Marchese di Varàno, a Nobleman of Tuscany, and was since dead.

A year rolled on without any new event, at the expiration of which, Verezio arrived at the chateau, and delivered to Madame de Villeneuve a packet and a casket designed for Cecilia, which he gave her permission to examine. Madame, finding by his manner, that any enquiries relative to this mysterious affair would not be answered, forbore to make any; contenting herself with assuring him that she would fulfil to this deserted child all the duties of a mother.

When Verezio had departed, Madame, calling her brother into the room, whom she requested to be present, proceeded to unclose the casket.

The first objects which met the eye of De Sevignac, on opening it, were two portraits set in gold, and enclosed with diamonds: one representing a young woman in the bloom of early beauty; the other a Chevalier, in a military habit, and wearing on his breast the cross of the Order of St. Louis. He turned hastily from this portrait to that of the female; but, ere he had examined it, it fell from his hand, and his countenance suddenly became pale.

"Oh my Leonora!" said he, "my poor Leonora!" and then sunk upon a sofa.

Madame, astonished at these emotions, eagerly seized the portrait; but the features of it were unknown to her. To her earnest enquiries De Sevignac kept a mysterious silence; and then, making an effort to recover his tranquillity, proposed that they should examine the remaining contents of the casket.

They found only a silver crucifix, a small ivory Madona, a pocket missal, a rosary, and such other religious mementos as are usually purchased at the *Santa Casa*, at Loretto. The papers were reserved for perusal on the following morning.

The contents of these were a secret to all but Madame de Villeneuve and De Sevignac; but, whatever was their import, the latter was so much affected by them, that he confined himself to his chamber the remaining part of the day.

For several weeks after this event, both De Sevignac and his sister appeared thoughtful, and, at times, much agitated; the former, from this period, never beheld Cecilia without great perturbation and anxiety. When gazing on her, tears would frequently start to his eyes; he would sometimes examine her features with a melancholy earnestness, as if he was endeavouring to trace a likeness to some beloved object, and then weeping aloud, exclaim—

"Alas! my unhappy—my poor deluded Leonora!—Could not

thy high sense of honour—of religion, preserve thee from an act so daring—and, I fear, alas! so impious?"

At such moments as these, his emotions almost overcame his reason.

His affection, however, for Cecilia daily increased. Her arrival at the chateau seemed to form to him a new epocha in his existence—a tie to bind him to the world, and to render life a source of new interested and more exalted pleasure. He was protecting one who, but for him, might have been left destitute. He had the power, and it was now become his duty, to form her mind by the simple and excellent precepts of virtue—to improve a disposition naturally sweet—to turn all its amiable sensibilities into sources of benevolence; and, whilst he taught her to feel for the unhappy, to support the friendless, and relieve the indigent, to preserve in her mind that fortitude, that elastic force, which resists sorrow on its first attack, and, when aided by the stronger power of devotion, fits it for the best and noblest enterprises.

Whilst De Sevignac's thoughts were more immediately employed in projecting future plans for Cecilia, those of Madame de Villeneuve were no less arduously engaged in contriving schemes for the present. Cecilia had now attained her fifth year; and having had as yet no companion, Madame turned her thoughts upon a little girl, the daughter of a cottager at Le Luc, a village only a few miles from St. Foix. The woman, whose name was Beatrix, had formerly been a housekeeper in the family of De Sevignac, and Madame had indulgently allowed her daughter to be called by her name. The little Louisette was accordingly brought to the chateau, and an attachment was soon formed between the two children.

CHAPTER III

Tous dans d'innocentes délices,
Unis par des nœuds pleins d'attraits,
Passoient leur jeunesse sans vices,
Et leur vieillesse sans regrets.

GRESSET.

THE æra of childhood, however fondly we may recur to it as the season of novelty and unmixed delight, seldom affords much matter for narration. The occupations of infancy, like the toy which supplies it with a casual amusement, are considered as too trifling for our riper years; and, unless the fading recollections of our juvenile pursuits are brought back upon the mind with the vivid colouring of genius, the analogy they may have borne to our own state, and our own feelings, are unobserved or disregarded.

We shall, therefore, omit some years in the life of our heroine; introducing her no longer as the little playful Cecilia, but as a lovely girl of eighteen, with a form and features of the most perfect symmetry, and a complexion for brilliancy scarcely to be equalled in the southern parts of Europe; with a disposition soft, yet ardent, and a mind stored with useful, and even fashionable accomplishments. She sung; she played upon the harp, if not with the skill, with the taste, at least, of a professor; she had some knowledge of drawing; and, with the assistance of De Sevignac, had made herself mistress of the Italian, the Spanish, and some other modern languages.

Such was Cecilia; but it was not these attainments which rendered her dear to De Sevignac—it was not the rapidity with which she gained every branch of instruction, nor the elegance it acquired under her delicate hands: it was the look which spoke to the heart—the ready tear—the softening sigh—the varied expression of a countenance true to the feelings of a soul, frank, noble, and elevated. It was her understanding, strong, yet feminine;

cultivated, yet not affecting superiority; correct in its discrimina-
tions, candid in its judgments, ready to suspend, to hear, and to
respect the opinions of others. Of the world she knew nothing;
all that had hitherto fallen under her notice were amiable, good,
and gentle. *Le Luc had formed the limits of her travels.*

The first serious uneasiness she had ever known was occasioned by the illness of Madame de Villeneuve, who expired at
length, after a confinement of some months, leaving De Sevignac
and herself inconsolable for her loss.

Shortly after her death, De Sevignac received a letter from the
Marchese di Varàno, intimating that Nobleman's intention of
paying him a visit at his chateau. De Sevignac, although his character was the very reverse of the Marchese's, prepared, nevertheless to receive him with respect, through affection to the Lady
Viola, his niece, the Marchese's daughter by his former marriage,
who had lately bestowed her hand upon Signor Boraccio, a noble
Genoese.

Immediately on this intelligence, De Sevignac, for reasons
best known to himself, sent Cecilia to the cottage of Basil and
Beatrix, at Le Luc. The silence preserved by him, with regard to
his guests, was extremely perplexing to Cecilia; but as she knew
him too well to believe him guided by caprice, even in his most
trifling decisions, she naturally supposed that there was some
reason, in which it was her duty tacitly to acquiesce; and accordingly, attended by Louisette, she set off for the cottage.

The village of Le Luc was sweetly romantic. It stood on an
ample plain surrounded almost with mountains; some cultivated
to their summits, others rocky and barren, their bases stained
only with lichens, or covered with mosses.

The cottage of Basil, which might be termed the seat of peace
and honest frugality, was separated from the village by hedges of
myrtle and laurestinus. A little wood wound round it, mingling
its rich entangled verdure with the brighter hues of the flowers,
evergreens, and rose-bushes which decorated the garden, and
overhung the casements; a few green pales, and a small gate,
overshadowed also with shrubs, adorned the entrance.

Cecilia often strolled into the wood, and sometimes to the
mountains, which commencing to the west of Le Luc, form an

almost continuous chain round the adjacent country: from these she could discern the spires of Marseilles, and the far off rocks of Toulon, melting into the blue and distant horizon; and farther still, towards the east, the tops of those precipices which compose a rude, but not ungraceful rampart to the beautiful islands of the Hyeres.

At the extremity of the garden was a small sweet bower of woodbine interwoven with laurestinus, planted on either side with lilac, ilex, and acacia; the path bordered with primroses, and the earliest flowers of the spring.

One evening, as the whole family were sitting in this little fragrant alcove, a party of villagers advanced, dressed in their holiday-clothes, their hats decorated with garlands; the youths bearing flagelets and oboes, and the damsels baskets of flowers. It was the celebration of a wedding. Claude and Adeline, the rustic bride and bridegroom, taking the lead, they arranged themselves on a green plat before the cottage; and the instruments being tuned to a lively measure, the dance began.

Cecilia, who found her spirits enlivened by the rural gaiety of the scene, took the hand of Louisette, and with light and sportive steps, tripped to join the dancers; Basil and Beatrix remaining in the grove, delighted witnesses of the sports.

The second dance was commenced, when their attention was withdrawn from it by a stranger, of a very elegant appearance, who, springing carelessly from his horse, gave it to his servant, and then stopped at some distance from the garden—his eyes fixed upon the peasants, and his whole attention engrossed by the mirth he witnessed.

Basil, imagining it was some stranger, who, as the country around was mountainous and wild, had mistaken his way, proposed, in the blunt hospitality of his heart, that he should go and invite him to the cottage.

"If I give him the invitation," said he, jocularly, "I shall not oblige him to accept it."

He then flew towards the stranger, more fearful of neglecting one act of real kindness, than of offending by what, in any other country than France, might be deemed impertinence.

The rustic urbanity with which the proposal was made, was

returned, on the part of the stranger, with an equal, but more polished courtesy.

"I am not," said he gaily, "as you suppose, a bewildered traveller. I ride about for my amusement, and without any settled plan. The country is new to me; and I extract as much pleasure from the beauty, as from the novelty of your scenes."

"It is a fine country indeed, Monsieur," rejoined Basil, "the best, I believe, in the whole world."

"I am not surprised that you think so," resumed the stranger; "you were not a true Provençal if you did not.—That tract of country to the left, I suppose, leads to Marseilles?"

"True, Monsieur. You are going then to Marseilles?"

"Not immediately," pursued the stranger, smiling at the curiosity of his interrogator; "I came here, as I told you, without any settled plan;—your music, and your dancing groups, have been my attraction. I am on my return to St. Foix."

"St. Foix!" exclaimed Basil.

"You are not acquainted with it, I find," said the stranger, mistaking the cause of the repetition.

"Oh! then you are at the chateau, Monsieur?" cried Basil, scarcely knowing what he said.

"True," answered the stranger; "M. de Sevignac is my friend, and, I may add too, my relation."

"And your name——"

"Varàno," replied the stranger.

Basil bowed; and, blushing deeply, discovered that he was conversing with the son of the Marchese di Varàno, and endeavoured awkwardly to apologize for his impertinence.

"Your behaviour," returned the Signor, mildly, "needs no excuse; on the contrary, I am much indebted to you for your hospitality; and to convince you how much I respect you for it, will attend you to your cottage. It is not, I presume, far distant?"

"No, my Lord," said Basil, pointing to his habitation, "it is there. Here is my wife; and that young girl among the dancers," pointing to Louisette, "is my daughter."

"And the other," cried Signor di Varàno, who had now obtained a full view of Cecilia; "is she your daughter?"

"That lady," said Basil, stopping, and lowering his voice, "is Mademoiselle de St. Bertrand."

"De St. Bertrand!" repeated the Signor, in an accent of surprise, "De St. Bertrand!"

"You know her then, my Lord?" said Basil.

"No," rejoined the Signor, hesitatingly; "but did not she once live at the chateau?"

"She was brought up, my Lord," resumed Basil, "by Madame de Villeneuve; and has resided, since her death, with M. de Sevignac."

"You will much oblige me by introducing me," cried the Signor.

Basil bowed low, as before; and then beckoning Cecilia and Louisette from the dancers, presented his new friend to the astonished Cecilia by the name of Signor di Varàno; and then conducted them into his cottage.

Madame de Villeneuve, in her frequent letters to her niece, the Lady Viola Boraccio, with whom she corresponded, had mentioned to her the circumstances of her having taken Cecilia; and it was from this correspondence that Varàno had obtained the knowledge of her name, and residence in the family of De Sevignac. Not seeing her at the chateau, he thought, if he thought of her at all, that she had been since removed; or, as was still more probable, that she filled some domestic department in the household.

Beatrix, entering the cottage with some fruit, was prevailed upon by Varàno to take her seat amongst them. The rank of her guest at first awed her into silence; but her confidence soon returning, she joined in the discourse, which was now supported by all except Cecilia, to whom this introduction was extremely confusing, with ease and pleasantry.

The dance was concluded, and the parties were beginning to disperse, before Varàno had even thought of returning. Recollecting, at length, his distance from the chateau, he arose, and, courteously complying with Basil's somewhat presuming invitation to call at Le Luc in his rides, mounted his horse, and attended by Benedetto, his servant, departed for St. Foix.

The fine person of the Signor, his easy and unassuming manners, supplied conversation at the cottage for the remainder of the evening. Basil, flattered by his condescension, spoke rapturously in his praise; Beatrix was not less ardent; and Cecilia already experienced one of those sudden prepossessions for which we cannot always account.

The next evening, Cecilia, accompanied by Louisette, set off for her favourite ramble through the wood adjoining the cottage; they had scarcely entered it, when they were overtaken by Varàno.

"Excuse," said he, "my having so soon availed myself of the permission afforded me by your friends, of visiting you at Le Luc. I was informed of your route, and have followed you."

Cecilia replied with her accustomed grace, but not with her accustomed composure, and they pursued their way together. On their road she enquired concerning De Sevignac, secretly surprised that he had not sent a message.

Varàno, already charmed with Cecilia, had longed to mention her to him; but as nothing which could in the least tend to this subject, was ever introduced, he was irresistibly withheld from naming her, or of acquainting the party at the chateau of their accidental *rencontre* at Le Luc.

Varàno's deportment at this interview was more frank, but not less respectful than before; and Cecilia, considering him as the beloved friend and relation of her revered benefactor, already regarded him with esteem. He praised the grandeur of the prospect; pointed out, with the eye of taste, the finest features of the landscape; and then, turning the discourse to a not less animated subject, gave a fascinating, though not too flattering a description of Italy, that part of it particularly to which he owed his birth.

Some knowledge of the classics, and a natural fondness for poetry, had created a strong interest in the mind of Cecilia in favour of that country, which may literally be called the birthplace of the Muses; and she listened with enthusiasm to the delineations of those scenes of natural and artificial beauty, which had called such powers into exertion. The attention she bestowed, while he expatiated with energy on the peculiar excellencies of their poets, delighted Varàno; and Cecilia could not help observing the unusual degree of animation which sparkled in his eyes when her sentiments were congenial to his own.

To find so much refinement united with such an elegance of form, and such a bewitching softness of manner—so much youth with so much information—such an engaging frankness with such a delicate sense of propriety, in a female living in an obscure village—unseen but by the vulgar eye, was a circumstance so new, so extraordinary, that he could not conceal his admiration. She appeared to him like a beauteous flower, formed and planted by Nature in one of her wildest, rudest scenes—

> "A blossom meek, which on the wild heath grows,
> Temp'ring the air, and loading it with sweets,
> More luscious far than all the gaudy gems
> Which grace the proud parterre, have power to yield."

The peasants had completed their tasks, and the low tinkling of the sheep-bell, with the notes of a distant flute, intermingled, at intervals, with the indistinct murmur proceeding from the village, were alone to be heard, when the party, emerging from the wood, returned to the cottage.

Cecilia's mind, when alone, wandered to Varàno: admiration had already ripened into esteem—and esteem promised soon to become affection. She recalled every thing which he had said to her on their last interview; and was struck by the similarity of their tastes, and the ease with which he had entered into all her sentiments.

Varàno, in the meantime, thought only of Cecilia. As conversation awakened the powers of her mind, he had viewed her with a mixture of tender admiration and astonishment, that insensibly tinctured his mind with a passion, the imprudence of which his reason, could he have exerted it, would easily have taught him. This passion, however, daily increased, and, when another week had passed on, he was almost constantly at Le Luc.

Cecilia, who had no idea that he could be so continually in her society without the knowledge of De Sevignac, received his visits and attentions with a sort of chastened delight, felt happy when they were resumed, and began to consider the hours spent in his absence as tedious and uninteresting. They read, they walked together; and discovered in each other, at every meeting, some new and more winning attraction.

Cecilia, who thought only of the present, was tranquil, and sometimes animated;—but Varàno, whose busy mind often rambled to the future, was frequently, when away from Cecilia, pensive and dispirited. He never spoke to her of his father; but oftentimes of his mother, and this with many marks of affection: he described her as a woman of a superior understanding, and of most sweet and polished manners.

The repeated absences of Varàno from the chateau, had greatly perplexed the Marchese, and he at length testified his surprise. Varàno's excuses, however, though they were merely such, were ever readily admitted; for though the Marchese sometimes rallied his son on his passion for retirement, he loved him too well to be seriously displeased with him.

Varàno, on his leaving St. Foix, was to proceed immediately to Dauphine, to visit a friend in that province, of the name of Le Chatre. Anxious, however, from the hope that Cecilia might be recalled to the chateau, to prolong his stay there, he proposed to delay his journey; but the Marchese insisting upon his accompanying him, the dutiful respect which Varàno paid to his father prevented his objections. The thought of being so soon separated from one, for whom he had formed so hasty, yet so tender an attachment, was, nevertheless, productive of such keen regret, that perhaps the Marchese had never exacted any thing from him in his life, with which it was more difficult to comply.

One evening, as Cecilia and Louisette, who had been joined by Varàno, were returning from one of their accustomed walks, they were overtaken by a shower, succeeded by a few claps of thunder, which echoing sullenly among the rocks, were returned, again and again, in repeated vibrations. Varàno, whose solicitude for his companions left him no thought for himself, having obliged each of them to take an arm, ran, or rather flew with them across a plain, when, striking into a narrow path, they were compelled to turn aside for the accommodation of two horsemen, who were hastily advancing.

The rain, which at first fell only in a light pattering shower, now descended in torrents. One of the horsemen, alighting, took shelter beneath a plane-tree, and, calling to Varàno, advised him to take advantage of it likewise.

When they had availed themselves of this shelter, Cecilia had an opportunity of observing the cavalier more minutely. He was considerably above the middle size, and there was much ease and grace in his deportment; his features were of Roman contour, large, and full of expression, particularly his eyes, which were dark and piercing, and seemed capable of announcing every emotion of the soul. His complexion was of a sunny brown; his address open and manly, though occasionally tinctured with an air of *hauteur*; and a smile, which he sometimes assumed, had something in it particularly fascinating. He addressed Varàno in French, and afterwards in Italian, and this, from the fluency with which he spoke it, seemed to be the language of his country.

Whilst the cavalier was engaged in conversation with Varàno, his whole attention was absorbed by Cecilia. She looked indeed more than ordinarily beautiful: her hair blown about by the wind, fell back upon her neck in the most charming luxuriance; her veil, which, in the general confusion, had been suffered to fall back, only partly concealed her face; whilst the soft bloom of her cheek, deepened by exercise and the remains of terror, displayed that full and glowing tint, which only exercise, or quick and exquisite emotion, could call forth.

Embarrassed by this notice, she drew her veil over her face, and endeavoured to elude his view; but the more she attempted to avoid it, the more assiduous he was to observe her, and, though his discourse was directed to Varàno, his looks were bent earnestly on her.

The rain at length abating, Varàno proposed their return. The traveller looked chagrined, and beckoning to his servant, who had stationed himself behind the tree, he bowed slightly to Varàno, who, taking the arms of Cecilia and Louisette within his, as before, soon hurried them out of sight.

Beatrix had awaited their return with the greatest anxiety, which Cecilia endeavoured gently to dissipate. Varàno, observing that she was wet, tore off her cloak, her gloves, and her veil, through which the rain had beat violently upon her head; but perceiving that it had penetrated through her dress, entreated her, with much earnestness, to change her clothes immediately.

"You are very anxious about my young lady, my Lord," said

Beatrix; "but perfectly careless about yourself;—your clothes are quite soaked with the rain."

"I meet with such accidents," replied Varàno, "too frequently to regard them.—I travel in all weathers—and am seldom subjected to any inconvenience by cold."

"You will certainly be in danger," cried Cecilia; "do be persuaded to take some precaution." She stopped, as if fearful of betraying too much solicitude.

"How happy am I," said Varàno, in a low voice, "to have become an object of your anxiety!—Who would not endure any possible evil to attain such distinction?"

Cecilia was disconcerted. Varàno perceiving it, respected his former injunction, and then took his leave, with more tenderness, because with less caution in his manner than he had hitherto preserved.

In the morning he returned to enquire after Cecilia, who was distressed on perceiving that he spoke hoarse, and looked unwell. He complained of a slight head-ache, which he said was of no consequence; adding, with great vivacity—

"Had I submitted to your request, it might have been avoided;—but a man is seldom in the presence of a lovely woman, without losing all anxiety for himself."

Cecilia forced a smile upon her features, and endeavoured to divert the discourse into a vein of raillery; but her trepidation betrayed the feelings of her heart. It discovered to Varàno that he possessed her esteem, and, he now ventured to believe, her love. As his attachment grew stronger, his fears of opposition became proportionally less powerful; and those obtrusive and uneasy sensations, which had at intervals assailed him, yielded to new and more pleasing reflections.

CHAPTER IV

—————————As the most forward bud
Is eaten by the canker ere it blows,
Ev'n so by love the young and tender wit
Is turned to folly: blasting in the bud,
Losing its verdure even in the prime,
And all the fair effects of future hopes.

SHAKESPEARE.

NEAR the village of Le Luc was a beautiful, but now decayed, structure, inhabited by a society of Cistersian Monks, called the Abbey de la Sancta Trinité. Varàno, who took delight in contemplating the now shattered remains of this once noble pile, had introduced himself to the notice of one of the Principals of the fraternity, a Monk of mild manners, and of a very courteous demeanour; who had conducted him through the Monastery, and shewn him the numerous relics and curiosities belonging to it. This Abbey was a favourite walk with Cecilia; and, accompanied by Varàno and Louisette, she had often rambled about the chapel and through the out-works with pleasure.

One evening when they were thus engaged, Varàno, pointing to an opening in the trees, that led to a retired spot among the mountains, which Cecilia had not yet seen, entreated that she would allow him to attend her thither on the following morning. Cecilia objected slightly to the proposal; but Varàno's persuasions overcame her scruples, and she promised to comply with his request.

In the morning, Varàno did not arrive. Supposing, however, that he would follow them, Cecilia and Louisette set off on their proposed ramble; but, to their astonishment, had concluded their walk without having seen him.—On their return to the cottage, they found he had not been there: not doubting but he would sufficiently excuse himself on his next visit, Cecilia took her work, and awaited with patience the expected eclaircissement.

When the morning had passed away, she began to be uneasy. She blushed to think how much Varàno engaged her thoughts, and was restless and disturbed.

Hour after hour rolled on, and still no Varàno appeared.—Every moment of delay increased her anxiety. She knew that visitors obtruded seldom upon the retirement of the chateau: for De Sevignac had but few acquaintance, and these were not likely to prevent Varàno from fulfilling his engagement.

Wearied with conjecture, she retired early to her bed; but could not sleep.—The moon shone into her chamber with uncommon brightness;—she arose, as was her custom when unable to rest, and opened the window. The night was more than usually serene; the air breathless; and, except the bark of a watch-dog, or the closing of a distant casement, not a sound was to be caught. The tranquillity which reigned around was awful;—she sat down, and resting her cheek upon her hand, viewed the adjacent woods.—She was lost in the contemplation of this moonlight solitude, when she perceived a figure emerge from among the trees, and then approach toward the garden. Cecilia drew back, but still kept her eyes fixed upon the object. It paced to and fro:——while she gazed, it glided amongst the shades, and she saw it no more.

After a pause, she thought she heard her own name pronounced!—she started—listened—but all was again quiet.—The casement was now closed; and, knowing that it could not be opened without noise, she suffered it to continue so.—In a few minutes she heard the garden-gate clap, and a noise like the sudden rustling of leaves; but she could see no one, neither could she hear any footstep.

This circumstance she imparted to Beatrix, and Louisette. The former supposed it to be some traveller, who had bewildered himself in the wood; Louisette thought otherwise; and the subject dropped, and was not again resumed.

The next day, and part of another were passed by Cecilia in a state of the greatest inquietude.—Varàno was certainly ill; he had taken cold; had neglected it; and was now, perhaps, confined to his chamber: and if it was indisposition which had detained him, his illness must be serious indeed.

Her books, her work became tedious to her; and she resolved

to take a stroll into the village.—She was met at the gate by Jerome, the postillion at St. Foix, who informed her that he was to convey her instantly to the chateau.

"To the chateau!" repeated Cecilia, greatly agitated.

Jerome replied that the Marchese and his son, the young Lord Lorenzo, had departed that morning, and that she must return directly.

"Gone!" exclaimed Louisette, "the Signor Varàno gone!"

Jerome confirmed the assertion.

Amazement now yielded to other sensations, and these of the most painful nature. Cecilia blushed—turned pale—and paced the garden and the house in visible emotion. She attempted to speak, but the words she would have uttered died away upon her lips, and the ready tear, which the consciousness of being slighted could not repress, started to her eye.

Beatrix took a reluctant adieu of her young guests, who discovered, on their parting, many symptoms of regret; and then entered the carriage.

The teazing conjectures of Louisette were not calculated to restore the perturbed mind of Cecilia to its wonted composure. The certainty that Varàno was gone from her, perhaps for ever, without once bidding her farewel—without breathing one prayer—one wish for her future happiness, was an idea too torturing to be endured: and when she compared this seeming inattention with his former behaviour—with his unceasing solicitude, his amiable assiduities, she could scarcely believe she was awake—so strange, so unaccountable did his conduct appear to her.

Considering, however, that she might have mistaken courtesy for esteem, and gallantry for affection, she determined to keep on guard against the possibility of a like deception for the future.

The smile which beamed from the benevolent countenance of De Sevignac, as he welcomed Cecilia to the chateau, was most soothing to her heart; yet she imagined that he looked thoughtful and melancholy.—The evening passed on, and no mention was made of the departed guests.—Cecilia, doubting not but he had heard of Varàno's visits at Le Luc, supposed he had adopted this mode of conduct, to try whether she was disposed to place in

him that confidence to which his undeviating kindness had entitled him. She accordingly resolved to seize the first opportunity
of making a full and open declaration of all that had passed at the
cottage.

She was quitting her chamber with this design, when she was
met by Louisette.

"I have strange news to tell you, Mademoiselle," said Louisette, as soon as she was seated; "strange news indeed!—Yet there
is nothing very wonderful in it neither—since all the good those
proud old men do, with their pretended sanctity, is to go about
doing mischief, and prying into other people's affairs—all for the
love of God!"

"I don't understand you, my dear Louisette," cried Cecilia;—
"of whom is it you are speaking with so much disrespect?"

"Why, of those ghastly looking Friars at Le Luc, Mademoiselle;—there has been fine work at the chateau;—all about you
too, and the Signor Varàno!"

"About me and Signor Varàno!" exclaimed Cecilia, with
amazement.

"Oh yes! all about you and the Signor Varàno!—There is such a
story to come out!—But I shall tell you all exactly as it happened."

"Then pray be explicit, Louisette;—I cannot—indeed I cannot
bear suspense."

"Well, you shall hear every thing just as Ursula told me."

"No, not so," interrupted Cecilia, "give me the substance only
now, and I will listen to it in any way you please afterwards."

"Oh no! I cannot—I must tell it my own way now, or never."

"Then pray be quick, Louisette."

"Holy Mother! you are always in such a hurry, you never give
one time to recollect oneself.—It was that very night when the
Signor Varàno persuaded you and I to take a stroll to the Abbey—
or was it down into the wood, Mademoiselle?"

"Indeed I don't know," said Cecilia; "but it is perfectly immate-
rial."

"True, it does not signify, as you observe; but it was that very
night, as I was saying, when Monsieur, and my Lord the Marchese,
and Signor Varàno were sitting together in the saloon, thinking
of nothing at all, that there came a loud rap at the great door.

Well, who should happen to be the nearest it but old Geraud, who, as he was tottering to open it, dropped the candle from his hand, and out went the light. The lamp which hung from the ceiling, however, though it was dwindling for want of oil, gave him a little light; and when he had opened the door, who should it be but a Monk, muffled up in his cowl, who demanded to speak with the Marquis. Now as Geraud knew it was not Father Pierre, my master's Confessor, he had a great fancy to get a sight of him; so he begged that he would just wait a moment in the hall, while he ran for a candle—Well, Geraud's quickest step was so slow, that before he could reach the kitchen for a light, that he might take a peep at the Friar under his cowl, my Lord's Swiss valet came down the great stairs, and settled the matter in a moment. When Geraud returned, which was not till the Monk had been closeted with the Marquis for some minutes, he looked around with amazement for the Father; and, forgetting that any person besides himself might have been there in the interval, he could not command his astonishment:—he first turned the candle on one side, and then on the other; still, however, nothing was to be seen; and it entered into his head that it must either be a spirit, or something worse. Whilst he stood crossing himself, therefore, in the middle of the hall, he thought he heard a voice which seemed to issue from a room adjoining the library. Now, as you know, Mademoiselle, that there is something very cheering in a human voice when one happens to be frightened, what did Geraud do but make up directly to the door. He had not been there long, when he distinguished the voice of the Marquis raised loud as if in anger, and soon after he heard him say something about his son, and a girl at Le Luc. The Monk then spoke, but his voice was low, and he could only catch here and there a word. Geraud's curiosity was now a good deal excited; so, dropping upon the ground, and applying his ear to the keyhole, he overheard all the discourse."

"Whatever was its import," said Cecilia, "Geraud's curiosity was unpardonable."

"True, Mademoiselle, it was not right, as you say, to listen; Geraud thinks so himself; but he says when he heard the Marquis speak of the young Lord, and the girl at Le Luc, it came into his head that it could be no other than either you or I; and so far you know, Mademoiselle, he was quite right."

"Perhaps so," cried Cecilia, hesitating; "but pray, Louisette, be brief.—I would hear no more of the conversation overheard by Geraud—tell me only what followed."

"Yes, I can soon tell you what followed: the Marquis, as I was saying, was in a violent rage, and this was the reason of his setting off in such a hurry from the chateau; for nobody, not even my master, knew of it, till the night before; and it was through this that the Signor was not permitted to walk with us, as he had intended."

When Louisette had concluded her recital, she withdrew, leaving Cecilia in a state of the greatest alarm.—De Sevignac was then acquainted with what had passed between the Marchese and the Monk; and either his suspicions did not light upon her, or he had waited, as she had imagined, for her purposed explanation.

Louisette's information was true: the Monk had frequently observed Varàno walking with Cecilia and Louisette about the Abbey de la Sancta Trinité. The rank of the former, the beauty of Cecilia, and her residence in a village among people, as much her inferiors in education as in natural endowments, had led to some conjectures respecting the nature of the connection seemingly subsisting between them. He accordingly took an opportunity of introducing himself to the Marchese. The motive this devout Monk openly avowed, was that of a zealous regard for the dignity of an ancient and honourable house; but the secret, and indeed the only one by which he was actuated, originated in those mean and selfish passions, which too frequently triumph over our best propensities.

The Marchese received him with that stately kind of reserve which was peculiar to his character; but, when informed of his business, so far from thanking him for his interference, or dropping any hint which might lead to the expectation of future favours, he insisted upon the impossibility of his son's acting in any respect derogatory to the dignity of his family; and, regardless of the many proofs which the holy Father had collected, dismissed him from his presence without farther investigation, and with many signs of displeasure.

Yet, notwithstanding the Marchese's conviction that Varàno would never so far forget himself as to act inconsistently with his hopes and those of his family, he did not reject indiscriminately every part of the Monk's intelligence, though his pride had prevented him from noticing while he was yet present. The bare possibility of his being seduced into a disgraceful connection, was sufficient to alarm his fears, and to determine him in his resolution of hastening instantly from St. Foix.

Previous to his departure, the Marchese had acquainted De Sevignac with the conference just held between him and the Father. De Sevignac, though he had suspected Cecilia to be the object of it, forbore to impart this suspicion to the Marchese; avoiding, as he had hitherto done, even the mention of her name: nevertheless, it deterred him from soliciting his stay, and occasioned him to look forward to the hour when the whole could be elucidated, with an eager impatience.

When Cecilia appeared at breakfast, which was soon after she had parted with Louisette, she endeavoured to introduce the subject which had so greatly disturbed her; but her heart fluttered so excessively, that she was obliged to decline it, and to touch upon others, in which her feelings were less interested. Recollecting, however, the impropriety of suffering an interruption in an affair of real importance, and summoning all her courage to her aid, she gave a full, though not an unembarrassed relation of the late occurrences at Le Luc.

De Sevignac fixed his eyes upon her, as she proceeded, with the air of a person who wishes to avail himself of what is passing in the heart of the speaker, without betraying the feelings of his own. Affected, at length, by her candour and sweet ingenuousness, he folded his arms around her, and breathing a secret prayer that no evils might accrue to her from an adventure which he had been thus active to prevent, hastily withdrew.

Relieved, by this disclosure, from a load of anxiety, which had wearied and oppressed her mind, Cecilia appeared composed and even cheerful; but these fits of animation became by degrees less frequent, and when resumed, more transient. Her imagination was perpetually engrossed by the image of Varàno. If she took up her pencil, it was to finish some piece which he had assisted her in the sketching. If she sung, which was now only when she was alone, it was some little melancholy Italian air, which he had taught her, and admired.—Her guitar she considered as hallowed, because he had touched it; and often, as she swept the chords with a disordered hand, would the recollection of those strains with which he had accompanied her, melt into involuntary tears.

De Sevignac was no sooner convinced that his scheme to prevent a meeting between Cecilia and Varàno (which was his sole motive for removing the former from the chateau) had proved abortive, than he discovered many tokens of uneasiness. That a young woman, who had hitherto been excluded from a common intercourse with the sex—born in mystery—and nursed in solitude—could hold an unrestrained converse with an object so dangerous, because so amiable, as Varàno, without experiencing the tenderest sentiments in his favour, appeared contradictory alike to reason and experience; and since an attachment, where the disparity in point of rank was so great, must inevitably be hopeless, he was anxious to oppose it.

This uneasiness, and these apprehensions, were soon greatly augmented: he perceived that a total revolution was taking place both in the health and mind of Cecilia.—She was at times, indeed, much more charming—more interesting than she had ever been; but she had lost that serenity, that evenness of temper, that guarded propriety, which had formerly mingled themselves in her every sentiment and action, and by which she had always been distinguished. What little amusements and recreations were proposed by him she acceded to, because she loved to oblige; and rejoiced when they were at an end, that she might take refuge in her own solitary ruminations.—When in his presence, she often assumed a cheerfulness it was extremely arduous to maintain; and an eye, less penetrating than De Sevignac's, might have discovered that her behaviour was unnatural, and her spirits forced. There were moments when even his society, once so dear to her, became irksome.

One day, the vivacity she had been endeavouring to support suddenly failing her, she took her work, and repairing to a rustic bench in the gardens, fastened between two trees which overshadowed it, she sat absorbed in reverie. Such was her situation, when looking up, she perceived M. de Sevignac, who was earnestly and tenderly regarding her.

"Pardon me," said he, receding, "I have disturbed you."

"Disturbed me, Sir!" cried Cecilia; "it is not possible *you* can disturb me. I thought—I was in hopes you was coming to sit with me."

"In hopes, my Cecilia!" repeated De Sevignac, "and why should you hope it—why desire to have those meditations intruded upon, which seem to be so dear to you?—Though I fear," added he, sighing heavily, "they are sad ones!"

"What meditations do you mean, Sir?" asked Cecilia, greatly confused.

"Oh my child!" exclaimed De Sevignac, "suffer me to call you mine, for not even the ties of blood could render you dearer to me,—how can I behold a melancholy, which seems to be stealing slowly, but irresistibly to your mind, without wishing to dispel it—without endeavouring to trace it to its sources, and, if possible, to administer a remedy?—Your spirits, my love, are sunk—your bloom begins to fade—and those eyes, which never failed to enliven me, and at those moments when consolation was most necessary and most grateful to me, have lost half their lustre.—Youth, my Cecilia, is the season of enjoyment; beware then that you cloud it not with premature sadness.—If we reject happiness when life is in its spring, at what period of our existence must we hope to find it?—How, my love, am I to account for this sudden change in your disposition?—a change so painful to you, and to me so perplexing!—Is there any thing in your situation here unpleasant to you?—If there is, only speak, and it shall be altered.—Nay, do not be thus distressed; for if it is within the verge of possibility to restore to you that tranquillity which you have lost, it shall be recovered; for, be assured, I have not a single wish beyond it."

"Oh Sir! it is your goodness only which overpowers me," said Cecilia; "I am, indeed I am unworthy of it.—But I will strive—I will pray to be better."

"Pray rather to be happier, my child," returned De Sevignac. "And Oh! may thy innocent prayers and mine, for the accomplishment of this blessed revolution, ascend together to the throne of Mercy!—Forgive my suspicions, my Cecilia; but I fear an attack, from which I had hoped to defend you, menaces your peace; and that I only am culpable.—For who knows but my zeal to save you from misery, may have precipitated you to the very brink of it!"

"Good Heavens! what mean you, Sir?" cried Cecilia, with amazement. "You—you precipitated me to the brink of misery! —Impossible!—You, who have been my protector—my father —my dearest, and now my only friend!"

"I will explain all hereafter," resumed De Sevignac; "but let me first propose a few questions.—The natural timidity of your disposition, and the reluctance with which women possessing less sensibility than yourself, usually unburthen themselves to those of our sex, even when the relationship is most near, would have prevented my enquiries, could I have found a female worthy of your confidence, and capable of directing your judgment.— Alarmed lest what I am about to say should be productive of two evils, which I would most strenuously avoid—that of wounding your delicacy, and of awakening the poignancy of regret by reverting to the cause from whence it springs—my anxiety, however, for your welfare, triumphs over every other sentiment. But tell me first, my Cecilia, whether, in consideration of the sacred title with which you have so lately invested me, I ought or not to take the liberty of interrogating you?"

"To that sacred title, by which you have condescendingly allowed me to address you, Sir," replied Cecilia, "is, and ought to be annexed that authority which might command, where it has submitted to request."

"True, my dear," cried De Sevignac; "but I had rather request than command.—You will allow me then to proceed?"

"Certainly, Sir," said Cecilia, "I am all attention."

"You was at Le Luc, my love, I think, somewhat more than three weeks?"

"I believe, Sir, that was about the time," returned Cecilia, blushing.

"And, during this period, there was scarcely a day," continued De Sevignac, "in which you was not visited by Varàno.—If he remained with us at the chateau in the morning, you say he generally returned to you in the evening; and that you often walked with him about the woods—that he assisted you in botany—formed your tastes for music—and, when the weather was unfavourable for walking, remained with you at the cottage. —Varàno, I allow, is versed in all the accomplishments of the age; his person is attractive, and his manners more than ordinarily pleasing; and, amidst all, his mind has escaped the contagion of pernicious example—I speak of the young men of his own country—and retains a grandeur of character, an energy of thought, not always connected with youth and nobility. You, my darling, are not yet nineteen—Varàno has, I believe, scarce entered his twenty-second year:—at this early age, the heart is more susceptible of tender impressions than at any other; and the romantic eye of youth, at that period, sometimes anticipates perfections even where they do not exist.—I have every reason to believe that Lorenzo, though he shielded his pretensions under the name of friendship, and derived his right of visiting you from his connection with me, was withheld only by the most worthy and discreet motives, from making a full and candid declaration of a tenderer passion. Yes, that Varàno loves you, my dear, I have no doubt.—May I not infer also, that you was not so indifferent to his attentions, as you would have been to those of a mere common acquaintance?—Would you not sometimes have excused yourself—sometimes, in defiance of solicitation, have given him reason to believe that his visits were not indispensable, if they had not been pleasant to you?—Young and delicate women, like yourself, do not like to be intruded upon by our sex when they can decently avoid it, unless they discover something in their conversation extremely prepossessing.—Are my arguments just, my dear?—or is there more in them of sophism than of sound reasoning?—Nay, do not be so confused, my love, but tell me, am I right, or has my anxiety for your situation led me into error?"

"Indeed I don't know, Sir," replied Cecilia, hastily covering her face to hide the deep glow which had mantled to her cheek; "I am sure—I believe the Signor Lorenzo is very amiable, and perhaps —it is very likely—I may have thought too much of him."

"That he is very amiable," rejoined De Sevignac, "I am convinced; but though we may approve, my Cecilia, we are not obliged to *love* all that are amiable!—You will say, perhaps, that there are certain impulses in our natures wholly involuntary, and I believe there are; but trust me, my child, much may be done by exertion. The strongest passion, as well as the most inveterate habit, will yield to effort;—and surely it ought to be the task of innocence and beauty carefully to guard all the avenues of affection till it shall be warranted by discretion. Think not that I am insensible to the attractions of Varàno; but, h my Cecilia! were his mind stored with all the collected graces and perfections that ever adorned humanity, I could have wished you to have been the last to have discovered them."

"Ah! why then, Sir," said Cecilia, "did you teach me to admire excellence, and shew me in yourself an example."

"I anticipated your answer, my dear Cecilia," interrupted De Sevignac. "You would demand of me why I directed you to the love of virtue—why I taught you to reverence and admire whatever is great and beautiful in the moral as well as the natural world, since it might become necessary to overlook it, even when presented to you under the most attractive form. You are not ignorant, my child, that Varàno is an only son, and, as such, the last surviving hope and support of an ancient and honourable House. He must therefore, probably, whatever pain it may inflict upon him, resign his inclination to his duty; and, in compliance with a popular prejudice, weak indeed, but not altogether resistible, bestow his hand when his heart is with another. This may be an arduous, and, I fear, a very affecting task. The mind naturally recedes with aversion from what appears to be compulsatory, and feels an unconquerable degree of inclination to become the modeller of its own happiness.——Forgive me then if I say that Lorenzo di Varàno, the child of tenderness and prosperity, is not likely to adhere to that path which his reason may point out. His wants have hitherto been prevented—his wishes anticipated. From disappointment he has been shielded from his earliest years—how then is he prepared to encounter it?—Does not an evil, which we have never taught ourselves to expect, fall with accumulated violence on our undefended heads?—And does not the mind naturally devise means to free itself from misfortune, as desperate as the misfortune itself?—Your birth, Cecilia, I believe

I need not remind you, though genteel, is not noble. You are not, I conceive, unacquainted with this, although, for reasons which may be hereafter disclosed to you, you are not fully informed of it.—Let me not wound your feelings when I add, that which makes you still dearer to me, by binding the tie of compassion round my heart, would be productive of the very opposite effect in the estimation of the world. Without fortune, for what little the claims of justice will dispense with in your favour, will not be sufficient to secure you from neglect—without, what in the present case would have still more weight, ostensible connections —is it probable, nay, is it not almost impossible that the Marchese should countenance an union so contrary to his intentions?"

"It is indeed impossible!" cried Cecilia, her tears flowing fast as she spoke; "but believe me, Sir," and she hesitated, "though I venerate and admire Signor di Varàno above every human being upon earth, except yourself—though I think of him as a dear friend and a brother, I have never, if I know myself, I have never aspired to his love!"

"Then still venerate—still think of him," said De Sevignac, "as a brother;—and Oh may thy innocent affection be rewarded only with fraternal tenderness!—But I have many things to urge. The arguments I have made use of were strong, but I have others to alledge still more powerful. I cannot, as I have before hinted, forbear placing more confidence in Varàno's attachment to you, than in his filial obedience;—not that I believe he would act decidedly in opposition to the will of his friends; but from the hope, not always ill founded, that paternal regard will not fail finally to triumph over the virulence of resentment. This, however, may incite him to the attempt of gaining your affections, and of persuading you to consent to a clandestine marriage; or, if he has too high an opinion of your delicacy to venture upon such a proposition, he may endeavour to succeed with you by a less formidable method. He may seek to inspire you with a vague hope that the obstacles which had alarmed you, are not wholly insurmountable—that a knowledge of your worth will endear you to his family, when he shall have prevailed upon them to see you; or, should this be ineffectual, may strive to wrest from you a promise of remaining single till he shall have become the uncontrouled master of his own actions—till the fear of paternal authority shall be removed, and he may take you to his heart without an opposing voice.—But bitter indeed would be my reflections, could I think my darling would be wrought upon by arguments so delusive; for, Oh my Cecilia! could you bear, with a mind so noble—so exalted as your's, to interfere with the interests of one, whose happiness is so essential to your own?—could you endure to be the means of clouding those prospects which are opening so fair?—No, you cannot—I am sure you cannot: you would not destroy the hopes of a proud, but noble House!—of a father, whose heart is in his child—and who looks up to him as the reviver and support of its ancient honours!—Oh no, you will not!—Cecilia has a soul above it!—She will listen to me—she will accord with my request."

"Name it, Sir," said Cecilia, "and, let it be what it will, it shall have the force of a command."

"It is then that you will deliver to me a solemn promise never to enter into any engagement with Varàno, however he may urge it."

"If such an assurance can relieve you, my dear Sir, from the solicitude my weakness has occasioned," said Cecilia, "you may depend upon my obedience. My heart is in your hands—you shall direct it henceforth as you please. Never, from this moment, will I think of Signor di Varàno, but as your relation—never will I even see him without your presence and approbation."

"Enough—enough, my child!" returned De Sevignac, "I rely now entirely on your rectitude; and may the consciousness of having acted virtuously be thy blessed reward! It was to save you from an evil which I could not but foresee, that I sent you to Le Luc; hoping, by your absence from the chateau, to prevent a meeting, I had a strange presentiment would be attended with some unhappy consequences."

A flood of tears had now relieved the overcharged heart of Cecilia, which De Sevignac allowed her to shed freely; and then, tenderly soothing her, he conducted her back to the chateau.

The admonitions, so tenderly delivered by her revered friend, sunk deep into the heart of Cecilia.——The illness of De Sevignac, whose health had long been gradually declining, added to her uneasiness and perplexity.—M. Langlois, a physician, and one of the oldest of his acquaintance, was accordingly sent for, who, having attended him some days, recommended the salubrious air of Italy as the only probable restorative; and exacted a promise from him, on parting, to commence his journey thither immediately.

One evening, as Cecilia was amusing De Sevignac with her harp, they were surprised by the appearance of two men, who alighted from their horses at the inner gate of the chateau, and one of them entering abruptly the room in which they sat, their astonishment was mutual and excessive on beholding Varàno. —He saluted De Sevignac with the greatest cordiality and politeness; and then, with an embarrassed air, and a suffused cheek turned to Cecilia.

"Nothing unpleasant has, I hope, happened to you, Signor," said De Sevignac, gravely, "to occasion your very hasty return?"

"Nothing," answered Varàno; "it was merely accidental; or rather it was one of those sudden whims which sometimes seize me.—My friend, whom I was to have escorted into Italy, has indispensable engagements at home: and, meaning to return into Tuscany by the route I came, I took St. Foix in my road."—He then addressed himself to Cecilia, adding—"I am more fortunate than I expected to have been, since I have the felicity of meeting Mademoiselle de St. Bertrand."

"I should have introduced you," said De Sevignac, coldly, "had it been necessary; but you are old acquaintance I find."

Varàno bowed, and taking his seat, the discourse turned upon his recent journey to Dauphine, and other general subjects of conversation.

Observing, at length, that Cecilia had been playing, her harp being by her side, he requested her to resume it. Cecilia hesitated; but a look from De Sevignac reassuring her, she drew it to her, and, accompanying it with her voice, performed an elegant little air with a simplicity and pathos of expression, which was truly enchanting. Her voice was at first tremulous and faint; but the encomiums of De Sevignac encouraged her endeavours, and it gradually regained its powers. Varàno was silent—but it was the silence of admiration.

She withdrew soon after to her chamber, where she was followed by Louisette.

"Ah! I guessed how it would be, Mademoiselle," cried she, the moment she entered, "when the Signor had discovered the trick. —Those wily old foxes always fall into their own snares?—But la, Mademoiselle, what's the matter?—You look as if you were not happy."

"I hope I have no great reason to be otherwise, Louisette," said Cecilia.

"Why, if you are not happy, I don't know who should be. Holy St. Agathe! if the Signor had come all these miles after me!"

"You don't suppose that the Signor's chief motive in coming hither was to see me, I hope," rejoined Cecilia.

"Why, what else could he come for," cried Louisette, "unless, indeed, he has fallen in love with my master? Besides, Benedetto says that his Lord would never have had a single thought——and Benedetto knows a great deal more than he chuses to confess to. —He says his Honour is quite another thing since he saw you; —that he can neither eat, nor drink, nor sleep; and he is sure——"

"I wish, Louisette," interrupted Cecilia, "you was less credulous."

"So that formal old Monk did not succeed at last, for all he thought he had laid his schemes so deep. He knew he was about no good, or he would not have come creeping out of his hole, like a tiger from his den, when he ought to have been in his cell, or at his prayers.—Geraud thought, he said, there was some mischief a brewing, or the lamp would not have burnt so blue; so he was determined to know the bottom of it.—La! the Marquis would no more have thought of going off, than he would have thought of clambering up to the moon, if it had not been put into his head."

Louisette might have proceeded in the same strain for hours, without a single interruption from Cecilia; her mind being now wholly engaged by the unexpected arrival of Varàno, and in considering in what manner she should act consistently with her late solemn engagement. This was a task so difficult to be performed, that, in spite of her joy in seeing Varàno again, she even wished for his departure.

She arose not in the morning so early as was her custom, and, on entering the breakfast-room, found De Sevignac and Varàno already there. The latter was in high spirits; the former appeared thoughtful, and said little.

After breakfast, Varàno proposed a walk over the grounds; but Cecilia declining it, he did not quit the room. Music, reading, and conversation divided the day. The next passed on nearly in the same manner; Cecilia still adhering to her resolution of not being alone with Varàno. On the third, she obeyed a message from De Sevignac, who desired to see her in his antichamber.

"You will be astonished, my love," said De Sevignac, as soon as she was seated, "when you shall be informed of the occasion of this summons.—Having resolved to take M. Langlois's advice of going immediately into Italy, I have determined to embrace the present opportunity of returning with Varàno. As I cannot leave you alone at the chateau, you must accompany me, and remain with my niece at Genoa, whilst I pursue my route into Tuscany. —I do not wonder that you are surprised; and it is painful to me that you should not only be under the necessity of seeing Varàno, but of becoming his fellow-traveller. But this trial of your solitude is unavoidable.—I wish, for your sake, we could have taken Louisette; but as this would interfere materially with our intended mode of travelling, we are obliged to decline it. You will therefore prepare for your journey."

Cecilia could make no reply;—a sort of confused pleasure rushed upon her senses:—she retired, and flew instantly to her apartment.

Varàno, when informed that Cecilia was to be of the party, was alive only to the impulse of immoderate joy, which he could neither restrain nor conceal: whilst Cecilia, tenderly susceptible of all he felt, endeavoured to retain the composure of a determined mind.

It was agreed that they should proceed in a cabriolet as far as Marseilles, on their arrival at which place, M. de Sevignac and Cecilia were to put themselves under the care of a *voiturier*, whilst Varàno prosecuted the remaining part of his journey on horse-back.

The day appointed for their departure at length arrived. Long before the carriage drew up, a number of the peasantry flocked upon the lawn to take and receive a last farewel. The melancholy so strikingly delineated on the countenances of his poor acquaintance, who were many of them pensioners upon his bounty, was touching, yet grateful to the heart of De Sevignac. As he stepped into the cabriolet, they crowded still nearer: some of them wept, whilst others addressed themselves to the Saints, to hasten the return of their benefactor.—Cecilia's voice faltered as she bade adieu to Louisette, Father Pierre, and the domestics——and the carriage drove off.

CHAPTER V

Bear me remote o'er Gallia's woody bounds,
O'er the cloud piercing Alps remote; beyond
The Vale of Arno purpled with the vine,
Beyond the Umbrian and Etruscan hills
To Latium's wide champaign, forlorn and waste,
Where yellow Tyber his neglected wave
Mournfully rolls.

DYER.

THE journey every hour became more and more enchanting; the scenery through which they passed, receiving new forms of beauty and splendour from the mellowing season, which now gave a riper lustre to every luxuriant object. About noon, advancing along a narrow plain, the beams of an unclouded sun, as it gilded the adjacent heights, and threw a trembling radiance on the vale below, presented to their sight the port and city of Marseilles. As soon as they arrived, De Sevignac and his party alighted, and enquired for a *voiturin*, whom they at length engaged to carry them on their way to Italy as far as Nice. Varàno then mounted his horse; and Cecilia and De Sevignac entering the *voiture*, they recommenced their journey.

They travelled leisurely along, often alighting from the carriage to contemplate the charming diversity that covered the landscape, which gradually softened, and soon began to exhibit scenes of varied elegance and beauty. These strolls were delightful to all of them, but particularly to Varàno, to whom it afforded more frequent opportunities of conversing with Cecilia; who, he knew, would extract as much pleasure as himself from the novelty and grandeur of the objects which would occasionally unfold themselves in the various progress of their journey. He loved to wander with her through the knolls and picturesque dells of the mountains, which arose in lofty masses above, and threw their giant shades across the path—to assist her in gathering every thing rare and beautiful among the flowers and trefoils which fringed the chasms of the rocks, or enamelled with their vivid hues the spreading pastures at their feet—to mark out the course of the rivers, now seen, and now lost amid groves of luxuriant evergreen, as they flowed away, in clear waveless expanse, to meet the pure and distant waters of the Mediterranean.

They renewed their course with little intermission; and, after some days travelling by easy stages, leaving Toulon and Hyeres to the right, reached the romantic village of Brigancieres. Leaving this, the country became more and more interesting; the road, which had hitherto fallen along the feet of the eminences, now winding among high and rocky hills.

After a few days' drive, passing through Brignolle and the little village of La Roque, the travellers turned their course toward the sea, in order to enter Italy by Nice. When they had reached Fregus, they were informed by the *voiturin* that an additional horse would be requisite to convey them up the mountain. De Sevignac desired him to procure one, and then to drive on, and station his carriage in some convenient spot, whilst they ascended the mountain on foot; Varàno having resigned his horse to Benedetto, who had orders to lead it slowly by his side.

Arrived at the summit of the mountains, they were struck with admiration at the magnificence and beauty of the prospect which now burst upon their view:—on one side, the ocean spreading away into immeasurable distance; on the other, a wide extended landscape, crowned at the very verge of the horizon by the lofty Alps of Piedmont, whose snowy peaks, lighted up and tinted by the rich colouring of an evening sky, were continually varying into new forms of sublimity.

"How striking," cried De Sevignac, "are these scenes! and

what a sensation of awe communicates to the heart as we survey them!—How sweet, yet how solemn are the emotions they inspire!"

"As to me," said Cecilia, "I feel so insignificant amid the lofty and majestic works of Nature, that I shrink into myself; and feel as if I, a mere speck in the creation, must be overlooked or forgotten in the general plan."

De Sevignac smiled.

"Look toward the sea, my love," said he, "and observe that vessel. It appears in the distance but as a point, and, as it glides away upon the vast space of waters, is as insignificant an object as you seem amid the gigantic heights which environ you; yet that vessel, my dear, shall be guided to its intended port.—Though Providence," continued De Sevignac, "in the works of Nature, delights to awe us to admiration with its stupendous imagery, the tree, the shrub, and even the smallest of its productions are alike the objects of its care. The stately cedar and the giant palmetto are not protected by it with more vigilance than the weed which blossoms beneath their foliage, unseen or unregarded.—Recollect, my Cecilia, the attention bestowed on every simple flower, frail and trifling as they may appear to us, to preserve them against the incursions of the weather, till the destined period for decay arrives. The smallest are consigned to the shade, where they are nurtured from the storm; others are destined to unfold themselves to the sun, but close up their silken petals at the hour when its beams are withdrawn from them. Some there are which scarce the tempest can shake; and these, by the peculiar formation of their parts, are disposed to brace it. If Providence overlooks and defends these, will it not protect us?"

"It was a childish idea, Sir," said Cecilia; "and deserved reproof."

"How often," replied Varàno, "when I have been wandering alone among these Alpine solitudes, have I felt the same!—You have pronounced my very sentiments!—How happy am I to have thought like you!"

"Not very happy," said Cecilia, colouring, and gently withdrawing her hand; "supposing the sentiment, as it really was, a very weak one."

"How sweet, how tranquil is this hour!" cried De Sevignac, rousing himself as from a reverie.

"Yes, and the calm motion of the sea," said Cecilia, "increases the general serenity—the wind scarcely agitates its surface."

"And observe too Fregus at our feet," interrupted Varàno, "perceptible only by the light wreaths of smoke rising, like clouds of vapour, and which serve to mark its place in the landscape. —And behold too," continued he, "on the banks of that noble inlet to the sea where stands St. Tropes, and farther on St. Maximin, half buried in a wilderness of pine and lentiscus; whilst far in the ocean appear the wide distant Islands of Corsica, tinted with ethereal blue."

He stopped, and looked tenderly at Cecilia, whose eyes had pursued his, and then changing the discourse, amused himself, assisted by De Sevignac, in discovering the situations of towns and villages, whose shadowy outlines, obscured by distance, were scarcely to be distinguished.

They had advanced some paces down the mountain, when De Sevignac, pointing to a little green recess formed in the hollow of two projecting cliffs, proposed that they should stop and refresh themselves.

The *voiturin*, who had engaged to convey their provisions, was called;—refreshments were spread upon the grass; and the party sat down to partake of a simple meal, which the situation and deep retirement of this lonely little dell rendered doubly delicious. A verdant carpet stretched at their feet, inlaid with flowers of every die, whose sweets were shaded from the sun and from the gales by thickets of myrtle and oleander, covered already with its lovely scarlet buds. Here, amid the glowing vegetation of grass and shrubs, they beheld patches of the pansy violet, the auricula, and the beautiful *anemone nemeroso*; whilst higher up appeared the heath-tree, the cistus, and the arbutus with its pale strawberry-like berry, mantling up to the crags above.

The next day conducted them along the margin of the sea, when, leaving Vannes and Anbibes, they gained the little town of St. Laurent, and fording the Var, entered the rich country of Nice.

On their arrival at the city, the postillion was discharged, and a *vetturino*[1] agreed with to convey them over the Alps. The *auber-gier*, to whom De Sevignac had spoke, observing that the passage called the *Cornich* was a rugged and difficult road, would have dis-suaded him from his purpose of proceeding farther by land; but De Sevignac persisting in his intention, in which he was joined both by Varàno and Cecilia, the host having afforded them all necessary directions concerning this formidable and very hazard-ous pass, they pursued their course along the Alps.

An emotion of indescribable awe seized the senses of Cecilia when she entered the track leading up into these stupendous boundaries. They presented, indeed, scenes calculated to suspend every effort of the mind in silent and enthusiastic astonishment! —and as she cast a fearful eye upon their impenetrable shades, their gloomy forests, and obscure caverns, her heart thrilled with sensations which partook equally of admiration and of horror.

As they approached toward the Italian side, the objects became more appalling, and the prospects still more irregular and vast. Mountains piled above each other, till they penetrated the clouds! —deep precipices, from which humanity recoils, falling beneath the massy blackness of the woods of pine and chesnut, which stretched along their base, or hung within their romantic val-lies!—the astounding roar of the cataracts bellowing among the cliffs!—these were the images presented to their view: yet often, amid the wildest horrors of these tremendous scenes, appeared some little green recess, shaded with fir, cedar, or mountain-ash; whilst, lower still, the eye caught beneath the opening vista the wide spreading pasture, where snowy flocks were seen cropping the luxuriant herbage of the summer, and the shepherd's pipe, echoing fainting among the rocks, reminded them of the scenes of tranquil beauty they had so lately left.

Descending lower, the vast plains of Lombardy stretching away on all sides into the remotest distance—the green vales of Piedmont—the long tract of Alps and Apennines, which here separate (one range running from thence to Calabria, the other to Constantinople) with the grand sweep of ocean, composed a rich expanse of beautiful and magnificent scenery; whilst on the

---

1 The driver of the Italian carriages.

slope of the gently rising hill at their feet, appeared the town of St. Remo, with its white houses and villas; its chapel overtopping all, its palms, its cypresses, and its olive-groves.

To the left of these, lifting high its threatening head, arose the lofty peaks of Mount Cenano, whose abrupt base, clothed with thickets of evergreen, oak, the Palirus fig, and the *arbor Judæ*, and bathed by the pure waters of the Nervia, contrasted well with the awful features of the rock above; which impending over in jutting masses of granite, or of black and white marble, bleak, and bare of vegetation, except what was afforded by a few scanty lichens, displayed a barren wildness assimilating with the tremendous region of the Alps, whose broken summits peered on every side in dreadful sublimity!

Having descended from those shelving ridges which overhang and guard the entrance into this enchanting country, the travellers alighted, and continued their way on foot; sometimes seating themselves on a romantic cliff, and sometimes at the foot of a little woody knoll, hid in the hollow of the projecting crags,

> ——————Till the moon,
> Rising in clouded majesty, at length
> Apparent Queen unveil'd her peerless light,
> And o'er the dark her silver mantle threw.

As they were descending into one of the most picturesque little vallies which Nature ever formed, the silence that had accompanied them was suddenly interrupted by the sound of a human voice, attended by an oboe and some other instrument, whose slow cadence was borne faintly on the breeze which arose from the lowlands. They paused in delighted wonder till the air had ceased, and the oboe, without its accompaniment, returned the strain. They soon found it proceeded from a little sequestered dell, sunk between two mountains, which they were about to enter.

While they yet listened, it touched a few simple notes, and then, attended by a female voice, low, but which seemed capable of unfolding itself in singing to every musical expression, shifted to a soft and mournful measure.

"Surely," said Cecilia, "it is some Fairy, who is seducing us to her haunts with mournful music."

"Listen!" cried De Sevignac; "I would not lose the cadence."

Scarcely had he spoken, when they beheld, at some distance from where they stood, a small cottage, or rather a cabin, surrounded on every side by rocks clothed with brushwood, at the door of which, on a turf-seat by its side, were assembled a group of persons of both sexes, regaling themselves with fruits: an oboe, and some other instruments of music lay beside them.

They arose on their approach, and an elderly peasant, whose aspect was expressive of great benignity, came forward to invite them to his cabin. The rest of the party disappeared, except a very lovely young girl, dressed in the simple habit of a mountaineer, who kept her place as before. The invitation was immediately accepted; chairs were placed for them by the door, and De Sevignac and his party sat down.

"We need not ask," said Varàno, as soon as they were seated, "whether it is to you we owe the melody which drew us to your valley; but to whom is it we are indebted for the air so tastefully and so very charmingly performed?"

"To my daughter, I believe," said the old man, pointing to the Paysanne: "she has a tolerable voice, Signor, as you say; but as to skill, she has had no opportunity of acquiring it."

"Your cabin is very commodiously situated," interposed De Sevignac; "these woods shade it from the wind, whilst those rocks form a sufficient defence against the incursions of the weather."

"Yes, Signor," returned the peasant, "we have, thank Heaven! no reason to repine. The storm which rocks the turrets of the castle, spares the humble cabin at its foot. It reminds me of the world, Signor: the great, held up to observation, are assailed by misfortunes from which we are exempt. The sweeping storm of ambition, and the biting blast of envy corrode their peace, and destroy their repose; whilst the poor shepherd, unenvied and unknown, and who has no thought but how to procure the food necessary to subsistence, and to secure himself a better rest when he dies, lives easy and tranquil, nor sighs to usurp the place of all those doomed to riot in splendid misery."

"You speak like a philosopher," said De Sevignac; "from

whence is it you have acquired these ideas?—These are not the sentiments, neither are they the expressions of an Alpine shepherd. How have you obtained this knowledge?"

"By the study of nature," replied the peasant, "and of man. Of books I know nothing; my opinions are, therefore, not formed from the precepts of others, but from my own observations——I was not always, as you say, a mountaineer shepherd."

"If your favourite study is man," continued De Sevignac, "what could lead you into a solitude which can afford you so few subjects for investigation?"

"Choice," returned the peasant.

"And could that determine you to a mode of life, for which it is evident neither Nature nor education designed you?"

"A thorough persuasion," rejoined the stranger, "that it was the happiest!—a persuasion which has since been confirmed to me by my own experience. I have now no care but for the present. I rise with the sun; and while the dew yet hangs upon the trees, lead my flocks from the vallies, to browse upon the cultivated knolls of the mountains. Thus the labour of the day begins. My daughter is my only companion: she manages my household, prepares my food, and assists me in the cultivation of my garden. In the evenings we sit, as you see, and spreading a bounteous meal at our door, supply a welcome repast to those who are still poorer than ourselves. Such is our life; it is simple; and, I hope, innocent."

"And you are content," said Varàno.

"Most happy!" returned the peasant.

De Sevignac, much pleased with his new acquaintance, whom he found both sensible and intelligent, would have continued the subject; but learning that the next village, which he enquired for, was more distant than he had imagined, having made all due acknowledgments to the peasants for their courtesy and attention, he arose; and the travellers again entered the carriage.

The moon, though not yet risen above the trees, which shaded on every side the rocks surrounding this solitary little glen, still afforded them light enough to discern the path which the shepherd had pointed out as leading to the adjacent village: and often did they stop to observe the influence of her mild and silvery beams amid these extensive deserts. The snow-capped summits of the rocks, which had lately been tipped with all the gold and purple of the setting sun, appeared as if crested with silver, which, contrasted with the obscurity that pervaded the woods and dreary caverns they overhung, displayed all the grace and magic of colouring, whilst often sunk beneath precipices, bare and bleak as the Alp which overtopped them, appeared glens so solitary, that they every moment expected to see the savage forms of banditti, such as Salvator Rosa gives to his assassins, stealing from the obscurity of the overhanging crags, ready to seize upon their prey:——the solitary figure of the chamois hunter, or the shepherd, pursuing his course over the bridge which united the two opposite cliffs, were, however, all that were to be seen.

They had passed St. Remo, and were on their way to Alassio, when they were informed that the road by the sea was so narrow as to admit only of mules. This was a circumstance which had escaped the recollection of Varàno, though he had so lately traversed the Alps, and the whole party was disconcerted and perplexed. De Sevignac, observing that the mode of travelling on mules would be extremely inconvenient, enquired of the *vetturino* if there was no method of avoiding it.

"There is only one way, Signor," replied the *vetturino*, "and that will cost us at least some hours' travelling; we must turn aside from the sea, and pass through an extensive forest, at the end of which there is a village and an inn."

"Proceed then," said De Sevignac, "we will pursue the path you have marked out."

The *vetturino* accordingly drove on.

CHAPTER VI

This is the place, as well as I may guess,
Whence even now the tumult of loud mirth
Was rife, and perfect in my listening ear;
Yet nought but single darkness do I find.
What might this be? A thousand fantasies
Begin to throng into my memory,
Of calling shapes, and beckoning shadows dire
And airy tongues that syllable men's names
On sands, and shores, and desert wildernesses.

MILTON.

THEY arrived about noon at the edge of the forest; and, proceeding with as much expedition as the unevenness of the road, shadowed by trees, and overrun with luxuriant vegetation, would permit, were soon within a league of the opposite borders.

The day was declining fast when the postillion, perceiving nothing before him but a gloomy extent of shade, endeavoured to gain a more open part of the forest. He had not succeeded in this intention before a drizzling rain, which had commenced soon afterwards, was followed by a rapid shower, which, impregnated with hail, descended with great violence. The sky suddenly became dark, and a rising wind, which swept along the forest with a hollow and tumultuous sound, made them fearful of proceeding.

De Sevignac, who had suffered no small inconvenience from the chill *mæstral* winds, which had occasionally assailed them on their journey along the mountains, and the humid texture of the clouds through which they passed, called to the *vetturino* to stop; and then pointing to a thickly embowered spot to the right, desired him to make up to it. The *vetturino* obeyed; but the place, shadowy as it was, was insufficient to defend them from the violence of the storm, which now burst upon their heads with augmented fury.

Varàno, observing that there might be some hut or cabin at

no great distance, dispatched his servants to different parts of the forest, to descry if any such were to be found. They returned soon after, with intelligence that there was a large dilapidated mansion not very remote; but, from the ruinous state of its appearance, they had little hopes of its being inhabited.

De Sevignac, observing that they were already wet, proposed that they should proceed, and make enquiries themselves.

The place answered exactly to the description given of it by the servants. It was a large, melancholy looking building, surrounded by a court, wild and grass-grown; a row of gloomy trees concealed one of its sides; the angles, with a considerable part of what had once been the out-works, were already in ruins; and several parts of the edifice had fallen to the ground, and now lay scattered in large masses on the area beyond. The main body of the building was, however, entire; and, a tall, meagre-looking figure, wearing the dress of a hunter, was seen crossing the court toward the entrance.

They stopped at an archway preceding the gate through which the person they had seen had just passed toward the house, when Varàno, calling to him aloud, demanded if he could accommodate them for the night. The man turned; and, eyeing them askance, was pursuing silently his way, when Varàno repeating the enquiry with some impatience—

"We admit no travellers," said he surlily; "you may come in, however; the storm will perhaps soon abate."

The invitation, uncourteous as it was, was gladly accepted; and the travellers alighting, followed their sullen guide over weeds and briars, through the court, and into a large half-furnished room, which appeared to be a kitchen, and which seemed to serve for every purpose to the hideous group of figures assembled in it.

It contained two windows in contrary directions, one on the same side as the door, the other opposite; a large table was placed under each;—near that which faced the entrance, were two men engaged in eating their suppers. They eyed our travellers attentively, but did not speak. One indeed noticed them with a slight inclination of the head; the other, after turning half round to survey them, stole a glance at his companion, and then bent down to resume his employment. A blazing fire, formed of turf and the withered branches of pine, relieved the desolation that surrounded them. The room was low, but extensive; various culinary utensils were disposed upon shelves, and the skins of chamoix, and of other animals taken in the chace, were suspended from the walls.

On the opposite side of the room were two women, busied in preparing some articles of cookery. They exchanged some significant looks as they examined their guests, whom they regarded from time to time with an air of seeming derision; but their discourse, which was a strange mixture of French, and what they meant for Italian, was delivered in such a low tone, and so imperfectly pronounced, that they could overhear only a small part of the conversation. They often laughed aloud, and the word *maledetto* frequently passed between them; but of the rest they could distinguish enough only to convince them that they had the misfortune to be considered by them as fit subjects for their mirth; and that the preparations in which they were occupied, were intended for the accommodation of some persons not yet arrived, but whom they appeared to expect with the utmost impatience. One of them went frequently to the door, as if to await their coming; whilst the other, after having employed herself for some time in various arrangements, spread a coarse cloth upon the table, which extended from the window nearly the whole length of the kitchen. The *pignatello di fuoco*[1] was then brought forward to receive a fresh supply of food; and a large dish of meat, mixed with *borago*[2] and some other sorts of vegetable, was heated at the fire; and all this, they were informed, was for the people, the Signors, as they called them, whose return was thus anxiously expected.

The men who had been engaged at supper now arose, and went out. Our travellers marked them, as they withdrew, with an eager intentness:—one of them was rather below the middle size, ruddy, and corpulent; the other was tall, thin, and bony, his visage long, his complexion sallow, his eyes black, melancholy, and expressive of mean cunning, one of which was somewhat contracted by the lid; a pair of huge eyebrows half concealed his

1 The pot used in boiling.
2 A plant reared in Italy, and which the Italians eat as spinage.

forehead, and gave a sullen and savage expression to his whole countenance; he was clothed in a faded red coat, much injured by time: his companion wore only a waistcoat.

The elder of the women, whom they called Pasquina, was the exact counterpart of Gil Blas's Leonarda:—she had the same features, the same fiery red hair; and though probably much younger than this celebrated Hebe, and from not being immured, like her, in the subterranean recesses of the *infernal deities*, she might be somewhat fairer,—not even Leonarda, engaged in her nocturnal occupations, could have excited more uneasy sensations in the breast of our travellers, than the two figures before them; for the other, if not equally masculine, was scarcely less hideous.

Each watched them in silence, undecided whether to remain there till the storm should abate, or to brave the fury of the elements and the long extended shade of a forest, darkening every moment with a falling twilight.

Whilst they were all ruminating in secret on what might follow, a middle aged man, somewhat better dressed than his companions, entered the room. He carried on his back a sort of sack, which he seemed to support with difficulty. He threw it down, and was proceeding; but started back with astonishment on perceiving the strangers.

De Sevignac, noticing his surprise, told him that they were travellers, who had been driven by necessity to seek shelter beneath his roof.

The man replied only with a familiar nod, and resuming his sack, passed on, often staggering as he went, beneath the weight of his burden. He was attended by two dogs, who, as they approached the hearth on which they sat, growled, and looked angrily at the strangers; but the hunter reproving them, they lay down, and stretching themselves on the hearth, remained quiet.

The man who had carried the sack, was not long absent. He took a seat beneath the window, on the side opposite to the door; the women, having completed their tasks, placed themselves by his side, and the whole party, as if a general mistrust had taken place, continued silent.

At length De Sevignac, observing the dogs appeared tired, demanded of the hunter what success he had had in the chace.

The man replied, that he had killed two chamoix about daybreak, but since then he had had little or no sport.

"These animals are very shy, I suppose," rejoined De Sevignac; "pray in what manner do you contrive to secure them?"

"The only way," replied the hunter, "is by lying in wait, concealed beneath thickets, or near their accustomed haunts, before dawn-light; for they are so swift, and have the sense of hearing to such perfection, that, except by artifice, it is not possible to succeed with them; since, without this, they would escape, and run to the precipices for security, where it would be death to follow them."

"You live here in a very solitary situation," continued De Sevignac; "but your table being furnished with provision for a much larger company than we have yet seen, there is probably a great number of you; all of whom are, I suppose, engaged in the chace."

"Yes, we find it more convenient," returned the hunter, "to live here several of us together, than apart in cabins, which afford a more indifferent shelter than even this, from the storms that sometimes annoy us."

Whilst De Sevignac was conversing with the hunter, Varàno perceived that both the man and women regarded them intently: he observed too that they frequently whispered; and, from the attitudes and gestures which attended their seeming remarks, it was easy to discover that they were the subjects of them. At length, finding themselves observed, the women stole off, and were soon followed by the man; leaving the party now, for the first time since they had entered, at liberty to communicate to each their suspicions.

It had occurred to Varàno that, disguised under the habit of an ostensible profession, it was at least possible that these people, into whose power they had thrown themselves, were enleagued with parties of those wretches who procure a precarious subsistence by rapine and plunder, and are known to infest, in large troops, the woods and forests of Italy. The savage countenances of the men corroborated the opinion; and their sudden retreat, as if to consult together in private on their previously concerted plans, united with the mysterious whisperings they had overheard, seemed to confirm it.

De Sevignac's apprehensions were scarcely less sanguine; and Varàno, observing that, since they could not continue there the night, it would be prudent to resume their way to the inn while it was yet light, he arose to call the servants, who had taken refuge in one of the buildings, forming a part of the out-works, and to give them such directions as might be requisite in case of an assault.

He returned in a few minutes, and the carriage being in readiness, Cecilia was assisted in ascending it. She had remarked an extreme trepidation both in Varàno and De Sevignac; but the haste in which they appeared prevented enquiries.

The storm was now over; and the carriage, driving from the gates, regained the path in the forest before the savage inhabitants of this desolated mansion had the smallest suspicion that their guests were departed.

Varàno alone remained behind; secretly determined to inform himself of their designs. The investigation would, he knew, be attended with hazard, if not with danger; but Varàno was a stranger to every species of fear.

Re-entering the building, he advanced with quick steps toward the door at which the party of supposed ruffians had departed: he listened to catch the sound of voices, if any of them were returned—he could hear none. He proceeded, and, advancing a few paces, found himself in a large square room terminated by a door. He opened it with caution, and descended by steps into a long straight passage, which branched out to the right and left on either side of the entrance.—Looking earnestly down the latter, he perceived, by the dim light afforded by a small grated casement at the farther end, a wide stone arch, which appeared to lead to some inner apartment in the mansion. Thither he bent his steps; for the path to the right was, he perceived, perfectly dark. It directed him to a spacious stone hall, which he at length entered.

The dusky gloom of the approaching night, piercing with a sad solemnity through the long rows of Gothic windows ranged on either side of the hall, shewed the frequent breaches in the roof, and the discoloured walls, in whose apertures the moss had fastened, and the ivy hung in many a fantastic wreath.

Varàno paused for a moment, and was proceeding, when he

stumbled over something, which, on stooping down, he perceived to be the sack which the hunter had just brought from the chace. He sunk down to discover its contents, but quickly started up with horror and affright!—For a moment terror overcame the exercise of his reason and utterance, for he perceived it contained the body of a newly murdered man!

The blood congealed about his heart as his hand rested on the forehead, on which the cold dews of death yet hung—he withdrew it from the touch with convulsive dread on perceiving the wounds yet bled, and, lifting his eyes to heaven, seemed to undergo a temporary pause in existence. It was recalled, however, by the sound of voices, as of several people speaking at once, and which evidently issued from a room adjoining the hall.

Terror again yielded to curiosity. Varàno drew his sword, and, armed with a desperate kind of courage, traversed the hall toward the door from whence these sounds proceeded: he stopped, and, as he listened, distinguished the following words:—

"You have nothing to do but mind the body—bury it deep enough, and see that you have no blood upon your face."

"D—n the body!" returned a voice, which he knew to be that of the man who had carried the sack, "what have I to do with that?—I've done his business for him—he'll tell no more tales now, I'll warrant him!—But what did you bring the knife here for —has not he gashes enough already, hey?"

"Hold your prating tongue," rejoined the other; "don't you know where you are?—Bury the body, I say, and wash the blood off your face. Would you confess yourself?—Would you shew your trade?"

"Confound the body and you too!" replied his comrade surlily; "bury your mangled carcases yourself—are you to do none of the work?"

"Aye, aye, you are a bold fellow, Lupigno," interposed another, "when you can meet with those who will second you. You don't mind being blown up—you don't mind hanging a little;—yet, I warrant thee, thou takest a look now and then at the edge of the forest. There was a bold fellow tucked up there as ever took knife in hand—he was made of good stuff; for he has hung upon that gibbet these five years, to my knowledge."

"Well, well, but to business," cried the first ruffian, "what are we to do with these?"

"Keep 'em till 'tis dark," returned another, "to be sure, and then let 'em go."

"But how are we to keep 'em?" asked his companion.

"Easily," replied the other; "tell 'em they may stay all night; and when you want to get rid of 'em, say you've altered your mind, and have no room for 'em."

"For my part," said he whom they called Lupigno, "I'm for detaining 'em."

"For what?" interrupted the other sullenly, "are not we sure of 'em?—Besides if we were not, you would not murder 'em here, would you?"

"Why not," enquired Lupigno, "when they are in their beds? ——Their ghosts won't rise to tell us of it."

"No, no," returned another of the ruffians, with a horrible oath, "I'm for giving 'em fair quarter; only mind they don't escape us. Our people will be here anon—so get you to the kitchen, Huberto, and tell 'em to wait—we can offer to get 'em a guide, you know."

Varàno heard no more.—Horror thrilled through every vein!—His limbs, influenced by fear, seemed to have forsaken their office, and though danger, which he had not the power to resist, awaited the delay, his feet appeared rivetted to the spot. The asylum they had sought was then peopled with murderers; and the hapless wretch, over whose mangled corse he had thus accidentally stumbled, had been sacrificed to the fury of these lawless assailants!

Recovering from the impression of instant dismay, he quitted the hall, and retracing the gloomy passages with quick disordered steps, reached the door of the entrance.—He turned for a moment to listen if he was pursued, and finding all was yet silent, mounted his horse, and striking into the most direct path, soon overtook the carriage.

De Sevignac had been alarmed by his absence, and Cecilia unwarily discovered to him, by her manner, the uneasiness which she had undergone through his delay. To their eager enquiries where he had been, he returned an evasive answer; not doubting, from the now decided character of the people from whom they had escaped, that detached parties of them could be abroad in the forest, with which it was too probable they should meet. Stopping, therefore, to enquire of the *vetturino* the exact distance to the inn, he desired him to make the best of his way thither; and ordering his servants to keep close, and to examine whether their fire-arms were in readiness, sought to facilitate their progress by slashing away with his sword the briars and underwood, whose trailing branches entangling the feet of the horses, threatened to impede their passage. This was rendered still more difficult by the falling of several of the largest of the trees, which, annoyed by frequent storms in the spring, or struck by lightning, had been torn from their roots, whilst the branches of others lay scattered along the path.

CHAPTER VII

—————————————Might we but hear
The folded flocks, penn'd in their wattled cots,
Or sound of past'ral reed with oaten stops,
Or whistle from the lodge, or village cock
Count the night-watches to his feathery dames,
'Twould be some solace yet, some little cheering,
In this close dungeon of innumerous boughs.

MILTON.

THIS part of the forest was more shadowy than any they had yet passed; the paths were intricate, and sometimes so narrow as scarcely to admit of a carriage. The scene was solemn, the night seemed approaching fast; and the thick and humid boughs which overhung the road, assisted to obscure the small remains of twilight.

Advancing farther, the deep recesses of shade grew more and more appalling!—Cecilia shuddered as she gazed, and frequently started at the sudden rustling of the leaves, occasioned by the accidental fluttering of some disturbed bird, who had sought refuge among the branches; and as she listened to the wind as it sighed among the foliage, sometimes sweeping along the trees in low and mournful cadence, and sometimes rolling in hollow blasts in the heavy tops of the pines, she thought with regret on the scenes she had left. In vain she gazed around, in hopes (as the distances between the boles of the trees, or the opening vista, admitted the faint light, and allowed a more ample perspective) of catching a view of a cottage, a cabin, or some kind of habitation, by which the haunts of man might be traced.

No such were to be seen.—No cheerful sound of pastoral flute, or mariner's song (such as had sometimes accompanied them along the winding shores of the Mediterranean, or had charmed them in those beautiful vallies they had just traversed) enlivened with their cheering notes the dreary prospect before them.

De Sevignac appeared thoughtful, and conversed little, and the mind of Varàno was yet too sensibly impressed with his late terrifying adventure, to allow him to support his accustomed vivacity.

They had advanced near a mile without meeting with any interruption, when, accidentally turning back, they perceived an equestrian making hastily toward them. He was habited as a hunter, and seemed to be well mounted. His dress consisted of a jacket and cloak of a deep crimson colour, with a cap such as is generally worn by those of his profession. He carried a gun, which was slung carelessly across his shoulder; and this, with a large bugle-horn, and a small net-bag suspended from his breast, comprised the whole of his accoutrements.—He addressed our travellers, while he was yet far distant, with a loud halloo, and then gallopped toward them.

Varàno calling to him, demanded who he was, and what were his intentions.

"I am a hunter," answered he, "accustomed to traverse the haunts of this forest. The paths are intricate—you are strangers, and perhaps little acquainted with them: will you allow me to accompany you?"

Varàno eyed him attentively as he spoke, and, being not much pleased either with his figure or address, felt inclined to reject an offer so abruptly proposed.

"You are probably not aware," continued the hunter, "of the

dangers which you may encounter in this place. The night darkens fast; and, should you lose your way, you may have reason to repent your temerity in crossing it at so late an hour:—parties of ruffians are abroad, and, if you neglect to make the best of your way through this forest, you will be likely to meet with them. My single arm can avail you nothing; but, as I am obliged to pass a considerable part of these wilds before I can arrive at my cabin, I shall be happy to be admitted into your party."

As he mentioned his cabin, Varàno turned and surveyed him, as before, with great attention—secretly wondering that a person so indigent as to be only the occupier of so humble a kind of mansion, should be in possession of a horse which appeared to be of some value.

De Sevignac paused upon the offer, and Varàno felt less and less inclined to accept it; for he imagined he saw in him one of those ruffians which he had represented as being then abroad in search of prey. But recollecting that, if he was really enleagued with this rapacious gang, he had it as much in his power to betray them to his associates then, as at a more distant period—and that, if his suspicions had wronged him, he might be an useful and even necessary assistant, he objected not to the plan, and the stranger slackening his pace, followed in the rear.

"If these wilds are so well known to you," said De Sevignac, "you can, doubtless, inform us how far we are yet from the nearest post-house. The night, as you observe, darkens fast, and we are anxious to gain it with all possible expedition."

The hunter replied that the *osteria*, or post-house, on the opposite borders of the forest, was at near half a league's distance.

"Ah!" said De Sevignac, "is it so much?"

"But should it be dark," resumed the hunter, without noticing the interruption, "there is a moon—she will soon be up, and her light will guide you.—You are armed, I suppose?"

"We are," rejoined De Sevignac; "but our number is small; and, should we be unfortunate enough to suffer an attack from one of those concealed parties you have mentioned, it might be insufficient to defend us from an assault, directed, perhaps, by skill superior to our's. But of this, since we are so near our destination, we are now, I trust, in no great danger."

"This wilderness," resumed the stranger, "is so extensive, and forms such a convenient receptacle for all kinds of villany, that you will have reason to congratulate yourselves on an escape from the many perilous adventures which may await you here; —there is scarcely a spot throughout Italy more notorious for murders than this forest!"

"And pray, friend," said De Sevignac, "if this tract is, as you have reported, so pregnant with dangers, what can induce *you* to venture alone through regions, which cannot be traversed without hazard?"

"You have forgotten, Signor," replied he, "one circumstance, which, had you reflected, was too obvious to have escaped you. A person who has nothing to lose, may venture in safety any where; few, if any, are so bloodthirsty as to murder for wantonness; revenge, or the prospect of gain, being the chief, and indeed only incentives to acts of atrocity. From the former I have a defence in my insignificance—from the latter in my poverty; for who would think of attacking a poor hunter, who lives in an obscure cabin, without any means of subsistence, except what is afforded him by his gun?"

"True," said De Sevignac, "I did not, as you say, recollect that."

As he spoke thus, Varàno again turned, and looked earnestly at his horse.

"If I imagined, as many others do," continued the hunter, "that the spirits of those travellers, whose tombs and crosses are erected at the edge of this forest, infest it in the night, I might probably be more averse than I am from exploring it."

"Perhaps so," said De Sevignac; "yet even then it might require as much, or more real courage to face the living than the dead; who, were they permitted to appear to us, we have no reason to imagine would be allowed to do us any essential injury."

"Yet I believe," replied the hunter, "if all those were to arise that have met their death-wound in this place, they would compose an army sufficient to appal a whole host of living ones; for, if we may give credit to report, there is scarcely a spot throughout the whole tract which has not been died in blood!"

"Enough, enough!" said De Sevignac; "the subject is an unpleasant one."

Again they were all silent, till Varàno at length proposed some enquiries relative to the occupation of hunting. De Sevignac also questioned him as to the manner of chasing the wolf and the izard among the steeps of the rocks; and how they contrived to defend themselves from the incursions of the before-mentioned animals, when they descended upon them in flocks in the winter —when

> "By wint'ry famine rous'd from all the tract
> Of horrid mountains, which the shining Alps,
> And wavy Apennine, and Pyrenees,
> Branch out stupendous into distant lands,
> Cruel as death, and hungry as the grave,
> Assembled wolves in raging troops descend,
> And pouring o'er the country, bear along,
> Keen as the north-wind sweeps the glossy snow."
>
> THOMSON.

They continued in this discourse till the broad avenue, in which they had remained some time, suddenly terminated; and the road, intersected into several smaller tracks, began to branch in various directions through the forest. The stranger perceiving this, told them to keep to the right, and then clapping spurs to his horse, he turned the angle of a rock, and disappeared.

De Sevignac, unsuspicious of his design, called aloud to him to stop. This was, however, in vain: he seemed to have plunged already into the depths of the forest—and the loud tone of his bugle-horn, which was re-echoed again and again throughout this vast extent of shade, was the only answer he returned.

The trampling of hoofs was now heard in the distance, and a loud rushing among the remoter foliage indicated the approach of numbers. De Sevignac started.

"We are betrayed!" said he.—The *vetturino* stopped.—"Drive on," pursued he, "our only refuge is in flight!"

Cecilia's heart thrilled with terror!—She grasped his arm convulsively, but could not speak.

"Courage, my love!" said De Sevignac, "we may yet escape."

Scarcely had he spoken, when the road opened upon a narrow plain, and a small troop of horsemen, consisting of four or five desperadoes, whose looks might have appalled the most adventurous spirit, darted across the space. The *vetturino*, notwithstanding his fears, would have obeyed the order, and lashing his horses, he strove with renewed courage to escape his pursuers, till one of the fiercest of the gang clapping a *musqueton*[1] to his breast, threatened him with death if he proceeded.

The ruffians now crowded about the carriage; and Varàno made a signal to his people to commence the attack. Two of the most daring of the assailants were armed only with stilettos—the others carried *musquetons*; but, on both parties firing, in which, fortunately for all, no mischief was done, each drew his sword, and, with fierce and random strokes, parried the blows of his courageous antagonist.

The travellers defended themselves for some time with the utmost bravery. One of the ruffians was wounded at the beginning of the encounter, and another had since fallen; but, though victory seemed to be declaring for our party, it was impossible they could have resisted long. Benedetto had received a cut on his arm, and De Sevignac was slightly wounded in the breast. In this critical moment a cavalier, attended by his servants, approached at no great distance. The villains immediately retreated, and retired with precipitation to the thickest part of the forest.

The cavalier now calling aloud, demanded who they were, and what had happened to them.

"We are travellers," returned Varàno, "and, passing along this forest, have been assaulted by outlaws. You had better not venture within its borders."

The cavalier enquired if they had sustained any injury.

"Yes, one or two of us are wounded," replied Varàno, "though I believe not materially."

The cavalier now approached; and ordering those of his attendants who were armed to hold themselves in readiness, in case the ruffians should return, and their number be reinforced, himself with one of his servants remained to assist them; and Varàno felt his regret as to his own unskilfulness in surgery instantly removed, on the information that the stranger was

1 A blunderbuss.

a surgeon, whom accident had called out, and who was then returning to his home on the other side of the forest.

De Sevignac's wound, which he had affirmed to be very slight, was at length bound up: Varàno, in the meantime, supporting Cecilia, whom he consoled with an assurance that all danger was at an end, and that De Sevignac's accident would be attended with no further inconvenience than a few days' delay. The agitation in which her spirits had been kept during the whole of the conflict, had prevented her from fainting; but the terrors she underwent now so completely overcame her, that, though the principal cause was removed, she seemed to feel them anew; and as she leaned upon the arm of Varàno, without being conscious of her situation—without feeling the trembling pressure of his hand as he grasped her sinking form, and scarce hearing the tender accents of his voice as he uttered the soothing words of love and pity, her imagination, tinctured by the gloom of night, suggested even more terrors than her situation could justify; and, as she gazed around her with dismay, she expected every moment to see the blood-stained forms of these desperate assailants start from beneath the shadowy pass, to complete the horrid devastation they had begun.

The surgeon, who was unable to afford any opinion concerning De Sevignac till he should have examined the wound, offered to accompany them, and to remain with him till he was in a situation to resume his journey. They accordingly proceeded, and alighted in a short time at the *auberge*.

"I am sorry to say," said the surgeon, soon after they had entered it, and Cecilia and De Sevignac were withdrawn, "that this *auberge* is not considerable enough to afford you those conveniences necessary to your comfort whilst you continue here.— Your friend's wound, though not deep enough to be dangerous, will demand, of course, much care and attention. He cannot be removed at present without incurring some risk, and there is no inn or post-house for the space of some miles. A lucky thought has, however, just struck me: in a castle, not far from hence, resides Signor di Rosalvo, a man of very melancholy manners, but of great benevolence of character. I have the honour to be known to him; and when he shall hear of your misfortune, and of the very limited accommodations that can be procured for you here, he will be happy to afford you an asylum in his castle. I will go, and myself explain to him your situation."

Varàno made a few slight objections, but these being over-ruled, he consented, though reluctantly, to the surgeon's pro-posal; determining in the meantime, not to acquaint De Sevignac nor even Cecilia with the plan, till he should have received an answer from the Signor.

Signor Tebáldo, for this was the surgeon's name, returned according to his engagement.

"We have been guilty of a great omission," said he, as soon as he was alone with Varàno. "Signor di Rosalvo, though he pos-sesses many estimable qualities, has some strange peculiarities, which have strongly tinctured his character: he will not consent to see you till he shall be informed of your quality and name—and these, you know, were enquiries I was not able to answer."

"He has undoubtedly a right to claim this proof of our con-fidence," said Varàno smiling, "before he admits us beneath his roof."

He then, although more averse than before from obtruding himself upon the notice of this singular stranger, wrote a note, in which he included all the information he conceived necessary respecting himself and his party, and committed it to Tebáldo.

The surgeon was not long absent.

"I have succeeded admirably," said he, to Varàno. "The Signor politely consents to receive you; and the Signora will be here immediately, to pay her respects to the lady, and to conduct you and your friends to the castle."

Varàno had no sooner acquainted De Sevignac with this arrangement, and gained, not without some difficulty, his consent to comply with it, when a carriage drew up, and a very beautiful woman, apparently about five-and-twenty, and whose manners were as elegant as her person was lovely, entered the *auberge*, and was shewn into the apartment of Cecilia.

Cecilia, who had never seen a face and form so immediately prepossessing, discovered, both in her looks and words, the high sense she entertained of the Signora's hospitality, and flew to apprize De Sevignac of her arrival, who was delighted with the charming, though not too flattering portrait which Cecilia had given of her.——In about an hour, they left the *auberge*, and proceeding slowly along, soon came within view of the castle.

The Castello di Montani, so called from its situation among mountains, was a large irregular pile of building, situated on an eminence in the vicinity of the sea.—It was built with Gothic grandeur; and its lofty towers still frowned in proud sublimity. The rock on which it stood, was surrounded by a moat, broad, and once deep, but now only half full of water, which was scarcely to be discerned from the number of aquatic plants that, spreading their vigorous leaves to the soil below, formed a refuge for various species of water-fowl, which had long lived there unmolested. Over this was a bridge with massive chains, now drawn up, and which led to the principal entrance of the castle. The building was constructed with great strength, and ornamented on every side with embattled parapets. A large gate-way, flanked with square towers, and crested with overhanging turrets, led to the grounds, which were encompassed, except a narrow opening to the sea, with high and ponderous walls. The turrets supporting the gateway, which was formed in the heavy Saxon-Gothic style, were strengthened with buttresses, and united by curtains, pierced and embattled.—From these the ramparts formed an extensive outline, as they communicated with other towers, overlooking a terrace, commanding on one side a view of the sea, and on the other a vast irregular prospect, terminated by the Alps; the forest, which they had so lately passed, with its dark thickets and deep shades, composed the foreground.

They crossed the court toward a hall, rudely magnificent. The roof, constructed of a singular kind of fretwork, was supported by pillars of marble, and crowded on every side with ensigns of chivalry. The high and narrow windows were decorated with figures, and devices in *arabesco*, and represented in a profusion of stained glass the illustrious achievements of some ancient House, blended with the heads of saints and martyrs.

The Signora conducting them to a staircase, which ascended beneath an immense arch to a spacious vaulted gallery, on one side of which was a long range of apartments, ushered them into a room, where sat Signor di Rosalvo.

"I have executed my commission," said the Signora, "and I am sure to your satisfaction."

The Signor bowed, and, after some polite enquiries, desired Varàno, whom he more particularly addressed, would consider his castle as his home, and not think of removing from it till his friend should have recovered from his late accident. This reception was such as the hints dropped by the surgeon had authorized them to expect. Traits of melancholy and eccentricity were perceptible even on a first acquaintance, and of these Rosalvo himself seemed painfully conscious; for, in spite of all his efforts to conceal it, a dejection, which appeared to be the effect of some deeply rooted sorrow, stole to his brow, and gave to it an expression of the deepest sadness. In conversation he was often visibly abstracted from the subject of discourse; and, when not immediately engaged in the duties of his family, it was his custom to ramble, unattended, for miles through the most unfrequented parts of the country. From these excursions his return was as uncertain as the cause was inexplicable. His wife he loved with an affection bordering upon enthusiasm; but, though his marriage had been attended with every possible advantage, she had dated his dejection from that memorable period.

Signor di Rosalvo could not be many years above twenty; yet was all the bloom of youth and health vanished from a countenance which, when possessed of them, must have been eminently distinguished for manly beauty. His large dark eyes, though they had contracted a languor, were yet full of expression, and when lighted up by momentary emotion, appeared brilliant. His stature was tall; and his figure, noble, graceful, and commanding, claimed that sentiment of respect which rank so often vainly flatters itself with inspiring.

Every attention which the most active benevolence could suggest, was bestowed upon De Sevignac, who was yet too much indisposed to continue long in the party. In the evening he was visited by the surgeon, in whose presence Varàno mentioned, for the first time, the conversation which he had overheard in the house inhabited by the supposed hunters, and the bloody testimony of their guilt he had there seen.

All were much shocked at this account; but Signor di Rosalvo,

on the mention of the warm and yet bleeding body of the murdered traveller, suddenly left the room, pale, and almost sinking
with emotion.

The second day passed on at the castle nearly in the same
manner as the preceding one. De Sevignac spent the morning
in his apartment, but joined the family at dinner. In the evening,
Signora di Rosalvo and Cecilia, attended by Varàno, took a walk
into the gardens: the former appeared charmed by her new
acquaintance. A gloomy castle, in which she seldom saw any one
but her own domestics, was ill suited to a disposition naturally
lively. Nobly born, and with a fortune more than adequate to her
birth, she had been accustomed to all the gaieties and all the ele-
gances of life; but, amid all the reverses of her lot, her heart was
bound to Rosalvo by an indissoluble bond: and not his resolute
adherence to his plan of retirement—not all his dejection—nor
yet his cruel resolution of not admitting her to any share of his
confidence, could loosen the hold of her affections;—his will was
the guide of her life—his tenderness the reward of her obedience. A female friend, like Cecilia, she had long wished for; and
oppressed by a load of anxieties, occasioned by the mysterious
conduct of her husband, she longed to pour them into the bosom
of her amiable and already beloved young friend: but the native
delicacy of her sentiments forbade such a disclosure, till it should
have received the sanction of a nearer intimacy.

The gentle attentions of the Signora were highly grateful
to Cecilia. She had desired her to write to her on her arrival at
Genoa; and had gained a promise from De Sevignac, that he
would renew his visit at the castle on his return from Italy.

Near a week had elapsed when the surgeon at length informed
De Sevignac that, as nothing further was to be apprehended from
his late disaster, he was now at full liberty to resume his journey.
A day was accordingly fixed; and the appoin

CHAPTER VIII

The mind not taught to think, no useful store
To fix reflection, dreads the vacant hour;
Turn'd on itself, its numerous wants are seen,
And all the mighty void that lies within.

MELMOTH.

THEY travelled leisurely toward Finale, and arrived the next day at Savona. When they had reached this port, De Sevignac dismissed the *vetturino*, and hired a *felucca*, to convey them to Genoa. They embarked, and Cecilia, for the first time, saw herself surrounded by the ocean. The day was serene, and the sun, yet scarcely in its zenith, threw a soft and silvery gleam upon the waters, tinting the rocks and far receding shores with a partial splendour; whilst many a tall vessel was seen gliding over the deep, their light sails scarcely curled by the breeze, as they floated away in the distance: and the sky, unobscured by the lightest cloud, exhibited that bright ethereal blue, peculiar to this genial and enchanting climate.

As the rays of the sun declined, its effects upon the waves and the shores became more and more interesting:—long lines of radiance coloured the rocks, and threw transient beams of light on the remoter perspective, leaving the shades and gloomy caverns of the nearer shores in obscurity.

De Sevignac grew better during the voyage;—his spirits revived, and he supported a conversation with Varàno on the political state of Genoa, its manners, customs, and other general subjects of discourse, till their attention was engrossed by the rapid succession of noble and magnificent objects which now opened to the sight. The stately city of Genoa, seated proudly on the margin of its gulph, which was filled with ships, and resounding with voices—its semicircular port—its splendid palaces, with gardens on the roof of each, all seen under the mild and enchanting influence of a delicious evening, afforded one of the most singular and delightful views they had ever beheld.

Having reached the shore, and disembarked, they proceeded on foot to the *Palazzo di Boraccio*. This was a modern and very magnificent structure, situated within view of the Bay, and which formed the centre of a grand sweep of palaces, belonging to the Nobles and principal people in the city. It was not supported by pillars; but painted in the Genoese manner, with the representation of columns of different orders:—the interior was furnished in a style of great magnificence.

Their arrival announced, the Lady Viola left her terrace to receive them. She embraced De Sevignac with much apparent affection, and then turning to Varàno, said—

"You are come most fortunately. Our cousin, the Lady Olivia di Montelina, is just arrived. You have not seen her of an age, and she is all impatience to be introduced to you."

"Allow me first to introduce another visitor," said Varàno, colouring, and presenting Cecilia.

"My aunt's *protegée,* I suppose," resumed the Signora, who till this moment had not seemed to notice her.

Cecilia curtsied; and Signora Viola leading the way, they followed her into a room where was Lady Olivia.

"I am bringing you a guest you little expect," cried the Signora, and immediately she ushered in Varàno.

De Sevignac took a seat, and then enquired for the Signor.

"He is at the villa, I believe," said the Lady Viola; "but he is much too fashionable to apprize me of his movements."

"And you, I suppose, are *much too fashionable* not to return the compliment," cried Olivia, with great archness.—"But where have you been burying yourself all this time?" added she, to Varàno; "my father has been expecting you at Naples: he says you are quite a runaway. How long is it since you left Italy?"

"Near two months," rejoined Varàno; "and my next route will be into Tuscany."

"Not immediately, I suppose," said the Lady Viola; "your engagements at home cannot be very urgent."

She then drew nearer to De Sevignac, with whom she conversed, taking little or no notice of Cecilia.

Varàno, when he wrote to his sister from St. Foix, knew not, nor was it indeed determined, that Cecilia was to be of the party; and as his next letter, written from the post-house on the borders of the forest, consisted only of a few hasty lines, simply relating the accident, and the delay it must occasion, she was consequently unprepared to expect her. That a child had been taken by Madame de Villeneuve, her aunt, from motives of charity as it was supposed, and that this child, now grown up, was still retained in the chateau, were circumstances with which she was before fully acquainted. But though the Lady Viola had always allowed that her uncle was, in some of his notions at least, strangely eccentric, she never imagined that he would place a little orphan girl, whom nobody knew, and about whom nobody cared, above the rank of a servant. The introduction of Cecilia, therefore, though she concealed her chagrin, was not more mortifying than displeasing to her; nor could the sweet ingenuous modesty of her manner deprecate her vexation.

Signor Boraccio did not join them till supper-time. He entered in high spirits, and expressed the greatest satisfaction on seeing his guests, particularly De Sevignac, whom he addressed with all that studied, though fascinating, politeness which marks the man of the world.—On beholding Cecilia he betrayed some surprise; and when informed by the Lady Viola, in a whisper, loud enough to be heard by the whole company present, who she was, he surveyed her with looks of mingled curiosity and admiration.

The collation withdrawn, Olivia, who had been engaged since the party arrived in discourse with Varàno, entered into conversation with Cecilia. She spoke to her with the greatest affability, and seemed desirous to atone, in her behaviour, for the coldness and neglect so perceptible in the Lady Viola's, who appeared to regard Cecilia as an indigent dependant, who had no right to expect from her even common attention.

The Signor Olivia was the daughter of the Conte di Montelina, a Neapolitan Nobleman, who had married a sister of the Marchese di Varàno. As she was an only child, and heiress to a very considerable property, it had long been the intention of the Marchese and the Conte to unite the possessions of the two families by a marriage between her and Varàno. Having been educated in a Convent, she had never but once seen Varàno; and that once, though she was not destitute of attractions, had not prejudiced him materially in her favour. Till that æra they had indeed been designedly kept asunder; the Marchese and the Conte having previously agreed that, if they met while children, their affection might be of too fraternal a kind to allow of a nearer connection. This meeting, eagerly as it had been anticipated, did not prove, however, in the sequel, quite so fortunate as was expected. The Lady Olivia, indeed, when speaking of her cousin, observed that he was handsome, and very highly accomplished; but Varàno, being either not very susceptibly inclined, or having suffered himself to underrate those perfections which an heiress, whatever may be her charms, is universally adorned, either never thought of her again, or, if he did, it was with an indifference scarcely amounting to an enquiry. With the views of his family, respecting this alliance, he was yet ignorant, or he would probably have taken some pains to destroy hopes which he could never intend should be realized. Frank and ingenuous himself, he suspected not artifice in others; and least of all could he suppose that the Marchese, whose affection for him had displayed itself in so many instances, would employ any thing like stratagem in the accomplishment of an affair, in which examination and prudence appeared to be the only requisites.

He had marked the behaviour to his sister with a sensible uneasiness, and, apprehensive of its consequences, procured a conference with her in the morning, the result of which was a promise that she would be more circumspect in her future conduct with regard to Cecilia. But though the Lady Viola had yielded to the entreaties of her brother, so far as to endeavour at least to disguise the illiberality of her sentiments from the observation of De Sevignac, whose favour it was necessary to acquire, there was an air of imagined condescension mingled with her courtesy when she noticed Cecilia, which could not be misunderstood, and of which, but for the delicate attentions of Varàno and the vivacity of Olivia, who was soon her almost constant companion, she would have been painfully conscious.

The mornings were usually employed by the ladies on a terrace, which extending from one wing of the building to another, displayed at its feet a luxuriant garden, rich in a diversity of the most gay and enchanting objects; and where the innovations of

Art were so successfully concealed, that they seemed to be called in only to assist the wild and simple graces of Nature. An awning of pale green silk shaded the terrace from the sun, beneath which the orange and the citron were seen blending their sweets with those of a thousand odoriferous shrubs, which, descending in beautiful gradation to the turf below, "gave an almost overwhelming fragrance to the gale that shook them."

The view from this terrace, which presented, on one side, the sea stretching into an ample bay—and on the other, the abrupt peaks of the distant Apennine, was so enchantingly beautiful, that Cecilia and Olivia often sat engaged in working or reading, after the Signora had retired, or in listening to Varàno, who would frequently play or sing to them some of those sweet expressive airs which he had so often performed at Le Luc.

Whilst the Lady Viola and her guests were thus engaged at the palace, De Sevignac, accompanied by Boraccio, and sometimes Varàno, amused himself with viewing the city; contemplating, occasionally, those wonderful works of art which exist in the Palaces of D'Oria, Balbi, and Durazzo.

In that part of the grounds which sloped toward the sea, and which was separated from the rest by a plantation of evergreens, was a room fitted up with great taste, and furnished with sofas, where the ladies usually retired, and sought there, under the canopy of waving trees, the most agreeable means of enjoying the *siesta*. Opposite to this building was a spacious platform, called the *Piazza di Pallone*[1], where the Signor, when surrounded by his friends, generally resorted in the evenings. At the game Boraccio, though he was but an indifferent player, often betted high; and it was to his success, or want of it, that his family was indebted for his good or bad conduct on the succeeding day.

After this diversion, which was either taken here, or in a square appropriated to the purpose within the walls of the city, it was the custom to take a walk to the *Piazza D'Aque Vende*, the fashion-

---

[1] The place where they throw the *pallone,* or great ball.—This game requires space, and is usually attended by a vast number of spectators.—The right arms of the combatants are guarded with a thick bracelet, set with points.

able promenade, or a drive to the *Viletta*[1], which was about half a league distant from the palace.—In these excursions they were attended by Signor Gerolamo Zuccato, a young Genoese, who was treated, and considered by all, as one of the family.

The Signor, who had been selected by Boraccio, on his marriage, to perform the important office of *cicisbeo* to the Lady Viola, his wife, was the son of a Noble of Genoa, whose revenue was so inadequate to his rank, as to oblige him to dedicate almost the whole of his time to the merchandise of wine. As his family, which consisted of four sons and two daughters, could not be otherwise provided for, consistent with their rank, the former supplied the office of *Cavaliero Servente* to the more opulent great, whilst the latter were left to lament the loss of all that was dear to them—their liberty; and to lament the occasion of it, at their leisure, in the solitude of a cloister.—To this honourable place, which he had filled for some years with credit to himself and his employer, Signor Gerolamo was indebted not only for the ease and tranquillity of his present life, but for that cessation from anxiety which must inevitably have pursued him concerning his future prospects.

His business was to assist the Lady Viola at her toilet; to await her orders when she wished him to accompany her to Church or to the Opera; to attend her to the Theatres; to sort her cards, present her sweetmeats, praise her person, if in danger of being eclipsed by some superior beauty; and to advertise the Signor if he saw, or imagined he saw, any thing in her attentions to others which might be construed into design, or was likely to lead to an assignation. In the latter case he had indeed but little room for the exercise of his abilities; for the Signora, though she had some faults, had, nevertheless, too strict a veneration for the state into which she had entered, to be wholly unmindful of its duties; but it was necessary sometimes to give hints, and relate little *rencontres* to the husband, when it could be done with discretion, as a proof that he was not unmindful of his trust. He had, however, art enough to conduct himself to the satisfaction of both; and, as he had no pursuit or employment to occupy his time, it

1 A small villa.

was consequently devoted to *friendship*.—When the family was alone, which was generally the case on the fore part of the day, as they seldom received or gave entertainments till the evening, he always breakfasted with the Signora, and dined with the Signor[1]. In evening, if their pursuits were so different as to not allow of his attending both, he was the constant companion of the lady. He was entrusted with all her affairs; and nothing was undertaken without his advice and concurrence. Every little vexation or disgust, which a sense of shame would have impelled her to conceal from others, was made known to him.—The pique her pride had sustained, in being obliged to wear an outward shew of respect to Cecilia, was a copious subject for complaint: she expressed her surprise to him that De Sevignac should think of introducing a person of her description into circles, from which the meanness of her birth ought to have excluded her; and she was still more astonished, she added, that her brother should participate in a proceeding, which a due regard for his family would have directed him to discountenance.

In person the Signora resembled her mother, but in disposition she was the counterpart of her father. Rank and merit were, in her estimation, as in his, inseparably connected. Her passions were strong, as her intellectual powers were weak; and, under a studied polish of manners, she united all the mean qualities of a little, and even of a vulgar mind. Warped by prejudice, and enslaved by custom, she never thought or acted but as directed by others; and though she would have shrunk with abhorrence from the commission of decided wrong, if she knew it to be such, it was easy for even a novice in sophism to deceive her.—Occupied in an almost continual succession of splendid and expensive pleasures, she had little leisure for reflection; and if she paused for a time from the giddy scenes of her amusement, the natural fretfulness of her disposition soon hurried her back to dissipation.

Boraccio, whose understanding was somewhat superior to that of his wife, yet applied himself to pursuits equally frivolous. He loved expence and shew with the fondness of a girl. Born and educated at Naples, he had acquired a taste for the manners

---

1 It is customary in Italy for the husband to dine alone with the *cicisbeo*.

and customs of that luxurious city; and during the period of his youth, and indeed before he had reached his twentieth year, had dissipated the greater part of his property in the most lavish indulgences, which he had soon no means of continuing. The death of an uncle, however, who died about this æra, relieved him from his embarrassments. He accordingly left Naples, and, having discharged the numerous debts which he had contracted in that kingdom, removed to Genoa; and as a Noble of the city, in right of his uncle (a member of the Council of this Republic) took possession, under the name of Boraccio, and the appellation of *Patrizio Genoese*, of the property and estates of his deceased relative. Here, had he followed the steps of his benefactor, and the example of many others in the State, in the economy of his household, and the disposition of his time, he might have possessed a revenue nearly equal to any in the Republic. But the natural indolence of his character (for the Signor possessed in an eminent degree all that indecision and imbecility classically attributed to those of his country) confirmed him in a state of continual embarrassment.

The palace formerly inhabited by his relation in the *Strada Balbi*, was exchanged for the more modern one he now occupied; and the furniture and decorations displaced for others, which had been purchased at an expence considerably above the produce of his annual income. Confined to gratifications like these, the Signor might, however, have been secured from any material inconvenience; but he had others, if they may be so styled, more pernicious than even these, the most unfortunate of which was an invincible passion for gaming—a mania which want of success, for he was seldom, if ever, fortunate, only tended to increase. He played, lost, became more desperate, ventured, and lost again; till his estates, so far from there being any likelihood of their descending unencumbered, as he had received them, to his next successor, were now mortgaged for above half their value. This known, his credit was declining fast; yet, though assured of this, and equally so that the Signora, whom he continued to delude with imaginary successes, was a stranger to the danger which impended over him, he had not the resolution to apprize her of it, or, though perpetually harassed by the representations of his agents, and the importunities of his creditors, to adopt himself a system of economical retrenchment. What had formerly supplied subject for unquiet reflection—the want of an heir to perpetuate his name and *virtues* to futurity, was no longer productive of uneasiness.—The estates, which he was now ruining fast, were to devolve, on his death, to a collateral branch of the family from which he had received them; a family with which he had little or no connection, and for whose happiness and welfare he was entirely unconcerned.—Thus undisturbed by apprehensions of what might be the fate of those who had the misfortune to succeed him, his mind was now wholly engrossed in suggesting plans for the present; and if a sense of the injustice he had been guilty of, did obtrude upon his thoughts, he strove to banish the recollection of it by a repetition of the very conduct which had induced him to practise it.

M. de Sevignac had known his character by report before he reached Italy; and that his niece, whom he loved, not so much for her own sake, as because she was the child, and the only one, of a beloved sister, should be so unhappily married, was not the least of his distresses.

In regard to Cecilia, as a dependant, who could have no reasonable pretensions to distinction or respect, Boraccio would have thought of her only as a very beautiful girl, whom he could not but admire, had not the paternal tenderness which marked the countenance of De Sevignac when he spoke to, or talked of her, suggested other ideas. As this became every day more apparent, he felt a strange fear lest she should be able to supplant his wife in the affections of her uncle; and, as the narrow and suspicious mind is ever fertile at invention, he imagined she had employed some arts for the accomplishment of this end.

Had Boraccio sufficiently studied Nature, his eye, however prejudiced, would have found as little in the charming countenance of Cecilia, as in the pure mind that informed it, to have justified the surmise; but as he seldom took the trouble to seek for truth when it required the labour of investigation, he was consequently compelled to substitute in its stead what was often infinitely more convenient to him—*supposition*.

Signor di Boraccio, as has already been observed, was solicitous only for the present; but as there are times when every man, whatever firmness he may possess, deviates, in some slight degree at least, from the general tenor of his conduct, he stepped from the line he had marked out, and began to consider in what manner he should act, in order to prevent the threatened evil.

M. de Sevignac's fortune was not ample, but it was considerable enough to be useful; and as it would be easy to enlarge it by his own report, it would at least assist credit. To ensure it therefore, if possible, to himself, was now his object; but as he saw that if he treated Cecilia with indignity or neglect during her continuance at his palace, it would be the means of precipitating the very measure he dreaded, he resolved to conduct himself toward her with respect, and even kindness for the present, and to trust to time and circumstances for the regulation of his future plans.

CHAPTER IX

As Thracian winds the Euxine sea molest
So wrath, and envy, from a human breast
Drive Halcyon peace, and banish kindly rest.

JACOBS.

THE Signora, whose wishes were always centered where gaiety and dissipation had convened a crowd, and who had suspended her amusements only out of compliment to De Sevignac (hitherto too much indisposed to mingle in the festivities of the place), now returned to her accustomed occupations with increasing avidity. Plays, Operas, and *Conversazioni*, divided the evenings spent from home, whilst those passed at the palace were devoted to the most gay and splendid amusements. But, alas! to the Lady Viola these once charming diversions were no longer, as before, sources of unmixed pleasure. She was no longer the idol of universal adoration. She saw, with envy and vexation, those fiends which destroy the repose of beauty—Cecilia, the humble, the despised Cecilia, as an object of general admiration; and it was not till she had convinced the wonderstruck admirers that the poor thing was a mere nobody—a plebeian, patronized by her uncle, and brought thither, as she supposed, on a vague prospect of advancement, that the gaze of curiosity was withdrawn from the interesting unknown, and fixed upon the less lovely, though not less animated form of the Neapolitan heiress.

Varàno, in the meantime, began to experience, in his turn, some of that peculiar species of distress which lovers only understand. That enchanting frankness—that sweet irresistible ingenuousness which had marked the countenance of Cecilia, when, listening to his discourse, she had rambled with him, unseen and unheard, amid the mountain solitudes of Le Luc, was no longer perceptible: she was guarded—she was reserved; and though he had attempted to draw her from the party, that he might converse with her alone, she had always cautiously withheld from him the opportunity he sought. Her motive for this conduct was wholly incomprehensible; and every day gave him more and more cause to apprehend that either he never had been regarded by her with any considerable degree of preference; or that by some fault, some inadvertency of his own, he had forfeited that partiality he once hoped he had inspired. The idea that he was no longer, or perhaps never had been dear to her, was insupportable. In vain he sought, by analyzing her words, her manner, to avail himself of her reason for a change so unaccountable and so perplexing to him.

Alas! he knew not at the very moment when he was lamenting his own imaginary want of success, Cecilia was struggling to conquer a tenderness which no arguments, no efforts could teach her to subdue.—Ah! little did he think, that while she clothed her charming brow in the smiles of a forced animation, her mind was secretly a prey to the most uneasy conflicts.

Hitherto Varàno had experienced only those rapturous, and oftentimes delusive sensations of delight, which await on an infant passion. Wrapped in visions of ideal bliss and present enjoyment, his busy thoughts strayed not to the future; or, if they did, it was to anticipate scenes of more refined and more permanent felicity than he had yet found. Sanguine, romantic, and impetuous, he had yet seen life but through the medium of the imagination; nor was he yet conscious how soon the vivid colouring in which Fancy decks the gay, unreal scene, must be effaced, or receive a melancholy contrast from the tame and sad realities to be encountered in the world.—But the time was approaching fast when these visions of self-created bliss were to vanish from his sight; and the certainty that happiness is not to be unalloyed with the bitter ingredient, pain, was to fasten upon his mind with all the force of conviction.

Cecilia, beautiful as when he first saw her, was now lifted to a sphere where her beauty would attract to her a crowd of admirers. To leave her thus, was to expose himself to the hazard of losing her for ever. But how to retract his promise of accompanying De Sevignac to Florence, was a circumstance equally distressing and perplexing; and an incident, which occurred about a week after their arrival, made him more averse than before from quitting Genoa whilst Cecilia was there.

The favourite Opera of Virginia had drawn the Lady Viola and her party one night to the Theatre. The piece was to be attended with every possible advantage. Signora di Palizo, a celebrated Venetian actress, was to take the part of Virginia; and a famous Sicilian dancer, newly imported from Palermo, to shew her skill in the ballet.—As the talents of these performers, which had been pompously announced to an admiring public, had entitled them to a considerable share of celebrity, a crowded and a very brilliant audience was of course expected.

To avoid the inconvenience incident to such occasions, the Signora and her friends repaired early to the Theatre. The house, as is usual at an Italian Opera, was lighted up, when they entered, with peculiar splendour. The *jalousies* were already let down; and the boxes, though the Opera had not yet commenced, filled with spectators; some of whom had resorted thither for the fashionable purpose of receiving and paying visits in their boxes, where cards form the principal amusement; others to witness the representation of an event preceding an important æra in the annals of Rome; whose despotism, destroyed by its own daring machinations, fell beneath the avenging sword of justice, and Rome, long bowed beneath the oppressive hand of arbitrary sway, rose from the power of a second Tarquin with the smile of freedom!

The characters of the Drama were supported with spirit; and the famous song of

Idol mio, quest alma amante
Sempre fido a te sara,

warbled in accents of such heavenly sweetness, as to draw from
the whole party an exclamation of surprise and rapture.

The first act concluded, the ballet, which seemed to be the
most approved part of the performance, and which commanded
what the action of the drama, and the voice of the singer were
unable to obtain—the united applause of the audience, at length
commenced. It was performed with a grace and sprightliness of
motion which was truly enchanting. *"Bravo & bravissimo!"* was
re-echoed at every step.—The dancers retreated, overwhelmed
with applause; and the Drama, which had been suspended by the
ballet, was again returned.

The second act concluded, Olivia, who had been engaged
for the greater part of the evening in receiving and paying visits
with the Lady Viola in the adjoining boxes, returned; and seating herself by Cecilia, she conversed with great sprightliness and
vivacity: then turning to Varàno, who was seated behind her, she
said—

"I have just been accusing your friend here," meaning Cecilia,
"of having lost at least one of her senses.—Her eyes are very dangerous to others, without being of any signal use to herself; since
she is unable to see across the Theatre a person who appears to
have seen nothing but her the whole evening:—had it been you, I
should not have wondered."

"Why me, Lady?" said Varàno, somewhat confused.

"The old adage you know—Florentini ciechi[1]."

Varàno smiled; and looking as she directed, his eyes encountered a person whom he recollected to have seen before, and
whom he at length knew for the identical stranger he had met
with in France, when he was escorting Cecilia and Louisette
to the cottage of Le Luc. He seemed to recognise Varàno in
the same moment; for he bowed, and then resuming his seat,
remained as before, his whole attention apparently engrossed by
Cecilia's party, in that sort of reverie which seems to absorb every

1 Blind Florentines.

faculty of the soul, and renders it invulnerable to the impression of the senses.—He was habited according to the custom of the place, in black; and his sable dress and reclining posture gave to his naturally fine figure an expression of great interest.

Varàno, turning to a young Signor who stood near, enquired if he was known to him. The Signor replied that he was a stranger of consequence; but of his family, or name, he could learn nothing.

Piqued by Olivia's remark and his own observations, Varàno felt chagrined and uneasy; but perceiving that his lively cousin was amusing herself at his expence, and suspecting, what was in fact true, that she had penetrated his secret, he strove to conceal, under an appearance of fictitious gaiety, those sensations of mortified tenderness which, though conscious of feeling keenly, he was yet unable to suppress.

The Lady Viola now entered her own box, from whence, with the majority of the party, she had been absent nearly the whole of the evening; and observing that the remaining part of the Opera would be insupportably tedious, proposed that they should make a table at cards. Boraccio was already engaged in this his favourite pursuit; and as De Sevignac, from a dislike of all kinds of gaming, and Cecilia from an incapacity of joining them, had each declined playing, there was some difficulty in completing the party.

"I must positively enlist some one," said Signor Zuccato, as he advanced with an unmeaning smile toward Olivia; "Mademoiselle St. Bertrand is cruel; but you, Lady—you positively must play."

"Not on compulsion, Signor," returned Olivia; "that *must* is so harsh, I would not admit it into my vocabulary for the whole world."

"Ladies are apt to be a little too nice about terms, Signor," interposed Varàno; "you must improve in your language, or——"

"And pray, cousin, who bade you speak?"

"Oh! I don't wait for bidding;—I am like the Lady Olivia, I speak much, and think little."

"*Mia padrona!*" rejoined Signor Zuccato, "you cannot, I am sure, be obdurate."

"I am not apt to be so, I confess," cried Olivia, disgusted by the ridiculous affectation which had accompanied his entreaties; "but in the present case——when one is not too wakeful, one is in no want of an opiate."

"An opiate, Lady!"

"Yes, an opiate, Signor.—Cards, very unluckily for *me*, have always this effect on me. My spirits too are somewhat weak to-night—I am subject, you know, to fits of *ennui*; and, should I be so unfortunate as to fall asleep, or relapse into one of my customary fits of melancholy in the very height of the contest, I am not sure that I could find a partner who would be inclined to bear with me."

The Lady Viola, seated at the upper end of the box, did not overhear the dispute which had engaged her friend and Olivia; but vexed that he had been detained by her, she sent a message by an attendant to summon him to the card-table; where she already presided, eagerly impatient for the commencement of the game, for which, however, the indispensable number was not yet provided. Finding Olivia determined not to play, Varàno offered himself in her stead. The party at length sat down; and Olivia, seating herself between Cecilia and De Sevignac, amused herself with alternately conversing with them, and in watching the progress of the game.

A silence, very unusual in such circles, had prevailed for some time, which was interrupted by Olivia, who, in a voice loud enough to be heard distinctly in the nearer range of boxes, called out—

"A very fortunate idea has just occurred to me—pray, my dear Cecilia, can you play at *moro*?"

The suddenness and oddity of the question excited an universal laugh. Cecilia answered in the negative.

"Strange—very strange!" continued Olivia. "Was you never at Naples?—Did you never visit St. Lucia—the Ponte della Madalina —or the Gran Piazza of the Olivetani¹?"

"No;—Genoa is the extent of my travels."

"Oh, I recollect you once told me so;—how unfortunate! for,

1 Places where the Lazaroni chiefly meet to play the simple game of *moro:* particularly the great square of the Olivetans, where they frequently assemble early in the morning, and present a hideous spectacle.

since we have no one to speak to, or to notice us, it would be a very charming amusement."

These words roused De Sevignac, who had been pursuing a train of thought infinitely more interesting than pleasing to him, and who now recalling his spirits, and apologizing for his abstraction, conducted himself so much to the satisfaction of Olivia throughout the remainder of the evening, that she proposed him as a model for imitation both to Signor Zuccato and Varàno, with whose gallantry she expressed herself greatly dissatisfied.

Signor Boraccio, who, by means of a gallery communicating with the pit and lower boxes, had been visiting his acquaintance in different parts of the house, now returned; and the company engaged at the card-table having waited to finish their game till the greater part of the audience had retired, now arose to depart.

Boraccio took Olivia's hand, and was leading her from the box, when he was accosted by a friend, who, pressing through the crowd, begged to introduce to him a guest of his, newly arrived at Genoa.

"Count Morsino," proceeded he, "has testified a desire to be known to you and your family;—I am happy to procure him so refined a pleasure."

The Count bowed; and Varàno looking up, beheld, with infinite vexation, the person whose sudden appearance at the Theatre had so much disconcerted him. Boraccio replied with his accustomed politeness, and was passing on, when Signor Gavino, hastily recalling him, said—

"Where shall you be to-morrow?—Have you any engagement?—If not, we shall have a party at the Gran Cervo[1]—will you join us?"

"I have no engagement, Signor," returned Boraccio, "at least none that I recollect. At what hour do you propose to meet?"

"At eight," resumed the Signor.

"I will not forget my appointment," said Boraccio.

The Count and his friend now took their leave, and retired; and the carriages being in waiting, the ladies, accompanied as before, returned to the palace.

1 The Great Stag.—The principal Hotel at Genoa.

The sweet manners of Cecilia soon penetrated the heart of Olivia, whose partiality for her amiable young friend daily increased. She took every opportunity of praising her in her absence, particularly to the Lady Viola, whose narrow mind and perverted judgment did not allow of a candid decision in her favour. The Signora, little expecting that Olivia would espouse the cause of so insignificant a being as Cecilia, was disconcerted and displeased; and she, one morning, conversed with some severity with her on this subject, in the presence of Signor Zuccato, with whom it had been frequently discussed; inveighing, with great bitterness, against the ridiculous practice of introducing people, born to herd with the *canaille*, into circles of fashion; and concluding with calling her a little indigent adventurer, who had intruded herself into her family and her palace, without any previous invitation, and who had been flattered into such an insufferable opinion of her own importance, that it was not possible to bear with her.

"Madame de Villeneuve's motive for admitting her into her family," continued the Signora, "was certainly a good one; and, had she detained her in it as a domestic, nobody could have had any possible objection; but to educate her as she has done, nothing surely could have been more absurd; and I wonder my uncle, who is certainly a very sensible man, should not see the impropriety of such a measure.—It is quite intolerable to see a girl of that kind giving herself such ridiculous airs!"

"Airs!" interrupted Olivia, with astonishment, "pray what kind of airs?—I protest I never saw any."

"Why the airs of a beauty," cried the Lady Viola, affectedly; "though I confess I am totally at a loss to conceive on what she grounds her pretensions."

"On more beauty and more sweetness than that niggard, Nature, has bestowed on half our sex put together," returned Olivia. "I do not know her equal; and were I a man——But 'tis better that it is otherwise, lest I should have more rivals than I could have the courage to attack in single combat."

"She has had art enough to ingratiate herself with you, it seems," said the Signora; "but as to the girl's person or manners, I protest I see nothing at all in either: she is too tall—too florid;

and then she is so reserved, that, were I not told so much of her *fine sense*, I should be apt to reduce her to the level of her real situation, by mistaking her for a rustic.—But what say you, Signor?" continued the Lady Viola; "is she so very handsome—so very charming as Olivia insinuates? For my part, I see nothing at all so extraordinary."

"*Dio mi guardi!* nor I neither," exclaimed Signor Zuccato;

> "But who, when gazing on the sky,
> Where constellations gleam afar,
> 'Mid such a blaze, would turn his eye
> To pause upon a single star?"

"An admirable and *well-studied* impromptu!" rejoined Olivia, laughing; "pray, Signor, when did you imagine that?—So fine a sentiment, so very elegantly expressed, must have cost you some head-achs;—how long is it since you assumed the character of an *improvisatore?*"

"Beauty is of such an inspiring quality," resumed he, languidly, "that it warms and animates even the most insensible!"

"I can most readily believe it," cried Olivia, "since it has warmed and animated *you*:—you have an exquisite knack at yawning, Signor;—and your conversation and manners are of so composing a quality, that I am in danger, every moment I remain with you, of catching the infection!—But to our subject: what should you think, my dear Viola," continued she, "if Varàno was to fall in love with Cecilia—this little *indigent adventurer*, of whom you have been speaking with so much respect?"

"Think!" reiterated the Signora, "good Heavens, Olivia! how can you hazard so ridiculous a proposition?"

"Only for the sake of an argument," replied Olivia; "but I say if such a thing was to happen, which is far from impossible, you know——"

"If you will have the goodness to confine yourself to probabilities instead of possibilities, Lady Olivia," interrupted the Signora, indignantly, "I may be disposed to answer you."

"Dear! what can be more probable," cried Olivia, "than that a fine young man, like my cousin, tenderly attached to our sex, full of sentiment, and highly susceptible, should be charmed with a very lovely young woman—a single glance from whose dark blue eyes would warm the heart of an Anchorite?——You don't imagine that people examine each other's pedigrees before they fall in love!"

"You speak of it as a thing you should much approve," said the Lady Viola.

"Why I confess I should have no very great objection."

"No objection!" repeated the Signora.

"None in the least;—on the contrary, I should most sincerely rejoice to find that Varàno had just spirit enough to cheat his father, and a few other members of his family, out of their unreasonable prejudices."

"And to accomplish this, you would have him marry a low-born thing—taken from charity, and retained by caprice, in a station which she has no right to fill.—Fortunately, however, Varàno has too much spirit, and too just a sense of propriety, to allow his reason to be seduced by the blandishments of an obscure and, I fear, a very insidious girl!"

"How far his sense of *propriety* may operate," returned Olivia, "I am not competent to determine—that is, if he conceives he is acting inconsistently.—But this, my dear Viola, is a mere matter of opinion, and when opposed to a violent inclination, is seldom a very powerful combatant;—and if Varàno does not love Cecilia —aye, and passionately too—I have been studying his countenance to very little purpose."

"Varàno love Cecilia!" cried the Signora; "Heavens! Olivia, are you mad?"

"No; never more perfectly in my senses. And, to declare my real sentiments, I think he has shewn more genuine taste, and more true discernment in this instance, than in any other in his whole life."

"I have too much confidence in his taste, his discernment, and the natural dignity of his character," said the Signora, haughtily, "to fear any thing of the kind; and you will much oblige me, Lady Olivia, by not imparting your suspicions to me—suspicions which could have no other existence than in your own creative imagination——"

She was proceeding; but seeing Cecilia enter the room, she checked herself, and remained silent.

"We were just talking of you, my dear Cecilia," cried Olivia; "where have you been concealing yourself—and what have you done with Varàno?"

"Done with him!—done with Signor Varàno!" said Cecilia, blushing violently.

"Yes, what have you done with him, I say?" rejoined Olivia, with a look and accent most provokingly arch. "Nay, nay, don't be so confused. I saw him, about a quarter of an hour ago, strolling along the orangery; and, observing that you went out soon after, I imagined you might have met with him, and had agreed to exchange a solitary ramble for the pleasures of a *tête-à-tete*."

"I have not been walking in the orangery," said Cecilia, endeavouring to compose herself, "neither have I seen the Signor."

"I wish," continued Olivia, "he had been fortunate enough to come in just when I mentioned his name; that blush became you so well, I would have given the world he had seen it!"

"Ridiculous!" cried the Signora, angrily; "Lady Olivia, this propensity to raillery is insufferable!"

Cecilia, looking up, perceived the Signora's eyes rivetted upon her's with a look of earnest indignation. Olivia observing it too, and that Cecilia was hurt by it, proposed that they should take a turn upon the terrace. They were met there by Varàno and De Sevignac.

"I have this moment been enquiring for you," said Olivia, addressing herself to Varàno; "where have you been all this time? —It was cruel of you to desert us. I have been wearied to death for these last three hours; doing penance, actually, in listening to the wearisome conversation of that ridiculous *petit maitre*, Signor Girolamo[1]. He certainly talks more nonsense in one half hour, than all the people in the city put together do in a week. Then he is so insufferably tedious with his *bellissima Signoras* and his *mia Padronas*, that it would require as large a portion of animal spirits as he has of impertinence, not to sink into absolute *ennui*."

"The Signor is much obliged to you for your opinion of him,

1 It is the custom at Genoa to speak of people by their Christian names.

Lady," said De Sevignac; "he has no chance, I see, of succeeding to your favour—you will not chuse him for a husband."

"Not unless there was a much greater scarcity of the commodity than there is at present, Sir," continued Olivia; "and if that was to be the case, and the Signor was to be my husband, I should be very choice of him——I would have him framed and glazed."

"Framed and glazed!" exclaimed Varàno.

"Yes, I would keep him as ladies do their favourite monkeys. He would want nothing but an Oriental appellation, as—the great *Tay-ouan-fou*—the non-descript monster from the deserts of *Tehama*—or the vast human baboon, just found among the mountain-wilds of Gabel-el-Ared, to make him pass for one of the most hideous of the species!—Thus caged, and accompanied by as many parrots and macaws as he should chuse, the only beings with whom he ought to converse, he might talk incessantly!—I could bear with him in the character of an ape; but in that of a man—he burlesques it so horribly, that it is quite intolerable!—and a woman must have more patience than *Griselda* herself, who could endure to see him a single moment without vexation!"

"Indeed you are too severe, I think, upon the Signor," said Cecilia; "he seems to possess an infinite deal of good-nature."

"More than any man in all Genoa," replied Varàno. "There is not a single particle of resentment in his whole composition;—I have attempted to provoke him in a thousand instances; but he is so incorrigibly stupid, that it is not possible to succeed with him."

"You mistake," resumed Olivia, "it is the lion, or rather it is the tiger, sleeping in the form of the monkey. See him among his inferiors, and he is a tyrant—a very Nero; see him among his equals, and he is scarcely less insolent; introduce him to his superiors, and he is their jester—their slave—their Macaroni—their any thing: but awake those dormant qualities his interest has lulled, and the fiercest animal you can encounter will not be more ferocious and revengeful!"

"*Non destare 'l can che dorme*[1]! then," said Varàno, "for here he comes."

---

[1] A Tuscan adage—"Wake not a sleeping lion."

"There is certainly some sort of witchery about me," said Olivia; "no name can ever pass my lips but the owner of it, as if I was indeed an enchantress, is sure to appear before me.—Signor, you was the very last man in my thoughts."

"You do me much honour," returned Signor Zuccato.

"We will not venture to declare what was said of you, Signor," cried Varàno; "ladies' favours must be sparingly bestowed, or they lose their value."

"Such favours always were, and always will be inestimable," said Signor Zuccato, bowing low.

Olivia was about to reply with her usual *naivéte*, but seeing Boraccio, who, with Count Morsino and another of his acquaintance, was approaching from the other end of the terrace, the discourse was diverted to other subjects.

The Count, since his introduction at the Opera, had been frequently at the palace; and though his attention had not been confined wholly to Cecilia, Varàno, who doubted not the motive of his visits, and who, amongst a thousand amiable qualifications, had notwithstanding as much jealousy in his composition as usually falls to the lot of a modern Italian, felt scarcely less uneasy than if he was already admitted as an acknowledged rival; and his disinclination to tear himself from a spot which contained all his soul held dear, was augmented by the dread of a competitor.

CHAPTER X

Forse se tu gustassi una volta
La millesima parte dalla gioie
Che gusta un cor amato riamando
Diresti ripentita sospirando
Perduto è tutto 'l tempo
Che in amor non se spende——

TASSO'S AMINTA.

————Wert thou but once to taste
Only one hundredth part of those rare joys
Which that heart knows that loves, and is belov'd,
Repenting, thou wouldst utter with a sigh—
Lost's every moment that's not spent in love.

VARÀNO having reluctantly consented to accompany De Sevignac to Florence, the time for their departure now grew nigh.—The latter dreading the consequences of an attachment so hopeless on a disposition like that of his young friend, violent from the excess of its sensibility, grew more and more anxious to separate him from Cecilia.—Cecilia, in her turn, became a subject most affecting to his thoughts; for though she strove to reassure him by a forced cheerfulness, the confused blush that coloured her cheek when addressing Varàno—the suppressed sigh, which, in spite of restraint, would escape to express the hidden secret of her heart, disclosed the nature of her feelings; and De Sevignac now trembled lest she should not adhere to her resolution—or, adhering to it, that her happiness should become the victim of her integrity.

Uneasy, irresolute, and perplexed, weary with awaiting an opportunity which no happy circumstance had afforded him, Varàno sought to make a full and open declaration of his passion to Cecilia. To leave her to support the contumelious conduct of his sister (who he much feared, however now guarded in her behaviour, would infringe the first moment of her power, on the resolution which his arguments and her own policy had imposed) was repugnant to every feeling of his soul. Yet how was it to be avoided?—By declaring his passion, he would draw down the Lady Viola's resentment, who he knew would be no advocate in such a cause, both upon himself and her. From his father every thing was to be feared. On his mother then—his fond, indulgent mother, rested all his hopes of future happiness. Yet should she dare to interfere, would she herself assent to his marriage with a young woman, of whose family nothing was known; and who was probably, as the Signora had frequently hinted in his presence, the daughter of a poor *villegeoise* at St. Foix.

Madame de Villeneuve had indeed mentioned, during her correspondence with the Lady Viola, that Cecilia was well descended; and that, owing to some very extraordinary circumstances in her story, which she was not at liberty to explain, she had taken her under her protection. But as this account did not arrive till some years after Cecilia had been received in the chateau, the Signora believed, or at least chose to insinuate, that her aunt had said this only an excuse for giving Cecilia an education above her rank, and as an ostensible reason for detaining her in her family, in a situation above that which propriety would have directed her to place her as the daughter of a peasant.

Presuming on the affection of his mother, Varàno resolved to disclose his unfortunate passion to her. But how could he do this without first knowing whether Cecilia would be disposed to encourage his addresses?—and would it not be dangerous to leave her with his sister till he should have succeeded in conquering the Marchesa's scruples—a work perhaps of many months, where she would be continually surrounded with admirers, ready to offer her independence and rank?—The day following was to witness his departure, and there was now no time to be lost.—To write to her was the only expedient. The project inspired him with the most lively hopes:—politeness would, he knew, dictate a reply; and that natural sanguineness of temper, which seldom wholly abandoned him, suggested that her answer would be propitious.

The moments which intervene between the formation and execution of a favourite project, are always devoted to the most flattering anticipations:—every difficulty disappears; and it is not till we are engaged in the task assigned, that we begin to dispute its success, or our own ability to perform it. The plan was not so easy in reality as it had appeared in perspective. Varàno had never composed a letter which had required so much thought—so much correction.

It was conveyed to Cecilia by one of the women of the palace, who had orders to take it to her apartment. But the messenger had no sooner retired, than Varàno began to have some doubts as to the rectitude of the measure. The difficulty of obtaining the sanction of his father's approbation returned with redoubled force; yet he flattered himself the Marchese, tenacious as he was of the dignity of his family, when convinced that his son's wretchedness would be the result of determined opposition, might be won by the mild persuasions of the Marchesa, finally to consent to the marriage.

Cecilia received the letter without the smallest suspicion from whence it came; but no sooner did she perceive the hand-writing of Varàno, than her fears informed her of its purport: and the trembling agitation with which she was seized, scarcely permitted her to unclose it. The contents were such as, under any other circumstances, would have afforded her the most ecstatic pleasure; but, thus situated, they filled her with grief and apprehension.

The conclusion of this epistle elucidated an event she had almost ceased to recollect, and which no former opportunity had allowed her to investigate. She found, as she had once feebly suspected, that the person, who had been seen stealing at midnight about the cottage of Le Luc, was Varàno; who, despairing of seeing her by any other means, had attempted to draw her to her window. Twice he had called upon her name, but received no answer; and, hopeless of success, had retired, silent and melancholy, to the Chateau de St. Foix; from whence, with his father, he had set off early on the following morning for Dauphine.

Cecilia's heart was too full to permit her to read with great attention what was sufficient to destroy all her natural composure. Tears fell slowly from her eyes as the expressions of impassioned tenderness, with which the paper abounded, met her view; and it demanded all her fortitude to resist the enfeebling softness that was stealing imperceptibly to her heart. The letter requested a reply; but she felt irresolute and perplexed as to the propriety of answering it. She did not hesitate long. De Sevignac was, she knew, competent to advise her; and to whom but to the monitor of her youth—the dear, disinterested friend who had supplied to her the loss of every nearer connection, could she apply for assistance and support?—To him, therefore, she flew, and putting the letter into his hands, she besought him, in a low voice, to peruse the contents, and then to decide for her in what manner she should proceed.

"It must be answered, my love," said De Sevignac, the moment he had examined it, "and it cannot be too soon."

Cecilia requested that he would dictate to her what she should write.

"By no means, my dear," returned De Sevignac, "I can rely entirely upon your own discretion. He has avoided, I see, all mention of his father; probably from a persuasion that he will be inclined to resist every importunity. An application to him should, on all accounts, have preceded this to you. Some allowances must, notwithstanding, be made for the ardour and impetuosity of a youthful lover. It is unnecessary to remind you what *ought* to be your reply."

There needed not *this* to convince Cecilia that De Sevignac remained steady and determined in his former purpose; and since it was evident that either she must resign all that ennobling affection which, commencing under more happy auspices, would have been her boast and her pride, or incur the reproaches of her own heart by involving Varàno in disobedience and ruin, she resolved to adopt the only plan by which her own approbation and esteem could be secured.

Cecilia, except in the supplied affection of De Sevignac, had never known a father's tenderness—a father's care. But, though bereft of these, she had yet a justness of principle, and a rectitude of understanding, which made her thoroughly comprehend, and resolutely adhere to, one of the most simple and compendious of Nature's dictates—the immutable obligations due to a parent; and her mind, unvitiated by those sophisms which seek to find excuses in a romantic passion for a direct violation of the most sacred duties, was unable to supply her with any plea which could authorize the sacrifice of such obligations, however strong might be the passion—however alluring the temptation. All that remained then was to convince Varàno that she could listen to no offers from him, till they should have obtained the warrant of his father's approbation; and, by refusing to afford him the interview for which he sued, to spare herself the trouble of fruitless altercation.—But might not gentleness—might not pity supply one cordial drop to heal the wounds of bitter disappointment?—She hesitated—she suppressed the tender sentiment which was flowing from her pen.

Her answer was brief, but explicit.—A sensation of joy, amounting to rapture, marked the features of Varàno the instant he received it; but despair succeeded to expectation the moment he perused it.—It was not that she had refused to listen to him without the sanction of his family; but it was the coldness which pervaded the whole, and her rejection of an interview that touched him to the soul: and the very idea that he was supplanted by some more fortunate rival, who, now that he was about to depart, would have opportunities for insinuation which *he* was denied, almost overwhelmed him.

Cecilia passed the night in endeavouring to strengthen herself in the resolution she had adopted. Varàno had not appeared at supper. He was then unhappy—unhappy by her means!—The thought was agony. In vain she sought to lose in repose remembrances so afflictive to her;—sleep fled her eyelids, and she arose in the morning pale and unrefreshed. On entering the room where the family met at breakfast, she found a servant engaged in cleaning it; and enquiring the hour, was surprised to find she had risen earlier than she had expected.

As a book, or a lonely walk, were her usual resources when her rest had been broken, she chose the latter, and stole with light steps into the library. She opened the door, and was proceeding, but receded some paces on beholding Varàno, who, with his hair dishevelled, and his countenance pale with anxiety, was lounging in a sofa at the farther end. Perceiving him, she would have withdrawn; but he started up, and prevented her.

Cecilia trembled. A trial, the most severe she had ever known, awaited her; for how could she bear to see Varàno pale, depressed, unhappy, and in tears at her feet, calling wildly on her name, and entreating her to revoke the dreadful sentence she had passed upon him—to behold despair settled upon features formed for the most lively intelligence—and to hear herself accused as the author and inflictor of all the miseries she witnessed? Every exertion which she had imposed upon herself was insufficient to support her through so trying a scene; and as, in accents of the most supplicating softness, she conjured him to compose himself, and to abide patiently by a decision she had not the power to reverse, her inarticulate expressions and unsteady voice shewed what conflicts she had sustained, and what support was now necessary to preserve her through those she had yet to undergo.

"Oh spare me these emotions!" said she, gently disengaging herself; "I beseech—I conjure you, Signor, to be more calm!"

"So gentle, and yet so resolute!" cried Varàno, rising from his knees, and looking earnestly in her face; "I do not—I will not complain. But to be rejected thus—to be denied a conference!—surely, Cecilia, surely I ought to have been heard!"

"Alas! for what purpose?" said Cecilia, faintly. "Are you not acquainted with all? Wherefore then seek an interview which can be productive only of pain to both of us?"

"Allow me but to speak," cried Varàno. "The Marchese will not—cannot persist in his opposition to my wishes, when he shall be convinced how entirely my happiness depends on their fulfilment. My father—my mother—both are too reasonable to insist on my sacrificing to a vain ambition that happiness, which it has hitherto been their pride and pleasure to promote."

"But would not such an acquiescence," rejoined Cecilia, "be constrained and reluctant?—And would you owe to the generosity of affection, what you cannot demand from reason and justice?"

"From reason and justice I may hope any thing; for which of their laws shall I have violated?—Oh! do not—do not, my Cecilia, permit an understanding so excellent as your's, to be obscured by the fallacy of vulgar opinion! Think not that an unworthy distinction, purchased by birth, but disclaimed by merit—an accidental superiority in a few trifling points, ought to weigh with more serious considerations."

"I am but an indifferent casuist," said Cecilia, "but I confess I think that there are some prejudices with which it is our duty to comply; and that a deviation from those laws which custom has imposed, may be attended with much positive evil."

"Ah! did you love me," exclaimed Varàno, "you could not reason thus coldly! Alas! my imagination deceived me not when I suspected I had a rival!—Yes, I am deserted—I am abandoned—Oh Cecilia! teach me how to bear with patience the horrors—the ever accumulating horrors of such a destiny!—You love—yes, it is too plain—you love Morsino!"

"Morsino!" repeated Cecilia.

"Yes; or why is he here?—Why do you smile upon him?—and why——".

"Moderate these transports I beseech you," interrupted Cecilia; "alas! into what inconsistencies may not this unhappy precipitation betray you!—Count Morsino never was—never will be any thing to me."

"I have been mistaken in my selection then, and there is some other—some still more formidable opponent, whom my suspicions have yet spared, whose purpose is to rob me of an heart, the only treasure the world can now offer me."

"None—none, I assure you!" exclaimed Cecilia; "none that I could place in competition with——"

She stopped, overcome with the consciousness that she was confessing too much; a crimson blush overspread her cheek, and she remained silent and embarrassed.

"Proceed—proceed!" cried Varàno; "Oh! tell me, may I dare —may I presume to hope, all objections—all interfering duties removed, Varàno—the then happy Varàno, might aspire to your love?—Convince me but of this, my adored Cecilia, and be assured that every interposing obstacle shall sink before us."

"Yes, I will be sincere: were there indeed no obstacles, no filial disobedience to be incurred——"

"You would be mine!—Yes, those blushes—those enchanting blushes confirm and conclude the unfinished sentence——and Oh what cannot a love like mine achieve!"

"Ah! do not be thus sanguine," cried Cecilia; "the Marchese never will—never can consent!"

"Think not so deeply," said Varàno, as he placed her beside him on the sofa, "nor let us cloud with uneasy anticipation the few short moments that remain to us. Rather teach me to support as I ought the tedious hours which must intervene ere I again see you, and, whilst I listen to those enchanting accents, revive in my heart the sweet hope that we shall meet again, free from those distressing apprehensions which have conspired to sadden our present interview."

"Yes, but does not disappointment derive its most poignant sting," said Cecilia, "from the indulgence of unwarranted hope? —and by preparing ourselves for the worst, shall we not be better enabled to encounter it?"

"I had no fears but for your love," answered Varàno; "and that preference obtained, am prepared to encounter every other difficulty: and thus," continued he, raising her hand respectfully to his lips, "thus let me seal the generous consent you have awarded me."

"That consent, Signor," resumed Cecilia, hastily withdrawing her hand, "was only conditional. Your obligations to your family precede every other; and relying on your honour, your delicacy, and the known rectitude of your principles, I expect you henceforth to desist from writing or speaking to me on a subject to which it is impossible I can ever listen, but on the terms prescribed; for never, never will I be your's under your father's prohibition."

Though this was a point in which they had both agreed, the collected tone and manner with which these words were delivered, raised anew those doubts as to the fervency of her affection, which the late tenderness of her manner had wholly dispelled. She found, to her confusion and regret, that he was in danger of relapsing into the same error from which her very candid avowal had so lately extricated him; and it required all her address to recal him from those transports of immoderate jealousy which had before so much alarmed her. Nothing indeed had elapsed to justify a change so sudden and so violent; but Varàno was a lover, and lovers are seldom consistent. Again he was at her feet—again he accused her of insensibility and unkindness; till the entrance of Boraccio, who receded with astonishment on beholding

Cecilia the companion of so extraordinary a conference, aroused him from his posture, and put a final close to the interview.

The above scene, though it may possibly serve to place the character of our heroine in a more determinate point of view, is certainly but little calculated for the amusement of the greater number of our readers. The cold, starched damsel of fifty-three, who, like the ancient Sicilian virgin, never bestowed a smile upon her lover till he had purchased it by the sacrifice of his youth and his health at the shrine of her beauty, and had performed as many vigils at her window as he had heaved sighs to the cruelty of his remorseless mistress, will find objections in the suddenness and openness of her declarations; whilst the sentimental Novel-readers of the present period, who have imbibed the accommodating maxim—that love, because the most powerful, ought to be the ruling principle of action, will condemn her as fastidious; and would have applauded her, as *infinitely more interesting*, had she sacrificed her integrity to her love, instead of her love to her integrity. But the historian, whatever deference he may be inclined to pay to this fair and respectable class of critics, must not deviate from his facts. Cecilia belonged to neither of these schools: her education was established on the very best of theories; and neither coquetry nor romance had been admitted in the system.

The nice observer, whose object it is to trace Nature, as he imagines, through all her imperfections and incongruities, may object to the character we have but attempted to delineate, as too perfect for imitation, and may wish to see in it some of those flaws which, like the opaque shades in a picture, improve, by giving greater contrasts to its lights, the effect and beauty of the whole. But Cecilia was not perfect. Education had indeed done much, and Nature, more lavish still, had done more. They seemed, however, to have separated at the very point where they should have met. She possessed a susceptibility of mental pain beyond her reason to subdue, though not to correct; and to restrain which, became the principal care and anxiety of her future life. De Sevignac was not insensible to this defect; but, satisfied with diverting its source into that channel from which she might derive the least positive inconvenience, he strove to convert a grace into a virtue, by making the natural sensibility of her heart subservient to the purposes of generosity and benevolence.

Cecilia, on quitting the library, fled to her apartment. The wild conduct of Varàno, and the sudden appearance of Boraccio, had greatly alarmed her; and the inference that might be drawn from the situation in which he had surprised them, filled her with confusion and mortification. She was met on the stairs by De Sevignac, who, perceiving her agitation, stopped to enquire the cause. Cecilia could not instantly reply.

"Something has disturbed you," continued he, as he leaned pensively against the balustrade, "or why this agitation?—You are pale, my darling, you are ill!—What has happened to distress you?"

"Alas! nothing, Sir," said Cecilia, bursting into tears.

"Nothing!" repeated De Sevignac, "and has *nothing* the power to produce such emotion?"

"Forgive me, Sir," said Cecilia, still weeping, "I meant to say nothing has happened which ought to excite emotion."

"Explain yourself," returned De Sevignac, as he led her along the corridor; "what is it you mean?—Speak—relieve me from this incertitude!"

"Signor Varàno, Sir," resumed Cecilia, throwing herself on a chair in the first apartment they entered, "Signor Varàno——"

De Sevignac shuddered; a thousand fears, a thousand undefinable sensations rushed upon his senses.

"Go on!" said he; "surely he has not dared—he cannot have presumed to offer terms that——"

He stopped; his countenance became stern, and fixing his eyes upon Cecilia with a look of earnest enquiry, he commanded her to proceed, and to disguise from him nothing which had occurred.

"My dearest Sir," said Cecilia, perceiving his mistake, "nothing has happened, or will happen, that can require concealment from you. The Signor is not less honourable than you expected."

She then related what had passed, concluding with the appearance of Boraccio, and the probable consequences of such an interruption. Reassured by this discourse, and satisfied that his surmises were not less injurious than they were humiliating to the person who was the object of them, De Sevignac felt little apprehension in regard to Boraccio; and Cecilia, in the caresses and approbation which her friend bestowed upon her, found an adequate reward for the obedience she had practised, and the strongest stimulative to perseverance.

He left her to compose herself, and to give some orders necessary to his journey. They met soon after at breakfast, which was scarcely concluded when the carriage, destined to convey the travellers on their road to Tuscany as far as Sestri, arrived at the gate. Distress, dejection, and something like disappointment, were visible on the countenance of Varàno. The last, loath adieu was with difficulty pronounced; and as he crossed the lawn toward the gate where the carriage was in waiting, his irresolute manner and unsteady gait evinced the tumults of his mind. At length they entered the carriage:—Varàno waved his hand, with a mournful air, to Cecilia; De Sevignac bowed, cast a look of tender solicitude upon his beloved charge, and in a few moments they were out of sight. Cecilia followed them with her eyes till they were no longer to be seen; when, leaning for support on the offered arm of Olivia, she returned dejectedly to the palace.

"Alas, poor Varàno!" cried Olivia, laughing immoderately, "this parting will cost him many heart-achs. If I wanted the picture of Melancholy, he should sit for the portrait. Oh Love—Love! how mighty are thy triumphs!—Medea herself never performed half the metamorphoses that have graced the victories of this spiteful little God."

"If you are convinced he is so spiteful," said Cecilia, assuming a vein of gaiety foreign to her heart, "beware how you tempt his revenge."

"Oh! I am armed so strongly in defiance, that the sharpest of his arrows, if aimed at me, would be blunted and repelled. I would rather be any thing than in love."

"But does it follow," answered Cecilia, faintly, "that because Signor Varàno is melancholy, he must be in love?"

"No; but it follows that because he is in love, he must be melancholy; for I never yet saw a lover that was not so. But you, who have had no *experience* yourself, can form no idea of the symptoms."

Cecilia, little disposed to enter into a disquisition on the nature and effects of a passion which she was too conscious of feeling, made no reply, and they entered the hall.

De Sevignac and Varàno travelled leisurely to Pisa, at which place, or at Leghorn, they were to embark on the Arno for Florence. Arrived at Sestri, they alighted; and proceeded in a *felucca* to Lerici. The weather was fine; and while coasting the high and rocky shores of the Mediterranean, they often landed on some abrupt cliff, or where projecting points of land formed a natural bay, to enjoy the grandeur of the objects, till they entered the *Golfa della Spetrira*, when resuming their course upon the waves, they continued to row along this enchanting gulf, under the influence of the moon, which, as it illumined some objects, and left others in deeper shadow, discovered scenes which painting cannot reach.

"Had Claude," said De Sevignac, "seen this picture, tinted as it is with the rays and shadows of moonlight, he would have resigned his pencil in despair."

The vessel, which scarcely seemed to touch the waves, glided silently beneath the crags; the moon yet shone in cloudless lustre; and at length the towers of the *Castello Porte Venere*, the wide extended harbour, with its lofty coasts crested with wood, became visible. Arrived here, they disembarked; and proceeding in a cabriolet through Venza, Massa, and Pietre Santa, reached the City of Pisa. They stopped at the Hotel L'Ussera[1], where they had scarcely arrived when De Sevignac was seized with symptoms of illness; and rapidly growing worse, the plan of proceeding was rendered wholly impracticable.

1 The Hussar;—the principal Hotel at Pisa.

CHAPTER XI

Can any mortal mixture of earth's mould
Breath such divine enchanting ravishment?
Sure something holy lodges in that breast,
And with these raptures moves the vocal air
To testify his hidden residence!
How sweetly did they float upon the wings
Of Silence, through the empty-vaulted night,
At every fall smoothing the raven down
Of darkness, till it smil'd.

MILTON.

A FEW days only had elapsed since Varàno and De Sevignac's departure from Genoa, when the Signora announced her intention of giving a *Gala* at her villa near *Campo Marone*. Nothing was to be omitted which could add to the gaiety and elegance of the intended spectacle; and the taste of the Lady Viola and of Signor Girolamo was for many days employed in the decoration of the grounds and of the rooms, which were to be adjusted in a style entirely new, and very magnificent.

Whilst the Signora and her *cicisbeo* were thus engaged in the country, Cecilia and Olivia remained at the palace. Here the lively spirit of the latter could indulge itself without restraint; and, in forming the most agreeable plans for the future, she succeeded in withdrawing the mind of Cecilia from those too tender recollections, which, though she did not culpably give way to, she could not yet wholly repress.

Olivia, from this arrangement, found herself restored to a degree of liberty, which, since her arrival at Genoa, she had not before known. Her walks, her visits were no longer prescribed: she was no longer reminded of her rank and possessions, or chilled with an indignant frown if she proposed to unite in any little scheme of amusement, supposed to be inconsistent with such advantages. For the Lady Viola was too fond of state to stir abroad herself without a numerous retinue; or to suffer those of

103

her family, who were under her immediate command, to deviate from her own established practice.

Boraccio, who was usually to be seen any where rather than home, seldom intruded upon his young guests; who now devoted the greater part of their time to pleasant rambles about the city, attended by a servant, who, acting as their *cicerone*, conducted them to the public gardens belonging to the Palazzo d'Oria, to the Stradi Nuova, and Balbi; where the novelty of the objects continually passing before their eyes, often detained them many hours. They loved to behold the simple *cittadini*[1], sitting on their house-tops, imitating, with ingenious art, the form and texture of the flowers, which uniting their paler hues with the spreading foliage of the orange, composed a luxuriant and fragrant umbrage.

In the evenings Olivia, in compliance with the request of her friend, would often accompany her to *vespro*. Sometimes they attended this ceremony at the beautiful Church of the *Annunciata*, and sometimes at the *Duomo*, beneath whose pointed arches Cecilia loved to wander in awful contemplation, occasionally prostrating herself, with holy fervour, before the shrine of *San Giovanni*, in that chapel where his ashes are said to repose, and where the never dying lamp holds up the symbol of immortality. At other times, when the long-drawn evening allowed a more extensive ramble, they repaired to the Church of *Santa Maria Carignano*; and ascending the lofty bridge which, thrown across the valley, unites the two opposite hills, would view the wide-extended bay, sparkling beneath the beams of a declining sun—the coast—the city, spreading in semicircular sweep round the edge of its gulf; and the various groups of figures, which fashion or devotion had directed thither.

The discourse during these walks usually turned upon Varàno; for Olivia being well convinced of his predilection in favour of Cecilia, sought to obtain from her a confession of reciprocal attachment. But Cecilia had too nice a sense of decorum to avow a partiality which, under such circumstances, she could not approve. Disappointed in this attempt, yet secretly persuaded

1 Citizens.

that Cecilia, whatever coldness she might affect, could not be insensible to such distinction, she endeavoured, by exciting her jealousy, to throw her off her guard. She informed her, therefore, that Varàno, during the last time he was at Genoa, had attached himself to a very charming *cittadina*, whom he afterwards supported in great splendour; and that on his leaving Genoa, which happened in the course of some months, she had removed to a house beyond the city, where it was generally supposed she was still maintained by him.

This handsome *cittadina*, whom Olivia had distinguished by the name of Ottavia, she had pointed out to Cecilia as they were returning from one of their evening excursions to the *Piazza del Annunciata*. Her face was so covered with her *mezzaro*[1], that they could gain only an imperfect view of her features; but the glance they had obtained was sufficient to convince Cecilia that Ottavia had beauty enough to justify any preference she might have acquired. Olivia's knowledge of this affair was very limitted: all she appeared certain of was, that Ottavia was the daughter of a Sbirro[2]; that she had appeared, about a year ago, on the stage, in the capacity of a singer; and that she now resided in a small house, or *casino*, in the suburb of *St. Pietre d'Arena*. But whilst Olivia, without the least intention of doing any essential injury to the reputation of Varàno, whom she really esteemed, was assisting, with no better motive than curiosity, to involve him in implicated guilt, by representing him either as the seducer of innocence, or as, what is scarcely less culpable, the patronizer of avowed and shameless depravity, Varàno had a sufficient defence from these unmerited attacks in the native candour of Cecilia. Yet the earnestness which marked the tone and manner of Olivia, whilst persisting in her assertion, made her doubtful whether or not there might not have been some apparent grounds for the report. However, this did not lessen her opinion of Varàno. She knew the most malevolent conclusions are often drawn from the best of purposes; and doubted not, could the affair be brought to a thorough investigation, that it would redound to his honour,

1 A kind of cloth made of printed linen, which partly covers the face. They are worn by the citizens at Genoa.
2 An Officer of Justice.

and serve only to confirm her in that high esteem which she had always felt for his character.

The day of the *Gala* arrived.——The ladies partook of an early dinner at the palace, and then, attended by Signor Girolamo, set off for *Campo Marone*.

The evening was ushered in with all that splendour and gaiety which mark the commencement of an Italian festival.—"Soft music pealed along the vaulted roofs;" lights were disposed among the trees, and alternate wreaths of lamps and of roses entwined the columns. The hall was hung with decorations; and the doors thrown back, admitted views of the rooms which fell in suites beyond, and in which lights, reflected on glasses of various colours and forms, were so placed as to present the gayest effect of illuminations. Curtains of Lyons silk, woven with the repre-sentation of fruits and leaves, ornamented the doors, and, from the manner in which they were disposed and drawn up, produced beautiful arcades. Beneath these, and under canopies of the same material as the drapery, which fell to the ground in ample folds, were placed statues of the most perfect sculpture, several of which were copies of the best antiques.

From these rooms, which formed a rectangle, the eye caught an extensive sweep into apartments adapted to voluptuous ease, and adorned with all the fascinating allurements of Italian art. Groups of figures in *basso relievo* formed a richly ornamented cor-nice round the edge of the roof; which rising into an open corri-dor, exhibited, in the manner of Guercino, the soft and beautiful tints of an evening sky. A lamp of rock-crystal, but of an Etruscan form, was suspended from the centre; lustres, cut with the most delicate art, were disposed on tables of marble, displaying all the beautiful varieties of Brescia and Carrara; and these, with the other numerous lights which adorned the pillars, and the lamps depending from the arches, were reflected in a blaze of splendour from the large Venetian mirrors that terminated the vistas, and which seemed to have no end.

The grand saloon, which was the principal place of assem-bling, was of a circular form, and adorned like the hall with a splendid dome;—around it was an orchestra, supported by col-umns of the Corinthian order, containing a band of vocal and instrumental music. The chapiters and architraves of these pillars were decked with lamps and other fanciful enrichments. The most blooming flowers were tastefully interspersed among the nicely sculptured leaves, whilst wreaths of myrtle and orange, gracefully twisted below, composed a simple and elegant decoration to the base of the pillars. The walls were painted in *fresco*; and around were sofas, on which those who, weary with walking or dancing, might repose. One side of this building was open to the gardens, in which temporary pavilions were erected, some for cards and dice, others containing seats for *conversazioni*.

The dance had not yet commenced when Signor Boraccio, Morsino, and two others of their acquaintance arrived at the villa;—and Cecilia and Olivia, who, with the younger part of the company, had been sauntering about the grounds, were called upon to join the dancers. This Cecilia would have declined; for her heart, amid all the gaiety which surrounded her, was not tuned to joy: but Count Morsino had seized her hand before her refusal was positive, and a look from Boraccio obliged her to accept him.

The dance continued for some hours; after which the company left the rooms for the woods, which were splendidly illuminated. Collations were spread among the trees, under bowers of luxuriant chesnut; where the murmur of a fountain, which threw up its bright spray among tubs of orange and citron-trees, was heard mingling with the notes of distant music, artfully concealed amid the groves; the performers having chosen the most obscure and retired spots, so as to elude the eye, and strike the imagination with the effect of enchantment.

The elder part of the company composed parties for cards; whilst the younger formed themselves into groups, which at intervals glanced from beneath the shades, and were again unseen. Among these were Cecilia and Olivia, who, with the Count and some others, had been strolling about the shrubberies; when having arrived at the end of a little shadowy defile, which opened abruptly to the woods, their ears were suddenly fascinated by the tones of a mandola, which performed the recitative parts of one of Pasiello's beautiful compositions with the most admirable execution and scientific exactness. They had not time to conjecture from whence they proceeded before the music stopped and then changing to the soft Sicilian measure, a voice, whose sweetness they had never heard excelled, accompanied it with the following air:—

SONG OF A DRYAD.

In caverns deep and glens unknown,
I hide me from the beam of day,
Nor venture from these shades so lone
Till twilight spreads her mantle grey;
And the last gleam of parting light
Gilds the mountain's distant height.

Then to deep woods and glades I stray,
By haunted stream, or shadowy bow'r,
And with some wildly thrilling lay
Beguile the lonely ling'ring hour:
Strains that soothing as they flow,
Charm away the sense of woe.

And oft, as in my airy round,
O'er wavy steep, or forest drear,
I wake the soul-entrancing sound—
The sound to TASTE AND GENIUS dear!
I hear some love-lorn pilgrim's prayer,
Sad mingling with the desert air.

Then, true to LOVE and PITY's voice,
I haste, I fly, with magic skill
To cull each herb and flow'ret choice,
Of power to cure the direst ill;
And o'er his burning lids diffuse
The balm of sweet oblivion's dews.

Awhile in soft repose he lies,
Nor hears the blast that sighs so drear,
Till swift before his wond'ring eyes,
A thousand beauteous forms appear!
A vision rais'd by DRYAD's skill
To charm away the sense of ill.

> But not such love, such care we shew,
> No fairy scenes HIS vision seek,
> The youth who, deaf to love or woe,
> Has stole the bloom from beauty's cheek;
> And late relenting o'er her doom,
> Weaves the cypress at her tomb.
>
> But Terror's band, an awful crew!
> From charnels deep and graves repair,
> And vivid flames of lightnings blue,
> Gleam dreadful in the lurid air.
> Forms wove in FANCY's airy loom,
> To lure him to his threat'ning doom.
>
> Aghast he wakes!—he starts!—he fears
> For future woes and terrors past,
> And oft he thinks my voice he hears,
> Loud shrieking in the midnight blast!
> Vision of ills to falsehood due,
> From DRYAD's skill, for love untrue!

They were all in raptures. The Count affected to believe it supernatural, and proceeded in haste to ascertain if possible from whence the sounds had issued. But the voice, after repeating the two last lines of the concluding stanza, sunk into silence, and the instrument which had accompanied it was alone to be heard. Whilst this continued, there was some guide for their researches; and, anxious to inform themselves in what part of her domain, in which of her caves or wizard glens the charming Dryad had concealed herself—whether or not she was one of those fabled nymphs to poets known, and by poets only seen, it was unanimously agreed that they should continue the search. But ere they had proceeded far, the music also ceased, and nothing was to be heard but the tones of a violin and tambarine at some distance, and the loud laugh and the buz of indistinct voices from the parties they had left. The Count smiled.

"We are wrong," said he; "the little Circe eludes us."

Scarcely had he spoken, when the path suddenly terminated, and the trees opening to light, discovered to them, not far remote, a kind of grotto, so embowered and shaded on every side with such deep and solitary woods, that it seemed designed by Nature for the very haunt of Superstition. But the visions of fancy, charming as they were, soon yielded to those of reality. No fabled goddess—no Circe—no Calypso was here enshrined; but a form and face that might have belonged to either, and which appeared not less lovely for being denied the dangerous gift of enchantment. It was a beautiful young female, apparently about eighteen, who was habited in a style at once simple and alluring: her arm supported her head, as she reclined with graceful ease upon a rustic bench, as if languid from the effects of her exertion.

Rosellina (for so she was called) had been educated a musician; and uniting to a voice uncommonly sweet, a thorough knowledge of the theory of her art, she had been engaged by the Lady Viola to secrete herself among the groves, which extended for a considerable way beyond the lawn, to sing and play, in the habit of a wood-nymph, such airs as were best suited to the character she had been hired to assume.

The dress of this visionary songstress tended to confirm the idea that she was indeed one of Diana's train. Her robe of airy gauze was confined by a golden zone, and looped up above the arm with a button of the same metal; her hair was tied up in knots of flowers, and a painted quiver depended gracefully from her shoulder.

The most lavish commendations were bestowed upon Rosellina, and the party retired, mutually pleased with an adventure which had afforded them so agreeable a variety in their evening's entertainment.

The Signora in the meantime, surrounded by the most illustrious of her guests, was presiding in a pavilion, covered with an embroidered awning, where also was Signor Girolamo. Nobody on this occasion could be happier than the Signor: he sung, played upon the piano-forte, and as an innumerable quantity of flying glow-worms[1] were seen gemming the air, and darting their momentary splendour among the trees, he amused himself with catching and entangling them in the hair of the ladies—bidding

1 The Lampyris Italica

the shining insects become jewels in their heads, and addressing them with those elegant lines of Tasso—

> *Cangia, cangia consiglio,*
> *Pazzarella che sei*[1]

The Count, during supper, was attentive only to Cecilia, recommending the greatest delicacies to her taste, and selecting for her the choicest morsels of the *ortolan* and *beccafiche*. The dessert was composed of creams, ices, cedar and water melons, and a variety of the most cooling and luxurious fruits. Rich liqueurs, in glittering cups, solicited the taste; the *lachrymæ Christi* rose in sparkling eddies to the top of the golden goblets. Etruscan vases, containing the most exquisite perfumes, supported on tripods of solid silver, filled the room with delicious odours; and from an opened window at the farther end, embowered with *clematis*, the breeze wafted the sweets of roses and jasmines, that bloomed beneath the shade of an extensive orangery.

The ruddy glow which marks the approach of morning, had begun to colour the east ere the assembly dispersed. The Signora and her party did not depart till the evening.——

We now return to De Sevignac at Pisa. His disorder, in the space of a week, increased to such a degree, as to allow but small hopes of his recovery; and the physician proposed that if he had any relatives or friends to whom it would be necessary to apply, such an application should not be deferred, since he could not answer for his life many days. Varàno, on whom the task of writing devolved, undertook to convey the melancholy intelligence to Genoa.

The letter dispatched for this purpose, was delivered to the Lady Viola on her return from the villa, who, on examining the contents, withdrew to consult on them with Boraccio.—Varàno had requested that they would proceed immediately to Pisa; and the Signor, being swayed by motives more powerful than any entreaties that could be offered him, instantly complied.

1 *Change, change thy purpose,*
 Little fool as thou art!

Cecilia's grief on this information can only be conceived. The greatness of the misfortune with which she was threatened, deprived her for the moment of the power of exertion; and it was not till she was reminded by the Signora that there was no time to be lost, and of the weakness of deploring what no foresight could prevent, and no affliction remedy, that she was enabled to arouse herself from her despair, and to make such preparations as her unexpected and melancholy journey demanded.

A servant was accordingly dispatched to procure a vessel; and the rapidity with which the order was executed equalling their desire of expedition, the whole party, including Morsino, who accidentally being present at the receipt of the packet, had agreed to accompany them, embarked, and pursued their course toward Tuscany.

After an easy voyage of near two days, the shores of Tuscany, with the ancient city of Pisa, its magnificent quay, its *campanile*, *battisterio*, and hanging tower rose at length to their view. Its melancholy and deserted aspect seemed to menace Cecilia with some impending evil; and, when arrived at the hotel, this terrible presentiment pressed so heavily upon her feelings, as to restrain all enquiries which could lead to a confirmation of her worst and most dreadful surmises.

Varàno, in whom the sight of Cecilia had revived an emotion of joy, which not even the presence of Morsino, unwelcome as it was, had power to subdue, discovered by his manner the unwilling truth his lips trembled to utter.

De Sevignac was still alive—he might survive some days; but his disorder was of so malignant a nature, as to resist all remedies, however skilfully administered. He had been prepared to expect the arrival of his friends; and Cecilia, somewhat recovered from her first shock, proceeded supported by Varàno, and accompanied by the Lady Viola and Boraccio, to his chamber.

CHAPTER XII

Tu frustra pius, heu! non ita creditum
Poscis quintilium Deos.

Alas! it is in vain that your tenderness demands from
the Gods a friend, whom they had lent you but for
a season!

The interview had lasted near an hour, when the Signora and Cecilia withdrew; and De Sevignac continued for the remaining part of the evening alone with Boraccio.—The subject of this conference was a secret to all but themselves; but whatever was its import, the result a satisfactory to the former: for the Signor had no sooner retired, than De Sevignac discovered more resignation and cheerfulness than he had evinced at any former period of his illness.

The night was passed by Cecilia in a state of sleepless anxiety. She arose ere the day had dawned; and while hope and fear throbbed alternately in her breast, proceeded to the apartment of De Sevignac. A smile of complacent delight irradiated his features the moment he perceived her. He stretched out his hand with an indulgent air, and desiring his attendants to withdraw, made a signal for her to approach.

She obeyed in trembling hesitation; but ere she had reached the bed, the ill-assumed fortitude with which she had hitherto supported herself, suddenly failed her.—Deep sighs impeded her utterance, and not till relieved by tears, could she attend to the entreaties of De Sevignac, who, bending over her with looks of the tenderest commiseration, attempted to console and reassure her.

"Forbear, my love," said he, "to give way to a despair so useless to me, and to yourself so injurious; and let us use, not waste in culpable regrets, the few short hours that may yet be spared to us. In death, my Cecilia, there is nothing new—nothing uncommon—and, to those who have anticipated its approach, nothing dreadful. Life, were it extended beyond its intended duration, would be replete with disadvantages; and the completion of the promises annexed to its fulfilled duties, being more distant, would become less the objects of our desire. The time allotted to us here is more than sufficient for the purposes for which we were sent. To most the world is, as it was designed to be, a scene of sorrow and of adverse accidents, and even to the happiest, a state which continually demands from them caution and effort. Does the competitor, when arrived at the goal, look back with regret on the labours he has passed, since it is there the prize, for which he sought, awaits him? Life, as the *means* of obtaining happiness, is desirable; but considered as an *end*, it would not be a gift of mercy."

The tone and manner in which these words were pronounced, and the confidence they implied, calmed the feelings of Cecilia. A glow of devotional enthusiasm lighted up the expression of her features, which despair itself could not destroy. A prayer faltered on her lips; she cast a look of supplicating earnestness toward heaven, as if enforcing a silent ejaculation; and then sinking on her knees, she covered her face with her hands, and remained speechless.

"Cecilia," at length said De Sevignac, with an expression of solemnity which he seldom assumed, "I have many things to say to you;—arise then, and while I have strength to speak, listen to what I shall unfold. Fear not but thy prayers will be accepted; and that He who is the friend of the friendless, and the father of the fatherless, will protect thee."

He stopped. Cecilia seated herself by his side, and De Sevignac continued.

"The story of your unfortunate parents which was conveyed to me in a packet, in your infancy, and which I have deposited in the hands of a friend to be delivered to you when I am gone, though not immediately on my decease, will elucidate some particulars with which you are only partially acquainted.——On the examination of these papers, all the mystery and obscurity in which every circumstance relative to your birth and family have been so long involved, will be instantly dispersed. But my Cecilia is yet to know to what it is she owes the affection I have always delighted to testify—why I took her to my heart, and cherished her with more than a father's tenderness. Often, indeed, ere you could lisp a sound, have you demanded of me why I wept, and wherefore I gazed on you so intently.—Alas! too young for reflection, too innocent for suspicion, little didst thou think I was recalling the image of thy mother—my beloved, and now lost Leonora!—whom time, nor absence, nor even death itself could teach me to forget. Oh that she had indeed been mine!—that I might have sheltered her in my arms, and thus have preserved her from all the miseries of her destiny!"

"My mother!" reiterated Cecilia.

"Yes, thy mother!—thy adored—thy angelic mother!—'Twas whilst looking at thee that I sought to retrace her features.—Her heart, too sincere to change its object, yet bled for the woes it had inflicted.——How noble—how disinterested—how irreproachable was her conduct! How soon was the impression first made by her captivating form, rendered indelible by the sweetness of her disposition, and the strength of her understanding!—— Though forbade to love, I still hung upon her idea;—and, though I pursued her not, the power which she had acquired over me remained undiminished.——To me she appeared all that I had imagined of perfection;—and Oh! if she has since erred——may Heaven, in consideration of what she once was, pardon her offences!"

Cecilia's looks seemed to demand an explanation of the concluding words of this speech. Thoughts rushed to her mind, which, if they had ever found entrance there before, she had dismissed as too affrontive to the honour of her parent to be entertained for a moment. De Sevignac observed her perplexity; but, as if unable or unwilling to afford a verbal explanation of this mystery, he referred her to the papers; and then changing the discourse to a not less interesting subject, he spoke to her of Varàno; mentioning him in terms of more decided commendation than any he had yet used.

"The mind of this young man," continued De Sevignac, "though somewhat tinctured with the impetuosity natural to youth, is yet ennobled by virtues which do honour to his situa-

tion and his heart. Would to Heaven they could be the means of
ensuring his happiness!"

Cecilia sighed.

"In the present instance," resumed De Sevignac, "nothing like
concealment can, I conceive, be requisite.—Varàno, my love,
has acknowledged his passion for you. I have remonstrated; but,
I believe, without effect.—You know my reasons for wishing to
discourage it;—you assented to the justice of them at the time
I disclosed them; and nothing has since happened which can
render them less forcible. Yet the arguments he has employed
to convince me that, through the successful meditation of the
Marchesa, these apparent difficulties may be removed, have not
been entirely ineffectual.—The Marchesa, by the power of her
virtues, is said to have acquired a complete ascendancy over
the mind of her Lord; and though the talk of undermining his
prejudices may be among the most arduous of her enterprises,
his opinions, insurmountable as they may at first appear, may
finally yield to the united powers of reason and affection. Let me
not, however, by a too implicit reliance on such an interposition,
revive expectations which, if too sanguinely indulged, may end
in the bitterest disappointment. Recollect that, whatever may be
your lot, whilst your conduct continues to be guided by the pure
principles of religion and virtue, a moderate portion of felicity
will always be your's; for none but the guilty can be completely
miserable.—Should the Marchese, swayed by the restrictions of
family policy, and his own avaricious propensities, continue deaf
to every application but that of interest—my Cecilia, assisted by
the energies of her own superior understanding, will be enabled
to exert that fortitude necessary to support her under such an
emergency.—It is the little mind only which sinks beneath misfortune;—the great one rises above it unsubdued, and claims its
affinity to Heaven, by shewing itself superior to the adversities
of its fate. Assure me then, my love, that, however this affair
may terminate, you will not fail to exert those principles which,
under every change that may await you, will be the best security
for your happiness. And should Varàno, urged on by a romantic
fondness, be induced to renew his addresses, without the concurrence of such circumstances as can alone warrant your accept-

ance of them, however prompted by affection, you will not listen to him, unless he can offer you his hand without incurring what would inevitably imbitter every moment of his existence—a parent's curse!"

Cecilia trembled. The emotions De Sevignac had betrayed when speaking of her mother—the hopes he appeared to entertain relative to the success of Varàno's application, through the influence of the Marchesa—and the last awful words with which the sentence was concluded, had excited such a variety of sensations as almost overwhelmed her; and it was not till after many efforts that she could so far command herself as to be enabled to repeat, with a firm and steady voice, her determined adherence to the conduct prescribed, and her resolution of fulfilling her former engagement.

The discourse then turned upon Boraccio, with whom, De Sevignac informed Cecilia, he had settled all particulars respecting his will. The Signor, he added, had promised to be her friend, and had offered her an asylum in his palace till she could be more eligibly situated. At the name of Boraccio—of the will, her spirits again failed her; tears, she could no longer suppress, streamed from her eyes, and covering her face with her handkerchief, she sobbed aloud.

De Sevignac was scarcely less affected. He took her hand, clasped it eagerly within his, and looked first upon her, with an earnestness which seemed to preclude the power of utterance, then toward heaven, and then at her again; and at length added—

"Oh thou who beholdest all things!—thou to whom the past, the present, and the future are alike known—and who seest, at one and the same moment, the spirit which still lingers in the body, and that which has entered the gates of immortality—bless, preserve, and keep this my adopted child!—And if it be thy blessed will to exercise with sufferings the patience thou hast in mercy bestowed upon her, may she, by a due observance and a faithful discharge of such duties as she may be called upon to perform, render herself worthy of thy protecting providence!—and Oh! let not the sins of those she has never known, be visited on *her!*"

Here his voice faltered, and, overcome with his own energy, he stopped, sunk back, and remained silent.

The ghastly paleness that overspread his face as he fell, apparently motionless, upon the pillow, impressed the mind of Cecilia with the most terrible imaginations. Starting wildly from her seat, she flew toward the door; but her trembling limbs refused to support her, and she sunk almost lifeless upon the bed. The convulsive motion this occasioned aroused De Sevignac; and the name of Cecilia, faintly pronounced, recalled her to a sense of her situation. He then requested that she would retire, and send Boraccio, with whom it was necessary he should have some farther conversations.

De Sevignac's conference with Boraccio, which took place immediately, was not so long as the former one. After this, his strength seemed to decline fast. The fever, which, during the first week of his illness, had returned only at intervals, arose to an alarming height; fits of delirium rapidly succeeded, and the physician at length pronounced the disorder to be of so infectious a nature, as to render it dangerous for any one to approach him without proper precaution. This ascertained, all were forbidden to enter the chamber where De Sevignac lay.

The Signora, thus relieved from the necessity of all future attendance upon her uncle, left the hotel; and, accompanied by Boraccio and the Count, sought to dissipate the gloom of her late solitary occupations by pacing the streets and piazzas contiguous to the hotel. The baths were now crowded with invalids; and the Signora, deprived of her accustomed resources, was prevailed upon to extend her walk to the foot of Mount St. Giuliano. —Here, whilst she courted a transient amusement in contemplating the alternately gay and feeble forms which occasionally presented themselves, the Count and Boraccio found food for investigation in attempting to descry where formerly stood the baths so anciently celebrated for their medicinal virtues, anxious to discover some vestige of the *Laconicum*[1], of which, however, no traces remained. Ascending to the summit of the mountain, they looked down upon the squares and grass-grown streets of this once splendid city; whose lofty towers, yet rising in sullen grandeur, told the triumph of solidity over the depredations of

1 A part of the ancient baths at Pisa so called.

war—the fury of civil insurrection—and even Time itself, whose destructive arm had threatened, but not yet destroyed those noble and stupendous edifices which remain a lasting and striking memorial of its ancient consequence.

Three days had elapsed since Boraccio and his party arrived at Pisa; on the fourth De Sevignac breathed his last.—He was attended in his last moments by Padre Tomaso, the Monk who had officiated as Confessor, and from whose pious hands he had received the last awful ceremony of the sacrament.

Cecilia, though designedly kept in ignorance of the physician's prohibition, had, however, been deterred by Varàno from visiting the chamber. By him she was informed of De Sevignac's demise, and from him received all the consolation a misfortune so great would admit. Her's was not that grief which discovers itself in the impatient utterance of exclamations and sighs—it was the sorrow of a virtuous heart, which, however oppressed, could keep its purpose of resignation. She retired dejected indeed, but not hopeless, to her chamber; and in the calm of reflection—in the comforts of religion, sought to combat a grief which every object she saw assisted to revive. She prayed—and her heart expanded to the impressions of devotion, as kneeling, with clasped hands, before an image of the Virgin, she supplicated the aid of Him, to whom the groan of affliction and the invocation of innocence ascend not in vain. Yet the tear, the scalding tear still flowed—the interdicted sigh yet heaved her bosom! But why did she weep?—De Sevignac was happy—he was removed from a state of sufferance and infirmity to the possession of happiness as exquisite as it was lasting!—The awful barriers which separate time from eternity were already passed—he had reached the goal of which he spoke, and his reward was with him.——Such were her consolations; but Cecilia, to a devotion almost saintly, had yet to contend with all the weaknesses of nature.

On the following morning, the Marchese, who had received from Varàno an account of De Sevignac's illness and apparent danger, arrived at the hotel. When informed of his death, he affected great surprise and uneasiness—lamented that circumstances he could not then explain, but which were notwithstanding very urgent, had obliged him to procrastinate; and bewailed the melancholy incident which had rendered his journey unnecessary, with more concern than could have been expected from the general apathy of his character. He then consulted with Boraccio concerning the place and time of interment, in which he was assisted by the physician, who confirmed his former assertion as to the malignity of the disorder with new proofs, deduced from the state in which the body then was. As, in cases of this nature, the rules of the place do not allow the deceased to be conveyed to the new *cimetiere* without the town, the attendant physician or surgeon may, by applying to the officers of the police, procure permission to have the body conveyed to the *Campo Santo*, the earth of which was brought from Jerusalem, for a considerable depth, and is said to have the *Sarcophago* property of corroding and reducing it to dust in the space of a few hours.

The result of this consultation was, that a certificate should be forwarded to the officers of the police, containing an account of the deceased with all possible dispatch; and that the corpse should be interred on the following night.

Whilst the Marchese and Boraccio were thus engaged, Cecilia confined herself to her apartment; here she was frequently visited by Olivia, whose generous mind, awake to all the duties of humanity and friendship, now disclosed traits which the thoughtless vivacity of her conversation had hitherto obscured. Her tenderness and assiduity toward Cecilia served to mitigate her distress; and, by seducing her into trifling occupations, she strove to divert her mind from those enfeebling retrospections, which, however, adhered to it too strongly to be thus immediately dispersed.

Varàno, in the interim, anxiously sympathizing in the distress of Cecilia, and the forlornness of her situation, remained in a state of the greatest inquietude. The behaviour of the Signora contributed to his uneasiness. He found, from a conversation with her, that she considered her as a designing girl, who had insinuated herself into the affections of her patron; and who was feigning an affliction for his loss, at the very moment when she was secretly rejoicing in the imagined fruition of her most extravagant hopes.

The mind, when once tinctured by jealousy, soon loses its

powers of discrimination, and events, casual and unimportant in themselves, are transformed into causes of disgust and displeasure. The Signora saw, or imagined she saw, a tenderer air in De Sevignac, when addressing himself to Cecilia, than he assumed to her; and indignant to be supplanted by an indigent dependant, she had pursued her since with an eye of jealous scrutiny. The impression made by the awful event she had so lately witnessed, was already completely erased; and the lesson it might have enforced, had departed with it.

Cecilia not appearing at dinner, Varàno, having partaken of a hasty meal, flew up stairs, and, pacing the gallery, waited there in the expectation of beholding her. Her door was closed; but as he listened, he had the satisfaction of hearing that voice, whose sweet tones had so often charmed him, discoursing with Olivia. He remained there for some time, till compelled to resign all hopes of seeing her, he returned, disappointed and reluctant, to the party he had quitted; where he was condemned to attend to a wearisome disputation between the Count and Marchese, on the hostilities carried on by the *Guelphs* and *Ghibbelines*[1], which, after despoiling and depopulating Pisa, extended their baleful and destructive influence over so many provinces in Italy. A disquisition on the effects of the not less unfortunate dissensions between the *Bianchi* and the *Neri*[2] succeeded; which had lasted near an hour, when Varàno, whose thoughts were divided between Cecilia and his venerable friend, quitted the hotel, and occupied by his own melancholy rumination, passed and repassed the borders of the Arno, and that side of the quay called the *della parte di mezzo giorno*, without noticing a single object he saw, or appearing to recollect that this once celebrated city,

1 The factions of the Popes and the Emperors: the first so called from Guelph, Duke of Bavaria; the other from a village in Suabia, given as a watch-word to the army of Conrad the Third, in the twelfth century.

2 These factions originated in a disagreement between two young men of Pistoia, of the family of Concellieri, one of whom was cruelly murdered by Bertuccio, the father of his opponent. The friends of the injurer and the injured immediately took up arms; and the whole city espousing the cause of one or other of the parties, the contagion soon spread to Florence, where it received fresh vigour from the ancient dissensions of the Cerchi and the Donati, and soon became tinctured with political enmity.

the favourite residence of a Cosmo, contained within its walls a single vestige of any thing that could have power to interest or amuse.

In the evening Cecilia left her room, in order to visit the apartment where the body of De Sevignac was laid to be in readiness for interment, resolved once more to see and weep over him; but when arrived at the door, she perceived it was fastened, and that the key was removed. Concluding it was in the possession of the hostess, she descended, and demanded to speak with her alone. —The woman instantly appeared; but, on her enquiring for the key, she was told it had been delivered to the Signor, who, having declared that the disorder was infectious, had issued a prohibition against any one's entering.

Cecilia's heart sunk within her at these words. She knew an application to Boraccio or even to the Signora, after such an injunction, would be useless.—The idea of beholding her beloved friend no more, was insupportable;—grief seemed to deprive her of all power of exertion, and she still leaned against the door, though hopeless of admission, as if unable to quit it. The hostess, who had received from Nature one of her best, though not least dangerous gifts—a highly susceptible heart, was greatly affected; and struck at once by the earnestness of her manner, and the despondent tone in which she spoke, endeavoured to console her.

"Would to Heaven," added she, "Signora, I could serve you!"

"You would much oblige me by attempting it," said Cecilia.

"But should the disorder be so malignant as it has been represented," replied the hostess, "the attempt may be fatal; and I, of course, should have cause to repent my interference."

"I am not inclined to believe it is so," cried Cecilia; "nor should I shrink from my purpose if I did.—My future happiness depends on the completion of my design; and if you will assist me, you will confer an obligation which will be ever gratefully treasured in my memory."

"I am much inclined to befriend you," continued the hostess, "could I do it with impunity."

Again she deliberated; and again Cecilia, fearful of an interruption, besought her to determine immediately.

"Have you courage," at length resumed the woman, "to visit the body by night?"

"I have courage to do any thing," returned Cecilia, "that can procure me this melancholy gratification."

"At midnight then," rejoined the hostess, "if I tap at the door of your chamber, will you be ready to follow me?"

"I will," replied Cecilia; "but how are we to procure the key?"

"About that time," said the hostess, "the bier and cear-cloths will be conveyed to the hotel:—the men who bring them must be admitted; and when they are gone, for I shall desire them to leave the key in the door, we can steal, unobserved, to the chamber."

Cecilia assented to the plan; and it was agreed that they should visit the room, where the body of the deceased was laid, by midnight.

END OF VOLUME ONE

WHO'S THE MURDERER?

CHAPTER I

——Is it not midnight?
Cold fearful dews stand on my trembling flesh!
What do I fear?

SHAKESPEARE.

As the appointed time drew nigh, Cecilia, who was alone in her apartment, approached her *balcon*, and throwing open her casement, sat lost in melancholy reverie. The day had been remarkably fine, and the evening had closed in splendid beauty; but a few lowering clouds were now seen flitting through the vast expanse, transiently veiling the moon, and shewing at intervals the trembling stars. While she sat, the sky became gradually overcast; and a rising wind, which blew hollowly around, announced an approaching form. As she gazed on the altered appearance of the heavens, she sighed, and tears gushed from her eyes.

"Ah! so," cried she, "vanished my prospects of happiness, and my future ones are like clouds and tempests that surround me!"

She was roused from these reflections by a light produced by a taper moving in an adjoining chamber, which projected beyond the main body of the building. While she observed it, it became stationary, and she perceived indistinctly in the neighbouring apartment, the figures of two people in deep discourse:—one was a female, and another glance convinced her it was the Signora: the other, by the peculiar style of his gestures, she discovered to be Boraccio. This incident surprised her. She knew the apartment, formerly appropriated to the Lady Viola, was at the upper end of the gallery, in which her's, and that hitherto occupied by

De Sevignac opened. She continued at the window anxiously watching the form of Boraccio, which changed into a variety of attitudes, till the rain had abated; when unclosing her casement, and shading her lamp, lest the light of it should betray her, she observed them more minutely.—The Lady Viola was sitting with her handkerchief to her eyes near a table, over which she leaned. Boraccio was traversing the room with slow and unequal steps —often stopping, and gazing earnestly at his wife. His looks were wild, and his manner, when he addressed her, commanding and impetuous. Cecilia's situation was too remote to enable her to catch a word of the discourse; but as the sudden gust allowed her to distinguish other sounds, a few heavy sobs were occasionally communicated to her ear.

At length Boraccio advanced to the window, and holding up a light, looked eagerly at the sky. Cecilia retreated, and apprehensive of being seen, closed, but did not fasten her casement. She watched the reflection of the light till it gradually died away on the opposite building, when she ventured to return to the window. Boraccio having replaced the taper, seated himself on a chair near the Signora; and folding his arms upon his breast, seemed lost in thought.—At length, as if suddenly actuated by a dreadful frenzy, he sprang from his seat, and seizing the light, hurried toward the door of the apartment.—The eyes of the Lady Viola pursued him—darting across the room, she threw herself at his feet, and endeavoured to detain him; but, with a violence which seemed to stun her, he flung her from him to the ground, and rushed instantly from the chamber.

This scene appeared so extraordinary to Cecilia, as to mock all her efforts to account for it;—the conduct of Boraccio toward his wife, though uniformly indifferent, had never before seemed tinctured with harshness. Whilst she was attempting to solve this mystery, she heard the steps of two people passing and repassing her door. One of them she soon found was Boraccio and in the voice of the other she distinguished that of Morsino. They spoke low and having reached the end of the gallery, she heard a door on the opposite side close after them.

The horrors of the night increased, and Cecilia felt equally to dread and desire the approach of the hostess. Loud peals of wind, which broke in sullen gusts over the building, were lengthened by the hoarse sound of distant thunder; while quick succeeding flashes of vivid lightning darted from beneath the thick volumes of heavy vapour, which had long been gathering in the sky.

The thunder advanced nearer, and the flashes of lightning became stronger and more intense:—Cecilia closed the *jalousies* of her windows, and withdrawing to the other end of the apartment, awaited the expected signal.—She heard the distant clock strike twelve, and began to fear that the host had either forgotten her appointment, or had been prevented from fulfilling it.—She had not remained long, when the voices of men, the sound of which seemed to approach, again arrested her attention; and immediately after a loud lumber on the stairs startled her. Instantly recollecting what the woman had said concerning the bier and grave-clothes, which were to be brought to the hotel at midnight, she concluded that the men, whose voices she had heard, were conveying them to the chamber of the dead.—As she recollected this, a sudden faintness came over her. The bier, the cear-cloths, and all the dismal trappings of the grave rushed irresistibly upon her senses, clothing death in new horrors.

When the men had gained the top of the stairs, one of them stumbled over something which accidentally lay in his way.

"Stordito!" exclaimed his companion, angrily, "what, can't you see your road?"

"Hold up the light," cried the other. "*Christo benedetto!* what a dreary length are these passages!"

"This is the tenth corpse I've taken out of this hotel within these five years," resumed the first speaker; "it was just such a night as this——"

"Hark!" cried his comrade; "did not you hear that crash?"

"'Twas the wind," replied the other.

"No! no! it was thunder—I see the lightning;—how dreadfully it streams and flashes along these galleries! *Santa Virgine mi guardi!* these are nights that will remind a man of his sins!"

"Lift up the bier," said the other, "and come along:—fool! coward! how thou tremblest! why, thy liver is whiter than thy face, blanched as it is with fear! Come, come, shew yourself a man: —what are you afraid of?—Do you expect to see a ghost, eh?"

"*Iddio vi perdoni!* Why should I?" returned his companion; "what harm have I done?"

"None that will have power to raise the dead, I'll answer for thee," rejoined the other. "Thou art an excellent workman, Giacopo, and hast made many a last dress; yet thou hast never seen thine own work twice, I'll warrant thee."

"Basto! basto!" answered he, "we lose time:—I'm no poltroon —I've as much courage as any man, but what signifies courage here?—Courage can't defend one from being blasted by a thunderbolt, though it may lead one to thrust one's head into danger by facing it.—*Sante beati!* preserve us—I wonder why we were obliged to come hither to-night!"

"Peace!" cried his comrade; "this is the door. Oh Lord! Oh Lord! how dreadful was that flash!"

Cecilia's heart beat violently as she looked through the chasms of the door on the figures of these men, as they passed to the chamber;—and as she listened to the awful sound of the thunder rolling over her head, fearful images of horror began to float upon her mind.

Ere she had leisure for reflection, they set down the bier; and she heard them insert the key in the door. A silence of some minutes succeeded, after which the men retired, and other steps, which she believed to be those of the hostess, were heard on the stairs.——For a moment Cecilia began to doubt her ability to perform the task she had imposed upon herself with becoming firmness, when she was recalled to the necessity of an immediate decision by the appointed signal. She opened the door, and would have spoken; but the woman, pointing to an apartment on the right, motioned her to silence:—"Be quick!" said she, "Signora! and tread light, or we shall be discovered."

Cecilia with swift but faltering steps, followed her conductor to the chamber.

As the hostess turned the key, her heart throbbed, and her feeble limbs almost sunk beneath the tremor of her agitation. —The woman seemed to tremble too; she grasped her arm, and would have dissuaded her from entering.—"The night is dreadful!" said she, "the place lonely; and to visit the dead, Signora, at such an hour as this——"

"I have no fears but of a discovery," cried Cecilia; "be quick! The moments are precious—even now we may be betrayed!"

The door was at length opened, the hostess advanced first, and descending together by a few steps to this chamber of death, they beheld the body of De Sevignac stretched on a bed at the further end, wrapped in linen, and partially covered with a pall. The bier, and other funereal apparatus, were placed by its side. —Cecilia shuddered, but advanced. How silent! how dreary! how solemn did every thing appear!—She made a sign for the pall to be removed, and then requested to be left alone. The woman would have expostulated, but a look from Cecilia commanded her to silence, and she withdrew.

As soon as she was departed, and the door closed, Cecilia's tremor increased. A gloomy terror took possession of her faculties; and as she listened with a thrilling anxiety to the footsteps of the hostess, as the echoes revived the sound in the distant galleries, she began to wish she was not alone, and felt irresolute whether or not to recal her.

She waited in dreadful hesitation till they were no more to be heard, when, resolved not to yield herself to a weakness she blushed to have discovered even to herself, she approached the bed. Here while she gazed with silent awe on that well-known venerable form, her terrors subsided, and were succeeded by emotions the most sublime. A placid smile yet irradiated the features; and whilst it seemed to confirm the happiness of the spirit by which they had so lately been animated, her thoughts ascended with complacent hope to him who gave it.

The state of the departed—the nature of that unalterable bliss which constitutes the enjoyment of the soul in its separation from the body—subjects where reason affords no guide, and where even faith leaves imagination to supply its power, was a topic on which De Sevignac had often expatiated; and as she strove to recollect what he had uttered with an energy that yet vibrated on her fancy, every idea of self vanished into air. She forgot that she was more than ever an orphan—without a relative, a friend, or one ostensible connection: De Sevignac, admitted to the possession of unalloyed and endless felicity, alone occupied her thoughts. But so unaccountable is the human mind, that, while she yet gazed upon that beloved countenance, whose benignity not grief, nor pain, nor the last pang of death itself could destroy, she could scarcely resign the vague hope of seeing it again animated. All he had ever said, all he appeared to feel, particularly on their last interview, recurred forcibly to her recollection. She remembered the tones of his voice so exactly, that she almost imagined they were repeated; and, in spite of her reason, started as the wind shook the casements, and looked around her with an awful intentness, as if she expected to see the body of him, over whose lifeless remains she now stood, suddenly revive.

The stillness which reigned throughout the building increased the melancholy of her situation.—But what could she fear? "If the spirits of the departed," cried she, "are allowed to visit us, it must be in mercy!"—The thought reanimated her; she took the hand of De Sevignac, and breathing a silent prayer, raised it slowly to her lips. It was pale, and cold as marble. She let it fall—it sunk nerveless by his side:—she shuddered—cast an imploring look toward heaven—and a deep sigh burst from her heart.

The rain continued to fall, and the lightning, which an opened *jalousie* admitted, now illumined the body and the chamber with a transient gleam, and now left it in shade.

As she stood gazing on the corpse, with a look expressive indeed of sorrow and dismay, but such a one as *Raffaello* might have given an angel, one of the strongest and most vivid flashes she had ever seen, darted in at the window; and as it threw its rapid radiance athwart the countenance of the dead, it seemed to give him life.——Cecilia shrieked—A louder peal of thunder, which broke over the building with a dreadful crash—the sudden bursting open of the door—and a slow moving figure bearing a lamp, completed the terror of her feelings. Cecilia saw no more:—horror thrilled through every vein—she sunk back, and was insensible of her situation, till she was recalled to it by a low hollow voice murmuring in her ear; and looking up, beheld, instead of the terrifying apparition which her fancy had portrayed, the benevolent hostess.—She revived, and again glanced her eyes toward the body. Cold, placid, and serene, it seemed gently to reproach her for the fears she had disclosed. Still, however, she trembled, and could with difficulty persuade herself that the dreadful scene, to which a disordered imagination had given all the horrors of supernatural interposition, was merely visionary.

As reason strengthened, these fleeting images died away; and when sufficiently recovered to attend to an eclaircissement—when informed that this transitory animation was produced by a sudden flash of vivid lightning—that the bursting of the door was occasioned by a violent stream of wind hurrying up the passages—that the figure bearing the lamp was the hostess, whom kindness and compassion had directed thither—reproached her for yielding to a superstition she had despised and pitied in others too much to apprehend the effect of it upon herself.

The hostess would have accompanied her to her apartment; but on Cecilia's assuring her that she had surmounted her fears, she locked the door, and retired.

Alarmed lest she should be seen either by Boraccio or the Count, who had probably not yet separated for the night, Cecilia passed swiftly to her chamber. She had not reached it when her own name, uttered by a voice which she instantly knew to be Morsino's, arrested her steps.

Before she had time to recollect herself, she heard Boraccio speaking; but in so confused and hurried a manner, that she was unable to catch a word of his discourse. For a moment she was dismayed; but an irresistible impulse prevented her from entering her chamber, and her attention was at length wholly engrossed by the following words.

"By Heaven! I love her beyond any other human being!—and if there are means——" He stopped.

"You may depend upon my exertions, my Lord," returned Boraccio; "there "is nothing—believe me nothing—"

The remaining part of the sentence was lost in the wind, which again hurried through the gallery; and the sudden moving of chairs, with the sound as of advancing steps, convinced her they were about to retire.

Scarcely had she entered her room, when she heard them approach toward the door;—they stopped, and again her fears were renewed. She knew, should Boraccio discover that she had disregarded his prohibition of not approaching the corpse, he would be seriously displeased; and were he to suspect that she had overheard any part of the conversation between him and Morsino, it might be difficult to persuade him it was merely accidental. Her door was unfastened; but as she perceived by their whispering that they continued near, she was irresolute whether or not to secure it. While she deliberated, they withdrew and she heard them descend slowly the stairs.

Too much agitated to sleep, she threw herself on the bed, and endeavoured to re-collect her scattered thoughts. From the few disjointed sentences that had met her ear, no positive inference could be drawn: but the certainty that whatever was the nature of the conference, she was the subject of it, inspired a curiosity almost painful.

The Count it appeared had been declaring his attachment to Boraccio. But why was it necessary to chuse an hour and place so secret for such a disclosure? There was an impropriety in this proceeding, on the part of the Count and Boraccio, that greatly distressed her.—At first she imagined that, though her name had been mentioned, Olivia might be the object of the Count's encomiums; but when she recollected that his attention had been directed chiefly to herself, she dismissed this idea as improbable.

To Morsino Nature and Fortune had been profuse. All the embellishments which reading, travel, and conversation could afford, were added to the rich store of personal and intellectual perfections with which he was endowed.—To these were united all the softer arts of gallantry, and an invincible ardour in his favourite pursuits:—but the graces of his oratory, and the studied polish of his manners, which veiled even from the most discerning eye, propensities apparently incompatible with the character he assumed, were unmarked by Cecilia. The intelligent countenance—the open address—the susceptible mind—the exalted sentiments of Varàno—the disposition, of which even the defects seemed beauties, were so impressed upon her heart, as to render it unassailable to every other attack. Yet so exquisite was her sensibility, that she felt unhappy to have inspired a partiality which she could not return.

The words dropped by Boraccio, evinced his design of employing his power over her; but to what this agency might

tend, she could not ascertain. Though bound by all the ties of
gratitude and duty to De Sevignac, she considered that she was
by no means subjected to the authority of his relations and since
to act consistently with her own ideas of propriety, she must
inevitably tear herself from Varàno, and that immediately, she
determined, when the ceremony of the funeral should be at an
end, to announce her intention of returning to Provence.

The thoughts of France—of her beloved country excited an
impulse of joy even in the midst of sorrow; but as her altered
state recurred again to her mind, these as suddenly died away.
She had now no home to receive—no friend to welcome her.
The Chateau de St. Foix was now the prosperity of the Signora:
—Ursula—Louisette, both would be discharged. These were
circumstances which her undivided attention to her late loss
prevented her from reverting to before, but of which, now she
had leisure to reflect upon them, she became painfully sensible.
Yet if the doors which had been always open to receive her, and
to which she had ever been welcomed with a smile of transport,
were now closed against her, some cottage in the neighbourhood
of the chateau might afford her a secure and tranquil abode.
There the scenes which had been familiar to her from childhood
—the haunts of her tender infancy might be traced.—"There,"
cried she, "if I cannot be happy, I shall at least, I trust, not be
wretched. I can view the bosom of that transparent stream on
whose delightful margin I have so often wandered in the mellow
moonlight—can bend with melancholy transport over the grave
of my maternal friend, and while I lament her loss, endeavour to
imitate her darling virtues."

These images, accompanied as they were with a resistless
sadness, were yet soothing to her heart; and her spirits gradually
sunk into a tender dejection, till sleep stole upon her senses.

The next morning being appointed for the opening of the will,
all the party, except Cecilia, who was indisposed, being assembled, it was produced and read by Boraccio, to whose hands it had
been consigned. It was short and succinct. It placed the Signora
in the undisputed possession of the chateau and domain at St.
Foix, and the estates contiguous. A small legacy to the Marchese,
another to Varàno, and a larger one to Boraccio, comprised the

whole of the amount.—Cecilia's name, to the apparent astonishment of all present, was not once mentioned.

The remaining part of the day was appropriated by Boraccio to those necessary arrangements which precede the solemn occasion on which they were to be used. He was assisted in this occupation by Pache Tomaso, De Sevignac's Confessor.

The hours passed slowly with Varàno till dinner, when he was again to behold Cecilia. She came, accompanied by Olivia, who was leading her to a seat, when Varàno arose, and with eager, but trembling solicitude, introduced her to his father.—The Marchese, who had been prepared by Olivia to expect a very lovely young creature, and by the Signora an affected, assuming girl, who fancied herself a beauty, and had been taught to adopt airs unbecoming her situation, surveyed her with astonishment and admiration. Her dejected air—her sable dress—her pale yet lovely features excited sensations of tenderness and pity beyond what he had ever felt; and, won to a temporary forgetfulness of her rank by the softening influence of her beauty, he received her with a complacency and respect which he seldom bestowed on those whom Fortune had not entitled to precedence.

The evening was far advanced, when Cecilia and the rest of the party prepared to attend the awful ceremony. The corpse, stretched on a bier, and covered with flowers, according to the custom of the country, was conveyed by six lay-brothers and followed by Friars to its last silent receptacle.

The officiating Priest walked first, holding in his hand a lighted taper:—next proceeded the bier, surrounded with torches and Madonas; and, lastly, the Dominicans, moving two by two, clothed in white, with hoods and scapularies of the same colour, bearing each a light.

When the procession had arrived at the *Duomo*, where the deceased was to receive benediction, the bell which had been for some time tolling, ceased. A distant chant rose through the aisles, which gradually grew louder till they had entered the Church, when the organ sounded a solemn peal, and the voices, rising all together swelled into a tone of exquisite grandeur! When they had reached the altar, the bier was rested beneath an arch, and the organ, with the voices that had accompanied it, suddenly stopped.—At length the Priest, arrayed in splendid habiliments, ascended the steps of the high altar; and the prayers for the occasion were read. These concluded, strains solemnly melodious pealed along the roof; and the Priest, with a loud voice and holy crossings, pronounced his awful benediction. The requiem was then sung; and the body, removed from the bier, and stretched upon a marble slab, committed to the vehicle in which it was to be conveyed to the place of interment.

During this and the whole of the ceremony, Cecilia leaned for support upon the arm of Olivia, and with an assumed tranquillity in her manner, the effect of many a painful effort, attended with reverential awe to these last solemn rites.—A veil of the slightest texture covered her face, and dimly concealed her tears. As the procession left the aisles, and proceeded on the northern side of the edifice, on their way to the *Campo Santo*, she drew it close and with feeble steps advanced slowly in the rear.

When they had reached the gate, the *vetturino* drove off, and the mourners, withheld by custom from witnessing the conclusion of the ceremony, returned to the Hotel.

The night was gloomy and dark. The funeral procession stealing slowly toward the consecrated spot—the immensity of the pile, amid whose dreary arches silence seemed to repose, save when they echoed to the faint receding step of some solitary Monk, whose shadowy form was seen dimly in the distance, excited sensations of the deepest melancholy.

Arrived at the *cimetiere*, the Priest advanced toward the grave; and with a motion of his hand commanded the awning[1] to be removed.

The congregation, all of which, except the friends of the deceased, had accompanied the body to the *cimetiere*, crowded about the spot. The Friars who had followed in procession, and those that had carried the bier, approached, and elevating their lights, the service for the dead, concluding with the awful words, *dust to dust*, closed the solemn pomp which awaits on the last melancholy incident in the eventful history of man.—The hour —the place, surrounded by the impending gloom of overhanging cloisters, well assimilated to the purpose; and as the glare

1 A grave is always kept open in this cemetery, covered with an awning.

of the torches and attendant tapers flared upon the remoter vaults, and discovered the silent mansions of the dead, the tomb —the sarcophago—the monumental stone—and other striking mementos of mortality, curiosity became fixed in attention, and attention soon brightened into the flame of devotion. Each felt disposed to ask himself, whilst with saintly exactness he numbered the beads upon his rosary, and listened to the last chant of the last hymn as it burst over the grave of the poor stranger, what it was he was pursuing?—since when the busy turmoil of life should be over, the same fate—the same uncontroulable destiny await alike the needy and the prosperous—when the revels of prosperity, and the groan of affliction shall be alike forgotten— when, immured within the precincts of that abode, at whose tremendous name nature recoils, and the hurrying pulse beats with redoubled quickness, the forlorn and the happy—the oppressor and the oppressed, repose together in equal security—where the sigh of penitence is fixed in fate, and Virtue awaits her promised immortality.

CHAPTER II

Levius fit patientia
Quicquid corrigere est nefas.
                    HORACE.

Patience renders supportable what
We cannot change.

THE next day the Signora acquainted Cecilia that Boraccio had determined to visit Florence, and that their journey was to commence in a few days. Cecilia, on this intelligence, resolved to apprize the Signora of her intention of returning to France—a measure to which she expected not the least opposition.

The Signora received this information with surprise, and Cecilia thought with some displeasure.

Her project of going immediately into France, she assured Cecilia, whatever she might think of it, appeared highly absurd and romantic; but as she seemed bent upon it, she must desire that she would consult with the Signor, who was much more competent to advise with her than she was.

"If you go, however," continued she, "you will at least accompany us to Florence?"

Cecilia thanked the Signora for her invitation, but observed that if she did return to France, she had reasons for not wishing it to be delayed.

"I cannot conceive," said the Signora, carelessly, "that there can be any real necessity for your leaving Italy so soon. You have no relation I presume—at least none that you know of?"

"No, Madam, I believe none," cried Cecilia, colouring with indignation at this unfeeling speech. "My parents died in my infancy, long, very long before I could estimate their loss; and till now, I have never had cause to lament them. Of my family I know nothing; I am even ignorant whether I have at this moment a single relative existing."

She stopped to wipe away the tears which had fallen plentifully on her cheek.

"Well, I did not mean to distress you," resumed the Signora, affecting a look of concern; "you know I have promised to be your friend, and it will be your own fault entirely if I am not so."

"A friend would indeed be valuable," cried Cecilia, struggling to suppress a sigh.

"The Signor is every way inclined to serve you," rejoined the Signora faintly; "and if you will consult with him, he will advise you; but he will not, indeed I think he cannot, approve of your going instantly to France."

Cecilia, not suspecting that either the Lady Viola or Boraccio considered her of importance enough to be at all interested in her decisions, was not a little piqued on finding that she must apply to the latter for permission to execute her purpose.—She immediately requested an interview, and Boraccio soon afterwards entered the room; who, supposing that her intention was to make enquiries concerning the will, after much unmeaning politeness, and many tedious circumlocutions, at length informed her of what must before have surprised the reader as much as Cecilia, that her name was nowhere inserted in it.—He was sorry, he added, extremely sorry, to be the harbinger of such unwelcome tidings; but he hoped his friendship, which he could assure her was very sincere, would relieve her from every disagreeable reflection on this subject.—Cecilia's amazement can only be conceived. The repeated assurances which she had received from De Sevignac, that he would leave her in the possession of an easy independence, and the impossibility of pursuing her favourite scheme without at least a competence, excited a degree of solicitude which, under any other circumstances, she would not have felt.

Boraccio, whose eyes had been fixed upon the will which he had brought with him, with much seeming intentness, now put it into her hands; observing that nobody could be more concerned than himself at this neglect, and nobody more anxious to make up for the deficiency by every possible attention to her happiness and interest—Cecilia would have declined the perusal; but on Boraccio insisting upon it, she cast her eyes carelessly over the pages, though without knowing what she read, except that she perceived, from the date of it, that the will had been made some years; and recollecting that, at the period from which it was dated, she had been only a few months at the chateau, she was less astonished than before at this extraordinary omission. Madame de Villeneuve had, however, bequeathed her a sum which would be more than sufficient for her present necessities. But what was her disappointment, when, on mentioning this to Boraccio, she was told that the five hundred *louis-d'ors* left by her friend, were deposited with him, and to remain in his hands till she was married, or had attained the age of one-and-twenty— that the power of guardianship was committed to him; and that this was so unlimited, as to allow of his determining as to her future residence.

All the airy dreams of comfort, which she had been indulging, vanished from her view at this unwelcome intelligence. She was now not only forlorn and unfriended, but dependant upon the bounty of a man, whom, short as had been their acquaintance, she felt she could not esteem; and whose late cruel treatment of the Signora, which she had witnessed from the window of her chamber, had excited apprehensions no recent explication had as yet erased.—She mentioned, nevertheless, her project of return-ing to France:—Boraccio heard her with patience, but objected to it with an earnestness which was sufficient to convince her that she had but little to hope from his future conduct. He represented the dangers to which so young and lovely a woman would inevi-tably be exposed, alone and unprotected in a solitary village; and the loss they should sustain if she withdrew herself from their society. He promised, however, on her consenting to remain with them till they reached Genoa, to reconsider her proposal.

Cecilia was reassured by this indulgence; and since there appeared no possible means of avoiding, what her nice sense of honour, and her own feelings convinced her she ought, all future intercourse with Varàno, she was compelled to assent to what she did not approve, and what, under her present uneasy feelings, could afford her but little satisfaction—a journey to Florence.

The Marchese, whose favour with the Minister, and strong political engagements, rendered his presence indispensable, was already on his way thither; and Boraccio and his party prepared to follow.—Count Morsino, though a perfect stranger to the Mar-chese, was included in the invitation, and a day was now fixed for their departure.

On the appointed day, the carriages being at the door at an early hour, Boraccio, the Lady Viola, and the Count entered the first, and Varàno, Cecilia, and Olivia occupying the other, they pursued their way toward Florence.

CHAPTER III

A transient calm the happy scenes bestow,
And for a moment lull the sense of woe.

JOHNSON.

THEY proceeded hastily along, and after travelling for several hours through the rich and extensive plain which leads from the *Pisano* toward Florence, descended into the celebrated *Val d'Arno* —spreading wide its superb and enchanting villas, and displaying the sweeps of its far famed river among features of unequalled beauty. Here they beheld the vine hanging in luxuriant festoons, now entwined with the maple, and now mingling its rich empurpled clusters with the paler green of the willow—there the golden glow of the orange contrasting with the deep scarlet of the pomegranate, or the snowy blossoms of the myrtle.—Every gale breathed fragrance, and every sound conveyed the touches of harmony.

These soft and magnificent scenes, at any other time, and under any other circumstances, would have soothed and delighted Cecilia; but her senses were now dead alike to the prospect that surrounded her, and to the gay and beautiful country through which they travelled. Sometimes she was compelled to smile at the *naiveté* of Olivia, and her lively remarks on what she saw; and sometimes to listen to Varàno, who endeavoured to amuse her by pointing out the different villas belonging to the Florentine Nobles; their white porticos and colonnades peeping from beneath the shade of poplars and cypresses, which fringed the borders of the river, and which seemed to give a more delicious coolness to the wave they overhung. But the recollection of her buried friend, whose presence would have added a new charm to all she saw, checked the momentary animation, and tears of tenderness and regret stole to her eyes.

Descending lower into the vale, they caught a distinct view of Florence, with the luxuriant plain beyond, closed on the north and on the east by the lofty region of the Apennines; their forms grandly irregular, and their sublime effect heightened by a rich glow from the west, which, spreading along their summits, touched them with a soft and saffron brilliancy.

As they drew nearer to the city, their curiosity was excited by the crowds of peasantry and others that were hastening to Florence, to witness the celebration of a *festa*.——Cecilia, accustomed to look with mingled concern and apprehension on the miserable figures which she had seen passing and repassing the streets of Genoa, beheld with astonishment the gay and opulent inhabitants of this delightful country—who, joining Arcadian manners to Arcadian scenes, completed the enchantment that surrounded her. The dress of the females was at once graceful and picturesque; some wore hats, others caps of netted silk, ornamented with gold and silver tassels; many of them had their hair adorned with pearls, and some with jewels.—Their conversation was as sprightly as their dress was fanciful; and her attention was often irresistibly attracted by the lively tones of the mandola and tambarine, which accompanied our travellers on their way, till they reached at length the gates of Florence.

Nothing could be more striking than their entrance into this city, now engaged in the celebration of a festival, in honour of its tutelary Saint, *San Giovanni Battista*, whose birth had been commemorated during the day by chariot races, stage horseman-ship, and a variety of entertainments held only at the Carnivals. —The evening had concluded, and the night was commencing with fireworks, formed in devices among the woods, and par-tially illumining the ruins of *Fiesole*, which towered in decayed grandeur above. The images of the Madonas that were scattered about the streets—the *Ponte della Trinita*, with its statues of the seasons, were hung with lamps of various colours—the heads of saints, crucifixes, and other emblematic representations of the objects of the Romish faith, adorning the tops of the houses, and decorating the squares, colonnades, and areas of the palaces, which were interspersed with lights and groves of evergreen.— The noble Church of the *Annunciata*, famous for the fresco of the *Madona della Sacco*, was also grandly illuminated; but nothing could exceed the effect of the *Duomo*, casting a mass of splendour upon the Arno, whole clear translucent surface reflected the glowing picture in all its colours.

The grandeur of the spectacles—the throngs of inhabitants in their dresses of *fête*—the sound of music, and the voice of singing girls chanting hymns to the Virgin and their favourite Saints, with the refreshing coolness of the breeze which wafted the sweets of the orange flower and other odoriferous shrubs from the long ter-races of the palaces, formed a combination of delights grateful to every sense.—In the streets, which were crowded with numbers, little distinction prevailed. The Nobles, regardless of their rank, associated with the *Cittadini*. The *Casinos* were filled with people of all descriptions, who left them only to traverse the streets in the habits of masqueraders, or to sail, on the pure streams of the Arno, now covered with pleasure boats, whose painted awnings, as they floated slowly on the wind, and caught the moving lights from the city, with whose lustre a brilliant moon seemed to contend, exhibited every beauty of form and colour.

The carriages at length stopped at the Palazzo di Varàno, from whence a servant of the Marchese crossed a terrace to the lawn, and immediately the party alighted.

They found the Marchese and Marchesa with a few of their friends seated on sofas in a vestibule, enjoying the coolness of the evening, and the splendour and gaiety of the objects.

The usual salutations being over, the Marchese took Cecilia's hand, and with an air of haughty affability, which he meant for condescension, introduced her to the Marchesa.

Cecilia, though prepared to expect an elegant and accomplished woman, was struck with the peculiar grace and beauty of the Marchesa's figure. She seemed to be not more than five-and-thirty.—Her complexion, though it had suffered from a delicate state of health, had gained in softness what it had lost in bloom. Her eyes retained all their lustre and the fine symmetry of her features, true to the line of beauty, ensured her the admiration of every beholder. Her deportment was lofty and commanding; but the dignity which high birth and conscious superiority had inspired, was so tempered with sweetness, and so judiciously blended with politeness, that she never failed to captivate.

From the vestibule they passed through a noble hall to a staircase of marble which led to a saloon, where a splendid supper was prepared.

The Palazzo di Varàno was a grand and spacious mansion, fitted up with all the heavy magnificence of former ages.—The servants, though the greater number of them, according to the Florentine custom, were hired only for the day, and discharged from their office at night, were gorgeous in their liveries, and profoundly servile in their manners.—Every thing announced state; but a state so impressive, that, while it inspired awe, it repressed pleasure.

The saloon in which they sat, overlooked the lawn, and afforded a view of the river.— The sofas and drapery of this room were of purple damask, embroidered, and fringed with purple and gold. The walls were hung with valuable paintings; and tripod lamps depended on chains of silver from the ceiling.

The guests spoke little during supper and Cecilia was surprised to find that ceremonious stiffness, which she had imagined was discarded from all the polished circles in Europe, prevail among the higher orders at Florence.—She found, though she was evidently considered as an object for curiosity by all present, none seemed inclined any otherwise to notice her. She once ventured to address herself to a lady that sat next her; but a smile, a gentle inclination of the head, or a monosyllable, was her only reply.— At the upper end of the table was a Noble of the city, with whom the Marchese seemed to be on terms of friendly intimacy; but the subjects discussed being chiefly political, were little calculated for the entertainment of the rest of the company. They lamented the extinction of the family of the Medici, expatiating in hyperbolical terms on the former reigning Dukes of that house; reprobated the measures of the present Minister, whom they represented as proud and tyrannical; and spoke of the party differences which at that period agitated the country, as the probable consequences of its altered Government. Morsino joined in this discourse and then, speaking of Naples, he boasted of its superiority over the rest of the Italian States.

His opinions, however; enforced as they were with all the studied graces of expression, were not generally received. The conversation again turned on the family of the Medici; and the Count, despairing to remove prejudices so rooted as their's, endeavoured to introduce a more agreeable topic of discourse by addressing himself to the ladies.

After supper the conversation became more general and more animated. The Marchesa frequently joined in it; and Cecilia was amused by the sprightliness of her wit, and the justness and delicacy of her remarks.—She saw in her, indeed, some portion of that pride which characterized the Marchese and his daughter, and which she had been taught to believe inseparable from the Nobles in Italy. But whilst in *them* it degenerated into selfishness and unfeeling arrogance, in *her* it was so softened with elegance, and so tempered by benevolence, that it served to elevate her character, without detracting from the ease and sweetness of her manners.

The Marchesa loved her son with an ardour at least equal to the Marchese's; and as their separation, since he had left her to visit France, was one of the longest she had known, she had anticipated his return with the greatest impatience, and was solicitous to be relieved from the restraints of society, that she might clasp him to her heart with maternal fondness.——From the penetrating eye of a mother nothing could be hid;—she saw in the anxiety of his looks, and the embarrassment of his manner, food for uneasy conjecture—she perceived too that he was paler and thinner than usual; and that there was an expression of sadness in his countenance, for which she could not account, but which she partly attributed to the late melancholy event. Considering Cecilia as a lovely girl, whom some of the best emotions of the soul had induced De Sevignac to patronize, and who was now deprived, by his death, of her last and only friend, she felt for her all that compassion and interest which, in minds unwarped by prejudice, soon ripen into esteem. She saw she was in want of those little attentions and kindnesses so soothing to tenderness and grief; and experienced an exalted pleasure in bestowing them. When, therefore, the guests retired from the Palace, she sent her woman to shew the Lady Viola and Olivia to their rooms, and took upon herself the task of attending Cecilia to her's, where she repeated the friendly welcome with which she had first met her, with an affability and sweetness that filled her with an instantaneous gratitude.

In the morning she repeated her visit before Cecilia was up; and, perceiving that she was languid and fatigued, excused her from joining the party below till she was recovered from the effects of her journey.—Cecilia, gratified by this indulgence, found her admiration of the Marchesa hourly increase.

CHAPTER IV

Here thy well-studied marbles fix our eye,
A fading fresco here demands a sigh:
Each heavenly piece unwearied we compare,
Match Raphael's grace with thy lov'd Guido's air,
Caracci's strength.—Corregio's softer line,
Paulo's free stroke, and Titian's warmth divine!

POPE.

THE two first days passed on at the Palace unmarked by any occurrence. On the third the party took a ride to the *Giardino di Boboli*, and on the morning of the ensuing day visited the Palazzo Pitti.

The paintings in the *Fabbrica degli Ufizi*[1] would have astonished Cecilia more, had she not seen pieces by the same masters in the different Palaces at Genoa. Its superiority, however, in point of sculpture was evident; and, contrasted with the transcendent beauty of a Niobe, and the grace and symmetrical perfection of that inimitable statue, which remains a lasting and wonderful memento of Grecian excellence, the Prosperine of a Baratti, and even the *Pieta* of a Michalagnolo, sunk into comparative insignificance.

In proportion as her spirits revived, her attention became fixed; and directing her discourse alternately to the Marchesa, the Signora, and Olivia, she strayed, hanging on the arm of the latter, through the *Salas* and *Gabbinettes* of this immense edifice.

They had reached nearly the end of the gallery, when the Marchese, drawing Morsino and Boraccio apart, reconducted them into the vestibule, to view the antique inscriptions on the walls, the oval vase famous for the *basso relievo* of Nero, and other valuable curiosities—Varàno remaining alone with the ladies, happy in the opportunity thus afforded him of conversing with Cecilia, without observation, or interruption from his imagined rival.

Whilst they were observing an angel by Guido, the Count,

1 This comprehends the Royal Gallery at Florence.

144

who had been reluctantly detained in the vestibule, returned, and begged leave to shew them a rare and much-admired painting, a *chef d'œuvre*, which adorned the centre of the Tribune. This was the *recumbent Beauty* by Titian.—They were joined shortly by the Marchese, who entered into conversation with Morsino on the merits of the piece.—The Marchese spoke of the wonderful effects produced by the declinations of light and shade—of the passing of the shadows into the demi-tints, and the imperceptible manner in which they were united to the *chiaro scuro*.—Morsino, whose nice taste could detect errors where they could scarcely be said to exist, observed that the artist, in the background of this picture, as well as in many others of his less celebrated performances, had neglected the rules of perspective.

"Do you not perceive, my Lord," cried he, "that the figures in that group are too small, and though obviously designed for waiting women, have the appearance of mere children?"

"A painter, without being accountable for a fault against the rules of proportion, may, I think," replied the Marchese, "make his figures somewhat above or below the common size: Nature, you will allow, has no exact standard."

"However Nature may deviate," said the Count, "the laws of beauty, and if of beauty, of painting, are more arbitrary; and a want of harmony in grouping, is not less perceptible and erroneous than an unjust gradation of colouring:—in the latter, Titian may be said to have no rivals—in the former he is certainly deficient."

"You do not mean to insinuate," rejoined the Marchese, "that if we except the works of Raffaello, that this justly admired master has ever met with a competitor?"

"Not in colouring, my Lord—there I am willing to allow him all due praise; but in every other department of his art, he has rivals, and these in his own manner: Guido surpasses him in grace, and Corregio in the grouping of his figures."

"Is it possible!" exclaimed the Marchese, "that you can speak of grace, and not recollect the famous Magdeline of Titian at Rome, nor that at the Palazzo Balbi at Genoa; and can persist that he is without skill in the disposition of his figures, when you observe the position of the angels in the latter, which form the group."

"I am willing to allow this picture," continued the Count, "all the merit it deserves—it has much, and the name of Titian will ever be held in honour by the lovers of this divine art: but whilst I recollect the beauty of his Magdeline, I remember too his Lucrezia, poorly finished, and without any thing which can indicate even the remains of genius."

If the Count was solicitous to ingratiate himself with the Marchese, he could not easily have hit upon a more unfortunate method. Unaccustomed to controul, and wrapped up in the conviction of his own imaginary superiority, he expected an implicit obedience to his own judgment; and discarded all who dared to oppose it.—As his character was well known at Florence, his society was consequently shunned by those who were unwilling to be subjected to this mental slavery; and courted in an equal degree by many, who, for the sake of pecuniary advantages, or high political preferment could bring themselves to submit to it. He had long considered himself as a *cognoscento* in painting and sculpture, and had been from time to time much flattered by the respect which had been paid to his decisions from people of his own rank in many parts of Italy.—It was therefore not without great mortification that he found his long received opinions combated, not rudely indeed, but with some spirit by his new guest.—
—Having surveyed the noble *busto* of Alexander, though without resolving the long contested point, whether the Conqueror was weeping for new worlds, lamenting for the murder of Clytus, or fainting from loss of blood after his adventure at Oxydrace, they entered the Tribune, where were the six Greek statues, the Faun, the Wrestler, and the *Arotino*.

Whilst the two *Virtuosi* were engaged in measuring and admiring the proportion of the Venus di Medici, and the ladies in examining a table of Florentine workmanship in the centre, adorned with *chalcedony* and other species of the onyx, set to imitate pearls, their attention was recalled by the entrance of a stranger, whose dress and figure declared him of some rank.— He advanced with a hurried step; and throwing his eyes carelessly around the Tribune, uttered an exclamation of surprise: and then, seeming to recollect himself, strode up to Morsino.

The Count drew back as he approached; his countenance

changed, and he gazed on him for some moments in speechless astonishment, till the deadly hatred expressed on the features of the stranger roused him from his posture, and he laid his hand upon his sword.

"Accident has at last befriended me," said the Signor fiercely; "my Lord, recollect I am no longer to be trifled with!—Is it thus you fulfil your engagement? Is this the conduct I have been taught to expect from you?"

The look of earnest indignation which Morsino had assumed, now changed to the paleness of apprehension;—he withdrew with him immediately to a remote part of the gallery, where they conferred for some minutes alone.

"Should your engagements be numerous," said the Count as they returned, "this eclaircissement may be deferred."

"However urgent may be my engagements," retorted the Signor, with a look of savage ferocity, "they shall not prevent me from taking advantage of an interview, for which I have long sought: you understand the rest."

The Count started.

"This, Signor, is not a time, nor ought it to be the place!"

"The time and place I leave for your selection," rejoined the stranger, sternly; "name them, and be not afraid I shall fail you."

"At the Casino, then, near the Libraria Laurenziano," resumed the Count, "meet me to-night at the hour of sunset."

"The appointment is sacred," cried the Signor, "and mind we have no witnesses.—You said at sunset?"

"I did," said the Count—"at sunset."

The stranger waved his hand, and retired; leaving all, except Morsino, in amazement at the eccentric and mysterious behaviour of this new comer.

The remainder of the day was employed by Cecilia at the Palazzo di Varàno in surveying the *gran Salas*, banqueting-rooms, and other splendid apartments, the walls of which were either ornamented in fresco, or covered with the paintings of some of the first masters of the Flemish and Venetian schools. Besides these were several statues:—one of them the Marchese pointed out to Cecilia as possessing extraordinary merit.

"If you admire, as you seem to do, the sculpture of the

ancients," said he, alluding to a figure which guarded the entrance of a room intended for *fiesta*, you will not be insensible to the beauty of that piece; it is the Faun, with the *syrinx*, or flute of reeds, and is an excellent copy of that celebrated statue at the Villa Ludovisi, near Rome: observe the expression of mirth delineated in the countenance!—Mark too the attitude—the gesture —can any thing be more admirable?"

"I am here amid such a scene of wonders, my Lord," said Cecilia, "that I scarcely know where most to bestow my praise."

"That too," resumed the Marchese, pointing to another, "is copied from the famous Flora beneath the arcades of the Palazzo Farnese;—it is not equal to the Faun, but the attitude is easy, the neck finely turned, and the countenance frank, open, and characteristic."

He then led her into a corridor to examine a painting there, selected from the affecting story of Pætus and Arria, the figures of which were in the Roman *costume*; and the design taken, like the statue that the Marchese had been commending, from the Villa Ludovisi.

The Marchese had also a cabinet supported by pillars of *verde di Calabria*, and other rare and beautiful marbles, with their bases and capitals finely wrought, and *bassi relievi* on their pedestals; containing a valuable collection of medals of antique gems in *intaglio*, with tripods of oriental crystal, and several articles in gold and silver sculpture.—Enclosed in this cabinet were also several vases, some Etruscan, and others supposed to have been found in the sepulchres of *Magna Grecia and Sicilia*.

The next day Morsino, observing that his former visits to Florence, though frequent, were too limitted to allow of his seeing any thing except the gallery, the Palazzo Vecchio, and a few other of the principal Palaces, proposed visiting the Churches.—The Marchese smiled on being told that the Count had never yet entered the *Duomo*.

"If you have viewed it as you say, only on the outside," said he, "you have a very inadequate idea of its magnificence. We must not let you depart with so poor an opinion of us. That our skill in designing is superior to our ability in executing, is indeed but too certain; and it will remain, I fear, a lasting reproach to us, that what our ancestors began, we are incompetent to finish. How strange that in a country so favoured as is our's with mineral production, we should be contented with it under its present imperfection!"

"The defect might be easily remedied," returned the Count.

"I believe not," continued the Marchese; "no individual will undertake it; and our Nobles are either too poor or too sordid to propose or assent to any other plan of execution.—They had rather see a wooden cupola, however it may disgrace the general uniformity of their city, than dedicate any portion of the annual produce of their merchandise to the replacing it with a marble one."

The Count lamented that so fine a design should remain unexecuted; and the Marchese having enumerated the particular Churches, and mentioned those most worthy of notice, it was agreed that they should continue at the Palace till the evening, and then proceed to the Church of *Santa Croce*, and afterwards to that of *Santa Maria del Fiore*. The ladies, at the request of the Marchese, consented to be of the party; and the evening arrived, they commenced their excursion.

Cecilia was amused as they drove along with the number of the carriages, and the extraordinary height and grandeur of the buildings.—The Arno seemed wider, its surface more transparent, and its sweeps more beautifully shaded than at Pisa.—The bridges, which the Marchese had asserted were the finest in the world, were not only infinitely superior to any thing she had ever seen, but to all she could have imagined. And having passed through some of the finest parts of the city, where Churches, Convents, and Palaces rise as if to outvie each other, it was not till she had entered the Church of *Santa Croce*, and saw the number of the aisles—the richness and extent of the arcades that separate them—the superbly ornamented windows—the frescos—and the quantity and variety of the marbles that inlay the pavement, and adorn the steps of the high altar, that she could believe it could bestow a beauty or a charm beyond what it had already afforded her.

To this elegant, and comparatively airy fabric, the Church of *San Reparata*, silent, gloomy, and deserted, formed a melancholy and decided contrast.—Cecilia shuddered as she passed along, for deeds of horror and desperation rushed instantly to her thoughts. She recollected the bloody tragedy performed by the *Pazzi* in the sixteenth century; and with a degree of superstition, which terror only could have inspired, almost imagined she saw the shade of the murdered Giuliano rising from among the cloisters.—A figure did move in the distance; but as it receded slowly through the arches, it was ascertained to be a Friar, who had been performing an act of penance in one of the chapels.

"Could I forget the sacrilege," cried Varàno, smiling at the apprehensions which she had betrayed, and alluding to the subject that had so recently engrossed her thoughts, "I should consider this immense Duomo as the place of all others fit for conspiracy and assassinations!"

"Yes, and the falling shades of the evening," replied Cecilia, "seem to add new horrors to what would be sufficiently impressive in the splendour of the day: yet the cupola is grand, and the architecture, though heavy, gives a striking, but certainly a very gloomy idea of ancient magnificence."

"It is solidity we affect here," cried Varàno, "not lightness;—it is Tuscan, you know, solid and durable as the world itself."

"You do not, I hope, Mademoiselle," interrupted the Marchese gravely, "despise our mode of architecture?"

"By no means, my Lord," said Cecilia, "I meant not to object to it."

"It was brought hither," resumed the Marchese, "by a Grecian colony which first settled in Tuscany, then Etruria, and discovers the exquisite taste and style of the ancients."

"Nothing can more surely evince true taste," cried Morsino, who had now penetrated sufficiently the Marchese's character, "than a renunciation of all trifling and meretricious ornament; as nothing so truly marks literary genius, as a dislike to gaudy and unmeaning metaphor."

"You are right, my Lord, very right!" returned the Marchese; "in poetry, in painting, and in architecture, our country has no rivals:—Tuscany is, you know, to Italy, what Athens was to Greece!"

The Marchesa, speaking of the Corinthian style of architecture, declared her preference of it to the Tuscan, which she described as too plain, too heavy, and too gloomy.

"I should greatly wonder, my dear," said the Marchese with some satire, "if you did not think so—women are fond of ornament, and often overlook perfection in search of it; nor is it strange that it should be so, since they are taught to estimate it from their cradles; and have seldom judgment enough to distinguish the gem from the counterfeit."

"An admirably turned compliment truly," said Olivia with her usual archness; "but you will allow, my Lord, that the Marchesa, once in her life at least, gave an incontestable proof of her judgment—and one too she will never forget, I'll answer for it."

"Indeed!" cried the Marchese, "and pray what was it?—Explain yourself, lady!"

"Could any thing but a nice judgment—a fine, discriminating taste," rejoined Olivia, "determine her to prefer the Marchese di Varàno to a whole phalanx of suitors, who were said to be dying at her feet, and to be forming daily invocations to the Virgin, lest, uninfluenced by the entreaties of her venerable sire, she should attain the important age of fourteen before she became a matron."

"I did not consider that, I confess," said the Marchese; "but how are we to decide whether the preference included was to my person, my rank, or my understanding?"

"Your person, my Lord, to be sure,—and your understanding!"

"These might have some influence, no doubt," said the Marchese, "but family, for you know, lady, mine is very ancient, might have more."

"To be nobly descended," cried Olivia, still more shrewdly, "is certainly one of the first of human blessings!"

"The virtues of our ancestors," resumed the Marchese, "remind us what ought to be our own; if we degenerate, we disgrace them."

"You have frequently told me, my dear uncle, and I have as frequently forgotten," said Olivia, "what was the circumstance by which you became related to the Medici:—the sight of this frightful old Church recals them to my recollection!"

"The only alliance I claim with that family," returned the

Marchese, "is through marriage:—if you will attend to me, lady, I will explain it.—Cosmo, the son of Giovanni de Medici, had two wives—the one Leonora di Tolede, who brought him two sons, Giovanni and Garcias—the other Camilla Martello, a Florentine, by whom he had a daughter married to Cæsar D'Este, Duke of Modena.—The Archduchess Camilla was a descendant from our house; and the uniting her daughter with the Sovereign of Modena, was the means of connecting it with two Dukedoms."

"I hope you reckon the virtues of Cosmo the first among those of your other ancestors?" said Olivia.

"By these he was made highly illustrious," replied the Marchese; "his power was uncontroulable, and his possessions splendid. It was he who purchased that immense repository of art, constructed with more ambition than prudence by Lucca Pitti, and which finally caused his ruin. Hurt by the commendations bestowed on the Palace of the famous Filippo Strozzi, he determined to build one, the court of which would be large enough to contain that of his rival. This he afterwards did; and expending the whole of his property, it was purchased, as I have before observed, by Cosmo."

"You have proved him to have been rich and powerful," cried Olivia, "but not virtuous. This is the first time in all my life, my Lord, that ever I heard riches and power confounded with mental excellence."

"These, however, may be more nearly allied than you imagine," rejoined the Marchese, indignantly.—"It is possible that virtue may exist without them; but if we are without the means of exerting these virtues, they lie dormant; and if so, of what use are they to the possessor?"

"Pardon me, my Lord," said the Marchesa, "you mistake, I think: the possessor, who is withheld by situation from bringing them more immediately to notice, derives, in that case, the only benefit.—Denied the ability of exerting them in a more extensive sphere of action, the public are the sufferers, and not the individual.—He enjoys them in silent complacency; and if he laments at all, it is only that he cannot render them more generally useful."

"Then you consider rank and birth, which are universally allowed to lead to noble emulation," said the Marchese, raising his voice, and regarding her with a look of stern contempt, "as mere fortuitous advantages, unworthy alike the attention of the great and good mind!"

"Excuse me, my Lord, I do not," replied the Marchesa; "if they lead to the attainment of excellence, they are highly estimable, and such, I am convinced, they often have done: if otherwise, as we have great examples before us in a wise and noble ancestry, the consequences are doubly humiliating—we are then unworthy the esteem even of the meanest!—In Cosmo we reflect upon a great, but wicked man—a man whose abilities would have added dignity to the most exalted station, and whose vices would have disgraced the lowest."

"True, Madam," interposed Varàno, "for he was an assassin! —the murderer of his son!"

"It was an act of justice!" said the Marchese angrily. "Garcias was the murderer of Giovanni the Cardinal, his brother; and who so proper to inflict the punishment he merited, as he who had suffered most by it, his father? By resigning him to the laws of his country, he would have disgraced himself and his house!—by avenging the deed with his own hand, he secured the honour of both."

"Neither honour nor justice," exclaimed Varàno, "could have demanded the perpetration of an act, at which nature and humanity recoil!"

"Brutus murdered his sons," cried the Marchese, "and he was esteemed noble."

"The sons of Brutus conspired against the freedom of the State, my Lord," returned Varàno.

"The deed was not more atrocious," said the Marchese.

"To the public it was, my Lord, though the private grief, in the case of Cosmo, might be more exquisite.—Besides, the fact was not proved; it never could be ascertained: where then was the justice—and what that honour, which could arm him against the life of his son, of whose guilt no testimony, no positive evidence at least could be procured?—a son too, who, in compliance with the entreaties of his mother, and with the permission of his father, came to throw himself at his feet, after a severe and unhappy banishment."

"It was only upon the ground that the punishment was merited that I have ventured to defend it," said the Marchese. —"Prove Garcias to have been innocent, and Cosmo sinks at once from the unbiased judge—the resolute avenger of cruelty, into the aggressor and the murderer. The fact, as you observe, was never absolutely proved; nevertheless, we have every reason to suppose his suspicions, formed as they were from the known character of his son, were not founded on conjecture."

"You may remember," said Olivia, "that when I began to enquire into the virtues of Cosmo, my uncle talked to me of his possessions—a proof that he thought not very highly of his virtues."

"Because I find both you and the Marchesa, by whom you have been tutored," returned the Marchese, "too apt to undervalue what you ought to estimate."

"Good my Lord," said Olivia, "what is it on which we ought to set so high a value?"

"On the state in which Providence has placed you—on your connections: they are noble, Lady, and as such, worthy your highest esteem and veneration!"

"If the Marchesa, my Lord, be as insensible as you have represented to the privileges and dignities annexed to rank," cried Olivia, "what greater proof can be required of her decided preference of your person and accomplishments to those of her other lovers?"

"Your sex, my dear Olivia," replied the Marchese, "decide sometimes from the heart, but much oftener from caprice:—the Marchesa and yourself may afford exceptions to this rule."

"Most true, my Lord; and if I had any judgment—but alas! I am but a woman, and we, unless like the moon, we are allowed to receive it by reflection from the superior planet *Man*, can have no pretention to it.—A faint dawn of reason, one degree only above mere animal instinct, is the utmost you can expect from us; and without reason, judgment, you know, cannot exist. But had I the power of discrimination—that is, were I of *your sex*, my Lord, I should consider the Marchesa's preference of you, assured as you must be of her entire exemption from every interested motive, as the highest compliment that could be paid you—I told you, if you recollect, that it was your person and understanding, and not your rank, which determined her in her choice—and now, my dear good uncle, you see I was right:—a man could scarcely have judged better—no, not even if he were a Duke!"

The sprightly and good-humoured manner in which these words were delivered, restored the contracted brow of the Marchese to more than its accustomed benignity.—They returned soon after to the Palace, where the evening was spent like the preceding ones, in a variety of conversations, which Olivia, who possessed that happy temperature of mind which resists every thing unpleasant, contrived to render easy, cheerful, and entertaining.

From the vivacity of her young friend, and the mild attentions of the Marchesa, who failed not to urge whatever benevolence could dictate, or politeness suggest to dispel her melancholy, Cecilia derived as much satisfaction as in her situation she could possibly experience:—but sorrow for her late irreparable loss preyed upon her heart; and she frequently withdrew to indulge the grief that oppressed her, in the solitude of her chamber.

The view from this room was singularly beautiful. It commanded the *Ponte della Trinita* with the remains of Fiesole on its banks—a range of Apennines towering beyond, now studded with convents and castles, and now frowning with forests of pine, cedar, and lentiscus; whilst a fine terrace beneath her feet, to which she could descend from a *balcone* covered with flowers, brilliant in colour, and fragrant in scent, mingled with myrtle and other evergreens, united all the young sweets of Spring with the maturer beauty of the more advanced season.—Here she loved to watch the declining orb as it sunk beyond the distant hills—to mark its last empurpled beam as it faded from the towers of Fiesole, partially disclosing the Cascine woods, now exposed, and now lost in the falling glooms of the night.

Here wrapped in that tender melancholy so soothing to fancy and to grief, she mused on her departed friend; and whilst she recalled to her memory his invaluable precepts, endeavoured to strengthen her mind with that fortitude, by which alone she could be enabled to practise them.

CHAPTER V

—————I never yet saw man,
How wise, how noble, young, how rarely featur'd,
But she would spell him backward:—if fair-fac'd,
She'd swear the gentleman should be her sister;
If black, why, Nature, drawing of an antic,
Made a foul blot; if tall, a lance ill-headed;
If low, an aglet very vilely cut;
If speaking, why, a vane blown with all winds;
If silent, why, a block moved with none.
So turns she every man the wrong side out,
And never gives to truth and virtue that
Which simpleness and merit purchaseth.

SHAKESPEARE.

AMONG some other guests engaged to dine at the Palace on the following day, was Signor Pandolfo, the stranger whom they had met with at the *Palazzo Pitti*, who had been introduced by Morsino to the Marchese the morning after he had fulfilled his engagement with him at the appointed Casino.

Neither the person nor manners of this Signor were at all calculated to ensure him a hasty prepossession.—He seemed to be upwards of fifty—his features were harsh, his complexion sallow, his figure tall, meagre, and ungraceful.—He spoke little during dinner, and arose immediately after, as did also the Count, who, pleading urgent engagements, retired with him to the *Curio*.

The dessert withdrawn, the ladies left the room for the gardens, the Marchese and Signora to enjoy their customary repose in an apartment used for the purpose, and Cecilia and Olivia to take a walk in an adjoining shrubbery.—As soon as they were alone, Olivia introduced the subject with which she had before so much perplexed Cecilia, relative to the connexion supposed formerly to have subsisted between Varàno and Ottavia.

"Your story is a very strange one," said Cecilia with a forced smile; "and the more I am acquainted with the Signor, "the more incredible it appears!"

"Why, were we to judge from appearances only," replied Olivia, "it might seem so; but men, my dear Cecilia, are so deceitful, and so easily flattered! Did not you mind my uncle the other day when I complimented him on his person and understanding, could a boy of fifteen have been more highly gratified?"

"But are not those who flatter, as culpable as those who are misled by it," asked Cecilia, "supposing it to be as you say, merely flattery?"

"Not always; for if it had not been for me, what would have been the consequence? The Marchesa dared to think for herself—nay, she had even the audacity to declare it!—The breach would have been irreparable if I had not interfered!"

"And does this prove that the report to which you allude," said Cecilia, "has any foundation in truth?"

"Not absolutely; but it proves men vain—and if vain, easily led into error.—No gudgeon can aim at the lure more greedily than they do at praise:—bait the hook with this, and you may catch them by dozens!"

"And to this rule you believe there are no exceptions?" cried Cecilia.

"A few, perhaps—my cousin Lorenzo, for instance, has more sense, and less vanity, than half his sex put together; and as to his affair with Ottavia, it was nothing—a mere nothing! He procured the girl a husband, and what could he do more?"

"A husband!" repeated Cecilia; "is Ottavia then married?"

"Undoubtedly she is!" rejoined Olivia. "But la, why do you blush so?—*Il cielo vi guardi!* if I had told you that Varàno had married her himself, you could not have been more confused!

"Oh! what would I have given," resumed she, laughing immoderately, "for Ottavia to have produced a young Sbirro!—What an honour to his papa—the Lady-mother—and the whole house of Varàno!—Methinks I see them now!—me, for I am determined the talk should devolve on *me*, introducing him to my uncle. —'This, my Lord,—give me leave, my Lord,—(on my knees, you know, for I kneel admirably), to introduce to you another, though remoter heir, to the ancient titles of Varàno.' ——Oh exquisite!

—Then the little urchin lisping grandpapa, for I should not forget
to teach him this!—What a scene for painting!—How it would
grace the old picture gallery where my Lord deposits his ancestors!——Behold my uncle, his brow contracting to a frown of
more than usual austerity!—'Take the brat hence—remove him
from my sight this instant! Is this your regard for your family, Lady
Olivia?'—Then rises the Lady-mother, blushing, yet assuming all
her dignity.—Now she sweeps across the room—and now she
pauses in suspense:—'Surely, Olivia—surely, my dear!'——'Yes,
my honoured Madam, nothing so sure!—Will you not kiss your
grandson?'——Then the storm rises again!—I kneel—I entreat
—I conjure!—Look on that brow—what dignity!—what majestic sweetness!—who can gaze on him, and mistake his origin?
—Observe, my Lord,—your very look—mark the expression
of that eye!—that countenance too, how finely illumed!—how
sweetly does it blend the angel smile of the Marchesa with the
manly but serene complacency which distinguishes that of her
illustrious consort!"

"You have charming spirits, Lady Olivia," said Cecilia, smiling
—"you can never have known sorrow."

"Now what will you give me," cried Olivia, "to convince you
that all I have been telling you is an absolute falsehood?"

"As much praise as the fabricator of such an ingenious story
deserves," rejoined Cecilia, significantly.

"No, seriously, I was not the inventor; the tale was fabricated,
as I have been told by Signor Girolamo, and had its rise in the
following incident.—It is the custom, you know, in Italy for the
actresses and singers to enter the upper boxes of the Theatre,
where they remain between the acts, and during the recitativo
parts of the performance. While there, they are often visited by
young people of distinction, who, if they happen to be pretty,
amuse themselves in talking with them till the Opera begins.
—Ottavia no sooner appeared in public as a singer, than her
talents and her beauty procured her a number of attendants,
among whom was Varàno.—Going one evening to her box
before the performance commenced, he found her alone, and
in tears; and, on enquiring the cause, drew from her, after much
sympathy and persuasion, the simple narrative of her sorrows.

—Ottavia had been designed originally for the son of a person of her own class; for so disreputable is the office of Sbirro, and so insurmountable the prejudices annexed to this profession, that none but the son of a Sbirro has ever been known to marry the daughter of one—the very lowest of the canaille being averse from forming any possible connection with this despised people, who are considered as involved by their office in disgrace and infamy.—Unfortunately, however, before the marriage could take place, one of the Nobles of the city, on seeing Ottavia at the Theatre, made proposals to her father, which, although dishonourable, in consideration of great pecuniary advantages, he consented to accept; and Ottavia was forbid, on pain of his displeasure, to receive the addresses of her former lover.—Varàno, who is a perfect knight-errant in the cause of distressed beauty, was no sooner apprized of Ottavia's disappointment, than he undertook, through an application to her father, to obviate the difficulties which opposed her marriage. This, by duly administering to his avaricious propensities, he finally effected; and the young couple, who had suffered a mutual uneasiness from their late cruel separation, were soon happily united. This," resumed Olivia, "is the whole of the adventure; and thus it was," said she, taking Cecilia's hand with an affectionate air, "that Varàno procured Ottavia a husband."

Cecilia's joy, as she listened to this account, was visible in her countenance; and she returned the friendly pressure with a look which shewed how greatly she was interested in whatever concerned Varàno.—After a few moments' silence, she demanded of Olivia how she had acquired her intelligence. Olivia informed her that, meeting with Lorenzo accidentally in the Marchesa's antiroom, she had rallied him on the subject of Ottavia, which was so displeasing to the Marchesa, that she had insisted upon his clearing himself from an aspersion it was impossible, she said, he could deserve; and from what passed between the Marchesa and her son at this interview, she was indebted for the above explanation.

The appearance of Varàno, who was followed at some distance by the Marchesa and Signora, put an end to this discourse. —They continued to stroll about the shrubbery till the evening began to close, when they withdrew to the *Padiglióne*.[1]—In about an hour the Count, who had been absent with Signor Pandolfo, returned, and accompanied by the Marchese, entered the gardens, where coffee was soon after served.—Morsino appeared more animated than usual; his conversation was sprightly and insinuating; and though his attentions were chiefly engrossed by the Marchese, he found many opportunities of speaking to Cecilia, to whom he sometimes directed the lively sallies of his wit, but now and then assumed an air of tenderness which it was impossible to misunderstand.

As the Marchesa seemed to derive pleasure from such arrangements as were most likely to contribute to the amusement of her guests, she proposed that they should make a party on the following day to visit the Convent and famous woods of *Val' ombroso;* which being instantly agreed to, it was determined that they should take an early breakfast at the Palace, and set off immediately after.

"You are no doubt informed, my Lord," said the Marchese, addressing himself to Morsino, "to whom this pious foundation of retired Benedictines owes its origin?"

The Count replied that he was not only ignorant of the circumstance which give rise to the institution, but even of the name of its founder.

"It was erected," continued the Marchese, "by a Tuscan Nobleman, called Giovanni Gualberto.—A descendant of his married a daughter of our house, which enables us to quarter the *Leoni argenti* of the Gualberti with the *Palle d'oro* of the Medici."

"A most glorious and honourable privilege indeed, my Lord!" said Olivia.

"You mistake, Lady," interrupted the Marchese; "the honour was on the side of the Gualberti."

"What, on the founder of the Convent, my Lord!" returned Olivia. "Alack! the pity he did not live to be sensible of it!"

"Signora, Signora, will you never have done with this childish—this invincible trifling?" resumed the Marchese. "I said the honour was conferred on the *Gualberti*—not on the erector of the Convent, but the family."

1 A Pavilion.

"Olivia, my dear," said the Marchesa, "is you know an only, and consequently a spoiled child. At present she has seen little of life, and the little she *has* seen, has served rather to increase than correct the natural levity of her temper.—A more thorough knowledge of the world, however, and of herself, will teach her the folly of indulging it, and the necessity of inuring herself to habits of discretion."

"It is that same thing called discretion," cried Olivia, "which makes all, except you, my dear Madam—my uncle, and a few others, so unaccountably stupid: though our country, as I have been told, is less annoyed by it than most others.—Yet thus it was for ever with the Lady Abbess of my Convent—'Lady Olivia, when shall I teach you discretion?—Do you recollect for what purpose you was sent here?'—Then comes one of the sisterhood, whose solemn aspect, because I suspect it of hypocrisy, makes me laugh.—She calls me wicked—drops her beads with a tear —and finishes her reproofs with an awful prayer to the Virgin to assist my reformation; though, if it had not been for me and my companions, who contrived, by a variety of manœuvres, to keep them from despondency, they would have sunk into *ennui*."

The Count regretted that so much youth and beauty should be condemned, as in Italy, to the unvaried monotony of a conventual life and expressed his disapprobation of those compulsatory methods by which thousands are enslaved—the devoted, not the voluntary victims of ambition and avarice.—The Marchese observed that, were no such measures employed, the dignity of many of the most ancient and honourable houses in Italy could not be supported; that the estates of the Nobles would frequently be subjected to so many divisions, as to leave little to the heir except the empty possession of a title and name—a circumstance which would bear hard upon the autocracy of the State, and tend to the subversion of peace and good order.

The Count agreed with the Marchese that no measures whatever ought to be taken which could lessen the power and respectability of the Nobles, whom he represented as the supporters and guardians of the State. No one, he said, could be more decidedly averse from that dangerous system of politics which tends to a general equalization of person and properly, than he was; and no one more desirous of dispelling those disgraceful and seductive theories which, disguised under the specious appearance of superior virtue, lead to anarchy and confusion.——A comparison between the republican and aristocratic forms of government succeeded, which was just decided in favour of the latter, when the Marchesa arose, and the party quitted the pavilion.

In the morning the Marchesa, complaining of indisposition, excused herself from accompanying her friends in their expedition to the Apennines; and Cecilia, who had a similar plea, besought permission to remain with her at the Palace.—This proposal was at first resolutely opposed both by the Count and Varàno; but on her assuring them that she was yet too unwell to undertake a ride of near six-and-thirty miles without considerable fatigue, they discontinued their entreaties; and the breakfast hour at an end, the Lady Viola and Olivia, attended by the Marchese, the Count, and the Signor, departed for *Val' ombroso*, leaving Cecilia to the polite attentions and refined conversation of the Marchesa.

Cecilia had written to Signora di Rosalvo an account of her journey and safe arrival at Genoa. To this letter an answer, enclosed with some others, directed to Boraccio, had lately been forwarded to Florence, full of the most affectionate enquiries concerning her and De Sevignac, and requiring the fulfilment of their promise of the Castello di Montani in their way from Italy. —Tears filled Cecilia's eyes as she perused this letter, which she read again with renewed anguish; till, recollecting that a more favourable opportunity than the present one might not speedily occur, she resolved to dedicate a portion of the morning to the duties of friendship; and by communicating the melancholy tidings she wished, yet dreaded to unfold, to spare herself the uneasiness of a future relation.

In her reply she promised, if permitted to leave Italy, to spend some weeks with her friend; but, alluding to the conversation passed at Pisa, added it was by no means certain that such an indulgence would be granted her; Boraccio being appointed her guardian, without whose permission and concurrence she had no power to act.—When she had concluded her letter, which abounded with many graceful acknowledgements of past kindnesses, she rung for Claudia, the young woman whose office it was to attend upon her, to convey it to the *Posta*.[1]

Claudia instantly appeared; but as Cecilia turned to speak to her, she perceived that she had been weeping: for her eyes were red and swoln, and the agitation of her manner indicated some new and great misfortune. As Cecilia spoke, she threw herself into a chair, fell back, and burst into tears.—Cecilia flew immediately to her assistance, and supporting her in her arms, demanded gently the cause of her emotions.

"Some great affliction has, I fear, befallen you," said she, in a voice the most soothing; "but do not weep thus; confide your sorrows to me, and if I cannot alleviate, I will endeavour at least to uphold you under them."

"Ah no, excuse me, Signora," rejoined Claudia, sobbing violently, "I am unworthy of your care! Miserable—ill-fated wretch! for what am I reserved? Was it for this I fasted—was it to be the victim of delusion I put up my prayers to our divine Prophet?—*O giorno infelice!*[2] why was I born? or if born, why did I survive that hour?"

Amazed at the import of these words, and urged equally by curiosity and compassion, Cecilia entreated that she would explain herself; and Claudia, consoled at length by her tenderness, related her simple and very artless story.

It was a tale which discovered an unhappy mixture of superstition and weakness. The poor girl, having resided for some years in the Marchese's family, had amassed a small sum in his service; but Claudia was ambitious, and the acquisition of a few *zecheens*, which were all that she had realized, was insufficient for the gratification of her darling propensity. The desire of becoming rich superseded every other; and she was induced to believe that by risking a few *paoli* in the purchase of *lotto* tickets, this end might be accomplished.—Her design was no sooner formed than executed. The *lotto* at Leghorn presented the immediate means of trial; and she embarked on this ocean of chance without fear or delay. The numbers, purchased at the low rate of six for a *paolo*, were some of them drawn prizes; and Claudia felt her inclination

1 Post-house.
2 Oh unhappy day!

for gambling rewarded. Her next essay was at Florence, where she procured tickets to the amount of five *zecheens*.—This was an adventure of some consequence to Claudia. Her dreams, however, presented no unlucky omen. She fasted during the usual time, six-and-thirty hours—prayed, and numbered *Ave Marias* to the Virgin; entreating for the interference of some saint or prophet, to declare to her the numbers destined for success.

Fortune, however, if we may allow of the intrusion of this classical personage among so holy a company, was less propitious than before. The *zecheens* were sunk in that abyss of imposition; and poor Claudia was convinced that all who sue for the patronage of this undistinguishing deity, are not to receive it indiscriminately. But as by hazarding something more, she might recover what was lost, she resolved to make another effort.—The tickets for this purpose were yet unpurchased, when the Prophet Jeremiah appeared to her in a dream in the dress of a Monk, and condescended to whisper to her in her sleep a list of numbers, which he promised should be fortunate.—To wait for the monthly *lotto* at Florence after such an interposition, (this son of Hilkiah, as an elegant[1] writer observes, having more influence in Tuscany dead, than he did, while living, in the land of Anathoth), would have required a degree of patience beyond what Claudia could now boast: she accordingly dissipated the remaining part of her wages in that of Leghorn.

The loss of her property, with which died all hopes of future advancement, was a severe stroke to poor Claudia: but this was not her only misfortune. Fabio, a young Florentine in the Marchese's suite, to whom she was shortly to have been married, either irritated with her losses, or disgusted with her temerity, had withdrawn his claim to her hand, abandoning her to the melancholy retrospection of her own imprudence.

Such was the account delivered by Claudia to Cecilia, who, having listened to her with great patience, though she could not always forbear smiling at the superstition she had disclosed, enquired how much she had ventured. Claudia hesitated, and at length replied, she believed that the whole would amount to about eight *zecheens*.

1 Lord Corke.

"Here then are ten," said Cecilia, presenting her with that sum; "take these, my good girl, and remember that time obliterates not from your memory the lesson experience has so severely taught you.—Fabio, should his addresses be resumed, may find you more worthy of them than before; if not, you will have little reason to regret a lover who could so easily resign you."

Claudia's astonishment can only be conceived. She gazed alternately at the *zecheens* and on Cecilia, as if doubting the evidences of her senses; and then throwing herself at her feet, burst into a fresh agony of tears. Cecilia, affected by this gratitude, raised her from her posture, and having requested that she would compose herself, and not forget her admonitions, she returned to the room where she had left the Marchesa.—The day was spent at the Palace till the evening, when they took a ride without the city, to enjoy the coolness of the hour in an open and extensive prospect.

The sun was departing from the scene, when, ascending one of the three hills which encompass Florence, they looked down upon its magnificent spires, rising on a brilliant horizon, and on the delicious plain below, gay with woods, and adorned with all the riches of cultivation. To the south of this appeared Mount Lupo, whose craggy summits, formed into cones, or exhibiting fantastic shapes, contrasted well with the bright green of the pastures, and with the woods which stretched at its foot.—Around on every side were seen only images of grandeur or beauty.—The long perspective of Apennines, tinged with ethereal blue—vallies filled with the most delightful verdure, where, surrounded with green slopes, separated by hedge-rows of almond and juniper, appeared cottages, gardens, and vineyards—all of these, tinted by distance, and covered with the softening veil of twilight, shewed like a picture touched by the inimitable pencil of a Claude, where tint steals into tint, till one soft harmonious hue pervades and unites the various colours of the landscape.

When they had reached the summit of the hill, they alighted from the carriage and the Marchesa, whose every look was intelligence, pointed out to Cecilia the different towns and villages it commanded, among which were Prato, Cajano, Pistoia, and St. Casciano.—Of these Cecilia was most struck, with Prato. The number and elegance of its villas—the Arno flowing at its feet —the Apennines towering beyond—the beautiful prospect the opening vista afforded of the more distant mountains—the luxuriant plantations of fig, date, and cypress that adorn the shores of the river, all mellowed as they were with the softening shadows of evening, composed a scene of beauty and romantic splendour she had never seen excelled.—From these the eye, glancing farther to the north, caught a view of *Poggio à Caiano*,[1] famous for the murder of the unfortunate Francisco and Bianca Capello, who there breathed their last. Cecilia recollected this dreadful and unhappy catastrophe; and as she withdrew her eyes from Poggia, and fixed them on the *Ponte della Trinita*, she recurred to the assassination of Buonsignori, the ill-fated husband of Bianca who, in consequence of his wife's beauty and his own arrogance, met his fate in that place.

The admiration with which the polished manners and delicate attentions of the Marchesa had impressed Cecilia, was considerably increased by a nearer intimacy. She found in her conversation and abilities sources of inexhaustible entertainment; and in every sentiment she expressed, something so congenial to her own, that almost every look they exchanged, and every word they uttered, announced the sympathy of their minds, and the pleasure they derived from each other's society. The *Lucciola* had begun to light its gem, and the evening to deepen into the shades of night, ere they thought of returning.

"If we are able to take such rides as these," said the Marchesa as she re-entered the carriage, "the plea which excused us from *Val'ombroso* will scarcely be accepted."

"I shall have the satisfaction of having spent the day as happily, and I am sure as profitably," cried Cecilia, "as if I had partaken of their excursion."

"How long, my love," said the Marchesa, smiling, "have those eyes of your's learned to flatter?"

"Ah, Madam!" rejoined Cecilia, "did you know my heart—"

1 A villa belonging to the Grand Duke of Tuscany, in the mid-way between Florence and Pistoia, built by Pope Leo the Tenth.—The Grand Duke, Francis the First, was here poisoned with his second wife Bianca Capello, by Ferdinand, his brother, who succeeded him in the Dukedom.

"I am sure it is a grateful one," cried the Marchesa, "and cold and insensible must be that heart which cannot sympathize in its feelings."

"Generous and noble Lady!" exclaimed Cecilia.

"Nay, it is your own merit, my dear, and not my partiality, to which you are indebted for this praise.—Had I a daughter, I should have prayed *that daughter* might have been like you."

Cecilia, whose countenance glowed with modesty while listening to commendations so grateful to her, found little difficulty in replying to these friendly professions; and she returned to the Palace with a mind less oppressed, and spirits more animated than at any former period of her visit.

As they were passing through the hall, they were informed that a stranger, which was Signor Pandolfo, had been there several times in great haste, and was now waiting in a saloon in much visible impatience. They had scarcely entered this room when the party returned; and Signor Pandolfo, whose business was with Morsino, took him apart.—When they returned, the Count looked chagrined and uneasy.

"I fear," said Boraccio, as soon as the Signor had withdrawn, "that the subject of your discourse has been an unpleasant one; you seem agitated, my Lord!"

"The only uneasiness I experience," replied Morsino, "arises from my disinclination to leave friends from whose society I have extracted so much pleasure.

"Is it possible!—You are not I hope going to leave us?"

"An affair of importance," resumed the Count, "hastens me to Venice. My presence there is indispensable; but my stay shall not be long:—I will see you shortly at Genoa—Florence I must quit to-morrow."

"To-morrow, my Lord?"

"I lament it; but business, which I cannot now explain, allows no alternative."

He then requested that Boraccio would indulge him with a few minutes' conversation; and they withdrew together through a door which led from a terrace to the lawn, which they passed and repassed several times, apparently in earnest discourse. When they re-entered the room, which was not till they had been absent near an hour, Morsino appeared more at ease than before. Cecilia shared, but did not engross his assiduities:—his discourse was directed as much to Olivia as to her; and though a tender and melancholy earnestness marked his manner when addressing himself to the former, he seemed anxious to avoid all peculiarity in his attentions, and to conceal a dejection which, from whatever source it might arise, he had not the power to resist. The next morning, after taking a polite adieu of the Marchese and the rest of his friends, and a more tender, though still a guarded one of Cecilia, the Count pursued his journey toward Venice.

CHAPTER VI

Deh pensa quanto falsamente piace,
Onore, utilitate, ovver diletto,
Ove per più s'afferma esser la pace.

LORENZO DE MEDICI.

Ah! think how false that bliss the mind explores
In futile honours or unbounded stores!
How poor the bait that would thy steps decoy
To sensual pleasure, and unmeaning joy!

ROSCOE.

THE Signora, meanwhile, though she joined in the amusements of the Palace, was thoughtful, spoke little, and seemed uneasy and dispirited.—The acquisition of a fortune, which had flattered her with so pleasing a prospect of independence and affluence, like many other prospects seen only in the distance, proved infinitely less alluring in reality than it had appeared in perspective. —In pursuing an expected good, she had encountered a real evil; and the moment which placed her in the possession of what she had long and anxiously desired, and promised to gratify and fulfil all her future wishes, was perhaps, the most unhappy one she had known.—It had discovered to her that the estates, which the will of De Sevignac in a summary, but regular manner had secured to her, were all she could call her's; that sums had been lavished by Boraccio, and the debts incurred to a considerable amount, which, except by the sale of these estates, or the adoption of some scheme of economical retrenchment, there appeared no means to discharge. Boraccio had received the will, as has been already observed, from the hand of De Sevignac, who, in consideration of his recent indisposition and declining health, had conveyed it with him from France.—To the period of De Sevignac's death Boraccio had looked forward with the greatest solicitude. His former irregularities and present expences had thrown him into difficulties from which he expected a temporary, but immediate relief; and his mind was wholly engrossed by a vague calculation of the value of the estates, and in fixing on the most advantageous means of disposing of them, when he found, to his inexpressible concern, that they were settled upon the Signora, without whose consent and approbation a small part only of what was contained in the will could be appropriated to his own immediate purposes. —The Lady Viola, however, by a single effort of her power, could secure the continuance of his pleasures for some time longer, and afford him an opportunity of regaining the immense sums which he had lost at *pallone, bigliardo*[1], and other games of chance.

For some weeks previous to their departure from Genoa, the Signora had importuned her husband's acquiescence to a scheme of alteration at the Palace, which, splendid as it was, she assured him would admit of improvement. This plan Boraccio, notwithstanding his inclination for novelty and shew, had the strongest reasons to delay, if not to oppose; the only person whom he could employ in the execution of this design, having already become clamorous for the payment of a debt long since contracted.—The Signora could not, however, abandon her intended scheme of improvement; and the disappointment occasioned by the delay of her hopes, served only to convince her of the indispensability of its performance.—No sooner, therefore, did they arrive at Pisa, than she renewed her entreaties, secretly wondering that Boraccio, who had always appeared too profuse, or too thoughtless to deny himself a present gratification from the apprehension of future consequences, should consider the sum necessary to its accomplishment, of importance enough to require a momentary hesitation.

1 Billiards

Boraccio heard her with patience; but, after listening to her, as before, with an affected complacency, dismissed her with a promise that he would think upon it on his return; adding, he had other affairs in hand, and till these were arranged, he wished to be spared all farther application and entreaty on this subject.—But no sooner had he perused the will, and found, to his unspeakable regret and mortification, that the estates were not devoted to his power, than he recollected that the Signora's request, unreasonable as it was, might be made subservient to his own interests. —He knew her passions were strong, but he knew also that her judgment was weak; and whatever difficulties he might have to encounter in his endeavours to bias the former, he despaired not, by flattery, promises, and persuasions, to gain an ascendancy over the latter.—Elated with this hope, he repaired to her apartment, and there mentioned to her the conditions on which her request might be complied with.

The Signora, who had till this moment believed Boraccio's circumstances so affluent as to make the estates in question a matter of no importance, was greatly surprised at this proposal. Whether they were confirmed to her or not by will, she had expected them to be solely and exclusively at her own disposal; and as to mortify by her magnificence, to overbear by her rank, and humble by her beauty, the gay circle with whom she mixed, comprised the whole sum of her gratifications, she had considered them as more than equivalent for the loss of her relative, to whose death she had looked forward without pity and without remorse. Indignant, therefore, at this attempt to deprive her of her rights, she refused stedfastly to concede to any terms that could be offered.

Disappointed in this attack, yet not despairing of success by more determinate measures, Boraccio now sought, by addressing himself to her feelings, to acquire from her that consent which he could no longer hope for from any further appeal to her vanity.—He assured her that if she continued obstinate in her resolution of not relinquishing the estates, he was a ruined man; that his debts, and the sums which he had lost at play, were beyond his ability to discharge; and it was only from the chance of regaining the latter, that he could have any hopes of satisfying the demands of his creditors, who were now become urgent, or even of maintaining his present establishment.

"A run of ill luck," added he, "has of late pursued me. This, however, cannot last long; and by the power of making future efforts, I acquire the means not only of repairing my late losses, but of supporting myself against future ones."

The Signora was so shocked with this intelligence, that it was long before she could recover herself, and not till after repeated assertions, could she believe that he was serious.—Weak as she was, she had nevertheless understanding enough to detect the fallacy of his arguments.

A man who had been so long in the habit of losing, was more likely, she considered, to increase than to lessen the deficiency. Thus what her pride had instigated her to withhold, her prudence determined her to detain.—Whilst these estates continued her's, she had a ready and certain security against actual poverty; and resolving that no persuasion nor perseverance on the part of her husband should oblige her to renounce them, she left him in displeasure, protesting that she would never, by any act of her's, relinquish her claim, convinced as she now was of the propriety of reserving it, as a resource against future evils.

Boraccio no sooner found that the Signora was departed, without affording him the signature so necessary to his wishes, than no sense of honour or of delicacy restrained the expression of his indignation.—He flew immediately after her; and threatening, if she persisted in her refusal, to take such methods as should in the end oblige her to comply, the scene which had so much astonished Cecilia, ensued.

Having arrived thus far, we recur, though unwillingly, to an incident that preceded it, and which may afford an awful and instructive lesson to those who, rioting in dissipation and luxury, imagine, whilst they obey the impulse of every irregular desire, that they can return at discretion to the path they have quitted, and thus spare themselves the commission of any atrocious crime.—Alas! how soon does the mind, enervated by indulgence, empoisoned by luxury, lose its powers of exertion!—how rapid is the transition from virtue to vice!—and the barrier once thrown down, who can limit its progress!

In De Sevignac's will, the name of Cecilia, according to Boraccio's assertion, was *no where inserted:* but at the time it was delivered to him, he received a codicil in her favour, which was, to place her in the possession of four thousand Louis d'ors;—it bequeathed also legacies to the amount of near three hundred more to be distributed amongst the domestics at St. Foix.—The four thousand Louis d'ors were to be paid Cecilia at the expiration of two years, or on her marriage, should that event take place before the term prescribed: the interest of this sum, with a quarter in advance, she was to receive immediately.—De Sevignac had desired likewise, that if Cecilia wished to return to France, a proper person might be selected to accompany her thither; and, should the chateau remain unoccupied during the first full year after his decease, that she might have the liberty of residing there till she could fix upon a situation more agreeable to her wishes.

With the assurances which he received from Boraccio on this subject, De Sevignac was in every respect satisfied; but the former was no sooner alone, than he conceived the horrible design of destroying the codicil, and seizing the contents.—He was going to tear it, when something like remorse flashed upon his mind, and prevented him irresistibly from fulfilling his purpose; till, recollecting that he might hereafter make a recompence for the fraud he was meditating—that the will would not betray him, should he secrete it—and as to the servants at St. Foix, a smaller sum than the intended one would reward sufficiently their services, and that this, by appearing to come from him, would heighten the report of his generosity, he yielded to a temptation which he had not the virtue to resist; and by tearing the paper into a thousand pieces, put an end to the contest, and confirmed the villany he had projected.—Yet this point gained, he was as restless as before. The estates were ensured to the Signora; and unless, by a skilful application of remonstrances and threats, he could prevail upon her to resign them, he promised himself no very considerable advantage from his late manœuvre.—The consequences of this solicitude are already known.

Though Boraccio had assured De Sevignac that Cecilia should either remain at his Palace, or return to France, according as she should decide, he had no intention whatever of performing this engagement. The terms of admiration in which Morsino had spoken of her—his tender and impassioned glances—and, above all, his proposition of accompanying them to Pisa, gave him little room to suspect the sincerity of his attachment; and since by detaining her at Genoa, he might have the satisfaction of disposing of her to so great an advantage, he resolved first to delay, and afterwards resolutely to object to her intended departure.

The expected declaration was made to Boraccio by the Count at the conference partly overheard by Cecilia as she was passing from De Sevignac's chamber to her own, soon after Boraccio had parted, with much apparent displeasure, from the Lady Viola, his wife.—The few words accidentally caught by Cecilia, as she was crossing the gallery to her apartment, have already been mentioned; but as the intimacy into which the Count and Boraccio had so suddenly entered, seeing that at the time of their introduction at the Theatre at Genoa, they were utter strangers to each other, it may be proper to explain it.

Morsino, as it will be remembered, had seen Cecilia at Le Luc. He was then much struck with her beauty; but as he left Le Luc that night, he had no means of informing himself who she was, nor of what nature was the connection between her and Varàno.

From Provence he removed to Dauphine; and after travelling through Languedoc, Auvergne, and a part of Burgundy, set forward for Italy.

At the time that he reached Genoa, he thought no more of Cecilia till his accidental rencontre at the Opera, when his former admiration was renewed. He seemed, as was observed by Olivia, to be insensible to the presence of every other object; and how to gain an introduction to so fascinating a young creature, now solely employed his thoughts.—Though a Neapolitan by birth, he had a numerous acquaintance in various parts of Italy, and particularly at Genoa. Of this he accordingly availed himself to circulate an enquiry concerning Cecilia and her party; and having acquainted himself with the residence and character of Boraccio, and solicited access, he betted, played, and entered into all those debaucheries which he conceived most likely to ensure him an admission into his company and his palace.

In the conference held between Morsino and the Signor at the

Hotel at Pisa, the Count, alluding with much apparent concern to the unexpected and repeated losses which the latter had sustained, mentioned the having by him a few thousands of which he had no immediate necessity, and which he begged that he would do him the honour to use, till the fickle Deity of whom he trusted, should become weary of persecuting him.

After a few scruples on the part of Boraccio, this generosity was accepted; and the discourse at length turned upon Cecilia.—The Count declared he could not live without her; but seriously objected to the subject being mentioned to her till he had some opportunity of insinuating himself into her favour.—Boraccio was convinced that she would be highly sensible of the honour of securing such a conquest, and did not conceive any delay necessary. The Count interrupted him by observing that he had the most urgent reasons for desiring that what had passed between them that night, might remain wholly with themselves, and on this condition he might depend upon the continuance of his friendship.—The Signor promised attention to this command, and they parted, mutually satisfied with the evening's adventure.

Having taken a retrospect of the events which occurred at Pisa, as far as is requisite for the elucidation of our story, we return to Florence.

CHAPTER VII

> What man so wise, what earthly wit so ware
> As to descry the crafty, cunning traine,
> By which *Deceipt* doth maske in visour faire,
> And cast her coulours died deep in graine,
> To seeme like *Truth*, whose shape she well can faine,
> And fitting gestures to her purpose frame,
> The guiltlesse man with guile to entertaine?
>
> SPENSER.

A FEW days only had elapsed since the Count's departure from Florence, when Cecilia enquired of Boraccio concerning the packet.—Boraccio acknowledged the receipt of it, but refused to relinquish it at present; urging that he had received positive orders from De Sevignac that she should not be permitted to examine it till the expiration of some months.—Cecilia was greatly perplexed by this intelligence, till recollecting De Sevignac's words, *"I have left it to be delivered to you when I am gone, but not immediately on my decease,"* her astonishment subsided; and she withdrew with a determination of repressing all appearance of curiosity till the time intended for its delivery.

Boraccio's mind had of late been too much engrossed to allow him to think seriously on any subject in which he was not materially concerned; and probably, had he not been reminded of it by Cecilia, the packet, and the admonition that accompanied it, would have been alike forgotten.—Supposing that it contained only letters of advice, he had neither the curiosity nor inclination to enquire farther; and as it formed no part of his present plans to disobey De Sevignac's commands when they did not militate against his interests, he resolved, by a pretended adherence to his most trifling request, to preserve an appearance of conscientious exactness, which he hoped would remove all doubts of his integrity.

Morsino, in his last conference with Boraccio, betrayed more uneasiness than he had done at any former interview, and seemed at times greatly agitated.—He spoke of Cecilia in terms of impassioned fondness; and after various enquiries, from none of which he derived any apparent satisfaction, confessed that he had no hopes of obtaining any preference in her favour while she continued in the same house with Varàno, since to her decided partiality to him, he could alone impute the coldness and restraint which marked her present behaviour.—Boraccio, who, since the adventure in the library at Genoa, had reason to acquiesce in this opinion, acknowledged that much was to be dreaded from so dangerous a competitor. But after enumerating the difficulties each would have to encounter, and stating the impossibility of the family consent ever being procured for such a marriage, he endeavoured to convince the Count that the coldness of which he complained, proceeded merely from her ignorance of his intentions; adding, he had no doubt that, when informed of them, she would accord with them with humility and gratitude: and whatever expectations she had formed, if indeed she was extravagant

enough to have indulged any with regard to Varàno, she would
see the propriety of resigning a distant and uncertain alliance, to
ensure one equally affluent, and almost equally honourable.—
The Count was reassured by this discourse, and having earnestly
recommended what he was particularly anxious he should practice, the strictest silence, he withdrew, having previously wrested
a promise from Boraccio that he would be guided entirely by his
directions.

Whilst Boraccio's thoughts were thus vigorously employed in
the prosecution of his newly concerted plans, the mind of Varàno
continued fluctuating between hope and fear. Little accustomed
to dissimulation, he could not so far command himself but that
the Marchesa saw something very extraordinary in his conversation and manners.—His spirits were now high and now low,
without any evident cause; and at times a total abstraction of
mind wrapped him in apparent thoughtfulness.—When accidentally alone with his mother, he seemed perpetually on the eve of
disclosing something, which he as frequently checked, and then
suddenly fled to some other topic of discourse. He arose much
earlier than was his custom, seemed fond of being alone, and
had often been seen rambling about the grounds long before the
family were up.—This change in the manners and habits of her
son was too conspicuous to pass unobserved by the Marchesa,
who now endeavoured, by a more scrupulous attention than
she had yet paid, to ascertain its cause. To this the good-natured
raillery of Olivia, or the more pointed sarcasms of the Signora,
unassisted by her own observations, would have been insufficient to direct her; but her suspicions once excited, the inad-
vertent remarks of the one, and the invidious ones of the other,
recurred to her thoughts; and those attentions, which, while they
appeared to her but as the effects of benevolence, or of a well-
bred gallantry, had secretly delighted her, were now converted
into sources of uneasiness and displeasure.

Yet, although convinced that the beauty and engaging manners of Cecilia had impressed the heart of her son, her kindness
and solicitude towards her suffered no abatement. Believing him,
as she did, to be irresistible, she would have esteemed, or at least
have loved Cecilia less, could she have received these attentions

with indifference: but perfectly aware of the delusion, and of the impropriety of suffering them to proceed in it, she embraced an opportunity of speaking with Cecilia alone on this subject, briefly explaining the Marchese's intentions relative to Olivia, and the advantages to be acquired by such a connection.

Cecilia listened to this discourse with surprise and apprehension. The Marchesa's motive for introducing it could not be misconstrued; and the effort she employed to conceal her embarrassment served only to increase the emotion she had been struggling to stifle.

"The objects of our fondest affection," resumed the Marchesa, her eyes rivetted upon Cecilia as she spoke, "are perhaps only the more endeared to us by the solicitude they occasion. The anxiety we are compelled to feel is, notwithstanding, too acute for our peace; nor is it easy to determine, the pains and pleasures summed up, which would preponderate.—The parents of Lorenzo di Varàno must feel in an eminent degree the anxiety I have described. The son of a noble and not opulent house stands in so many relative situations, that it becomes every member of that house to unite in promoting a marriage equally advantageous and honourable.—In the Signora Olivia di Montelino we behold a lady every way calculated to sustain its dignity:—noble alike in every branch, lineal and collateral, the proudest house in Italy might sue for her alliance.—The friendship which has long subsisted between our families, and the immense possessions to which Olivia is heiress, render her a match in every respect desirable.—The Count is not less eager than ourselves to conclude this marriage; and though as yet they are unsuspicious of our intentions, our confidence in their affection leaves little doubt of their obedience: nevertheless, these are moments of great anxiety! When this is removed, and Lorenzo is established to the satisfaction of his family," continued the Marchesa, her eyes still fastened upon Cecilia with a look of penetrating earnestness, "no care will remain to disturb me; nor will my heart retain any wish half so ardent, so anxious, and so sincere, as that of promoting the happiness of my Cecilia."

She then tenderly embraced her; and perceiving she was almost sinking with confusion, spared her the effort to reply by hastily quitting the room.

The shock of this intelligence completely overpowered the spirits of Cecilia. The colour faded from her cheek, and a sudden faintness came over her, from which she recovered only to a painful consciousness of having discovered a passion she trembled to have betrayed, and the impropriety and even danger of its farther indulgence.

She retired to her chamber, where, being once more alone, the tears, which her pride had repressed, found vent, and she suffered them to flow unrestrained.

"So ends my dream of happiness," said she; "that deceitful illusion of bliss, portrayed by the flattering pencil of Hope, is now vanished from my sight for ever!—Oh Varàno! was it just—was it generous to deceive me thus? Was it likely a family so proud, so noble, would condescend to receive me, poor and dependant as I am!—and do not the credulity and presumption I have practised, merit the punishment they have incurred?"

She was startled from these reflections by the appearance of Claudia, who, since the accidental affair of the *lotto*, had been a frequent visitor in her chamber.

Cecilia was much pleased with the mild attentions of this girl, which seemed to flow from a gratitude as fervent as sincere. She sometimes conversed with her, but oftener listened with a patience and sweetness so peculiarly her own, to little anecdotes of her family, or to the narration of certain events which had occurred at the Palace, both before and since her arrival.—Flattered by this notice, Claudia would often linger in her apartment beyond what her duty required, appeared pleased when detained, and was observed to perform the little offices in which she engaged, with something more than a common zeal to oblige.—As her reserve wore off, she grew more and more communicative; and Cecilia became unintentionally acquainted with some circumstances relative to the Marchese which excited her surprise and curiosity.

The Marchese, she was told, had married his present Lady a short time after the death of the first, to whom his conduct had been so uniformly unkind, that it was thought by many to have occasioned the disorder of which she died.—In the last stage of her illness she was persuaded to try the baths at Lucca, and the

Marchese, at her request, agreed to accompany her.

Finding little benefit from this prescription, she was ordered to pursue her way along the shores of the Mediterranean toward France. The Marchese closed eagerly with this plan; and having an estate and chateau in one of the southern provinces of that country, proposed their removal thither.—Whether the Marchesa assented or not to this proposition, had never been ascertained; and what became of her afterwards nobody knew, as the domestics who attended them were dismissed, and a *laquais de place* hired in their stead.

The Marchese remained abroad some time, and then returned, bringing with him a child about six months old, whose birth, he said, had occasioned the death of his wife.

Several months passed on without any extraordinary occurrence, during which the Marchese seemed restless and unhappy; but going soon afterwards to Naples, he saw the present Marchesa, to whom he was shortly united, and in his affection for her soon lost all traces of his former uneasiness.—The same mystery, however, concerning the late Marchesa still continued. As her remains were not conveyed into Tuscany, nobody could surmise whether she died in Italy or in France.—Several reports were circulated about the neighbourhood, but it was difficult to know what ought to be believed;—some indeed went so far as to say she was still living; but as there appeared no grounds for this conjecture, it was almost universally discarded as an idle suggestion.—The general opinion was, that she had died in France; and that her death, agreeably to the Marchese's deposition, had rapidly succeeded the birth of her daughter.—This information was conveyed to Claudia by her mother, who resided at that time in the family.

Cecilia had often ruminated upon this account. At first it suggested unpleasant ideas, but these were almost immediately dismissed; and if an uneasy suspicion did intrude upon her mind, she had the prudence to repress the expression of it.

The look of tenderness and compassion which marked the countenance of the Marchesa when she parted with Cecilia, left her nothing to apprehend from *her*; but though assured of her esteem, it was not possible to appear before her with her accustomed composure.—The restraint visible in her manners did not escape the Marchesa, who endeavoured, by every little art which kindness and gentleness could devise, to restore her to cheerfulness.

Boraccio joined the party at supper, which, as usual, was splendid and profuse; and declared afterwards his intention of quitting Florence in a few days.—The Marchese seemed surprised, and would have entreated his stay; but on Boraccio's assuring him that he had engagements at Genoa, which admitted not of delay, he desisted from the attempt.—A deep sigh at that instant drew the attention of the Marchesa to her son. Varàno's eyes met her's, and, startled at the observation he had drawn, his features, vivid but the moment before with hope and pleasure, suddenly became as pale as death. Her look, at once scrutinizing and severe, penetrated his soul, and he arose and left the room in evident embarrassment.

The next day was employed by Boraccio in making all due arrangements for his journey, and in considering how he might most effectually carry on his designs respecting Cecilia. The Marchese, it was obvious, was yet entirely unsuspicious of his son's attachment to her; but it was necessary to the success of his schemes that he should not long remain so.—Here, however, a new difficulty arose;—it was scarcely possible to open the Marchese's eyes without betraying the knowledge of his interference to Varàno, who of course would be highly incensed at the discovery.—Hints, nevertheless, might be given, which circumstances might confirm; and thus, without subjecting himself to censure by a voluntary and open interposition, his design might be accomplished.

It had long been Boraccio's opinion that Cecilia and Varàno formed assignations in the gardens. What suggested this conjecture was, that Cecilia frequently took a ramble at an early hour in the morning, and sometimes remained absent from the Palace some hours. This circumstance, which he had formerly attributed to her fondness for walking, and her admiration of the beautiful and picturesque scenes through which she passed, now operated forcibly on his imagination; and he scrupled not to decide that the motive of these rambles was an assignation with

Varàno.—Secretly persuaded of this, he determined to watch her steps; and when he should have discovered the place of their visitation, to draw the Marchese thither, not doubting but something would occur in the course of their observations, to confirm the justice of those suspicions which he meant only gently to excite.

He was passing and repassing the corridor while he was thus musing, when a footstep on the stairs roused him, and looking up, he perceived the Marchese.—The opportunity for which he sought, now offered; and he was revolving in his mind how the subject might commence, when the Marchese put an end to his deliberations by leading to it himself. He informed him that he had that day received a letter from his friend and relation, Count di Montelino, requesting the return of his daughter, and entreating that he, (the Marchese) and Lorenzo, would conduct her to Naples. Olivia, he added, on the receipt of this letter, had determined to set off immediately; and agreeably to the invitation contained in it, he had determined to be her escort:—but, contrary to his expectations, and much against his inclinations, Lorenzo had refused to accompany them.

"He says he has affairs at Genoa," continued the Marchese, "and must return with you."

"With us, my Lord!" repeated Boraccio with astonishment—"with us?"

"With you, Signor," rejoined the Marchese. "But why this surprise?—It is by your desire—from your invitation, I presume?"

"From mine—from my invitation, my Lord!—No, pardon me; I should be the last—I have reasons indeed which——"

"He goes not by your invitation—you should be the last—and you have reasons!" cried the Marchese. "And pray, Signore, what do you mean that I should understand by all this?—Very inexplicable upon my word!"

Boraccio, whose embarrassment arose chiefly from the idea that the Marchese had at last discovered the cause of his son's unwillingness to comply with this measure, and meant to accuse him as an accomplice, now perceived his mistake. He saw, instead of being gratified, as he had expected, by the disapprobation so openly, though so inadvertently, expressed to Varàno's scheme of returning with them, he was seriously displeased; and it required all, and more than his accustomed address to deprecate his chagrin.

"My son," said the Marchese, "independent of his rank, has talents, virtues, and acquirements which may justly entitle him to the most distinguished favour.—Wherever he visits, he confers an honour; and you, Signor, who have been so often befriended by him, ought to be the last to be insensible to the favour he meditates."

"I am well aware of the distinction," cried Boraccio, recollecting himself, "and shall be solicitous to deserve it.—When I hinted I had reasons to oppose the Signor Lorenzo's design of returning with us to Genoa, I meant only to signify my wish of promoting, by every exertion in my power, an alliance so long and so anxiously desired: and by sacrificing my own pleasures to his interests, to clear myself from the imputation of selfishness that your words conveyed."

"If this was all," said the Marchese with mildness, "you are not culpable."

"I had no other, my Lord—I am incapable of any other motive."

"Olivia," resumed the Marchese, "has birth, beauty, and accomplishments, which would add lustre to any station. Her family is unexceptionable—her fortune splendid!"

"The Signora has perfections both of mind and person," interrupted Boraccio, "to which few could be insensible."

"She is thought to bear some resemblance," continued the Marchese, "to the portrait of the wife of Francisco di Varàno, first Count of that name, who flourished in the fifteenth century. A remarkable story, of which I can give you but the outline, attends this lady."

Boraccio, impatient of delay, would have spared himself the vexation of attending to a wearisome narrative; for such, from the Marchese's fondness for reciting long anecdotes of his ancestors, he expected it to prove. But he knew the danger of interposing, and was compelled, therefore, to remain a courteous, though reluctant auditor.

"She is said," proceeded the Marchese, "to have flown from her husband in consequence of an intrigue; after which, to avoid discovery, she hid herself in a cavern. In this retirement she was attended by a Friar, who protected her, and conveyed her food. —The deep solitude of this place, and the appearance of lights from the remotest part of the cavern, induced some travellers, who were performing a pilgrimage to the shrine of San Giovanni, to explore its recesses. They entered the cavern, and were proceeding, when they beheld the lady attired in a white robe, and covered with a veil, sitting alone at the extremity, the Friar being absent on his customary occupation at the nearest town.—Her dress, her figure, and the singularity of her situation, assisted by the weakness and superstition of that remote period, defended her from insult.—They advanced with trembling awe; and as the light shone full upon her features, which her veil, and the darkness that pervaded around them had hitherto concealed, believed they saw a vision.—She arose. Her majestic step concurring with the power of her beauty, aided the surmise. Imagination kindled —they took her for the Virgin; and throwing themselves at her feet, besought her pity and protection.—The lady, perceiving their mistake, and apprehensive of the consequences of this visit, should her concealment be made known, suffered them to remain in it.—She confirmed them in the opinion that she was indeed the Virgin; and after affording them her blessing, assured them that they would prosper so long as they concealed this extraordinary event from all others, and never again ventured to explore the sacred and mysterious depths of that cave.—They agreed to these conditions, and were departing, when they were startled by the appearance of the Friar, who receded with astonishment on beholding the recess he sought, peopled with pilgrims.—The devotees crossed themselves, and were retiring, when they were recalled by the voice of the lady.—'Stay, noble strangers,' said she, with a presence of mind truly admirable, 'and receive the blessing of the holy Prophet Elijah.'—The Friar, amazed at the import of a speech, not a word of which he could comprehend, stood silent and aghast.—The pilgrims at length returned, and prostrating themselves before him as they had done before his companion, entreated also his benediction.— The Friar, reassured by a look from the lady, stretched forth his hand, and laying it upon the forehead of his supplicants, delivered it with much emphasis and solemnity.—'Hence now,' cried the pretended Virgin, 'and intrude no more into the awful and secret recesses of this cavern; for in the hour that you return to it, or dare to disclose what you have seen and heard in this place, you die, and your souls partake the sufferings of the damned.'—— The strangers trembled as she delivered the dreadful mandate, and departed for Florence!"

"The contrivance was, indeed, an ingenious one," said Boraccio.

"Women—women, Signor, are famous for them.—The Monk, before he could have thought of personating the Prophet Elijah, would have perplexed himself for ages; chance, indeed, engendered the idea: but who but a woman could have continued the deception, and have turned it to such an advantage?"

"If the lady is to be commended for her sagacity," rejoined Boraccio, "she lays claim to an equal share of admiration on the score of courage. But how did it end, my Lord?"

"Contrary to her intentions," cried the Marchese, "and yet happily.—Attend, Signor, and you shall hear.—Francisco was no sooner informed that his wife, whom he yet tenderly loved, and whose crime he had already forgiven, had escaped from his Palace, than he ordered a proclamation to be issued throughout the city, offering large sums to the acceptance of any one who could procure news of the fugitive.—Parties were also dispatched among the different provinces of Italy, to Switzerland, and to France, as far as Lyons, in search of her: but, notwithstanding the utmost diligence and enquiry, no account of her whatever could be procured.—Affairs were in this train when the pilgrims arrived at Florence.—The figure of the lady, her garb, and that of the Friar, who was suspected as an accomplice, were minutely described; and aware of their folly, and of the deception which had been practiced upon them, they acknowledged the rencontre in the cavern, and were the means of restoring the lady to her husband."

"A strange story, my Lord, truly!" said Boraccio; "but a legend, I suppose—a mere legend?"

"The account is too well attested," continued the Marchese, "to admit a doubt of its authenticity. It is recorded in the annals of Tuscany, and is now in the archives of its Convents."

The Signor made no reply, and they paced the sides of the corridor for several minutes in silence.

Boraccio, proceeding with his plan, at length enquired of the Marquese, whether he did not think the repugnance expressed by Varàno to his proposal of attending them to Naples, originated in some other attachment.

The Marchese looked surprised.

"I may be mistaken, my Lord," resumed the Signor; "I confess, however, from some circumstances——"

"Explain yourself," interrupted the Marchese.

"Pardon me, my Lord, if I do not," cried Boraccio; "my suspicions, whatever they are, may be groundless; and my zeal for the welfare of your house——"

"Speak quickly, and to the purpose," said the Marchese, "if you intend to be understood."

Boraccio hesitated.

"Could I be assured, my Lord, that what you now tempt me to unfold would be confined to your own breast,—that Signor Varàno——"

"I understand you," cried the Marchese; "Lorenzo shall not know of it. Be quick then, and let me be acquainted with your thoughts."

"Speak low, my Lord, I conjure you!—Signor Lorenzo—— We will remove, my Lord, if you please, to the other end of the corridor."

"You trifle," said the Marchese, angrily; "if you have any thing to disclose, say it here; I am in haste!"

"You will promise then, my Lord——"

"I have already promised," interrupted the Marchese; "this delay is unnecessary and ridiculous!"

He then commanded him to proceed; and, drawn at length by his enquiries to be more explicit than he had at first intended, Boraccio confessed that he had long suspected Varàno's predilection for Cecilia; and that he had the strongest reasons to believe that she was the chief, and indeed only motive of his intended journey. He then hastened to inform him of several little instances of attachment which he had observed at Genoa; the surprise which he had occasioned to Cecilia and Varàno on his abrupt appearance in the library; with a number of others too numerous and too trivial to relate.

The Marchese, though he checked the expression of his displeasure while Boraccio was speaking, was yet greatly incensed at this discovery; and as he revolved every incident he had described, and compared them with others which had fallen under his own notice, though he had forborne to remark them at the time, his uneasiness increased.—Ever hasty in his resolves, he determined, therefore, to insist upon Lorenzo's abandoning his scheme of returning to Genoa, and conceding to his of accompanying Olivia and himself to Naples; a resolution which he put almost immediately into practice.

In the evening the Marchesa and her party took a drive along the *Via Cassia*, and from thence to the royal *Cascina*[1], and repaired at night to the *Pergola*[2].—When they entered this Theatre, the Marchese, contrary to his custom, conducted Cecilia to the box, and resigned Olivia to the care of Varàno, who seemed little calculated to sustain his part in the trifling but animated conversations which she occasionally introduced.—The performance was long and uninteresting.—On their return, the Marchese took his seat in the same carriage with Cecilia, and compelled Varàno to enter the other.—In this manner they drove on, and soon reached the Palace; the Marchese preserving in his deportment an air of haughty reserve, which the Marchesa, by a constrained vivacity of manner, vainly endeavoured to dispel.

1 Farm—the Grand Duke's farm—the fashionable drive at Florence.
2 The Opera-house at Florence.

CHAPTER VIII

——————Dubita un poco
Quinci l'onore il debito le pesa,
Quindi l'incalza l'amorose foco.

Ariosto.

——————Awhile he doubted,
Here honour and duty sway'd him—
And there the tender passion urg'd him on.

The next morning the beams of a splendid sun which shone full upon her chamber, invited Cecilia to the gardens.—She had just sprung from her *balconé* to the terrace, when she discerned some one walking thoughtfully along the shrubbery which fronted her window.—At first she imagined it to be Varàno; but an opening in the foliage affording her another view, she perceived it was Boraccio.

There was an air of mysterious sadness in Varàno's manner on the preceding evening, which had greatly interested Cecilia; and probably had she obeyed the impulse of her heart and of her feelings, she would have sought, instead of shunned an interview, which might have afforded her the explanation so necessary to her wishes; but prudence and a delicate pride restrained her, and she determined to avoid the probability of throwing herself in his way, by forbearing to visit that part of the gardens where he usually walked when alone. She shunned, therefore, the path leading to the pavilion, where, with no other companion than a book, she knew he often remained for some hours; and striking into an avenue which led by a gentle descent along the back of the Palace, wandered on in silent reverie till she reached the borders of a lake, when the shades opening to light, discovered to her a scene so sweetly romantic, that she seated herself on a bank to contemplate its beauty.

As she inhaled the fresh breeze which came scented with the

delicious odours of the flowers which fringed the borders of the lake, and listened to the soft carols of the birds, her spirits gradually revived, a sweet and varied emotion of delight diffused itself over her mind, and she sat lost in the rapture it inspired.

She was interrupted by a rustling amongst the trees; she turned her head, and perceiving Varàno, arose to depart.

"Pardon me," said he, greatly agitated, "that I have dared to follow you; I wished to see, to speak with you once again:—a few days, a few hours only, and you may be lost to me—perhaps for ever."

As he uttered these words, he drew her arm within his, and hurried her along the grounds.

They had arrived about half way down the avenue, when they discovered Boraccio moving slowly along at some distance. He turned, but without seeming to notice them, and then walked swiftly toward the lawn.—He was met there by the Marchese, who immediately joined him.

"The fineness of the morning, my Lord," said Boraccio, "has I see tempted you from your studies."

"Yes, Signor," returned the Marchese, "yet even here they may be resumed. In my cabinet I enjoy the beauties of art—here those of nature; each presents an endless variety."

"Your Lordship penetrates all things," continued Boraccio, "and can reduce any thing to a science.—How highly are you favoured!—a strong and comprehensive mind is one of the first of blessings!"

The Marchese bowed, and graciously smiling, enquired for his son, who he was told had been up some hours.

"The Signor is more than ordinarily studious this morning," cried Boraccio; "I saw him from my window reading, and traversing the grounds as early as daybreak."

"Abroad so soon as daybreak?" said the Marchese.

"It could not be long after, my Lord," replied Boraccio; "the sun was not up, I think."

"It is very extraordinary that he should be out so early," cried the Marchese; "this boy is strangely altered, I fear."

"Not materially so," resumed Boraccio; "the Signor, you know, was always fond of retirement."

"Always inclined to it, perhaps; but never so madly, so enthusiastically attached to it as at present," said the Marchese.

"It is like all other passions, my Lord, I suppose; it grows by indulgence."

"Or rather it is the consequence of another passion," cried the Marchese, reddening, "which may cause him and his family some trouble."

"I hope, my Lord, the circumstance to which I alluded," rejoined Boraccio, "has not been the means of——"

"I wish I had known it sooner," interrupted the Marchese; "and excuse me, Signor, when I say I ought to have known it sooner. The girl has been thrown in his way; she knows her power, and will exert it."

"She cannot surely presume," returned Boraccio.

"There is no answering for the vanity of a girl, Signor.—But she must be removed—you understand me—she must not remain in your house."

"Our suspicions are, I hope, unfounded," replied Boraccio.

"I wish they may be proved so," said the Marchese.

The Signor was silent; and they continued their way for several paces in mutual thoughtfulness.

When they had arrived near the edge of the lawn, the Marchese would have turned into a path which wound along the front of the Palace; but Boraccio remarking that the avenue they had quitted was more shady, and therefore more pleasant, he consented to return to it.

They had proceeded only a few steps down the avenue, when the sound of voices from a distance roused the attention of both. They listened;—the sound returned at intervals, but without seeming to approach.—They advanced, and again stopped.

"Hark, Signore!" said the Marchese, "did you not hear?"

"What, my Lord?" asked Boraccio.

"The voice of a woman," replied the Marchese.

"The Marchesa, perhaps, or the Signora," cried Boraccio.

"Olivia rises not so early," said the Marchese, "and the Marchesa has not yet left her chamber;—it is Cecilia!" resumed he, with a look of piercing indignation.

He attempted to proceed—the Signor restrained him.

"Not yet, my Lord," cried he; "stop and we may overhear them."

"Had you ever experienced one half of what I now feel," said a voice which they knew to be Varàno's, "you would know what you enjoin is no longer in my power:—when I see you, when I hear you speak, all your precepts are forgotten, and my soul loses all its former energy."

The Marchese started.

"It is as I feared," said he, "but by Heaven——"

"Be calm, my Lord, I conjure you!" cried Boraccio.

"Peace!" reiterated the Marchese, "and unhand me!—Rash degenerate boy!"

"Yet hear me, my Lord."

"For what purpose?" interrupted the Marchese, angrily.

"Command yourself but for the present, my Lord," continued Boraccio, "and all shall end answerable to your wishes.—Cecilia shall be disposed of; the time and manner must be discussed hereafter."

The Marchese looked less indignant.

"An hour hence, my Lord, if you will condescend to confer with me, I will explain myself more fully:—here, and at this time, I cannot."

"Signor," said the Marchese, fixing an eye of earnest regard upon him as he spoke, "I think I may depend upon you."

"I have no views, no desires, my Lord, beyond your interests; nor have I ever, I hope, given you cause to dispute my sincerity."

"I recollect nothing that should induce me to suspect it," cried the Marchese—"You will promise then to meet me in the course of an hour at this place, my Lord?"

"Where you please," returned the Marchese; "but Olivia—remember, Olivia must not hear of this——you understand me? She must be kept in ignorance of the discovery accidentally made here. Women are vain—neglect is insupportable—and to be supplanted by a base-born girl! ——"

"Right, my Lord," interposed Boraccio; "the Signora, as you observe, must not hear of it."

They had reached an opening in the groves, and were issuing

through a vista to the pavilion, when they perceived Olivia sitting alone upon the steps, amusing herself with a little Bolognese lap-dog belonging to the Marchesa.

"Is it on such animals as these, Lady," asked the Signor, "you mean to bestow all your caresses?"

"Why, yes, till I can find some object more worthy of them," cried Olivia.

"I fear you are difficult, Signora."

"A little, no doubt; but are not men more so?"

"Of the merits or demerits of my own sex," answered Boraccio, smiling, "I am not perhaps competent to judge, both of which are, I believe, better discriminated by your's; as the perfections and defects of your's, (forgive the ungallantness of the latter expression), are allowed to be better understood by our's.—But how is it you consider us as more difficult?—Produce a reason, Signora."

"Easily," replied Olivia. "I have been in this world upwards of sixteen years, the greater part of which has been spent in numbering beads, and repeating paternosters to the Virgin within the limits of a Convent.—More than five months have now elapsed since I was emancipated from my prison; and yet, during all that time, I have never made a single conquest:—does not this prove men *difficult?*"

"Were it true," pursued Boraccio, "it would prove us at least highly insensible. But you mistake, Lady; you have captives doomed to wear your chain, and condemned to suffer it in silence."

"How is it that you have risen so early, Olivia?" said the Marchese, recollecting himself, and endeavouring to end a conversation which he began to think tedious.

"Oh! I have been up a long time, my Lord," rejoined Olivia.

"Indeed! and alone a long time, Lady?"

"Yes, till I was heartily weary of it, when happening to take a turn into the orangery, who should I see but——"

"But who?" vociferated the Signor.

"The Marchesa's macaw."

"Pshaw!" said the Marchese.

"It is really a wonderful bird;—you would be astonished at the facility with which I have taught it to speak French; never was so apt a scholar!—It can pronounce the names of Cecilia and Lorenzo too with the most admirable exactness. Its gift of articulation is amazing!"

"And why not Lorenzo and Olivia?" cried the Marchese, colouring highly.

"I tried them together, my Lord, but they would not do; they did not slip smoothly off the tongue—the macaw absolutely stammered at them."

The Marchese frowned; and, unable to support the conflict which this discourse, artless and innocent as it was, had raised in a bosom already torn by contradictory emotions, withdrew toward the Palace, leaving Olivia to amuse herself with her little Bolognese favourite, on which she appeared to be lavishing all her fondness.

The Marchese, as was his custom when any thing happened to discompose him, resorted immediately to the Marchesa's apartment. He found her in her closet, attended only by her woman. She turned as he approached, and perceiving that his countenance was inflamed with anger, tremulously demanded what had happened to disturb him.

"Dismiss your woman," said he, sternly; "I would speak to you alone."

The Marchesa desired her attendant to withdraw.

"Your son, your son, Madam," resumed the Marchese, throwing himself into a chair, "has disgraced himself!—he would marry a beggar!"

The Marchesa trembled, drew a seat near his, and in a soft but agitated voice, desired him to explain himself.

A few words, though dropped in the very height of refinement, were sufficient to acquaint her with the purport of those which had so greatly alarmed her.—What she had before only feebly suspected, was at last confirmed; her heart sickened, and she found those consolations which she was constrained to bestow upon her husband, necessary to herself. Anxious, however, to check that impetuosity of which she dreaded the effects, she besought him to leave the management of Lorenzo to her, urging that gentleness and persuasion were the only arts that could be employed with any chance of success. The Marchese consented, though reluctantly, to this measure, and the family soon met at breakfast.

This meal, but for the thoughtless hilarity of Olivia, would have been a silent one. The Signora only was absent;—she sent word she was unwell, and desired that breakfast might be prepared for her in her own room.—The Marchesa was grave, said little, and when she spoke to Cecilia, it was not with her former kindness.

This change in the conduct and behaviour of her friend was too sudden and too obvious to escape the observation of Cecilia; and being noticed, it occasioned an anguish it was very difficult to support.

Boraccio and the Marchese removed immediately after breakfast; Olivia likewise withdrew, and Varàno and Cecilia were left alone with the Marchesa.

A silence of several minutes ensued after the rest were retired, which was interrupted at length by Varàno, who, taking up a harp, offered it to Cecilia. She received it, but refused to play; and presenting it with a slight curtsey to the Marchesa, besought her to favour them with a song.

"My spirits are but ill attuned to music," cried the Marchesa, returning it with an air of marked indifference; "but if my son wishes you, Madam, to play, I can withdraw; my presence is, I suppose, a restraint upon you."

"Alas, Madam!" said Cecilia, greatly disturbed, "how have I deserved this?"

"Ask your own conscience, Cecilia," replied the Marchesa; "if that accuses you not, neither do I."

"If it is to that I am to refer, Madam," said Cecilia with dignity, "I am acquitted."

"The affection which outlives the merit of the object," continued the Marchesa, without noticing her defence, "is a disgrace instead of an honour to both parties!"

"I am still unable to comprehend you, Madam," said Cecilia.

The Marchesa was silent; but Cecilia was so much hurt with what had passed that tears streamed from her eyes, and she hid her face with her handkerchief.

"There is some strange misunderstanding, I fear," said Varàno, who had been an uneasy spectator of what was passing.

"Whatever it is," cried Cecilia, rising to depart, "I am unable to rectify it."

She withdrew, and the Marchesa arising also, desired Varàno to attend her in her anteroom.—He obeyed, and dismissing her attendants, she entered upon the subject of her concern.

Varàno listened to her with anxiety, with grief, with apprehension.—He dreaded the displeasure of his father, and discovered that all his fondly cherished hopes relative to the interposition of his mother, were now wholly at an end. Yet solicitous to make at least one effort to engage her compassion, he threw himself at her feet, hung upon her robe, and avowing his passion for Cecilia, besought that she would interfere—would entreat—would save him from the misery that awaited him.

While he proceeded in his importunities, he endeavoured to anticipate in her countenance the answer preparing for him; but from this her derived no satisfaction.

"Should I encourage you in your disobedience," said the Marchesa, scarcely less agitated, "by suffering you to involve in your transgression the distinction of your family, would it not be sacrificing my own sense of duty to a mere feminine weakness? —Oh my son! my son! why will you thus agonize me? Endeavour to reconcile yourself to a necessity which you know to be inevitable. The efforts of virtue and fortitude are always successful; and how can they be more nobly exercised than in striving to conquer an attachment so humiliating, and which must be hopeless!"

"Would to Heaven it were indeed conquerable!" said Varàno.

"While you continue to believe it unconquerable," said the Marchesa, "it will remain so. Consider it as surmountable, and every obstacle will be subdued. Exert only that fortitude with which nature has endowed you, and you will find the conquest not so arduous as you imagine.—Lorenzo, you was once capable of acting nobly: to what then am I to impute this strange degeneracy?"

"If to love a being pure and innocent as an angel——" cried Varàno.

"No more, Lorenzo," said the Marchesa; "this is the very

height of romance:—I expect, nay, I insist upon it you speak rationally.—You must forget Cecilia!"

"Forget her!" exclaimed Varàno, "forget her!—Oh Cecilia! Cecilia!"

"Endeavour only," said the Marchesa, "and you will find it practicable. My words are not merely those of course; they are the result of experience, and, as such, are entitled to your attention. At the time I married your father, he was not the object of my affections: I loved a person whose rank was inferior to my own; and, like you, believed happiness unattainable but through the gratification of my wishes. Time, however, and reflection convinced me of the contrary. I saw the Marchese; he declared himself, and my father, ever resolute in his determinations, insisted on my compliance. Well instructed in the obedience ever due to a parent, I disputed not his power; and to *you* I may acknowledge it, though, till now, it has been carefully undivulged, was led a patient but unwilling victim to the altar. The consciousness of having acted virtuously served, however, to support me in the hour of trial; my regrets gradually subsided, and I soon regained that cheerfulness which is the reward of rectitude.—A short time discovered to me the precipice from which I had escaped: my former lover, of whom I received occasionally some accidental information, evinced himself incapable of a serious attachment; he proved gay, thoughtless, and dissipated; and I had soon reason to congratulate myself on our separation."

"But had your affection, Madam," said Varàno, "been unsubdued—had you dared to follow the dictates of your heart, his might have expanded to the precepts of virtue, and he might have lived to have been a blessing to thousands!"

"We can judge only from effects," cried the Marchesa.

"We may at least be allowed to trace them to their causes," said Varàno.

"Causes are not always self-evident; and if we judge from suppositious ones, we are leading ourselves into error. But I am receding from my purpose:—your father has commissioned me to inform you that he means to escort the Lady Olivia to Naples, and insists upon your attendance;—we expect this concession, and do not doubt but you will give it."

A deep blush passed over Varàno's cheek as the Marchesa expressed her confidence in his acquiescence. He knew if he withheld it, he should draw upon himself an increased share of that displeasure he feared, the weight of which he was in no condition to bear.—He declared nevertheless his inability to comply, adding—"Why that inability exists I am not bound to explain: it is but just however, to assure you, Madam, that, whatever pain I may inflict by my apparent disobedience, what I must inevitably feel myself, will be infinitely more acute.—But my resolution is taken, and it is, and must be unalterable."

"Since my embassy is discharged, and answered then," said the Marchesa, rising from her seat with an air of ineffable dignity, "why should I intrude farther?"

"Ah, Madam!" cried Varàno, starting up, and throwing himself at her feet, "will you then leave me?—are you, too, inexorable? —will you abandon me to misery?—If I have incurred the resentment of my father, let me not incur your's also.—Oh! ever till this moment treated with maternal tenderness, how can I support this coldness?"

Tears now streamed fast from his eyes; he seized the hand of the Marchesa—it trembled with emotion.

"Rise, Lorenzo," said she, "rise; it is I, not you, that must assume the suppliant. It is your mother, anxious for the honour of her house, must kneel to sue for its continuance—for the restoration of her own peace, for the comfort, nay, perhaps, the very existence of a husband, dearer to her than life itself."

"Your husband!—my father!" exclaimed Varàno. "Oh, never, never! the consequences could not be so fatal!"

"Your delirium tempts you to overlook those consequences," continued the Marchesa, "which, were you disposed to be rational, would be but too obvious. The Marchese, solicitous to secure you a safe and honourable marriage, will never hear of any other; and should you rashly dare to disobey him in a point in which his interests and happiness are so nearly concerned, the effect is at present unanswerable.—His constitution might enable him to survive it, but his prospects of felicity would be annihilated.—Would you be the destroyer of your father?"

"Heaven and earth!" reiterated Varàno, rising half way from

his knees, and then sinking to the ground as if overcome by the violence of his emotions; "is it, can it be possible!—You—my father!—Oh exquisite misery!——But proceed, Madam, proceed —I have interrupted you!"

"Reflect," resumed the Marchesa, "and let your resolution be speedy. Will you spare your parents—your parents who have so dearly loved you?—Ah! did you know, Lorenzo—did you know what belongs to that sacred appellation—had you experienced the anxiety, the tender sorrow which wound the paternal breast when it fears for the honour of its object—did you know what it is to have those hopes—hopes so sanguinely indulged, so implicitly confided in, extinguished for ever—you would not, nay, I think you could not hesitate."

"What were my sensations at that moment!—even now, at this distant period, I recall them, when, daring to follow nature in defiance of custom, I nursed you at my bosom, and hung over you with all a mother's fondness. 'Blessed,' said I, 'blessed be the babe thou hast in mercy sent me!—He will be the glory of his father—the joy, the delight of his enraptured mother!—He will uphold the honour of his house—he will transmit to posterity the ancient virtues of his ancestors!—Oh Lorenzo! my child! my darling! my only one!—what were the transports of that moment! I blessed the hour of thy birth!——Oh teach me not!" throwing herself into his arms, and bursting into an agony of tears, "Oh teach me not to curse it!"

"No more, I conjure you," said Varàno, springing from his seat, and pacing the apartment with hasty and agitated steps; "you have conquered, Madam; dispose of me as you please."

"There spoke my son!" cried the Marchesa. "Oh Lorenzo! great then as have been our expectations, unlimitted as were our hopes, you will fulfil them all; you will see Cecilia—you will at least think of her no more."

"I know not what I can, what I ought to promise," said Varàno; "allow me but a moment to reflect; all within is tumult and distraction! You are too generous, too good; my mother would disdain the thought to draw from a moment of agitation—a sensibility roused to an excess of agony, an assent which should be the consequence of deliberation!"

"You will strive, however, to obey us—you will exert your reason, Lorenzo?"

"I will attempt, Madam—I will endeavour. But to see her no more——"

"We will discuss that hereafter," said the Marchesa; "you will at least try the effect of absence. I exact nothing at present, nor will I, but your own exertions; except this, you will accompany your father to Naples?"

At the mention of Naples, to which the miseries of a long and painful absence from Cecilia gave accumulated bitterness, all the fortitude which he had been struggling to preserve, failed him. Sighs again agitated his breast; and covering his face with his hands, he leaned against the wall without having power to utter a word.

"Alas, my son!" said the Marchesa, "your purpose is, I fear, but half fixed."

A long interval of silence succeeded.

At length, by a strong and sudden exertion, Varàno assumed a composed and steady aspect.—The scene below flashed upon his mind; and, persuaded that the alteration which he had witnessed in his mother's behaviour to Cecilia, originated either in some unfortunate mistake or wilful misrepresentation, he attempted, by a thorough elucidation of her former and subsequent conduct, to eradicate from her mind the painful and erroneous impression it had imbibed.—The conversation which succeeded, convinced him that she had been deceived relative to the supposed assignation in the gardens. The Marchesa had been informed that they had appointed a meeting; and the imprudence and indelicacy of such a step, and the appearance of design which was conveyed with it, had so greatly offended her, that the confidence which the extreme innocence of Cecilia's deportment and manners had invited her to repose in her, was entirely withdrawn.—What was then her astonishment, and what her remorse, when she found so far from having received Varàno's addresses with pleasure, she had studiously avoided them; and, influenced by a promise more than once repeated in the lifetime of De Sevignac, had resolutely refused to listen to any overtures that could be made to her.

The Marchesa's breast now glowed with emotions of renewed

tenderness for Cecilia. She sighed to think that she had given pain to a mind so noble, so exquisitely susceptible of unkindness; and having assured her with an energy evincive of the sincerity with which she intended to adhere to it, she assented to his entreaties of allowing him another interview with Cecilia in her presence, previous to his departure for Naples.—Consoled by these promises, Varàno withdrew; and the Marchesa, actuated by sensations which she could no longer oppose, flew in search of Cecilia.

CHAPTER IX

Oime Fortuna fella!
Che cambio e questo che tu fai!

ARIOSTO.

Oh base Fortune! what a reverse is this that thou makest!

SHE found her alone in her chamber, and in tears.

"Alas! it is I that should weep, my love," said the Marchesa. "Oh, how could I offend such goodness?—how ever, when looking at my Cecilia, believe her capable of a conduct to which her every action and word proclaim her superior?—Forgive—Oh forgive!" added she, "an error which, though I bitterly repent, I cannot recall: and if the sincerest contrition, the truest admiration of your virtues, and the most unalterable affection can obliterate the past, be assured they are engraven on my heart."

The confusion of Cecilia's thoughts, whilst listening to a concession so extraordinary, prevented her from demanding an explanation. The Marchesa did not keep her in suspense. She confessed, though with evident embarrassment, the mistake she had fallen into; she blushed, she said, that she could harbour a suspicion against her noble young friend, the adopted child of her affections; and concluded with assuring her that she might rely for the future on her friendship and exertions.

She then related what had passed between her and Varàno in their late interview, including his determination of attending his father and the Lady Olivia to Naples, and his resolution of endeavouring at least to surmount a passion, the indulgence of which, situated as he was, would be followed by the severest malediction.—In compassion to her feelings, for, assailed at once by pride, tenderness, and confusion, Cecilia was almost sinking to the earth, she avoided all mention of the emotions which Varàno had betrayed when she first addressed him in her antechamber; but expatiated at large upon the persuasions he had employed to engage her friendship and protection for her.

"The former you have indeed possessed," continued the Marchesa, "ever since I was acquainted with you, though a more thorough knowledge of your virtues has contributed to strengthen it. —My protection, if I cannot offer you with propriety an asylum in my Palace, I would most willingly afford, could I do it with impunity; but as Signor Boraccio is appointed your guardian, he would doubtless be offended at such a proposal. The Lady Viola, though I am ignorant of the cause, never loved me; and as she invariably turns every thing to my disadvantage, she would interfere rather to irritate than to appease his resentment. Domestic disturbances were always displeasing to me; I would therefore avoid gladly every probability of incurring them, though in the present instance could I, by taking you to my care, render your situation more eligible, I would encounter some hazard. My obligations to you are infinite; they are beyond what I can ever repay. I would fain give you some proof of my gratitude. If I can serve you, only speak, my love; prefer your request, and it shall be granted."

Cecilia sighed, and looked up at the Marchesa as if she would have spoken, but could not.

"Speak, my dear!" resumed the Marchesa; "recollect how much I am indebted to you:—it is a debt, indeed, too vast to be discharged."

She gazed earnestly in her face, as if expecting her reply; but Cecilia was yet unable to articulate.

"Take some time for reflection," said the Marchesa, rising; "I will retire; and you will acquaint me with the result of your deliberations on our next meeting."

Saying this, she withdrew, leaving Cecilia, who had not the power to recall her, in a state of uneasy irresolution.

The Marchesa's offer, as it would free her from any future apprehensions concerning Boraccio, demanded her consideration; and she found it difficult to suppress those feelings which would have directed her to relinquish his protection, and accept that of the Marchesa. But recollection suggested that such a conduct, notwithstanding these apprehensions, would be equally rash and unjustifiable. It was not possible to withdraw herself from the authority of Boraccio without assigning some reason, which, if it had no connection with truth, would be vague, and if otherwise, eventually expose her to the animadversions of the family.—She resolved, therefore, after proper acknowledgments of this generosity, to mention, and finally adhere to her resolution of rejecting it.

The Marchesa soon repeated her visit, and having heard Cecilia's decision in respect to her proposal, she desired that she would often write to her from Genoa, and inform her, should any thing occur there to induce her to alter it.

"I am sorry," continued the Marchesa, "since my son leaves us to-morrow, that we are to lose you also:—the Signor departs the next day. It is unnecessary to add how keenly I shall regret the loss of your society.—To-night we are to have a company of select friends at the Palace; the engagement has been made for some time, and must therefore be fulfilled—I need not say on my part how unwillingly. Should you wish to continue in your chamber, in preference to joining the party below, which will be merely a private *conversazione*, we will not insist upon your attendance.—Remember, whilst you are here, you are released from all forms."

Cecilia thanked the Marchesa for her consideration, and preferred remaining in her apartment.—The Marchesa left her with an assurance that her every request should be granted, and soon afterwards sent Claudia, on whom devolved the duties of attending upon her in her chamber to receive her commands.

To relieve her mind in some degree from the painful recollections that obtruded on it, Cecilia busied herself in preparations for her journey; an occupation in which she was frequently interrupted by the entrance of Olivia and the Signora, the latter of whom came to confirm the Marchesa's intelligence relative to their intended departure.

At night she retired early to her bed; and in the morning was recalled from harassing and uneasy dreams by the voice of the Marchesa.—It was yet early.—She started.

"Ah, Madam! is it you?—Why so soon?"

She looked up.—The Marchesa's eyes were red with weeping.

"Dress yourself in haste, my love!" said she; "there is not a moment to be lost!—The Marchese is impatient to be gone. Lorenzo wishes to see you, and now waits for you in my closet. Recall your fortitude, my Cecilia, this one trial: I would have spared it you, but I have promised, and my word, you know is sacred."

Cecilia obeyed, but trembled excessively.—The Marchesa assisted her; and in a few minutes leaning upon the arm of her friend, she was ready to leave the room; but ere they had reached the corridor, the certainty that this was intended for the final interview, struck cold upon her heart; and when arrived at the door, she stopped, shuddered, and was unable to proceed.

"Resume your courage, my love," said the Marchesa; "remember how much I expect from you."

Cecilia fixed her eyes upon her with a look of piercing anguish, but could not speak.—The Marchesa opened the door.

Varàno, who had been traversing the room for some time, now turned round, and with a countenance in which agony and despair were faithfully delineated, yet illumined with an expression of momentary joy on beholding Cecilia, he flew to meet her, and seizing her hand, pressed it to his burning forehead.

"My Cecilia," he said, "and do I—do I see you once again?—But, Oh God! for what is it I see you?"

"Signor," said Cecilia, her voice low and tremulous, "may Heaven preserve and bless you!"

"Ah that voice! that voice!" cried he, "on the accents of which I have hung delighted in happier days!"

Convulsive sobs again impeded his utterance; he sunk upon a chair, and putting his hands before his face, hid the tears which flowed down his manly cheeks.

"This interview must be shortened," said the Marchesa, greatly moved, "Cecilia, my love, we will retire."

Varàno started.

"Not yet, Madam," cried he; "you may be cruel, but you shall not be unjust."

"Look, Lorenzo," said the Marchesa, "look at thy mother; wears she the aspect of unkindness?"

"No, forgive me—I will be calm. Cecilia, my love! my angel! we must part.—The stroke of death itself is not more arbitrary and decisive than the prejudices annexed to rank: I have yielded to them—I have sacrificed my own hopes, my own happiness, to secure the tranquillity of my parents.—Cecilia, I am now worthy of your love."

"Oh, be less agitated!" said Cecilia; "I am, indeed I am unequal to these moments."

He gazed wistfully in her face.

"To part so soon," said he, "so very soon, and to part—but it must not, it shall not be for ever!"

"Nor will it," cried Cecilia; "we shall meet hereafter in a world where no duty shall forbid our attachment, and where we shall enjoy together an eternity of blessedness!"

"Excellent woman!" exclaimed the Marchesa.

"And yet it is from such a woman you would separate me!" cried Varàno.

"No, Lorenzo, it is not I."

"True, Madam, it is not you—it is my father."

"Lorenzo, remember I hear nothing against your father."

"Let us say it is my destiny then," rejoined Varàno, "and you and my father its ministers."

The step of the Marchese was now heard from the corridor:—Cecilia started, and looked at the Marchesa, who arose, and flew to meet him at the door.—The Marchese entered, threw a look of stern regard around the room, coldly saluted Cecilia, and then blaming Varàno for delay, insisted upon his immediate attendance.—The Marchesa accosted him for some minutes aside.

"We will not, my Lord," said she, "intrude upon your patience. Lorenzo will attend you instantly."

The Marchese retired.

"Our time is now limited, my dear," cried the Marchesa; "why then should we prolong an interview productive of so much pain to both of you?" Saying this, she led Cecilia to Varàno, adding

—"I would willingly have spared each the uneasiness of a formal parting:—let it, however, be short."

"A few moments, Madam, but a few moments," said Varàno; "why indeed should it be protracted?—I must not bid her think of me—must not hope——" He paused, overcome with agitation. —"Yet to you—to you, Cecilia," he continued, "the talk of forgetting may be easy; to me, the very effort will be torture!—But Oh! whatever you do," his eyes filled with tears, as with a deep sigh he raised them toward Heaven, "may God protect and bless you!— and if a knowledge of my sufferings would occasion one pant to a bosom which I would shield with my life from the very shadow of misfortune, never, never may it reach you!"

"The rewards of virtue," cried Cecilia, "will be your's, and these shall uphold you; they will support, they will comfort you under every trial:—the blessings of Heaven will be upon you, and the prayers of your parents will call down mercies on their son! —Adieu, Varàno! adieu!"

Lorenzo pressed her to his breast in speechless agony.—Faint and trembling, she would have departed, but he still gently withheld her.

"Not yet, not this instant!" he cried; "one moment—one word only!"

Here his voice faltered; and again she turned, and looked on him with unutterable anguish.

The Marchesa now took Cecilia's hand, and led her from the room; but scarcely had she entered her chamber ere she turned so pale, that the Marchesa, believing that she would faint, rang her bell violently for assistance.

"I am not ill, Madam," said Cecilia, "and yet——"

Before she could finish the sentence, a faint sickness came over her, and she sunk upon the bed, apparently without sense or motion. The Marchesa was much affected:—she chafed her temples, applied hartshorn, and, with the assistance of her woman, restored her at length to reason. As soon as she revived, the Marchesa threw her arms around her, and sobbed upon her bosom.

"I am better, Madam," said Cecilia, rising, and disengaging herself from her embrace; "I am quite well.—Ah! why do you weep so?"

"For your sufferings, my love," returned she, "so unmerited, and yet borne with such angelic patience."

"Be happy, be happy," said Cecilia, "and you will make me so."

"Noble-minded girl! how shall I ever recompense you?"

"By forgiving me all my weakness," said Cecilia.—"Oh shame! shame!" continued she, "that I should have discovered so much!"

"You have discovered nothing, my love," cried the Marchesa, "but a sensibility which gives a brilliancy to your other virtues. —You have behaved, you have done every thing I could desire."

"Oh then I am most happy!" said Cecilia.

"Olivia is enquiring for you," resumed the Marchesa; "shall I convey your excuse, or would you wish her to be admitted."

"By all means, Madam," returned Cecilia; "I am now able to see any body."

She had scarcely spoken when Olivia rushed into the room, and before she had time to recollect herself, she found herself in the arms of her friend, who kissed her cheek on parting, and with many tender adieus assured her that she should often think of her with regret.

As soon as she was withdrawn, the Marchesa informed Cecilia that the Signora Viola being in want of some one qualified to assist her in the decoration of her person, she intended to recommend Claudia.

"She has been educated," continued she, "above most in her condition; and her conversation may perhaps sometimes enliven you."

Cecilia was much pleased with this plan; and it was at length determined, much to the satisfaction of Claudia, who had relinquished all hopes of regaining the lost affections of her Fabio, which not even the *zecheens* could restore, that she should be admitted into the suite of the Signora.

Cecilia spent the remainder of the day in her chamber till the evening, when she stole into the gardens, to take a last farewell of scenes to which she experienced a sudden and strange attachment.—As she wandered on, the bitterness of grief subsided, and was succeeded by a soft and not unpleasing melancholy. The playful breeze refreshed her, and she pursued her way, interrupted only by the Marchesa's lapdog which frolicked around her, or the ceaseless din of the *cicada*, immersed in the trees and low groves which were scattered about the grounds, till she entered upon the spot where she had met, and parted with Varàno on the preceding morning; when recollecting that they were now separated, perhaps for ever, her spirits sunk as memory revived, and she turned hastily away from the object which had awakened it.—She was followed and joined by the Marchesa, who reconducted her to the Palace.

Nothing could exceed the compassion and kindness of this truly amiable woman.—She knew the attractions of her son, and their effect upon Cecilia, and could estimate the important sacrifice she had enjoined.—Might she have been permitted to pursue the dictates of her own reason and feelings, she would probably have yielded her ambitious interests to her sensibility by espousing Lorenzo's cause with the Marchese, had she not been sensible to the impossibility of obtaining his consent to a marriage with a person, whose origin was obscure, and even doubtful.

The grief and wild expressions of Varàno had, however, so unhappy an effect upon her through the night, that she arose more than once from her bed, and paced the room in much agony of spirit.—She dreaded lest he should draw comparisons between Cecilia and Olivia; and that the Marchese, irritated by this late unfortunate adventure, should be less gentle than he ought; and now wished, since Cecilia was so soon to depart for Genoa, that she had used her influence with her Lord to detain Lorenzo at Florence.

Cecilia passed a sorrowful and unquiet night.—She was called early from her chamber, and the carriages being in waiting, she took an affectionate but mournful adieu of the Marchesa; and with a heavy heart prepared to enter the chaise destined to convey her to her future home.

As she entered it, the idea of Varàno glanced instantaneously to her thoughts, and she sighed at the probability she might never see him more. This probability so completely depressed and saddened her, that nothing but the consciousness of being surrounded by domestics, and exposed to the supercilious remarks of those who might be disposed to put the most invidious construction possible on her conduct, could have tempted

her to proceed without stopping to weep and to pray for him.
—Denied this melancholy consolation, the only one that could
have imparted any portion of comfort, she flung herself into the
chaise, and leaning back, drew her veil over her face, and thought,
as the carriage drove off, that her last hope of earthly happiness
was annihilated.

CHAPTER X

————Incedia per ignes
Suppositos cineri doloso.

HORACE.

Fires hid in treach'rous ashes glow,
On which, with heedless feet, you go.

WHILST every idea which love and tenderness could suggest,
pained and agitated Cecilia, and Varàno, still more wretched,
because less able to command himself, was pursuing his way
silently toward Naples, Boraccio's mind was responding only
to images of delight from the success of his newly-invented
schemes. Secure in their termination, he had now, he conceived,
placed an insurmountable barrier between Varàno and Cecilia.
Morsino was to join them shortly at Genoa; and he resolved,
should he be sincere in his professions, which he believed he had
little reason to doubt, to conclude an almost immediate marriage
between him and Cecilia.

A small share of penetration was indeed requisite to convince
him that she experienced more repugnance than attachment to
her new lover; but as he seldom allowed a sentiment of compassion, or even justice to come into competition with his interests,
this afforded him but little uneasiness. He had given the Marchese
an assurance, at their appointed meeting in the gardens, that he
would place her beyond the reach of his son—a promise which
could be performed only by her marriage with another, or her
removal to a Convent. The emolument which he might exact as
the price of his agency, should the intended marriage take place,
combined with the little prospect there appeared of his obtain-

ing such pecuniary resources by any other means, would alone
have decided him; and having silenced that busy monitor within,
whose obtrusive though salutary admonitions had formerly pursued him, he resolved, by the adoption of that system of conduct
best calculated to screen his duplicity, to commence and conclude
his projected machinations.

Boraccio, although he could not be said to have penetrated,
like many others, into the innermost recesses of the heart, was
not totally unacquainted with its intricacies.—He knew that
gentleness and persuasion were more likely to be successful with
a mild and ingenuous nature, like Cecilia's, than their contrary;
and therefore determined to have recourse to importunity rather
than force, to accelerate the accomplishment of his wishes, since
it would be easy to exert that authority with which his guardianship invested him, should this continue inefficacious.—He
was not, indeed, without hope that the impossibility of marrying Varàno, united with the rank and fine person of the Count,
would triumph over the indifference he had witnessed; in which
case all interference, except what might be employed by him as a
friend, would be wholly unnecessary.

It was not till the evening of the fourth day that they arrived
within sight of Genoa. When they alighted at the Palace, Boraccio demanded of Giacomo, one of his attendants, whether any
body had enquired for him in his absence. Giacomo replied that
a Signor, whom he never remembered to have seen before, had
called more than once at the Palace.

"Describe his person," said Boraccio.

"He is tall," returned Giacomo, "has a dark complexion, and
stoops very much in the shoulders.—He did not enquire for you,
but for the strange Count your Honour knew before you went
into Tuscany."

"It is Pandolfo," cried Boraccio; "did he leave his address?"

"He lodges, your Honour, in the Strada Balbi."

"Find him out," continued Boraccio; "I would see him immediately."

Giacomo departed on his embassy, and returned soon after
with intelligence that the Signor was engaged, but that he would
wait upon him at an early hour in the morning.

Boraccio appeared satisfied with this reply; and seating himself between the Signora and Cecilia, he conversed alternately with each till supper was announced; after which the Signora pleading indisposition and fatigue, they separated, and retired to their apartments.

About noon on the ensuing day, Signor Geralamo Zuccàto, with all that disgusting familiarity which marks the Italian *petit maitre*, came to pay his most respectful *devoirs* to the party at the Palace.—The Signor was, as usual, in the best humour imaginable. He congratulated them on their return and on their looks, which he assured them were very visibly improved by their late journey; and having exhausted all those hacknied phrases and unmeaning compliments with which his conversation, if conversation it could be called, abounded, declared he had been almost dying with chagrin in their absence, and that nothing but the promise of an antediluvian existence should persuade him to renew the sufferings he had undergone—sufferings which, but for the hope of again speedily conducting them to the vortex of fashion and gaiety, would have been utterly insupportable.

He was proceeding in this rhapsody when Signor Pandolfo, in consequence of Boraccio's message on the preceding night, came to await his commands.—Boraccio arose immediately on his entrance; and having conducted him into a private room, and shut the door, he eagerly demanded of him if he had heard from the Count, where he was, and if he knew of what nature was the business which had called him so suddenly to Venice. The Signor replied that he was entirely ignorant of the Count's having left Florence till that morning, when he had received a letter from him, in which he desired him to depart instantly for Venice, as he had some business upon his hands there, which could not be transacted without his advice and assistance.—In pursuance of this order, he had therefore determined, he said, to commence his journey immediately, though he was unable as yet to form any opinion whatever as to what might be his friend's motive for desiring it.

Here the Signor was silent; and Boraccio, finding that he could draw no further particulars from his new acquaintance relative to the Count and his concerns, desisted from his enquiries; and

having courteously entreated his stay, which was as courteously
refused, the Signor took his leave, and retired.

The Signora, though she affected to be at ease, was, nevertheless, a prey to the most tormenting anxiety.—In what manner to
conduct herself so as to keep the estates her's, without exposing
herself to the resentment of her husband, was a subject still
uppermost in her thoughts; and, apprehensive lest measures
more arbitrary and more cruel than any she had been yet threatened with, should oblige her to relinquish them, she shunned
every opportunity of being alone with him; to avoid which,
and her own secret disquiet, she plunged into dissipation.—Her
parties at her Palace were numerous and frequent; she joined
the *conversazioni* at the Casinos, played deep, betted high, and
assumed a gaiety which it was often extremely difficult to support. The Signor, however, contrary to her expectations, neither
plied her with arguments, nor wearied her with entreaties.—He
knew, though she had the will, she had not the power to resist;
and having discovered another spring, which would afford him a
more immediate and not less copious supply, he considered the
estates in France as a kind of dernier resort, to which he might
have recourse on some more pressing emergency.—To the Lady
Viola he unfolded so much only of his plan relative to Cecilia,
as he conceived necessary to its accomplishment. He desired
that she might be considered as a friend, and not as a dependant; observing that he had reasons, which time would at length
explain, for enforcing this command.—The Signora, though not
admitted into his confidence sufficiently to make her thoroughly
comprehend his intentions, promised obedience to the injunction—a promise she would have been reluctant to perform, had
she not been assured by Boraccio that Cecilia, whatever might be
the event, could not long remain an inmate of their house.

The conduct prescribed being resolutely adhered to, Cecilia
soon found her situation in the family of Boraccio infinitely more
eligible than she had any reason to expect. She was treated not
only with respect, but with attention; and her soul, ever tenderly
susceptible of the kindness of others, repaid with profuse gratitude the favours she experienced.

The Signora, thus acting a part which, while her policy

approved, her pride secretly condemned, but which she performed nevertheless with all the address and ability of an experienced practitioner, was compelled in her turn to feel for this once hated dependant a respect which her virtues inspired, and an admiration which her understanding imposed.

Accustomed as she was to look with a jaundiced eye upon the beauties of her person, and the varied accomplishments of her mind, she could not forbear acknowledging that the former, lovely as it was, owed its principal attraction to the embellishments of the latter: and, while she beheld with mingled envy and astonishment the operations of that invisible power which informs and animates with its all-potent influence features, which, devoid of this ennobling emanation, would attain no higher an appellation than mere faultless inanity, she felt the justness of that axiom by which philosophers have endeavoured to support the connexion between physical and moral excellence —that beauty is not, as is sometimes vulgarly supposed, a mere abstract quality confined to partial rules, and subjected to arbitrary definitions, but a perfection acquired from the mind which, having the power of impressing upon the features, the countenance, and the whole person, such dispositions as inspire love, produces beauty.

A fortnight passed on in a round of dissipation and company; and Cecilia, who attended the Signora in all her visits, was sometimes amused, but oftener wearied.—Among several other families on terms of intimacy at the Palace, was that of Signor Gavino, of whose party was Madame Le Marne, who, with her daughter, a lively French girl of eighteen, had newly arrived at Genoa.—Madame Le Marne had been twice married; and being in possession of a splendid jointure, which enabled her to reside in a style of almost eastern magnificence at her chateau in Languedoc, she had determined to devote the remaining part of her days to the sober decencies of widowhood.—This resolved, she now turned her whole thoughts upon her daughter, who being heir to an estate to the amount of near fifty thousand *louis d'ors*, which the good-natured world, in pity to her poverty, had kindly augmented to above thrice its value, was considered by her mother as a sufficient and even eligible match for any Nobleman in the land, whatever might be his connections or his rank.—Yet, although bent as she was upon ennobling her hitherto obscure family in the disposal of her daughter, the antipathy which she experienced to that frequent attendant upon greatness, poverty, occasioned her many a severe struggle between her avarice and her pride, ere she could make her election.—The Noblesse of France were poor—those of Italy were not less so; and having heard and rejected many whom the fame of the fair Le Marne's fortune had drawn to her parties, she at length prudently determined to sacrifice her interest to her ambition, by securing her the possession of a title, wishing rather to see her an indigent Countess, than the wife of an opulent and respectable Commoner.—With a pretty person, a disposition naturally inclined to gallantry, and a few superficial accomplishments, which she had address enough to employ to their consequent advantage, a temper the most pliant, and a deportment the most engaging, the gentle Emily prepared to make her public *entrée* into the gayest circles in Genoa, where her vivacity, her figure, and, above all, her fortune ensured her an universal attention.

But though impressed in some degree with the wise precepts of her mother, there were moments when Emily began to doubt whether distinction and happiness were synonymous; and when she even ventured to believe that, could she meet with one of those irresistible heroes, whose actions she had seen recounted in the Romances of her country, she had rather the possessions which she enjoyed were devoted to his aggrandizement, than appropriated to the rebuilding the once splendid, but now dilapidated mansion of some needy patrician.

She had passed two winters at Paris without meeting with this all-accomplished youth, whom her imagination had portrayed as destined to conduct her to the Temple of Love and Hymen, when she was raised at length to the very pinnacle of hope and expectation by the proposed route into Italy; that dear—that enchanting country, which abounded, as she conceived, with every thing that was great, wonderful, and attractive.—The splendour of its climate, the magnificence of its cities, and the gaiety and luxurious habits of its inhabitants, assisted the delusion which was stealing upon her senses. She panted to become

an inmate of a place, the customs and manners of which united all that was fascinating and alluring. —Great was her admiration, and unbounded her expectations, when the Signora undertook, at the joint solicitation of her friends, a few days after her return from Tuscany, to introduce her to the world of fashion at Genoa. —This engagement performed, she attended the *conversazioni* at the Palace; and Cecilia, as the only companion of the Signora, was usually present.

The strange mystery concerning her birth, as related by the Signora, who now condescended to insinuate that it might not be quite so contemptible as she had at first imagined, had rendered her an object of curiosity both to Madame Le Marne and her daughter.—The lively Emily, in whose character the love of the marvellous was the predominating feature, scrupled not to decide that she was the orphan daughter of some Prince, the next heir to whom had concealed her birth, and usurped her kingdom; observing, on beholding a smile of incredulity on the countenances of her auditors, that the circumstance she had alluded to was by no means so rare as they imagined, since she had read in many books, well known to be authentic, of the cruelty of Princes who had concealed or murdered their relatives, to secure the possession of their rights.—Whatever might be Cecilia's opinion of her new friends, she returned their efforts to oblige with the utmost courtesy. With Emily she was sometimes pleased, and always amused; but the continual rotation of routs, operas, and *conversazioni*, so effectually impeded private conversation and friendly intercourse, that she could form no very accurate opinion as to her real sentiments and character.

The frequency of these meetings, the exertion they imposed, and the little amity which appeared to subsist between those invited to partake of them, rendered them extremely irksome to Cecilia. She longed to exchange the dissipation of the Palace for the retirement of the villa, and the quiet of domestic life: but of this retirement, this quiet, there was no hope. The Signora could exist but in a crowd; and her mind, harassed by the conflicts it had so lately sustained, was less than ever disposed to reflection and solitude.

Several weeks rolled on without bringing either the Count or

the mention of him, in the interval of which Cecilia wrote to the Marchesa, and received a letter from her friend and correspondent, Signora di Rosalvo, expressive of the utmost sorrow and regret for De Sevignac's demise, and containing many affectionate enquiries concerning herself.

"I scarcely know," continued the Signora in another part of her letter, "how to offer consolation to others, who am so much in need of it myself.—The Signor alarms me more and more. He is evidently suffering under the influence of some deep and hidden grief; and the more solicitous I appear to penetrate its cause, the more determined he seems to conceal it.—Sometimes my imagination soars into the regions of improbability, and I tremble lest he has involved himself in guilt.—In his sleep he starts, and sometimes weeps; then laughs, and utters incoherent sentences; and once—Oh that night! never, never shall I forget it!—he spoke of murder!—said that he had imbrued his hands in blood!—I screamed—I called to him!—Oh God! what were the horrors of that moment! when, trembling, speechless, agonized, his eyes wild, his cheeks pale, and his whole frame distorted by emotion, I flung myself before him; and repeating, with clasped hands and streaming eyes, the awful words, the horrible recollection of which still harrows up my soul, conjured him to reveal their dreadful purport!—As I spoke, his looks became more and more wild; he seized my arm, and grasped it convulsively.— Again his countenance changed; and gazing on me for a moment with an expression of such tender sorrow and commiseration as no language can describe—'Giuliana,' said he, 'I am wretched—I do not deny that I am so; but what I have uttered is nothing; it was a dream—a strange, a wild, a very troubled dream! But be at rest —all will soon be over:—yet never ask—never, I command you, enquire of me the cause of my misery: so long only as you are ignorant of it, can you know the blessings of repose; for, believe me, virtuous and innocent as you are, you could not survive the recital!'——What, my Cecilia, can I think of these words?—How dreadful must be the secret he dares not impart to me! Oh that you were here—that you would fly to your unhappy Giuliana! —Society would, I am convinced, be beneficial to him. He says, if he survives this year, he will return to it.——If he survives this

year!—what can he mean by this? Alas! how terrible is my situation! when a single word, a particular emphasis, has power to rob me of my peace!—He often talks of you and of the Signor di Varàno; and sometimes I imagine seems to wish you were here: —it is unnecessary to add how much I should rejoice, would you consent to return to us."——

Cecilia wept as she perused this letter; nor was the melancholy account contained in it of her friends, her only cause for distress. To behold her own name united with Varàno's, was a circumstance too painful not to awaken her regrets; for, though she strove to banish from her mind all anticipation and all retrospect, it was not possible to forget that their separation would now, in all possibility, be for life: and since to remove from a place where every scene she encountered was fraught with some tender recollection, and to administer the balm of consolation to her afflicted friend, was now the first wish of her soul, she determined to acquaint the Lady Viola with the invitation which she had received, and to consult with her on the propriety of accepting it.—She availed herself of the earliest moment of leisure to enter upon her purpose; but the Signora, after giving her a patient hearing, referred her to her husband; and Boraccio, less than ever disposed to part with her, refused to accord with her request.

Cecilia, when she could excuse herself from attending upon the Lady Viola, frequently took a walk, accompanied only by Claudia, along the margin of the bay.—The proximity of the sea to the Palace, which commanded from its lofty terraces a view beyond the walls of the city, of the port, and of the ocean, rendered it peculiarly delightful to Cecilia. The sight of that immense tract of waters inspired her with the most sublime emotions.—She loved to sit upon the beach listening to the melancholy moaning of the waves, and watching them as they rolled in regular succession to the opposite shore. Here the image of Varàno would often recur to her thoughts; and recalling the recollection of past happy events, sink her into pensiveness and despondency.

One evening, on her return from one of these her favourite excursions, she found the Lady Viola in her dressing-room, splendidly attired, accompanied by Paulina, her woman, who was busied in assisting her at her toilet. Cecilia enquired of the Signora if she was dressing for the Opera, and was told that a party was expected that night at the Palace, and that she must prepare herself to receive them.

"Count Morsino," resumed the Lady Viola, "is just arrived from Venice; and happening to call here on his way to the Strada Nuova, the Signor was absurd enough to invite him and the Gavinos to supper, though he knew that the charming Opera of *Artaserse* was to be performed at the Theatre della Croce, and that all the world is to be there:—but this is always his way; he is perpetually destroying my plans.—As I knew that Madame Le Marne and her affected daughter would be ready to die with vexation if we had nobody to meet them, I was obliged to dispatch cards to two or three other families, all of whom, as I supposed, are engaged."

The mention of the Count and his return was so embarrassing to Cecilia, that she was unable to attend to the concluding words of the speech. The Signora stopped to adjust her bracelet, and then proceeded.

"And so, my dear, as this delectable Count is to be here to-night, who, they say, is the envy of all the men, and the admiration of all the women, you must display all your graces and attractions to counteract those of our little Gallic coquette, who, I understand, was brought over into Italy for the sole purpose of procuring herself a title, though I have no doubt but she will be disappointed, for she is a low-born thing at the best; and as to her fortune, it is not, I am told, so large as has been represented."

Cecilia replied that she had not the smallest intention of rivalling Mademoiselle Le Marne, nor any design upon the Count, whose situation was equally above her wishes and expectations.

"You must allow, however," continued the Signora, "that he is most enchantingly handsome; though, were he a few years younger, he might appear a more suitable match for a girl of your age:—as it is, there are few women that would refuse him; and, situated as you are, I have too high an opinion of your prudence to suppose you of the number.—They say he is immensely rich; and that, though nobly descended, he has imbibed none of the aristocratical notions of his high-born progenitors, who would have scorned to mix the pure fluid which flowed in their veins with the blood of the canaille. His estates in Naples are numerous and extensive; and he has others too in France he inherits from his wife, with whom he lived but a year, and who is lately deceased."

Cecilia having never received any hint either from the Lady Viola or Boraccio of the Count's former marriage, betrayed some surprise at this intelligence, which the Signora perceiving, said—

"Some unhappy circumstances in this marriage, for it appears to have been an unfortunate one, accounts for the silence which he has so uniformly preserved; and probably but for Signor Gavino, who has been long acquainted with him and with his family, they would never have been known to us. These seem to have originated in the gallantry of the lady, who, in consequence of a dispute between her and the Count, eloped with her lover, with whom she afterwards resided."

Here the Signora paused to give some directions to her woman; and Cecilia taking advantage of her silence, withdrew to her apartment, where she had not remained long ere the guests were announced, and she descended to the saloon.

The first person she saw on entering the room was the Count, who, with eyes that sparkled with delight as they fixed with eager admiration the beauties of her form and the timid graces of her manner, arose; and having uttered some inflated compliments delivered in the hyperbolical diction of love and gallantry, led her to a chair. Cecilia, without appearing to notice them, though she could not prevent the glow of indignation from rising to her cheek whilst listening to language she despised, took her place by a card-table at which the Signor and his Lady, with two others of the party, were already assembled.—Scarcely was she seated, when raising her eyes from the ground, she perceived Madame Le Marne, who was steadily and earnestly regarding her. Mortified by the attention which she had drawn, and the remarks it had excited, she remained silent and disconcerted, till she was relieved from her embarrassment by the voice of Boraccio, who, without seeming to notice it, offered her a card, and entreated that she would make one of their number at *Ombra*.—Cecilia hesitated, and would have complied; but the Count insisting that, as he had already engaged Mademoiselle Le Marne, it was unfair he should monopolize all the beauty to himself, proposed that they should make another table. Another was accordingly brought; and Cecilia, the Count, and few of the remaining part of the company, sat down to play.

The cards ran excessively high; and Cecilia, who had been drawn rather by necessity than inclination to partake of an amusement which she had hitherto avoided, soon found herself a loser by several *zecheens*. The Count, being the chief winner, proposed that, by way of affording an opportunity to the losers of refunding their losses, they should redouble their stakes.—The proposal was unanimously approved; but the whimsical Goddess, who usually bestows her favours where they are the least wanted and regarded, continued blindly unpropitious; and Cecilia, after having played several succeeding games without any prospect of success, was compelled to rise from the table with the humiliating acknowledgement that she had lost all her money, and consequently that she could play no longer.—The Count smiled at her confusion; and then declaring that it was impossible they could part with her, insisted upon becoming her banker. Cecilia started at the proposition, and refused for some minutes to accede to it; but perceiving that he was absolute, and that the eyes of the whole company were rivetted upon her, she resumed her seat at the table. But what was her astonishment, and what her distress, when, after playing several more games, she found, instead of recovering her late losses, that she had considerably augmented them; and that by the time they arose to supper, the Count was actually her creditor for the sum of thirty *pistoles*.—This was a species of distress entirely new to Cecilia, and of which she never before had had the smallest conception. The anxiety which she experienced was depicted on her countenance; and it demanded all her firmness to support herself throughout the evening with a tolerable share of address, and to answer the various questions and remarks of Mademoiselle Le Marne, who, as the Lady Viola had predicted, was displaying all her attractions and accomplishments to engage the attention of the Count.

The company did not separate till a late hour, or rather till an early one, for it was long past midnight ere they left the Palace. As they departed from the door where the carriages were in waiting, Boraccio, addressing himself to the Count, desired that his visits might be frequent and without ceremony; an invitation which was very graciously accepted.

The party withdrawn, Cecilia, with a beating heart, and spirits more than ordinarily oppressed, retired to her room, though not to sleep; for uneasy thoughts pursued her.—A debt, such as she had just contracted, to a mind unaccustomed to, and unvitiated with fashionable excesses, appeared monstrous; and she accused herself of rashness for having yielded to persuasions which, her reason returned, she felt she ought to have withstood. —To acquire such a sum without an application to Boraccio was impossible; and from this her delicacy and her pride alike revolted. As it was, however, there was no other part to take: and since at all events it was better to owe an obligation to him than to the Count, she left her room with the resolution of acquainting the Signor with her perplexity, and of entreating his assistance.

Boraccio laughed heartily at the adventure, and assured her that the sum she had lost was not of importance enough to occasion even a momentary anxiety: adding, he much wondered that a girl of spirit and sentiment like her, should consider it as such. —Cecilia reminded him that it was not the largeness of the sum, but her inability to repay it, which had occasioned this anxiety.

"Well, I admire your prudence," resumed Boraccio, "though in the present instance it is a little *outré*. The Count was a happy fellow to have it in his power to befriend you; and if I augur right, you will have much less difficulty in acquiring the money to repay him, than in obliging him to accept it."

Saying this he withdrew, and returning soon after with a purse, containing about fifty *pistoles*, he desired she would discharge the debt, and dispose of the rest as she thought proper.—Cecilia would have remonstrated against appropriating the whole; but without waiting for her reply, he retired, leaving her in admiration at his generosity and kindness.

CHAPTER XI

—————If powers divine
Behold our human actions, as they do,
I doubt not then but innocence shall make
False accusation blush, and tyranny
Tremble at patience.

SHAKESPEARE.

THAT Boraccio was actuated by any motive in serving her, but what proceeded entirely from a disinterested regard for her welfare and happiness, never once occurred to Cecilia: and whilst the purity of her mind held her completely ignorant of his intentions, she ran with avidity into the very snare that had been preparing for her.—The suspicions his former conduct had excited, his subsequent behaviour had ultimately erased; and she felt that pain which the mind of sensibility must ever eventually experience at the idea of having formed a hasty and erroneous judgment.—The man, she considered, who, without the smallest prospect of reward, could patronize and support an unprotected orphan, maintain her in affluence, and raise her into importance by introducing her as his equal, whatever might be his defects, must at least be entitled to the praise of humanity. Thus reasoned Cecilia, too ignorant of the world and its wiles to suspect its frauds, detect its sophisms, or fear its allurements.

She was busied in these reflections, her cheek reclining on her hand, and her arm resting on a table, when the door opened, and turning her head, she beheld the Count. He advanced with a careless air, and, apologizing for his intrusion, added, that, having heard she was alone, he had ventured to enquire after her health, which he feared might have suffered from her last night's fatigue. —Cecilia bowed, and offering him a seat, requested that he would accept her acknowledgements for the assistance he had offered her, presenting at the same time the *pistoles* she had procured from Boraccio.—The Count, affecting surprise, protested that the circumstance of which she spoke, had entirely escaped his memory; but if it really was as she represented, he must entreat that she would so far oblige him as to avoid all future mention of it.

"Pardon me, my Lord," said Cecilia with dignity, "the *pistoles* are your's, and I must insist upon your receiving them."

She then counted them upon the table; and taking up her work, walked to the other end of the room.

"Charming Cecilia," at length continued the Count, "why this solicitude about trifles?—why deprive the man who adores you —who lives but in your smiles, and who has no hopes, no wishes unconnected with your happiness, of the power of assisting you?"—He paused.—"I know you will condemn me," resumed he, "for this premature declaration. I meant not—I ought not to have been thus precipitate; but your scruples—your angelic beauty—the present moment——" (He now placed himself by her side, and seizing her hand, would have smothered it with kisses.) —"Add then to this obligation one more, that of empowering me to raise you from dependence to affluence. Consent but to be mine. Let me lay my person, my fortune at your feet, and the day shall dawn only to witness our joys, and depart envious of our mutual happiness."

Thus far he had proceeded without any interruption from Cecilia. The sudden and unexpected avowal of his passion, the vivacity of his manner, the vehemence of his language, conspired to overwhelm her. The Count, translating her silence into an approbation of his suit, continued.

"Free from those restrictions by which thousands are enslaved —with a mind noble and independent as your's, what should preclude my charming Cecilia from giving and receiving mutual felicity?—from raising the lowest of her slaves, the most adoring of her lovers, to the extreme of earthly bliss!—the man whose assiduities and whose fortune shall be devoted to the anticipation of her wishes. Complete then the rapture you have inspired; and while hope revels in our hearts, and irradiates our prospects, let us seize the happiness which awaits us; and, regardless of the world and its forms, fly where splendour and delight court us to their arms—where every luxury shall be your's, and where the

whole globe shall be ransacked to contribute to your gratification!"

Cecilia heard with unutterable pangs a declaration so wounding to her pride, so insulting to those high-wrought principles
of virtue that glowed indignant in her bosom.—Shocked and
mortified by a proposal which it was impossible she could misunderstand, her cheeks pale but the instant before, were suddenly
suffused with crimson; and summoning all her spirits to her aid,
she thus addressed him.

"My Lord, this is unworthy of a reply; nor will I condescend
to answer a conversation I ought not to have heard, and which,
but from the supposition that I was poor and friendless—a supposition which should have been my defence against insolence
and inhumanity, you would never have insulted me with. Neither
your person nor your fortune, important as they may appear to
you, have ever been the objects of my pursuit: and had my ambition or my partiality been such that I could have overlooked the
inequality of our situations, and the still greater disparity in our
minds, the baseness of your heart, and the depravity of your principles, would have directed me to spurn the one, and despise the
other:—as it is, I receive the degradation you have inflicted with
the disdain it merits."

She then burst from his arms, which he had folded about her
waist; and looking on him with eyes which shot mingled contempt and indignation, darted from the room.

The Count stood transfixed in astonishment and perplexity.
Thrown completely off his guard, he had ventured, in a fit of passion, and, as it had proved, in an unlucky moment, to throw aside
the mask with which he had hitherto concealed the blackness of
his intentions; for though, under the specious pretence of honourable attachment, he had engaged the agency of Boraccio, whose
embarrassments had rendered him the easy dupe of his arts,
nothing was farther from his thoughts than marrying Cecilia, or
even of deceiving her with the shew of it. By obtaining an admission to her at all times, which would afford him such repeated
opportunities of pleading his cause, of displaying his eloquence,
and calling up all the studied blandishments of his conversation,
he considered his triumph as complete:—that, however reluctant

she might appear at first, she would finally yield to his importunities, and consent to an elopement, his former successes did not
suffer him to doubt; nor would he have considered the agency of
Boraccio at all necessary to the undertaking, had his confidence
in her partiality been greater, or his apprehension of Varàno's
predilection less sanguine.—To meet with a repulse from a being
so destitute as Cecilia, without friends to protect her, a fortune
to support, or any obvious means of subsistence, except what
she derived from the bounty of strangers, was a circumstance
not more hostile to his intentions, than mortifying to his pride.
—A humiliation so extraordinary, so unlooked for, to one who
had been accustomed to consider the world and its inhabitants as
mere creatures of his will, amenable to his power, and subservient
to his gratifications, seemed the very acme of earthly torment;
and he experienced a malignant kind of satisfaction in the hope
of transmitting a portion of the mortification which he had thus
deservedly incurred, into the innocent and unsuspecting bosom
of her who had inflicted it.—But the resentment these reflections
had called forth was only momentary. Base as were his designs,
he could not bear to see, even in his mental view, the woman he
had adored, and whom, notwithstanding what had happened, he
still passionately loved, under circumstances of distress. To shield
her from these, there was scarcely an indignity or a danger he
would not have surmounted. To lose her, if by remonstrances
and assiduities it was possible to obtain her, would, he concluded,
be madness; and he departed from the Palace with a determination of renewing his suit, not fearing by address and perseverance
to accomplish his purpose.

Cecilia, on leaving him, flew immediately to the Signora, to
whom she instantly unfolded all that had passed, conjuring her
with tears to dispense with her attendance when the Count was
there, whom it was impossible she could see again without the
utmost pain and displeasure.

The Signora appeared greatly concerned.

"I am all astonishment," said she, "at what I hear. I think, however, you must be mistaken in your judgment on the Count's conduct: on the motives of his actions I am convinced you are so. The
Signor, I know, has long expected him to declare himself; and but

for his interdiction, I should have prepared to have congratulated you on your conquest."

She then desired that Cecilia would repeat the conversation; which she accordingly did, though not without evident uneasiness, and many marks of confusion discovering themselves in the detail.

"Well, my dear," said the Signora, with a smile, as soon as she had concluded, "and what does all this amount to? The Count has offered you his person and his fortune, which he intends to secure to you by marriage; and because, in pity to your feelings, he has avoided all the wearisome parade of settlements, &c. you have construed it into an insult, and have refused to listen to him."

Cecilia replied with some spirit, that the Count's behaviour was such as could not admit of a mistake: she must therefore request permission when he next repeated his visit, to confine herself to her chamber.

"To absent yourself," continued the Signora, "because you have received an offer from him, not dictated exactly in the terms you could wish, would be extremely ridiculous; neither, I am sure, would the Signor consent to it. As his friend, the Count is entitled to respect from every member of his family; and so palpable an omission on this point would justly expose you to his resentment.—To comply, however, in some measure with the prejudices you have imbibed, unreasonable as they appear, I shall desire the Signor to inform himself of the Count's intentions concerning you, which, notwithstanding your assertions, I believe will redound to his honour. Should it be otherwise, the Signor has too just a sense of decorum to suffer an insult such as this to escape with impunity."

The appearance of Signor Zuccato, who came to conduct the Signora to Church, put an end to the conversation.

The Count did not return to the Palace till the following day, when he consented, at the request of Boraccio, to stay dinner. —He saluted Cecilia with his former confidence, declared she looked more enchanting than ever; and on her withdrawing her hand, which he yet struggled to detain, protested that she was not only the most charming, but the most obdurate of her sex, and that he was justified, by all the laws of love and gallantry, in detaining that angelic hand till it was confirmed to him for ever by the most sacred of bonds.

As soon as dinner was concluded, he retired with Boraccio, with whom he remained absent some time. On their return the Signor appeared agitated, his countenance looked stern, and he walked about the room in much evident perturbation.—To the Count he seldom spoke; and when addressed by him, his answers were short, peevish, and repulsive. Morsino seemed scarcely less uneasy: he did not stay supper, nor did the Signor invite him so to do: it was plain some disagreement had taken place; but nothing had transpired which could afford even the remotest hint as to the subject of it.

The next day and the next passed on without any new event, during which Cecilia never saw or heard any thing of the Count. —From this period she remarked that the Signor was more frequently at home, and that he seemed thoughtful and unhappy.— She often found him alone with the Signora in close conversation, which, at her entrance, they suddenly broke off. Not doubting but she was the subject of it, and that the Count's absence, his altered manner when he had last parted from him, and Boraccio's indignation, owed their source to a full explanation of his insidious views upon her; and that these had met with the reception which they merited, she felt anxious to make an acknowledgement of her gratitude to the Signora for her services, and to sue for a continuation of her favours: but the Signora was seldom alone, even for a moment; and when she was, she studiously repressed every effort at communication by sending for her woman, her *cavaliere servante*, or by pleading indisposition or engagements.

Near a week had elapsed, when the Count, to the astonishment of Cecilia, appeared again at dinner, gay and insinuating as before, and more than ever in favour with Boraccio, whose gloom seemed to have evaporated with his return, and whose countenance was once more arrayed in the vivid smiles of joy and welcome.—Each succeeding day produced a repetition of the same visits. He was their constant attendant on their rides, at the Operas, and the Casinos; and in the interval of other employments, sat, or walked with them on the terrace.

One evening, when they were thus engaged, they were met by

Boraccio, who, drawing Cecilia aside, entreated that she would indulge him with a few minutes' conversation in private; and then without waiting for her reply, he conducted her into a room, and having closed the door, he thus addressed her:—

"I have requested this interview, Madam, to inform you of what, in your situation, must give you pleasure. The Count has solicited me to inform you of the honour he designs you—he offers you, by my means, his fortune and his hand. As he knows you have neither connections nor expectations, his proposal is at once flattering and disinterested. An alliance so much above your hopes, merits your warmest gratitude—you will receive it as becomes you."

Cecilia, all astonishment at an overture she had so little reason to expect, remained silent: but, lest Boraccio should imagine that she was deliberating upon the offer, she desired he would inform the Count that she was obliged to him for the honour he intended her, but at the same time that she absolutely declined accepting it. Boraccio, laughing aloud, told her this answer might do very well for one of her plebeian lovers, but certainly not for the Count, whose fortune and whose character were alike unexceptionable, and whose rank in life was such as might entitle him to an alliance with the most fastidious woman in Europe. Cecilia entreated he would be satisfied with an answer which it was impossible she could change; and on his remonstrating with a mixture of surprise and discontent on the motives of it, besought him that he would spare her the enumeration of unnecessary objections, and instantly and implicitly acquaint the Count with her determination, who, whatever might be his qualifications, was entirely and in every respect disagreeable to her.

Boraccio, who seemed to have considered her acquiescence as a matter of course, listened to her rejection with mortification and perplexity; and having in vain endeavoured to persuade her to consent to a marriage which would instate her in affluence, and raise her into consequence, refused to afford any final answer to the Count, till she had taken some time for consideration.

The following week had neither event nor disturbance, except some little vexations occasioned by the behaviour of Boraccio, who seemed to entertain no doubts of the ultimate success of his legation, and the unwearied attentions of the Count, who continued to conduct himself with the ease and familiarity of an accepted lover.—This impertinent confidence she could alone attribute to the officious encouragement of Boraccio, and therefore she resolved to seek rather than avoid an explanation.—She was revolving upon the most effectual means of releasing herself from his provoking assiduities, when one day, the Signora Viola and Boraccio having designedly quitted the room, she was left alone with the Count.—He arose as they retired, and taking a seat near her's, besought that she would favour him with a few moments' attention; having been informed by the Signor that she had entirely mistaken his intentions, which he hoped it was now unnecessary to convince her were as honourable as disinterested. Cecilia interrupted him by observing that all further conversation on this subject was useless; and then referring him to the discourse lately held between her and Boraccio, she entreated, as he valued her esteem, that he would desist from all future importunity.

"I know not, Madam," said the Count, reddening, "what you would teach me to infer from the conversation you mention."

"If you have been deluded as to the purport of it, my Lord," returned Cecilia, "give me leave to recite it."

She then repeated the most particular parts of the conversation, concluding with the answer which she had returned expressive of her obligation for his very flattering proposals, and her resolution of rejecting them.

"Impossible, Madam!" cried the Count, "these were not the words."

"Not exactly, my Lord, but they would admit of the same interpretation."

"Then I have been deceived," replied the Count, "miserably deceived!"

"Not by me, my Lord," said Cecilia, mildly; "by yourself and by the Signor you may; but as to me, the whole tenor of my conduct has been such as could not lead you to mistake my meaning."

The Count bit his lips in anger, but made no comment; and Cecilia, eager to escape from all further altercation, would have quitted the room; but, aware of her intention, he arose, and locked the door.

"No, adorable Cecilia!" said he, "I will not lose an opportunity which I have so long anxiously awaited.—Though you disdain to pity, you shall hear me."

"My Lord," said Cecilia, "this conduct is insupportable; it is cruel, and permit me to add, unmanly.—Release me this instant; or, unprotected as you think I am, a supposition on which you ground your security for insulting me, be assured you shall repent your temerity."

She then withdrew herself from his grasp, and unlocking the door, walked calmly out of the room.

Hitherto her pride, and the conscious dignity of virtue, had sustained Cecilia; but no sooner was she alone, than the little spirit which she had exerted, yielded to grief and indignation, and she burst into tears. That is was the Signor's intention to unite her to the Count, his recent behaviour did not permit her to doubt; and she trembled at the idea of the persecutions she must inevitably encounter, although resolutely determined to submit to any evils her wayward destiny might have in store for her, rather than consent to connect herself with a man she despised. —The misfortunes to which her now destitute situation might expose her in her passage through the world, pressed heavily on her fancy; and she deplored with renewed anguish the loss of De Sevignac, arraigned the cruelty of death, which had robbed her of all that was dear and valuable to her on earth; and a thousand times in earnest prayer entreated that he would look down and protect her.

Boraccio having made all due arrangements with the Count, though not without many arduous struggles with himself, the cause of which will be hereafter explained, dispatched at length a message by the Signora to Cecilia, informing her that, as every thing was now settled, she must prepare to become the wife of the Count in the course of a week, as the nuptials could not possibly be delayed beyond that period.

Having executed her commission thus far, the Signora presented her with a casket containing jewels to a considerable amount, designed as a wedding present from the Count to Cecilia.—They were set in the most elegant devices, some forming necklaces, others zones, with a variety of the most costly ornaments for the head; among which was a comb for her *chignon*, painted in the representation of an Etruscan border, set on either side with topazes formed into stars, and interspersed with diamonds.

"These jewels," said the Signora, "though useless to you here, the laws of our Republic forbidding us to wear gems except as rings, may be worn at Naples, where you are to remove on your marriage, and where no person of rank can appear without them. In regard to your clothes, I am authorised to provide you a suitable wardrobe, which will be ready by the time appointed."

She then closed the casket, and gave it to Cecilia, who immediately returned it, observing that, as she had already determined never to marry the Count, she could not be justified in accepting his presents. The Signora smiled satirically; but having too much of what the Italians call *buona creanza* to betray the natural asperity of her temper when it was possible to conceal it, she placed the jewels upon the table, and retired silently to give an account of her mission to her husband.

Morsino was absent at dinner; and Boraccio, as was his custom when no company was present, dined alone with Signor Zuccato. When coffee was prepared, he joined the ladies in the pavilion; but he seemed in haste to be gone, looked angry, and never once spoke to Cecilia, whose pale countenance and embarrassed air would have softened any heart not goaded by passion or deafened by avarice, like those of her persecutors.

The evening was devoted, like many of the preceding ones, to the amusement of the Theatre; but neither Boraccio nor the Count was there.—The play was the *Aristodeno* of the Abate Monti, where pathos and sublimity, portrayed by the vigorous pencil of genius, unite their powers to touch the heart, and nerve the imagination.—Cecilia, whose ready conception of every thing great and beautiful made her peculiarly susceptible of the charms of dramatic excellence, was often drawn from scenes of melancholy reality to those of fancy and fiction; and while she repressed the ebullitions of that grief which weighed heavily upon her bosom, she disdained not to drop the tear of sympathetic sorrow at the shrine of fabled, but well-imagined woe.

On the following morning she received a message from the Signor, requesting to see her in his library. She obeyed in trembling expectation; and on entering the room, found him busily engaged in the perusal of some papers, which, on her approach, he threw aside.—The authoritative severity of his countenance alarmed her:—she doubted not but the Signora had acquainted him with her resolution, and that the occasion of this summons was to insist upon her compliance with his wishes.

"I sent for you, Madam," said he, as soon as she was seated, "not to avail myself, as you may imagine, of the real motives of your conduct, but to inform you of its consequences.—Of the motives of it, could I have been weak enough to misinterpret them, your late heroic refusal of a man every way your superior, would have rendered it obvious: it is therefore incumbent upon me, as your guardian and friend, to expose the fallacy of those hopes which have so strangely deceived you, by convincing you, if you are not so far gone in error as to be insensible to the dictates of reason and truth, of the impossibility of forming an alliance with a family, the heir of which is designed for the husband of a lady, whose connections are nearly equal to his own, and whose fortune is indeed superior."

"This is a subject, Signor," said Cecilia, colouring, and rising half way from her seat, "I thought your delicacy would have spared me."

"It must, therefore, be sufficiently obvious to you," continued Boraccio, "that common policy will not allow the Marchese, believing, as he must, that you are proceeding in an insidious and clandestine correspondence with his son, to permit you to remain in my palace, or indeed any where, without the severest restrictions, till that son, the last support of his noble and uncontaminated house, shall be settled to his wishes, or till there are some hopes that he will become so. The Marchese, however, ever noble and lenient, offers you proposals which are at once generous and considerate.—He purposes to afford you a suitable and ample portion on your union with the Count; or, on your rejection of him, with any husband whom you shall yourself appoint, provided the marriage he designs takes place immediately."

Cecilia raised her handkerchief to her eyes, but made no answer, and Boraccio proceeded.

"On your non-compliance with these terms, you are to be removed to a Convent, the Superior of which is not unknown to the Marchese, and who will receive orders from him to treat you with distinction and kindness. Here too is another instance of his justice and benevolence:—he compels you not to take the veil, nor has he the most distant intention of secluding you longer from the world, than the peculiar exigencies of the case may require. Supposing a Convent might be your choice, an application for your admittance preceded the necessity of it.—The rules in that selected for you are by no means rigid: every gratification which can be procured for you within the limits of a Convent, you will enjoy unrestrained. All the Marchese demands from you in return for this lenity is, that you will never, either directly or indirectly, acquaint his son with your situation; not fearing, when informed that a Convent has been your choice, that he will give a ready and unlimitted consent to those measures, by which alone the peace and honour of his family can be secured. To this retirement, which is situated in a small village in France, in the Province of Languedoc, on your obstinate refusal of the above-mentioned terms, I have orders to convey you immediately.— Thus acquainted with the basis of my authority, you see to what extent you are dependant upon my power. Feeling nevertheless, as I do, as much regard for your happiness as for your interests, I would solicit your acceptance of the honour that awaits you; and on that condition only can I endure your continuance in my family. I shall allow you three days to decide upon it; at the expiration of which I shall expect your answer."

Cecilia, in whose bosom grief and indignation had been struggling for pre-eminence whilst listening to this speech, conscious that she ought to attempt something like a vindication of her conduct, spoke as follows.

"I shall not, Signor, by any appeal to your compassion or your humanity, endeavour to deprecate a decree which, though I know it to be unjust, I believe also to be unalterable. It is, however, a duty I owe to myself to clear away, if possible, the invidious and ingenious aspersions which have been cast upon my character—aspersions which are at once cruel and unmerited.—To the Marchese's accusation, that I am proceeding in a clandestine amour with his son, I reply that, after the suspicions he has betrayed, and the conduct he has accused me of, nothing short of overtures from him, and these the most pressing, could tempt me to ally myself with a family which, undeserving as I am of it, has subjected me to insult, and loaded me with opprobrium.—When I speak of the family, I would be understood to except the Marchesa, whose generosity and whose virtues have justly entitled her to my esteem and admiration. With the promise which the Marchese exacts me in return for his *lenity*, I shall accede unconditionally:—what I have further to add may be conveyed in a few words. With his views reflecting the Count, I never *can* comply; nor will I do so great a violence both to my feelings and my delicacy, as to accept a husband of *his* or *your* providing. To the alternative, since he has graciously allowed me a choice of evils, I must of course submit: with patience I will, and I hope with dignity.—For the hospitality and kindness which I have experienced beneath your roof, Signor —kindness which, while I believed it to be genuine, I received with transport, and repaid with gratitude, I thank you:—the child of poverty and misfortune ought not, cannot be ungrateful. All I have now to request is, that I may be conveyed to my Convent. Had my inclinations been consulted, I should have chosen the retirement of one endeared to me by early remembrance, and by its proximity to the spot which witnessed the happy and ever to be regretted æra of my childhood—a spot which a sensation within tells me I must never more revisit; but I scorn to solicit favours from those who are ignorant of the happy art of bestowing them. —For a situation like that I am destined to fill, no preparation can be wanting: I shall therefore await your orders."

Saying this, she arose to quit the room, but was recalled by Boraccio, who, putting a packet into her hand, said—

"Since your resolution, Madam, is taken, permit me to deliver to you this packet. The restrictions under which I received it are already known to you; with the contents, as you must suppose, I am wholly unacquainted: you may peruse it at discretion.—Respecting your passage to France, I shall ensure you the protection of Madame Le Marne, who is fortunately going thither in the course of a week, and who will engage to accompany you through Languedoc as far as Beziers, from whence she is to embark on the Canal Royal for Tholouse.—A letter to the Superior from me will secure you a reception in her Convent, and the care of some Religieux, whom she will of course dispatch immediately on the receipt of it, to conduct you to Beziers.—As to the Count, he waits only to be acquainted with your decision to receive your hand, or fly instantly from Genoa—a place his despair and your scorn have rendered hateful to him.—Whatever may be the event, nobly resolved to confine his sorrows and his injuries to his own bosom, he seeks not to pursue you with useless importunity. To-day he departs; and, quitting Italy and his hopes, proposes in another country, and in society less dangerous than your's to court the return of that peace of which you have so cruelly deprived him.—Go then, Madam, and if you can, enjoy the proud triumph you have obtained; a triumph worthy of the heart that designed it, that of rendering the man who adores you, and who, in spite of your disdain, would still glory in calling you his, wholly, though, I trust not lastingly, miserable."

"Of any attempt to injure the peace of him you speak of," said Cecilia, "my conscience acquits me.—If the Count had deserved my esteem, he would probably have had it: the injuries I still think he once dared to meditate against me, I have already forgiven him." Having said this, she withdrew.

As she was passing through the hall, on her way to her apartment, she was met by Emily Le Marne and Signor Zuccato; the latter of whom, with his usual *mia padrona*, stopped to accost her. —Too much oppressed to attend even to the common forms of politeness, Cecilia only curtsied, and passed on to her chamber, where alone, and unobserved, she endeavoured to collect her thoughts, and to arm herself with fortitude to bear the increasing evils of her lot with resignation and calmness.

The melancholy retirement of a Convent was repugnant alike to her principles and her inclination. Though educated in all the rigour of the Catholic faith, a seclusion from the world and its enjoyments to a mind like her's, capable of deducing pleasure from innumerable sources, was an infliction as severe as it was arbitrary.—However zealous as to her religion, she reflected too

much, and thought too accurately, to consider a total renunciation of society and its blessings as indispensable to the attainment
of eternal happiness. She knew that a grateful heart, rejoicing in
the innocent gratifications an infinitely great and good Being has
mercifully provided for us, is the most acceptable of all sacrifices,
and an useful life the best proof of obedience.

Released, however, from the anticipation of future mortifications and future insults, her spirits insensibly revived; but when
she recollected the length of time which must elapse ere she
could be emancipated from her confinement, and the probability
that she might be secluded in it for life, and that, at all events, she
must inevitably remain there till Varàno was for ever lost to her
—these as suddenly forsook her, and she wept the fate she could
not deprecate. That fate so cruel, so unmerited, again roused
her from the torpor of inactivity and despair, and she formed a
fluctuating design of claiming her privileges, and asserting her
independence: but reflection soon convinced her of the futility
of this plan, and of any other she could devise to cope with the
authority of her persecutors, who, if driven to desperation by a
well supported opposition, might open to her a new source of
dreadful and hitherto unimagined evil.—The packet containing
the melancholy story of her unhappy parents she still held; but as
yet she had not the courage to unseal it. She knew it was to unfold
a tale

"Whose lightest hearing would harrow up the soul."

For a task so mournful the present moment was inimical—the
succeeding ones might be equally so: at all events, she determined
to delay the examination of it till after she should have arrived at
her destination.—Convinced that this was not a season for the
indulgence of sorrow, but for the acquisition of fortitude—an
æra which called for action, and not for tears, she endeavoured,
by drawing a comparison between what was, and what might
have been, to renew her spirits, and recover her firmness.

She succeeded so well in this attempt, as to be enabled to join
the party below with some degree of composure.—The Count
was departed; but they had a party in the evening, and at night

a concert, at which Cecilia, to avoid peculiarity, consented to be present.—Several pieces were performed; after which Emily Le Marne, who had a sweet and powerful voice, accompanied Cecilia on the piano-forte. They had sung and played all Marcelli's most beautiful airs, when the rest of the company joined; and Signor Gavino, who was an enthusiast in the art, and himself a scientific performer, leading the band, the amusement was concluded with the sublime choral compositions of Mozart.

In the interval of these performances, Madame Le Marne conversed alone with Cecilia on the subject of her intended journey into France, expressing her surprise that so young a creature should prefer the solitude of a cloister to the pleasures that surrounded her; and then, on Cecilia's returning only short and slight answers to her numerous interrogatories, turning the discourse upon herself, she informed Cecilia of her reasons for quitting Italy, which she assured her she should not have done without having first visited Rome, Naples, and Florence, but for the illness of a relation of her's at Tholouse, whose disorder, though not so dangerous as to threaten him with an immediate dissolution, was, nevertheless, attended with symptoms not altogether favourable.—The state of her friend would not, however, she said, have occasioned so speedy a removal, but from the apprehension that he might have neglected a very necessary precaution respecting some writings, which were of the utmost consequence to *her*; since, without a due attention to this point, his property, the most considerable part of which would devolve to her daughter, could not be legally secured to her.

She then spoke of the Count, who, she informed Cecilia, was almost universally considered as her lover, though few who knew him believed he had any meaning in his attentions beyond casual amusement.—She hoped, therefore, it was not owing to any disappointment regarding him that she was going to immure herself from the world, as she was too young and too handsome to have any real cause for despair.—Men of rank and merit, like him, were always, she said, profuse of their assiduities, and unsteady in their attachments: she had always found it so, though she believed few (bridling as she spoke) had been more successful with them than she had; as few, she might now acknowledge without a blush, had been more celebrated and admired.

Having concluded this satire upon others with this eulogy upon herself, she entreated that Cecilia would not delay her preparations, as she waited only for a letter, which she now daily expected, before she commenced her route into France.—The presence of the Signora, who came to propose a song, in which Cecilia was to join, interrupted the conversation: it was resumed, however, on the ensuing day by Boraccio, who informed Cecilia that Madame Le Marne had received the expected letter from Thoulouse, and that she had determined to set off on the following day.

Cecilia, on hearing this, withdrew to collect her books, her trinkets, and such of her clothes as she conceived might be useful to her in her Convent: the rest, except two suits newly purchased, she bestowed on Claudia, whose grief at being separated from her amiable benefactress, admitted not of alleviation.

Having arranged her little wardrobe, she sat down to write to Signora di Rosalvo, to whom she related all that had happened since the time of her quitting Florence, beseeching her that she would still honour with her friendship an unhappy and now isolated being, who, except her, had no one to look up to for consolation and sympathy. As she was yet ignorant not only of the situation, but of the name of the Convent to which she was about to retire, she was unable to enclose her address; a deficiency which she, however, promised to remedy on her arrival at the Convent, from whence she meant immediately to write.

To the Marchesa she would also have written; but, contrary to her expectations, she had received no answer to her letter; and, had she resolved to address her, the satirical smile which she had observed upon the features of Boraccio, when she was speaking of the Marchesa, would probably have deterred her.—It is true she had offered her her protection, and had even said she would incur some domestic disturbances, displeasing as they were to her, rather than abandon her; but, although she had declared this, it was evident that she was either not very zealous in the cause, or that she had been irresistibly prevented from putting her former intentions into practice.—Nothing then was to be hoped from

any future application; and even were it so, it was scarcely probable that a letter would be allowed to reach her. It was, however,
some consolation that there were yet a few beings in the world
who loved and pitied her. There is a degree of pride in human
nature which upholds us in suffering, while we believe we are
objects of interest to some, and of affection to others. While we
continue to feel this, we are not wholly miserable: the energy of
our sufferings abates, the horizon of our prospect clears, and a
beam of hope, or something like it, breaks through the obscurity
that surrounds us.

Cheered by this reflection, she took up her packet, her *port-
feuille*, and drawing implements, which, together with a few
valuables presented to her by De Sevignac, she placed in a small
box with her books and clothes.—These adjusted, assiduous to
employ every moment of her time, she amused herself in reading, sketching, and working, occasionally going down to sit or
walk with the Lady Viola till night, when she repaired again to her
room and to her bed, from which she was recalled by a servant,
who came to convey her *valigia*[1] to the vessel, and to inform her
that the passengers were in readiness, and impatient to embark.
—Cecilia, on this intelligence, dressed herself in haste, and then
flew to take leave of the Signora, who, after gently chiding her
for being such an enemy to her own real interests, as to prefer
a life of solitude and seclusion to one of splendour and delight,
graciously offered her hand, which Cecilia, solicitous to convince
her that she retained no enmity against her, pressed to her lips.—
She then tenderly embraced Claudia, and recommending herself
with fervency to the protection of Heaven, departed, accompanied by Madame Le Marne and her daughter, and preceded by
Boraccio, to the quay, from whence, a vessel being in readiness,
they accordingly embarked.

1 Portmanteau.

CHAPTER XII

Far as the eye can trace, a sombre hue
That seems to mingle with the distant skies,
Darkens the surface of the placid deep
Full many a league. The seamen know it well,
And with fantastic whistlings from the deck
Invite the coming breeze. It speeds along,
And near and nearer now on fluttering wings
Hastes o'er the intervening space. Anon it sings
Most grateful music to the seaman's ear;
Shakes the flat cordage, and with friendly breath
Expands the bellying sails.

GOODWIN.

THE sea was unusually calm; and Cecilia having placed herself on deck, gazed for the last time upon the city of Genoa, surrounded by its lofty walls, its *fanala*[1], its Palaces, and its magnificent port, till it sunk gradually from the view; and the spires and turrets of the Churches, the adjacent Convents, and the distant points of the *Bochetta* remained alone on the horizon, when, reverting to the gay hopes with which she had entered it, the memorials of Varàno and De Sevignac returned to her thoughts, and she melted into tears.

The present moment of her fate had something in it peculiarly affecting to Cecilia. It seemed to separate her for ever from all her earthly connections, from all she had loved, revered, and confided in; and forming a new epoch in her existence, fancy was left to portray the scenes beyond, yet hidden in obscurity. She now shrunk from the perspective with terror, and now again the sanguine pencil of youth tinted it with more lively colours; the shades became softened, and a calm resignation took possession of her faculties: the sweet confidence that she was under the eye of a Being whose power is equal to his mercy, renovated her hopes, and strengthened her fortitude. She blushed that she had

1 Lighthouse.

suffered herself to doubt his care; and in silent supplication, and with entreating looks, besought his pardon and protection.

It was now the excellency of those precepts which had been so early instilled into her, were fully elucidated.—She found that an unlimited reliance on a Supreme Protector has power to enlighten the darkest hour, and to support in the severest and most trying periods of our lives; and that the certainty of this support has efficacy to bestow refuge and consolation in the midst of calamity, when the most subtile reasonings might have proved vague and unavailing.

She remained the greater part of the day upon deck, marking the motion of the ship, and listening to the low dashing of the wave beneath, or the song of the pilot supporting himself at the helm as he was seen steering his unequal course along the waters. As the day declined, the solemn uniformity of the scene was unbroken by any intervening object, except one solitary vessel, which was discerned cleaving the ocean at the remotest distance, whose sails were now seen, and now lost, as the lights fell upon their summits, or the rising vapour allowed them to be distinguishable.

Evening at length advanced: the sun sunk in refulgent beauty on the western main; a dimmer obscurity began to draw over the unfathomed deep, and the moon rising proudly in the east, cast her silvery light upon its surface, throwing the scene into still deeper repose, and making silence more solemn; whilst above the planet Venus burnt with a steady lustre, reflecting a tremulous gleam upon the wave below, which, unruffled by the lightest gale, flowed away in clear, gentle undulations.—Cecilia watched the moving radiance as it twinkled upon the surface till other planets appeared; and innumerable stars, spangling the heavens, were reflected in the deep sable of the waters.

Toward morning the wind arose:—about noon it was unusually high, the sea became rough and boisterous, and the clear blue of the heavens was suddenly overcast with a dense, dark vapour which, rolling over the disk of the sun, now discovered, and now left it to darkness. The sea-fowl clamoured in the air, often dropping to dip their light pinions in the wave as they fled screaming to the shore to seek for shelter among the rocks. Cecilia trembled as she gazed; and recollecting, as the vessel alternately sunk in the abyss, and rose again on the foaming wave, that a plank only divided her from death, and that she was now exposed to encounter all the dangers, all the horrors of a storm, her terrors increased, and she sat silent and appalled.

At length the rain began to descend, the wind to subside, and ere sunset all was still and serene.—This calm continued near two days with little intermission, notwithstanding the united efforts of the Captain and his crew, who wearied every Saint in the calendar to promote and precipitate their intended passage.

On the fourth day a brisker gale arose; and the pilot, observing that the wind was in their favour, steered for the coast of Provence. Cecilia's heart beat quick at the sound.—"Oh France! Oh my country!" said she, "and shall I see you once again?"— But who may describe her emotions, when, casting an eager eye toward the north, she beheld in a gleam of the declining sun the high shores of Provence dark with wood, and gay with a variety of pasturage—the scenes of her earliest delights which, though veiled in distance, memory, ever faithful to her task, brought back upon her mind with the most affecting accuracy.—Lost in tender recollections, she gazed on the beautiful islands of the Hyeres, smiling with vineyards, and glowing with orange-groves, and upon the spiral summits of the mountains that ascend beyond them, which she had so often seen from St. Foix, till these and Toulon receded, and the twilight deepening into the gloom of evening, the perspective sunk again into obscurity.

After a pleasant voyage of a few days, the vessel, drawing gradually near the coast, reached at length the Gulph of Lyons. As they approached toward the mouth of the Rhone, the shores of Provence receded, and those of Languedoc became visible, and the sailors drew near to the port.

They disembarked at an obscure town called Port St. Louis, from whence a *voiture* was procured to convey them to Beziers.

When they arrived at this place, Madame Le Marne dispatched a servant from the *Auberge* at which they alighted, to acquire intelligence respecting the packet, which she was told was to set sail in the space of an hour.—Whilst Madame Le Marne was thus engaged in her enquiries about her passage, Cecilia interrogated the *Aubergiere* concerning the person to be sent thither by the Abbess for the purpose of conducting her to her Convent. —This person, who had already been there, was, she was told, a *Religieux*, probably a lay-brother belonging to a Convent of Carmelite Friars, in the vicinage of St. Michael. He had called there on the preceding day; but as Cecilia was not then arrived, he had then removed himself to a Capuchin Monastery without the town, where he remained to await her orders.—Cecilia, on hearing this, desired that some one might be commissioned to apprize him of her arrival, and of her readiness to accompany him.

This matter adjusted, she partook of a hasty meal with Madame Le Marne and Emily, which was scarcely concluded, when a servant appeared to inform the latter that the packet was about to sail; and that if it was their intention to embark, they must depart immediately. The party arose at these words; and Madame Le Marne and her daughter having each made their fashionable *congées* to Cecilia, though without betraying any visible signs of uneasiness at the thoughts of parting with her, bent their way to the canal.—As soon as they were gone, the messenger employed by the *Aubergiere* on an embassy to the Monastery, returned, attended by the *Religieux*, who proposed, as the day was far advanced, that they should delay the prosecution of their journey till the ensuing morning. Cecilia acquiesced in this arrangement, and the Father having acquainted her with his plans, respectfully retired to perform a promise he said he had made, of attending the service of vespers at the adjacent Convent.

The evening was spent by Cecilia in gloomy anticipations and melancholy remembrances. Never had she felt so forlorn, so friendless, so comfortless as at this moment:—alone, in a strange place, going she scarcely knew whither, among people who, notwithstanding Boraccio's assertion, might be disposed to treat her with severity, or, what was still worse, contemptuous pity. The very occasion of her removal, the ostensible one at least, was sufficient, she considered, not only to preclude esteem, but to excite sensations of mingled contempt and abhorrence; for, had she not been accused of maintaining a secret correspondence with the

heir of a noble house?—and would not this be given as a reason
to the Superior for her hasty and certainly involuntary seclusion
in her Convent?—Guiltless as she was, she felt a faint suffusion
of shame colour her cheek as she found herself subjected to a
suspicion, from the reality of which every principle of her soul
revolted with horror and detestation.

"And is it ever thus?" said she. "Has rectitude no shield to
defend its adherents from the united stroke of cruelty and
oppression?—innocence no resource against malevolence and
falsehood? Shall guilt triumph, whilst virtue feels the lash of
shame it scorns to merit?"

"*Mon Dieu!*" cried the hostess, whom the energy of her expressions, as she uttered this affecting apostrophe, had attracted
unseen to her side, "are you too the victim of undeserved sorrow?
—Alas, poor lady! the world, as you observe, is a scene of oppression, from the effects of which no innocence can shelter us!"

Cecilia started.

"I am not indeed very happy," said she, "but a moment of
dejection has, perhaps, made me unjust."

"Pardon me, Mademoiselle, I guess but too well the cause:
your will has been overruled, your inclinations unconsulted; you
have been prevailed upon, perhaps arbitrarily constrained, to
adopt a mode of life your heart recoils from.—The sacrifice of
a willing mind is acceptable to God; but he spurns the service of
that, compelled reluctantly to approach his altar."

"You are right," said Cecilia, "Heaven lends an ear of mercy to
the unadulterated oraison of the devoted heart; but the invocation of insincerity must never hope to reach it."

"Holy Maria!" exclaimed the hostess, crossing herself, "how
strange that two such circumstances, and these so similar, should
occur in one short week!"

"What is it you mean?" cried Cecilia.

"Why, Lady, a very astonishing incident happened here a few
nights since;—God, they say, cannot prosper wickedness, and
yet——"

"Pray proceed," said Cecilia; "you have strangely interested me."

"A few nights ago, as I was saying," resumed the *Aubergiere*;
"but you will be secret, Lady?"

"As you can wish," replied Cecilia.

"We were roused from our beds by an unusual knocking, which, in spite of repeated callings, continued with little intermission till we had gained the outer gate of the hotel, which was no sooner opened, than two figures wearing masks, one a female, the other a man very singularly accoutred, appeared at the entrance. The man, advancing first, demanded horses for Lodeve, whilst the lady remained a few paces behind, apparently absorbed in grief, now sighing, and now weeping bitterly. They were shewn into a room, which they had no sooner entered, than we heard the door bolted within, and the travellers in earnest conversation, sometimes speaking loud, and at others low, as if fearful of being overheard.—The extraordinary appearance of the man, the magnificent habiliments of the lady, which declared her to be a person of distinction, the circumstance of their being masked, and their anxiety to be gone, as if to elude pursuit, (though it was long past midnight when they entered the hotel), excited the curiosity of my husband, who, whilst the horses were preparing, endeavoured, by taking his station at the door, to acquaint himself with their schemes. Little, however, was to be acquired by this manœuvre—the man, as if suspicious of his intention, speaking lower than before, whilst the voice of the lady was often lost in sighs and profound lamentations:—all he could discover was, that she was accused of having broken her matrimonial engagement—a crime for which she had already been confined, and that this confinement was now about to be exchanged for the religious one of a Convent. To the invective employed by the man to intimidate her into this measure, his companion made but little defence. Her destiny was, she said, decided beyond human interference, and her wrongs beyond all hopes of redress; but her cause was in the hands of God: she had submitted it to him, and would await his deliverance.—When the horses were in readiness, they mounted them in silence, and rode off; the lady dropping in her haste a bracelet, probably of great value, which, as no word passed the lips of either, by which we could inform ourselves of their residence and name, we have no clue to return."

When the *Aubergiere* had concluded her narrative, she arose,

and opening a boudoir, took from thence the bracelet, which she
delivered to Cecilia, who was much struck with the lustre and
beauty of the gems which adorned it:—it was composed of several rows of Venetian gold chains, united at the ends with clasps
of the same metal, set round with rubies, the largest and the most
brilliant she had ever seen.

Cecilia having examined it attentively, returned it to the *Aubergiere*, who, depositing it as before, left her to reflect at leisure
upon the extraordinary and mysterious adventure she had been
recounting.

The day had just dawned when Pere Baptiste (for this was the
name of the Religieux), came to convey Cecilia in a carriage as far
as Lodeve. On their way thither, she enquired of him concerning
the Abbess; but of her she could learn nothing, except that she
was a lady of high rank, who presided in a Convent of Carmelite
Nuns in the neighbourhood of Cevenna.

They travelled with unremitting speed, stopping only to
change horses till they arrived at St. Michel; having passed which,
the aspect of the country which, till now, had exhibited only features of beauty, suddenly began to change. A dreary perspective
of mountains bounded the horizon; their summits, either bare,
and jutting out into immense crags, or covered with a scanty
vegetation, such as dwarf oak, holly, and phillyrea, whilst forests
of gloomy pine, larch and chesnut, hanging from steep to steep,
descended to their base in dark and shadowy masses.

They followed the track among the hills till they entered a
narrow defile bounded on either side by rocks, which sometimes
receding, discovered small but richly cultivated vallies, whilst
in other places they so nearly met, as to exclude all views of the
country beyond.—They proceeded in this path, which gradually
ascended a precipice for some miles, when it suddenly opened to
extensive prospects over fields, and to more distant mountains.
The woods now began to stretch on all sides; but from these
some natural vista often afforded scenes of peculiar elegance and
beauty; and Cecilia having ascended one of the highest of those
eminences which precede the gloomy mountain region of the
Cevennes, beheld far to the west the pleasant hills of Gascony
stretching in the remotest distance, whilst far beneath her feet

extended the wide plains of Languedoc, rich with harvests, and gay with clusters of the purple vintage.

They proceeded for several hours through rough and unfrequented paths, seeing only now and then in the distance the solitary residence of the hunter or the shepherd, and listening only to the hollow murmur of the wind as it swept the high tops of the pines which waved over them, till the day began to decline, when they distinguished the note of a bell which the rocks feebly prolonged; and soon after arriving at a village, they stopped to procure a guide. The road continued to wind along the side of the woods, till they descended at length into a valley overhung with deep shades, and surrounded by rocks of almost Alpine magnificence, when their ears were suddenly assailed by shouts which rose and died alternately upon the wind; and soon after they perceived a blaze as of distant fires, which they found was occasioned by a band of Gipsies, who, having concluded their depredations, were regaling themselves with the spoils.—As they approached toward the centre of the valley, the *Religieux* commanded the guide, who was armed, to discharge his musket in the air; which he had no sooner done, than the affrighted itinerants betook themselves to flight, screaming as they went, as if the fate they expected had already overtaken them.

"We have now," said the Father, "nothing more to apprehend. These mountains, though infested by these outlaws, are not the haunts of banditti, though the numerous cavities they contain, well known as the disgraceful retreats of the Huguenots in the beginning of this century, seem to mark them for their purpose. We have now only another league to pass; we will therefore stop and refresh ourselves. The night approaches fast, but the moon will guide us, and we shall soon be in safety."

Cecilia, whose strength and spirits were nearly exhausted with the speed they had used whilst traversing these uncultivated tracks, instantly alighted. A pleasant bank was before her, and she seated herself upon it: the evening was serene, the wind had sunk into gentle murmurs, and no sound broke the stillness of the air, except the melancholy note of a thrush which was warbling its last farewell from a neighbouring tree, and the noise of a distant waterfall.—The calm retirement of this spot, environed on

every side with scenes of solitary grandeur, the mountain wild
above her head, the torrent rolling at her feet, tended to raise in
her mind emotions of sublime awe, and to lift her from the contemplation of Nature and all her splendid diversities, to the hand
which formed and combined them with such exquisite grandeur
and beauty!

She was roused from her reverie by the sound of voices: it
approached, and instantly three men of a ruffian like appearance
darted from the woods. Cecilia started, and would have retreated;
but she was followed and secured by one of them, whilst another
flew in quest of her companions, who had availed themselves
of the opportunity to escape. A musket was discharged; but it
was unnecessary, for they were already beyond the reach of its
consequences. The two not engaged in this pursuit remained
with Cecilia. The man who had seized her, still held her arm; she
shrieked vehemently, but to the cry of terror, or the plea of pity,
the hearts of her assailants were alike inaccessible.—The first
ruffian, as if apprehensive of a rescue, endeavoured to stop her
mouth; while his confederates, after binding her hand and foot,
placed her upon a mule, which one of them had just brought for
the purpose.—The most daring of the villains now seated himself before her; and his comrades taking possession of another
mule, they rode off at full speed, often galloping among the crags
with the most dangerous velocity.

The men neither spoke, nor endeavoured to stop her career;
but urging on the mules, who continued to gallop without
restraint, soon convinced Cecilia that their destruction was inevitable. They pursued the track among the rocks for some time,
and then entered a wood: the pathway was narrow, and the trees
which hung over it almost excluded the feeble remains of light.
Suddenly the moon arose, and gleaming over the shadowy pass,
discovered to the terrified Cecilia the dreary and gloomy wood
that surrounded her. No view of any habitable mansion, or of a
path likely to terminate in one, animated her hopes; the partial
light as it slept upon the scene below, giving only the fading outlines of rocks, pine-forests, and glittering torrents, sparkling in
unison with the lucid moonbeam.

From these and from the savage countenances of her conductors, she shrunk appalled; and when she recollected that she was in the power of wretches, whose desperate conduct proved them capable of any act of villany, however atrocious, it was with difficulty that she could keep her seat: resistance, nevertheless, would avail her nothing, nor had she the power to contend with those whose purpose, from whatever cause it might arise, was evidently the result of some settled plan.

The pass now became more difficult, and the moon being again obscured, the horror of her situation became almost insupportable, when she was instantaneously and unexpectedly relieved by one of the men crying out—"Thanks to St. Peter, we are nearly at home, for I see the bridge!" and in a few minutes they were actually before some building, and soon heard a bell they had rung, whose deep tone and hollow sound reverberating in sullen echoes through a long extent of arcades, aided the solemnity that surrounded them.—In a moment the chains of the gate fell, the portcullis was drawn up, and the creaking hinges gave way: the gate was opened, and the figure of a man, whose features were shaded into an expression of horror by the dim light he carried, stood before them.

Cecilia trembled, shrunk back, and involuntarily laid her hand on her nearest companion, as if to implore his protection.

"You have nothing to fear, Lady," said one of them in no very soft voice; "we have executed our office; you may now enter the court."

A court indeed appeared, wide, solitary, and almost overgrown with weeds and brambles, surrounded on every side with buildings of an amazing extent, whose ponderous turrets, as they rose above the woods in sullen but mutilated grandeur, seemed to frown defiance on all who should dare to invade them.

They entered, through a portico, a hall barbarously magnificent.—The lamp gleamed dimly on its vaulted roof: one of the men walked first, carrying a torch; Cecilia followed mechanically, often shrinking with affright as the light flaring across the space, discovered to her the extreme desolation and wildness of the room they passed through. Figures painted in the representation of chivalric exploits, but which time, and the humidity of the place, had now nearly obliterated, hung in tatters from the walls, which were adorned on either side with *bustos* and gilded pilasters: the floor was tessalated, and rows of windows, high, narrow, and arched to correspond with the rest of the building, displayed in the numerous devices, and in the vivid colouring of antiquity, the feats and gambols of the heroic ages. A gallery with iron rails ran round it: the hall was terminated by a staircase, at the bottom of which stood two women, one apparently about fifty, the other several years younger, the only female part of the establishment Cecilia had yet seen. The countenance of the elder was harsh and forbidding, she spoke civilly; and Cecilia felt a faint emotion of joy communicate to her heart on perceiving the men had left her, and that she was now unexpectedly consigned to the care of women; for she had yet to learn that there are fiends even among her own sex, whose principal aim it is to practise with success upon the credulity and security of unsuspecting innocence.

A large and spacious apartment, to which they ascended by a corridor, formerly one of the grand saloons in the chateau, hung with crimson velvet, and surrounded by sofas formed in the ancient *costume*, and covered with the same material as the walls, tended not to solve the enigma of her situation. Every thing was superb, but it was grandeur in decay: loose fragments of tarnished gold hung from every part of the furniture, which, like the drapery that surrounded it, was worm-eaten and impaired. The frescos that ornamented the ceiling, probably the *chef d'œuvres* of antiquity, were scarcely more perfect, the colouring being in some places nearly withdrawn, and in others so entirely lost, as to exhibit only the faint outlines of saints and heroes, whose actions and whose sufferings they were intended to perpetuate. Small dilapidated figures in black marble occupied, but did not adorn the recesses; and two large Venetian mirrors in gilt foliage, the frames of which were in part gone, descending nearly to the ground, reflected the blaze of the lights, and of a fire which had been kindled for her reception.

Faint, trembling, and nearly sinking to the earth beneath the horror of her surmises, Cecilia threw herself almost lifeless on a sofa. One of the women remained with her; the other withdrew, but returned in a short time with some wine and a few cakes: she poured out a glass of the wine; Cecilia took it—it refreshed her, and she was soon sufficiently recovered to be enabled to sit up. Agnes (for so the elder of the women was called), now offered her some cakes; but fear and fatigue had so entirely overcome her, that she was unable to taste any food. Her companions then placed themselves by her side: Cecilia looked on them alternately, and then conjured them to inform her to whom the chateau belonged, and by whose orders, and for what purpose she was brought thither.

"We are forbid to answer enquiries," said Agnes; "it may not, however, be long before you have complete satisfaction on a subject which appears to have occasioned you much unnecessary disturbance. This place must be your home; every wish you can form within the limits of these walls will be indulged indiscriminately—beyond them you must not hope to go."

When she had uttered these words, she arose, and desired Cecilia to follow her.—She conducted her through a number of unoccupied chambers, to one which appeared to be the last of the suite; and this Cecilia was informed was to be her apartment.

It was large, as were those which she had already passed, and scarcely less ruinous.—The wainscot was of cedar, or some other dark wood, curiously carved: the floor was of the same colour, and seemed decayed. All the cornices and mouldings were involved in dust; and the cold chill of the room proved it to have been long uninhabited. The curtains of the windows were of dark green Lyons damask fringed, and ornamented with silver trimmings. A canopied bed of the same stood at the farther end of the room; and at the other end was a large projecting chimney of Parian stone, over which was suspended a mirror supporting two reposing figures in white marble. A table, a cabinet constructed like the wainscot, and a few high-backed stuffed chairs, covered also with damask, and trimmed with silver, completed the furniture.

Cecilia gazed around her with astonishment: every thing she saw contributed to her perplexity. Her sudden removal to a chateau, which she was told to consider as her future home— the strange event which had preceded it, and the mystery that seemed to involve every part of her destiny, appeared to her rather as the effects of supernatural, than of mortal agency; nor was the attention which had apparently been paid to her comfort and convenience the least extraordinary part of the adventure. —"Heavens!" exclaimed she, with amazement, "where am I, and to what can all this tend?"—Scarcely had she spoken, when recollection returned, and terror, indescribable and unresisted terror, rushed upon her senses. It was then to the Marchese she was a victim, and it was by Boraccio she had been delivered up. The servile duplicity with which she had formerly taxed him, was now fully proved. This was doubtless the estate, and this the chateau in which the first Marchesa was thought to have died, or, as many imagined, where she still lived. To reflections such as these, emotions the most agonizing succeeded. To condemn her to the perpetual retirement of a dreary and isolated mansion, instead of the temporary one of a cloister, seemed to have been the grand object of the Marchese's intentions, and of Boraccio's treachery.

The words of Agnes, *"beyond these walls you must not hope to go,"* returned to her recollection with augmented energy; and her imagination, strengthened by the conflicts which she had so lately undergone, suggested even more evils than her situation, dreadful as it was, could justify.

END OF VOLUME TWO

WHO'S THE MURDERER?

CHAPTER I

——————————'Twas but a dream:
But then so terrible it shakes my soul;
Cold drops of dew hung on my trembling flesh—
My blood grows chilly, and I freeze with horror!
                                        SHAKESPEARE.

CECILIA was traversing her chamber with the footsteps of despair, now yielding to the anguish which oppressed her heart, and now endeavouring to reason herself into some degree of tranquillity, when she stumbled over something which accidentally lay in her way, and stooping down, discovered, with mingled surprise and satisfaction, the travelling trunk she had conveyed with her from Italy. Her alarm at the time it was removed, was too great to permit her to be assured of its safety; and the distracting tumult of her thoughts ever since her arrival, had prevented her enquiries; and she now sincerely rejoiced that she had been spared the solicitude which the supposition of its loss must inevitably have occasioned her.

The slow and heavy clock of the chateau had numbered four, ere Cecilia took possession of her bed. Previous to this she determined to fasten her door; but the lock, as is customary in France, was on the outside, and the bolt within so covered with rust, that it resisted all her efforts to turn it. Compelled, therefore, to remain there without any actual means of security, she threw herself upon the bed in the clothes she wore, which she had scarcely done, when the anxiety of her mind yielding to fatigue, she fell into a fast sleep; but the images of her waking thoughts pursued her in her dreams—her slumbers were uneasy and disturbed, and she awoke in terror and apprehension. Again she turned to court the gentle influence of sleep, and again images of horror flitted before her mental vision.—She thought she was in bed in a dismal old chamber, similar to that in which she slept, when a gradual light imperceptibly shone around her, increasing into brightness, and a tall spectre-like figure by degrees became visible. Streaming robes of celestial whiteness played about her form in alternate foldings, spangled over with stars which shone like various gems. A veil depended from her head, and devolving to the ground in an ample expanse of train, increased the majesty of her movements. As she approached toward the bed, the light insensibly died away, and the trembling beams of the moon alone illuminated the chamber. The face of the apparition was paler than death, and marked with an expression of the deepest sorrow. Her right hand was crimsoned with blood, and several drops of gore stained her robe; on the finger of the other was a wedding-ring, to which, with a solemn and significant gesture, she thrice pointed: she spoke not, but looked earnestly on Cecilia; and then waving her arm, beckoned her to follow her. As she rose to obey, she thought the features of the spectre suddenly became animated. A smile of ineffable sweetness played about her mouth—a soft and humid lustre swam in her eyes—and her whole countenance assumed an expression of more than mortal beauty and benignity. Whilst she gazed on this vision with speechless transport, a panel of the wainscot flew open, and in a moment she was conveyed, as if by the spell of an enchantress, through the most secret recesses of the chateau.

To dismal passages and extensive chambers, where no ray of light broke through the almost midnight darkness which pervaded them, a gallery more dreary still succeeded. Sounds of fearful and portentous import ran along its sides. The wind howled with a dismal moaning as it rushed through its weedy cavities, mingling with the dank vapours of the air, among which a thousand nameless objects flitted by, and were again involved in the deep but ineffectual gloom of night and silence.

At length the wind dropped, the sounds were hushed into repose, and the jarring of a distant door, which moved slowly on its grating hinges, alone disturbed the almost deathlike stillness that prevailed. It opened as they approached;—they entered, but could discern nothing, for the darkness was thicker, and more impenetrable than before. Suddenly a light streamed through a crevice, brightening by degrees into a thin blue flame, and in an instant the whole place was illuminated, and Cecilia perceived she was in a vault surrounded with coffins and tombs; some supporting crucifixes—others grim and ghost-like figures holding tapers. Cecilia stepped back—her blood was chilled, and she turned to regain the door; but before she could seize it, it shut to with a thundering clap, and she was left alone among the dead. As she advanced again from the door, she thought the figures on the coffins began to move, their marble features became fleshy—the lights they held waxed pale—a strong sulphureous vapour rose from the tombs—and a loud crash of thunder, like the noise of a thousand pieces of artillery, reverberated, and shook the inmost bowels of the earth. Horror again overwhelmed her, and again she made an effort to depart; but her feet, when she would have moved, sunk imperceptibly into the ground—a hot boiling fluid seemed to be gathering around them—and in a moment she was involved in a sea of blood!

As she was struggling to save herself, a stream of music, so low—so dulcet, that it seemed like a symphony of spirits in the air, rose gradually on the ear in the silence of the night, and then swelled into numbers of such enchanting sweetness, that fear was charmed into ecstacy! Again the bright vision appeared—her countenance more lovely than before, and her figure dilated to a size more awfully majestic!—A lambent flame of beamy purple played around her forehead, and mingled with her flowing hair; she waved her hand in token of friendship to Cecilia, and smiling as she went, vanished slowly from her sight. As she fled, the strains which accompanied her melted into air, sinking into a tone that could hardly be caught: the celestial radiance faded into darkness—the tapers in the vault glimmered, and expired—and the whole scene sunk again into chaos.

In an instant, with the inconsistency so common in dreams, she was transported to a scene more sweetly romantic than fancy can suggest, or the pencil paint. The path on which she trod, was bordered with roses, and the rivulet that refreshed them was resplendent as silver. The dew that gemmed their leaves, and hung upon their blooming petals, mocked the lustre of the diamond—and the groves which overshadowed them, with the luxuriant space beyond, overlooking woods and gaily tinted vallies, presented to the astonished sight all that the most poetical conception and the most exuberant imagination can conceive of Elysium.

As she was stooping to gather a nosegay of the flowers which sprung at her feet, she thought she was seized by Boraccio, who, in spite of her screams and struggles, precipitated her to the edge of a rock, which he was about to force her down, when Varàno appeared on the opposite side, and by wild looks and frenzied gestures evinced his despair at being unable to pass the chasm, to save her from the destruction that menaced her.—Just as she gave herself up for lost, she was instantaneously transported to the other side of the abyss by a female in the habit of a Nun, who, after pressing her to her heart with delighted fondness, gave her hand to Varàno, whose rapturous expression in receiving it, awoke her from the enjoyment of fancied bliss, to the contemplation of real and unavoidable misery.

The day had already dawned;—she arose, and opening her *croisée*, inhaled the pure air of morning. The window was low, and she had a full view of the woods and nearer mountains. The sun had just risen beyond the eastern hills; light and airy clouds spread over the horizon—here streaked with crimson, and there variegated with gold and silver tints. In the west the ethereal blue of the heavens enlivened the landscape, and the dark precipices of the Cevennes seemed for once to smile. The precipices were broken into immense crags, which in some places impended far beyond their base, and in others rose in huge misshapen points near the walls of the chateau—shaded by larch, or darkened by lines of gloomy pine, suspended along the rocky chasm, from whence the eye reposed on the thick woods which sunk abruptly to the vale beneath, uniting in a mass of deep and indistinct foliage.

The chateau she perceived was completely moated, and a bridge, which she did not recollect having passed, the only means of access. The grounds enclosed were extensive, and appeared formerly to have been laid out in blooming parterres; but, like the mansion they surrounded, they were now ruinous and despoiled. Her chamber was a turret in the western wing of the building, on one side overlooking the court—on the other what had once been the gardens. From an avenue which fronted her window, she discovered a lawn—and a little to the left, through another opening, a clear sheet of water. The sun, emerging from a cloud, glittered on its unruffled surface; the air was chill, but breathless;—a solemn tranquillity pervaded every thing around, and it seemed like an "awful pause in nature," to convey a soothing serenity to the inhabitants of the earth.—"How calm, yet how tremendous!" thought Cecilia, "are the objects which surround me! How grand the waving outline of those mountains—how beautiful the woods that sleep in silence at their feet! What a peaceful tranquillity is diffused over the whole animated world! Alas! the repose I view dwells not in my bosom: this landscape, which to a heart at ease would have a thousand beauties, only adds terrors to mine!"—Tears streamed fast from her eyes; she turned from the window, and seating herself on the bed, wept unrestrainedly.

The day was divided between silent lamentation and impotent attempts at resignation. The women were attentive to her wants, and seemed even solicitous to prevent her wishes; but for the grief which she experienced from the hopelessness of her situation, she could awaken only a small portion of sympathy in the breasts of these whose feelings had been blunted into an habitual torpidity; and for the long captivity she dreaded, she strove in vain to excite any.—But the mind, unworn by repeated calamities, soon regains its elasticity. Her spirits, if not her fortitude, returned; and that composure which solitude augments, communicated to her heart. The chateau, though desolate, was not wholly without its comforts, nor to the mind of sensibility totally devoid of interest. In rambling amongst its decayed outworks, or tracing the intricate windings of its dreary labyrinths, she found amusement and consolation. Here were objects for meditation more striking, more impressive than any she had yet met with; and whilst she viewed the melancholy pile sinking slowly into oblivion, certain interesting situations arose to her mind in their strongest energies.

"In this place," cried she, as she crossed the hall, whose faded banners waved slowly to the passing wind, "the proud banquet has been spread, and here the gay dance has resounded. Where are now the Knights, and where the dames who led the festive group over this broken, but once finely chequered pavement! Gone—mingled with the dust, as though they had never been! —Long is it since the martial band, the warlike trumpet, the shrill-toned flagelet, the soft strain of the clarinet, and the still softer lute echoed along these vaulted roofs. The shout of the victor, and the groan of the vanquished have ceased to be heard. Consigned to the dreary mansions of the grave—'that bourn from whence no traveller returns,' to tell the fate he met with, the conqueror and the conquered sleep together in peace! The record of mortality, the proudly sculptured stone, only tells they once were; and even this, the perishable memorial of departed greatness, like the hand that erected it, shall crumble into dust, and be soon no more seen!"

Adjoining the room in which she sat, was another filled with books. Curiosity directed her to examine them; they were covered with dust, and several of them were written in a language she did not understand. Her indefatigable researches, however, to find some which might beguile the lingering moments into speed, were not eventually unrewarded. She discovered, amongst a number of others, a few volumes of the best French and Italian authors—treasures of which she joyfully availed herself. This study insensibly engaged her mind, and soon meliorated those feelings it could not subdue. Two days of uniform solitude and confinement had nearly passed away, when she was startled by a loud noise in the corridor, and rising to enquire the cause, discovered Agnes lying apparently senseless upon the stairs, attended by Berthe, who was vainly endeavouring to restore her. Cecilia flew instantly to her assistance; and believing she was dying, if not already dead, no symptoms of life appearing on her countenance, called loudly for help.

"You need not cry out so, lady," said Berthe, "for there is not a creature in the chateau except Roland and Benoit, and the men that have been working at the fosse; and I believe if Agnes was to die, there is not a single soul among them that would bestir himself. But don't be too frightened, Mademoiselle; these fits are very dreadful, to be sure, but she has always been used to them, and many and many a time, when no help was nigh, have I thought she would have died, and that every gasp she took would be her last. Ah! now she stirs:—Jesu Maria! how ghastly pale she looks!"

"Oh! fly—fly this instant," cried Cecilia, more and more alarmed, "whilst you deliberate, she may be lost!—Run—call!— Is nobody within hearing?—Will no one come to her assistance?"

"Holy Virgin! what a bustle is here!" returned the girl, with the most provoking *sang froid*; "why, you could not be more terrified, Mademoiselle, if you were in danger of dying yourself. I can call, to be sure; but of what use is it, when there is not one of them that will answer me? If I was to scream loud enough to awaken the dead, they would not hear me, they are so engaged in drinking, and singing, and carousing; and as to bringing them, I might as well attempt to bring the statues in the great hall:— la! they think no more of people's dying, than of their going to sleep!"

"And is there—can there," said Cecilia, "be wretches with such hearts as these? Look up, poor creature! there is at least one that can pity thee!"

"Who are you?" cried Agnes in a deep and hollow tone, as she slowly unveiled her eyes, which she almost immediately closed again; "I do not know that voice."

"Thank Heaven! she revives," resumed Cecilia, in an accent of delight; "help—help me to support her."

"Ah! is it you?" cried Agnes, her dim eyes again fastened upon her face with a look of speechless agony; "you—you that would save me! Oh!—Oh! I have not deserved this!"

"Poor soul!" said Cecilia, "she raves—alas! her head is affected! —Assist me to convey her to her chamber."

The woman continued to gaze upon her for some moments with an expression of mingled pity and astonishment, but without uttering a word; and then heaving a profound sigh, which seemed to relieve her almost bursting bosom, she was enabled to stand up, and, supported by Cecilia and Berthe, to walk to her apartment. When in bed, she became gradually more composed, and soon evinced tokens of amendment. Cecilia remained with her the greater part of the night, and on the succeeding day was her chief, and sometimes only attendant.

In the evening, as Agnes rapidly grew better, Cecilia took a stroll in the gardens. These were yet unexplored, and she experienced a melancholy sort of pleasure in rambling amidst their gloomy and deserted avenues, whose darkened vistas were not unfrequently embellished with some weedy grotto, or half-decayed temple, their walls only remaining, but which, in the days of their early strength, might have been selected as models of antique beauty.

She wandered on in silent thoughtfulness, sometimes over lawns overrun with entangled vegetation, and sometimes beneath the canopy of hanging woods; when, having traversed a considerable part of the grounds, she discovered to the left a grove of luxuriant cypress. The sombre hue of its colouring, aided by the coming gloom, was congenial to the present temper of her feelings, and she entered the grove. It was thick—but not extensive. She passed hastily along, and soon reached its termination. A narrow winding defile, bordered also with cypress, succeeded.—The trees of this walk were of older growth, and their shades deeper, and more awful than those she had already passed. She paused—she hesitated—a fear of she scarcely knew what tempted her to return; but an unaccountable impulse urged her on, and she proceeded. The defile led into a large area overgrown with nettles and brambles, on one side of which, over a range of half decayed arches, ascended the east tower, and a lofty part of the edifice she had never before seen—the other side was open to the woods. She crossed the area with a hurried step; but what were her emotions when, having entered one of the loftiest of the arches, she found herself in a chapel, the desolate appearance of which denoted it to have been long consigned by humanity to the silent and unconscious dead who slept undisturbed within its hallowed precincts. She started as she surveyed the awful fabric: —a dreadful recollection obtruded on her senses: it was a chapel, and not a vault; yet was its similarity to that which her imagination had shaped in that feverish and appalling dream, which still haunted her perturbed mind with sad and gloomy presages, too evident to remain unnoticed. Every step she advanced increased its resemblance; she trembled—but proceeded, often shrinking with superstitious dread as the bat, the only tenant of its walls, flitted silently by, or the wind their frequent cavities admitted, shook the drapery of the high altar, where saints, crucifixes, and Madonas, the pride of Monkish devotion, mingled with tombs, monuments, and headless statues, called forth the awful faculty of meditation.

"And thus," cried Cecilia, as she passed and repassed the pavement, where the yarrow and the nettle grew high and rank amid the stones, "ends the proud dream of human greatness. It is in the contemplation of scenes like these that the frivolities of life are detected, and we blush that we have suffered ourselves to be misled by them. Here the warrior who pursued 'the bubble reputation even in the cannon's mouth'—the proud beauty, inaccessible but to the allurements of grandeur, formed for triumph, and fated to move with *eclat* within the glittering vortex of a throne— the meek divine, and the still meeker penitent are promiscuously mingled. And here too in a few, perchance a very few years, the dust of the poor moralist, whose sacrilegious feet have intruded themselves over their mouldering and unconscious ashes—the child of misery and misfortune may be consigned in peace."

She had wandered over the different aisles in the chapel while she was thus ruminating, and was approaching toward the end, when turning accidentally round a pillar, she descried a low door, which appeared from its situation to lead either to vaults beneath, or to communicate, by means of a descending staircase, with the subterraneous parts of the chateau. The probability was on the side of the latter, and she ventured to unclose it. The exertion requisite to accomplish this, occasioned her first to perceive that it was constructed of iron; and the force with which it shut to, the instant she quitted it, again reminding her of her dream, struck her with dismay.

It opened to a passage, lighted by loopholes at the upper end, to the left of which was another door, and farther on, to the right, a steep stone staircase. She endeavoured to unclose the door, but her utmost efforts to this purpose were finally ineffectual; and stooping down to observe it more accurately, she perceived it was nailed up—a circumstance which confirmed her in the sugges-

tion that this, and not the former one, as she had before imagined, was the door belonging to the vaults. Disappointed in this
attempt, she bent her way toward the stairs, moving quickly, but
lightly through the passage, for the echo of her steps startled her.
The stairs were narrow and winding, and interrupted by frequent
breaches, and loose fragments of stone; they grew narrower and
narrower, and at length terminated in a wide stone gallery. A faint
glimmering of light, issuing from a window above, just discovered its extent. She proceeded fearfully and cautiously along; for
the floor was in many places broken, and the sort of twilight the
high opened window admitted, was scarce a guide to her steps. A
low and melancholy moaning seemed to creep along the walls,
and the dews that discoloured them struck upon her a cold and
chilling blast. Two doors presented themselves at the extremity.
She hesitated, but at length turned to the right. She opened it;
and descending a few steps, discerned a small square room, communicating with another by a door fastened across with a slight
bar of iron. Cecilia removed it with ease, and lifting up the arras
on the other side, found herself in a large half-furnished room,
nearly as spacious as her own, the whole appearance of which
denoted it to have been recently inhabited. A dark blue velvet bed
with a high canopied tester stood at the upper end; and near it,
beneath a window, a table, on which lay a musical instrument, a
missal, a small crucifix of ebony, some crayons, with a few other
implements for drawing, and a *port-feuille*, containing a number
of landscapes in aquatint which, though torn and unfinished,
bore tokens of their having been executed by the hand of taste.

Over the arm of a settee, covered also with velvet, hung a
long white robe, and a veil, with various other articles of female
dress, lay scattered about the room. These habiliments—the solitary situation of this gloomy and now desolated chamber—its
prison-like windows, through which the evening twilight pierced
—its proximity to the chapel—and the melancholy that pervaded
every part of it, evinced it had formerly been selected as a place of
confinement for some unfortunate and perhaps guiltless woman,
who, in all human probability, had expired beneath the miseries
of hopeless captivity. That the chateau, and the estate belonging
to it, were the property of the Marchese, Cecilia had never suf-

fered herself to doubt; and though the proofs she had collected by no means amounted to conviction, she had little difficulty in persuading herself that the rumours so prevalent in Tuscany, both before, and subsequent to his last marriage, were not, as she had once candidly believed, the asseverations of falsehood, but reports founded upon just and reasonable circumstances, and that the person confined there was the first Marchesa.

A nameless dread came over her when she recollected that she was alone in the apartment where this amiable and ill-fated woman, the beloved sister of De Sevignac, breathed her last agonizing sigh. Imagination repeated it to her ear, as, throwing aside the curtains, she leaned over the bed, as if to behold the feeble but angelic form of its late owner, whose fine eyes were now closed for ever on all sublunary objects. She shivered;—it was but fancy; yet a sigh, or something like one, struck her upon her sense with all the force of reality. Again it was repeated;—she turned, and looked wildly, but deliberately around the room: nothing living except herself was present, nor could she then distinguish any sound but the low groaning of the wind behind the tapestry. Ashamed of her fears, yet unable to combat them, she threw herself upon the settee, scarcely daring to breathe, and much less to move, when the robe which hung suspended from the arm, instantaneously caught her eye, and she ventured to lift it up; but in an agony, to which fainting would have been a relief, almost immediately let it fall again, for she perceived that it was spotted with blood! For a moment she almost doubted her existence, and the reality of the scene before her—so completely was she overpowered with horror and astonishment. The Marchesa was then murdered—privately, and most barbarously murdered! The Marchese, ever jealous, implacable, and revengeful, for some venial or imaginary wrong, had doomed her, as it appeared, to a lingering imprisonment, and afterwards to a cruel and unmerited death; and the garment she had touched was died with the blood of this innocent and unoffending victim to his cruelty!

Yet strong as were the evidences, she could scarcely imagine that the Marchese, despotic as he was, revengeful as he seemed, could be the perpetrator, or even the abettor of a deed so atrocious. Could the father of Varàno, whose breast was the seat of every virtue, and who shrunk, as well from education as through principle, from the very shadow of dishonour, degrade himself so far beneath the very lowest of his species, as to become the assassin of his wife? Reason suggested this improbable, and she now ventured to believe it impossible. Yet to whom, if not to the Marchese, could she owe a death so dreadful? Who else could meditate such a scheme of villany against her?—Bewildered with her conjectures, she remained fixed, and scarcely daring to look around her during several minutes. The room was silent as the grave, and her blood seemed to freeze with the horrors which assailed her. Impelled at length by fear, by her terrors, and by the obscurity that surrounded her, she arose to depart, when something her dress had disturbed, fell slowly to the ground, the low rustling sound of which made her start involuntarily. She stooped to take it up, and discovered at length, with more pleasure than the occasion seemed to authorize, a small roll of paper tied round with string, and almost buried in dust. Possessed of this treasure, which, if the means of elucidating the dark and almost impenetrable mystery of that eventful chamber, she considered as inestimable, she rushed toward the window; but the light it afforded was sufficient only to convince her that it consisted of a number of detached papers, thickly written over, but so injured by the damps, that the characters were in several places illegible, and in others totally obliterated. Impressed, notwithstanding, with the idea that the little which remained intelligible, would supply her with some clue at least for her researches, she determined to reserve them for a future inspection, and having rolled them up as before, she secured them in her pocket.

Not venturous enough to explore any other part of the edifice, she was advancing hastily toward the door, when an approaching step startled her, and she as hastily receded. It passed distinctly along the gallery, pausing, as if to listen between every step, and then entered the opposite chamber. The door of the apartment was no sooner closed upon the person who opened it, than another footstep was heard, pacing slowly from the stairs to the upper end of the gallery. It stopped at the same place. The door of the chamber was opened, though with caution, and a loud and angry voice fiercely demanded who came there?

"A friend," quoth the other surlily.

"Oh! Oh! it is you, Jacques," said his comrade, "you may come in then;—but what did you leave that door unfastened for? Would you have your master——"

"Stop, stop," interrupted Jacques, "I can lock it now."

"No, no, let it be for the present," said the man who had first spoke; "I have other business for you; we can attend to that afterwards."

Cecilia's heart beat quicker at every word;—she imagined herself surrounded by dangers from which an immediate and almost supernatural exertion could alone extricate her. Darting, therefore, from her concealment with the velocity of an arrow, she soon entered the gallery, and as soon reached its extremity. As she was hastily descending the stairs, she descried something of a shining appearance, lying upon a step some distance before her, as if accidentally dropped there. She seized it as she passed; but her apprehensions of pursuit prevented her from stopping to examine it, till she had paced the passage and the chapel; when, holding it up to the light, she beheld, to her inexpressible astonishment, a small gold bracelet, evidently the fellow to that which she had seen at the *auberge*. Scarcely could she credit the evidences of her senses, scarcely believe she was not under the deceitful fascination of some delightful dream, as she gazed upon this precious—this invaluable relic.

"She lives then!" she ejaculated in a voice of transport, "the Marchesa lives, and the father of Varàno is not a murderer!"

All the evils she had undergone—all the future ones she had anticipated, seemed amply repaid by this one interval of joy. She forgot that she was herself a prisoner—an orphan—an outcast; —deserted by him who ought to have protected her—deceived by those in whom she had most confided. In that one single discovery every grief seemed to have evaporated; hope again renovated her frame, and she experienced for a moment what may be termed the sublime of human happiness.

Lightly she tripped along the avenues;—they were dark and cheerless, but never to Cecilia had they appeared less gloomy. The lively emotions of joy that impressed her heart, and played about her bosom, tinted every scene through which she passed with the most enchanting verdure: nor could the lustre of the dawn, or the meridian splendour of the day, whilst under the domination of these impressions, have added to their beauty. So vivid is the colouring of joy—so sombre that of sorrow.

A repast, consisting of several sorts of confectionary, was spread for her on her return, of which she slightly partook, and then hastened to her apartment, not more solicitous to peruse the papers so singularly found, than to develop the melancholy and apparently eventful circumstances under which they were written.—Of these so many were defaced, and so many in all probability entirely lost, that it was not possible to connect them into a regular series of events, though this had evidently been at first the intention of the writer. The deprivations of health, of spirits, and that habitual melancholy inseparable from a long and hopeless estrangement from society, had conspired perhaps to prevent the accomplishment of this plan. Years seemed to have elapsed, of which no note had been taken; and even where the narration was most perfect, the sudden transition from local to imaginary circumstances, from scenes of reality to those of fancy and fiction, contributed to render the language obscure and always doubtful. They were obviously addressed to some lover, to whom, previous to her marriage, she had been long and tenderly attached.

The difficulty of arranging these torn, detached, and at best unconnected papers, was even greater than Cecilia had expected. At length after much attention and much time, she succeeded so well, as to form them in the order in which they are now placed.

———

"Impossible as it appears that these papers, the frail memorials of my misfortunes, can ever meet the eye of sympathy, I experience, nevertheless, a melancholy satisfaction in retracing them. —To you, St. Louis, I address them—to you would I unfold the sad story of my wrongs! But, ah! how torturing is the conflict I am destined to endure between affection and indignation, when every word will be a volume of guilt, every expression will convict the writer, and stamp indelible disgrace on the parent who

deceived her!—Yet perjured as I am,—for, ignorant of the infernal combination that was formed against our peace till involved in its consequences, I swore (at that ever to be regretted æra of our separation) to live only for your love,—I would fain clear myself from the imputation under which I labour.—But, alas! how vague—how unavailing must be every effort I can employ to reinstate myself in your esteem! How hopeless—how ineffectual appears the task of vindication!—Never can this scroll reach you —never can it meet the eye of him, who, if he lives, lives but to load me with unmerited opprobrium. You believe me guilty:—I am so; for who that has committed a sin so heinous as that of perjury, can stand acquitted by conscience? A self-convicted criminal, I venture not to lift my hands toward Heaven—I dare not supplicate its mercies!—I can only deprecate its justice with the tears of penitence and submission! But is the deceiver less guilty than the deceived?—Are these who spread snares to entrap the innocent and unsuspicious, to be exculpated, whilst the deluded victim to their arts sinks, without an arm to bear her up, into the lowest abyss of shame and misery?" * * * * * * * * * * * * * *
* *
* *

"How strange! how complicated! how incomprehensible appears the progress of my destiny! Accused of a crime, the bare mention of which fills me with horror and indignation, I yet live to experience further trials:—but for what is it I live? To be the companion of the dead—the inhabitant of a dreary and deserted turret—to watch the faint radiance of the sun as it dawns through its grated aperture—to chide its lingering beams as it sets beyond the high and trackless mountain—to hear no sound but the wind as it breaks in sudden gusts over my head, or the hoarse voice of my keeper as he stalks across my chamber. * * * * * * * * * * *
* *
* *

"Already I have strayed from my purpose. I meant to have begun a narrative of my misfortunes from the earliest period of their commencement; but my brain is confused—my hand trembles—my tears flow in torrents. Again I make the attempt. —Listen then to a tale, which, if it cannot justify me, may lessen the magnitude of my offence.—Taught to believe you dead—a martyr to the cause of your oppressed and much-injured country, my days were spent in sighs and lamentations for your loss, and the nights returned only to witness the severity of my anguish. My father appeared penetrated with sorrow on the news of your death;—he passed whole nights in my apartment; and often, taking me tenderly in his arms, would entreat me not to add to his sufferings, already insupportable, by leaving him to bewail the loss of an amiable and beloved child—the delight of his soul—the support and solace of his declining years.—Alas! how unsuspicious was I then of the deceit he had been practicing!—His tears, his importunities at length restored me to composure, though not to health; for my form was wasted, my strength gone, and I seemed sinking fast to an untimely grave.—Months passed on; —I recovered, though slowly;—change of air was prescribed, and my father, agreeable to this prescription, proposed a journey into Italy. Oh horrible epocha of my fate!—scene of all the varied transactions which have conspired to overwhelm me with disgrace and infamy! *

"It was in the spring of the year that we commenced our journey. The season was propitious, the scenery delightful, and the society we mixed with elegant and enlightened; but our grief for your supposed death pressed heavily on my bosom; my spirits fled, and all my energies seemed buried in the cheerless gloom of inanity. Our destination was Naples—that emporium of every thing which is great, noble, and splendid—that terrestrial paradise where every heart, mine only excepted, seemed to throb with happiness, and every eye to beam with affection and transport!—My father, for the few first weeks after our arrival, appeared cheerful and collected. He visited the Casinos, attended the libraries, and made frequent excursions on the bay, and to the adjacent villas. But the change I contemplated in his disposition and manners, for till then he had been uniformly melancholy, was of short duration.—He was pensive even to sadness; his arms were perpetually folded; he was restless, though thoughtful. Sometimes he sighed profoundly—at others he seemed transfixed by grief, and talking to himself in a kind of whispered rumination. My uneasiness on witnessing this sudden transition from cheerfulness to despondency, the cause of which appeared inexplicable, could only be equalled by my curiosity.—I listened to catch the faintest sound of his voice, as he paced to and fro in his apartment; but the low key in which he spoke, rendered it indistinct even to the ear of mute attention.

"Every succeeding day contributed to my perplexity, and increased the power of my apprehensions.—The most terrible conjectures darted across my brain, and were again repelled from their seat with the velocity of lightning; and, unconscious of what he was meditating, unsuspicious of the artifice which was employed to entrap me, I entreated to be made the partner of his sorrows.—The consequence of this requisition was a confirmation of my worst and most terrible surmises. He informed me that, owing to a number of circumstances, and these the most complicated, nearly the whole of his property was irrecoverably lost; and that if I was solicitous to save myself from dependence, and him from the humiliations incident to poverty, I must consent to unite myself in marriage to a person of distinction, from whom I had formerly received overtures, and who, having heard I was released from the engagement, on the plea of which he had been rejected, was now ready to receive my hand.

"The consternation into which I was thrown by this intelligence, cannot be delineated by the power of words. Pale, speechless, convulsed, I leaned upon the arm of my father, and faintly articulating your name, sunk senseless at his feet. When I recovered, I found him looking earnestly in my face;—his features were unmoved, and I thought I perceived a concealed joy sparkle in his eyes as he exclaimed—'He is dead!—to you and to the world he has long been so; nor from that grave of which he is now a tenant, can your boasted constancy recall him. The grief we experience at the loss of friends, untimely snatched from us, is virtuous, and ought not to be too suddenly repulsed; the tear of sympathetic sorrow is a tribute due to their ashes, which nature and custom alike demand from us:—but grief indulged beyond a certain season becomes impious.—Rouse then from this lethargy of despondency, and embrace the happiness that courts you.'

"I raised my eyes ere he had finished speaking, but almost immediately withdrew them; for the severity which was marked expressively on his countenance alarmed me: and had he not supported me in his arms, I should have relapsed into torpor. Oh St. Louis! What were the agonies of that moment? All the horrors of dependence stared me in the face! My father too—my father in danger of becoming the melancholy inmate of a prison!—Imagination could not add another pang:—my brain maddened—I fell upon my knees, and clasping my convulsive hands, with eyes upraised, and drowned in tears, exclaimed—'Oh God! whatever ills my hard destiny may have in store for me, be thou the guardian of my father!—Thou hast been his defence in youth—forsake him not now, when he has none but thee to fly to.'—

"My voice, the tone of which was marked with agony, seemed to strike him to the soul with the force of electricity. The tide of parental tenderness rushed back to his heart: he could not speak —he could only gaze on me in silent sorrow.—I hid my face on his arm; he wept—his pale cheek streaming with tears, met mine. He clasped me to his breast; he kissed my cold and quivering lips; and then, replacing me by his side, besought me to save him from destruction, and myself from the miseries of contempt and poverty.

"Oh! wherefore dwell I on the recollection of a scene so painful? My vows to you were yet fresh in my memory; ah! why did I break them?—why suffer myself to be deluded by the sophistry of persuasion? Alas! what misery have I not incurred by it!——I must relinquish my talk for a short time.—The blood flows chilly through my veins—my pulse throbs languidly, and my eyes are dim with weeping:—suffice it that the hard wrung reluctant consent was at last obtained, and in three days I became of the wife of——" *
* *
* *
* *

The word which should have terminated this interesting fragment, to the infinite disappointment of Cecilia, was torn off.—She looked carefully among the remaining ones; but the precious morsel, so necessary to the concluding sentence of this paper, was no where to be found; and she proceeded to examine the rest, not doubting but the curiosity which the former one had excited, would in that be fully, if not immediately, gratified.

"I resume my pen.—Several succeeding weeks passed on in a series of sorrow. My melancholy, in spite of all my efforts to conceal it, became more and more apparent; and the altered manners of my Lord, who began to construe its indulgence into a tacit avowal of my indifference, augmented its power upon my heart.—My father waited only to witness the solemnization of our nuptials, and then returned to France. He had left Naples but a few months, when a letter (penned by an unknown hand) informed us of his illness and apparent danger, and commanded our immediate attendance at his chateau in Provence.

"In obedience to this injunction, we accordingly embarked, and the wind being in our favour, soon landed at Toulon; from whence we proceeded by land, and by the swiftest conveyances to our place of destination.—But how shall I find language to portray the conflicts of my soul when I entered this house of mourning—how paint the wild distraction which seized and possessed my mind, when I beheld my revered parent stretched upon the bed of death, his eyes rolling with agony, and his limbs distorted with convulsive pangs.

"There is an extreme grief, having obtained which, our faculties become deadened, and we lose the sense of our miseries in the torpor it inflicts. But the hour which was to take from the sensation of acute anguish was not yet arrived. It was not till that terrible moment of my fate when, bending over the emaciated form of my then dying father, I heard him declare you lived— lived to claim the fulfilment our mutual promises, and to heap curses on our destroyers—till I was informed that the report of your death, and the infamous allegation which succeeded it, were the fabrications of falsehood—promulgated for the invidious

purpose of drawing me into a splendid, but indiscreet marriage, that the measure of my woes was full, and I could anticipate no climax more refined in misery!—Oh St. Louis! how dreadful are the reproaches of an awakened conscience!—and awful are its effects in the hour of dissolution! The groan which accompanied this horrible confession, scarcely perhaps to be paralleled in the annals of iniquity, still vibrates on my ear.—I thrill with horror at the recollection—my blood runs colder than ever—my limbs tremble;—again I resign my pen. * * * * * * * * * * * * * * *
* *
* *

"Nothing but the hope of obtaining an interview with you in private, unsuspected by my Lord, who, in spite of the known sincerity of my nature, was a continual spy upon my actions, could have supported me under the heavy and repeated calamities under which I then laboured.—But, ah! how painful were my struggles ere I could resolve to endure the reproaches of him, whose mildest censure my trembling heart convinced me would be infinitely too mild for the enormity of my offence—before I could bear to meet those eyes which would read in my burning cheek the consciousness of error. Equally solicitous with myself to unfold the enigma of my situation, you flew to assist my endeavours—less eager to reproach than to unravel that mysterious web of circumstances which had led to our final separation. But, alas! how terribly fatal did the concerted confidence I have hinted at, prove to our murdered peace!—How little did we imagine it in the power even of diabolical malignity to wrest the meaning of two hearts, susceptible as were our's to the faintest impulses of virtue!—I saw your tears—I heard the melancholy utterance of your sighs as they burst from your overcharged heart;—but I saw—I heard no more:—an invisible hand arrested my arm as I threw myself, like a convicted culprit, at your feet, and fainting with my fears, I was borne unresistingly from your presence.

"When sensation returned, I found myself in my chamber: —somebody still grasped my arm; I turned—it was my husband; who I was now fatally convinced had been prompted by jealousy to plead an engagement elsewhere, for the purpose of detecting us, should we project and accomplish our intended interview. His darkened countenance, in which pride and resentment struggled for pre-eminence, awed me into silence.—Aroused and terrified, I attempted to depart; but he still grasped me firmly.—'Think not to escape me, traitoress!' exclaimed he, in a voice scarcely human, 'or to escape the exemplary punishment due to your guilt! The sword of justice is in my hands—prepare then to meet the stroke your crimes have merited.—The ministers of my will are at hand, and wait only my commands to bear you to your fate—a fate which, severe as it may seem to you, is in no degree proportioned to the enormity of your offence. I seek not to deprive you of your existence; though could I, by so doing, preserve you from infamy, and myself from dishonour, this sword (pointing his stiletto to my breast) should take the forfeiture of your crimes!'

"When he had proceeded thus far, he arose, and rung the bell; and in a moment two men, whom I never remember to have seen before, rushed into the room. They gazed on each other alternately.—'Do your office!' said my Lord, sternly; 'you are acquainted with the place;—by to-morrow night——' He stopped: one of the men hesitated: 'No parleying,' continued he angrily, 'you know your business.—The east tower—see that every avenue be secured:—if she escapes——you guess the rest: —this instant she departs!'

"I heard the mandate with a calmness of soul with evinced its innocence. Not a sigh escaped my bosom—not a tear betrayed the weakness of my heart.—I felt conscious that the reprehension that I had incurred was unmerited, and my pride towered above my sorrows. The known futility of every assertion I could make against the imputation of guilt from so powerful an accuser, prevented me from hazarding his indignation by any attempt to justify a conduct which, strong as circumstances were against me, appeared scarcely to admit of vindication.—Resigning myself, therefore, without reluctance to the plan of my persecutors, I followed my conductors to the portal, where a carriage was in waiting to convey me instantly from thence. I flung myself in;—one of the men took a seat by my side; the other placed himself with the postillion, and we drove off.

"We travelled with all imaginable speed, and soon arrived

at the chateau, selected for me by my husband for my place of future confinement.—The room, and the only one appropriated to me, was on the eastern side of the edifice, adjoining the chapel, where several of my ancestors, (the chateau having been the property of my ancestors) lie entombed.—A woman attended me at first, who treated me with respect, and seemed to feel for the distresses incident to my situation; but as she was suspected of being in my interest, she was dismissed, and another engaged in her stead. With the former one I was supplied with books; she also procured me implements for writing and drawing; and my mind becoming gradually more composed, the amusement I drew from these sources rendered the dreariness of my confinement less irksome.—Her successor I see only at stated periods; my food is conveyed by men; and twice in a year I am visited by a Signor, deputed by my Lord to regulate and overlook the affairs of the household. I know not his name; but every evil passion of which the human heart is susceptible, is delineated on his countenance. His voice, whenever he speaks, alarms me almost to fainting:—I cannot look on him without horror! * * * * * * *
* *
* *

"Three years, three dreary and melancholy years have passed on, and still I am a prisoner. Some secret, some instinctive power informs me that in this solitude I am doomed to perish—in early youth to perish! I shudder at the thought; but there is something in it so awfully prophetic, that I cannot shake it from my mind with all the force and energy of reason.—Oh St. Louis! pity, if you can, the unhappy victim to your love, to whom every succeeding year brings only an accumulation of the deepest anguish! I sink beneath the weight of my sorrows—I have no friend near me to participate its pressure. Oh God! thou knowest my heart! I have sinned—but I will yet look to thee for consolation! * * * * *
* *
* *

"I rise from my bed feverish and depressed. I have dreamed—dreamed of all my soul holds dear! Oh, that the illusion had continued—that thus dreaming I could have slept till the last sleep of death had overtaken me!—What can these ceaseless tears—this burning brain portend? My bosom palpitates, and my pulses beat more rapidly than ever.—I tremble as I look around; the sound of my own footsteps, as I pass and repass my chamber, startles me. *

* *
* *
* *

"The dawn is dreary and tempestuous—the rain descends in torrents—and the strong towers of the chateau seem to shake from their foundations as the thunder rolls over them. The lightning glares through my chamber, and the flame of the lamp I hold, is every moment rendered invisible by the vivid and intense flashes. Something screams against my window—it is the eagle, frighted from her nest among the rocks by the unusual light. * *

* *
* *
* *

"The rain abates—the thunder continues; but its effects are less awful. The elements are returning to repose; they storm for a while—then are at peace:—Oh! that the calm air their abating violence portends, could be transmitted to this breast!—Vain wish! never—never again can it know the blessings of repose! * *

* *
* *
* *

"What is that spell which attaches us to life long after we have taught ourselves to despise it, and from whence does it derive its power to subdue us? It is because we fear to die, that we still cling to existence as to the choicest of our treasures,—or does the deceiver, Hope, in contradiction both to our reason and experience, succeed in persuading us it may be yet a blessing? How often, in the anguish of my soul, do I question it! Does the wearied traveller, who has surmounted a long and toilsome journey, dread the sanctuary where he may find comfort and repose? Does the recently condemned wretch, on the eve of encountering a painful and ignominious death, avoid the reprieve which is to restore him to liberty and joy?— Does the thirsty lip close when the invigorating draught presents itself? Wherefore then should I wish to linger on the wreck, when the yawning gulph around me

menaces destruction? Why check the anticipation of that hour when this lacerated bosom shall freeze in the sepulchre, whose gloomy confines I have so often contemplated from my prison? Surely the idea, awful as it is, ought to bring consolation:—I ought to rejoice when I reflect, the tempests of this wintry life at an end, our union will be certain and indissoluble.—No storms can visit the deep sleep of death—no human arm have power to disturb our ashes, or to extinguish that pure spark of ethereal essence which the Almighty has given us to burn for ever. * * * *
* *
* *

"An awful stillness reigns throughout my chamber:—my keeper has been in only once to-day; he looks more than usually savage.—Something has, I suppose, happened to disconcert him.
* *

"Hark! I hear a noise!—some one knocks loudly at the outer gate—a voice calls—it is my husband's agent! What can this mean? He has been absent but a month; some unexpected event must have hastened his return.—His presence alarms me more than I can express!—I have no claim whatever to the character of a physiognomist; but if I read this man right, he has a villain's heart.—He comes—I hear his footsteps pacing deliberately along the gallery; it is like the step of the assassin stealing through night and darkness, to commit a deed 'the day would blush to look on!' I shrink with horror from his approach. * * * * * * * * * * * *
* *
* *
* *

"His manners are less ferocious, but more disgusting than formerly. Twice already has he visited my chamber.—He affects to compassionate my sufferings, and has even made some attempt to abate the rigour of my punishment. This morning, by his orders, I was permitted to leave my prison, and to take a walk along the grounds; but not without being continually crossed by one or other of the domestics, who were doubtless employed to watch me. Alas! how needless this precaution, when every avenue to escape is so carefully guarded. * * * * * * * * * * * *
* *

* *
* *

"What a day have I passed—and what a night of agony has succeeded it! When will my persecutions be at an end—these tears of bitter recollection cease to flow—and this heart to palpitate with the anticipation of future evils? Oh St. Louis! this man is, as I suspected, a villain—a confirmed, a deliberate, and most abandoned villain! the insulting familiarity of his addresses overwhelms me with confusion, and yet I have not the power to avoid him. Yesterday when he entered my apartment, he seized my hands, and had I not prevented him, would have carried them to his lips.—The indignation I experienced from this treatment was excessive, and my terror became infinite. I shrieked involuntarily; still, however, he persevered in detaining me; and throwing his arms around my waist, would have proceeded to still greater insults: but with an effort almost incredible, I tore myself from his grasp, and snatching up his stiletto, which, in the hurry of the conflict, had fallen from beneath his cloak to the ground, threatened him with instant death if he persisted!—In the midst of my struggles to recover it, one of my arms was wounded so deeply as to render me totally incapable of further resistance, and in a moment I was covered with blood, and so agonized with the wound I had received, that I had scarcely the power to implore his assistance. The anguish I appeared to suffer, and the sight of the blood, which streamed over every part of my dress, rendered him sensible to the feelings of remorse, if not of pity. —Compunction for the mischiefs he had occasioned, fastened irresistibly on his heart; and he endeavoured to remedy as much as possible the injury I had sustained, by applying his handkerchief to the wound, which, on a minuter inspection, was found to be not so deep as was at first imagined.—When he retired, he sent a woman to attend upon me, who has since been an almost constant visitor in my chamber.—Heaven grant that the remorse he testified may be my defence against any future attempts which the malevolence of his nature, and the baseness of his heart my prompt him to! *
* *

* *

"Do I live?—am I awake?—or is all around me visionary?—Yes, I live—I breathe—I can discern objects—distinguish sounds —and have all the faculties of sense and reason unimpaired. Yet every thing I see—every thing I hear, contributes to my perplexity. To-day, St. Louis, I depart; but whence, and for what is it, I depart?—All is mystery, astonishment, and confusion. * * * * * *
* *
* *

"I am unable to analyze my feelings; but a dreadful presentiment—an awful foreboding, I have generally found prophetic, clings insurmountably to my mind. Perhaps——but I dare not think; my brain maddens—an icy chillness arrests the circulation in my veins—a strange tremor comes over me!—Adieu, St. Louis, adieu!—ere long we may meet again to part no more! In this world we have been arbitrarily and most barbarously separated; but in that which is to come our union will be perfect and indissoluble."

CHAPTER II

Have you the heart—When your head did but ache
I knit my handkerchief about your brows.
* *
* *
And with my hand at midnight held your head;
And like the watchful minutes to the hour,
Still and anon cheer'd up the heavy time,
Saying, "What lack you? and where lies your grief?
And what good love may I perform for you?"

SHAKESPEARE.

THE melancholy contents of these papers, so exactly calculated to excite sympathy and esteem for the fair and unfortunate writer, and the various conjectures which they inspired, impressed the mind of Cecilia with the most uneasy sensations.—Impelled by a curiosity which became every moment more rational, she would probably have sought an explanation by an application either to Agnes or Berthe, had her confidence in their sincerity been greater, or her apprehensions of future consequences less ardent.—The struggles she was fated to encounter ere she could determine to confine the extraordinary effects of her researches to her own bosom, were, notwithstanding, too powerful not to occasion her a considerable degree of irresolution, which it demanded all her prudence to surmount. The conflict this imposed, the mental fatigue she had undergone previous to the examination of the MS, and the distress she had suffered whilst perusing it, conspired to give an added dejection to her manners on the ensuing morning, which was too apparent to escape the notice of Agnes, who, having recovered from the debility consequent to her late alarming indisposition, had resumed her occupation of attending upon her.

This woman, though she had exhibited some very strong symptoms of insensibility on the arrival of her guest, was, nevertheless, unable to behold a lovely young creature like Cecilia, whose humanity and unequalled sweetness of disposition had so recently been made manifest in her amiable attentions to her, under circumstances so addictive, without experiencing some degree of pity for her situation. And probably had she been empowered to rescue her from the contemplation of future misery, without any essential injury to herself, she would have embraced the opportunity of repaying the obligation thus incurred, and of relieving herself from that oppressive load of remorse, which, in the moment of supposed danger, seemed to press heavily upon her mind, by some spirited exertion in her favour.—From this period, however, a decided alteration took place both in Agnes's conversation and manners. She appeared thoughtful and agitated; and often, when pressed by Cecilia's enquiries, abruptly left the room to avoid interrogatories, which she was evidently restrained only by fear from answering satisfactorily.—This agitation spoke more powerfully in her favour than she could herself have done, had she been ever so cool and recollected. That confusion proceeding from duplicity and conscious guilt, Cecilia imputed to the sensibility of a benevolent heart, on witnessing sufferings which she could not alleviate; and she began to flatter herself, her mind thus softening by degrees from asperity to kindness, she might be disposed ere long to assist her escape from a confinement, the dreariness and solemnity of which, independent of the melancholy idea of being secluded in it for life, rendered it insupportably irksome to her.—Once beyond the walls of the chateau, she doubted not of protection and support; and even within them, could it have been possible to gain access to the train of domestics that filled it, she despaired not of finding some one who would be inclined to pity and befriend her.

Another day and night had passed on nearly in the same manner as the foregoing ones, when, at the conclusion of the second evening, as Cecilia was sitting alone in the saloon, she heard a sort of unusual bustle in the hall, as of a number of people moving backward and forward, and the clamour of several voices. Her heart fluttered; hope, however, rekindled for a moment in her breast as she distinguished an approaching step, which was almost immediately succeeded by a gentle knocking at the door. She sprung from her seat; but the sudden effects of surprise and apprehension took from her limbs the power of motion; and she had sunk into a chair, almost breathless with agitation, when her own name, hastily but distinctly articulated, caught her ear, and in an instant the door was thrown open, and a figure resembling Count Morsino, burst into the room, rushed to the window near which she sat, and fell at her feet. She shrieked —she trembled;—a quickened second glance convinced her this was no error of her sense, and she fainted!

Her sensations may be better conceived than described, when, on recovering, she found herself alone with, and apparently in the power of a man, whose mind she believed capable of any machination, however daring, and whose ungenerous conduct on a former occasion, left but little room for hope at the present juncture.—A confused and trembling stupor threatened again to overpower her senses:—she raised her eyes toward Heaven as if to implore its protection, her bosom surcharged with sighs, and incapable of giving utterance to the anguish which oppressed her. Her distress brought the Count immediately to his recollection:—he execrated his own folly in intruding himself thus abruptly into her presence; and repeatedly in the most earnest manner entreated her forgiveness.

Several minutes had elapsed before Cecilia could command her resentment sufficiently to demand of him by what means he had acquired a knowledge of her residence; and with what view, since she had given him such an unequivocal answer to his late overtures, he had had the temerity to follow her.

"Is it possible," returned the Count, affecting a tone of surprise, "my Cecilia can have been so long and so strangely deceived as to the real circumstances of her situation? Have my orders been so punctually obeyed then, that she has yet to learn where she is, and who is the proprietor of this mansion?"

"How, my Lord?" exclaimed Cecilia indignantly; "is it to you I am indebted for the outrages I have received?—you who have authorized such acts of violence on my person? Is it by your orders I am kept a prisoner here?"

"For Heaven's sake suppress your resentment, my dear Cecilia —hear me; though I cannot exculpate, at least I may palliate my conduct.—No motives, be assured, but such as are in their nature the purest, the most laudable, and the most honourable, could have induced me to take a step which the established, but somewhat fastidious customs of the world might condemn as arbitrary.—Impelled by the sincerest affection, and by the truest regard for your happiness, I designed and executed a project, which, while love urged, reason disapproved, well knowing that your displeasure would be the consequence. But, ah! did you know," added he, softening his voice, and gazing upon her with a look full of tenderness and contrition, "what were my sufferings!—Could you have witnessed the pangs I endured ere I could resolve to execute my design—before I could bear to subject that angelic form to the rude grasp of an hireling—that mind to the horrors of unexpected captivity, you would pity, you would even be induced to pardon me!—Think what must have been the situation of a man who loves as I do, when he found himself in danger of losing you for ever—when he heard, fatal determination! that you had decided to renounce the world—to bury yourself eternally in the depths of solitude, and to waste your hours, unregarded and neglected, in the gloomy shade of a cloister!"

Here he ceased to speak; but Cecilia was so much shocked and aggravated by this discovery, that it was not till after repeated exertions, that she was enabled to afford any answer. At length, recovering herself, in some degree, from the effects of her displeasure, she said—

"Forbear, my Lord, to attempt to justify a measure your utmost efforts can neither palliate nor excuse; nor hope by a few penitential expressions, so foreign to your heart, to regain that place in my esteem which you have so entirely and so justly forfeited.—True contrition shews itself in actions, and not in words: proceed then to convince me of the sincerity of these professions, by restoring me to that liberty of which you have so basely deprived me. Persist in refusing me this, and your hypocrisy will only deepen the colour of your offence, and render it more conspicuous to the eye of discernment."

"At present," rejoined the Count, somewhat piqued, "I know of one request only with which it is impossible I can comply. Let my charming Cecilia mention any thing independent of this, which can contribute to her ease, and my fortune, and even my life shall be sacrificed to procure it!"

"I require no sacrifices from you, my Lord," she replied. "I demand only what you have no right to withhold from me—my liberty. Without meriting such a misfortune, I am become a prisoner in your house; my residence here is equally disgraceful both to myself and you, and I cannot consider you as my friend while you persevere in detaining me."

"Let us fly then," exclaimed the Count eagerly, "let us abandon for ever this hated place, and taste in happier regions, and under more friendly auspices, those supreme enjoyments, which youth and sweet affection may secure to us!—There living only for each other, we will tread together one continued round of pleasure. The changing seasons shall but vary our delights; Nature and Art shall unburthen all their stores to administer to our gratifications; and ages of never-ending felicity shall be our portion!—Promise but to be mine—let to-morrow's sun witness our vows; and my whole life shall be dedicated to the promotion of your happiness: and while sheltered in these encircling arms from every external danger, those who once called themselves your friends, shall not presume to charge you with the consequences of their own neglect and brutality."

Cecilia heaved a deep sign, and her cheek reddened with indignation.

"All I ask," said she disdainfully, "is an asylum from the dangers which await me here. Once beyond the reach of your persecutions, I can defy every evil my malignant stars may have in store for me. No misery I can experience beyond these detested walls, can be comparable to what I now feel—no danger so appalling as that which now threatens me."

"Great Heaven! my Cecilia," exclaimed the Count, "whither does your imagination lead you?—what evils do you dread?—and where are the dangers you are thus solicitous to avoid? Wrong me not, I conjure you, with these heartrending suspicions! Are you not in my power? and do I not disdain to take advantage of your situation? What proofs of esteem, of affection, and of self-denial would you demand from me, which I have not already given you? Can my charmer suppose I consider empty words only a sufficient atonement for the sufferings I have occasioned her—and that I would add to these sufferings, so unwillingly inflicted, by fresh insults upon her person? Never while she permits me to hope that, by my unremitting assiduities, I may remove the aversion which she has so unjustly conceived for me—never, unless driven to desperation by her scorn, can I attain that extremity of depravity with which I am charged!"

He would have proceeded, but she arose; and while the tear of indignation rolled down her cheek, she approached the door of the apartment, and was prevented only by her excessive agitation from retiring.

"Wherefore these tears, Cecilia?" said the Count, springing forward, and seizing her hand, "whither would you go? I entreat—nay, I insist upon being heard. Are not the proposals I have made at once splendid and honourable? Do I not offer you my fortune and my hand—to make you mistress of some of the noblest villas in Italy—to surround you with grandeur and opulence—and, by introducing you to the world as my wife, to free you from those unmerited and degrading epithets which malice or misrepresentation may affix to your name?—Consent then to ensure your own safety, and my honour, by allowing me henceforth to become your guardian and protector—the only means now left you of regaining your liberty, and preserving your yet stainless reputation from the shafts of envy and detraction!"

"Were it envy and detraction only that I feared, my Lord," said Cecilia, blushing, and hastily withdrawing her hand, "your arguments might have some weight."

"And what other reprehension should the loveliest of her sex fear?" resumed the Count, interrupting her. "Can the suggestions of her conscience, in contradiction to reason, accuse her of acting wrong when she is only obeying the dictates of honour and virtue?—Has my charmer so little candour in her composition, that she can imagine, because I once had recourse to arts, which I own to have been both cruel and degrading, my principles are debased, and my heart is contaminated?—Injure me not, I entreat you, with such a supposition!—Your example has inspired me with the love of goodness, and your inimitable excellencies have fixed for ever those affections which were before, I acknowledge with regret, wavering and uncertain.—By the gentle influence of your example you will correct my errors, and strengthen my virtues. From those lovely lips I shall receive lessons of wisdom and instruction, and you will soon become a sharer in the felicity you bestow."

"If you intend I should construe what you say into a renewal of your former offer, my Lord," said Cecilia rather haughtily, "I must repeat what I formerly declared on that occasion.—Your proposals, in point of liberality, as I then assured you, exceed my utmost wish. It is evident, then, that my reason for declining them is of a nature not to be overcome, and ought, therefore, to be an obstacle of as great weight with you as it is with me. Had your first offers been such as I could have accepted with honour, you might have possessed my esteem, and certainly would have been entitled to my lasting gratitude. More it was never in my power to bestow; and esteem and gratitude from me would have been a poor and very inadequate return for the sincere and ardent love you professed. Convinced, therefore, as I trust you now are, that no warmer sentiments than these ever could have been excited, had you never deviated even in thought from the strictest rules of decorum, what inducement can I now have for accepting your proffered hand? By a stratagem the most daring that can be conceived, I am made dependant on your power; and, presuming on the authority you have obtained over me, you would persuade, or rather terrify me into a measure which my reason and my heart alike condemn. My unsuspecting nature, which ought to have been my guard against insult and oppression, was made the means of ensnaring me; and the proud, the high-born Morsino now stoops to efface from my mind the remembrance of one infamous act by another equally ungenerous."

She fixed her eyes upon the Count ere she had finished speaking. The simple eloquence of her manner rendered him susceptible to shame, though not to remorse; and he threw himself upon a chair, and leaned his head upon his hand to conceal his confusion.

"After such an avowal, I rely entirely on your mercy, my Lord. Situated as I now am, it may perhaps be deemed madness in me to dispute your will. But as I scorn to have recourse to dissimulation, I again repeat, I hope for the last time, my unalterable determination never to connect myself with a man of your character —a man whom I never could love, and whom, after what has passed, it is impossible I ever can esteem."

These words, which were uttered in a tone at once firm and indignant, aroused the Count from his posture;—wild and angry glances darted from his eyes; he struck his clenched hand upon his forehead, and while his lips were distorted by a disdainful smile, he said—

"Since you brave my power, Madam, and execrate my character, you cannot wonder that I avail myself of the one, and attempt not a vindication of the other. If by depriving me of all hopes of reinstating myself in your good opinion, you drive me to extremities, you have yourself only to blame, and must take the consequences of your own rashness.—I ordered you to be conveyed hither, to hear the avowal of a flame which destroys me, to renew my claim to your affections, and to receive your favours as a gift: but if goaded on to frenzy by your hate, I am urged to commit an act of desperation the fault is ultimately your own—you teach me what to do, and I shall profit by the instructions you give.—If then you value your life, or what is perhaps dearer to you, your liberty—if you are not careless of reputation, you will consent to become my wife without further procrastination; aware as you must be of the outrages which will attend upon a rejection so obstinate."

There was a look of profligate assurance in his countenance while he spoke, which greatly disgusted Cecilia, and at the same time unequivocally indicated the meaning of his words. With a degree of terror she was unable to conceal, she arose from her seat, and in silent anguish walked to a distant part of the saloon. —Deep sighs burst from her heart; and almost fainting, she leaned against a window-frame for support.

The Count followed her, and again in a softened tone, and in accents of earnest supplication besought her to consent to his wishes. He then threw his arms around her waist; but with an energy springing from despair, she disengaged herself from his hold, and hastening to her own apartment, sunk upon a sofa in a transport of grief and indignation.

His avowed resolution of detaining her, even though she should persist in opposing his intentions, his threats, his entreaties, and the various inconsistencies of his conduct, annihilated every hope which had sometimes floated on her mind; and whilst the anxiety she felt taught her to put the worst interpretation possible on his motives and designs, she imagined her disgrace to be inevitable, and her destruction certain. That Boraccio had been an active instrument in betraying her, a number of till then unnoticed circumstances left her little room to dispute. This suspicion, apparently so well grounded, greatly aggravated the horrors of her situation; and she felt extreme pain from the persuasion that the person who had bound himself in the most solemn manner, and on the most awful occasion, to be her guardian and friend, had ultimately proved himself her most decided foe.

"Oh De Sevignac!" she exclaimed, "my beloved—my more than father! how deep even now would be your regret—how severe your remorse, were you permitted to know the heart of the man to whom you ventured to delegate a trust of such magnitude—the care of your adopted child! Could you behold me forsaken by every friend, and beset as I am with a thousand dangers?"

The adventure in the turret, which the sudden intrusion of

the Count had driven till this instant from her immediate recollection, now recurred to her thoughts; and with it a persuasion that the person recently confined there was not, as she had before supposed, the former Marchesa, but the wife of the Count, the report of whose death had probably been circulated in order to assist his nefarious designs upon her—a persuasion which soon ripened into conviction.

While she mused, she heard the sounds of a step, and in an instant Agnes appeared advancing towards her. At the sight of her attendant, on whose gratitude for past favours rested her every hope of emancipation, a gleam of consolation returned to her mind; and aware that if she was at all inclined to befriend her, there was not a moment to be lost, she conjured her with tears, and with the most urgent importunities, to assist her in forming some scheme for her deliverance.

"Be consoled, Madam," said Agnes; "your prospects are not so gloomy as you imagine. If your happiness depends upon your removal from this chateau, your wishes will be indulged:—to-morrow, if you please, you may depart."

"If my happiness depends upon it!" interrupted Cecilia. "Oh deceive me not!" she wildly exclaimed; "if you would save me from a fate the most dreadful that can be conceived, this instant inform me by what means I can escape!—instruct me what to do, and I will execute your orders at the peril of my existence!"

"The Count waits but to receive your hand," resumed Agnes; "after which he will convey you immediately from hence to a very splendid abode, which he intends you should consider for the future as your home."

"Oh Agnes!" cried Cecilia with a look of mingled sorrow and disappointment, "do you excite hope only to render despair more poignant? Think, were our situations reversed, how would you bless the hand which would extend itself for your deliverance! To you—to you, Agnes," added she mournfully, "I could not have been thus unkind. When stretched upon the bed of sickness, pale, shivering, convulsed—almost dying with your fears, did I not support you in my arms, and bend over you with a friend's affection? Whole hours have I sat by, and watched you, and with cautious zeal stilled every sound which might disturb your slumbers. How fervent—how ingenuous—and apparently how sincere were those expressions of unmerited praise which then flowed from your lips! Alas! how greatly was I deceived!—A novice in every species of dissimulation, I suspected not their motive. Little—little did I imagine them to be the ebullitions of a heart so fortified against the feelings of humanity and justice!"

"Spare your reproaches, Madam," rejoined Agnes, "I am not perhaps so guilty as you suppose. Heaven is my witness that, had I the power of assisting you, I would joyfully participate in any scheme for your advantage. But my actions are under the dominion of a power I must not—dare not controul. My Lord is the only friend I have left; and I should be a monster of ingratitude if I were capable of deceiving him."

"But are there not certain situations," continued Cecilia with earnestness, "in which our faith becomes criminal, and our zeal disgraceful?"

"That may be true," answered Agnes, "but there are also certain situations in which it becomes our duty to act up decisively to the part we have taken, however it may terminate. My comfort —perhaps my life, depends upon my submission; for my Lord, though unexampled in generosity to the few he respects, never omits an opportunity of taking exemplary vengeance on those who disobey his mandates.—By a fruitless attempt to frustrate his plans, I should expose myself to his resentment without advancing my cause; and probably involve you as well as myself in the effects of his severest displeasure.—Let me entreat you then to accept the terms he now offers you. By the ascendancy which you have gained over him, you may mould him to your wishes; and making the ardent love he professes for you, subservient to your gratifications, may enjoy every pleasure which rank and countless wealth can procure. The resentment his late conduct has excited, it will be the study of his future life to remove. Reflection will convince him of his error, and teach him to deserve you by the sincerity of his repentance."

"Never!" cried Cecilia. "His mind is too depraved to reform it, or even for my forgiveness!—Long practised in every art of deception, he does not even try the power of rectitude over those whom he would vanquish."

"You mistake," resumed Agnes; "my Lord, though he may have indulged himself in some foibles, possesses nevertheless many qualities truly estimable, which time and a more thorough knowledge of his disposition will amply unfold to you. —He is fascinated with your beauty, and would fain elevate you to a station where that beauty would appear to the highest advantage."

"The Count has not the smallest intention of fulfilling his professions," cried Cecilia, "and even were he so inclined, I am convinced he has not the power."

"You amaze me more than I can express!" returned Agnes. "Is it possible you can doubt his word? Has he not sworn——"

"Most vehemently," said Cecilia; "but oaths and protestations are the subterfuges of guilt, which serve only to confirm the weakness of the cause they are intended to promote. The asseverations of falsehood may deceive for a time; but reason returned, the fraud is ultimately detected, and we view the act and the actor with equal abhorrence."

Agnes paused, and looked despondingly.

"To what do you allude?" said she. "What act has my Lord committed which can authorize the suspicions you seem to have betrayed?—You know his happiness or misery depends entirely upon you; and being conscious of your influence over his feelings, you should endeavour to use it with discretion.—That his views are in every respect honourable, I have never permitted myself to doubt. He has no wish, no hope beyond those of making you his wife. To convince you of the sincerity of this assertion, he has commissioned me to inform you that he has already engaged a Priest, who waits but your acquiescence to perform the rites of that ceremony which may make you, if you please, the most envied among women."

Cecilia interrupted her with a request that she would desist for the future from all useless expostulations on this point, as she had long since resolutely decided never to marry the Count, her prepossessions against him being such as she could not surmount.

"For the love of Heaven determine not so rashly!" said Agnes; "you know not the consequences of such a decision."

"I have prepared myself for the worst, and am resolved to

encounter every thing, rather than submit myself to the will of this detested tyrant."

"My Lord is not of a nature to be trifled with with impunity; and should you persist in opposing his wishes, your punishment may be even greater than you imagine. This chateau is large, solitary, and filled with dungeons, through whose melancholy grates no cheerful beam of day can ever enter. I shudder at the recollection of what may be your situation should you continue refractory.—Reflect then, I beseech you, before your refusal becomes absolute; and by a timely submission to a will which must be obeyed, save yourself from a destiny so full of danger."

Cecilia trembled; and her face was instantly overspread with an ashy paleness.

"And does the monster threaten me with imprisonment too?" exclaimed she tremulously. "Oh holy Heaven! in what a net of misery am I now entangled!"

"I have heard no hint of that kind at present," resumed Agnes; "but my Lord is inexorable in his displeasure; and should his love by repeated provocations be converted into hate, there is no answering for the consequences. Let me hasten then to inform him that you have reconsidered his proposals, and are now solicitous to accept the honour he would confer. A conduct such as this will restore you to his confidence, and be attended with the most durable advantages to yourself."

"No advantages," answered Cecilia, "are equivalent to the difficulties which a connection inconsistent with honour would involve me in—present suffering would not be its worst effect."

"What is it you mean?" cried Agnes.

"The Count is sufficiently convinced," said Cecilia, "that the marriage he proposes would never be deemed legal. Base in every purpose of his soul, he has determined on my destruction, and is resolved, by every stratagem he can devise, to effectuate his design."

"I am unable to comprehend you," continued Agnes with some impetuosity; "and since your language is so ambiguous, I must insist upon an explanation."

"The Contessa della Morsino," cried Cecilia, "still lives."

Agnes started.

"The mysterious secret is discovered then!" said she.

"Look on this bracelet," rejoined Cecilia, displaying at the same time the gem she had so providentially found; "know you not these jewels? Observe them well;—they are rare; and when once seen, cannot easily be mistaken: this was your Lady's!"

"My Lady's, sure enough!" cried Agnes. "Good Heavens! Mademoiselle, where and how did you obtain the possession of that bracelet?"

Cecilia then briefly recounted her late incident in the turret; having concluded which, her companion remained for several minutes silent, as if overwhelmed with confusion. At length recovering herself from her embarrassment, she said—

"I am a guilty and unfortunate woman; but what I do is from necessity!—An instrument in the hands of a man by whose arts I have been ensnared, I scarcely dare to think, and much less to act, but as he shall dictate. Conscious as I am of having assisted in this deception, I must not hope for your forgiveness; nevertheless I shall always have an interest in your welfare and happiness."

Cecilia, touched by these words, assured her of her readiness to overlook the part she had acted, on condition that she would immediately concert some plan for her enlargement—a measure which her late interview with the Count had determined her to attempt, were it even at the hazard of her life.

Agnes shook her head, in token of the impracticability of this enterprise. The gates, she said, were constantly kept shut, and the bridge was drawn up, so that no one could pass to and from the chateau without the knowledge of the Count. She would make some enquiries, however, she said, of the porter, with the result of which she would acquaint her immediately. This said, Agnes withdrew, and having been absent near an hour, returned to give an account of her mission, the ill success of which was faithfully delineated on her countenance. She was going to speak, but Cecilia interrupted her.

"There is then no hope!" said she; and she burst into tears.

"It is as I feared," replied Agnes; "my Lord has issued a pro-hibition against the gates being opened; he has penetrated your design, and is determined to counteract it."

Cecilia wrung her hands in agony, but could not utter a syllable. Agnes, moved by her distress, remained with her in her room till the supper hour was announced, when she withdrew to obey an order from the Count, who desired to see her in the saloon.

Having proceeded thus far, it may be proper to take a retrospective glance at those circumstances which occurred at Genoa previous to Cecilia's departure.

CHAPTER III

> My shroud of white stuck all with yew,
>   Oh, prepare it!
>   * * * * * * * *
>   * * * * * * * *
> Not a flower, not a flower sweet
>   On my black coffin let there be strown;
>   * * * * * * * *
>   * * * * * * * *
> A thousand thousand sighs to save,
>   Lay me, Oh where!
> True lover, never find my grave,
>   To weep there!
>
> SHAKESPEARE.

THE decided and very spirited manner in which Cecilia had repulsed the advances of the Count when he first hinted his designs upon her, having compelled him to relinquish all hopes of obtaining her on the terms proposed, he had been induced to offer her his hand.—On her positive rejection of this also, his very *honourable proposal*, his vexation was excessive; and resolved that, in some shape or other, she should be his, whatever danger or guilt might attend the accomplishment of his desires, he consulted with Boraccio on the means of forcing her into a marriage, the day for which ceremony was actually fixed upon, unknown to Cecilia, when an unforeseen event put an end to this scheme, and suggested another equally and even more atrocious than the preceding one.

From a conversation lately held between the Count and Signor Gavino, it appeared that the report of the Contessa's death, however industriously propagated by the partisans of the former, was not generally believed throughout Italy. Alarmed, therefore, for what might be the issue of this marriage, should the fact be ascertained, he determined to make a full avowal of it to Boraccio, from whose necessitous circumstances, and apparent disposition to befriend him, he derived the most flattering expectations as to his future services. This confession, and the proposition which succeeded it, were the cause of a very serious altercation between Morsino and the Signor; after which the Count, as it may be remembered, refrained from visiting at the Palace for several days together. The perturbation of Boraccio's mind during this interval of his absence, was such as is scarcely to be described. Depraved as he was, he could not view himself in the light of a pander to an innocent and unsuspecting girl, whom he had already defrauded, and who had no resource from his power, no protection but his honour, without the severest self-reproach. He was reluctant, nevertheless, to lose the friendship of a man, whose unprecedented generosity on a former occasion was yet fresh in his memory, and whose countenance was so essential to his future credit.

The Count, perceiving his irresolution, endeavoured to remove it by representing that in a short time the bonds which united him to a woman he despised, and whose conduct had disgraced the name she bore, would in all probability be dissolved by death; when he would make an ample restitution for the injury done Cecilia, by publicly acknowledging her as his wife. The arguments thus employed were finally victorious; and a plot, which, but for the interposition of the Marchese, who had really written to Boraccio to desire that he would either marry Cecilia off immediately, or place her in a Convent as a boarder, could not so easily have been carried into effect, was accordingly laid.—The man who personated the *Religieux* was the Count's valet, who, possessing talents for intrigue, well suited to the office, was selected as an accomplice. The guide was his brother; and the musket which was discharged on the road between St. Michel and Cevenna, the signal of attack to three other of their colleagues, conveniently ambushed near the spot.

By the artful management of Boraccio, the Signora was kept

in ignorance of the whole of the transaction; and Mad. Le Marne made the innocent abettor of a stratagem, in which, could she have divined its termination, she would never have participated. We now return to the chateau.

As soon as Agnes was dismissed from her imposed attendance upon her Lord, she returned to the apartment of Cecilia, and, in compliance with her entreaties, consented to continue with her the night: Cecilia's apprehensions having suggested the impropriety of remaining alone in a chamber, where she was without any apparent means of defending herself from the intrusions of the Count.—Reassured by her compliance, she ventured to take possession of her bed; but the repose she sought, exhausted as she was by grief and vexation, refused to befriend her.—If she closed her eyes for a moment, in the next she awoke in some fancied danger. Every step in the corridor made her start—every noise in the more distant gallery filled her with terror and apprehension.

This mental agitation was succeeded in the course of a few hours with some strong symptoms of indisposition. She complained of thirst, and was restless and feverish throughout the night. These feverish indications were augmented on the ensuing day;—her pulse beat quick, though feeble; her cheek was flushed —her respiration grew short and laborious—and the hasty transitions she experienced from heat to cold, denoted the approach of a disorder equally alarming and dangerous.

Agnes continued with her in her room till a late hour in the morning, when, perceiving that her malady was rapidly increasing, she became seriously uneasy; and less fearful of disturbing the Count by an avowal of her supposed danger, than of leaving her to struggle with it unassisted, she hastened to inform her Lord of Cecilia's situation.

The Count had no sooner received information of Cecilia's illness, which he was conscious might be attributed to the atrocity of his own conduct, and the vehement and unguarded protestations he had used on the preceding night, than he penned a hasty note, which he dispatched immediately by Agnes, replete with expressions of remorse, and full of promises of amendment, should he be fortunate enough to obtain her forgiveness. He acknowledged the cruelty he had been practicing, in thus forcing her into his power; lamented that the ardour of his affection had induced him to commit an act so degrading to himself, and so injurious to the object of it; and concluded with an assurance that he would refrain from any further expostulation which his unhappy passion might suggest, and even from visiting her till she should be perfectly restored, or till he had her permission so to do.

Cecilia having read, returned only a short verbal answer to this billet by Agnes, signifying her wish that she might not be persecuted for the future by any letters or messages from him, and containing a positive command that he would forbear from any attempt to see her.—This she did from a conviction that the pretended concessions and unsubstantial promises with which the letter abounded, proceeded not from a real compunction for the fault he had committed, but to his newly arisen apprehensions of what might be its issue.

The Count was greatly incensed at this reply; but he had the policy to suppress every appearance of his indignation, not doubting but, when sufficiently recovered to admit him into her presence, that her resentment would be subsided, and that he should then acquire some degree of influence over her.—That she was really ill he could have no reason to dispute. But he flattered himself that, after a few days' retirement, which seemed to him as so many ages, she would be perfectly restored to him; and though he had given her a solemn assurance, that he would on no account repeat his importunities without her permission and concurrence, he looked forward to this epoch as to the summit of all his expectations and all his wishes. To beguile the melancholy hours till he could again see her, he employed himself in examining the different apartments in the chateau, in alternately passing and repassing the rampart wall, and in conversing and giving directions to the men occupied in repairing it.

Whilst the Count was thus engaged, sometimes yielding up his mind to ungovernable chagrin, and sometimes indulging himself in the most extravagant hopes, Cecilia, attended only by her two female domestics, was suffering under the united attacks of mental and bodily pain, equal, and perhaps superior to what she had ever before felt. In the evening she grew materially worse;—her pulse beat more and more rapid; she was delirious the greater part of the night, and in the morning was so alarmingly ill, suffering occasionally from delirium and successive fits of stupor, that her attendant having already decided that, without the timely interference of some medical proficient, she must inevitably perish, returned to apprize the Count of the nature of her surmises, and to entreat that he would procure for her all necessary assistance.

The Count, who had voluntarily deluded himself into the suggestion that Cecilia's malady was in no way dangerous, listened to this account with amazement and perplexity; and his desire of concealment yielding at length to his fears of losing her, he was about to dispatch an express to Cevenna, requiring the immediate presence of an eminent practitioner, when he was informed that in a village scarcely a league and a half from the chateau, dwelt a once celebrated physician, newly become resident in Languedoc; who, notwithstanding he had for some time relinquished the regular practice of his profession, never refused his assistance in cases of emergency.

The Count availed himself gladly of this very welcome intelligence. A servant was instantaneously commissioned to wait upon the *medecin* with a polite message from his Lord, which was no sooner delivered, than the good old man, for he was near seventy, with all that active benevolence for which he was so eminently distinguished, arose, and mounting his mule, followed his less eager guide through the various passes among the mountains, till he arrived at length, after about an hour's travelling, at the chateau. He was met in the hall by one of the principal domestics, who having received due orders for his admittance, ushered him into a saloon, where the Count usually sat, and where he had been for some time impatiently awaiting the return of his emissary.

As soon as they were alone, and the Count had exhausted every term which the most fervent gratitude for this attention, and the most high-wrought courtesy could suggest—anxious to do away every appearance of mystery relative to Cecilia, he proceeded to inform his new guest (having previously fabricated a tale for his purpose), that the invalid was a young lady of character and consequence, consigned to his guardianship by an uncle, who, dying suddenly in Italy, had left her to his friendship and protection. On the demise of this her relative, he had placed her, he said, in a Convent, where it was his intention to have detained her during the first few years of her minority;—but having escaped by night from two or three of these seminaries, in consequence of a mean and disgraceful connection, he had been necessitated to take her under his more immediate inspection. Baffled, however, in every attempt he had used to keep her within bounds, he was finally obliged to confine her in that chateau; having no other intention in so doing, than to prevent an unsuitable and disgraceful marriage! The horror excited by her present transient confinement, and the despair she felt at being thus unexpectedly separated from her delectable admirer, had, he added, he believed conspired with the extreme delicacy of her constitution, to bring on the malady under which she now languished. He wished, therefore, that he (the physician) would use his utmost endeavours to compose and quiet her mind, cautioning him at the same time against giving credit to any thing Cecilia might say, whom he represented as equally artful and indiscreet.—Here he stopped speaking; and the physician having promised a due attention to these rules, and the Count conjured him again and again to have recourse to all possible means in his power to hasten her recovery, he gave orders that he should be conducted to her chamber.

She was sitting up in bed when he was introduced, supported on one side by Agnes, and on the other by Berthe. Her fever ran high, for she was sometimes laughing, and sometimes talking incoherently. She did not notice his approach till he had reached the side of the bed, when she suddenly drew back, screamed, and then seizing the arm of her attendant, attempted to hide herself.

It was evident from her motions, and the alarm they expressed, that she had mistaken him for the Count, but after a short interval of silence, during which she sighed deeply, and seemed to respire with difficulty, she raised her head from the pillow, and looked very earnestly at him. In a few minutes a gleam of imperfect recollection seemed to light upon her mind, for she smiled sweetly, and holding out her hand, said—

"You are come at last then; but why were you detained? Why

did you not come sooner?—Did they not tell you I was here, that the bloodhounds had pursued and overtaken me, and that the monster was about to kill me? Oh, no, they forgot—they could not tell you; you would have hastened—you would have flown to rescue me!—But why are you so pale? You were not wont to look so:—ah! I remember now," (pausing, and gazing mournfully in his face), "you died, and was buried: I followed you to the grave myself! But how did you get out again?—It was cold and deep, and they told me you would soon be dust.—Poor soul! it was winter too;—the winds blew bleak and chill, and the rain pelted hard upon thee, and thou hadst nothing but a sod to cover thee with. —It was right to get away, for there will be no spring nor summer now. The flowers are beat down by the storm, and there is no sun to revive them. I see what you would say:—ah! those were happy days!—but they are all withered away now, save one poor willow-branch! I wonder he did not take it with him; he might have worn it for my sake,—for he loved, and would have cherished me like one of those poor pretty flowers we used to tend.—But there are tyrants over him also.—Ah! you may well weep; it was a grievous sight! He pitied me, and wept too! His tears fell upon this hand —see, it is wet with them even yet, for they were precious drops, and I loved him too well to wipe them off.—But what do we wait for? Come, come, it grows late; the moon will be down, and there are no stars to guide us.—But how are we to pass the gates? Have a care—we must be swift as lightning, and secret as the dull cold grave you came from, or they will detect and overtake us!—Mind too that you have a dagger ready:—the tyrant wears one, and if we do not instantly escape him, he will murder us both. He has destroyed one already.—He thought I should not find it out; but there was blood spilt, and I traced it to the very chamber.—It was a sorry act——but quick—quick—or we shall be discovered!"

The physician gazed on her intently, but could not articulate a word, so absorbed was he in astonishment, perplexity, and admiration. She presented, indeed, a figure which could not be looked upon with indifference. Her fine auburn hair, escaped from the confinement of her cap, had fallen in glossy ringlets upon a neck scarcely to be excelled in whiteness by the robe with which it was only partially concealed. Her arms were whiter than either; and the glowing hectic of her cheek heightening the natural radiance of her eyes, till they had acquired a sort of wild and humid lustre, added at once to their expression and their beauty.

To check the progress of a disorder so appalling in its aspect, the good Doctor was sensible that his utmost skill and assiduity were no more than adequate. As the first step to this, it was requisite that she should lose some blood; but having been informed, on enquiry, that these fits of transitory derangement were always regularly succeeded by long intervals of stupor, he deemed it prudent that the operation should be deferred till her spirits had recovered some degree of composure. Ordering her, therefore, to be kept cool and very quiet, he returned to the room where he had left the Count, who, half-distracted with impatience, flew eagerly to meet him, and as eagerly demanded what he thought of his patient.

"Her situation is precarious in the extreme," replied he;—"the visible perturbation of her mind has produced every alarming symptom, and nothing but repose can present a chance of her recovery."

"Good God! then you really believe her life to be in danger!"

"In imminent danger!" rejoined the physician, while the expression of his countenance spoke the exquisite feelings of his heart; "a few days in all probability will terminate this unfortunate affair; for unless we can succeed in tranquilizing her mind, death, or what is still worse, a decided derangement, will be the consequence."

The horror of the Count's feelings as he listened to this report, was such as is scarcely to be conceived. He raved, stamped, swore, and having practiced every species of frenzy with the rapidity and wildness of a maniac, declared that she was infinitely dearer to him than his existence; that life without her would be no longer supportable; and that he would joyfully lay down his, if by so doing he could ensure the preservation of her's.

This conduct, had such a testimony been wanting, would have confirmed the *medecin* in his belief that the story which he had been attending to, was neither more nor less than an artful and very ingenious fabrication invented to mislead him. He had, however, discretion enough to forbear from any verbal remarks upon it; secretly resolving that if Cecilia, as he had every reason to suspect, had been trepanned into the Count's power, to strain every nerve to accomplish her deliverance. In pursuance of this plan, he determined to call a little policy to his aid; and the more easily to avail himself of the motives and designs of the Count, prepared to answer with assurance, and to make of him such enquiries as were best calculated to screen his intentions.

In the course of a few minutes the Count becoming gradually more composed, proposed visiting Cecilia in her chamber; but to his earnest and very urgent request that he might be permitted to see her, the *medecin* returned to an immediate and decisive negative, observing that unless certain positive injunctions were unconditionally acceded to, his prescriptions would be unavailing, and his attendance unnecessary.

The Count demanded what these injunctions were, protesting at the same time his willingness to comply with any terms he might propose, at all likely to promote the restoration of his patient.

"In the first place then, my Lord, it is expedient for the young lady's health, that she be instantly removed from a place where every object seems to awaken painful recollections.—My house, which is at only a short distance from this chateau, will afford her every requisite accommodation during her confinement. Here, though you cannot see, you will have frequent opportunities of hearing of her, and here she may be safely, and even easily conveyed. On your acquiescence with this plan, if you have a sufficient reliance on my skill to confide her to my care, my utmost efforts for her recovery shall not be wanting; but if, on the contrary, you reject the only conditions on which that recovery can be effected, since my further continuance here will only subject me to the mortification of witnessing griefs I cannot assuage, and pangs which you have forbid me to alleviate, I must positively take my leave."

"Great Heaven!" exclaimed the Count, starting from his seat, and pacing about the saloon with an anxious and disturbed air, "how am I to decide in this distracting situation?"

"There is but one way, my Lord; if you love her—if you would preserve her life——"

"If I love her!" repeated the Count, "if I love her!" throwing himself upon a chair.

"If you love her," pursued the physician, "you will not purchase a mere trifling gratification at the price of a whole life of despair—you will subscribe, in short, to the conditions I have proposed!"

"Never!" exclaimed the Count fiercely, "unless——"

"Then, my Lord, I have only to lament that the life of a very charming, and apparently a very amiable young creature must be sacrificed to an obstinacy you would fain, I perceive, dignify with the name of affection."

"You have interrupted me," continued the Count, less angrily; "I meant to add that, on my compliance with your terms, it is necessary for my own satisfaction that I should exact others, to which I shall of course expect you to concede unequivocally."

The physician bowed; and it was at length agreed, though not without much tedious hesitation and obvious reluctance on the part of the Count, that Cecilia should be conveyed to his chateau. Agnes was to accompany her; and the physician to receive, should the affair terminate to their wishes, a considerable sum on her return as the price of her restoration.

There, placed under the care of a skilful duenna (for as such the Count considered Agnes), he had not a doubt as to her safety; whilst the very ample reward with which he had bribed, as he imagined, the physician to his interests, from the persuasion that there was not a man in existence weak or mad enough to forego a certain advantage for the sake of indulging himself in an act of romantic generosity, left him perfectly at ease as to his future proceedings.—This assurance, and the unsuspicious avidity with which his now wary guest seemed to enter into his wishes and designs, dissipated every fear which Cecilia's departure had suggested;—resigning him, however, to the more acute apprehension that Death—that tyrant whom no gold can bribe, no prayers pierce, and no entreaties soften, might eventually deprive him of his prey, and render every precaution for her preservation vague and ineffectual.

The remainder of the day passed on in silence, and Cecilia's malady seemed every moment augmenting.—She raved and talked incessantly; sometimes calling upon Varàno, sometimes upon De Sevignac, and sometimes upon Boraccio. In the evening her delirium began to abate, though slowly;—the operation of bleeding was performed, and she fell into a state of stupor, which held her, without any intermission, for near an hour, leaving her apparently bereft both of sense and motion.—When she recovered, she looked around; and seeing the physician, made a signal that he should approach. As he advanced, she shook her head significantly, and then pushing up her sleeve, so as to expose her arm, and the fillet which bound it, said—"I did not think you would have used me thus cruelly. I thought you was come to take me home again, and that I might love, and hope, and confide in you, as I was wont to do when I was your poor, dear, prattling little Cecilia! But I have found you out at last. You are a traitor! —But no matter—the world is full of them."

She stopped a few moments.

"Why do you deliberate?—Men that make a trade of blood, should be resolved. Fear in such as you is but a baby feeling. Come, come, dispatch—'tis time to be in motion—the monster will grow impatient! Mind, though, that you have a covering ready, and that you have no blood about you!—Have a care, too, that my grave be made secretly—bury me deep enough; for if he should find it out—if he should once hear that I have been murdered—and by you, though he will not move a step to protect me living, he will rouse Heaven and earth to revenge me dead!

"Poor creature," added she sorrowfully, again pausing, and looking piteously upon him, "you are irresolute: you have been compelled then, and would not, but that you must commit a deed you shudder at! A ruffian's talk should have a ruffian's heart, and your's is tender. Well then I'll help you—bring me a dagger. —Why should you fear to strike? I'll neither cry nor struggle;—a shallow wound will do, and when it's done, the wretch will have his will, and you your bribe.—Come, be not so tardy—the night will wear away, and day has tell-tale eyes.—It were best it were done quickly!"

She continued to ramble in this manner for several minutes, when, as if overcome by the violence of her exertions, she threw herself back, and fell into a profound sleep. The physician, judging this to be the crisis of her disorder, dismissed her attendants from the room, and watched by her himself during the remainder of the night.—She continued in this sleep till the following morning, when she awoke tranquil and composed, her reason perfectly restored, and already in a state of convalescence.—But who can portray her astonishment, her gratitude, and her joy, when the first object which she encountered on opening her eyes, was the benevolent physician, in whose features she almost immediately recognized those of M. Langlois, the well-known friend of De Sevignac!

Her sensations, on finding a friend to solace her, may be imagined, but cannot be described. M. Langlois was scarcely less affected. In vain she plied him with enquiries:—he could answer none; he could only bend over her like a father over a fondly beloved child!

As soon as she was recovered from her surprise, though her exhausted state would scarce admit of her speaking, she felt the necessity of accounting to him for the singularity of her situation, and would have entered upon the detail; but M. Langlois, being now sufficiently assured of the truth and justness of his surmises, requested that the communication might be deferred till she was enabled to afford it without further injury to her health. He then briefly recounted the particulars of the discourse lately held between him and the Count; the insidious tale which the latter had recited, and the resolution that he had taken, in consequence of a succeeding conversation, that she should be conveyed to his chateau; the distance of which, he added would be no impediment whatever to her speedy removal, and where she would be secured for the present from the addresses of the Count.

Cecilia was delighted with this arrangement, and with the fresh assurances of her friend, who informed her that he had already been concerting a plan for her enlargement, which he doubted not would be easily and happily accomplished.

"We have only one thing," added he, "to apprehend. The Count is obstinately determined that you shall not go hence unless your principal attendant may be allowed to accompany you; and as he seems naturally suspicious, and is probably tolerably acute in discovering the motives and designs of others, any attempt to thwart him in an affair on which he seems to have decided so confidently, would be impolitic and even dangerous."

Cecilia acquiesced in this remark; but observed that if the imposed attendance of Agnes was the only probable bar to their project, she could be answerable for its success; since she was already in her interest, and was prevented only by severe necessity from aiding her escape.—M. Langlois was reassured by this intelligence; and having requested that she would desist as much as possible from all such exertion, as in the present weak state of her frame might have a tendency to injure her health, and retard her recovery, he withdrew to recal her attendants to the room, and to give all necessary orders for her removal, which he had every reason to believe might take place on the following day.

Before night all was ordered within the chateau to favour the departure of Cecilia, and in the morning she was conveyed, wrapped up in blankets, and accompanied by Agnes, to the Chateau de Langlois, where her newly recruited spirits supporting her through the fatigue of a short but harassing journey, she arrived without having suffered much visible inconvenience.

The Chateau de Langlois was a neat and elegant mansion, situated at the extremity of a village, encircled on one side by woods, and on the other by a range of lofty mountains.—Above these and at some distance arose others, still more majestic, and almost equally regular, forming in the whole a spacious and magnificent amphitheatre.—The area it enclosed was rather beautiful than extensive. It was divided into groves, pastures, and meadow-land, intermingled with vineyards of grape and olive.—A branch of the Loire, which, after forming a variety of *jets d'eau*, as it fell with clear, pauseless melody from the rock above, wound through the various recesses of wood and shade, giving fertility to the soil, and beauty to the landscape.

The chateau was preceded by a lawn, on either side of which, separated by thick hedges of myrtle and pomegranate trees, were gardens filled with fruit, and blooming with *parterres*.—The grounds were disposed with taste; and the whole constituted a retirement at once romantic and picturesque. It had been bequeathed by will to M. Langlois by a distant relation; and on the news of his decease, he had removed immediately thither:

having previously declined the practice of a profession which, though habit had endeared, age had long since rendered irksome to him. Here it was his intention to remain resident till the commencement of the winter, and then to return to Vence; for so great was his partiality to his own native province, that no advantages whatever could have induced him to abandon it.

Madame Langlois, his sister, and only relative, presided in his absence at his chateau in Provence. She was an amiable and sensible woman; and though her character and manners were somewhat tinctured with caprice, the mildness of her disposition, and the goodness of her heart had extremely endeared her to M. Langlois; and the impatience which she expressed for his return in her frequent and very affectionate epistles, had almost tempted him to relinquish his plan of continuance.

To the same estimable qualities of heart and mind by which Madame was distinguished, M. Langlois united an understanding at once solid and penetrating.—Unpractised in the frivolities of fashionable intercourse, he was a stranger to every species of insincerity; he lived but to do good, and felt in an eminent degree that supreme felicity which the practice of virtue will always regularly ensure to us.—In conversation he was generally lively, and sometimes humorous; but his mirth, like his discourse, was always temperate and unassuming, never degenerating into buffoonery, or rising into satire. But a kind and amiable attention to the wants and feelings of others was his most striking characteristic; and never did this appear more conspicuous than in his behaviour to Cecilia, who, ill as she was, could not refrain from the expression of her astonishment when, on entering the house, she found every thing in readiness for her reception; M. Langlois having dispatched a courier from the chateau to apprize his domestics of her arrival, and to desire that an apartment might be immediately prepared for her.—To this she was accordingly conveyed; and, the hurry of her spirits subsided, soon began to give tokens of amendment. M. Langlois seldom quitted her room; and the next day, Cecilia being able to sit up and to converse, he imparted to her, at her earnest request, the scheme which he had devised. This was to send her, as soon as possible, under the protection of Homfroi, an old and faithful domestic, to the Chateau

de St. Foix, to which place, as it was his intention to depart shortly
from Languedoc, he was to follow her, and himself escort her
to his other residence at Vence. Meanwhile, he added, the more
effectually to free her from the artful manœuvres of her pursuer,
he should spread the report of her death—a report which would
the more easily gain credit, as he had assured the Count on their
departure that, though her fever was abated, the extreme debility
it had left would, in all probability, occasion a relapse, in which
case there was little or no hope but the termination would be
fatal.

"The only reluctance I feel to this measure," continued M.
Langlois, smiling, "arises from the necessity which it imposes of
propagating and supporting a falsehood which nothing but the
peculiar exigencies of the case can excuse. The circumstances
under which I report it will, however, justify me to myself; and
since the opinion which the world may form of me, should the
imposition be detected, is only a secondary consideration, I shall
have little to apprehend from the malevolence of those, who,
deciding from false premises, or through the medium of popular
misrepresentation, may be inclined to condemn me."

Cecilia received this fresh testimony of M. Langlois's attention
to her future as well as present prospects with the gratitude it
merited; and having assured him of her unlimited approbation
of his intended plan of proceeding, she hastened to unfold the
above scheme to Agnes, omitting only the name of the person
selected for her escort, and that of the place destined to be her
asylum.

The woman readily promised every thing; demanding only
that, if the fraud should be discovered, M. Langlois would defend
her from the resentment of the Count, whose power she dreaded,
and whose indignation she trembled to excite.—M. Langlois
acceded willingly to her requisition, and it was agreed, after some
previous conversation, that Cecilia should escape from thence
in the habit of a peasant girl: M. Langlois having suggested this
method as the only one likely to secure her from the effects of an
idle and impertinent curiosity.

In the space of a few days, in the interim of which the Count
had been several times at the chateau, departing each time in a

state of mingled hope and apprehension, though without seeing Cecilia, she gained strength so rapidly, that the intended route was marked out, and a day fixed for her journey.

The appointed—the long wished-for time at length arrived. About an hour before daybreak Homfroi came with a carriage to the gate; and Cecilia having hastily attired herself in her simple but becoming habiliments, her luxuriant tresses bound up, and covered with a large straw hat, in the manner of the country, prepared to depart.

M. Langlois embraced her tenderly on parting; and as he lifted her into the carriage, pronounced a blessing upon her with so much warmth and earnestness, that her eyes insensibly became filled with tears.—She pressed his hand in speechless gratitude as she bade him adieu; while her swelling heart mentally ejaculated the sincerest thanks to Heaven for the wonderful interference of its protecting providence.

Her look—her gestures conveyed more to the heart of M. Langlois than the most eloquent expressions could have done without them. He turned away to conceal, if he could, the fine emotions of his soul; and in a few minutes the carriage drove off, and was soon out of sight.

CHAPTER IV

Care selve beate!
E voi solinghi e taciturni orrori
Di riposo e di pace alberghi veri!
O quanto volontieri
A rivedervi io torno!

GUARINI.

Ye woods beloved! Ye sacred glades!
Ye silent, solitary shades!
The true abodes of peace and rest,
Again I see you, and again am blest.

THE travellers proceeded cautiously along the mountains, and meeting with no adventure on the road, reached the town of

Lodeve, where Cecilia having exchanged her peasant's dress for that which she had formerly worn, they renewed their course to Montpelier. Having passed Lodeve, leaving Nismes to the left, they gained the banks of the Rhone, and crossing the river, arrived at length, after several days' journey, in Provence.

That rich, that fertile, that enchanting country now burst at once upon their view; and never was a lovely prospect so delightful to the enamoured eye of the enthusiast, as the towers and buildings of Marseilles to the now exhausted Cecilia.—They were not long in reaching it. Her guide conducted her to an hotel; and on the ensuing day they commenced their journey to St Foix.

Hitherto Cecilia's thoughts had been so entirely engrossed by the subject of her escape, as to preclude every other reflection: and it was not till they were within a few stages of the chateau, that she recollected the possibility that it might be sold, or otherwise disposed of, or, as was still more probable, that the former domestics were discharged, and others placed in their stead. Nothing, indeed, had transpired during her residence at Genoa to favour this opinion; and the continual hurry of dissipation in which the Signora lived, and her great apparent inattention to pecuniary concerns, afforded her every reason to hope that no such arrangement had as yet taken place. The apprehension, however, faint as it was, was sufficient to harass her mind; and the pleasure which she experienced from the sight of objects so long known, and so tenderly endeared to her, was almost immediately superseded by the most cruel anxiety.

Homfroi was civil, and uniformly talkative; and he frequently stopped to point out to her some particular features of the scene, which had irresistibly attracted his notice.—Cecilia was sometimes pleased with his remarks, and sometimes wearied by them; but as they approached toward the neighbourhood of St. Foix, her mind became too much occupied by melancholy rumination, to permit her to attend to the conversation of her guard, so that they soon travelled on in profound silence.

The night was far advanced, when the road winding round the edge of a mountain, they came within sight of the chateau, which was shewn to them in the deep perspective of the valley by a gleam of moonlight, and then vanished into shade.—As they approached, the moon arose higher in the horizon, shedding an undulating gleam upon the woods; and every part of the fabric soon became visible.

Cecilia felt her heart sink within her as her eye reposed on the turrets of this well-known mansion. The fields which surrounded it, the groves, the gardens, the distant mountains, all brought with them a thousand interesting recollections of her hours of youthful felicity; and these objects of her former enthusiastic admiration now excited only sorrow and regret.

Whey they had arrived at the gate of the chateau, they alighted from the carriage, and traversing the lawn, proceeded to the principal entrance. But expectation was succeeded by despair the moment they reached it. No light was seen from the windows. They knocked; but no passing foot answered to the summons. A silence deep and universal reigned throughout the building; and from the general symptoms of neglect which pervaded every part of it, it had no longer the appearance of an inhabited mansion.

"Holy Virgin protect us!" exclaimed Cecilia, in whose bosom every ray of hope was refracted by this unlooked-for disappointment. "Where can we go?—and what are we now to do? Alas! I am too much exhausted to proceed further to-night!"

"Be patient, lady," returned her companion; "by the blessing of St. Benoit, we are not so badly off as we might have been. I have a purse of good Louis d'ors in my pocket, which, I doubt not, will ensure us some very tolerable accommodations in the next village."

Cecilia proposed that they should first endeavour again admittance on the contrary side of the edifice; observing that if the chateau, as was very likely, was committed to the care of one or two domestics, they would in all probability occupy that part of the building which had formerly been appropriated to the use of the servants.

Thither they accordingly repaired; but Homfroi having rapped several times with the end of his stick upon the door, accompanying every stroke with a loud halloo and a fresh survey of the building, they were compelled to relinquish all hopes of success, and were returning despondingly to the carriage, when, to their mutual astonishment, a light was seen gleaming through the shutter of one of the upper apartments; and in a few minutes the door was slowly unclosed, and a female, holding a candle in her hand, her figure half concealed by the door she yet cautiously held, tremulously demanded who came there.

"Oh, Oh," exclaimed Homfroi, "so you are come out at last then; I thought verily you had every soul of you been dead. Here have we been knocking and hallooing for this last half hour, and not a man of you would stir to let us in. A little longer, and we should have been off again, and a fine wearisome journey we should have had on't; for the poor beasts are as jaded as we are, and have hardly a foot to set to the ground."

"I know nothing of either you or your beasts," returned the woman. "Who are you?—and what is your business here?"

"Oh, as to my business here," answered he, "I can soon explain that. I have brought you a young lady."

"A young lady!" repeated two voices at once, (for a man was now added to the party)—"a young lady!"

"A young lady," continued Homfroi; "whom you are to admit and treat kindly till the arrival of my master, who will amply reward you for any trouble she may occasion you."

"And pray who is your master?" enquired the peasant, who now came forward.

"The best man in the whole country," answered Homfroi, "let the other be who he will.—He has a better heart and more noble blood in his veins than half the Lords in the province; and will go farther, St. Benoit befriend him, to do a good Christian action, than many of the proudest of them will commit a bad one."

"Has he no name?" demanded the other.

"Yes, and one he has no reason to be ashamed of:—his name is Langlois."

"Langlois!" repeated the peasant; "Langlois! I think I have heard that name."

"Mayhap you may; but we have no time for parleying, so be so kind as to let us in, and shew me to some good stabling for my mules; for if they have not a fresh feed of oats, and some good clean straw to lie on, all the whips and spurs in the country won't get them on to-morrow."

Cecilia, whom anxiety and mortification had hitherto kept silent, now advanced; and having explained in a few words who she was, and what were the real circumstances of her situation, she enquired if they were the only people then resident at the chateau, and if so, to what place Ursula, Louisette, and the remaining part of the establishment were removed.

"Ursula and Louisette," replied the woman mildly, "are both gone; but if you are indeed the young lady that used to live at this chateau, I am willing to afford you an asylum in it for the present, and to acquaint you, on your permission, with what has happened since you left it."

Cecilia expressed her gratitude for this offer, and immediately entered; while the man, who was more pleased than offended with the blunt manners of Homfroi, accompanied him across the lawn to the place where the carriage was situated, where he readily contributed his assistance in the care of the mules.

Those only who have been separated, like Cecilia, from a fondly beloved home, and have returned to it under circumstances equally afflictive, can form an adequate idea of her sensations as she entered this once cheerful abode. How melancholy—how silent—how solitary did every thing appear! Not an object on which her eye reposed, but what led immediately to the subject of her grief, and recalled, Oh, how affectingly! to her memory that happy period of her life when she had friends to receive, to love, and to cherish her.

She was conducted through a passage to a room adjoining the kitchen, formerly the servants' hall, where Susanne, for so she was called, usually sat, and where the animating beams of a cheerful fire served to dispel in some measure that gloom which time and neglect had given to its now altered aspect.

She took a seat by the fire, and Susanne having placed herself by her side, and made such observations and enquiries as her curiosity suggested, she said—

"You have been informed, Madam, without doubt, that this chateau, and the large estate surrounding it, have become the property of a Nobleman of some consequence in Italy, who, though he has no intention whatever of retiring to it himself, has ordered it to be repaired, with a view, as it appears, of either letting or selling it, according as he shall hereafter determine; though if his Honour, M. de Sevignac, God rest his soul! had a single thought of its being sold, he would, in all probability, have bequeathed it elsewhere."

Cecilia enquired by what means she had obtained a knowledge of the Signor's intentions, and whether any person had been deputed by him to visit the estate.

"About a month after the death of Monsieur," continued Susanne, "my Lord's steward, attended by two others of his suite, arrived at the chateau for the purpose of examining what repairs might be requisite, and to discharge the servants, all of whom except Ursula were immediately dismissed.—As his Honour, M. de Sevignac, had assured them on his departure that, providing his illness should prove fatal, he would leave a token of his regard to all such of his domestics as had served him faithfully till death, they were all greatly disappointed at not receiving a legacy. The steward, however, by the express desire of his Lord, presented each with a small sum, with which, though it was in no degree proportioned to what they had been authorized to expect, they retired tolerably well satisfied.—From that time till about three weeks ago, Ursula remained alone at the chateau; but being old and infirm, and the house very lonely and remote, she left it to reside with a relation of her's at Vence, and engaged Vincent and myself to live here in her stead."

"And Louisette?"

"Louisette procured a service somewhere in the neighbourhood; but on the death of Beatrix, her mother, she left the family she was with, and repaired to Le Luc."

"Is Beatrix then dead?" interrupted Cecilia; "Good Heavens! when and where did she die?"

"She died suddenly at her cottage after a few hours' illness; and Basile being inconsolable for her loss, sent immediately for Louisette, who has continued with him ever since."

Cecilia thanked her hostess for her intelligence, and then demanded whether the Signor, his steward, or any other part of the family were expected shortly at the chateau. Susanne replied, she believed not at present; but as they had forborne to give any orders whatever concerning the repairs, there was every reason to suppose that some of them would return to it before the commencement of winter.

The entrance of Homfroi and the peasant put an end to this discourse; and Susanne having prepared a little repast for her exhausted guest, who willingly partook of this welcome refreshment, conducted her to her chamber.—A train of melancholy reflections occupied her mind, till weariness overcame her, and she fell asleep.

In the morning she enquired of Susanne whether Father Pierre was still living, and if he ever visited the chateau.

"The remains of the good Father Pierre," returned Susanne, "were interred about a week since in the *cimetiere* of his Convent. He had been going off some time; but till within the few last days of his illness, he was able to creep about, and used frequently to come here, and walk upon the terrace.—The news of Monsieur's death went very hard with the poor Monk. He mourned deeply for his loss, and would often sit for hours and hours, as old Ursula told me, talking about him and you, and enquiring whether she had heard from you, and if you was likely to return to St. Foix, or to continue in Italy. The last time he was here he looked very sadly, and wandered about the house as if he was greatly disturbed in his mind;—the day following I was told that he was ill, and the next account I had, was that he was dead and buried."

Cecilia was so affected by this account of Father Pierre, as to be totally unable to continue the conversation; and she abruptly quitted the room. About noon she took her leave of Homfroi, by whom she dispatched a letter to M. Langlois, acquainting him with her safe arrival at the chateau, and the kind reception which she had met with from its now hospitable inhabitants.—As soon as he was departed, she wrote also to her friend the Signora di Rosalvo a brief but circumstantial account of the several events which had befallen her since she left Genoa. The humane attentions of this lady, and the solicitude which, short as had been their acquaintance, she had always testified in her behalf, were yet strongly engraven on her memory; and she resolved, should she repeat the very pressing invitation which she had formerly given her, to embrace the present opportunity, the only one that might ever occur, to pay her long expected visit at the Castello di Montani.

In the evening, though extremely languid and indisposed from her late illness and exertion, she was able to take a walk with Susanne about the environs of the chateau; and the next day was enough recovered, and had regained a sufficient degree of tranquillity to enable her to peruse the packet consigned to her by her mother, and delivered by Boraccio, which a number of occurrences, as extraordinary as they were unforeseen, had hitherto prevented her from examining; and which with the MS that she had discovered in the chamber of the chateau which she had been so providentially delivered from, had been carefully conveyed with her from Languedoc.—Many and arduous were her struggles ere she could resolve to unclose it; till curiosity triumphing over disinclination and mournful presentiment, she prepared to enter upon her task.

It was composed of several sheets; some written by her mother previous to the demise of her husband, and the remainder by Madame de Villeneuve.—Those by the latter contained the whole of the intelligence conveyed by Verezio on his last visit to St. Foix, and formed the sequel to the melancholy story before recited.

From the perusal of the first page of this MS, Cecilia learned, to her astonishment, that the name of St. Bertrand, by which she had hitherto been called, and the only one she had ever known, was given to her by Blanche de Coucy in consequence of her having been consigned to her care near a town of that name in the province of Gascony, and that her real one was D'Arnaud, being the daughter of a Chevalier of that name, the particulars of whose story we are now about to recount.

As the voluminous contents of this packet, if recited at large, would not only extend our narrative considerably beyond the bounds prescribed, but would be defective moreover as to some of the principal incidents of the story, we shall arrange them in the order in which they occurred, and recapitulate the substance of what was inserted, as briefly as possible.

CHAPTER V

Why should the lover quit his pleasing home,
  In search of dangers on some foreign ground;
Far from his weeping fair ungrateful roam,
  And risk in every stroke a double wound.

HAMMOND.

JULIEN D'ARNAUD was descended from a genteel but not opulent family in the province of Auvergne. His father, whose only surviving son he was, was a man not more eminently distinguished for his loyalty to his Sovereign, than for the superiority of his intellectual endowments, and great personal bravery. He had entered, when very young, into the service of his country; and having acquitted himself in several campaigns with the utmost courage and success, was raised, through the interest of the Prince of Condé, under whose banner he fought, to a post of some eminence in the army. But the laurels which he had gained in his wars with Spain were doomed to wither in a succeeding enterprise.—His attachment to Stanislaus, who had been raised to the throne by the victorious arms of Charles XII. of Sweden, formed at once his glory and his ruin.

After the death of Augustus, King of Poland, and Elector of Saxony, the free-minded Poles, endeavouring to liberate themselves from the shackles of despotism imposed by the Nobles, recalled Stanislaus, whose daughter had lately been united to the young King Louis XV. to that throne from which he had already descended with true Roman magnanimity. But his election was opposed by the Emperor of Germany and the Ruffians, who, under the invigorating influence of Peter the Great, had buried their primitive obscurity, and having broken the power of the Swedes, sought to give laws and discipline to the neighbouring States.—The successor of Augustus having entered into a confederacy with the Emperor and the Russians to support the nomination of the late King to the Crown of Poland, war in the year 1733 was rekindled throughout Europe and Poland, and the unhappy scene of contention was deluged with the blood of the contending parties.—Louis warmly espoused the cause of his father-in-law; but his forces were overpowered by numbers, and the unfortunate Stanislaus, besieged in Dantzick, was compelled to escape in disguise from the battered walls of that city, and to take refuge in France.

He was accompanied in this expedition by the Chevalier D'Arnaud, and a few of the most faithful of his followers, who, having sustained a series of hardships and fatigues, scarcely to be paralleled in the records of history, arrived with him at Versailles, where the young King was impatiently awaiting the success of the enterprise.—D'Arnaud scarce survived his return. A wound which he had received in an engagement, previous to the succour afforded them by Cardinal Fleury, though not expected to prove mortal at the time it was inflicted, put a final period to a life ever cheerfully devoted to the service of his country.—He expired in the arms of him in whose behalf he had contended with unabating ardour, solemnly conjuring his son, then only fifteen years old, never to abandon the cause in which his father had bled.

The successes of Ann of Russia, in conjunction with those of the Emperor Charles, who as eagerly espoused the cause, soon placed Augustus III. in the long disputed possession of the kingdom of Poland. The distance of the former was a complete security against the resentment of the French; but the less remote dominions of the Emperor were not equally unassailable: and France, once more resuming her arms, prepared to revenge the outrage which had dispossessed Stanislaus of Poland.

The young Chevalier D'Arnaud, who had been trained to every military exploit beneath the eye of his father, and who, in consideration of his services, had been raised, though scarcely sixteen years of age, above the rank of a subaltern, now commenced his career of martial glory.—He hastened to join the confederate armies on the banks of the Elbe; and having signalized himself by a valour approaching to rashness in a short but very desperate engagement, was on the eve of gaining a rapid and complete victory, when the army of the enemy being unexpectedly reinforced by an ambuscade of the Imperial troops, the attack was resumed, and being continued for near three hours with the utmost courage and intrepidity, success seemed to be declaring for the Emperor.

D'Arnaud defended himself bravely throughout the whole of the contest. But the violence of the assault had so weakened those already harassed by the toils and dangers of the field, that they were obliged to surrender; and D'Arnaud and his party, after having been immured for some weeks in one of the enemy's forts, were conveyed prisoners to Vienna.—There compelled to remain without any prospect of enlargement, suffering alternately from the pining miseries of want, and the insulting taunts of the foe, they lingered out a wretched existence for the space of six months; when an emissary being dispatched by the King to the Court of Vienna, to negotiate with the Emperor for an exchange of prisoners, their emancipation was effected; and the transported captives, thus happily and unexpectedly restored to their freedom and their friends, returned triumphantly to Paris. —D'Arnaud continued there a few days only, and then hastened to Versailles, to express his gratitude for this deliverance at the feet of his Sovereign, who dismissed him with many marks of his esteem. He then proceeded to Bourdeaux, where his regiment was ordered, and where it was expected to be quartered during the whole of the ensuing winter.

The fame of his father's exploits, his recent and very hazardous engagement on the banks of the Elbe, and the hardships which he had encountered in his subsequent imprisonment, obtained him an immediate introduction to many families of the first rank in that province. Among these was the Chevalier D'Aubigne, a man of parts, and a soldier, whose family consisted of one son, then absent on his travels; a daughter, at that time very young; and Donna Leonora, his niece, the daughter and heiress of Don Pedro de Velasquez, who having formerly been united to the Chevalier's sister, had sent her, on the demise of her mother, on a visit to her uncle at Bourdeaux.

To a disposition remarkable for its sweetness, an understanding the most correct, and a figure the most graceful, Leonora united all the allurements of beauty, and all the accomplishments of her sex.—Her complexion was the most lovely that can be conceived:—her eyes either sparkled with animation, or languished with sensibility beneath their long and silken lashes; her voice spoke to the heart; and the mild expression of her countenance, the elegance of her conversation, and the polished ease of her manners ensured her the admiration of all who saw her.

Such an assemblage of charms could not long be overlooked. A number of opulent admirers contended for her hand; and the Chevalier D'Arnaud, who had obtained repeated opportunities of seeing and conversing with her, through the medium of her uncle, soon confessed himself her slave, and received from the lips of his too beautiful mistress the most unequivocal assurances that this affection was reciprocal.

The attachment of these lovers soon became too obvious to escape the notice of D'Aubigne; and, apprehensive of the indignation of Don Pedro, should he allow it to continue without his consent and approbation, he wrote immediately to Toledo, the present residence of his brother-in-law, to inform him of his suspicions, and to solicit permission to bestow his niece upon D'Arnaud, who, though greatly inferior to her in point of fortune and expectations, he represented as in every other respect worthy of Donna Leonora.

Don Pedro having predetermined to ally his daughter on her return to Don Manuel de Roderigo, an old Spanish Grandee, who had recently made overtures, no sooner received intimation of her partiality to a young soldier, with no wealth but his commission, no dependence but his sword, than he departed for Bourdeaux, in order to separate her effectually from the object of her choice, and to unite her to the man whom he had thus arbitrarily selected for her, and whom he commanded her, on his arrival, to consider for the future as her husband.

In vain were all the tears, all the incitements of his daughter to win him from his purpose.—In vain she represented to him the disparity in their years, and the inhumanity of sacrificing her to a man whom she despised, whose person and manners were alike displeasing to her, and with whom it was impossible that she could be otherwise than wretched.—Her tears, her importunities only exasperated him the more; the most violent and dreadful imprecations issued from his lips. He swore he would never see her but as the wife of his friend; and conveyed her with him from Bourdeaux with the avowed resolution of espousing her to Don Manuel, though not till she had obtained a private interview with D'Arnaud, with whom, after having given him every possible assurance which love and tenderness could demand from her, she concerted a plan for a correspondence, which, with the assistance of a friend, then resident in Guienne, was to be established between them.

Consoled by this measure, and by the hopes which it afforded him of sometimes hearing from Leonora, D'Arnaud appeared tranquil and reassured. But no sooner was she departed, than, fearful of what might be the event of such a conduct, should Don Manuel be dismissed, and not less so lest the menaces and incitements of her father should eventually precipitate her into a marriage with his antiquated rival, he formed a fluctuating resolution of following her into Spain; and was about to make an application to his Colonel for permission, when his project was put an end to by an unforeseen occurrence.

Charles Emanuel, King of Sardinia, the successor of Victor Amadeus who had resigned the throne to his son, having concurred in the views of Versailles and Madrid, the confederate armies had begun already to pour their troops into Italy, and on the borders of the Rhine. D'Arnaud's regiment, therefore, instead of being stationed at Bourdeaux, was ordered to Strasburg; from whence it was conjectured it was to proceed immediately into Germany, and from thence into Italy.

Previous to the commencement of this route, D'Arnaud wrote to Leonora, in answer to which she informed him that, owing to the cruel treatment of her father, and the persecutions of Don Manuel, she had been necessitated to quit Toledo by night, attended only by her maid, and to fly for protection to Donna Almeria, her aunt, the Abbess of a Convent of Dominican Sisters in the vicinity of Madrid. Don Pedro, she added, had traced and pursued her to her sanctuary; and, after loading her with menaces and reproaches, had threatened her with the heaviest maledictions on her rejection of Don Manuel: but having been swayed from the immediate prosecution of his purpose by the repeated expostulations and friendly admonitions of the Abbess, he had agreed to her continuing there a year; at the expiration of which time, she was either to consent to this marriage he was yet resolutely determined upon, or to be admitted into the institution of which she was then a member.

D'Arnaud's reply was calculated to dispel every uneasy reflection which the situation of the now persecuted Leonora could in any way authorize. He assured her that peace, owing to the successes of France on the borders of the Rhine, would be speedily concluded; that Rhiel, Trierbach, and Phillipsburg were already reduced; and that the Emperor, bending beneath the storm, was ready to accede to any conditions they might exact. This settled, he should repair, he said, instantly to Madrid, where, presuming on the promise which she had given him on parting, he would lay his laurels at her feet, and claim, as the reward of his exertions, the hand of his Leonora.

The æra which he had so ardently anticipated, at length arrived.—A cessation of hostilities commenced, and peace was shortly proclaimed throughout Europe.—D'Arnaud, thus released, as he imagined, from every military engagement, returned to Versailles; and having been presented by his Sovereign with the Cross of the Order of St. Louis, as a recompence for his services in several successive contentions, now resolved to bend his course toward Spain; impatient to rescue his beloved mistress from the tyrannic power of her father, and to confirm her his by the nearest and most tender of all ties.—But a new and still severer disappointment awaited his hopes. Don Carlos, second son of the King of Spain, having attained to the government of Naples and Sicily, (which was ceded in the late treaty from the house of Austria), the Chevalier, instead of being at liberty to commence his journey to Madrid, was compelled, by an order from the King, to attend the Ambassador to Naples; an expedition which was designed at once to instate Don Carlos in his possessions in that country, and to secure Barr and Loraine to the crown of France.

From the ease and celerity with which the whole of this arrangement was completed, D'Arnaud had time only to dispatch a few lines to Leonora, acquainting her with his hasty and unexpected removal, and beseeching her to continue stedfast in her affection, till the business which had called him so suddenly from France should be finally adjusted; when he would avail himself of such steps for her deliverance as could not fail of being successful.

On the day appointed for the expedition the Ambassador and his suite set forward for Italy, and arrived in due time at Naples, where they were conducted, amid the ringing of bells, and the joyful acclamations of the delighted populace, into the presence of the new King, in the Castello di St. Elmo, who, having loaded them with presents and other distinguishing tokens of his approbation, commanded that apartments should be allotted them in the Palazzo di Monte, to which they accordingly repaired, and where they were served and attended by the royal domestics, and entertained in a style of suitable magnificence.

D'Arnaud was much struck with the beauty of this city, and spent the greater part of his time in examining its libraries, alternately conversing in imagination with the most celebrated poets and historians of Greece and Rome, and with those whom a refined taste, and an inclination for classical and literary researches had collected around him.

It was during his repeated and almost daily visits to the *Libraria Studia*, which contains perhaps more of the rare and valuable MSS of antiquity than any other library in Naples, that he commenced an acquaintance with Signor di Speroni, a Neapolitan of some rank, who, as the successor of a numerous and wealthy ancestry, possessed estates to a considerable amount, not only in the *Terra di Lavora*, but in various other provinces in Italy.—This Signor was genteel in his deportment, and insinuating in his manners. The conversation of D'Arnaud, which was at once polished and rational, drew him often into his company. This partiality was strengthened by a more durable intercourse;—the Chevalier received a general invitation to visit him at all times; and finding him an agreeable companion, as well as an instructive *Cicerone*, a friendship, which promised to be as permanent as the occasion of it was accidental, was cemented between them.

In a Piazza, contiguous to that in which the Signor resided, lived Maria D'Olivetto, his sister, a widow of about two-and-thirty, who having early married advantageously, presided in great splendour at her Palace in Naples.

This lady was handsome, fond of company, and delighted with admiration—had a gay and brilliant wit, and was skilled in all the arts of coquetry. She played and sung enchantingly. Her concerts were more crowded than any other in the city; and D'Arnaud, allured at length by the blandishments of beauty, and the charms of music, passed many of his pleasantest, as well as most dangerous, hours in her parties.—His figure and address had captivated her at first—this captivation was increased by a nearer intimacy; —she panted to inlist him among the number of her admirers; and having been flattered in her youth on the fancied power of her charms, no witchery was unemployed to try to the utmost their dominion.—Vain, however, for some time was her every attempt at fascination.—The charming form of his Leonora —her looks—her parting accents were engraven indelibly on his memory; and the languor of melancholy, notwithstanding all his efforts to restrain it, would steal at intervals from beneath the thin disguise of cheerfulness, and diffuse over his features an expression extremely interesting.

When several weeks had passed away, these fits of transitory dejection became more frequent and more obvious. He had hinted more than once his wish to be gone; blamed the tardiness of the Court in delaying the completion of the business which detained him at Naples; and even applied to the Ambassador for his permission to depart.

"Ah, too amiable Chevalier!" said the Signora one day, as he was expatiating on his projected departure, "wherefore this impatience to leave Italy and your friends? Is it," added she, sighing heavily, and regarding him with looks expressive of all the tenderness and animation which played about her heart, "that you have some nearer and dearer connection in your own too happy country?—Yes, I see I can no longer be deceived; or why that dejected air—these sighs—these abstractions—and these various tokens of an anguish which seems to have penetrated to your very soul? —Alas, you love!—Your affections have been entangled—you are the slave, perhaps the dupe, of an inauspicious attachment! If so, permit me, I entreat you, to become the sharer of your sorrows;

—confide them fearlessly to this breast—this breast which throbs with an affection as pure as it is ardent!"

She pronounced these words in a tone so soft, so tender, so energetic, that D'Arnaud was at once flattered and interested. Were it possible that he could have withheld his confidence from so lovely a woman, one who had professed so much, and who was in reality so charming, he would have esteemed himself a monster of insensibility. He avowed, therefore, unhesitatingly, his passion for Leonora, whom he described as endued not only with beauty, youth, wit, and accomplishments, but with every other quality requisite to perfection. The Signora, although inwardly chagrined, affected to be in raptures with the portrait which he had given of her; and curious to discover whether she possessed in such a very eminent degree the extraordinary intellectual embellishments of which he had spoken, was allowed, at her very urgent request, the perusal of her letters, from which, and from the short and imperfect explanations afforded by D'Arnaud, she obtained all the information she required on the subject of their connection.

From this period the Chevalier's visit to the Signora at the Palazzo d'Olivetto became more and more frequent. He attended her in all her parties, escorted her to the Parade, the *Gran Corso*, and the *Terazzo Nuova*, and made various excursions with her about the environs of the city. These excursions led them sometimes to Caprea, to Puzzioli, Baia, or the woody steeps of Pausilippo; and as, on their return, they glided along the pure waters of the bay, a mirror, over which the rays of the retiring sun threw all the grace and magic of colouring, the strains of Italian instruments, and Italian voices, seemed to give enchantment to the scenery that adorned its shores:—and oftentimes, when all was hushed except the distant call of the fishermen, or the Lazaroni in the strand, the groan of the now far-off mountain, or the low trio of the vinedressers reposing on some promontory beneath the pleasant shade of their poplars, D'Arnaud would accompany with his flute the soft voice of the Signora in one of her sweet Sicilian airs, where love, as was usual, was the subject, and of which the tender and impassioned looks she involuntarily bestowed upon him, proved him the object.

Week after week passed on in the same routine, in the course of which D'Arnaud, who had been in daily and hourly expectation of intelligence from Spain, heard nothing from Leonora. This circumstance perplexed him. The letters which he had last written to her from Bordeaux contained his address; and this, with her former promises of punctuality, seemed to offer no excuse for so palpable an omission.—He was tormenting himself with conjectures on this extraordinary silence, when he was engaged by the Signora D'Olivetto to meet a party of her friends at her villa at Portici.

The company was brilliant, though select. It consisted of two families from Naples, a third from Casserta, a French Marquis and his son, and a young Castilian cavalier, who appeared to be a stranger to every one of the party.

The Marquis talked much, and observing that the Chevalier was from France, he spoke of the war which had depopulated Europe, of the late Regent, of Cardinal Fleury, whom he distinguished by the appellation of the Solon of France, and on various other topics, in which he seemed anxious rather to receive than to give information. An old Italian Count, who sat next him, cut the discourse short by enquiring if the Marquis had not lately been in Spain. He had made that tour, the Marquis answered, with his son, and had spent his last winter at Madrid.

"Apropos of Madrid," interposed the cavalier, who had hitherto kept silence; "know you Don Manuel de Roderigo, formerly of Saragossa, the relation of the illustrious Don Manuel de Cassasonda, Governor of Quito?"

"Don Manuel de Roderigo," rejoined the Marquis, "is a resident of Cuenca.—His person is unknown to me; but I am told that he is nobly allied, rich, still more generous, and in high favour with his Sovereign, from whom, though of Moorish descent, he had obtained the rank of a *Grandee*, and the tile of *Most Illustrious!*"

"You have probably been informed too," resumed the stranger, "of his marriage with the beautiful Leonora, daughter of Don Pedro de Velasquez, and Hidalgo of Toledo, which was solemnized a few months since at the Church of the Monastery of the Escurial, near Madrid?"

"Impossible!" exclaimed D'Arnaud, his cheeks glowing with indignation, and his limbs shaking with uncontroulable emotion, "recall your words, Senor; or by Heaven——"

"And who are you, Sir?" retorted the Castilian angrily, "that have dared to implicated in your suspicions the veracity of a true cavalier?—I tell you, Senor, that Don Manuel de Roderigo is united to the incomparable Leonora de Velasquez. I was present at the Monastery of the Escurial when the nuptials were solemnized, and cannot be mistaken."

"His Eminence," said the Marquis smiling, and not appearing to notice the disorder of D'Arnaud, "seems to have entered into a very extraordinary engagement for a man of his age. He was not young when he left his Castle at Saragossa, and has been many years a courtier."

"Don Manuel," rejoined the Castilian, "has already completed his thirteenth lustrum, which he has devoted, like a true disciple of Venus, to the composition of Sequidillas, and the performance of serenades beneath the different windows of his mistresses.— All the beauties in Castile have been honoured in their turn with these testimonies of his approbation; and it was probably with a view of avenging himself for the cruelty of some, and the disloyalty of others, that he determined to marry.—And now," added he, laughing aloud, "if the illustrious Donna Leonora intends to shew him at Bourdeaux, where I am told she has friends, she has only to embellish her *caro sposo* with the capo and *sambrero*[1] to make his pass for an exact specimen of Spanish antiquity; for a more risible looking animal, on two legs, I never saw."

The Marquis enquired if he had ever seen Donna Leonora, and if she was really so handsome as report had represented her. The cavalier replied that he had seen her only for a few minutes as she was passing along the Prado; but from the casual glance that he had obtained, she appeared to be young and very charming, and in every respect the opposite of Don Manuel, her husband.

D'Arnaud listened with agony to a detail every word of which struck like a dagger to his heart. Leonora—the perjured Leonora, was then the property of another! The event had been too con-

1 The *capo* is the flapped hat, and the *sambrero* the cloak worn by the ancient Spaniards: a mode of dress now retained only by the people of Arcas.

fidently attested—too circumstantially related to admit of incredulity; and, overwhelmed with disappointment, embarrassment, and vexation, he arose, and returned hastily to his lodgings.— The business of his whole life appeared now to be accomplished; for all that remained of it seemed only vacuity and gloom.—In vain he looked around; the prospect thickened as he gazed, and death presented the only possible termination of the misery which assailed him. The next day he received a letter. It was from Leonora. He opened it, and read as follows:—

———

TO THE CHEVALIER D'ARNAUD.

"Before these lines, which I send by Father Niccolis de Pedrosa as far as Capua, can reach your hands, I shall be the wife of Don Manuel. This determined, your own prudence will sufficiently suggest to you that I cannot receive with impunity any future visits or letters from you.—Such a conduct would be too injurious to my interests and honour to be thought of. Feeling, however, as I trust I always shall, the highest esteem and veneration for your sentiments and character, I subscribe myself with pleasure,

"Your sincere, and still affectionate friend,

"LEONORA DE VELASQUEZ."

———

"Base and perfidious woman!" exclaimed the injured and unfortunate Chevalier, and he read in these cruel words, from a hand he could not doubt to be Leonora's, a confirmation of all which the stranger had asserted; "what demon could have urged thee to so hateful a sacrifice? What but interest and ambition, those iron-hearted monsters, who stalk over the earth to subdue it, and erect their altars on the miseries of the vanquished, could have debased and contaminated a heart so pure, so innocent as thine was? But I will forget," added he, sighing, and tearing the paper he yet held into a thousand pieces, "what she once was; and remember her only as the wife of Don Manuel.—Then, as I must cease to esteem, I shall in time, I hope, cease also to love."

Such were his resolutions; and if the triumph of reason over sensibility was not instantaneously completed, his exertions to this end were not ultimately unsuccessful. The world again resumed its charms; it contained at least two beings interested in his fate; and one of these, though a female, that did not blush to feel and to acknowledge his virtues.—But friendship as well as love has its attendant anxieties. That friend, whose admonitions and endearments had been his principal and indeed only support under the heavy pressure of his misfortunes, soon opened to him a new source for apprehension and regret. She became thoughtful and retired. Her eyes were either perpetually suffused with tears, or bent on him with an expression of the deepest melancholy.—When she spoke, her articulation was often arrested by sighs; and she sometimes secluded herself for days together at Portici, where, attended only by her Confessor, and occasionally by her brother and D'Arnaud, she resigned herself to sorrow and reflection.

One morning the Chevalier took a ride to the villa, and being told that the Signora was at home, proceeded without ceremony to her dressing room.—She was warbling a charming little air from the *Amor Timido* of Metastasio, where he so feelingly and so sympathetically describes the cares and agonies of love.—As he entered she stopped, and with a soft and insinuating smile, desired him to come forward. Her harp was by her side; she drew it to her, and performed at his request, the two following stanzas:—

> T'intendo sì, mio cor;
> Con tanto palpitor,
> So, che ti vuoi lagnar,
> Che amante sei.

> Ah! taci il tuo dolor,
> Ah! soffri il tuo martir,
> Tacilo e non tradir,
> Gli affetti miei.

I read thy meaning, Oh my heart!
By thy throbs too well I see
Thou mourn'st thy deeply rooted smart—
Thou mourn'st that love has conquer'd thee!

Hide, my heart, Oh hide thy anguish!
Bear thy pangs, thy wailings stay!
Be silent, and in secret languish!
Nor one tender thought betray!

As she repeated the words—

Tacilo e non tradir
Gli affetti miei

her voice faltered, and she burst into tears.

"Maria—dearest Maria!" cried D'Arnaud, throwing himself on his knees before her, "to what am I to impute this strange emotion? You alarm—you shock me! Is it that *you* feel the symptoms of a disorder——But pardon me," added he, recollecting himself, "I ought not to be thus urgent—but would to Heaven it were in my power——" He stopped.

"I will be sincere, Chevalier!" said the Signora, sobbing, and covered with blushes; "you deserve my confidence, and I will candidly acknowledge that—" She hesitated—"that, disguised under the insidious name of friendship, I have imbibed a passion too powerful both for my happiness and health!"

"Amiable and adorable creature!" interrupted D'Arnaud, rising, and clasping her to his breast with unaffected transport, "how shall I reward you for this enchanting frankness? Look up, my Maria; if I have involuntarily been the destroyer of thy happiness, I will endeavour at least to establish it."

An interval of rapture succeeded, and in a few weeks D'Arnaud became the husband of Signora D'Olivetto.

Months passed on in a variety of amusements and avocations. The Signora was more animated, more charming than ever; and the birth of a son, which event was celebrated at Portici about a year after their marriage, heightened the felicity they mutually enjoyed.

To watch over this gradually unfolding blossom of infantine innocence, thus expanding like a flower beneath the eye of his parents, was the dearest care of D'Arnaud; and the Signora, attracted by its beauty, and the resistless eloquence of its endearments, professed an equal attachment.—Time, however, shewed that the destructive habits of dissipation, in which she had always indulged, were not easily to be surmounted; for the novelty at an end, she returned with avidity to the gayest circles in Naples, where no allurements were omitted to obtain in them the admiration she had formerly ensured.—Often did D'Arnaud represent the folly and even danger of these nocturnal assemblies; and by inventing amusements for her at the Palace, endeavour to detain her with her child.—These arguments, these projects were alike unsuccessful; and as they were usually productive of some unpleasant retort—a severe witticism upon his gravity, or, what was infinitely more distressing to him, of sullenness and tears, he desisted from any further attempts to reclaim her; not, however, without some latent hope that time and reflection would convince her of her error, and restore her more effectually to the home she had now almost entirely abandoned.

Four and even five years elapsed, and no such change had taken place, when the Signora, whose constitution had been for some time declining, was assailed by a malady, under the influence of which she languished for near six months, and then expired; having previously divided the small remains of her property between the Chevalier and her son.

In her last interview with D'Arnaud she acknowledged, with many symptoms of contrition, that the letter he had formerly received, and which he had imagined to be Leonora's, on the subject of her marriage with Don Manuel de Roderigo, was forged by her hand; and that the stranger, the pretended cavalier, who had so confidently declared himself an eye-witness of the transaction, was an agent of her's from Capua; who, in consideration of a very ample reward, had agreed to attest it, after she had herself put a period to their correspondence by intercepting and destroying the letters they mutually sent.

D'Arnaud's astonishment at this confession may easily be imagined. He had long since ceased to esteem his wife; even the impression she had made upon his senses was considerably diminished;—yet he heard not without pain that she had been the contriver of a scheme which, were it possible she could have been restored to him, was of too atrocious a nature not to tend to the destruction of their future peace.—That pardon, for which she so earnestly entreated, he was nevertheless too humane to withhold from her; but her remains were no sooner interred, than, anxious to make every reparation in his power to his beloved and much-injured Leonora, he took an affectionate leave of his son, whom he recommended to the protection of his uncle, Signor de Speroni, and accompanied by Carlo Verezio, his servant, set out for Madrid.

CHAPTER VI

Thy rage shall burn thee up, and thou shalt turn
To ashes! * * * * * * * * * * * * * *
Look to thyself!—thou art in jeopardy!

SHAKESPEARE.

WHEN the Chevalier had proceeded on his way to Spain as far as Bourdeaux, being ignorant whether Leonora was at Madrid, or her former residence at Toledo, he enquired concerning her relation, M. D'Aubigne, of whom, as he was doubtless acquainted with every particular incident in her story, he despaired not of obtaining the intelligence he wanted. D'Aubigne, however, to his infinite disappointment, had removed with his family from Bourdeaux to a distant part of France, and was not expected to return thither till the beginning of the ensuing winter.—Vexed and disconcerted, he was about to renew his route, when he recollected Mad. de Bouiloise, the confidential friend of Leonora, by whose means they had corresponded; and being acquainted with her address, he went immediately to her Hotel, and having procured an audience of her in private, falteringly demanded if she had lately heard from Leonora, where she lived, and whether she was yet unmarried.

"Leonora de Velasquez," returned the Mad. de Bouiloise, "is

still under the patronage of Lady Almeria, her aunt, the Abbess of a small Convent at Fontcarrel, a village near Madrid, and has been more than five years a Nun."

"Then all is over!" said D'Arnaud, and he pressed his hand upon his forehead.

"Her year of initiation expired," continued Mad. de Bouiloise, "she was compelled, on her rejection of a match proposed to her by her father, to substitute the eternal veil for the novitiate one, having assumed which, the fate of the person professed, is supposed to be fixed; few, if any, being permitted to return afterwards to a world, the cares and pleasures of which they have thus solemnly renounced. Leonora, however, who had always a decided repugnance to a monastic life, found means to declare her aversion in a legal form.—Before she took the veil, she had a protest drawn up against it, which she delivered to Father Antonio, a Dominican Confessor, and Superior of the community, and immediately after the ceremony, she repeated it in form, and gave it to a second person, affirming at the same time that, as she considered the vows which she had taken, to be extorted and nugatory, it was not her intention to confirm them by any subsequent act; and that she should always reserve a right of availing herself of that her solemn protest, whenever she should see occasion. If, therefore," added Mad. de Bouiloise, "you can invent such excuses for your conduct as may serve to justify you in the opinion of my amiable young friend, and your affection for her is unchanged, I hope soon to have an opportunity of congratulating you mutually upon an event, which I foresee is at no great distance."

The Chevalier D'Arnaud's eyes sparkled with rapture; he took her offered hand, and pressed it to his lips in speechless transport.

"It is necessary, however, that you should be informed," continued Mad. de Bouiloise, "that the estates which ought to have been Leonora's, owing to her having entered into the institution previous to the demise of her father, have devolved to the male heir; every *religieuse* in that country, whatever may be her rank, and to whatever order she may belong, being prohibited by the ecclesiastical laws the possession of every species of property, not legally secured to her before the assumption of the last veil."

"Her father is dead then?" said D'Arnaud.

"Don Velasquez experienced a sudden and very melancholy death about four years ago, in consequence of a fall he had from his carriage, as he was traversing that immense ridge of mountains which separate the French from the Spanish Navarre.—As he died without a will, the whole of his property, with the exception of a genteel, but not an ample annuity, before settled upon his daughter, is in the possession of Signor Garcelles, a merchant of Oviedo, and a discarded lover of Leonora."

D'Arnaud, whose affection was so entirely disinterested that, had Leonora been reduced to a situation the most abject that can be conceived, and himself elevated to the highest, he would have gloried in the alliance, attended to this relation without the smallest degree of uneasiness; and having procured a direction from Mad. de Bouiloise to the Convent she resided in, love and impatience urging him to flight, he crossed the Garonne, and proceeding through a part of Gascony, and along those dangerous passes among the Pyrenees which intervene between Bayonne and Navarre, gained the town of Pampeluna, and from thence pursuing his way through Calahora, Almanson, and Sequensa, arrived at Madrid.

He stopped at a *Posado* in the *Plazuela de los Affigidos*.—The evening was drawing on, and the winter advanced—it had even commenced with a rigour unknown to this climate: but his anxiety to reach that Convent which contained within its walls the beloved object of his search, admitting not of restraint, he resigned his mule to Verezio, and passing the gate of *San Bernardino*, took the road to Fontcarrel.

At Uzeda, the last post but one between Seguensa and Madrid, he had addressed a letter to Leonora, in which, after affording her every requisite explanation on the subject of his marriage, and the events that had preceded it, he renewed his former suit; earnestly conjuring her to take advantage of her protest, and by investing him with the legal right of protecting her, to free herself effectually from her present confinement:—and this he hoped to have an opportunity of presenting to her at the grate of the Convent.

But the happiness which he experienced from the idea of

seeing and conversing with her, was imbittered by a succeeding recollection.—Habit might have reconciled her to the retirement she filled; it was even possible she might be attached to it—a suggestion which was the more probable from her having forborne to avail herself of any steps in her power at all likely to tend to her future enlargement. He dreaded the scruples of delicacy, and even those of religion—doubted whether the explication which he had attempted, was sufficient to exculpate him from the charge of inconstancy—and began utterly to despair of that forgiveness which only a few hours before he imagined that he had ensured. These doubts, these apprehensions sunk him into thoughtfulness; and he had traversed the brow of that hill which leads on one side to the *Prado*, and on the other to Fontcarrel, without noticing the path, when he perceived a little below in the valley the village which he sought, and soon afterwards the Convent.

As he slowly approached the gate, the chapel bell tolled one, paused, and then tolled again. It was the *Ave Maria* or *Angelus hour*. The Chevalier stopped—drew back:—again the note was repeated; and in a few minutes a small troop of Nuns, preceded by the Abbess, and followed at some distance by the Novices and Boarders of the Convent, crossed the court toward the chapel. They were dressed in white, with scapularies and hoods of the same colour. The elder of them wore cowls, the younger only veils, and each held suspended from her arm a large chaplet of beads. As they entered, the bell stopped; and the door of the chapel was closed after them. A silence of near half an hour succeeded, when a low soft chant issued faintly from the walls; it grew louder and louder, and then swelled into a tone of exquisite sweetness—D'Arnaud listened; a tear of sensibility trembled in his eye; for he thought amid the voices in the choir he distinguished the well-known accents of Leonora.

Again all was hushed.—The doors of the chapel were thrown open, and the procession proceeded slowly, as before, to the door of the Convent. D'Arnaud pursued them with his eyes till they had entered the portico, when he was startled by the sound of a step, and looking round, perceived the portress with her keys, who gently demanded who he was, and with what intention he came there. Confusion for a moment obstructed his utterance; but quickly recovering himself from the stupor of his embarrassment, he put the letter into her hands, and with it a purse containing about twenty *piastres*; entreating her that she would deliver the former immediately at directed, and accept the latter as a gratuity for the service he required.—The Nun took them, and withdrew; and D'Arnaud returned pensively to his lodgings, having determined to repeat his visit to the Convent early on the following evening.

The hours which intervened were devoted to silence and reflection; and the Chevalier found his retirement at the Posado insupportably tedious. He took up a book, but the subject was inimical to his thoughts, and he as hastily laid it down again; for such was the present temper of his mind, that the production of a *Calderoni*, a *Lope de Vega*, or a *Cervantes* would have been perused without emotion, and relinquished without regret. The day passed slowly to its close; evening at length advanced, and the Chevalier repaired again to the Convent.—The Nun met him at the gate; she curtsied meekly as she approached, and drawing a letter from beneath her robe, motioned him to depart. D'Arnaud received it with delight, and turning the angle of a wall, and fixing himself in a spot where he might continue unobserved, he broke the seal, and found, what to his transported imagination appeared the very height of human happiness, that Leonora, though altered in fortunes, was unaltered in affection—that she loved, pitied, and forgave him; and that, as the most convincing proof she could afford him of the steadiness of her attachment, she had resolved to escape with him at a stated time from the Convent, to throw herself upon his protection, and to unite her destiny to his by the most sacred of bonds.

The time appointed for this enterprise at length arrived.— Disguises, through the assistance of the portress, were without difficulty provided; and Leonora soon perceived with delight that she was already some miles beyond the walls of Fontcarrel.

The Chevalier, as he was travelling among the Pyrenees on his way toward Spain, had accidentally passed a night at the cottage of a peasant, situated in a small hamlet on the Spanish side of this tract, a few leagues only from Estella; and in this place, since it was indispensable to their safety that they should be for some time concealed, he determined to seek refuge from the emissaries of the Church, who, if acquainted with their flight, would doubtless endeavour, by every artifice in their power, to discover their destination.

Thither they accordingly shaped their course, and after a journey, including in the whole near two hundred miles, gained the foot of the Pyrenees, and presently afterwards the hamlet; and a monastery being near, an ecclesiastic was engaged, and the rites of marriage were performed.

When Leonora was settled in her new abode, she wrote to Donna Almeria, her aunt, the Superior of the Convent at Fontcarrel, to inform her of her marriage, and of the name of the person in whose hands she had deposited her protest, which she requested might be read publicly in the *refectoire*—the only form she conceived requisite on the present occasion, and that her name might be erased from the list of the community.

The Abbess was no sooner apprized of Leonora's escape, than she betrayed many symptoms of indignation, and afterwards of uneasiness. Immediately, however, on the receipt of this letter, she dispatched another to Padro Juan de Centelles, the Abbot of a Monastery at Madrid, the person to whom Leonora had delivered her protest, demanding its resignation, and requiring his attendance at a fixed hour in the morning.

The Abbot, in obedience to this injunction, hastened to the Convent, and continued for some hours in deep discourse with the Abbess.—From what passed at this conference, it appeared, from some particular circumstances in the case, that the ceremony of reading over the protest, was insufficient for the purpose for which it was intended; and after various interviews and consultations, it was decreed that a representation should be made by the Abbot to the Court of Rome, of the force under which Leonora had been obliged to take the vows.

The Pope's answer was to the following effect:—

That the Sister must await a summons made to all the parties who were in any way interested in the abolition of her vows; wherein, should there be no cause discovered which might instigate the proper Court of Madrid, in conjunction with the Superior of the Convent, and the community of Nuns to which she belonged, to confirm her religious engagements, they were to be absolved, and the marriage might be considered as legal. But if any reason could be adduced by the opposite parties why her vows should be held sacred, after the act intended to annul them should be publicly examined, the affair was to be determined by the Inquisitorial Powers of Madrid, by whose decisions, however terrible, they were hereafter to abide.

When the substance of this intelligence was communicated to the Abbess, the protest was read aloud in the *refectoire* of the Convent, in the presence of the Abbot, of Padro Antonio, the Monk to whom it had formerly been consigned, and several others of the fraternity; and no cause appearing throughout the whole of the investigation why Leonora's religious engagements should not be repealed, it was decreed that the marriage should be declared lawful, and that her name should be erased from the archives of the Convent.

D'Arnaud, who had nothing further to apprehend from the tyrannic powers of the Church, now removed to Estella; and having written to Signor di Speroni, his brother-in-law, to request the presence of his son, all that was now wanting to complete his felicity, enjoyed in the society of an adored wife, and amid scenes of domestic tranquillity, a more refined and exquisite sensation of happiness than he had ever yet known.

The arrival of the little Julien in Spain had been long confidently expected, when the Chevalier received a packet from Naples, in the enclosure of which the Signor was so extremely urgent in his entreaties to detain him, that D'Arnaud, yielding to his eagerness, consented that he should remain for some time longer in Italy.

More than a year had passed away, when to fill up every thought and moment, a daughter was born to D'Arnaud and his beloved Leonora. They baptized her Cecilia, after her maternal grandmother; but often as the enraptured father gazed on her perfect features, fine blue eyes, playful locks, and vermeil-tinctured cheek, in the wild enthusiasm of the moment he would press her to his heart, and call her his Leonora, in sweet affection to her whom she so strikingly resembled.—Imagination can scarcely conceive a more interesting *trio*, or a finer figure than Leonora, when bending, with the look and softness of a Madona, and in an attitude of grace which Praxiteles might have imitated, over the cradle of her child, or conveying it, assisted by D'Arnaud, amid the flowery recesses of the mountains they yet sometimes visited.

Whilst the happy pair were thus enjoying without interruption all the grandeur of nature, Fortune seemed to promise not utterly to abandon them. It appeared upon inspection that Leonora, being thus released, as it was supposed, from her late monastic engagement, was the lawful heiress to the estates, formerly, and for many years in the possession of her ancestors; and the Abbess of the Convent of Fontcarrel, partly with a view of establishing her in her rights, and partly with that of revenging herself upon her nephew for having employed emissaries to propagate reports about the city highly injurious to the character of the order, dispatched an express to Estella, to summon D'Arnaud to Madrid, for the purpose of filing a bill of recovery against Signor Garcelles.

The Chevalier immediately set off, and prosecuted his journey with so much rapidity and success, that he arrived in Castile on the same day as his opponent.—The cause, after much tedious preparation, and many voluntary delays on the part of the defendant and the Council was accordingly brought forward; and being terminated eventually in favour of Leonora, D'Arnaud returned shortly to Navarre, eager to congratulate her on the success of an enterprise, from which they had neither of them derived any very flattering expectations.

But the satisfaction which they experienced from this unlooked-for acquisition, was superseded ere long by the most cruel anxiety; and D'Arnaud was compelled, by another order from the Abbess, to hasten back to Madrid; Signor Garcelles, under the tuition of a Monk, and two other of his agents, having recommenced a suit, in which he endeavoured to make it appear that the dissolution of Leonora's vows had been unlawfully obtained; and this he afterwards proved by a clause in an act to that purpose, not always enforced, which says that monastic vows made above five years, cannot in any case, or on any pretence whatever, be annulled. This was a circumstance which the

Abbot, in his representations to the Court of Judicature at Rome, had neglected to mention; though it was more than six years since the protest drawn up for that occasion, was committed to his care.—On this ground the cause was again brought before the Grand Council of Castile, where, notwithstanding the decisions of a former Court, the eloquence of an eminent pleader, and several precedents in point being produced, the marriage was declared void; and D'Arnaud, convicted by this inhuman decree of having stolen a Nun, was summoned by a written mandate, issued by Don Ignacio de Santos Aparicio, Alguazil Mayor of the Supreme and General Inquisition, signed and sealed by the Inquisidor General, to surrender himself at the *Casa*, there to be privately interrogated, and afterwards to stand the examination of the Inquisitorial Court.—Couriers were also to have been dispatched throughout the different provinces of Spain in search of Leonora, whose life, like D'Arnaud's, was at the mercy of the Tribunal. But pains having been taken privately to explain the leading circumstances of the case to some of the principal Fathers of the Council, it was at length determined, through the mitigating influence of the Abbess, the Abbot, who was the chief of the Order, and the community of Nuns, that, on condition she returned voluntarily to her Convent, performed a weekly penance during life, and resigned her daughter to the institution, to be educated under the directions of the Superior, for a lay-sister in the monastery, she was to obtain pardon and absolution; but on her rejection of these terms, and farther concealment, to receive the punishment due to the supposed magnitude of her crime, in the dungeons of the Inquisition.

To further this view, an edict was accordingly published throughout the streets of Madrid, the provinces of New and Old Castile, Navarre, Arragon, and Catalonia, and a reward offered to those who should convey a proper knowledge of the offenders to the Court of Conscience.

The particulars of this transaction were conveyed to Leonora by a letter from the Abbess; in which, after bitterly lamenting her own error and want of foresight, and acquainting her with the very dangerous predicament in which she stood, she entreated her to return immediately to her Convent, the only protection she could now offer her and the only possible condition on which her preservation could be ensured.

The agony of Leonora's mind as she perused this fatal paper, exceeds the power of conception. She sunk lifeless on a couch; and but for the care and assistance of her servants, in that posture she had probably expired.—Grief like her's cannot be delineated by the power of words, for to words it gave no utterance.

Let us draw a veil over this melancholy pause in our narration, and attend upon D'Arnaud, who, after a confinement of some days in an inner apartment in the *Casa*, was conducted by the Ministers of the Tribunal to the hall of examination, where, at the head of a long table covered with a black cloth, and surrounded by a balustrade, sat his Excellency the Inquisidor General, with his *Fante*, and six of his Assessors, three on each side the chair of State, the Alguazil Mayor, and two Notaries, attending in their places.

The prisoner was placed behind a bar at the lower end of the table, between the messengers who brought him; and the charge against him being read, was called upon, according to the usual forms of proceeding, by one of the junior Judges of the Council, to make his defence. D'Arnaud looked indignantly around, and with a firm and collected voice, declared himself innocent of any crime whatsoever.

The Judges gazed upon each other in silent astonishment.

"Recollect yourself," said his Excellency the Inquisidor General, sternly, "and in the presence of this our righteous and equitable Tribunal, confess openly the offence with which you stand charged; an offence which, partaking in its form of the dangerous nature of heresy, makes you amenable to its laws, and dependant upon its mercy."

D'Arnaud persisted in his declaration that he had no confession to make.

"You swear then," rejoined the Inquisidor General, in an awful and elevated tone of voice, "that you are guiltless of any known crime or misdemeanour against the laws of this Court."

"I swear," replied D'Arnaud, "that I am innocent of any intentional offence, as well as to your laws, as to those of the Civil Government of this country."

"Hear him!" cried another of the Fathers, crossing himself, "the unholy wretch holds the stealing of a Nun to be no crime against the Church!"

"Are you aware," resumed the Inquisidor General, "of the power of this Tribunal, and the authority it possesses over you, standing, as you now do, accused before it?"

"I am," replied D'Arnaud impetuously, "and I am also aware that no mercy, nor even justice, is to be expected from its decisions."

"Away with him to a dungeon!" said the Inquisidor General; "he has insulted both us and our laws; break up the Court; we must take an examination of him in private!"

The Court adjourned; and D'Arnaud conducted as before by two of the messengers of the Auditory, was led through passages, and vaults, and melancholy cells, till he was delivered into the dungeon, where he was finally abandoned to his own solitary reflections.

Verezio, meanwhile, who had accompanied the Chevalier to Madrid, but had waited there only to learn the event of the trial, arrived at Estella; and was soon ushered into the presence of his unfortunate mistress. But, alas! he arrived only to confirm the heart-breaking intelligence which had already reached her. —Anxious, however, to suppress every part of his information which might add to her affliction, he cautiously concealed from her the very hazardous situation in which he had left D'Arnaud, who, he assured her, would be ultimately released; though, as he was undoubtedly at the mercy of the Inquisitorial Court of Madrid, it was probable that he might undergo a temporary confinement.

The sinking spirits of Leonora were revived by these words; and Verezio having urged her by every incitement in his power to return immediately to Fontcarrel, extorted from her a promise that, if he would provide a situation for her child, whom she had determined, whatever might be the issue, not to sacrifice to the severity of a monastic education, to surrender herself at her Convent; and by publicly asserting there that Cecilia was dead, to free herself effectually from any future enquiries.

But where was this unfortunate to be placed?—and who

would undertake a charge, which would subject them, if known, to the severest reprehension? The rumour of this inhuman requisition had penetrated already every part of the province; none, therefore, would offer refuge either to her or her child. France presented the only eligible asylum, and to France it was determined she should be conveyed. Verezio accepted the trust: but the period at hand when the wretched mother was to bid adieu, as it should seem for ever, she formed the sudden resolution of accompanying them herself; nor could the prayers, the remonstrances, nor even the tears of Verezio deter her from her purpose.

As, from the commencement of this journey till their arrival at the fortress to which Blanche de Coucy was conveyed, nothing essential occurred, we shall proceed to the more material parts of our narrative.

A storm had driven them to its shelter; and it was whilst Verezio was reconnoitering the spot, in order to discover some cottage or cabin where they might repose for the night, that he perceived the habitation to which they afterwards removed.—The owner of it wore the habit of a Monk; but he proved to be a layman, who had been driven by misfortune to a life of melancholy and seclusion. On being told that the lady was on her way to France, to seek a protection for her daughter, actuated by that compassion which the unfortunate always feel toward others suffering like themselves under circumstances of distress, he united his entreaties with those of Verezio to prevail upon her to remain there till a person could be procured to take the charge of her child. Leonora assented to their wishes; and Verezio having provided himself on his way with the dress of a hunter, the better to defend him from the assaults of banditti, proceeded rapidly toward France; and stopping only for refreshment at the different villages in his road, arrived at St. Bertrand.—What happened from the time of his entrance into the *auberge* till Cecilia was consigned by him to the protection of Blanche de Coucy, has already been related.

The sequel of the story of this ill-fated pair may be given in a few words.

D'Arnaud, after having suffered all the tortures and inflictions which human, and even infernal cruelty can invent, continuing stedfast in his resolution not to acknowledge himself a wilful offender against the established and unrelenting laws of that tremendous Tribunal, before which he was again summoned, received sentence of death; and was executed with several other victims, and in the presence of a number of witnesses, who, urged on by the spirit of superstition and fanaticism, poured execrations on them as they passed at the next succeeding spectacle of the *Auto da fé*.

This dreadful account, with that of the death of Leonora, who expired, as it was supposed of grief, a short time afterwards, was communicated by Verezio to Madame de Villeneuve, to whom he also gave the casket of which we have formerly spoken, and the packet which is the subject of the present memoir.

M. de Sevignac, to whom Leonora was well known, having been one of the unsuccessful candidates for her favour during her last visit to Bourdeaux, no sooner unclosed the casket containing her portrait, and that of the Chevalier, than he expressed much astonishment and uneasiness; but when he opened the packet, and read, in the papers, written by herself, the sad recital of her misfortunes, injuries, and persecutions, horror and resentment toward those who had been the authors of them, were the only lasting impressions which remained on his mind.

The casket, as it may be remembered, was delivered to Cecilia by De Sevignac on the death of his sister; but judging it more prudent that she should remain ignorant for the present of her birth and connections, he wilfully detained the packet; nor was it without an exquisite sensation of uneasiness that he relinquished it at all, well knowing what she must suffer on the perusal.

CHAPTER VII

Lieve arboscel, cui debil aura siede,
Lieve augellin, che geme o che si move
Lieve foglia che cade o che si scote,
Di terror doppia il dubbia cor percote.
                                        ARIOSTO.

The light bush where the faint gale sits and sighs,
    The light bird's moan, that does not move or start,
The light leaf's fall, that quivers as it flies,
    With double terror strikes her doubtful heart.

CECILIA closed the manuscript. The fate of her father had wound
up her feelings to a pitch of inconceivable agony; but when she
thought of her mother, the wretched victim of a destiny almost
equally deplorable, her grief became more tender, though not
less exquisite than before; and she bitterly lamented that, she
thought, culpable solicitude for the security of her happiness,
which had prevented her from participating in the anguish she
had suffered.—"Oh, why," said she mentally, "was not I permitted
to remain with her? The presence of a beloved daughter would
have lightened the pressure of her affliction, and she might have
lived—Oh transporting and yet torturing idea!—to have been a
blessing to her child, who must never—never know the sweets of
maternal affection!"

She was startled from these reflections by the voice of
Susanne, who, observing her ruminating look and dejected air,
had viewed her with concern.

"Alas! Mademoiselle," said she piteously, "you seem very
sorrowful and unhappy.—To be sure you have lost a great
friend; and the sight of this chateau, and every thing about it,
must recal him to your recollection.—But death, you know, is
common to all; and if we suffer ourselves to grieve immoderately for those whom we have lost, our grief becomes injurious
to ourselves, and is of no use to the departed. So do not weep

thus sadly; Monsieur is happier than we are—he is an angel in Heaven!"

"I hope—I trust he is!" said Cecilia energetically.

"But I come to tell you, Mademoiselle, that we have had a little surprise, though I hope nothing that——for I would not for the world that any thing should happen to you here. But this house is so silent and solitary; and as we seldom see a Christian soul except ourselves, and now and then an old Monk from the Abbey, stalking among the trees of the avenue, with as much solemnity and deliberation as if he was going to confess them, the appearance of a stranger——"

"Of a stranger!" interrupted Cecilia, whose curiosity was now visibly excited.

"Last night," returned Susanne, "as Vincent was retiring from his work at the other end of the forest, a little to the right of that wood which overhangs the western side of the lawn, he spied two people in very earnest discourse, who, as they proceeded leisurely along the path, often turned, and looked attentively at the chateau.—As it occurred to him that they had been commissioned by the Signor to review the estate, and that their business was with him, he struck directly into the road, in the expectations of meeting them; but as soon as they perceived him, they retreated through a gate to the woods, and he saw them no more.—This morning one of them returned, and was seen sauntering about the grounds for near an hour before sunrise; sometimes walking slow, and sometimes quick, as if fearful of being overtaken.—Vincent pursued him as before; but in the most ingenious manner imaginable he contrived to escape him, always turning into a different path from that he had taken. From this it appears that, though a stranger to us, he is not so to the place, with every winding and outlet of which he seems perfectly acquainted."

This incident, trifling as it was, was sufficient to alarm Cecilia; and the information she had obtained heightening her impatience to know more, Susanne departed on the enquiry.

On her return, she learned that the strangers had been seen in every part of the village; but who they were, and from whence they came, no one could conjecture, though their dress and appearance, which indicated them superior to a common rank of life, had rendered them objects of attention to all the neighbourhood. It was evident, nevertheless, to Cecilia that they had no connection with Boraccio; since, if delegated by him to overlook the repairs, they would have come openly and immediately to the chateau.—But the circumstance of their having visited the gardens with so much secrecy and design, roused equally her curiosity and her terror, and she could not dismiss it from her thoughts.

The two following days passed on nearly in the same manner as the foregoing ones, in the interval of which they collected no information whatever relative to these extraordinary intruders. —On the third, as Cecilia was sitting alone in an apartment overlooking the terrace, a carriage drew up to the gate; a glance from the window convinced her it was M. Langlois, and she ran with joy to receive him.

When he had alighted from the carriage, and the customary salutations were exchanged, he followed her into a room, where, as soon as they were alone, he said—"Permit me to congratulate you, my young friend, on the completion of our project, which has terminated even more fortunately than we expected.—The Count believes you dead, and has left the country, as I am told, in no very enviable state of mind. At first he affected to discredit it; but my assertion being corroborated by that of a Monk, who, from his having really interred a female, with whose family and name he was entirely unacquainted, became a ready and highly useful assistant, he has not the smallest suspicion whatever of the fraud we have been practicing."

Cecilia was so much delighted with this intelligence, and with the kind attentions of her friend, that it was some time before she could give utterance to words marked with equal gratitude and joy, and which M. Langlois in vain endeavoured to suppress.

"The Count's offer," pursued M. Langlois, "having met with such a decided rejection, may I hope, presuming on your situation, that the one I am about to make, may be more favourably received? Nay, do not be alarmed," added he, smiling; "I have no intention, I can assure you, of proposing myself as a husband. Were I young indeed, I am not certain that I have enough stoicism in my composition to render me invulnerable to the fascinations of so much innocence and beauty. But will you permit me to make such overtures as a crazy old fellow like myself may venture upon with impunity?—You had once a father, an adopted one I mean; though a real one could not have been more fondly attached to you.—I loved him equally with yourself—he was the friend of my youth;—the grave has closed over him—allow me to be your father:—permit me at least to hope that I may in time become the friend, which your extreme youth and engaging appearance render so necessary."

"Ah, Sir!" said Cecilia, in a voice so faltering that her words were with difficulty pronounced, "how am I to support such unmerited kindness? By your exertions I have been emancipated from dangers the most menacing that can be conceived!—To your benevolent interference I owe the comfort and security I now enjoy.—To benefits such as these no gratitude can be adequate;—how then am I to recompense as they deserve, such unparalleled goodness and generosity?"

"By consenting," rejoined M. Langlois, "to make me your debtor. Age, you know, is accompanied by infirmities, whims, and absurdities; and a man who has lived to the age of threescore years and ten, must have some one on whom to vent at his will the idle effusions of his spleen, petulance, and caprice. To those who will submit to them, he is of course infinitely obliged; and his utmost gratitude is insufficient for the forbearance they impose."

"And are you sure," said Cecilia with an enchanting *naiveté*, "that I have patience enough to qualify me for the situation you mention?"

"I fear rather," he answered, "you possess too much. A little salutary contradiction is wonderfully efficacious. It gives a zest to our enjoyments—is an admirable antidote against *ennui*—and by supplying us with new subjects for declamation on the wayward passions of youth, serves to elevate us considerably in our own estimation.—You will then return with me to Vence;—my sister knows you by name, and will receive you with pleasure. She is a little whimsical, perhaps, but a good woman in the main; fond of retirement, books, and knitting;—acquire but a little knowledge of drugs, and you will be excellent companions."

Cecilia expressed much pleasure at the thoughts of seeing

Mad. Langlois; but having written, she said, to the Signora di Rosalvo, from whom she had formerly received repeated and very urgent invitations, it was necessary, before she ventured to determine upon any plan for the future, that she should await the event of her letter.

M. Langlois requested that she would be directed in this and in every other instance by her own feelings and discretion; and the next day, having recompensed Vincent and Susanne for their hospitality to their guest, he departed for Vence; having previously obtained a promise from Cecilia that, should any circumstance intervene to prevent her intended journey into Italy, she would proceed immediately to Vence—a promise she very readily bestowed; her apprehensions lest Boraccio's steward or servants should revisit the chateau, being too sanguine not to suggest the inconvenience of her present residence, and the dangers which might accrue to her from her longer continuance.

Towards evening the objects of her alarm having forborne to intrude upon her retirement for the space of some days, she took a stroll to her favourite haunts.—The tranquillity of the hour, of the place, and of the scenes she passed through, led her insensibly on till she had reached an opening to the woods; when a slight noise among the bushes caused her to start, and retreat some paces back. It was occasioned by a young man of no ungraceful appearance, who, with a gun in one hand, and a small net bag in the other, stood on a small eminence within view of the gardens, and was earnestly gazing on her.—The stranger saw he was observed, and pulling off his hat, addressed to her some hasty salutation, to which she was about to reply, when he turned suddenly away; and springing lightly over the fence which divided the gardens from the woods, was out of sight in an instant.

Cecilia was surprised, but collected.

This doubtless, was the person of whom Vincent had spoke, whose alarm, on his first appearance in the gardens, now seemed groundless, since there was nothing either in his countenance or address which could authorize the suspicions he seemed to have caught.—This adventure for a time solely engrossed her thoughts; till other and more interesting recollections usurped their place in her mind.

The sun was hastily declining, and as it threw a fiery gleam athwart the woods, softening by degrees to a bright golden glow, every spot as it opened upon her became more and more interesting. It was *here* she had often rambled with De Sevignac: at the foot of *that* declivity which the partial, uncertain light scarce permitted her to trace, she had first parted with Varàno.—Together they had ascended the hill—together viewed the landscape as it broke upon them from its summit in all its beauty and magnificence. An emotion of renewed tenderness communicated with the recollection; a sigh, she strove to suppress, agitated her bosom; and she became sensible to the features of the scene only as they served to bring Varàno more immediately to her fancy.

"Oh, why, why," said she, weeping, "were we separated?—Why in these shades must we never hope to meet again?"

She was stopped by a voice speaking near her in the grove;—she shrieked;—it spoke again;—she turned her head and perceived the figure of a man at some distance from her among the trees. She looked earnestly at him; but the decline of day, and the obscurity of the place permitted her not perfectly to distinguish his features. She approached a few steps, and hearing others pursuing her, trembling, and hardly knowing what she did, she ran or rather flew toward the lawn; but in the eagerness of advancing, the trailing branches of the underwood entangled her dress, and she fell to the ground. Her pursuer overtook her; and supporting her tenderly in his arms, her emotions of terror were converted into those of joy when, as he tremulously pronounced her name, she distinguished the well-known tones of Varàno. It was indeed Varàno that now pressed her to his heart! For the joy, the surprise, the tender agony of that moment, there were no words: Varàno himself shed tears as he lifted her from the ground; and it was some time before either was sufficiently collected to enquire of the other by what strange chance they thus met once more. —Varàno would have entered upon the explanation; but perceiving that she yet suffered pain from an accident of which he justly considered himself as the cause, his anxiety would not allow him to proceed till they had entered the chateau, when the first transports of this unexpected meeting having in some degree subsided, at her very earnest request, he began as follows:—

"I shall not trouble you with a description of my journey, which, from the time of our quitting Florence till our arrival at Rome, was marked only by mere common occurrences.—Our approach to this city was by the ancient *Via Flaminia*, which winds between the Pincian and Marian hills. We entered it about noon, and took our station at an Hotel in the Piazza di Spagna; where my father, on the plea of indisposition, but I believe with the view of writing and receiving letters, having ordered some to be forwarded to him whilst at Rome, proposed to remain resident some time.—Olivia, though uneasy at this delay, affected to be pleased with it; and the Marchese, assiduous to afford her every possible gratification, commanded me to accompany her to the Corso, the Theatres, none of which she had yet seen, and to point out to her the various curiosities and antiquities most worthy of her notice.—I obeyed, though reluctantly, for my spirits were depressed; and those scenes which had formerly created interest, enthusiasm, and delight, presented nothing to me in their stead but satiety and disgust. I endeavoured, nevertheless, to amuse and be amused; but the effort it demanded was inconceivably painful to me.—Olivia appeared grateful for my attentions, though she knew them to be constrained; and as I conducted her amongst the many noble, but now shattered remains of Roman magnificence, the vivacity of her conversation, the extraordinary facility of her comprehension, and, above all, that disposition to extract pleasure from the most inconsiderable of its sources, often drew me from myself, and my melancholy began slowly to abate.

"We prolonged our stay for near a week, and then continued out route.—When we reached our destination, we were told, to our astonishment, that the Conte and Contessa had quitted Naples in haste a few days before.—A letter, penned by the latter, to be delivered to us on our arrival, explained the motive of their absence. The Baronessa della Pinetta, a near relation of the Conte, who resided on a Baronial estate in the county of Molise, had been seized with an illness at Tarento; and in consequence of a message from her, immediately on her return, informing them of her danger, and soliciting their attendance, the Conte and his Lady departed instantly for Molise, leaving orders that we should either follow them thither, or remain at Naples till their return; which, as it depended entirely upon the fate of their friend, was yet very uncertain.

"The Marchese did not deliberate upon the proposal. The beauties of the more southern parts of Italy had fascinated his imagination; and we set off on the day following for Molise.

"The Baronessa's Castle is an ancient and majestic edifice, situated at the lower end of the valley of Bojano; a tract of land so fertile, so luxuriant, that the flowers spring up spontaneously, and yield an odour superior even to those which grow in our gardens. The valley is closed on the right by woods, and on the left by a projection of rocks, crowned with fox-glove and other wild plants.—Vineyards and thick groves embellish the recesses, whilst around it for many a mile, with graceful undulation, wander the Tiserno and Trigno, which, with the range of Apennines on one side, and the distant points of the Abruzzo on the other, compose a landscape more singularly beautiful than any I remember to have seen.—The Conte was overjoyed at our appearance; and the fine eyes of the Contessa sparkled with delight as she flew to welcome our approach.—The Baronessa, though recovered, was still invisible from debility; but she joined our party below in the course of a week. She was yet, however, too much indisposed to venture from the Castle; and as the Contessa seldom quitted her side, Olivia and I, whilst the Conte and Marchese were otherwise engaged, often strolled into the valley, or ascended the rocks, which being overshadowed and almost concealed by the mantling shrubs and wild flowers that spread their foliage around them, reminded me of those so beautifully described by Aelian in his charming valley of Tempe.—Whilst wandering with slow, unequal steps amongst the picturesque varieties of these enchanting solitudes, how often, my Cecilia, has your dear image accompanied me! How many times an hour have I thought of you—and how many bitter tears have I shed since our last cruel separation! Olivia has seen my grief; she has pitied the anguish she could only faintly alleviate! But she loves—she reveres—she appreciates you as you deserve and the commendations she has bestowed have endeared her to my heart.

"It was on my return from one of these solitary excursions

along the borders of the valley, that I received a summons from my father to attend him in his anti-chamber.—He was pacing the room as I entered, and seemed absorbed in rumination.—A table scattered over with papers and other implements for writing stood in the centre of the room, and near it a chair, from which he seemed to have risen.—He addressed me with much tenderness, and after applauding my late conduct in regard to Olivia, informed me that it had long been his intention to form an alliance between us; and my submission on this point being essential alike to his interests and happiness, he had no doubt of obtaining it.—I stood, I believe, for some moments the very picture of astonishment. My father looked earnestly on me for a minute, and then proceeded.

"'The Conte's circumstances are even more affluent than we expected.—Independent of a very considerable property in and about Naples, he has an estate to which he has only lately succeeded, in the Tavogliere di Puglia, which he designs as a marriage portion for his daughter.—The others will be her's on his decease; and her expectations being equal, and indeed superior to her paternal rights, the alliance we propose is in every respect desirable.'

"'How, my Lord!' I exclaimed, interrupting him, 'and have these arrangements been made without the consent and even knowledge of the parties chiefly concerned in them?'

"'They were made through the joint concurrence of our wishes,' said the Marchese, 'and your obedience to them will follow of course.'

"'Impossible, my Lord! Olivia has my friendship—my esteem; but as to love, we have never either of us indulged a single sentiment of the kind.'

"'Love,' said he disdainfully, 'is not essential to happiness, and if it were, Olivia has beauty enough to inspire it to its fullest extent.'

"'I mean not,' said I, recovering myself, 'to depreciate her excellencies; but no bond but that of friendship shall ever unite us.'

"The energy with which my last words were pronounced, convinced him of my steadiness and inflexible perseverance; and

a very distressing altercation almost immediately took place:—
he called me proud, stubborn, romantic: such were the terms he
affixed to my conduct, and even the epithet of ingrate was not
forgotten, but cruelly subjoined.—I shall pass over the conversation that ensued; a recital of which would serve only to awaken
me to a fuller sense of my misfortunes. Suffice it that, after an
interview of some length, he informed me, by means of a letter
which he had that day received, written by Boraccio, that you was
gone into a Convent in France, and that your abode there was
to be for life. Conjecturing, if this was really the case, that your
seclusion was involuntary, and imposed merely to favour and
promote the ambitious views of my family, I determined to go
immediately to Genoa, where, by a calm and thorough investigation of every circumstance attending it, I hoped to fathom the
mystery which seemed to involve you.—My resolution being
taken, I accordingly made ready; and acquainting no one with
my design, set off, attended only by Benedetto, from the Castello
della Pinetta.

"We took the road to Isernia, the way by which we came,
and travelled on for some leagues without interruption or delay.
The steps of travellers seldom broke in upon the silence of these
regions; and during our journey we were met only by a few
solitary *vettarini*, conveying goods imported from Santa Maria
Capua, Foggia, and the neighbouring Abruzzo, with here and
there a mean, low constructed carriage, employed in carrying the
wines and legumes of Ifernia from the banks of the Volturno, or
laden with the famous oil of Venafro, on the way to Rojano.—It
was my design to make the best of my way to Naples, and to take
shipping from thence to the shore of Genoa.—Having reached
Ifernia, we crossed the Volturno, and arrived shortly after at
Venafro, proceeding from thence to Capua, and afterwards to
Naples. It was at a late hour in the evening that we entered this
city, which we perceived to be lighted up, on our approach, with
peculiar splendour. The bay was crowded with pleasure-boats,
and the coasts with Lazaroni. The Strada dell Toledo was lined
on either side with carriages, and the loud ringing of the bells
proclaimed the eve of a festival. I alighted at the Palazzo di Mon-
telini, near the Church of San Gennaro; and having dispatched

my servant and a facchino¹ to hire a vessel at the quay, I entered an apartment; and throwing myself in a chair, gave way for a time to the most tormenting anticipations. I had not been there long, when the door of the apartment suddenly flew open, and Le Chatre, the beloved companion of my childhood, and constant companion of my studies, rushed into my arms. The expressions of mingled joy and surprise with which I received him, augmented the pleasure which he experienced from our meeting. He told me that he had lately been at Florence, but on hearing that I was at Naples, he had followed me thither. He then observed I looked unwell; and on my frankly acknowledging that I was so, plied me with such an infinitude of enquiries, all of them leading unsuspectingly to the subject of my chagrin, that I was compelled to make a candid avowal of all that had befallen me. Formerly I could assuage and console my heart by confiding all its griefs to my friend; but they appeared now so cruel, that I could not even describe them without aggravating that sorrow which no human consolation could at that time alleviate. Le Chatre was as much affected by my recital as he had been by my manner; and having given his unlimited approbation to my avowed plan of proceeding, promised to accompany me himself on my intended expedition to Genoa.

"We spent the night at the Palace, and in the morning, a vessel being engaged, walked together to the quay. The wind was contrary, but I persisted in my resolution of embarking; and as it changed, and became high, though not boisterous, in the space of a few hours we were borne swiftly, but safely along, and reached, even earlier than we had expected, the destined port. We disembarked, and proceeded directly to the Palace.

"We found Boraccio at home, and without any engagement. Having sent my name to him, and requested an interview, contrary to my expectations, he readily granted it; and in a few minutes after, entered the room into which we had been shewn.—He greeted us with politeness, and without any appearance of embarrassment, till I mentioned your name, when his countenance began to change, and my suspicions of course to

¹ A porter.

strengthen.—To my eager and repeated enquiries where you was, and by whom, and whose orders you had been placed in a Convent, he answered that he knew but very little about the matter—from some sudden pique, to which he was unable to attribute any probable foundation, you had withdrawn yourself from his protection, and was gone into France, with the intention, as he had since found, of residing in a Convent. But in what province it was situated, to what order it belonged, and whether you designed to continue there for life, or only to remain there as a boarder, were circumstances with which he protested, and in the most solemn manner imaginable, that he was utterly unacquainted.—Suspicious, yet unassured as to the extent of his villany, I affected confidence in his assertions; and withdrawing with Le Chatre, we consulted together in private on what was next to be done.

"After much deliberation and debate, we determined to direct our course toward France; and by propagating our enquiries among the Convents in the different provinces we passed through, to gain intelligence, if possible, as to your residence and fate.—On our way to it, I recollected Father Pierre; and flattering myself that he would afford me some clue that might lead to the information for which I was thus anxiously seeking, I resolved to bend my way to St. Foix.

"Hither we accordingly came; but on enquiring at the Abbey for Father Pierre, we were told, to our unspeakable disappointment, that he had been dead some weeks; and thus appeared to terminate every hope which had directed us to his asylum.—We were, however, fortunate, notwithstanding, in gaining an introduction to the Abbot, who received us with politeness; and being acquainted with our plans, generously, and without any previous solicitation, undertook himself the task of writing to the Convents in the various towns and villages of Provence and Languedoc; and even offered us a residence within his monastery till he should have obtained for us the intelligence so necessary to their accomplishment.—These proposals were too eligible not to be accepted with pleasure; and Le Chatre having provided himself with a gun, amused himself with traversing the woods, whilst I experienced an equal though a more melancholy sort of gratification, in frequenting the domains of the chateau; where every object I saw, or that my imagination presented to me, served to impress me with recollections at once gloomy and fascinating.

"One evening after our arrival, and which was one of the most charming ones I ever saw, I took a walk to the cottage of Le Luc. —The moon was just rising; and the beauty of the surrounding groves—the charms of the moonlight scenery—the delicious fragrance of the roses and jasmines which hung about the windows—the season of the year, and the hour of evening, conspired to wrap me altogether in one of those luxurious reveries, where sensibility seems to have dispossessed reflection—where no other faculty but that of feeling exerts its power upon the mind, and the heart enjoys an exquisite and delicious tranquillity.—'Twas there, by that soft light, and through those fragrant bushes which so sweetly embalm the air, that I first saw Cecilia; 'twas there I conceived that enchanting hope of happiness which her presence has revived, and which I still cherish with delight.—I cannot describe all I have felt in revisiting these scenes, or what I suffered on leaving them. Every moment revived some image of what my terrors suggested I had then irrecoverably lost: the illusions, which my fancy had conjured up, vanished from my sight; and that sensation of pleasure which I still lingered to resign, was but converted into an increase of torture.

"The next day, and the next, early in the morning, and pretty late in the evenings, I resumed my rambles about the chateau; seldom seeing any one except a peasant, who sometimes attempted to meet, and at others to pursue me, but whom, as I was well acquainted as himself with the premises he seemed to guard, I always carefully avoided.—This wearisome curiosity, for I did not impute it to fear, became at length so intolerable as to deter me from visiting the interior part of the grounds for several days together; but I walked constantly about the wood, and sometimes ventured to cross the barrier into the adjoining shrubbery.—Here I could continue unobserved; and by opening the wicket gate, and ascending the bank, obtain a full view of the gardens.—This evening I entered the shrubbery; but seeing the peasant employed amongst the trees, at some distance from where I stood, I retired as before, without attracting his notice, or

drawing his attention from his work.—But what was my astonishment and what my delight when, on re-entering the wood,
I was informed by Le Chatre that a female figure answering so
exactly to the description which I had formerly given of you,
as to leave little doubt as to your identity, had been seen by him
only a few minutes before, and was then in the gardens.—My joy
was as excessive as my despair had been infinite. Amazing and
mysterious as it appeared, I imagined it to be you; and springing over a hedge into the path into which I had been directed,
commenced anxiously my search.—I had paced several of the
avenues without meeting or seeing any one in my way, when I
thought I discerned something white among the trees; and quick-
ening my pace, eager, yet dreading to be convinced who it was
that I was pursuing, followed you into a grove. You paused near
the entrance, and still keeping near, though concealing myself
from your observation among the boles of the trees, I remained
fearful and perplexed; for the lateness of the hour, and profound
obscurity of the shades did not allow me a distinct view of
your figure. But when these again opened to light—when you
stopped, and, disturbed by the light rustling of the leaves, gazed
anxiously around—when I caught the thrilling accents of your
voice—when I heard you—Oh moment of unutterable ecstacy!
—speak of me—of me whom you believed lost to you for ever
—my doubts vanished; and losing the apprehension of alarming
you in the excess of my emotions, I could no longer be silent.
—Oh my Cecilia! these are indeed moments which make amends
in their enjoyment for whole ages of misery!"

Here he stopped: and Cecilia, in compliance with his solicitations, gave a short though (fearful of irritating a spirit naturally
impetuous) not an unembarrassed account of the persecutions
which she had undergone; but with every possible palliation
of the conduct of Boraccio and the Signora, against whom
his resentment, she well knew, would be more immediately
directed, of the means which had been employed to decoy her
from Genoa, and her memorable meeting with the Count at his
chateau in Languedoc, where, in the ungoverned state of his
feelings, he was incapable of reflection, and insensible to pity
—of the humane interference of M. Langlois, including also the

considerate and very flattering offers of protection which he had since given her—and her resolution of accepting them, when she had made her intended visit into Italy.—But, however guarded in her expressions both as to Boraccio and his wife, Varàno found sufficient grounds for his resentment even in her account; and the patience with which she spoke of her oppressors and of her sufferings, and her fortitude in supporting them, while her pale cheeks and colourless lips evinced their power upon her health, at the same time that it increased his love and admiration of her to a degree of idolatry, roused his indignation against Boraccio and his nefarious employer; and the manner in which he named them, particularly the former, alarming her as much for his safety as for her own, she was now only anxious to prevent the consequences of his resentment.—This she endeavoured to do by urging the impolicy and even danger of forcing Boraccio into an explanation which would reflect so much dishonour upon his relative, and might be productive of the most serious effects to both of them.—"At any rate," said she, "declaring yourself his enemy will only make him more actively your's, and justify him in some measure for being so, and can do no good."

Varàno listened to her entreaties with attention, but replied to them only with looks of tenderness and despondency, disguising as much as possible the sentiments he felt both as to Boraccio and the Count, that he might sooth the apprehensions that distressed her. But the violent internal conflict he underwent between his solicitude for her, and his indignation toward her enemies, was too apparent, notwithstanding all his endeavours to conceal it, not to occasion her some fear; and she became so strenuous in her remonstrances that he would forbear to insist upon an eclaircissement, or even to exact another interview with Boraccio in the present temper of his feelings, that, touched as much by her manner, as by the warmth and energy of her expressions, he promised to remain calm, and to submit himself entirely to her guidance, though it was evident that nothing but his extreme anxiety for her peace could have determined him to overlook injuries which appeared, every time he recurred to them, to be more and more atrocious and unpardonable.

The subject of their mutual concern was scarcely discussed

when they were surprised by a loud rapping at the outer gate
of the chateau; and in a few minutes Susanne entered, ushering
in a stranger, whom Cecilia soon discovered to be the Chevalier
she had encountered near the wood, and who was immediately
introduced to her by the name of Le Chatre.

He saluted her with an air at once easy and respectful; and
having slightly apologized for his intrusion, and for the alarm his
first appearance had occasioned, said—

"I ought not, however, to lament an accident which has made
me instrumental to a *rencontre* productive of so much happiness
to my friend, and which will be the means I hope of terminating
an anxiety I have long witnessed with pain."

Cecilia curtsied, and Le Chatre, taking a seat near Varàno, conversed with him for some time on indifferent topics of discourse,
in which Cecilia sometimes joined, but oftener remained silent,
being too much agitated by what had passed between her and
Varàno, and too much embarrassed by the sudden entrance of
his friend, to be enabled to take her part in the conversation.—In
about an hour Le Chatre, observing that the Monks of the Abbey
of Sancta Trinité retired early to repose, and that it was even then
probable that the gates of the Monastery might be closed, they
arose and withdrew; leaving Cecilia to reflect at leisure upon the
extraordinary and unlooked-for occurrences that day had produced.

Varàno went to bed, but could not sleep, nor even enjoy the
least repose.—How far his father was implicated in this late infamous transaction, he was wholly incompetent to determine, and
not less unwilling to discuss. The certainty, however, that he was
in some way or other concerned in it, was equally mortifying and
afflictive to him.—Nor did the conduct of the Marchesa appear
materially less culpable; every promise which he had drawn from
her, and that she had herself given Cecilia, having been either
totally neglected, or wilfully violated: and considering himself as
freed by this omission from the performance of that which she
had once mildly and authoritatively exacted from him, and which
he very fortunately recollected was only conditional, he had little
difficulty in conquering those scruples which, while duty suggested, love urgently opposed; and having surmounted his own,

he resolved to spare neither argument nor entreaty to remove those of Cecilia, and to convince her, if possible, of the indispensability of a union, which only could ensure his happiness, or properly atone to her for the sufferings she had so undeservedly undergone.

Hoping, yet dreading lest her resolution of not entering into a clandestine engagement might be too unalterably fixed even for his entreaties to move it, he awaited impatiently the return of morning, when he arose, and repaired eagerly to the chateau.

He found Cecilia alone, and in a profound reverie, her head reclining on her hand, and her hair falling in luxuriant tresses on the arm that supported it, of which it concealed a part.—Her eyes were bent earnestly to the ground, and as, startled by his unexpected appearance, she raised them with emotion to meet his, he perceived they were filled with tears.

Varàno seated himself in silence; for, struck by the extreme dejection of her looks, he seemed at a loss how to address her. But when, smiling and blushing through her tears, she gently accosted him, elated with hope, and no longer able to command himself, he fell at her feet, and seizing both her hands, proceeded to propose an immediate marriage, and that at an early hour on the following morning she should quit the chateau, and be conducted by him to the Church of the Benedictines, where a Friar would await to unite them.

Cecilia shuddered at the proposal; for though she could not suffer herself to hesitate, a painful sense of an impropriety even in having listened to it, and which the recollection of her late vow more immediately suggested, flashed across her mind, and betrayed itself upon her countenance. And aware that, after the assurances which she had received from him at their former interview at Genoa, nothing but his excessive anxiety about her, and utter despair of obtaining her with the approbation of his family, would have tempted him to make it, and also that her answer ought at all events to be decisive, she conjured him not to continue to deceive himself, and to give her pain, by indulging hopes which she was now more than ever convinced never could be realized; and which, while unsanctioned by an authority to which he owed so much, were scarcely to be even mentioned with impunity.

Varàno loved too tenderly to venture the language of reproach; but a profound and exquisite sensation of sorrow seized upon his heart. He could neither controvert the truth of what she said, nor bear the thoughts of parting with her; and having exhausted at length every argument with which his passion, his apprehensions, and that an excess of tenderness could supply him with, compelled to respect even while he condemned the delicacy of which he was doomed to be the victim, and fearful of increasing an uneasiness he could not witness without pain, he desisted from any further solicitation, though not till he had obtained permission from Cecilia to accompany her into Italy; a measure which he pressed with so much earnestness, and with such an impressive energy of manner, that she thought she ought not to refuse.—And then, as if desirous to conclude an interview which tortured them both, and perceiving all the danger of trusting longer to her resolution in the presence of Varàno, she arose and withdrew.

When alone, the idea of going a journey of that length in the society of two young men, it being determined that Le Chatre was to be of the party, appeared so inconsistent with delicacy and her own nice sense of propriety, that she resolved to send immediately to Louisette, of whose ready acquiescence in any scheme she proposed, the various proofs of attachment which she had formerly received from her left her little reason to doubt.—This she accordingly did; and Louisette, whom nothing but her ignorance of Cecilia's being then resident at the chateau could have absented so long, returning with the messenger, accorded so joyfully with the proposal of attending her into Italy, that every obstacle being removed, Cecilia waited only for a letter from the Signora di Rosalvo to determine the time and manner of their journey.

Varàno, though he spent his nights at the Abbey, was generally at the chateau during the day; sometimes coming alone, and sometimes with Le Chatre, whose spirits being seldom depressed, gave cheerfulness to the little party now assembled within it. Le Chatre, although a native of France, had resided chiefly in Italy, having been educated by an uncle, a member of the *Academia della Crusa* in Florence, at whose house he had lived.

In this city he remained, going only occasionally into France, till the death of his father, at which period he quitted Italy, and had since resided with his mother on her estate in Dauphine.—Similar in tastes, and alike in principles, in sentiment, and in education, a friendship at once ardent and sincere was early formed between him and Varàno; and though since the time of Le Chatre's quitting Florence, months and even years had elapsed without either seeing the other, through the medium of a correspondence long established between them, the most trifling as well as the more important incidents of their lives were always regularly transmitted.

Though much inferior to Varàno in person, manner, and accomplishments, the conversation of Le Chatre was at once lively and intelligent; and Cecilia soon discovered that it was not to the partiality of Varàno only that he was indebted for the esteem with which he had inspired her.

Day after day passed on, when one evening, as Cecilia was sitting at work in her apartment, attended only by Louisette, Varàno being then absent with his friend, she received her long expected letter from the Signora di Rosalvo, whose expressions of esteem and kindness were very necessary consolations to her heart, awakened as it was in her late interview with Varàno to images of sorrow and regret.—It was conveyed to her by a servant dispatched thither by the Signor to escort her into Italy; and as there was now no further cause for delay, early on the ensuing morning, every arrangement being made, the travellers commenced their journey; proceeding in two carriages to Toulon, at which port they embarked, and coasting the shores of the Mediterranean, gained the county of Nice. From thence, stopping only a few hours, they continued their way by land; and having traversed the *Cornich*, and a part of that forest rendered awful to Cecilia by the recollection of a former dreadful event, and whose dreary woods and almost impenetrable recesses, although seen only under the influence of a noonday sky, and notwithstanding she was protected by one so dear to her, yet struck her with dismay, they soon after arrived at the castle.

CHAPTER VIII

Oh Melancholy!
Who ever yet could sound thy bottom—find
The ooze, to shew what coast thy sluggish carrack
Might eas'liest harbour in?

SHAKESPEARE.

THE Signora di Rosalvo was playing an elegant air at her piano when the carriages with Cecilia and her friends entered the courts. She ran immediately to receive her guests, and having tenderly embraced her, and expressed the utmost pleasure and surprise at the appearance of Varàno and his friend, she conducted them into a room, where they were shortly joined by Rosalvo. He entered with a dejected air; and as he courteously addressed them, seemed to be struggling to divest himself of a despondency, of which he appeared painfully conscious. "Alas!" thought Cecilia, to whom his pale, emaciated, though still finely proportioned figure had never appeared more interesting, "how deep must be that sorrow which time cannot obliterate—how agonizing that anguish which admits not of friendly participation!"—She sighed as she meditated, and fixed her eyes upon the Signora, who, comprehending their meaning, endeavoured to conceal the uneasiness which Cecilia had thus inadvertently excited, by interrogating her concerning their journey and mode of employment whilst in Provence.

"Tell me," said she, smiling, and directing an arch look at Varàno, "were you not in some danger at St. Foix from the attacks of melancholy. Lonely walks, Italian poetry, and Italian music are calculated to make us susceptible of this uneasy malady:—and you, my Cecilia, if I judge right, have not escaped its contagion. —Why, Signor," added she, to Varàno, "do you not teach her to be less thoughtful? Your country-women are renowned for their vivacity."

"They are, Madam," returned Varàno; "but were I to succeed

in the effort of making Mademoiselle de St. Bertrand any thing but what she is, would she not be less amiable?"

The Signora di Rosalvo rewarded this compliment to her friend with a benignant smile. Cecilia's cheek glowed, but it was with a glow of pleasure—that sweet feeling which praise deserved bestows.

Whilst this conversation passed between the Signora and Varàno, Le Chatre endeavoured to support one with Rosalvo.— He spoke of the laws and manufactories of the Italian States, particularly that of Genoa, which he commended for its superiority over many others with regard to its Police. On his happening to mention Naples, the Signor changed colour; his eyes assumed a peculiar wildness, and a convulsive sign escaped his breast.

"You have been at Naples then?" said he.

"For a short time," replied Le Chatre; "but as Nature has been more lavish of her beauties in these charming regions than in any other in the world, I would willingly explore some of those romantic scenes which have stored the imaginations of our poets with such enchanting imagery! I would not merely see—I would enjoy the Elysium of Virgil."

Whilst Le Chatre was expatiating on the beauties of Naples, Rosalvo has relapsed into one of his accustomed reveries, from which he at length started, and demanded of Le Chatre whether he had any acquaintance amongst the Nobles of that city.—Le Chatre replied in the negative. Rosalvo leaned back in his chair, heaved another sigh, and was silent.

The next day Cecilia made a full disclosure of her melancholy adventures to the Signora, who, deeply affected by them, embraced her with more tenderness than before; and lamenting her promise to M. Langlois of accepting his offers of protection, insisted that she should remain with her at the Castle, at least during the winter.

Varàno, since he had suffered from the apprehension of being separated for ever from Cecilia, had become more and more infatuated. He could now scarcely bear her from his sight— counted with impatience even the moments in her absence, and blamed equally the rapidity of those passed in her presence. The uneasy idea of his father, and the still more insupportable one of his mother, would often intrude upon his thoughts. He knew the former would reflect upon him with indignation, and the latter with sorrow. His abrupt departure and mysterious absence would be variously accounted for, and such measures employed for his discovery as nothing but the gloomy secrecy of his present residence could render abortive. To the anguish which his conduct would inflict upon his parents, he was not insensible; the thought perplexed and disturbed him, but had not power enough to determine him to return.

Whilst Varàno, torn by conflicting sensations, was now happy and now miserable by turns, as he was more or less sensible to the uneasiness of his family, or enjoyed the converse of Cecilia, the Marchese, who remained with Olivia and her father at Molise, unable to obtain any intelligence of his son, felt his pride and his tenderness suffer equal attacks. He now trembled lest he should be involved in the disgrace which an alliance with Cecilia would inflict, and now shuddered lest the child of his affection, whom scarcely and deviation from rectitude could make him reflect on without an excess of tenderness almost painful, should be driven to desperation.—The plot which he had concerted with Boraccio, of forcing Cecilia into a Convent, and endeavouring to deceive Varàno into the supposition that she had voluntarily retired thither, seemed to have drawn upon him the evil which he had endeavoured to avoid.

Olivia, though less interested, was not less perplexed than the Marchese.—She had no doubt but that Varàno was gone in search of Cecilia. But why he had quitted them so abruptly, what route he had taken, and with what view he was gone in quest of her, were propositions not easy to be solved. Though hopeless of succeeding, she endeavoured to divert the Marchese from his plan of pursuing him. The Marchese, notwithstanding, set off immediately for Florence, with the design of consulting with the Marchesa, intending to go from thence to Genoa, where he despaired not but he could inform himself of the situation of Cecilia, and from whence he might dispatch couriers into the southern parts of France in pursuit of Varàno.

The most tormenting apprehensions, and the most uneasy surmises agitated him throughout the way; and after traversing the mountain-region of Abruzzo, he had arrived at Celano, indisposition overtook him, and he was unable to proceed.

From this place he wrote to the Marchesa to acquaint her with his own illness and Lorenzo's departure, desiring her to waste no time in sending emissaries into France, particularly Languedoc; left Varàno, driven on by his passion, and by the resentment which he had lately conceived against him (the Marchese) and Boraccio, should frustrate their design by an immediate and disgraceful marriage.

The Marchesa was at her villa at Prato when she received this intelligence.—Her fears concerning Lorenzo were still more acute than the Marchese's. Dreading lest he should fall a victim to this unhappy attachment, she felt half inclined to use her influence with her Lord to persuade him to consent to his wishes; but convinced that such a proposal would be rejected with asperity, the idea was almost instantly discarded.

Returning immediately to the Palace, she was surprised in a few days by the arrival of the Marchese, who, notwithstanding his illness, had pursued his journey. Her still beautiful features were overcast with the deepest sorrow as she approached to meet him; and this expression was considerably heightened when she learned from the Marchese the plan devised by himself and Boraccio relating to Cecilia; nor could her affection for her Lord suppress her indignation at the tyranny of the measure. The absence of Varàno was, however, the subject which pressed most heavily on her thoughts; and she agreed with the Marchese that it would be right to pursue him before his purpose could be accomplished.—The Marchese's designs when once formed, were always executed with rapidity. He accordingly embarked upon the Arno, and arrived shortly at Genoa.

When he alighted at the Palace, he found, to his disappointment, that Boraccio was then absent, and the Lady Viola entirely ignorant of every thing relative to Varàno and Cecilia. All she could communicate was that the former had been there; but whither he was gone, unless to seek Cecilia in Languedoc, she was unable to devise. It was a pity, she observed, that her uncle had ever brought the girl into Italy; obscure young women like her were better at home, or with those of their own class.

The chit, it seemed, was destined to be a trouble to her and her family, who were now requited for their condescension in having suffered her to intrude into it; adding, that nothing but her presumptuous hope of drawing Lorenzo into a marriage with her, would have determined her to refuse the Count; and nothing, this refusal excepted, could have astonished her more than that Nobleman's intention of uniting himself to a person of her fortune, and whose birth, the very circumstance of its being unknown proved to be disgraceful.

The Signora might have proceeded for hours in this unfeeling harangue without a single interruption from the Marchese, whose mind was too much occupied in conjecture concerning the late conduct of his son, to permit him to attend to it, and who, had he been in a situation to have listened to it, would have been convinced that exertion, in the present urgent state of his affairs, would be more prevalent than invective.

Boraccio soon arrived, and unprepared for this encounter with the Marchese, conscious of duplicity toward him, and of guilt toward Cecilia, his replies to his interrogatories were confused, and his voice faltering.—The Marchese perceived it; and, both suspicious of deceit, and resentful of his evasions, commanded him to give a brief and explicit relation of this affair.

Boraccio gave the recital in nearly the same words in which he had delivered it to Varàno; concluding by observing that he had little doubt of Cecilia's being then in her Convent, or if not, it must be owing to some secret correspondence with Lorenzo, which all his vigilance could not prevent, or to the artful machinations of the Count, whose mad passion no repulse could overcome.

"Had he," the Marchese enquired, "heard of her since she left Italy?"

Boraccio replied that he had not; but as he had forborne to give any particular orders, or even to intimate a wish to receive information of her immediately on her arrival, he was not surprised at the omission.

"Where was the Convent situated?—Who was the Superior?" demanded the Marchese, "and to what order did it belong?"

Boraccio believed, he answered, that they were Carmelites;

but the situation, the name of the Abbess, and even that of the Convent were points with which he declared himself totally unacquainted, having consigned her to the protection of a Monk of the same order, who acted as Confessor to the community, and who had orders to introduce her to the Abbess as a young lady who was desirous of passing her minority in her Convent as a boarder, and to whom he was to deliver a prohibition against any person's being admitted to her at the grate, or her having the means of writing or speaking to any one without the presence of the Superior.

These, the Marchese remarked, were good precautions, and in the present case very necessary ones. He intended, however, that Cecilia should be treated with mildness and that she should not be compelled to remain there beyond the time prescribed.

"She is a fine and very sensible young woman," added he; "and had she been as richly endowed by Fortune as by Nature, I know no one, Olivia excepted, that I should prefer to her for my son; but he is the last of his line, and he must not unite himself with a beggar."

"Certainly not," cried Boraccio; "the ancient house of Varàno would suffer the severest degradation from such a union."

"The few remaining members of that house," pursued the Marchese, "ought therefore to unite to prevent the evil which threatens it. Should Lorenzo descend from his dignity, and marry this girl, he is less accountable to himself than to his house: the honour of his family is in his hands, and his own depends upon its continuance. The blood which fills his veins has descended to him in an unsullied stream from an illustrious and self-ennobled ancestry; let him beware that he mingles it not with baser matter!"

He pronounced these words with a peculiar emphasis, and traversed the room with measured steps.

"You are still ignorant, my Lord, that is, you are not fully informed," resumed Boraccio, "as to the circumstances of Cecilia's birth:—may not her descent be less humble than you imagine?"

"In respect to most things," said the Marchese, still pacing the room, "I can place an unlimited dependence upon my own judgment. At present I have not hinted my surmises, but the oftener I recur to them, the more I am convinced of their probability. She is certainly the daughter of De Sevignac by a peasant of the neighbourhood of St. Foix, the widow of a soldier, a Gascon, in the service of France, and whose name I think was De Coucy."

Boraccio observed that, since his Lordship was seldom wrong in his conjectures, undoubtedly it was highly probable as he had stated it. The conversation then broke off.

The Marchese, obliged to await the return of his emissaries from their expedition to Languedoc, continued at the Palace, where he received frequent letters from the Marchesa, none of which were, however, satisfactory as to the subject of their mutual disquiet.

Hitherto Boraccio had heard nothing from the Count. But as the plot was too ingeniously conducted to admit a doubt of its miscarriage, he was persuaded that Cecilia had been delivered into his power; and since, amid the solitudes of the Cevennes, she could ensure no other protection, that she was still his captive. He wondered indeed that the success of his project had not been confirmed to him by a letter or messenger from the Count; but attributing this omission to the excessive joy of his situation on the completion of his base designs upon Cecilia, and willing to conclude any thing rather than that she had escaped, his mind regained its former composure, and he now thought only of reassuring the Marchese, and deluding Varàno, who if he had actually discovered that Cecilia was not in any of the Convents in Languedoc, would probably return to Genoa.

Varàno had yet not given any hint as to the time of his departure from the Castle—he had, indeed, scarcely thought of it; for, sensible only to the happiness of being in the same house with Cecilia, every thing else was forgotten:—the distress of the Marchesa occurred less frequently to his thoughts; and firmly persuaded that Cecilia could be safe only from the artifices of his family as long as she was under his immediate protection, his love, his policy, and, above all, his high sense of what was due to injured innocence, conspired to detain him.

Cecilia's uneasiness increased as his stay was protracted. She knew if it was ascertained that she was under the same roof with

Varàno, she should be exposed to the censure of having encouraged his addresses. Her pride was mortified at the reflection; and she resolved frankly to explain to him her reasons for wishing him to quit the Castle. She accordingly represented to him the anxiety which his long absence from him family would occasion his father, the grief of his mother, the cruelty he was practicing in thus lengthening their suspense, and the humiliating suspicions to which his stay would expose her as well as himself.

These arguments, though they could be neither controverted nor evaded, had nevertheless no tendency to subdue his reluctance to the thoughts of parting from her. He acknowledged the force of them, and lamented and even wept with her at the recollections her remonstrances had awakened; but was unwilling, or, as he confessed, unable to yield to them implicitly: and the discourse was interrupted before she had obtained from him any positive assurances that her entreaties had not been in vain.

Entertaining little hope of his compliance, and more than ever convinced of the indispensability of the measure, she now thought of employing the agency of the Signora, and now of Le Chatre. The latter she knew possessed some authority over his friend; and she determined to incite him instantly to employ it, to hasten his departure from the Castle.

An opportunity for the execution of her purpose was not long wanting. She saw Le Chatre from her window walking alone upon the terrace, and immediately joining him, enquired whether Varàno had mentioned any thing of his return to his friends.

"Not a word," cried Le Chatre; "he is, I believe, too happy:— but what must that man be who could not be happy—who could not, in short, forget every thing in such society?"

"I have much to say to you," said Cecilia, rather gravely; "but you are perhaps engaged."

"When with you I am, and most happily," returned the Chevalier still more gaily.

"You are very gallant, and an adept, I find, at compliment," rejoined Cecilia; "but it is your advice I came to ask, and not your praise."

"You shall have both," cried Le Chatre; "the former you may command—the other *will* come when it *will* come."

"And is often bestowed where it is the least merited," said Cecilia, laughing.

"In larger portions, perhaps, and the reason why it is so, is evident. Women of sense are epicures in their praise; to them, therefore, it must be temperately and very judiciously administered: there are even those whose minds are so delicately modelled, that they will bear none, except that which results from their own hearts; others are too greedy of it to be nice as to the quality—they will digest any thing, however coarse."

"It is well," cried Cecilia, carrying on the comparison, "that the extremes of gluttony and epicurism do not meet in the same person."

"True," said Le Chatre, "an Apicius in praise would be a very perplexing character. But am I indeed so favoured as to be the motive of your walk? How is it that I have been honoured with your thoughts?"

"I came," answered Cecilia, "to solicit your assistance."

"What is it Mademoiselle de St. Bertrand can ask, and I refuse?"

"No more of this," said Cecilia; "I would speak seriously.—Your friend——"

"What of him, Madam?"

"Will incur, by remaining here, the anger of the Marchese and of his family; it is proper that he should remove from hence. Can you not persuade him?"

Le Chatre looked surprised.

"Whilst he is here," cried she, "I am unhappy, because I know him to be the cause of unhappiness to others. The Marchesa adores her son. What then must be her feelings when she is ignorant where he is, and when even this is the least of her distresses."

"By informing them of his residence, might we not," replied Le Chatre, "prevent the necessity of his return?"

"Even this," resumed Cecilia with hesitation, "would be insufficient."

She then earnestly desired that he would urge these reasons to Varàno. Le Chatre, whose penetration perceived in this request motives which her delicacy forbade her to explain, promised to obey.

At a little distance from the Castle was a deep dell sunk

between two opposite hills, and terminated by a clump of dark trees, immersed in which was a lonely little summer-house, built with rough marble in the Saxon Gothic style, and ornamented in the interior with *alto relievo* figures, representing the labours and sports of the vintage. The grotto-like coolness of this place, the romantic wildness of the dell itself, and of the high trees which waved over it, rendered it the favourite retreat of meditation and melancholy. One evening as Varàno was strolling thoughtfully alone, he accidentally entered this glen. He advanced leisurely along the path, often pausing to listen to the breeze, and sometimes to the liquid melody which floated through the foliage of the overhanging shades, till he reached the summer-house; when a deep sigh arrested his attention, and he paused in suspense. —"Ah, beloved and unfortunate Chevalier!" said a voice which he instantly knew to be Cecilia's, "could I have known—could I have administered to thy sorrows!"—Another sigh succeeded these words, and he perceived that she wept. Varàno started. A thousand fears—a thousand agonizing presages flashed to his mind! The most torturing and improbable suggestions usurped the empire of reason; and that he had a rival—a secret, but successful rival, was the first which offered itself to his fancy. Distracted with this surmise, he rushed into the summer-house; his respiration short, his looks wild, and his whole frame disordered with agitation. Cecilia, who was sitting with her eyes fixed upon a picture which she held with an expression of mournful tenderness, started from her posture, and gently demanded the cause of his emotion. Varàno replied only by enquiring whose was that portrait. Cecilia dried away her tears, and faintly smiling, delivered the picture into his hands.—"Can you not," said she tremulously, "trace a resemblance to these features?"

Varàno gazed upon it with astonishment, then at her, and then again at the portrait—a shade of suspicion crossed his mind: his eyes were lighted up with new fire, and his cheeks suffused with burning blushes.—"I think I can," returned he, breaking silence; "but if it belongs to you, from whom, or by what means did you obtain possession of it?"

"Is it surprising," resumed Cecilia, "that I should have the portrait of my father?"

"Of your father?"

"Yes, Varàno, it is indeed my father! the most unfortunate—the most injured of human beings!"

"Great God! is it possible?" cried Varàno, half frantic with joy. The mystery of her birth elucidated, all obstacles to his happiness seemed, in his imagination, removed.—"Does he live?" exclaimed he with deeper emphasis, and regarding her with looks of transport unutterable.

"Ah, no," said Cecilia, "his destiny was severe—his death dreadful! Till lately all the incidents attending it were unknown to me."

"Oh, let me know them!" interrupted Varàno; "repose them fearlessly in a breast which will willingly become the repository of all your sorrows."

"Spare me—Oh, spare me!" replied Cecilia, with an affecting energy, as she paused upon the propriety of disclosing them, "there are reasons——"

"Forgive my curiosity," cried Varàno; "I have done—I will not press you to gratify it; tell me only the name of your father, his rank in life, and how you have attained the knowledge of this secret."

"His name," continued Cecilia, "was Julien D'Arnaud:—he was an officer in the armies of Louis XV, and was signalized under the severe discipline of one of the most renowned Generals of the age, in the war at that time carried on by France against the united powers of Germany and Russia. I became acquainted with his fatal story from some papers left for me by M. de Sevignac in the possession of Signor di Boraccio, which I have only lately examined; till my perusal of these papers every part of his history was concealed from me."

"And why then," said Varàno impatiently, "do you not assume the name of your family?"

"Particular circumstances in this story," replied Cecilia, (who had been induced, by the arbitrary decree of the Inquisition that the child of Leonora should be devoted to a religious life, to retain the name of St. Bertrand) "have rendered it unadvisable."

"And these, too," said Varàno significantly, "are to be concealed from *even me*."

Cecilia, affected by this remark, and desirous to spare herself the pain of a recital which it appeared even cruel to withhold, promised him, after a little previous deliberation, the perusal of the papers.

As they were returning to the Castle, they were met by the Signora di Rosalvo and Le Chatre, whom she was rallying with great sprightliness on his gravity, his anxiety for Varàno having checked his natural vivacity.

"He is positively," said she, "the most stupid Frenchman I have ever met with. I have been sauntering with him for this half hour, and concise remarks and abstracted answers are the utmost I can gain from him. Such a man at Paris would be a prodigy:—tell me, Chevalier," continued she, "are you not considered as a curiosity in your own country?"

"France," rejoined Le Chatre, "and particularly Paris, abounds with curiosities; a silent woman, or a black swan, would there scarcely be deemed a rarity."

"Indeed! What superiority can France boast beyond the neighbouring kingdoms on the Continent?" cried the Signora.

"Great originality, or rather great variety of character," resumed Le Chatre. "The mild temperature of our climate, and the gaiety of our manners, attract to us numerous visitors. Here the Spaniard buries his solemnity, and the Englishman his *ennui*; the Dutchman forgets his commerce to mix in the gaiety of our assemblies; and the Italian, animated as he is, derives an additional vivacity from the same source."

"But you have not discovered, Chevelier," said the Signora, "from what source you have imbibed your gravity."

"If the disease is epidemic, I have not caught it of Signora di Rosalvo," returned Le Chatre.

The presence of Rosalvo put an end to this raillery, and they entered the Castle.

Varàno, impatient to be alone, hastily quitted the party, and eagerly perused the papers given to him by Cecilia. He was now as anxious to depart, as he had been before reluctant; and prepared to fly to the Marchesa with the welcome intelligence that Cecilia's birth was at least genteel. Le Chatre offering to accompany him, they agreed to set off on the following day.

Cecilia, from whom, through motives of delicacy, he concealed the real cause of his departure, forgot the pain of a separation in the pleasure she felt from the idea that the Marchesa's anxiety concerning her son would be now at an end.—In the morning the two friends, attended by Benedetto, set off for Florence.

Cecilia, on their departure, retired immediately to her chamber, where she was soon followed by Louisette; who, imagining that she looked ill, and attributed this supposed indisposition to her parting with Varàno, endeavoured to offer her consolation.

"I am not ill," said Cecilia mournfully, "I am only low, Louisette."

"If you were not low," continued Louisette, "I am sure I know who is. Poor Signor Varàno, my heart aches for him! Ah! if you had seen him one day when we were talking about you!"

"About me!" cried Cecilia.

"Yes, we often talked about you, Mademoiselle; the Signor is always so affable and so free—he has no more pride than Benedetto; and then he carries himself with such a grace!—Once when I happened to meet him in the corridor, he asked me how I liked the Castle.—'Louisette,' said he, 'you was very kind to come with your young Lady;' and then he put a ducat into my hand, and said with one of his sweet smiles, for you know, Mademoiselle, how charming he looks when he smiles—'I hope you will have no reason to repent your journey;' and then he enquired whether I liked Italy as well as France."

"And what was your answer, Louisette?" returned Cecilia.

"Why, I told him, Mademoiselle, that to be sure I could not say it was quite so pleasant, because there was no music, nor singing, nor dancing under the trees, and nothing to be seen but those dreary looking mountains; and as to the Castle, I thought it was but a great wilderness old place at the best, and so gloomy, that it looked for all the world as if it was haunted. When I said this, the Signor laughed out, and said he hoped I was not superstitious.— 'Why, as to that, your Honour,' said I, 'I am no more fanciful than other people; but the rooms are so large, and so ruinous, and run in such long suites, and the passages so winding and so bewildering, that one is in danger of being lost every moment.'

"'Your objections are very strong, Louisette,' said the Signor; 'but you love your Lady, I hope, too well to leave her?'

"'Yes, Signor,' says I, 'and I hope *you* love her too well to leave her. Holy Maria! I shall never forget how she laid it to heart when your Honour set off without taking leave of her; she used to sit by herself for hours when my poor dear master was in his study, thinking about you, and singing mournful ditties.'"

"Good Heavens! Louisette," interrupted Cecilia, "how could you be so imprudent?"

"La, Mademoiselle, why, what can it signify? The Signor must know you like him; and I am sure there is not a servant in the Castle that does not say how fond he is of you; for Benedetto says, that when his master left Bojano, he hardly ever ate or drank till he got to Naples, and he is sure, he says, it was all along with you."

"Louisette," said Cecilia solemnly, "I must entreat, nay insist upon it, that you never more speak to the Signor of me."

"Never speak to him of *you*! What, never mention your name, Mademoiselle? Holy Saints! the Signor could no more see *me* without thinking of *you*, than he could fly over the southern turret; and I am sure if you had seen what pleasure it gave him when I told him how sadly you lamented him, you would never have forgotten it—his eyes sparkled so, and his colour came and went——"

"No more, I command you, Louisette," continued Cecilia, still more gravely; "and remember that no temptation for the future must induce you to talk thus with the Signor. You know not," added she, "how much this conduct has distressed me.—The Signor and I must never meet again but as *friends*!"

"The Virgin forbid you ever should meet but as *friends*!"

"I mean," rejoined Cecilia, "that nothing more than friendship can ever subsist between us. I know not whether we ever shall, or indeed whether we ever *ought* to meet again."

"La, Mademoiselle, sure you have not quarrelled?"

"We have not," returned Cecilia; "but remember my injunction. I shall judge of your attachment to me, according as I am obeyed."

"Well, who would have thought it?—What strange things

come about! It was but yesterday that Benedetto was saying
—'Louisette,' says he——"

"Once more," cried Cecilia, with more severity than was usual
to her, "I conjure you to be silent!"

"Holy Virgin protect me! You are so particular, Mademoiselle!
I was only going to say that Benedetto told *me*——"

"Hush!" said Cecilia; "I will not hear you:—leave me——I
have my reasons for wishing to be alone."

She pronounced these words in a manner which admitted
not of reply; and Louisette was obliged, reluctantly, to withdraw,
vexed to be prohibited a subject she would have discussed so
eloquently, and not a little mortified at being chid for what she
considered as harmless.—Fondly partial to Cecilia, she believed
no match could be superior to her deserts, and consequently to
her expectations; and as her beauty, and Varàno's attachment to
her had been the popular theme in the kitchen ever since their
arrival, she could not controul her inclination to disclose what
had probably been as instrumental to the support of her vanity
and anticipated importance, as if the panegyrics bestowed upon
her mistress had been confined to herself, and the prospect of
aggrandizement wholly her own.

END OF VOLUME THREE

WHO'S THE MURDERER?

CHAPTER I

O somme Dio! como i giudici umani
Spesso offuscati son da en nembo obscuro!

Ariosto.

Oh mighty God! how often are human opinions
given in a dark cloud!

From the period of Varàno's departure, the Signora became more and more attached to Cecilia, who continued to recommend herself by an affectionate assiduity, and a diligent attention to the most minute circumstances that might contribute to her happiness. When alone with Rosalvo, the Signora had frequently expressed her astonishment that Cecilia had never mentioned her family; observing that when any thing was hinted relative to the subject, she had always changed the discourse with some appearance of embarrassment. Cecilia's real motive for this conduct originated not in any fear of being betrayed by her friends, but from the idea that the Signora di Rosalvo might be as rigid in her religious principles as De Sevignac, and consider her mother's infringement of her monastic vows as criminal and impious.

Rosalvo, when his guests had quitted the Castle, relapsed into his former despondency. This dejection, in the course of a few weeks, became more rooted than ever. He would sit at times for hours in the cold torpor of despair, till new and more torturing recollections brought with them an accession of agony, and he would then plunge into the woods and thickest shades of the forest, where, in defiance of danger, and devoid of feeling, the unhappy wanderer passed many of his wretched and lonely hours.

Cecilia was sometimes afraid of increasing those symptoms of a distracted mind by appearing to notice them; and at other times she ventured cautiously to unite her remembrances with those of her friend, to detain him with them at the Castle.

The only person with whom he loved to converse was the Abbot of a neighbouring Convent, a profound and able theologist, with whom he frequently held long conferences on subjects of religious controversy, which often lasted till midnight. It was in one of these discourses that Rosalvo demanded of the Abbot his opinion concerning supernatural interposition.

"This is a subject," returned the Abbot, "on which no human mind is competent to judge."

"I asked only for your opinion," interrupted Rosalvo.

"I think then," said the Abbot, "that if ever the unimprisoned spirit is permitted to revisit the regions of mortality, it must be on great occasions only."

"And what do you suppose those occasions to be?" asked Rosalvo.

"In cases of murder perhaps," replied the Abbot, "where the perpetrator has been undiscovered, the unappeased spirit may be allowed to return again to the earth, for the purpose of obtaining retribution."

Rosalvo fixed his eyes upon the Abbot, and a ghastly smile overspread his features.

"But though this may sometimes be the case," continued the Abbot, "the credulity of ignorance has led to frequent imposition. Fancy has in all ages peopled the world with apparitions; and the goading stings of an awakened conscience have oftentimes given birth to the most dreadful superstitions!"

A gust of wind at this moment blew hollowly through the room. Rosalvo shuddered—looked around him with an expression at once of terror and awe, and springing wildly from his seat, darted from the room.

The Signora, observing the astonishment of the Abbot, endeavoured to frame some excuse for a conduct which she was unwilling, and indeed unable to account for, but her voice faltered, and the Abbot, taking advantage of her confusion, retired.

This incident occasioned the most horrible surmises both to the Signora and Cecilia. The former, anxious as she had before been to investigate the cause of her husband's secret distress, now seemed rather to dread than to desire the explanation. But whatever were her suspicions, she confined them to her own breast.

The beauty of the season was now rapidly declining. On one of the long chill evenings which forerun the approach of winter, the small party at the Castle were assembled in a large gloomy apartment, which, from its being furnished with a few old books, was denominated the library. The night was stormy, and the wind so loud, that the Signora and Cecilia often started involuntarily, as it broke in lengthening squalls over the building; whilst Rosalvo, his arms folded, and his eyes fastened upon the fire, seemed utterly unconscious of all that was passing. The storm continued to howl, and the rising gusts shook the casements.

"I never hear the wind groan, and then burst again into sudden violence, as it does to-night," said Cecilia, "but I think of the poor mariners at sea, or the houseless wanderer who has do defence against its fury."

"'Tis a melancholy reflection," cried the Signora.

"It is so," pursued Cecilia," but while I think of the miseries of others, I feel less inclined to repine at my own."

"But what pleasure can we derive," rejoined the Signora, "from the idea that there are others more wretched than ourselves?"

"It may teach us to make a more proper estimate of our own situations," answered Cecilia, "and feel ashamed to murmur at those little ills which must unavoidably be our lot."

The Signora made no remark, but continued her work in silence. She was engaged in drawing the figure of a Magdalen, but had failed in her attempt to catch the peculiar style of countenance necessary to her subject. The forehead was too low, the hair too little exposed, and the uplifted eye had not in it the characteristic devotion. Requesting Cecilia, therefore, to finish it, she took up a book, rather as an antidote against thoughts, than an amusement.

The storm was abating, but the evening was so intensely cold, that the party drew still nearer the fire. The boisterous motion of the sea became less and less awful; and the silence which succeeded the tremendous warring of the elements, was interrupted only at intervals by the loud screaming of the owl, from an adjacent turret, or the flutter of the night-raven.

"These descriptions," said the Signora, closing her book, "are too, too horrible!"

Rosalvo, starting from his reverie, enquired what she meant. The Signora demanded if he had ever been in Spain:—on his answering in the negative, she turned over a few pages, and was again silent. Rosalvo, roused by this enquiry, rose half way from his seat, stirred the fire, and then crossing his arms upon his breast, relapsed into his former abstraction.

Cecilia was thoughtful too. Her mind, ever faithful to its object, was fixed upon Varàno. She wondered where he was at that moment, what was his employment, and whether he was then thinking of her. It was sweet to be remembered by him, and to remember him; though recollection served only to convince her that she must never be his.

"Good Heavens!" exclaimed the Signora, "it cannot be true!"

Rosalvo, again rousing himself from his abstraction, like a man newly awakened from sleep demanded what she was talking about. The Signora put the book into his hands. He opened it in the middle, and casting his eyes carelessly over the pages, said, with a forced smile, "If it has amused *you* so much, you will, perhaps, favour us with the contents."

It was a celebrated French Romance, written by an author of some eminence in the fifteenth century; remarkable only, like the other productions of that period, for its wild and extravagant adventures. The scene of action, commencing in Andalusia, after a thousand untoward circumstances and marvellous disasters, terminated at Madrid. The author, from a full conviction that terror is a principal part of the sublime, had collected all the circumstances best calculated to inspire it. Not contented with combining such as the principal masters in the *school of horror* have delighted to delineate, he had struck into a less trodden path; and mingling a small portion of truth with the witcheries of fiction, had pierced into the gloomy recesses of the Inquisition. As he proceeded in his descriptions, he seemed to have acquired new powers:—the mock trials were supported with wonderful ingenuity—and the racks and tortures, brought in as the auxiliaries of terror, were extraordinary in their effect!—It was by this the attention of the Signora had been fascinated; and this chapter, which contained, perhaps, the most affecting incident in the story, she read as follows:—

"Almeyda was led on, as if by an invisible hand, till she had reached the walls of Madrid. The dawn yet lingered, and the piercing wind penetrated her bosom. She drew her *mantilla* close, and hurried on, till she was seized by a cavalier, masked, and muffled up in a *sombrero*. Almeyda shrieked, and attempted to free herself, when a well-known voice sounded in her ear, and she paused in thrilling wonder!

" 'Come on,' said the cavalier, in a voice of thunder, 'wretch! monster! inhuman parricide!'

" 'Oh spare me!' exclaimed she.

" 'It is too late,' cried the cavalier; 'the hour is already come!'

"As he spoke, a distant chime struck her ear. The cavalier started, and throwing his cloak over his shoulders, hurried her along the city.

"The sun arose over its spires, and the chiming of the bells in all the churches of Madrid proclaimed the commencement of the *Auto da fé*.—The cavalier stopped at the gate of the *Sancta Casa*, and obliged Almeyda to do the same. The populace assembled, and shouts and murmurs, mingled with the heavy tolling of bells, filled the air. At length the procession began, and a pause of silence ensued. First appeared the Dominicans, who advanced two by two with a slow and solemn step, preceded by the banners of the Inquisition. Next to these moved the victims, attended by their *Parains*, each holding a taper in his hand; one wearing the *sambenito*, or yellow scapulaire, sprinkled over with crucifixes, and ornamented with the bloody Cross of St. Andrea—the other bearing the *carochas*, or pasteboard bonnet, in the form of a pyramid, marked with flames and diabolical devices. Horror froze the blood of Almeyda! As her eye caught the last of the victims, she

screamed aloud:—'It is my father!' exclaimed she; 'Oh save him
—save him!'

"She fell pale to the ground as she uttered these words—and
again the death-bell tolled!"

———

The Signora had been too intent upon the story to mark its
effects upon her auditors; but when she had proceeded thus far,
she was roused by the voice of Rosalvo, who, with a countenance
of terror and wonder, was supporting Cecilia, who had fallen
back senseless in her chair. She flew immediately for assistance,
leaving Rosalvo to support Cecilia, whom he watched over with
looks of anxious astonishment. After a short interval of silence,
she opened her eyes, and looked earnestly, but fearfully around
the room; and then heaving a heavy sigh, exclaimed, "Where am
I?—Oh! tell me, was it indeed my father? Did he perish? Was he
sacrificed in those flames?—Yes, I know he was!—those dreadful
papers!"

Rosalvo started at this exclamation, and his features assumed
an expression of deeper wildness.

The Signora, who had attributed Cecilia's disorder to the
increasing heat of the room, now entered with restoratives, and
she was conveyed to her apartment.

In the morning, her slumbers having restored some portion of
her former tranquillity, Cecilia took her accustomed solitary walk
to a wood within view of the Castle. Turning back, she perceived
Rosalvo, who was hastily following her. There was something so
strangely mysterious in his looks as he falteringly addressed her,
that she involuntarily receded.

"You must not leave me," cried he with embarrassment; "I
have something to say to you."—He took her arm.—"Let us
retire into this wood," said he; "no passenger enters it; it is solitary—a retreat most fit for private intercourse."

Observing her astonishment—"What is it you fear?" added he.
"Were it possible that danger could overtake you, I would defend
you with my life!"

Cecilia blushed at the reproof, and allowed him to lead her

to the wood. They passed through a romantic glade; and having reached the centre of the wood, Rosalvo seated himself upon a bank, and placed Cecilia by his side.

"Forgive me," said he, "if I have alarmed you. I know my manners—my strange, eccentric manners must have prejudiced you against me. But if you knew all, thought you might condemn, you would pity me. Some circumstances which occurred last night have strangely interested me. A story, accidentally read, produced an effect upon you, scarcely attributable to any common cause. Your reason forsook you, and in the moment of delirium you spoke of the Inquisition—of your father. Answer me, then, this question:—Was the idea but the phantom of the moment? —or did your father really fall a victim to this impious tribunal?"

"He did!" cried Cecilia, clasping her hands together in an agony of distress.

"His crime?"

"He was accused of stealing a Nun from her sanctuary."

"His name?" pursued Rosalvo, breathless with agitation.

"Julien d'Arnaud."

"Great God!" exclaimed Rosalvo, "thy ways are unsearchable!"

"Oh! did you know him?" said Cecilia—"did you know my father?"

Rosalvo groaned, struck his hand upon his forehead, and paced the glade with perturbed steps.

"Oh stop!" cried Cecilia; "I conjure you stop—Did you indeed know my father?"

"I did;—but question me no farther."

She fixed her eyes fearfully upon him; a sort of confused idea rushed across her senses: she grasped his arm—it trembled!—his countenance was pale, and marked with contending emotions!

"Leave me!" said he; "begone!—I can endure no more."

Cecilia's curiosity was now almost insupportable; her feet seemed rooted to the spot. "Yet hear me," said she; "I entreat you hear me!—You knew my father;—here is his portrait," putting the miniature into his hands, "is the likeness exact?"

Rosalvo gazed on it intently.—"It is his very look," cried he; "but I must forget him—forget, if possible, that——"

"Forget what?" interrupted Cecilia; "your words are paradoxes. Is it kind, Signor—is it generous to excite a painful curiosity, which you seem determined not to gratify?"

"Remember no more what I have said; let that, and the dreadful past, be eternally forgotten, lest you wrest from me a secret that may cause my ruin!—Oh that deed—that deed! Till then I was guiltless!"

"What would you say?" cried Cecilia. "Oh torture me no longer!"

"You have seen my distraction, Cecilia," pursued Rosalvo; "you have felt for—you have pitied me!"

"Heaven knows most truly!"

"Were it then possible that I could disclose to you the cause of my remorse—of that long hidden grief which has fastened upon my soul, would you promise, solemnly promise, never to divulge it?"

"Alas! what can be this mystery?" said Cecilia, in a tone of uneasy irresolution, "and whom does it concern?"

"Those most dear to me," returned Rosalvo. "Can you be firm?—Will you swear?"

"I will!" said Cecilia.

Rosalvo took a small gold cross which was suspended from her neck, and pressing it to her lips, repeated the word *swear*. Cecilia shuddered.

"Why this solemnity?" cried she; "I have already sworn."

"You will then be secret?"

"As the grave itself," said Cecilia.

"Did you ever receive any particular information," resumed Rosalvo, "concerning your parents? I speak chiefly of your father."

"Yes."

"And by what means was this intelligence conveyed?"

"By means of some papers written by Madame de Villeneuve and my mother."

"What did these papers contain?"

"A brief account of the life of my father, both before and after his marriage."

"With your mother; but was there no mention of a former alliance—no account of Signora d'Olivetto, a widow of Naples?"

"Yes, she was my father's first wife: they were married at Naples; but she survived her marriage but a few years."

"Did these papers give no account of the fruit of this alliance?"

"They mention a son," said Cecilia, eagerly; "a son called Julien."

Rosalvo groaned, and covered his face with his hands.

"Does he live?" cried Cecilia.

"He does," replied Rosalvo, rising, and throwing himself at her feet; "I—I—am that Julien!"

Cecilia shrieked; and sinking into his arms, exclaimed, "Great God! do I behold my brother?"

"You do. I am that unfortunate, that guilty, that devoted wretch! But be secret—disclose it not! You will not—you dare not, for you have sworn!"

"And have I then," said Cecilia, "who never knew the ties of kindred, found a brother—and Oh! may I not acknowledge him?"

"Your vow," continued Rosalvo, "was solemnly taken; and so long only as you hold it sacred, I am safe. *Break* it, and you destroy me!"

"Explain but your motives," cried Cecilia, "and again I swear that I never *will* violate it."

"Meet me at this place to-morrow," replied Rosalvo, "and you shall know all: at this hour."

They were startled at this moment by the appearance of a woodcutter, who, attended by his dog, was traversing the wood, and who, with an impertinent kind of curiosity, stopped to observe them.

"This fellow seems inquisitive," said Rosalvo; "we must avoid him."

They accordingly turned into another path, and hastened to the Castle, Cecilia trembling with emotion, and Rosalvo still more agitated than when he had first met her.

The Signora saluted her young friend with the tenderest enquiries concerning her last night's indisposition. Cecilia endeavoured to recover her composure; but the astonishing discovery that had been unfolded, and the mysterious incidents which were yet untold, completely overwhelmed her.

At breakfast Rosalvo's usual melancholy abstraction was con-

verted into the wildest agitation; and Cecilia, finding herself in
the society of those not only connected with her by the bonds of
friendship, but by those of the nearest relationship, was torn by a
conflict of contending sensations.

CHAPTER II

One part, one little part, we dimly scan,
Through the dark medium of life's feverish dream,
Yet dare arraign the whole stupendous plan,
If but that little part incongruous seem.
Nor is that part, perhaps, what mortals deem:
Oft from apparent ill our blessings rise.
Oh then renounce that impious self-esteem,
That aims to trace the secrets of the skies,
For thou art but of dust—be humble and be wise!

BEATTIE'S MINSTREL.

CECILIA, passing the day in the presence of a brother whom she
was condemned to treat only as a friend, could with difficulty
support the severe restriction. The wished-for, yet dreaded interview robbed her of even a broken repose. Why did he not dare
to confess his relationship?—why, under an assumed name, in a
lonely solitude, take refuge from his fellow-creatures?

The sun shot a slanting ray through her casement; she arose,
and hastened to the appointed place. At the entrance of the wood
she met Rosalvo. She would have spoke—she would have called
him by the endearing name of *brother*;—the word trembled on
her lips. Struggling to command his feelings, Rosalvo led her in
silence to the wood, and, as if eager to conclude his painful task,
immediately began as follows:—

"The first melancholy event of my childhood was the death
of my mother. The agonizing fate of him who was the parent of
us both, is still more lively in my recollection. On his departure
to seek your mother, I was left with my uncle, Signor di Speroni;
and through his wife, who was jealous of her husband's affection
for me, was sent, under the care of my tutor, to a seat of his at
the foot of Mount Soracte, situated about nine leagues from

Rome. As it is not my design to enter into the minute particulars of my story, I shall pass over the season of my banishment, till the æra when I lost my beloved tutor. This to a youthful mind, already torn by misfortune, was a most serious affliction. Alas! I was now bereft of the only friend to whom I could look up for hope and consolation. I felt as if I was left alone in the world; and with the enthusiasm of that early age, would have gladly followed him to the tomb. The sensations of that moment remain fresh in my memory, as though they were still present with me. I remember his simple grave bound over with osiers, and daily decorated with flowers—a tribute duly paid by devotion to the memory of departed excellence. The *cimetiere* in which he was interred, belonged to a Convent. The Prior was known to my tutor, and had been often the companion of our solitude. He felt for my misfortunes, and undertook to inform my uncle of my loss, whose wife being now dead, soon arrived, and conveyed me to Naples.

"Years rolled away without any remarkable occurrence. My uncle was affectionate,—he was even vain of me; he spoke of me with rapture, and introduced me into the most brilliant circles. In these, though I had many acquaintance, there was none except Signor Guidotto, a young favourite of the King, by whom I had been distinguished with any particular marks of esteem. His Palace joined our's; and our acquaintance, although he was some years older than myself, improving gradually into friendship, we soon became inseparable. The partiality with which the warmth and sprightliness of his disposition directed him to speak of me, procured me various introductions, and amongst others to Conte Minotti, an elderly Nobleman, who, on his second marriage with a Sicilian lady, had lately become resident at Naples.

"The Contessa was young, lovely, and fascinating. It might be difficult to assert she had the perfect beauty; but her form was proportioned by the exactest rules of symmetry, and there was an expression of airy lightness and exquisite grace in her movements not easily to be described, but such as we sometimes see in the nymphlike figures of the Italian painters. Guidotto, who was alike charmed with her person, behaviour, and discourse, soon artfully insinuated himself into the favour of the Conte;

and as conversation unfolded the early culture of his mind, he often congratulated me on my good fortune in having chosen an acquaintance, whose merits he was never weary of appretiating. Whilst the Conte was conversing with Guidotto, politeness obliged me to direct my attention to the Contessa. Little did I think these attentions could have been misconstrued.

"I had been some days absent from the Palace, when one evening as I was strolling along the Bay, the Palace being situated on its borders, I bent my steps thither. I entered, and as the family usually spent the evening in a rotunda in the gardens, I hastened toward it. The doors of this building were of glass; and as I drew near, I perceived the Contessa and Guidotto. He was reading to her. I stopped, and heard him repeat a passage from the sonnets of Petrarcho. While I observed him, he closed the book, and raising his handkerchief to his eyes, exclaimed—'Oh wretched bard! how deeply do I feel thy woes!—for have I not shared thy fate? —My Laura,' added he, looking tenderly upon the Contessa, 'is devoted to another!'—I heard no more—I fled.

"Guidotto was then a traitor, who had ingratiated himself with the Conte only to procure interviews with his wife;—a husband so unsuspicious, that, like another Marcus Antoninus, he had been often heard to return thanks to Heaven for having bestowed on him a consort so faithful, and possessed of such an engaging simplicity of manners. But whilst the Contessa was violating, like Faustina, every moral obligation, she remained unsuspected by others. The dissolute Empress, on the contrary, had skill only to keep from her husband the knowledge of her excesses.

"My indignation was too violent to be concealed. The Conte was then absent. I awaited not his return to accuse Guidotto of perfidy; but openly taxing him with his duplicity, disclaimed his friendship, and finally threatened to ruin him with the Conte, whose virtues should have been the safeguard of his honour.

"Guidotto listened to me with astonishment, but not with indignation. He expressed his surprise that an inhabitant of Naples should be alarmed at a little harmless gallantry, which had no meaning, and which malice itself could scarcely interpret to his disadvantage; assured me that the Conte's honour was not less dear to me than his own; and by the eulogiums which he passed upon him, made me imagine that I had been too severe in my conjectures on his conduct; and my affection for him undermining my judgment, we parted without further explanation. Feeling, however, from this disclosure, to what extent he was in my power, he became from that moment my most decided and implacable enemy.

"After this the Contessa distinguished me from all the rest of her acquaintance; her attentions were so marked, that I was often oppressed by them. She accused me of ingratitude when I affected to overlook them, and never failed to redouble them in the presence of her husband, who, notwithstanding his former confidence in her affection, soon began to regard me with an eye of mistrust. I perceived it; and, anxious to vindicate myself from the implication under which I evidently suffered, requested an interview with him in private.—'Meet me,' said the Conte, sullenly, 'to-night at the entrance into St. Lucia.'—The air with which he pronounced these words convinced me that his suspicions were more deeply rooted than I had imagined. I received, nevertheless, with pleasure this opportunity of clearing myself.

"I repaired, at the time fixed, to the appointed place. The Conte met me. 'Villain!' exclaimed he, in a tone of desperation, 'prepare to receive the reward of thy crimes!'

"'What crimes?' repeated I. 'Convince me that I have injured you, and I am willing to afford you satisfaction.'

"'Base wretch!' interrupted the Conte, 'what satisfaction can you give? Would you not seduce my wife? Have you not lurked like an assassin, secretly to destroy me? Defend!' added he, drawing his stiletto.

"He rushed forward. I drew mine. It pierced his breast! He groaned, and fell! I shuddered, screamed, and sunk nevertheless to the ground!—When I recovered, I found myself supported by Guidotto. I enquired wildly of the Conte.

"'Alas!' cried Guidotto, 'he has breathed his last!'

"The horrors of my situation can only be imagined. To stay would be to suffer infamy, perhaps death! I had no time for deliberation: Guidotto assisted my flight, and promised to be the guardian of my secret.

"After leading a wandering and unsettled life for near two years beyond the Neapolitan territories, meeting with a Venetian vessel, I took refuge in the Island of Marano. The exhausted state of my finances threatened shortly to add to the severe mental miseries under which I laboured. My uncle, from whom I might otherwise have received supplies, I was informed was dead; and having heard no tidings of me, had endowed a monastery with his possessions. Thus was I, by a sudden and unexpected calamity, exposed to penury and distress, with this aggravation, that ease and affluence were become habitual.

"The manufactory of the island presented the only honest means of subsistence; and from having revelled in the luxuries of fashion, a favourite in the Court of Naples, I became a labourer in a glass-house."

Cecilia, whose mind had been variously agitated whilst listening to this relation, now grasped her brother's hand in silent sympathy. Her own misfortunes appeared little in comparison with his. Rosalvo seemed to feel the consolation of sisterly affection. A faint smile shot across his features.

"One day, whilst working in this manufactory," continued he, "not being yet completely skilled in my profession, as I was endeavouring to open the blown globe, one of my fellow-labourers undertook to assist me. When he had performed the operation, and extended the plate, looking earnestly at him, I thought I recollected his features. He recognized mine at the same moment, and our astonishment was mutual. This was Giobbe, an old servant of Conte Minotti. In the evening, when we had completed our work, he requested to speak with me alone; and, Oh what a tale of horror did he unfold!—Guidotto, from the hour in which I had accused him of a private intercourse with the Contessa, had been planning my destruction. Dreading lest his own treachery should be discovered, he had secretly inspired the Conte with a jealousy of me. The Contessa was the chief auxiliary in this scheme. Passionately fond of Guidotto, he could mould her to his wishes; and stimulated to proceed resolutely in an intrigue, of which I was doomed to be the victim, the Conte was deluded by her into a conviction that I had a design upon his life: and, supposing that for this purpose I had requested the interview he had appointed, had come armed to avenge himself. Giobbe had acquired a knowledge of these circumstances from a conversation accidentally overheard between Guidotto and his confidential servant.

"'Base dissembler!' exclaimed I, 'but I will be revenged! Yes, the villain shall be unmasked!—he shall be brought forth! By Heaven, he shall not escape my vengeance!'

"'The attempt might fail,' returned Giobbe, 'and you would be regarded as an assassin.'

"I shuddered as he spoke: death I could have borne; but an ignominious death a heart, like mine, which had never wilfully deviated from the path of rectitude and honour, wanted firmness to encounter!"

When Rosalvo had proceeded thus far, the Castle clock struck nine.

"Some of the most material incidents of my life," said he, rising from his seat, "are yet untold. Hitherto you have pitied. When you hear the rest, you may condemn me!"

"Fear not," said Cecilia, "misery, you know, is sacred; and are you not my brother?"

"How kind—how good!" cried Rosalvo. "Will you then consider me as a brother?—though——" He stopped.

"I will," answered Cecilia, "though you have cruelly forbid me to acknowledge you!"

"Heaven, I thank thee!" said Rosalvo; "the cup thou hast hitherto offered me has been dashed with bitterness, but thou hast sweetened it with one cordial drop."

His manner, as he pronounced these words, acquired a more affecting energy. Cecilia's tears streamed fast; she put her arm within his, and they returned to the Castle.

The Signora had twice observed Cecilia and Rosalvo walking from the woods; and suspicious that he was imparting to her that secret which he had refused to confide to herself, was disconcerted and distressed. Cecilia perceived it, and a new occasion for perplexity crowded on her mind. The idea of appearing to possess that confidence which was denied to an amiable wife, was agonizing to her delicacy; yet how could she disclose that *she* also had the claim of a tender relationship?

The next morning Cecilia and Rosalvo repaired again to the wood, and the latter thus continued his relation.

————————

"The agitation produced in my mind by the discovery of Guidotto's villany, united to my being unaccustomed to the heat of the furnaces, soon affected my health, and rendered me totally unable to continue my employment. A few jewels, which I had hitherto forborne to sell, because they were the gift of my father, were my only resources, and these my necessities induced me to borrow a sum upon at a lapidario's. To Venice I accordingly hastened; but apprehensive of imposition, should I appear in the simple garb of a glass-blower, I resolved to procure a genteel Venetian dress at a shop in the Guidecca, to which I was directed. I fixed upon one, and offered the Rigattiere a jewel, as a pledge till I could pay him; but, to my astonishment, he insisted that it was a counterfeit, and refused to accept it. This passed, to my mortification, in the presence of a stranger, who generously relieved my distress by offering to lend me the sum required. I availed myself of the proposal, and appointing a place and time to repay him, repaired to take my lodgings at an hotel.

"When alone, the degrading circumstances of this incident pressed heavily upon my feelings. I took a retrospect of the past, and my agony was increased. 'Where,' said I, 'are those scenes of joy which the visions of my youth presented? Alas! They have vanished like a dream of the night, and have left no trace behind! —Persecuted and forlorn—bereft of my friends—menaced by want, and goaded by wrongs, I wander a wretched outcast, in a world which has long since disclaimed me!'

"The night advanced—I was alone. I paced my chamber at intervals; all was still in the house. The melancholy that reigned around—the idea of being in a rich and populous city, without knowing a single being that would interest himself in my behalf, conspired with my degraded situation to overwhelm me. I passed the night in the most gloomy despair. The dawn yet lingered, when I arose, and opened my window. It overlooked a canal. Twilight yet hung upon the scene, and the lucid mirror of the waters was overspread with that cold, grey tint which foreruns the rising of the sun. The city was yet still, and no sound, except the song of the Barcaroli,[1] and the low rippling of the oars, met my ear.—'Happy souls!' said I, as they continued their responses, 'your wages are the reward of your labours, and you enjoy them in thankfulness. The miseries of those you envy are unknown to you; your hands are unstained with blood!'

"The contrast which I had drawn between my own situation and that of the Barcaroli augmented my despair. The morn brightened—I quitted my casement, and again traversed my chamber. I threw myself upon a couch. My dagger lay beside me: —I took it up, and a horrible idea shot across my senses. I looked at it intently;—all my griefs, all my wrongs rushed instantly upon my mind.—'One moment—one short moment,' said I, 'and all may be at end!'

"Again I paused, and again the angel of destruction hovered over me. I sunk upon my knees; they knocked together with the violence of my emotions! Oh God! never shall I forget the agony of that moment—when meditating upon the most daring of crimes, I seemed to stand upon the verge of eternity!—I would have prayed, but the power of articulation was denied me!—My hand still grasped the dagger. I had pointed it to my breast, when my arm was forcibly arrested, and a female, in the habit of a Nun, stood before me.

" 'Stop!' said she, in a voice which seemed to proceed from the lips of an accusing angel, 'stop, misguided wretch!'

The dagger was in my hand;—she snatched it from me, and threw it with violence against the wall. I attempted to speak, but the cowardice of guilt prevented me.

" 'Unhappy man!' exclaimed she, earnestly regarding me, 'what is it that has plunged thee into despair so impious?'

" 'The machinations of a villain!' said I, recovering myself, 'the treacherously concealed baseness of those in whom I most confided.'

" 'And for this, mistaken wretch!' resumed she, 'thou hast

---

1 Kind of watermen at Venice. They sing as they wait for customers; and being joined by others of their profession, perform in responses the most known and celebrated passages from the Italian poets.

dared to venture upon an act which would have doomed thee to everlasting torments!—Oh man! weak at the best, but most fragile when thou hast most need for firmness, and most daring when thou shouldst be most humble, thou shrinkest from the biting of the blast, and wouldst face the whirlwind!—thou tremblest at the imbecility of man, and darest to challenge thy Creator!'

"'Wherefore, then,' said I, 'did the God that made us, form us so frail!—why give us passions keen and insurmountable?'

"'Shall the thing made,' cried the Nun, 'accuse the Maker?—Shall the being, into whose breast he has breathed a portion of his everlasting fire, question the goodness of his Creator?—Rather let the winged inhabitant of the air, as he performs his lofty course among the clouds, arraign the justice of his providence,—or the monster of the waves as he tosses himself in the flood, and sees the storms collect above him, say, 'Wherefore hast thou made me thus?' To them mercy has been limited—to *thee* it is infinite!'

"'Did you know,' cried I, 'the wrongs I have sustained—the miseries to which I have been reduced by an inveterate foe!'

"'It is yourself,' interrupted the Nun, 'it is yourself who are your greatest enemy!—But grant you have been injured—who has not suffered from the inhumanity of others? Shall the eternal law of wisdom be perverted, that thou mayest be happy? Are not thy enemies instruments in the hands of the Almighty to punish thee for thy sins? And may not the punishments inflicted by him, who bears the chain which connects all mortal events, permit them for thy soul's eternal welfare? But allow it otherwise—a few short years, and the bonds of humanity shall be dissolved; and either thou shalt cease to remember them—or, remembering, shall wonder how they ever vexed thee!'

"'Your words,' said I, 'breathe the sentiments of an Anchoress, and your precepts are the precepts of virtue!—They have conquered—you have saved my life, and I thank you!'

"'Promise, then,' replied the Nun, 'never to forget them: and should desperation again urge you to lift your arm against your life, thank of the Nun of Misericordia[1], and be patient!'

1 The Nuns of the order of Misericordia visit the sick, and not unfrequently enter the Hotels, in search of distressed objects, who are relieved, and sometimes supported at the expence of the Convent.

"'Ah! well-earned appellation!' said I; 'thou art indeed a sister of mercy!'

"She glided past me, and disappeared; but her accents still vibrated on my ear—her form still floated before my fancy. Astonishment in her presence had arrested my faculties; her beauty, her sudden appearance in my chamber, left me doubtful for a while whether she was a mortal or a celestial visitor. I felt as if escaped from a dreadful precipice. The horrible presumption of the act—my own puerile defence, opposed to the elevated devotion which breathed in the energetic language of the Nun, filled me with confusion.—'Can a being like myself,' said I, 'framed in the same mould, and disposed to the same propensities, display a soul which can claim affinity to Heaven by rising above human weakness? Is the Promethean spark, which she told me had been infused into my breast, extinct?—or to what is it I owe my imbecility?—Shall a woman, composed of frailer materials than man, whose fragile form speaks her dependence, and whose still softer mind, untutored by science, hangs upon the decisions of our's, as upon an eternal mandate—shall she speak the language of truth, and with a peerless elevation hush the warring of the passions, while I sink beneath their pressure?—Ah! where is the superiority, the boasted sovereignty of man?—the dupe of his desires, the creature of imagination!—Take him out of his sphere, deprive him of those precarious advantages which he believes he has secured, and calls indispensable, because they have been his for a season, and he is wretched. Let the syren voice of Hope stop her enchanting melody, and every string in the vast human machine is unstrung—and despair, misery, and death complete the picture!'

"I arose, and went into the city, and reached, without designing it, the Convent of St. Ursula. This being the school of the Misericordia, an involuntary expectation induced me to stop, in the hope of beholding my beautiful monitress; but no one appeared. I passed thoughtfully on:—my jewels were in my pocket; and taking advantage of a gondola, I entered the Piazza di San Marco; and turning into one of the little streets leading from the piazza, made my way to a Lapidario's. A decent looking person in black drew my attention to his shop:—he appeared to have been observing me; and bowing obsequiously, seemed to expect my entrance. I returned his salutation, and followed him into his shop. He examined my watch and the rest of the jewels, and offered me a loan proportioned to their value. I was not displeased with my bargain; and having committed them to his care, walked on to the Piazzetta. I was pacing the colonnade of the Librario Publico, when the bell of San Marco tolled for vespers. I entered the Church, and joined in the service. When it concluded, I passed slowly through the aisles; and the Gothic beauty of the building arresting my attention, walked toward the altar. I was approaching it, though at some distance, when by accident I went round a column to a door which led into a side chapel, decorated with some little statues and pictures of saints. I entered, but had proceeded only a few paces down the chapel, when I heard a soft whispering; and turning toward the spot from whence it issued, discovered a small altar, and about two steps from where I stood, a female figure richly dressed, kneeling before a crucifix. Her face was shaded by her veil, which descended nearly to her feet. One of her hands touched the crucifix, while she rested her head on the other. She continued for some minutes in the most fervent devotion, and then arising from her posture, discovered to me a face of the most bewitching beauty.

"She blushed on observing me; and hastening from my view, quitted the Church. I rushed after, and would have followed her; but was prevented by a fresh crowd of devotees, who came thither to prostrate themselves before the famous Virgin of San Lucca, in order to procure fine weather for the approaching Carnival.

"Departing slowly from the Piazzetta, I returned to my hotel, where, amid all the distresses of my condition, the charming image of this stranger perpetually haunted my imagination.

"The next evening I repaired again to San Marco, and again beheld the object of my admiration. I placed myself near her, though unseen; and her veil being thrown back, every lovely feature was exposed. As she was rising to depart, her eyes, which had been fixed earnestly upon the ground, accidentally encountered mine, which were riveted upon her; while my unexpected glance was repaid with a look so frank, so innocent, yet so animated, that it struck immediately to my heart. I had seen many females distinguished for their attractions, but it was now only that I began to love—it was now only that I had discovered that archetype of perfection which my vivid imagination had portrayed. My attendance at the vesper service at the Church of San Marco was from this time frequent and even daily. Yet who was it I was pursuing?—Poor, a fugitive, and without a single connection—my life marked with peculiar misfortune, and even stained with blood!—obliged to vegetate in obscurity—with a person clouded with care, and a mind worn by unmerited wrongs—could I hope for her love, even were she at liberty to bestow it?

"One evening, having followed her through the Piazzetta, I was accosted by the generous stranger whom I had met with at the shop of the Rigattiere. He saluted me with great cordiality; after which, pointing to the lady, who, attended by her servants, was then entering her gondola, I enquired if he knew her. He answered that she was a young widow of great fortune and rank; —'and these,' resumed he, 'are not all—she has benevolence, generosity, and virtue.'

"'You speak with authority,' said I; 'the lady, I presume, is well known to you?'

"'It would be strange if she were not,' cried he, smiling; 'for I have the honour to be her Maggiordomo.[1] Her name is Signora di Villetto.'

"Delighted with this intelligence, I renewed my thanks for his kindness, and invited him to my lodgings. He shook my hand at parting, saying, with an expressive look, 'I shall not forget your enquiries concerning my Lady.'

"At our next meeting, Cariello (which was the name of the Maggiordomo,) ventured to interrogate me concerning my first appearance at the Rigattiere's; hinting his suspicions that, notwithstanding my disguise, I was a person of distinction. I evaded these enquiries, informing him only that my name was Rosalvo (which name I now assumed), and that my life had been marked with melancholy disasters, which I was not at liberty to disclose.

"With a polite apology for his curiosity, he then mentioned the jewel which he had seen me offer the Rigattiere. I was surprised

[1] A kind of steward.

at the question, but nevertheless acquainted him with whom I had deposited it.

"On the ensuing evening, as I was returning from my usual walk to the Church of San Marco, I was addressed by the Lapidario who had furnished me with the loan on my jewels. He asked me if I was inclined to sell them, adding, that there was a lady now in his shop who was much pleased with the ring, and desirous to purchase it. We entered the shop before I had returned him with an answer; but guess my astonishment, and the awkwardness of my situation, when in the intended purchaser of the ring, I beheld the object of my attraction. My presence seemed to act as powerfully upon her feelings as her's did upon mine. Her cheek was suffused with blushes, and her faltering voice betrayed her emotions.

"'This is the Signor, Madam,' said the Lapidario, addressing himself to the lady, 'of whom I spoke. Some pecuniary embarrassments, as he has before told me, have obliged him to deposit them in my hands. It was not his design to sell them; but noble offers are not always easily to be withstood. The ring is not unfashionable, and the diamonds are of some value.'

"The mortification which I endured whilst the Lapidario was speaking, is not to be conceived. To have my indigence exposed at the very moment when I would have appeared to some advantage, was torturing in the extreme.

"The lady, perceiving my embarrassment, observed that if the ring was a favourite one, she ought not to request me to part with it, but entreated me to allow her to have one set in the same manner. My reply was awkward and confused; she gave directions concerning the ring, and then withdrew, glancing on me, as she went, with a look of such unutterable sweetness, that all my senses were absorbed in rapture. I returned to my lodgings, enchanted with the manners of Signora di Villetto, and chagrined that I had not the presence of mind to present her my ring."——

The sound of voices in the wood here interrupted Rosalvo. It drew nearer—and in a moment, to their mutual and unspeakable astonishment, Varàno, followed by the Signora, sprung forward.

Cecilia's spirits, already agitated by the deep interest which she had taken in Rosalvo's story, could scarcely support her under this sudden meeting; nor was Rosalvo himself less visibly perturbed. She observed an unusual appearance of joy in the expressive features of Varàno while he tenderly saluted her, heightening into rapture. Never did he address her with so much warmth—so much confidence!

After breakfast the Signora withdrew, and was soon followed by Rosalvo. Varàno instantly started up, and seizing Cecilia's hand with an ungovernable transport, her perplexity was converted into emotion, when, putting a letter into her hand, with a casket containing a small miniature of himself, attached to a rich necklace of the most valuable diamonds (a present from the Marchesa), he informed her that their marriage was agreed upon, and that he was now come to demand that consent which, every difficulty surmounted, and the claims of duty fulfilled, she had now no pretence to withhold.

Cecilia, pale with astonishment, could not demand an explanation. She opened the letter (which was also from the Marchesa); but in the excess of her surprise, was unable to comprehend its contents, or to reply to the passionate expressions of Varàno till she was relieved by a copious flood of tears. This change, so wonderful, so unexpected, seemed more like illusion than reality. She could scarcely believe she was awake.

"My mother," resumed Varàno, "is now solicitous for our marriage. My father has consented, but cruelly insists on its being deferred till the expiration of a year."

Cecilia's incredulity was not yet removed, till Varàno, when his transports had a little subsided, gave a full relation of the circumstances by which the Marchese's consent was obtained.

The meeting between Varàno and his mother, after his mysterious absence, was embarrassing and affecting on both sides. She had no doubt but if he had really discovered Cecilia, that they were already married; and it was not till assured of the contrary, that she would enter into any conversation on the subject. Varàno ingenuously confessed that, irritated by his father's plan of forcibly confining Cecilia in a Convent, he had made proposals, which had been nobly rejected. He then recounted all the intelligence relative to her birth which he had gained from the papers. The Marchesa listened attentively to the relation; and after a pause,

during which the feelings of the mother seemed to be triumphing over those of offended dignity,—"If your happiness," said
she, "depends entirely upon your marriage with this girl, Heaven
forbid I should oppose it!"

"Did I hear right?" exclaimed Varàno.

"Yes," resumed the Marchesa, "I will promise to exert my
influence with your father."

Varàno fell at her feet, but could not speak. Never was silence
so eloquent.

The Marchese, whose indisposition, occasioned by fatigue,
had settled into a serious illness, soon after arrived from Genoa.
His mind, humbled by a near prospect of death, and softened by
Varàno's filial attentions, had assumed a more accommodating
character; and the symptoms of danger abated, the Marchesa
and the Lady Bianca, the Marchesa's favourite sister from Venice,
whom the former had already engaged to her interest, judged
this a proper time to endeavour to vanquish his scruples concerning Varàno's marriage.

The Signora Bianca, like the rest of her house, had formed
high expectations for her nephew; but yielding to the solicitations of the Marchesa, she had consented to unite her influence
to her's, to aid his cause with the Marchese.

This lady was an adept at argument; though in her it was rather
the gift of nature than of art. Her logic was not the result of
reading, but of reflection: she could solve a proposition without
knowing the parts of a syllogism, and detect sophism under its
deepest and most artful disguise. Thus enjoying all the pleasure
which results from reasoning without the labour of study—without involving herself in the obscurities and mazes of science, she
resembled the intuitive admirer of nature, who can see beauty
in a flower without analyzing its parts, or embarrassing himself
with a dry, uninteresting speculation on genera and species. Thus
armed, she prepared to dart the arrows of her eloquence at the
heart of the Marchese, representing, as the most powerful of all
arguments, that if Lorenzo was disappointed in an affair apparently so essential to his peace, he might probably refuse to marry
at all, and thereby the name and ancient title of Varàno become
extinct—that Cecilia, if not nobly descended, was of a genteel

and respectable family, perhaps equal to that into which the Marchese himself had first married. As she urged this latter argument, she carefully suppressed the mention of the fatal death of Cecilia's father, which he might probably consider as disgraceful. The contest was a long one; but although supported on both sides with equal art and address, neither of the combatants was completely successful; and the attack was at length suspended, to be resumed at some future opportunity.

If the Marchese was not wholly overcome, he, however, suffered something like a defeat. The shield of prejudice, by which his opinions had been hitherto defended, was no longer invulnerable—the shafts of conviction had pierced it. In her absence he began to reflect seriously upon those arguments to which his pride, his own imaginary importance, and a thousand other motives had prevented him from allowing due weight. All hopes of an alliance between Varàno and Olivia had been long since extinguished; and his regret at having been made an instrument in the hands of Boraccio (with whose villany Varàno had now acquainted him) of Cecilia's being thrown into the power of Morsino, inclined him more immediately in her favour. Agreeing, therefore, with his sister that it was better that his son should marry ill, than that he should refuse to marry at all, he gave a vague and reluctant consent to her admonitions that he would not oppose the marriage at the end of a year, secretly hoping that in that space some unforeseen occurrence might intervene to prevent it. Varàno, to whom information of this acquiescence was immediately brought, flew to convey these tidings to Cecilia at the Castello di Montani.

CHAPTER III

And after him she *went* * * * *
    * * * * * * but all in vaine,
For him so far had borne his light-foot steede,
    Pricked with wrath and fiery fierce disdaine,
That him to follow was but fruitlesse paine;
    Yet she her weary limbes would never rest,
But every hill and dale, each wood and plane
    Did search, sore grieved in her gentle breast,
    He so ungently left her whom she lov'd best.

SPENSER.

VARÀNO ended his relation.—"And now, my Cecilia," said he, exultingly, "*there are no obstacles; no filial disobedience is to be incurred*—and you will be mine!"

Cecilia's cheek was overspread with blushes. The idea of being the wife of Varàno with the consent of his family—the prospect of her whole life being devoted to the charming task of contributing to his happiness, was an excess of joy almost painful. The restored tranquillity of her brother, and permission to be acknowledged by her beloved friend by the endearing name of sister, was all that was now wanting to complete her felicity.

This sudden transition from despondency to hope rendered her thoughtful, and at times agitated. She longed to impart to the Signora the strange occurrences of the morning; but Varàno had anticipated the disclosure the moment of his arrival. Rosalvo was yet, however, unacquainted with it; and conceiving that her brother had the strongest claim upon her confidence, she awaited eagerly and opportunity of speaking with him alone. In the evening she perceived him walking slowly beneath the ramparts which enclosed the court; and stealing from the saloon, instantly joined him.

"This is kind," said he. "Ah! how unlike the world! You leave the fortunate and the happy, and go in quest of the wretched!"

"You must promise to be happy too," returned Cecilia;

"endeavour at least, and your exertions will not be unsuccessful."

Rosalvo shook his head.

"When the mind has been long harassed with care," said he —"when it can no longer look into itself for consolation—when all the energy which governed its earlier pursuits is extinguished, never more to be rekindled, the effort is too—too much for human weakness!"

"Throw aside this despondency," rejoined Cecilia; "think— hope at least, that there are many comforts in store for you."

"For *you* may there be many!" said Rosalvo. "Oh Cecilia! But for you and Giuliana!—and yet it is her—it is that——"

"You must not, you shall not give way to these uneasy reflections," cried Cecilia; "permit *me*—allow your Giuliana, however, to be your comforter."

"Allow her—Giuliana to be my comforter!—Oh were *she* happy!"

"She would be so, were you tranquil," resumed Cecilia: "her disposition is, you know, lively in the extreme, and nothing but her invincible affection for you could have reconciled her to this solitude."

"And like a base, unworthy wretch as I am," exclaimed Rosalvo, "I have sacrificed her inclination to mine!—Cecilia, that woman is an angel! —Strange and unaccountable as has been my conduct, she has never reproached me with it. Though I have repaid her efforts to oblige with all the apathy of despair—though I have denied her my confidence, and often in the dead hour of night have affrighted her with my convulsive terrors, she clothes her face in smiles, and sooths me with the most bewitching tenderness!—Ah, Cecilia! your sex, say what they will of our's, possess a greatness of soul which we in vain aspire to!"

"Indeed you overrate us," said Cecilia; "but Giuliana——"

"Shames me with her goodness," interrupted Rosalvo. "Young, rich, beautiful, born to noble expectations, she left all, gave all for me!—a wretch spurned from the civil haunts of man! —a vagabond!—the murderer of——"

"Forget—forget it all," cried Cecilia, "if your own peace, mine, and that of Giuliana are dear to you!"

"Forget it," said Rosalvo, lifting up his hands and eyes to Heaven with melancholy earnestness; "yes, so you will say when you shall have heard the sequel of my story!"

"I am impatient for the conclusion," said Cecilia; "but in the meantime would request your advice on a subject which concerns me nearly."

She blushed, hesitated, and stopped.

"What would my sister say?" cried Rosalvo.

She was going to reply, but checked herself on perceiving Varàno and the Signora, who now approached.

"Unkind Cecilia," whispered Varàno, "thus to deny me your society!"

"The only way in the world to make it valuable," said the Signora, who had overheard him, and who felt as little able as Varàno to guess why Cecilia was engaged in such frequent and private conversations with her husband.

Varàno smiled, but appeared chagrined. He was not of a disposition to bear that any particular marks of preference should be shewn to others by the object of his tenderest affections. Twice already had he seen her alone with Rosalvo. These conferences he could not think indispensable, particularly whilst he was in the Castle.

Yet though the fever of jealously raged at intervals in his bosom, reason instantaneously returned to counteract it. He could not conceive that Cecilia, to whatever lengths she might be disposed to carry her somewhat romantic ideas of gratitude, could be so regardless of that decorum her situation demanded —"so unprincipled in virtue's book" as to entertain an improper partiality for a man circumstanced like Rosalvo.

These uneasy sensations of mistrust of course immediately died away; and the Signor's friend, the Abbot, joining the party at the Castle at supper, the day passed on to its close in uninterrupted harmony.

Louisette's joy on seeing Varàno was only to be equalled by Cecilia's.

"We shall be quite another thing, Mademoiselle," said she as she entered her room at night, "now the Signor is returned. *Sancta Maria!* I shall never forget how delighted I was to see him!—We were sitting, that is Brigitta and I, looking at a fine old picture of my Lady's father that hangs in a closet in one of the turrets, when who should come prancing over the bridge but Benedetto. 'There he is!' said I; for I knew who was behind him. Oh how my heart began to beat! I thought verily I should have leaped out of the window!"

"The Signor is much obliged to you for your high opinion of him, Louisette," said Cecilia, smiling; "I hope he is aware of it."

"Yes, he says he is very much obliged to me," continued Louisette, "for I have told him over and over again that if I was you, I should soon know where to chuse; and then Benedetto is so kind, and so handsome too, he is the very model of his master!—Holy St. Peter! I thought this very night, if it had not been for him—— But he is surely the civillest creature in the world."

"And what did Benedetto?" asked Cecilia, who now began to perceive that Louisette's joy on seeing Varàno, arose partly from her partiality to his servant.

"Why, to be sure, as Benedetto said," resumed Louisette, "there was nothing much to be frightened at; only in such a place as this, one is apt, you know, to be full of fancies. As I was passing, about an hour ago, along the gallery on my way from your chamber, I heard a sudden noise upon the stairs, at a little distance from where I was. The wind was high, as it is now; and you know it is an old saying, that when a fire or candle burns blue, it is a sure sign that one shall see a ghost. Well, the flame of my lamp did burn blue; and as I stopped to listen when the wind was a little still, I heard something behind me go pod, pod—for all the world like a spirit. I was too frightened, as you may suppose, to look behind me, and so down stairs I went, more dead than alive, and there met Benedetto."

"I thought you said the steps were behind you," cried Cecilia: "how then could it be Benedetto?"

"Oh, it was not he!" answered Louisette; "but you shall hear, Mademoiselle.—I was so frightened, as I was saying, that down I went to the bottom, where stood Benedetto, who seeing me look ghastly pale, caught me in his arms, thinking, as well he might, that I was dying, when who should leap after me over the balustrades but old Lupo, the Signor's favourite spaniel. Poor fellow,

I dare say he was as much terrified as I was, for I gave a hideous scream!"

Cecilia could not refrain from smiling at the superstitious credulity of Louisette, and after a gentle reproof dismissed her.

The next morning, Varàno being alone with Cecilia, full of the idea which now solely engrossed his thoughts, spoke with animated fervour of their marriage and future prospect.—Cecilia, more composed than before, listened to him with delight; but reflecting that she had now discovered a relation nearly interested in her concerns, and forgetting for the moment that she was under a solemn engagement to conceal this relationship, she mentioned something about consulting Signor di Rosalvo on their intended plans.

"And why Rosalvo?" said Varàno, throwing himself upon a chair.

"Is he not your friend as well as mine?" cried Cecilia.

Varàno sighed, and continued for some minutes silent. Suspicions, such as he had never before felt, glanced athwart his mind. But although they were admitted for a moment, they were soon rejected with disdain; and as if imagining that she could read his heart, and find there the surmise ere it was uttered, he earnestly entreated her pardon.

"Forgive me," said he, with a look beaming tenderness and contrition—"forgive my too hasty expressions. That impetuosity of which you have always complained, is for ever urging me to offend!"

Cecilia accepted the apology, though wholly unconscious of its motive; for as guilt is ever suspicious, so is innocence decidedly otherwise. The sweetly engaging manner with which she overlooked his retort restored Varàno to his tranquillity, and increased, if possible, his admiration; but in the evening his surmises were again roused by the affectionate looks which Rosalvo and Cecilia involuntarily bestowed upon each other, and which did not entirely escape the Signora. Uneasy and disconcerted, he quitted the room; and scarcely knowing whither he went, took the path that led to the wood. A peasant with his axe passed near him. Varàno stopped; and anxious to take refuge from his own unquiet reflections, entered into discourse with him.

"This wood is not very extensive," said Varàno, "but seems to be of ancient growth. You reside, I suppose, on its borders?"

"I have lived within a mile of this place, your Honour," returned the woodcutter, "man and boy, near fifty years. 'Tis a grand old wood, as you say; and the time has been when it was kept in fine order."

"And how happens it to be neglected now?" asked Varàno.

"Because there are no such doings in the Castle now as there used to be formerly," resumed the woodcutter. "When my Lord the Count was alive—God rest his soul!—those fine chestnuts yonder used to be hung with lights; and when evening was set in, and my Lady was here, the villagers, dressed in their holiday clothes, and as merry as crickets, used to dance beneath their shade. Those were happy days, your Honour; I shall never see the like again!"

"And are the present inhabitants of the Castle," continued Varàno, "less hospitable than their predecessors?"

"Why no, I can't say they are less hospitable," replied the peasant; "for my Lady, the Signora, to whom this fine estate belongs, is beloved by every body: but they live so solitary, and nobody comes now to walk here but the Signor and a young lady. They, indeed, often say here for hours before the rest of the family are up."

Varàno turned pale.

"*Santo Padre!*" exclaimed the peasant, "you seem surprised! But as to their walking and sitting together, nobody can say there's any harm in that."

"None in the least," cried Varàno, in confusion.

"But yet, your Honour, when one sees two people meeting each other at the same time and in the same place, one cannot help having one's thoughts. Twice, Signor, have I seen them in this wood, and both times they were in earnest discourse—she crying, and he with his arm round her waist: and once I heard her tell him she would do any thing to make him happy; and then he kissed her cheek, and said she was sent from Heaven to be his comforter!"

"Villain!" exclaimed Varàno. "Oh Cecilia! Cecilia!"

"And yet after all," continued the woodcutter, "there may

be nothing in it; or if there is, as they say she is nobody, and has no friends, it's no matter, so long as my Lady does not know of it."

Varàno walked away with a distracted air; and then returning to the peasant, said fiercely—"The lady to whom you allude is neither friendless nor unknown!—Take heed what you say; those who dare to defame her, shall not escape punishment!"

So saying, he hastened from the wood, leaving the peasant, who little expected such a rebuff, in the utmost amazement.

The agitation which was perceptible in the countenance of Varàno when he returned to the Castle, was visible to all the party. The astonished Cecilia eagerly and tenderly enquired what had disturbed him. A cold, evasive answer converted her surprise into distress.—Rosalvo, by the indignant glances which he received from him, and the expression of sorrow and indignation which were blended in his looks to Cecilia, began at length to suspect the cause. He recollected, for the first time, that his fraternal attentions had been particular; and since it was not to be wondered at that a lover should be jealous of such a mistress, resolved not only to be more circumspect himself, but to intimate the reason of his precautions to Cecilia. He had promised to give her the remaining part of his story the next morning in the wood; but as they had been once met there by Varàno, he desired her to rise an hour before her usual time, and meet him in the most retired spot in the gardens, requesting her to leave directions with her woman to say that she was engaged, should Varàno enquire for her.

Cecilia was punctual to the hour of appointment; and having committed the papers for his perusal, bequested to her by her mother, which she had before had no opportunity of delivering, Rosalvo conducted her to a thick grove of ilex and arbutus, and piercing into its thickest shade, thus concluded his narration.

———

"The next day I received a visit from Cariello, whom I was surprised to find acquainted with the adventure at the Lapidario's. —'I know not,' said he, after a little previous conversation, 'how sufficiently to congratulate you on your extraordinary conquest! My Lady has refused offers from some of the first Nobles in the city, whilst you, whom she has only accidentally seen, and in situations where you could have no opportunity of conciliating her esteem, have impressed her with the most lively sentiments in your favour.'

"I looked seriously at the Maggiordomo to be assured that he was in earnest; but was unable to give a reply, I was so overcome with astonishment. He paused for a few moments, as if awaiting my answer, and then continued—

"'If you are insensible to your good fortune, you are certainly the only man in Venice that could be so. My Lady's beauty and riches entitle her to the first alliance in the State; how happy then must be the man who can attain such a treasure!'

"'Deceive me not,' said I, 'with hopes which can never be realized!'

"'What does he deserve,' rejoined Cariello, 'who can reject blessings when they offer, and even court his acceptance?'

"The manner in which these words were delivered left me no doubt of their sincerity, and I hastily demanded by what authority he spoke.

"'My Lady's woman,' replied the Maggiordomo, 'who is shortly to become my wife, is in her confidence; from her I obtained this information. Had you offered her your ring, the event might have been hastened. If she admired it before—now, that she knows it to be your's, she considers it as infinitely more valuable.'

"I took the hint, and with a strange mixture of surprise and delight flew to the Lapidario's for my ring, which I committed to Cariello, with a polite note to his Lady. An answer was speedily returned, and accompanying it was a ring of thrice the value of mine. This led to an introduction to the house of my charmer. Nothing could be more animated, yet more delicate, than the reception I met with—nothing more frank, yet more innocent, than her conversation!—To be brief, in spite of my poverty and my disgrace, the passion which I had conceived for her could not long be concealed. She drew from me a confession of the tenderest attachment, and promised to reward it."

"And this," said Cecilia, fixing her eyes upon him with an expressive gaze, "was Giuliana?"

"The same," returned Rosalvo; "she whom I loved to madness —whom I have injured beyond redress!—She is not my wife!"

"Not your wife!" repeated Cecilia.

"No—by that Heaven, in whose sight I received her at the altar, she is not legally my wife!—I plighted my vows by a name not my own!"

"Oh why—why," said Cecilia, thunderstruck with this declaration, "did you deceive her?"

"Listen," resumed Rosalvo, "and excuse, if you can, a conduct which has been the cause of all my anguish!—Trusting to her love, her tenderness, her pity, I meant to have unfolded all my crimes; but a discovery, as fatal as unexpected, prevented the confession.—Going one evening to her Palace, I found Giuliana in tears. The ardour of my enquiries denoting how greatly I was affected by them—'You have no doubt been surprised,' said she, after a deep sigh, 'at the silence which I have preserved concerning my family, and particularly those to whom I owe my birth. This conduct, sanctioned by your own, which has been equally reserved, originated in an event which I cannot recollect without the severest anguish!—It is two years this fatal day since my father, Conte Francisco di Minotti, met his death at St. Lucia near Naples, from the stroke of an assassin.'

"Had the poniard of a murderer been at that moment pointed at my breast, the horror of it would have been nothing to what I then suffered. Giuliana perceived it, but mistook the cause; and after a few minutes' hesitation, proceeded to relate the dreadful affair in which I had been the principal agent.

" 'I have every year,' continued she, 'set apart a considerable sum for masses to be said for the repose of my father's soul: and since the Church is so soon to witness the vows we have already exchanged, let us repair together to-night to the Church of San Geminiano—the intercessions of his children may sooth his departed spirit!'

"To refuse was impossible. I attended her thither; and whilst before the sacred altar she knelt with a look of devotion almost saintly, my soul was alive only to the horrible idea of being the murderer of her father!—I could not pray—I could not even utter a word—I could only lift an imploring eye to Heaven to supplicate that forgiveness which, had not the deed been involuntary, I dared not hope to have obtained. Dreadful were my struggles! —To discover the truth would be to torture her; to marry her by a fictitious name was dishonourable—was base! One moment I resolved to leave her, and bury myself for ever in my former obscurity—the next to declare openly the necessity under which I acted; but to lose her, which must be the inevitable result of either, would be agony—would be distraction!—Oh Cecilia! the trial was a severe one, and I yielded. The little virtue I possessed was insufficient to uphold me in the hour of contest; the dreariness of a perpetual retirement—poverty, dependence, with all their store of accumulated evils, threatened to weight me to the earth. On the other hand, by burying the fatal secret in my breast, this invaluable woman might be mine.

"Awful were my emotions while at the high altar in the Church of San Marco, where I had first seen this charming woman, I received her hand. The same delicacy which had prevented her from being minute in her enquiries concerning my family and connections before marriage, actuated her afterwards; and her silence was a safeguard to my secret.

"But, ah! never let any man imagine that happiness, or even ease, can be attained but through a steady and determined perseverance in the open path of sincerity. Though pleasure may enchant, and interest may allure, if denied that heavenly whispering within, the possession of all which they can bestow, will be found vain and unsatisfactory. Never, from the hour I married Giuliana, have I tasted tranquillity. Harassed as I was by my own remorse, Venice soon became insupportable, and we exchanged it for Genoa. This city, too, soon became irksome; and having visited this Castle, I prevailed upon Giuliana to reside with me here. Time seems to have reconciled her to my eccentricities without impairing her affection; but while it tends to convince me of her virtues, it heightens my sense of her injuries.—Oh my Giuliana! mayst thou never know how thou hast been wronged! May the dreadful mystery that involves me still cast an impenetrable veil over the events of my ill-fated youth!—for would not thy gentle nature recoil with horror from an act which covers me with confusion?—Wouldst thou not abandon a wretch who dared to bestow upon thee a hand crimsoned with the blood of thy father, —and who, by concealing from thee his name, has continued to abuse they unsuspecting confidence?—Never, I charge you, then," resumed Rosalvo, rising, and throwing himself at Cecilia's feet, "if you would save Giuliana from distraction, and me from all the horrors of madness, reveal the secret with which I have entrusted you!"

"Never, never shall it transpire!" cried Cecilia, bursting into an agony of tears.—Oh most *unfortunate marriage!*"

"Would to Heaven it had never taken place!" said Rosalvo; "for then, though I might have been unhappy, I should not have been criminal!—But spare me the sight of those tears—they seem to reproach me!"

"They are tears of compassion—of the tenderest affection," replied Cecilia, "not of reproach! Would I could save you from the dangers which may yet await you, should Giuliana discover——"

"You, too, foresee danger then!" pursued Rosalvo, throwing his arms around her waist, while his head sunk unconsciously on her shoulder. "Explain—tell me what you fear!"

While he spoke, he felt his arm forcibly grasped, and turning around, beheld Varàno. Rosalvo arose in disorder, and after eyeing him a moment in silence, demanded with confusion why he was intruded upon.

"Rather ask why I did not intrude upon you sooner!" retorted Varàno. "When we once suspect a man to be a villain, it is no matter how soon we prove him so!"

"A villain!" reiterated Rosalvo—"a villain!"

"A base, insinuating villain!" returned Varàno, in a voice of thunder.

"Signor," resumed Rosalvo, gravely, "this is language to which I have not been accustomed."

"'Tis such as your conduct merits," cried Varàno: "think not you shall escape with impunity."

"What chastisement am I to expect?" demanded Rosalvo; "and from whose hands am I to receive it?"

"From his whom you have most injured," answered Varàno.

As he spoke, he clapped his hand upon his sword, and Rosalvo involuntarily did the same. Cecilia shrieked, and rushed between them.

"Forgive him," said she, seizing Rosalvo's arm, "he knows not what he says.—Nor you," added she to Varàno, "whom you accuse."

"And you would plead for your seducer," cried Varàno, "the villain who——"

"Oh stop—for Heaven's sake stop!" exclaimed Cecilia, "he is my *friend*!—and not only my friend, but——"

The word *brother* trembled on her lips; but a look from Rosalvo arrested her tongue.

"But what?" vociferated Varàno disdainfully, "your *most disinterested adviser*! But, Madam, since *you* are satisfied," (greatly agitated), "*I*, of course, am so. If the *unfortunate marriage* you have been lamenting can be dissolved, you are at liberty—I have no further claim upon your affection. Farewel!"

"Oh stay—stay!" cried Cecilia.

Before she could utter another word, the powers of articulation and sensation together forsook her, and she fell senseless to the ground.

"Eternal Powers!" exclaimed Varàno, rushing forward and raising her in his arms, "what is it that I have done?—Oh Cecilia! even now, lost as thou art to me and to thyself, I could take thee to my heart, and weep over thee! But we must part. Close then those eyes—look not upon me—I would not see them—I would not hear thy voice! Oh God, protect her!"

"Help—support her," cried Rosalvo; "she is an angel, and——"

"Unhand her!" retorted Varàno, fiercely. "Base, dissembling wretch! she was an angel once!—and you——"

"Moderate your indignation," interposed Rosalvo, "and assist me to convey her to the Castle. She has never wronged you."

"Touch her," cried Varàno, "and your life shall be the forfeiture of your rashness!—Yet why—Oh why," said he, as he carried her in his arms toward the Castle, "should I protect her?"

The Signora flew to meet them; and terrified by the wild countenance of Varàno, and the situation in which she saw Cecilia, eagerly enquired what had happened. Varàno, without replying, rushed by her, and entering the first apartment he came to, laid Cecilia upon a sofa, furiously fastening the door upon Rosalvo, who was hastily following.

Cecilia instantly revived.

"Thank Heaven you are here!" said she, observing Varàno. "But where—where is Rosalvo?"

"He is safe," returned Varàno, sullenly—"the coward is safe!"

"Ah! how little do you know him!" said Cecilia; "his heart is as honourable as your own:—trust not to appearances!"

"*Appearances!*" interrupted Varàno, "*appearances!*—Your eloquence, Madam, will be in vain till you can teach me to discredit the evidences of my senses—till you can teach me to believe that the words you uttered at the moment when you were weeping in each other's arms, were the cold expressions of friendship instead of the confirmations of guilt!"

"Guilt!" repeated Cecilia, raising her streaming eyes to heaven.

Varàno was staggered. Her countenance spoke her innocence.

"Speak!" cried he, breathless with expectation—"unravel this mystery!—Oh tell me we may yet be happy!"

"At a future time," rejoined Cecilia, remembering the solemnity of her promise to Rosalvo, "all may be explained. Were I to confess it now, I should destroy one whose peace is dearer to me than my own!"

"Yes," cried Varàno, again roused to fury by her words, "you would *destroy Rosalvo!*"

He said no more; but bursting open the door, instantly disappeared.

Cecilia, terrified by his impetuosity, and utterly unable to recal him, sunk back motionless on the sofa; but a sudden impulse of despair roused her from her stupor, and she flew to follow him. She ran through the apartments, then into the gardens, calling wildly on his name, till her strength was almost exhausted. At the edge of a thick grove which led toward the wood she was met by Rosalvo.

"Where is he?" cried he; "I will disclose every thing—I will confess that I am your brother!"

Cecilia took his arm, unable to speak; but her looks expressed eloquently the gratitude she could not utter, and they fled together in search of Varàno.

They again traversed the gardens, the wood, and again returned to the house. A servant met them at the door. Rosalvo hastily enquired for Varàno.

"The Signor is gone," returned the servant; "he has quitted the Castle this half hour."

CHAPTER IV

——————"Where will you I go
To answer this your charge?"
"To prison, till fit time
Of law, and course of direct session
Call thee to answer."
SHAKESPEARE.

ROSALVO, to whom no reflection could be so agonizing as that of having been the cause of a separation between Varàno and Cecilia, dispatched servants immediately from the Castle in search of the former. To the Signora the occurrences of the morning had appeared strangely perplexing; and, agitated by uneasy surmises, she remained alone in her chamber till dinner, when, surprised by the precipitate retreat of Varàno, she enquired the reason of it. The confused replies she received both from Rosalvo and Cecilia increased her astonishment, and she became thoughtful and reserved. This change, and the motive of it, was too obvious and too sudden to escape the notice of Cecilia. The Signora, she perceived, partook of Varàno's suspicions; and the impossibility of vindicating herself to her, though, by Rosalvo's intended disclosure, she might to him, wounded her to the soul.

The servants returned in a few hours, but brought no intelligence of Varàno. Rosalvo, more than ever distressed, resolved to write to him, promising, if he would return, a complete elucidation of his suspicions. A faint hope sustained Cecilia on the execution of this plan, which at length sunk into despondency, when several weeks had passed, and no answer arrived from

Varàno. Rosalvo was equally wretched, and the altered behaviour of the Signora, who seemed to have lost in her conjectures all the ardour of her friendship, added to their mutual distress.

Day after day rolled on, yet brought no tidings of Varàno. Cecilia, dashed in a few short hours from the summit of happiness to the abyss of misery, could with difficulty support the sudden transition. Her fortitude declined, and there was a melancholy expression in her features—a composed, but settled dejection in her manner, which greatly alarmed Rosalvo. He feared she was sinking into a gradual decay; and accusing himself as the cause, endured the most poignant distress.

Anxious to amuse her mind, he often proposed short rides about the country, but not without the Signora was in the party, aware that she too had imbibed the poison of suspicion.

Louisette, who was also an uneasy spectator of Cecilia's melancholy, frequently endeavoured to amuse her by relating all the little stories which she had gleaned during her stay in the Castle.

"La, Mademoiselle," said she one night, as she was laying some wood upon the fire in her apartment, "if all is true that is said about this Castle——"

"About this Castle," said Cecilia, faintly; "why what is said of this Castle?"

"Nay, nobody knows much about it," returned Louisette; "it was old Rogero that told me one night when we were sitting together in the kitchen after you, and the Signor, and my Lady were gone to bed——Do just sit down, Mademoiselle, and I'll tell you how it was.—They were all gone out of the kitchen, as I was saying, but old Rogero and me. It was one dreary and bitter cold night, about a month ago, when the rain was beating against the windows. Rogero had been asleep for some time, notwithstanding the storm, when he suddenly started up. The wind had just then blew very horribly; and thinking there might be something the matter at sea, he went out upon the rampart wall to see if any ships were in sight; for the bridge was drawn up, and he could not get beyond. The sea continued to rage, but nothing was to be seen; so Rogero came back again, and took his seat in the corner as before.

"He had not been there long when a sudden gust shattered the casement, and burst open the door. It came with such force, and then hurried up the passages with such a shrill sound, that we both quaked, and drew nearer the fire.

"'Lord have mercy upon the wicked!' said Rogero, rising and crossing himself.

"''Tis a dismal night,' said I, 'for those that have done no crime. Lord have mercy, as you say, upon those that have!'

"'I'm sure,' said Rogero, 'if it was not for being certain that I have never harmed any body in word or deed, I would not stay in this Castle for all the Signor's riches.'

"When Rogero said this, I began to think he had some meaning in his words; so drawing my chair close, and looking carefully about to see that nobody was behind me, I asked him what he meant.

"'Surely,' said I, 'Rogero, you don't think that any thing has been done in this Castle more than in another. It's a grand old place, and I dare say time was when there were fine doings in it.'

"Rogero shook his head as if he did not care to say more; but this, as well it might, only made me the more curious to know his thoughts; so after a great deal to be said, and a great deal to be done, I got him to tell me what he knew.

"'My Lady's father was, as you may have heard,' said Rogero, 'the owner of this Castle. When my old Lady, God rest her soul! died, my Lord the Count married a young wife from Calabria. This lady was so beautiful, that he could not bear her out of his sight; and as she married him only for his riches, she liked every body better than her husband.

"'Well, to be brief,' continued Rogero, 'though the story is somewhat long, my Lord the Count was missing.'

"'Missing!' said I.

"'Yes, my Lord the Count was missing,' said Rogero, 'and it was soon found out that he was murdered!'"

Cecilia trembled, but concealed her alarm, and Louisette proceeded.

"'Many stories,' cried he, 'were told about it at Naples, but nobody knew what to make of 'em; some thought that the murderer was employed by his wife, and others by one of her lovers.

This seemed the more likely from his having hurried away from Naples, and nobody ever hearing of him since.'"

"And what became of the Countess?" asked Cecilia.

"Why one of her gallants," answered Louisette, "a Signor, I forget who, was to have married her; but somehow or other before it came to, it went off, and so they never came together at all."

"Your story," said Cecilia, "or rather Rogero's, is a very wonderful one, but amounts to little, and certainly can have no connection whatever with the present inhabitants of the Castle; any thing, therefore, which may happen to alarm you here, can have nothing to do with this murder."

"Why that's what I told Rogero. 'What can that signify to the Castle?' said I, 'when the Count was killed at Naples. If his spirit, Holy St. Peter protect it! can't rest where it is, what should he do here?—Unless, indeed, as his Honour used to live at this Castle, he chuses to stalk about the old galleries for his own pleasure.'"

"Tales of this kind," cried Cecilia, "have seldom much foundation in truth. How did Rogero obtain his intelligence?—and where was he at the time all this happened?"

"He was here," replied Louisette, "and so was Brigitta; for their Lord liked the Castle, and would have it kept open. Strange noises they tell me were heard in it the night he died. Rogero says the owls screeched, and flapped their wings dismally against the windows; and there were such deep groans and doleful rumblings upon the stairs, and the neighbours talk of bloody hands that were seen moving about the casements. But, la! Mademoiselle, you look pale—sure I have not frightened you?"

"I am sadly fatigued," returned Cecilia, still more agitated. "What is the hour?"

"It is near one I think," said Louisette; "I heard the clock just now striking the quarters."

"It grows late," resumed Cecilia; "and really, Louisette, I have listening to your improbable tales till I begin to think I shall be weak enough to be infected by them."

"Then pray, Mademoiselle," cried Louisette, stirring up the fire, "let me stay with you till you are asleep. This is a dismal time of night, and I always think if any thing is to be seen——"

"No more," said Cecilia with quickness; "I am weary, and would be alone. Good-night, and may the Holy Mother guard you!"

Louisette remonstrated, but withdrew; and Cecilia, with a sensation not entirely devoid of superstitious terror, took possession of her bed, where she lost in a broken repose those fears for her brother which the artless conversation of Louisette had unintentionally excited.

The remainder of the winter passed on, and the returning spring began to put forth its blossoms. But the charms of this delightful season, which approached with the most smiling aspect, lost their effect upon Cecilia; she appeared like a beautiful flower bent beneath the storm. Yet keen and unmerited as were her suffering, she reproached not Varàno.

"When he shall hear of my death," said she, weeping, "he will perhaps think of me without resentment; nay, who knows but my justification may be accomplished, and he may remember me with affection! Yes, when the grave has closed over me, he may shed a tear—a tear, perchance, of sorrow and contrition over my unconscious ashes."

To gaze upon his portrait, the last, and now only relic of his tenderness—to wander, in mournful rumination, through the darkest shades of the wood—to climb the barren heights of the precipice, whose uncultivated tracks afforded only a scanty herbage for the marmotto,[1] or playful capretto[2]—to view, from its projecting brow, the dashing wave, rising and bursting against the shores, and throwing its white foam among the rocks, were now Cecilia's favourite occupations—occupations which at once soothed and saddened her mind.

The Signora, softened by her distress, which had already visibly impaired her health, felt her tenderness revive; and perceiving nothing either in her conduct or Rosalvo's which could confirm the suspicions she had unwillingly indulged, her generous heart, ever candid to her husband and her friend, attributed the strange departure of Varàno to some sudden impulse of his own impetuous temper. Cecilia, in the returned affection of the

1 The marmot.
2 The young mountain-goat.

Signora, found one great cause of anguish removed; but though she rejoiced in this change, and repaid her efforts to console her with the most expressive sweetness, there was a despair at her heart, when she thought of Varàno, which nothing could subdue.

Time had not diminished her distress when her attentions were engrossed by the indisposition of the Signora, which at length confined her to her chamber. In her anxiety for the restoration of her friend, Cecilia lost the immediate sense of her own sufferings; and as she reflected upon the possibility of being deprived of so valuable a relative, she found it was in the power of circumstances to make her still more wretched. The solicitude which she discovered was gratefully acknowledged by the Signora, who frequently expostulated upon the necessity of her being more attentive to her own health.

"Ah, Madam!" Cecilia would say, "my life can now only be valuable to myself in proportion as it may be rendered useful to others."

"This is despondency, my love," cried the Signora. "Where are those noble sentiments you have so often expressed, and which I have so greatly admired? Have you not assured me that the good must be happy, and *that* sorrow, that fixed kind of dejection which is better termed despair, can be attached only to positive guilt?"

"Alas!" said Cecilia, "this is, I fear, a maxim of speculative morality, promising in theory, but not always confirmed by practice. That there are some species of intellectual distress confined solely to the vicious, no one will dispute; but it is not equally certain," added she, sighing, "that virtue is efficient to happiness."

The Signora's health was now gradually amending; but she was yet too weak to leave her chamber.

One night as Cecilia and Rosalvo were sitting in one of the lower apartments, they were alarmed by a loud ringing at the outer gate, and immediately Rogero appeared with intelligence that a Nobleman, attended by a numerous retinue, having been bewildered in the neighbouring forest, requested admittance.

"Enquire his name," cried Rosalvo.

He had scarcely spoken, when the stranger, muffled up in his travelling cloak, and with his hat drawn and slouched over his face, rushed into the room. He started as he entered, and offered his hand to Rosalvo, and then threw off his cloak.

"Guidotto!"——"Morsino!" exclaimed Cecilia and Rosalvo at the same moment.

Cecilia shrieked; and darting from the room, fled with terror to her apartment.

The sudden appearance of her persecutor, in whose unsuspicion of her existence she had grounded all her hopes of security, struck her with indescribable horror!—and that Morsino should prove to be the perfidious friend of her brother—that Guidotto who had so basely betrayed him, filled her with astonishment equal to her horror. She knew that he only possessed the dreadful secret on which hung the life of Rosalvo. Her own danger, now that Morsino had discovered the feigned tale of her death, imposed upon him by M. Langlois, was disregarded in her alarm for his safety.

She continued in a state of inconceivable perturbation till her ears were assailed by a loud tumult from below, as of the voices of a number of people together contending in the hall. She sprang into the gallery, and leaning over the balustrade, heard distinctly the clashing of swords in the apartment below, where she had left the Count and Rosalvo; and in a moment Rosalvo rushed out, pale and bloody.

Her cries brought him instantly to her relief; and seizing her arm, whilst he tremblingly and with difficulty supported her —"We must fly," said he; "my life and your safety depend upon our instant departure!"

Then hurrying her into the Signora's chamber—"Giuliana," cried he, "I must escape—a moment's delay will be fatal to me; and not only to me, but one dear to us both. You shall know all —prepare to follow us!"

Observing that they looked with speechless terror upon the blood which stained his clothes—"I am safe—I am unhurt!" added he, bursting from them with the rapidity with which he had entered, leaving the Signora and Cecilia in terrified astonishment.

Cecilia, as soon as she could speak, informed the Signora of Morsino's strange arrival.

"But are you not safe under our protection?" cried the Signora. "The villain, daring as he is, cannot insult you here!"

"But Rosalvo—your husband!" interrupted Cecilia.

"What endangers him?" replied the Signora.

Rosalvo returned before she had finished speaking; and, regardless of the tears and exclamations of his wife, bade her an incoherent adieu, and forced Cecilia from the apartment.

The horses were in readiness at the gate of the outer court. Rosalvo committed an account of his route to the trusty Rogero; and assisting Cecilia to mount, he vaulted upon his horse; and crossing the bridge, they soon lost sight of the Castle.

The rapidity with which they proceeded scarcely allowed Cecilia to breathe till they reached Noli. They stopped at a post-house till the servants who had followed them arrived. Rosalvo, commanding them to convey the horses back to the Castle, and to be in readiness to attend the Signora on her journey in the morning, ordered a *vetturino* to be instantly prepared. As they were entering it, a post-carriage and four, with two gentlemen, attended by their servants, drove into the court. One of them was Varàno, who, accompanied by Le Chatre, was returning from France, whither he had flown in despair, to confide all his miseries to his friend. He saw Rosalvo alone with Cecilia; he saw him hand her into a carriage, and drive off with all the speed of a disgrace-ful elopement!—while the travellers, intent only on their flight, were unconscious that he whom they had so eagerly sought, was so near. Varàno's frenzy was ungovernable; and it was with diffi-culty that Le Chatre could prevent him from pursuing them, and plunging his sword into the breast of his supposed rival.

At the last post but one between Briancon and Turin, the Count's people had accidentally met Varàno's; and learning from Benedetto that Cecilia was then living, and at the Castello di Montani, they communicated this intelligence to their Lord. The Count instantly flew thither, intending to introduce himself as a benighted traveller, little expecting to behold in the owner of the Castle, his old acquaintance D'Arnaud.

Rosalvo and Cecilia travelled rapidly along. Each endeavoured to support the other; but both were so much oppressed by the present gloominess of their prospects, as to be equally unfitted for the task of consolation. They arrived in the evening at Casal, where they were to wait for the Signora, and then to renew their route into Switzerland, where Rosalvo meant to take refuge from the fury of the Count, who had threatened, on his refusal to deliver Cecilia into his power, to give him up to the Neapolitan laws as the murderer of Conte di Minotti.

Cecilia being unable to resume her journey, they were compelled to remain at Casal a whole day, engaging lodgings at an obscure inn. At night, the Signora not being arrived, Rosalvo, though alarmed at this delay, resolved to proceed to the next post, and wait there till she should overtake them.

They had gained the suburbs, when Cecilia, looking from the carriage, beheld it surrounded by armed men. They had no time for conjecture.

"Seize him!" cried one of them as he opened the door of the carriage.

Rosalvo drew his sword, and fiercely demanded their business.

"You will soon know it," cried another, whom Rosalvo now perceived to be an Officer of Justice—"you are our prisoner."

A crowd soon gathered around them, and several voices at once enquired the cause of the disturbance.

"This Signor," replied one of officers, "has been guilty of an assault upon Count Morsino, a Nobleman who took shelter beneath his roof, and who now lies at his Castle mortally wounded."

"I deny the charge," said Rosalvo firmly; "his wounds are not mortal!"

"His absconding," cried the first Sbirro, "is a sufficient proof of his guilt. Whoever, therefore, shall oppose our authority in this town, must answer for it before the Council of Genoa. This lady is the wife of the Count, and an accomplice in the act."

"Wretch!" exclaimed Cecilia, "how dare you utter such a falsehood! I the wife of the Count!"

"A pretty wife to deny her own husband!" rejoined the other officer.

"You had better be silent, lady," interposed the first Sbirro; "as to the Signor, he must go with us."

It was in vain to resist. The atrocity of the deed seemed to have

palsied the powers of all the spectators; and Cecilia, with a sensation little short of distraction, saw Rosalvo, in the last struggles
of desperation, dragged from her sight. At the same moment a
party of Morsino's servants gallopped towards them; and placing her again in the carriage from which she had leaped, two of
them seated themselves beside her, and ordered the postillion
to drive on. They travelled all night with inconceivable velocity,
without stopping, or even speaking either to her or each other.
Cecilia now found, what she had scarcely believed possible, that
her miseries still admitted of aggravation. Rosalvo was torn from
her, doubtless to be dragged to the scaffold; and she was again in
the power of Morsino! The Signora, when she should hear the
dreadful tidings, would probably sink under this accumulated
weight of calamity!

Morning at length dawned; and the light gleaming faintly
upon the countenances of her companions, Cecilia, recoiling
with horror, exclaimed, "Do I see Pere Baptiste?"

One of them was indeed the pretended Monk, the Count's
favourite valet, who had been employed by him to decoy her
to the Cevennes. The wretch replied only with a sarcastic smile
indicative of his villany.—Cecilia, though more and more
alarmed, summoned courage enough to enquire whither they
were conveying her.

"To Venice," returned he, sullenly.

As they advanced, the closeness of the carriage, and the
increasing heat of the day, affected her almost to fainting. The
other man perceiving it, let down one of the windows; but the
valet reproving him, he instantly drew it up.

They travelled on day after day, stopping only for refreshments, till they reached Ferrara, proceeding from thence to the
little village of Francolino, about five miles distant. Here they
alighted; and embarking in a barge upon the Po, resumed their
course toward Venice. The men took their place by the rowers;
and Cecilia, to whom every change in her situation appeared an
augmentation of her misery, saw herself enclosed in a little cabin,
close, gloomy and lighted only by one solitary *bougie*. The oars
dashing at regular intervals, or the coarse laugh of the rowers,
only broke the silence. About midnight, overcome with fatigue,

and harassed with conjecture, she flung herself upon a kind of mattress which one of the men had then brought, often starting from her perturbed slumbers as the recollection of Rosalvo's danger rushed confusedly on her mind, or the keen bite of the moschetto awoke her to the acute, though less agonizing tortures of bodily pain.

The morning had just dawned over the Adriatic, when she perceived the city rising gradually from the bosom of the ocean, its lofty spires tipped with the brightening crimson of the rising sun; and passing the *Laguni* near the little island of *Santa Chiara*, entered the *Canal Grande*.

The barge stopped at a flight of steps; and Cecilia, with terror and indignation, found herself landed at a magnificent Palace, constructed, like the rest of the buildings, of white marble, and in the most finished style of architecture. They entered a hall. One of the men remained with Cecilia—the other ascended a staircase: he returned in a few minutes; and Cecilia, trembling with apprehension, was commanded to follow him.

They entered an apartment, where, seated on sofas at the farther end, were three ladies elegantly dressed. The valet introduced her, and withdrew. The elder of the ladies, who appeared to be about fifty, and whose face, though it bore the ravages of time, exhibited nevertheless the remains of great beauty, arose to receive her, introducing herself to her notice by the name of Madame Schellinsburg, being the widow of a German officer, and, as she herself informed her, the aunt of Count Morsino. She addressed her with a polite, but sort of studied salutation; for there was a natural loftiness in her manner, heightening into *hauteur*, which it seemed impossible to conceal. The younger ladies, whom she presented as her daughters by a former marriage with the uncle of her relation, Count Morsino, had all the frankness of their country. They ran over a profusion of compliments which confused and overwhelmed Cecilia, who felt no small embarrassment from her situation.

"My nephew," cried Madame Schellinsburg, "has entrusted you to my protection. Conscious that he has injured you, he is now solicitous to render you all possible reparation. Of his former conduct I know little—this may have been reprehensible;

but the anxiety he has testified to reinstate himself in your favour, proves the sincerity of his repentance. Disengaged by the recent death of his wife, and hearing accidentally of your residence, that affection which neither time nor your indifference could subdue, urged him to pursue you. The very tender regard which I have always felt for my nephew, united to the conviction that his intentions are honourable, induced me to accept the charge."

The faded cheek of Cecilia underwent frequent revolutions during this speech;—grief and indignation struggled at her heart; but her mind, harassed by fatigue, denied her strength to give it utterance. Madame Schellinsburg then hinting that repose might be necessary, rang her bell for refreshments; after which, with many promises of protection, she desired an attendant to conduct Cecilia to her apartment, where she found change of apparel and every comfort her unpleasant situation required.

Cecilia threw herself upon the bed, and yielding to excessive fatigue, procured a transient repose; but the agonizing recollection of Rosalvo again awoke her: and recoiling from the idea of remaining with people in any way connected with the Count, though probably unacquainted with the baseness of his character, she resolved to express her detestation of it openly, and to insist upon returning to her friends. She found Madame Schellinsburg and her daughters in the room where she had left them, and instantly and briefly related the infamous treatment she had experienced from the Count and his agents, and his base attempt to criminate Rosalvo on the false charge of having mortally wounded him.

The exclamations and astonished looks of the ladies during this recital convinced Cecilia that the most objectionable parts of the Count's character had been hitherto concealed from them; and she summoned courage to declare her resolution of instantly quitting Venice.

"I am not surprised, my dear," said Madame Schellinsburg, "at your repugnance to remain with those who have the misfortune to be related to a man capable of such villany. Good heavens! is it possible that this can be my nephew, whom I have loved with all the fondness of maternal affection?"

"That you have been deceived, Madam, strangely deceived,"

cried Cecilia, "I cannot doubt it; let me then intercede for your protection. Alas! I have no dependence but on you!—it is you only that can save me from his schemes!"

"Here, at least," she answered, "you are safe from them; and though his having placed you beneath my roof convinces me that his intentions are now honourable, I do not request, I do not even wish you to accept him, or to continue here; however, after the proofs I have had of your discretion, I may be inclined to value your society, longer than till an opportunity can be found of restoring you safely to your friends. His reasons for seizing upon Signor Rosalvo must be too palpable to occasion you any serious uneasiness. The letter which I received from him is a strong evidence that his wounds, though probably considerable enough to delay his intended journey to Venice, are not mortal. What surprises me most is, having sent you to me, as if he imagined that I too could be deceived into a participation of his stratagems. This is a conduct I shall not fail to resent; while in my protection of you, I shall take care to defeat all his projects."

Cecilia thanked her with her tears. Her observation relative to Rosalvo, and the recollection that he was not arrested concerning the affair of Conte di Minotti, consoled and reassured her; and she yielded to the request of her new friend, to continue with her at her Palace till she could fix upon some safe plan of returning to the Castello di Montani. Madame Schellinsburg then retired, leaving Cecilia with her daughters.

The young ladies, though both handsome, bore no resemblance to their mother. Clarice, the elder, was of a low stature, and had that style of complexion which the French call *clair brun*. Her eyes were large, dark, and penetrating—her carriage light, easy, and graceful. Ippolita was the exact size of Cecilia; and being near two years younger, promised to be still taller. Her figure was rather striking than elegant, her complexion fair and glowing, and her eyes of a mild blue. She was less volatile than her sister; but the minds of neither seemed to have been much cultivated.

At dinner they removed to a spacious *salla*, the walls of which were hung with damask, and covered with a profusion of pictures. The sofas were ornamented with drapery of the same, and trimmed with silver. The windows, covered with awnings, opening to balconies overlooking the canal, and lustres of various coloured glasses were suspended from the ceiling. They were attended by a number of domestics, whose appearance coincided with the general magnificence.

After dinner Cecilia recollecting that Cariello, the former *intendante* of Signora di Rosalvo, resided at Venice, and thinking it probable that when informed of her connection with that family, he would himself convey her back to the Castle, she requested that enquiries might immediately be made concerning him, to which Madame Schellinsburg instantly consented. A messenger was accordingly dispatched to several parts of the city, who returned shortly with intelligence that a person of that name had resided in a small house near the *Ponte dei tre Archi*; but he had left that, and another which he had since purchased in the island either of Burano or Mazorba, and was gone no one could tell whither; nor was it certain that the person in question was the same who had formerly supplied the office of Maestro di Case to the Signora di Rosalvo.

Cecilia was chagrined at this account; nor could she recover from her disappointment till Madame Schellinsburg informed her that she had an acquaintance at Venice who had connections in the Genoese State; and that it was probable she should soon find for her a respectable escort thither.

CHAPTER V

With restless oar, while night embrowns the skies,
   The gondoliers still cleave the foamy way,
   All jovial singing by the moon's bright ray,
How through the forest's gloom Erminia flies.

And whether harsh or sweet the note they claim,
   They hope no plaudits, and no censure gain;
   They sing because they love the tuneful strain,
Nor tries their song the surges wild to tame.

ZAPPI.

The Humours of a Carnival—a Surprise—and an Adventure.

COULD Cecilia have divested herself of expectation or retrospection, the attractive novelty of her situation, the beauty of the objects, and polite attentions of Madame Schellinsburg, who endeavoured, by suggesting every thing which could lead to hope, to relieve and tranquillize her mind, would have restored her to cheerfulness; but the dangerous state of her brother, and her apprehensions concerning the Count, whose arrival she now daily expected, were a continual check upon her spirits.

Anxious to change the current of her thoughts, Madame Schellinsburg invited her to take an excursion with her into the city, pointing out to her, as they glided on, the most striking features of the scene. Yet, though drawn at intervals from the contemplation of her own immediate misfortunes, Cecilia felt an oppressive weight at her heart, which prevented the expression of her admiration, and which the contrasted gaiety of the inhabitants tended to increase.

Having viewed a number of the *stradas* and stately *piazzas* in the *Canal Grande*, turning into one of the lesser intersections of the canal, they passed the bridge of *San Giobbe*, and proceeded by the *Bersaglio* to the School of St. Theodora. Advancing from thence to the north-east side of the city, a noble and extensive sea view, with the islands of Burano and Murano, and the main land beyond, crowned by the lofty Alps of Carinthia and Carniola, and the distant mountains of Friuli, skirting the northern shores of the Adriatic, expanded to their sight; and Cecilia's attention was for a time irresistibly engrossed.

Returning home by the Rialto, Madame Schellinsburg left her gondola to purchase some gold and pearl ornaments[1] for her daughters, with some of which she politely presented Cecilia, entreating her to receive them as a token of her respect: but perceiving, by Cecilia's manner of declining them, that her delicacy would be hurt by their acceptance, she repeated not her request.

The Carnival was to commence in the course of a few days; and Clarice and Ippolita endeavoured to amuse Cecilia with the most lively descriptions of the approaching festival.

"All restraints," cried Clarice, "are thrown off at this season. We consider it as a principal part of our religion to join in the sports, and as great a breach of duty to neglect them, as to fail in the observance of the penances inflicted upon us for our supposed irregularities at the conclusion of the Carnivals."

Cecilia smiled.

"You seem incredulous," continued she. "Is it possible that you, who have been so long an inhabitant of Italy, should know so little of our manners?"

"I was thinking," said Cecilia, "that religion, as you seem to understand it, admits of some very curious contradictions. By your account, it imposes dissipation, and then penance, as the punishment of dissipation, from which it seems we are counselled what to do; and having done it, are in danger of being whipped for our pains."

"You French people, as I have frequently understood," rejoined Clarice, "are but half Catholics."

"We, at least, imagine ourselves to be good ones," resumed Cecilia, "though we have no Carnivals, and, comparatively speaking, few penances. But perhaps you think it necessary for us to sin, that we may have an opportunity of asking pardon?"

---

1 Beneath the arcades of the Rialto are shops filled with brilliant and costly ornaments, nothing being sold there but gold and pearls.

"Then you believe that our Carnivals must necessarily be sinful," cried Clarice.

"I should suppose, by the penances that ensue, they are generally thought so," replied Cecilia, "though many, no doubt, visit them without being guilty of irregularities;—to believe otherwise would be both illiberal and absurd."

"You are just in time," cried Clarice to Ippolita, who now entered, "to assist me in a religious controversy."

"Pray proceed then," said Ippolita, laughing; "I shall be infinitely edified by such a discussion."

"We have exhausted all our arguments I fear," cried Cecilia pensively; "and, what is very extraordinary, without either of us having suffered a defeat. The subject in question is—whether it is better to sin, that we may repent—or not sinning, to need no repentance."

"The former, undoubtedly," rejoined Ippolita; "we are solemnly commanded to repent. If we commit no sin, how can we repent?—and if we repent not, how can we obey our teachers?"

"I must refer you to your Confessor," answered Cecilia, "he, I think, will resolve the question differently."

"You may depend upon my enquiries," continued Ippolita; "I shall see him to-night, and will not neglect to ask him."

She did not neglect it. The Father assured her that the sins committed at the Carnivals were of a *venial* nature; and as such, could be of no real importance.

On the first day of the celebration of this festival, Madame Schellinsburg and her daughters prepared to unite in the amusements of the city, and Cecilia was with difficulty prevailed upon to accompany them. They were dressed in dominos, according to the custom of the place, wearing half masks of black velvet; and entering a magnificent gondola, the cabin of which was carved and gilt in devices, and ornamented with curtains of purple silk, fringed and drawn up with tassels of gold, set off, attended by servants, for the Piazza di San Marco.

The countenances of Clarice and Ippolita glowed with delight; nor was Madame Schellinsburg herself much less animated.

As they advanced, the clear waters of the canal, flanked on each side by grand sweep of Palaces, lengthened into perspective, terminated by the elegant arch of the *Ponte di Rialto*. Passing the Rialto, instead of turning into the smaller canals, they continued their course along the serpentine windings of the *Canal Grande*, and issued into the open sea by the *Dogano di Mare*. Here a spectacle of unequalled grandeur burst at once upon their view: the Giudecca, with its spires stretching to the left, and farther on the beautiful island of St. Giorgio Maggiore; its lofty campanile; the dome of its Church adorned with statues; and the Convent of the Benedettini Fathers.

The Adriatic was overspread with numberless gondolas and zendalettos; some containing cabins, carved and gilt like their own in various devices—others lined with blue and purple silk, hanging in festoons round their sides, rowed by gondolieri in white jackets, with caps of scarlet or dark blue, with blue trowsers. In the open boats were seen reclining, ladies attended by their cavaliers, and some by Friars in long robes. People of all ranks and descriptions moving beneath the piazzas of the Broglio, or gliding in gondolas, their habits of various colours brightening in the moonbeam, formed a grotesque appearance.

The gondola at length stopped, and the party proceeding through the two famous Grecian columns, walked down the Piazzetta, where the gay group were already assembling. It is impossible to portray the astonishment of Cecilia at the grandeur and novelty of this scene. To the left extended the Libraria Publica with its two stories in arcades, and its range of statues crowning the balustrades on its top; to the right the *Palazzo Ducale* with its Gothic colonnades; in front, a long perspective of buildings, which the campanile, and part of the noble Church of San Marco —the whole terminated by the *Orologio* in the Grand Piazza. They had not advanced far, when a strain of music, proceeding from several instruments at once, floated upon the waters in tones of melancholy, but entrancing sweetness! They listened as if afraid to lose a note of this soft minstrelsy, till it paused, and then changed into one of those light and airy measures which Italian art and Italian taste know so well how to express. It issued from a gondola which was making for the shore. It stopped, and four gentlemen in the habits of masqueraders landed at the Piazzetta. They walked swiftly along. The foremost of the party, perceiving

Madame Schellinsburg, looked on her intently, and immediately unmasked. She instantly recollected him, and they discoursed for some minutes aside; the rest of the party remaining with their eyes fixed upon Cecilia and her youthful companions.

"I thought," said Signor Orcello, "that you had left Venice; how is it that I see you here? Are you an inhabitant still?—or do you only return to it at the Carnivals?"

"I am too much attached to a place in which I have resided so long," replied Madame Schellinsburg, "to have the least inclination to quit it. How is it that you have fallen into so palpable a mistake?"

"How!" exclaimed he; "you—you a long resident at Venice! Did not I see you at——"

Madame Schellinsburg's cheek was suffused with crimson; and she laid her hand upon her lip in a token of silence. The Signor bowed, and seemed to understand the signal. This little occurrence was unmarked by Cecilia, Madame Schellinsburg having desired her and her daughters to walk on, herself and her friend following them at some distance. The other young men often intercepted Cecilia and her companions, sometimes turning to observe them with a look of familiarity extremely shocking to Cecilia. One of them, with an insolence equally distressing and provoking, stooped down to obtain a view of her face.

Orcello was now formally introduced to Cecilia and the two young ladies. He expressed himself much pleased with the evening's rencontre, and proposed that they should make one party. This Madame Schellinsburg at first gently opposed; but yielding at length to his persuasions, it was determined that when the ladies had taken a few strolls in the Piazza, they should partake of an entertainment that was to be prepared for them in the Signor's *Casino*. The other gentlemen declared themselves delighted with this plan; their number, they observed, was a fortunate one; there were four of them, and each must claim a lady. Orcello accordingly proposed himself as a chaperon to Madame Schellinsburg; and the rest, determined not to be outdone in gallantry, prepared to follow his example. One of them, who was somewhat taller than his companions, advanced towards Cecilia, and with an air at once easy and unassuming, offered to be her *cicerone*.—The respectful gravity of the address drew upon him the raillery of his gayer associates, who, regardless of decorum, burst into a loud laugh.

"This is admirable!" said one of them. "Pray, Raymond, how long have you been in the habit of attending Princesses? No, no, by Heaven the lady is too good for you!"

Saying this, he took Cecilia's arm within his, and would have hurried her down the Piazzetta; but, disgusted by his boldness, she refused to proceed. They were overtaken by Raymond. He rebuked him sternly for his impertinence.

"Attend the others," said he; "this lady is my care!"

They were joined in a moment by Madame Schellinsburg. She threw a severe look upon the young man who had insulted Cecilia; and commending her for her spirit, said—"I ought, how-ever, to have warned you of what might be expected here. The Signor had no intention of offending you. These little gallantries are so common at this place, that nothing is thought of them!"

She did not wait for her reply; but stepping back, rejoined her former acquaintance, Orcello, leaving Cecilia a few paces before with her new escort.

They now entered the Piazza; and turning round the campa-nile, came in full view of the superb Church of San Marco, with its rich assemblage of domes decorated with crosses, its porticos, its bronze horses, and its pinnacles; whilst opposite, at the end of an immense square of piazzas, appeared the small elegant church of San Geminiano.

The sports which had been practiced during the day were now about to be resumed to a more respectable audience. The crowd had retreated from the Piazzetta, and the grand Piazza was become the scene of universal attention. The young stran-ger who had taken charge of Cecilia, offered her his arm; she declined it, but the crowd pressing upon them, finding it impos-sible to proceed without assistance, she ventured to accept it. He seemed gratified by her acquiescence; but whenever he regarded her, there was an expression of anxiety and solicitude in his coun-tenance which greatly perplexed her.

"May I ask, Madam," said he with an air of earnestness, "if you have been long in Venice?"

Cecilia replied that she had not.

"You are doubtless acquainted," continued he, "with the lady in whose party you are?"

Cecilia looked surprised.

"Forgive my curiosity," resumed he; "your appearance has so much interested me, that I can scarcely believe it possible——"

He paused in confusion.—Cecilia, at a loss to comprehend his meaning, requested that he would be more explicit.

"Perhaps, Madam," said he, recollecting himself, "I may have been deceived; and you, should I explain myself, might have cause to condemn me. You do not, I presume, reside here?"

"My present residence," returned Cecilia, "is in the family of the lady under whose protection I came here; and while I do remain at Venice, the Palace of Madame Schellinsburg will be my asylum."

"Pardon me," said he, colouring; "I ought not to be inquisitive."

He was silent and thoughtful.—Cecilia, struck by the words —"*you are doubtless acquainted with the lady in whose party you are,*" would have demanded their import; but being at that instant overtaken by the party, which had lingered a few paces behind, there was no opportunity.

The gaieties of the scene were now commenced. Here *Arlequine*, animated by the loud shouts of the populace and the merry tones of the tambarine, intermingled with the sound of drums, trumpets, and other noisy instruments, was performing his feats of agility. There the actor, elevated on high, was arresting the attention of his auditors with the thunders of his eloquence, supplying the place of pathos by rant, and gesture by grimace.

"If you have never been present at our Theatres," said Raymond, smiling, "you will have an admirable idea of Venetian oratory. Can any thing be more disgustingly absurd?—That fellow is attempting the Torrismondo of Tasso! Observe his attitudes!—mark the tones of his voice! Who would not mistake him for the conductor of a puppet-show rather than the hero an of admired tragedy?"

"Yet hark how he is approved!" cried Cecilia. "The most celebrated of your performers could scarcely be honoured with a greater concourse of spectators, or louder bursts of applause! Did you hear that shout?"

"Yes, that was occasioned by the entrance of Rosmonda. Admirable!—now he is to discover that she is not his sister.— Alas! ill-fated Poet, what would have been thy feelings wert thou doomed to be present at the murder of thy offspring!"

"It is well he is spared so humiliating a contemplation," replied Cecilia.

"Were I the author," continued he, "I should be tempted to revenge myself upon the actor; the anecdote of Ariosto and the potter[1] would be my excuse. His execrable decorations of paste-board, and other ingenious contrivances, would be in danger of destruction."

"What pity," said Madame Schellinsburg, who had heard a part only of the discourse, "that these itinerant performers, who have seldom any skill in their profession, should attempt tragedy! Comedy, as more easy, would be better suited to their powers, and more proportioned to the capacities of the greater part of their audience."

"And did the man who has assumed the part of Torrismondo," rejoined Raymond, "rate his abilities by your estimate, he might think so too; but Nature, you know, has some strange caprices, among which it is not the least that, while she endues the superior mind with a sense of deficiency, she permits the vulgar one to exult in imaginary superiority, thus supplying by vanity what it wants in energy."

"The pantomime," cried Orcello, "is infinitely more amusing; —that Arlequine has some merit; and the clumsy imitations of the Clown are far from contemptible; if we step back, we shall see him to more advantage."

"Observe that Macaroni," said Ippolita; "can any thing be more ridiculous, yet more laughable than his gestures? He has more humour than the rest; and though he has performed but few feats, seems not to be without his admirers."

"That fellow is a juggler," resumed Orcello, "and waits but

---

1 The same anecdote is preserved of Ariosto as of Hesiod, who, overhearing a potter most barbarously murdering his verses, instantly revenged himself by breaking his pots.

for the conclusion of the pantomime to introduce himself to notice. He has promised to turn *zecheens* into *paoli*, and *paoli* into *zecheens*—to eat fire—to foretel future events—and, finally, as the last effort of his genius, to revenge himself upon Scaramouch, who is continually opposing him by securing him in a bottle. He has with him a duck which sings, a pig that can dance, and a goat who, under the directions of his son personating a Knight, is to perform all the various evolutions of the ancient *menage*.—That figure in the immense capo is Pantalone; and the other, at the farther end of the Palco, who has been unburthening the Doctor's pockets while listening to his quotations from Plato, Galen, and Hippocrates, is Caviello."[1]

The feats of Arlequine suspended, the juggler, who, during the whole of the representation, had been only partially observed, commenced his wonderful achievements. The party now resorted to the promenade, where a number of masqueraders, some assuming characters, and others wearing dominos, were displaying their sprightly manœuvres. They often stopped to let them pass, and were sometimes amused by the lively strokes of repartee occasionally exchanged among these fanciful actors. Turks, Indians, and Mandarins were plentifully disseminated. Here a Jew, with his characteristic pack, was seen vending his commodities to a credulous multitude—there a Pilgrim, leaning on his staff, related the hardships which he had encountered on his return from Jerusalem, the immense space which he had trod, the miracles he had seen performed, and the difficulties interwoven with the observance of his vow. Fruit girls, Macaroni-men, and Magicians formed the rest of the assembly.

The juggler, who had been hitherto holding forth to the no small entertainment of his wonder-loving audience, now rested from his labours, and another candidate for praise mounted the scaffold. The suspended attention of the multitude was again fixed; all crowded round the new comer, who, in a theatrical tone

1 There are four standing characters which enter into every piece that comes on the Venetian stage—the *Medico* or Doctor, *Arlequine, Pantalone*, and *Caviello*. The Doctor's character comprehends the whole extent of a pedant—Arlequine's is made up of blunders and absurdities—Pantalone is a sort of fool—and Caviello a sharper.

of voice, and a correspondent style of gesture, entered upon his harangue. It was an introduction to a story which he promised to relate. His appearance and address were strangely imposing: curiosity was excited, and the reiterated sounds of *bravo!* and *bravissimo!* offered encouragement to his exertions. The Orator threw back his cloak, and pressing his hand upon his breast, continued as follows:—

"Noble Venetians! what I have to recite abounds with marvellous and shocking incidents! It is not, as you may suppose, a mere fiction, contrived solely for your amusement; but a tale founded upon facts the most wonderful, the most extraordinary that were ever yet known! To avoid prolixity, I shall illustrate it only with a few comments. 'Tis marked with many strokes of original humour—'tis also extremely pathetic, and contains a striking combination of incidents at once novel and beautiful —'tis capable, too, of embellishments from the graces of oratory. You, noble Venetians, are famous for the cultivation of this art. 'Twas known to you from the earliest ages; and the proficiency you have made in it, declares the estimation in which it is held; insomuch that the Venetian Senate-house is not more renowned for the wisdom of its decisions, and the wise regulation of its laws, than for the peculiar graces of expression in which these wise and just laws are delivered. I don't mean," continued he, "that these graces are, or ever have been, confined to the Nobles —far from it; I consider you, my countrymen, as models of excellence in this art; since, although you may have neglected the practice of it yourselves, your looks declare your admiration of it in others. Born in your country, and initiated in your customs, I have imbibed the same sentiments with which you are animated! To these the story which I have promised you, is perfectly congenial. It will elucidate the superiority of your laws, the wisdom of your Senate-house, the mildness and justice of whose decrees will be fully exemplified;—it will supply motives not merely for content, but triumph—it will convince you that your city is not only the finest, but the best regulated in the world; and that you are the happiest and most envied among nations!"

He was here interrupted by the shouts of the surrounding spectators.

"The story!" reiterated many voices at once, "we would hear the story!"

The orator bowed.

"That you should be thus importunate, my friends," resumed he, "for this astonishing narrative, is a conviction of the truth of what I before urged; it will indeed repay you for your attention. The marvellous, the pathetic, and the terrible are judiciously combined: instruction is coupled with amusement, and interest with delight."

"The story—the story!" was again loudly repeated.

"A short prelude is, however, necessary," returned the orator. "It was not the custom of the ancients to enter immediately upon the detail. Solon, Demosthenes, and even Cicero, whose followers we are, were remarkable for the contrary. Nevertheless as you, noble Venetians, are so impatient for my recital, you shall be obeyed; but, as I have before observed, a prelude is necessary."

He then took off his cap, and presenting it to his audience, added, bowing as he spoke—"It is needless to appeal to your liberality; if you are not generous, you are not Venetians!"

"This rascal is a knowing one," cried Orcello; "he has attracted the curiosity of all present, and will make it subservient to his own purposes. He has more art, and of course will succeed better than the rest of the competitors."

"I wonder what he has to relate," said Clarice; "he has prepared us for astonishment, and cannot have the audacity to disappoint us."

"I suspect that he has no story at all," replied Orcello; "but let us wait the event."

All were eager to prove their title to the praise of generosity. The cap was accordingly returned, laden with the beneficence of the attending parties. The eyes of the orator sparkled with delight; he took it, and leaped instantly from the scaffold.

"Seize him—seize him!" was re-echoed from every side.

"It is as I expected," cried Orcello, laughing; "the scoundrel has escaped; and if his heels are as light as his head is fertile, he will have nothing to fear from his pursuers."

The bustle occasioned by this ridiculous incident did not immediately subside. Some execrated, whilst others applauded the ingenuity of this comic deceiver, who, retreating amongst the crowd, was not afterwards to be found.—Cecilia, unable to make her way through this vast concourse of people without the assistance of Raymond, still hung upon his arm. He spoke frequently to her, but took little or no notice of her companions. The air of respect with which he at first addressed her, and which he still continued to preserve, made her amends for the mortifications she had so recently suffered; and the amiable and delicate solicitude which his every action discovered, made her cease to recollect that they were yet strangers.

When the crowd, which had been gathering about the orator, began to disperse, accidentally turning round to speak to Madame Schellinsburg, she found to her astonishment that she had left her, and that a new party—a party which she had not before seen, had taken her place at her side. The person who stood next to her was tall, and wore a blue and silver domino; an elegant looking girl, masked, and dressed in a white domino, was leaning upon his arm. Cecilia turned eagerly from this party in search of her own.

"They are gone! Oh Heavens!" exclaimed she, "where—where are they?"

"Be not alarmed," cried Raymond; "the crowd has separated us, and they are probably on their way to the *Casino*; there, at least, we may hope to find them."

These words caught the attention of the group which stood next to them. The Signor in the blue domino turned first, and hastily unmasking, recoiling from her astonished gaze as if he had encountered a basilisk, she beheld Varàno. He started, and disappeared amongst the crowd, leaving Cecilia in a state of unconceivable agony. She could not move, she could not even breathe; a mist seemed to be gathering before her eyes; and but for the assistance of her attendant, who gently supported her, she would have sunk motionless at his feet. Raymond, though unable to divine the cause of such extraordinary emotions, was scarcely less agitated.

"You are ill," said he. "Good God! you are, I fear, very ill!"

He threw his arms around her, but sobs and heavy sighs were her only reply. More and more alarmed, he took her into his arms, and pressing forcibly through the crowd, conveyed her to the *Casino*, which was fortunately at no great distance, and where Madame Schellinsburg and her party were already arrived. Attributing her indisposition to the oppressive bustle of the scene, the former offered her some wine; and the Signors, all equally officious, selected for her the most cooling and luxurious fruits of the season.

The graceful manner in which the collation was disposed, the simple elegance of the *Casino* itself, furnished with chintz, and hung with Indian paper, its situation under the colonnades of the Piazza, still thronged with masqueraders, seen at any other time, and under circumstances less afflictive, would have enchanted Cecilia. But the attractive beauty of the place had lost its power upon her senses; nor was she conscious, as gliding on their return, amid groups of figures, to which the pencil of a Cannaletti could scarcely have done justice, of the sweet strains from the gondolas and of the *gondolieri* themselves, warbling, as they skimmed the moonlight sea, and dashed the sparkling tide, the poetry of Tasso, Ariosto, and Guarini, and which accompanied them on their way till they reached the Palace.

CHAPTER VI

Are there no poisons, racks, and flames, and swords,
That Emma thus must die by Henry's words?
Yet what could swords or poisons, racks or flame,
But mangle and disjoint this brittle frame?
More fatal Henry's words—they murder Emma's fame!

PRIOR.

IF Cecilia's grief was before acute, it was now exquisite! Varàno's sudden appearance before her—his retreat without deigning to notice her, apparently to deprive her of every opportunity of vindicating herself, agitated her almost to frenzy!—even Rosalvo was forgotten; and, in the idea of Varàno, enraged by a combination of strong circumstances beyond the possibility of reconciliation, the anxiety occasioned by her own still doubtful situation was for an instant suspended.

When she arose in the morning, she was informed by Madame Schellinsburg that, having learned that her friend had determined to depart for Genoa in the course of a few days, she had ventured to make arrangements for her journey. Cecilia was reassured by this plan; but the expression of deep sorrow which was visible in her countenance as she rendered her acknowledgments, roused the curiosity of her companions, who now found that her fears concerning the Count were not her only cause for distress.

In the evening, whilst Clarice and Ippolita were engaged in their remarks on their last night's amusement, Madame Schellinsburg being then absent in the city, a gondola stopped at the door and in a moment a servant entered with a message to Cecilia, acquainting her that a lady, splendidly dressed, and accompanied by two *lacchè* and a *paggio*, desired to speak with her. Cecilia, who had no time for surmise, followed him into the hall.

"Your name," said the lady in a voice that chilled her, "is, I suppose, St. Bertrand?"

"The name by which I am generally known, Madam," replied Cecilia, greatly disconcerted, "is St. Bertrand."

"Your real one, if that is not your real one," resumed the stranger haughtily, "is of no consequence: you, I presume, are the person to whom I was directed; you will therefore oblige me by an interview—I shall not intrude upon your patience."

Cecilia conducted her up stairs, and opening the door of an unoccupied apartment, ushered her into it.

"You are no doubt surprised," said the lady as soon as they were seated, "at receiving a visit from a person of my rank, and who is an entire stranger to you?"

Cecilia bowed, and said she was indeed at a loss to account for so great an honour.

"My name," rejoined the lady, "is Bianca di Bellania; I am of the house of Varàno, and sister to the present Marchese."

Cecilia turned pale.

"My nephew," continued she, "to whom you have been long known, and whose ill-placed attachment to you has involved himself and his family in the most poignant distress, has solicited me to wait on you. You have a picture, he says, of his; and since all hopes of a connection with him must be now at an end, you are desired to return it. The jewels which belong to it you may keep; they will be a resource to you when you have no other."

"Neither the picture nor the jewels, Madam," said Cecilia, untying the portrait from her neck, "shall be detained. As the gift of Signor Lorenzo di Varàno, they were, and still are most precious to me; and Oh! may he never know," cried she, bursting into tears, "the pang with which I part with them!"

"Poor young creature!" said the lady, "you are indeed to be pitied! Have you no relatives—no friends—none that will snatch you from the miseries of vice and infamy?"

"If your purpose is to insult me, Madam," interrupted Cecilia with a look which expressed the triumph of offended dignity over sensibility, "your visit, much as I am honoured by it, might have been spared."

"Pardon me," said the Lady Bianca, "I did not mean to insult you—no, Madam, erroneously as you have acted, ill as you have conducted yourself towards a family which would once have condescended to receive you, I came not to reproach you."

The tone of contemptuous pity in which she delivered these words excited fresh sentiments of indignation in the breast of Cecilia. As she arose—"Accept," said she, "our thanks for the portrait; the jewels which are attached to it are of value; be persuaded, and keep them."

"Simply as jewels, Madam," cried Cecilia, "they are of *no* value; and if Signor Varàno thinks it improper for me to detain his portrait, it is equally so that I should wear the jewels."

"Since you are resolved," returned the Lady Bianca, "I shall importune you no more; but this is not my only commission. On the recovery of the portrait I was to present you with this letter; it is from my nephew, and requires, I believe, no answer."

Saying this, she put a paper into her hand; and hastening down the stairs, re-entered her gondola.

The letter was indeed from Varàno; that dear, that well-known hand could not be mistaken. Her heart beat high with expectation. She broke the seal—another paper was enclosed. It was a draft upon his banker for the sum of a thousand ducats. A glow of resentment crossed her cheek.—"Never, never," said she, tearing it, "will I avail myself of this insulting generosity!"—She turned from this to the letter; but it was written in such apparent agitation, that it was with difficulty she could understand the purport.

The first part contained an apology for the enclosed paper.

"I cannot," said he, "support the agonizing idea of your being reduced to penury. Yes, in spite of all your indiscretions, I am unable to think of you, poor, miserable, and destitute, without a throb of compassion. It is my design to secure to you a more ample provision. But how, when I recur to the scenes I have just witnessed, can I expect you to comply with the conditions I must impose? Oh Cecilia! when I think of you as you once was, chaste, artless, and beautiful, how insupportable are my feelings!—the past, the dreadful past appears to me like a troubled dream! I start—I can scarcely believe it to be real; and, inconsistent as it seems, I can almost persuade myself that you are innocent. But new and sadder emotions awake me to a sense of my irremediable misfortunes; the visions of hope die away, and the agonies of despair succeed. I would fain, by thinking of you as you now are, drive from my too faithful recollection what you once was; but the captivating form, the ingenuous air of her I once loved, is still pictured to my imagination; the peace I would regain is withheld, and my life becomes a series of sufferance and exertion. But for whom is it I am cherishing these distracting memorials?—For her who, while feigning a friendship for the wife, was seducing the affections of the husband—for the companion of courtezans, the deserted mistress of Rosalvo! For her——Oh Cecilia! do I still live? Have not my senses deceived me, who has since sold herself to luxury, infamy, and Morsino!"

———————

The dreadful secret of her situation was now fully unfolded. The paper fell from her hand, and emotions of terror—terror more decided, more appalling than she had ever before felt, crowded to her mind. The people she was then with were the minions of the Count, and an escape from their power was her only means of preservation. But to whom, surrounded as she was by the infernal agents of his villany, could she apply for assistance?—and was it possible, should she write a letter to Varàno, to clear herself from his imputations, and solicit his protection, that it could be conveyed to him? The porter who had admitted her, was the only one of the domestics whose appearance had pleased her; and being generally at the door, she had frequently seen him, and recollected, what she had scarcely thought of at the time, that he once looked at her significantly as she was passing through the door, as if he had something to say to her. Could she see him alone, she doubted not by promises and entreaties to prevail upon him to convey a letter to Varàno; and to meet with him was now the great aim of her endeavours: but, to her unspeakable disappointment, he had quitted his post, and the remainder of the evening passed away without her having once seen him.

Arduous as was the task, she determined to appear before the pretended relatives of the Count without betraying her resentment; but though she affected to seem composed, to avoid giving them any cause to suspect that their artifices were detected, her agitation was generally perceived. She was accompanied to her chamber by the two younger women of the party, who soon retired to their own, which was divided only from that appropriated to Cecilia by a slight partition.

They had withdrawn about an hour, when she heard the door of their apartment cautiously opened; and listening attentively, thought she heard them stealing slowly down the stairs. An impulse, more pardonable perhaps than curiosity, directed her to their chamber, and she opened the door. All was silent. She advanced toward the bed; and drawing aside the curtains, found, as she had suspected, that they had both left it. She retreated in haste; and re-entering her room, threw herself upon a chair. She had not been there long, when she distinguished the sound of voices in an apartment below, and again quitted her room. Advancing toward the stairs, she heard it more perfectly. The accents of the women were plainly to be caught; sometimes they spoke loud, and at others so low, that a kind of indistinct murmur was alone to be heard, intermingled with peals of frequent laughter. From this and the unusual bustle among the servants, who were passing and repassing in different parts of the Palace, it instantly occurred to her that the Count was arrived; and she was retreating hastily to her chamber, when the door of a saloon opened, and the Count, attended by a person masked and habited in a domino, entered the hall. They stopped near the door, and seemed in earnest conversation. The figure in the domino spoke louder than the Count, and she soon found it was Pandolfo. As he was departing from the door, he took a dagger from beneath his habit, and presented it to the Count. The Count looked at it intently, and then delivered it to Pandolfo, who, having replaced it within his dress, quitted the Palace.

Returning to her chamber, which overlooked the canal, she saw him enter a zendaletto, and proceed, attended by two *gondolieri*, toward the *Piazza di San Marco*. The mysterious gestures she had observed while they were speaking at the door, and the significant looks of the Count on the delivery of the dagger, accompanied by words too indistinct to be overheard, excited a confused sensation of horror, which surmounted for a time every other consideration; but if the terrors of anticipated danger were for a moment superseded, they soon returned upon her mind with augmented force.

In the morning Madame Schellinsburg came to announce to her the arrival of the Count; requesting, after various apologies and intercessions for her nephew, that she would indulge him with an interview.

"I feel," said she, with an assumed concern, "that your resentment is just; but conscious that his errors have proceeded entirely from his affection for *you*, your pity, if not your love, should dispose you to pardon them."

Cecilia, irritated by her duplicity, deigned not to reply; but on her repeating her importunities in a manner so pressing as to convince her that no excuse would be admitted, aware of the impolicy of suffering her to suspect that she had availed herself of their designs, and animated by a faint hope of hearing something concerning Rosalvo, she accompanied her into a room, and in an instant Madame Schellinsburg having retired, the Count rushed in.

The look of triumph which was manifested in his countenance as he entered, made her tremble; and forgetting, in the indignation of the moment, the danger of exasperating him, she expressed again, in open terms, her detestation of his conduct and character, demanding by what authority he had sent her thither—why she was detained—and insisted upon being safely and immediately conveyed to her home and her friends.

"To your home!—to your friends, Cecilia!" repeated the Count, energetically; "where is your home, and where the friends you would return to?—Your brother, amenable, by my power, to the civil police of his country, can no longer protect you! Suppress then, I command you, the expression of your reproaches, and let me hope, the past consigned, as it ought to be, to oblivion, I may yet aspire to your love!—Oh Cecilia, Cecilia!" softening his voice, and throwing himself on his knees before her, "still, still your slave, let me entreat, let me intercede for your pity!—let my actions, not my words, speak the ardour of my affection! Condemn me not to the tortures, the regrets of losing you!"

"Rise, my Lord," said Cecilia; "this attitude but ill becomes you. If I am to be your prisoner, let me be treated as such; mock me not with a shew of respect which serves only to awaken me to a keener sense of my misfortunes!"

"Never, never," cried he, "will I rise till I have obtained your forgiveness! If, hurried on by my passions, by despair, by my love, I have dared to commit acts from which your delicacy revolts, and which I myself condemn, consider the necessity under which I laboured, and let my violent, my sincere, my insurmountable attachment plead my excuse. What restitution can you demand which I am not anxious to afford—what concessions require which I am not willing to make? Have I not placed you under a safe and noble protection?—Are you not in my family—a family in consequence and connections equal to any in the city, and which is ready joyfully to receive you? Obscure in your birth, and without any dowry but your beauty, never have I pursued you but with intentions the most honourable, or with any motive in view beyond the security of your happiness."

"If your intentions were so honourable, my Lord," said Cecilia, interrupting him, "why, let me ask you, were such contrivances necessary?—Why was I immured by them in a desolate and ruined mansion?—Why, when happily escaped from *thence*, and placed under the protection of friends—friends whom a nearer tie than that of friendship had bound to my interests, was I driven from them?—When I consider the arts that have been employed by you and your's to ensnare me into situations the most appalling that can be conceived—when I reflect upon the society into which I have been thrown, and the treatment I have met with, I must needs confess myself happy, and you, my Lord, both in your intentions and practice, *most honourable!*"

"Proceed, Madam," said the Count, piqued, yet endeavouring to conceal his chagrin, "disdain becomes you; and since I cannot obtain your smiles, I will strive to think you more lovely in your frowns. When you have made me sufficiently contemptible by your censure, you will perhaps deign to listen to me."

"Censoriousness, my Lord," continued Cecilia, "whatever errors I may have fallen into, is not naturally my fault. I have delighted always to draw favourable, rather than unfavourable conclusions; and often, as it has proved, from very bad hearts.—If I had confided less, I had been less unfortunate. Had I judged with the discretion of age, and not with the candour of inexperience, the man who first delivered me into your power would not so basely have deceived me; though, when I reflect on the strata-gems he had recourse to, I am compelled to acknowledge them such as were not easily to be withstood."

"Signor Boraccio," pursued the Count, "was as much your friend as mine. He wished to procure you an ample and splendid establishment."

"And yet such noble designs," returned Cecilia, indignantly, "were obliged to be carried on with the most scrupulous conceal-ment; the most detestable falsehoods, the most illegal methods were employed for their accomplishment."

"Unjust and cruel!" exclaimed the Count; "and will no entreat-ies, no concessions induce you to forgive wrongs which time and my contrition ought long since to have obliterated?"

"Had your persecutions been confined to me," said Cecilia, "much as I have been injured by them—cruelly as I have been insulted, I could have forgiven them; but when I recollect the disgrace in which you have involved one so deservedly dear to me —one whom you once acknowledged as your friend, tell me, my

Lord, whether I can—whether I ought to pardon the man who has been the author of such complicated mischiefs?"

"Rosalvo's safety," said he, significantly, "may be purchased by your smiles. The charms of the sister may ensure the preservation of the brother."

He then forcibly seized her hand, and amid her struggles to disengage herself, pressed it to his lips. At his touch she shuddered; all caution forsook her—she drew her hand hastily from him with an exclamation of aversion, and commanded him to leave her. Irritated, but not confounded, the Count remained for an instant suspended between love and rage; but the indignant glances she shot upon him soon roused the fire of his resentment; and starting up in a fury, he admonished her not to provoke him too far.

"The worst you can do," said she, "wretch! cannot exceed your perfidy to my brother!"

"Have a care—have a care," cried he vehemently, "lest, actuated by a revenge more deadly than you can imagine, I make him answer for your cruelty!"

"Oh, Heaven protect him!" exclaimed Cecilia, who comprehended but too well the meaning of this dreadful menace; "he is then your prisoner!"

"Your perception is tolerably quick, and it may be equally just," retorted the Count; "you, you alone can preserve the forfeited life of Rosalvo; I give his fate into your hands, and the issue of your decisions must be upon him."

These words, and the import of them, alarmed her almost to fainting. The Count looked earnestly in her face.

"Oh why, why," said he, "will you drive me to these distressing extremities? Speak—let me know your resolves—let me instantly dispatch orders to procure his enlargement;—every moment of delay increases his danger; even now, while thus suspended, the mandate may be signed, and officers delegated by the Police to drag him to justice!"

The dreadful, deadly apprehension that had seized upon her heart was now confirmed. Her brain maddened; bitter and frequent exclamations of sorrow burst from her lips; sobs, violent and unrestrained, agitated her bosom; and losing all the acrimony of her indignation in her terrors for Rosalvo, she besought him to be merciful.

"Oh spare him, spare him!" said she in agony; "he has never injured you!"

The Count, softened by her distress, renewed his former remonstrances; and having offered her some time for consideration, persisting, however, in his resolution of criminating Rosalvo, should she continue firm in her rejection of him, he promised to dispatch a messenger immediately to Genoa to suspend the proceedings of the Police, which had already received orders for his removal to Naples.

Cecilia was somewhat tranquillized by this assurance; and indulging, amid all her terrors, a vague hope that he had no meaning in his threats beyond that of alarming her into an immediate compliance with his wishes, she withdrew to her apartment, having previously obtained a promise that she should not be intruded upon whilst there by any part of the family, or receive any future visit from the Count till she should be herself disposed to grant it.

CHAPTER VII

Con cor tremante, ed con tremante piede
Fugge la tapinella, et non sa dove
In cio'chi' intorno ascolta in cio che vede,
Vede di nuova orror sembianze nove.

ARIOSTO.

With quiv'ring feet that scarce can touch the ground,
And trembling heart the wretched virgin flies;
In all she hears, in all she sees around,
She finds new terrors—new alarms arise.

SHE remained alone in her chamber till the evening; when venturing cautiously to descend the stairs, she discovered old Carlo, the porter, standing at his post within the vestibule, and made a motion for him to follow her; but Morsino's valet accidentally crossing the hall, he walked away without speaking, or appearing to notice her. In about an hour she again left her room; but on advancing about half way down the stairs, she perceived he was gone; and although she made several other attempts to speak with him, they were all equally unsuccessful. She look anxiously from her window; it was possible—it was even probable that Varàno, having discovered her abode, might frequent that part of the canal which the Palace overlooked; but one solitary gondola, returning from its customary occupation to the island of *Santa Maria*, was alone to be seen.

Night at length advanced; and the noisy tumult subsided, which seemed to issue to her affrighted ears from every apartment in the house, she heard the Count and his companions retire severally to their beds; and was about to repair to her's, when she was surprised by a gentle tapping at her door; and instantly unlocking it, a figure, which in the haste and surprise of the moment she was unable distinctly to ascertain, thrust a letter into her hand, and disappeared.

She started—she trembled; it was the tremor, however, of joy, of hope, of expectation—it was doubtless from Varàno. Varàno, still interested in her fate, still resolved to protect her. Eagerly she tore it open, and as eagerly would have devoured the contents; but the sudden emotion of delight which had communicated to her heart, as immediately subsided, when she perceived, instead of the signature of Varàno, that of Raymond St. Aubin. The letter was indeed from Raymond—the noble, the interesting young stranger whom she had met with at the Piazza di San Marco. Enchanted with her beauty, and not less so with her manners, he determined to leave no efforts unexerted to discover, if possible, the real circumstances of her situation; and having, with the joint influence of Orcello, succeeded in his endeavours, and engaged the agency of his mother, who had offered to accompany them, he promised, after many apologies for his abruptness, that a gondola should be in readiness in the space of an hour to convey her to Padua, from whence he would himself procure her an escort to conduct her to her friends.

Cecilia could not deliberate upon the proposal—the presence of his mother was a sanction to her flight; and losing the apprehension of pursuit in the excess of her gratitude, she wrote a few hasty lines with her pencil, which she had scarcely completed, when the messenger returned, and she perceived it was Carlo. Enjoining him to caution, she committed it to his care, earnestly requesting that he would acquaint no one with their plan. Carlo replied that there was no danger of its miscarriage, himself and Launcelotto, a young servant of the Count, being the only persons concerned in it, who had both rather die than betray her.

The open sincerity of his countenance while he assured her of her safety, convinced her of his fidelity; but the bare mention of the Count's servant was sufficient to excite fears as to the ultimate success of their project, and she eagerly demanded why he had been entrusted with it.

"You need not, lady," said Carlo, "have any doubts respecting Launcelotto; he is an honest fellow, the only one indeed in the Palace worth the toss up of a piccolo; and were he inclined to betray us, as we are both to decamp to-night, he would have no opportunity. He knows my Lord too well to wish to continue with him. A Neapolitan by birth, and much attached to his country, he has long resolved to return to it; but whenever he hinted his intention, the Count raised so many objections against it, that poor Launcelotto was obliged to stay, though not without many signs of discontent and reluctance. Wearied at length with his remonstrances, and more than ever averse from remaining with him, an altercation ensured between him and his Lord, the result of which was a determination on the part of Launcelotto to depart secretly from the Palace."

"And why secretly?" said Cecilia, whose curiosity was somewhat roused by this account; "what motive can the Count have for detaining him contrary to his inclinations?"

"As to his motives, lady," returned Carlo, "I know no more of them than you do: but to tell you the truth, I think there have been some black doings which Launcelotto is privy to; and as they are all quiet in their beds, I may venture to speak out.—An altercation, as I observed, took place this evening between Launcelotto and the Count, a part of which I overheard. Meeting soon after with Launcelotto, I enquired what had happened. Launcelotto made no reply, but shook his head, sighed deeply, and seemed greatly disturbed in his mind. I repeated my question.—'The Count,' said he, 'is a villain—I will quit his service to-night.'

"Astonished at his resolution, I requested an explanation, which he, however, refused to afford, commanding me to be secret as to his intended departure, as the Count, if apprized of it, would immediately interpose to prevent it.

"'He is blind, nevertheless,' added he, 'to his true interest in wishing to detain me. If I stay, I shall betray him; if I go, his infernal secret may be safe in his keeping.'

"Amazed at these words, I pressed him to be more explicit; but he continued cautious and reserved. I then enquired concerning the Signor who had attended the Count to Venice, and whom I had seen set off masked from the Palace soon after their arrival. He told me he knew little of him; but that he was a bloody dog, and little better, he believed, than a common assassin. He then repeated his resolution of leaving Venice to-night; and finding him sincere in his protestations, I ventured to unfold to him our plan, in which he agreed to participate, consenting to accompany me to Padua, and afterwards to Naples."

Carlo, having now sufficiently calmed her fears, withdrew from the chamber; and returning shortly with intelligence that the gondola was arrived, encouraged by the profound stillness which reigned throughout the Palace, with quick steps, and a beating heart, she followed him into the hall, the door of which was no sooner opened than Raymond sprung forward.

At the sight of her young and noble deliverer, whose dignified mien, intelligent countenance, and open address would have dissipated every doubt, could she have imagined any, the grateful emotions of her heart could no longer be suppressed, and she endeavoured to give them utterance.

"Cease, Madam," said Raymond, "to overrate services to accept which must confer an everlasting obligation on the unworthy bestower."

He then conducted her down the steps, and lifting her into the gondola, a genteel, matronly looking figure, with all the frankness of benevolence, and all the ease of polished life, offered her her hand, and was immediately introduced to her by the name of Madame St. Aubin.

Cecilia, who, by the rapid succession of hope and fear, had hardly had time to recollect her scattered thoughts during the last few hours, now looked around her; and perceiving the city with its isles sinking gradually from her view, saw herself in comparative security, delivered from the unrelenting power of the count, and under the protection, as she could not doubt, of a man of honour.—But it was amongst the peculiar infelicities of her lot never to enjoy hope without a proportionate degree of pain. Rosalvo, dependant, as had been proved, upon the merciless will of his persecutor, was still in danger of destruction. Varàno had condemned, had forsaken her; he had even refused to listen to her vindication. Recollections such as these, her anxiety for her own personal safety removed, grew every moment more agonizing; her tears flowed in silence; and Madame St. Aubin, moved by her extreme youth and dejected air, found the grief she would have alleviated but too infectious.

Crossing the *Laguni* with its stone ramparts, they reached the city of Fusina, and Cecilia again found herself on *terra firma*. Morning had just dawned, when, embarking in a *burchio*, they entered the Brenta; and pursuing their course along its borders, crowned on either side with Palaces and Palladian villas, the most elegant of the former of which were those of Foscari and Pisanio, gained the village of Doglio, and then proceeded on their way by land toward Padua. They entered this city near the Church of San Giustina, and passing the *Prato della Valle*, stopped at length at an Hotel.

Immediately as they alighted, Madame St. Aubin, with the same kind air with which she had first greeted her, presented Cecilia to M. St. Aubin, her husband; and then conducting her to an elegant apartment, entreated her to be there entirely at home.

M. St. Aubin was a descendant from one of the noblest families in Switzerland, where he chiefly resided. Having sent Raymond, his only son, to complete his education at Padua, himself and his lady were come purposely to convey him home; and their journey, as Madame St. Aubin informed Cecilia, was shortly to commence.

Cecilia, whose native ingenuousness told her in a moment that the smallest reserve, the least appearance of mystery, would involve her in suspicions equally humiliating to herself and the friends who protected her, would have unfolded to Madame St. Aubin some of the most material incidents of her story; but she had not proceeded far before the resolution she had been struggling to acquire failed her, and she burst into tears. Madame St. Aubin, affected by her distress, requested that she would conceal every thing which it would be painful to her to disclose; and after a previous consultation with M. St. Aubin, offered to convey her with them to Switzerland—a situation which appeared to her, she assured her, much more eligible than any in Italy, where she would be still liable to discovery, and new dangers from the Count.—That the Count, learning from Madame Schellinsburg that it was her intention to return, if possible, to the Castello di Montani, would immediately pursue her thither, was indeed but too probable. This objection to her remaining in Italy was sufficient to counterbalance in her mind every other; and, encouraged at length by the promises and importunities of Madame St. Aubin, she acceded to her request, resolving, immediately on her arrival in Switzerland, to place herself in a Convent as a boarder, till she should have heard from the Signora di Rosalvo, to whom she meant to write. Carlo, who had been engaged by M. St. Aubin to fill one of the most important posts in his establishment, was to accompany them. Launcelotto was already on his way to Naples.

Cecilia, amongst all her gratitude to her new friends, forgot not what was due to the services of the good old Carlo, and recollected with pain that, except a few jewels singularly precious to her, she had nothing with which to recompense them. Too generous not to reward favours which no reward could overpay, she took him apart, and leading him into a private room presented him with a ring, which she requested him to accept as a small acknowledgment of her esteem. Carlo refused it; but as she was replacing it on her finger, he hastily drew it back, and perplexed her with the question how she came by it. Cecilia hesitated—she looked on him with surprise. There was something in his voice, in his countenance expressive of more than curiosity.

"Speak," said he eagerly, and with a trepidation which alarmed her; "that ring was——"

"My mother's," cried Cecilia, scarcely less agitated.

Carlo threw himself at her feet, but could not articulate a word.

"And do I—do I," said he, at length recovering himself, "behold the daughter of my revered master? Has the unfortunate Verezio, in his zeal to protect a stranger, rescued his beloved young mistress?"

Cecilia started; her eyes wandered wildly over his figure, while the anxious feelings of her heart seemed to demand a confirmation. It was, however, Verezio, the steady adherent of her mother, the faithful attendant of her father through all the vicissitudes of his fortune. The names of those dear, those unknown relatives inspired her with the tenderest regret that filial affection could experience; and as soon as her emotions would admit of words, she required from Carlo some account of them and of himself since he had last parted from them.

"But little," returned Carlo, "remains to be proved. The packet I deposited with Madame de Villeneuve, and what I afterwards communicated, the substance of which must be known to you, contained every particular incident in the lives of your unfortunate parents. The packet and the casket were delivered to me by a Nun, who was your mother's confidential friend. I resided at that time at Madrid:—Madame D'Arnaud was then living; but on my return to Fontcarrel, though I had been absent but a week, I learned that she was dead and buried. My grief was exquisite. I visited her remains—I wept over them; and then, anxious to fulfil her wishes, flew to execute my commission. The death of this beloved lady dissolved at length every tie which had attached me to Madrid, and I repaired to Naples. Here, however, though I had promised myself repose, new griefs assailed me. The ravages of time, of affliction had robbed me of my friends, and I grew melancholy and disconsolate. Years softened, but did not subdue my disappointment. I married; and the necessitous state of my circumstances, by inspiring activity, served to dissipate my despondency. My wife was amiable and affectionate; our attachment seemed to increase as we grew older; and in the simple occupation of a fisherman I supported her with decency. On her death, which happened about fourteen years after our marriage, I engaged myself as a servant to a Venetian gentleman then at

Naples. I attended him to Venice, but had scarcely arrived there, when he was seized with an illness which soon proved fatal. Alone in a strange city, I again sought a situation, and, through the recommendation of a fellow-servant, was introduced to Madame Schellinsburg, who I was told was a widow of great family and importance, who had lately become stationary at Venice. Accidental as this seems, the hand of Providence," continued Carlo, "must have directed me to the asylum I found, to preserve you, by my means, from the arts of a libertine who, I soon found, to my astonishment, was the owner of the Palace, the women being only the instruments of his will, the ready tools of his power."

While Verezio was speaking, Cecilia was agitated with various sensations:—pity, gratitude, and affection took their turns in her mind; his griefs, his misfortunes endeared him to her heart; that reverend figure which she had before admired, was regarded with an added interest; and they parted with mutual expressions of joy, sympathy, and esteem.

When M. St. Aubin was informed by Madame of the Count's designs upon Cecilia, and his artful measures to accomplish them, his indignation was excessive.

"It is such wretches as these," said he, "that disgrace our natures, and make us blush to acknowledge that we are of the same species.—As to you," added he to Raymond, "you have acted like a man; remember it is your duty to protect the unfortunate, and that the ample fortune you will one day possess, can be said to be used only so long as it is dedicated to the most worthy purposes."

"Oh my father!" said Raymond, "was this necessary?"

St. Aubin looked tenderly at his son—a tear trembled in his eye.—"You are a noble boy," said he, "and will not disgrace your situation."

The contrast which St. Aubin had drawn between Raymond and Morsino, while it flattered his feelings as a father, increased his resentment towards the Count, and his partiality to Cecilia. Cecilia he indeed regarded with more than common compassion:—already was M. St. Aubin and his Lady embarked in her fate; and while they recoiled with abhorrence from the hated character of her betrayer, to his intended victim they promised unalterable friendship and paternal affection.

The Count, when informed that Cecilia had escaped, was seized with rage so violent, that it had the appearance of distraction. He uttered innumerable oaths and execrations in a voice that was scarce human—reprehended Madame Schellinsburg for retaining, in so important a post as that of porter, a person on whom no dependance could be placed; nor would the creatures of his will have escaped exemplary punishment, had they not declared with one voice that they knew not where she was—that they had attended her to her room on the preceding night—and that no one had since, to their knowledge, passed in or out of her apartment.—To be disappointed in his last attempt at the very moment in which he had imagined he had ensured success, fired him to a degree of madness. The flight of Launcelotto too, whom he suspected to be an accomplice, formed another subject for vexation.

To have Cecilia conveyed to Venice had been a long concerted plan; there he flattered himself the intoxicating influence of that splendour with which he meant to surround her—the force of novelty and the charms of music—the solicitations of tenderness —of a love the most impassioned, would concur to pervert those principles he had laboured in vain to undermine. Such were his hopes, and such his expectations, when, by an open acknowledgment of his passion, he endeavoured to facilitate its gratification without disclosing its object. This, guarded as he was, he however failed to effect; the sentiment he would have stifled, acquired new energy from restraint; and the expression of it, by drawing upon him a resentment which all his subterfuges could not avert, destroyed for an interval the completion of a project which an entire confidence in its success had tempted him to adopt. But though delayed for a time, it was by no means abandoned; the plot of decoying her into Languedoc being intended only as a prelude to its immediate execution. To precipitate the accomplishment of this eagerly concerted scheme as to the effect of it upon Cecilia, the intervention of Madame Schellinsburg and her daughters was deemed indispensable. They accordingly, at his desire, took possession of his Palace, and presided there some months in a state of constant expectation, and, to their unspeakable astonishment, without once hearing from the Count. This silence originated in the supposed death of Cecilia—a supposition which, condemning himself as the cause, was so agonizing to the Count, that he had no power to convey the tidings of it to the women whose agency he had ensured, or to displace them from the situation they then occupied. From the suspense which his absence and total neglect of them had produced, they were relieved at last by a letter penned for him by a servant from the Castello di Montani, and the arrival of Cecilia, on whom they had orders to impose themselves as the relations of the Count, till, alluding to his late accident, he should be enabled to follow her.

Madame Schellinsburg had been known to him previous to his having assumed the title and name of Morsino—an honour which had been conferred upon him by the King of Naples, as a recompence for some trifling service done to the State about a year after his memorable parting with Rosalvo in the Island of San Lucia.—She was a famous Roman courtesan, and had spent her youth amid scenes of dissipation and debauchery. At the death of the Count's uncle, the father of Clarice and Ippolita, with whom she lived, and whose name she had been allowed to take, she was united to a German Officer of the name of Schellinsburg. On his demise, being in the possession of a small annuity, bequeathed to her by her former lover, she returned to Venice, in which city he had resided, and where, when surrounded by all the trappings and allurements of vice, she had been approached with confusion, and loaded with adulation. Here accidentally meeting with the Count after his precipitate retreat from Florence, in consequence of a violent contest he was then engaged in, concerning the legality of his claim to an estate in the Island of the *Santo Spirito*, she assented with rapture to his proposal of reinstating her in that Palace, from whose shelter, as the luxurious dissipater of that property which he might otherwise have enjoyed, she had been driven by him, only two years before, with contempt and indignation.

The success which the interposition of so experienced an auxiliary as Madame Schellinsburg seemed to promise him in his base attempts upon Cecilia, increased in due proportion his sense of failure. To pursue her, if pursuit was practicable, was his immediate determination. All the *gondolieri* in the city were accordingly questioned, bribes offered, and such prevailing measures employed by them for the recovery of the fugitive, as nothing but the cautious management of her deliverer (who, avoiding all connection with this people, had been assisted only by his servants) could have rendered utterly abortive. In their account that no person of her description had escaped from thence by night in their gondolas, they all persisted without variation; and having filled the Palace with alarm and confusion, the Count, unable to gain intelligence by what means he had been baffled, or on whom to turn his resentment, stung with rage, and bewildered amongst the innumerable possibilities which might have produced his disappointment, experienced a degree of agony little inferior, perhaps, to what he would have inflicted upon the object that occasioned it. That diabolical fruit of revenge which love, though it might appease, could never thoroughly repel, ruled and agitated his breast; and he felt a horrible gratification in the idea of sacrificing to his resentment, and the defeat of his licentious views upon Cecilia, the life of Rosalvo. He knew in a Court of Judicature like that of Naples, his evidence alone would be sufficient to criminate him; and, yielding to the infernal impulses of his nature, prepared to take his measures accordingly.

Leaving the Count to pursue his purpose, and Cecilia to perform, under the guardianship of her worthy friends, her intended journey to Switzerland, we return to Varàno.

CHAPTER VIII

————Had she been true,
If Heav'n would make me such another world
Of one entire and perfect chrysolite,
I'd not have sold her for it!

SHAKESPEARE.

ON the night of his first appearance on the promenade at the *Piazza di San Marco*, Varàno had been only a few days at Venice. Having met with Cecilia and Rosalvo at Noli, he concluded that they had escaped secretly from the Castle, and, on seeing Cecilia at the Piazza, that their destination was Venice. That Rosalvo, under such circumstances, should permit her to appear publicly at the Carnival, attended only by a stranger (for such he supposed Raymond), afforded ample scope for his surmises; and although stung as he was to the soul with a full conviction of her falsehood, impelled, perhaps, by curiosity, or, as is more probable, by some latent spark of tenderness yet remaining in his breast, he resolved to trace her to her residence. His perplexity on discovering it, was considerably augmented. The Palace she lived in was undoubtedly the Count's, and her companions (for his enquiries were not confined to her) wretches with whom guilt only could take refuge—only infamy associate.

The Lady Bianca di Bellanio, through whose successful mediation the Marchese's prejudices had been overruled, and his consent to his marriage obtained, was a silent but not an uninterested spectator of an anguish which, in spite of all his efforts to conceal it, was nevertheless too obvious; and which, had she not been acquainted by Le Chatre of the strange occurrences at the Castle, would have greatly disturbed her. Learning from his conversation that Cecilia had been seen at Venice, and the place of her abode, she insisted that she should herself demand from her the restoration of Varàno's portrait, alledging that, having forfeited by her conduct all claim to his affection, she ought not to be suffered longer to detain it.

The recovery of this pledge of an apparently ill-requited attachment required not the aggravating circumstances attending it, to rouse every indignant sensation of which he was capable, in the tortured mind of Varàno. He dashed it instantly to the ground; and, as if with that odious resemblance he could have annihilated in his breast the dearer image that reigned there, stamped it to atoms.

To his letter containing the draft no answer, as we have before observed, was returned: and as the Lady Bianca, more politic than minute, had forborne to acquaint her nephew of the time and manner of its delivery, or to afford Cecilia any hint how a letter might be conveyed to him, he interpreted her silence into a tacit rejection of the terms which, on her acceptance of the enclosed draft, he had promised to propose; a rejection arising, he imagined, from the persuasion that the conditions which he meant to exact, would be such as she should be averse from, and perhaps, unable to accede to.

To return immediately to Florence was now his determination. That return had, however, a consequence so humiliating, that on his arrival at Bologno, he remained for several hours irresolute whether or not to proceed; for how could he acquaint his father—how unfold to his mother the hateful tidings he must communicate?—how declare to her that the woman he had adored—her to whom he would have sacrificed every thing—whom he had hitherto held forth as an example of all that was excellent, and for the loss of whom, had she been true, not even worlds could have compensated, had proved unworthy of him? —How disclose to her that, after a duplicity of conduct which had degraded her in his eyes beneath the very lowest of her sex, she had eloped secretly, and by night, with the husband of her friend, and had since voluntarily embraced a life of infamy and prostitution?—Would not his veracity be suspected? Would not the lovely image of his Cecilia, as she once was, rise in judgment against him?

To the Marchesa, indeed, an account of so extraordinary and sudden a change of character appeared so contradictory to reason, so contrary to all she had ever thought, and to all she could have imagined, that she could scarcely persuade herself she was not listening to the wild ravings of delirium rather than to a received and well-attested fact.

Happy, thrice happy would it have been for her, could the delusion have continued; but, alas! in the haggard cheek, the sunken eye, the fixed despair, interrupted only at intervals by the wild start of emotion, observable in her son, she read a melancholy confirmation of all that he had asserted. But not even into the bosom of that beloved mother could he pour all his griefs; though often, when starting from the imperfect slumbers her fondness sometimes soothed him into, would he imagine he saw in her a benignant angel descended to snatch him from the miseries of his own fate. Hour after hour did she watch by him in silence, while the sighs and groans which escaped him, when he believed himself unheard, pierced her very soul.

The Marchese, though he shared in her assiduities, and sympathized, as much as it was in his nature to sympathize, in the sufferings he witnessed, saw, nevertheless, in the disappointed feelings of his son, and supposed disgrace of Cecilia, every wish he had ever formed accomplished. The moment which was to unite the heads of two noble houses seemed now to his delighted fancy to be at no great distance. That Varàno, with so keen a sense of injury, of duty, of honour, would prove himself so deficient in point of spirit, so regardless of decorum, as to allow himself to continue the dupe of an improper and now humiliating predilection, was a decision his partiality would not suffer him lightly to adopt.

To the Marchesa every project, unconnected with the restoration of the health and peace of Varàno, appeared vague and uninteresting. She had concluded upon the impossibility of this alliance, till she had ceased to wish for it; and the period which seemed to threaten her with evils to which no acquirements could be adequate, was that she deemed least favourable to the renewal of her Lord's hopes on this subject. She therefore expostulated with him on the propriety of avoiding all mention of it to Varàno, at least till he should have recovered some degree of composure; suggesting the impossibility of his compliance in the present temper of his mind, and alluding to the indelicacy of the measure, and the effects which such a conduct would inevitably produce. In this she, however, judged not with her usual discernment. There is an energy in despair, which despair only can give. The shipwrecked wretch shrinks not at the light blast that succeeds the warring of the tempest, nor the mind to which misery is become familiar, from the contemplation of evils which, under impressions less agonizing, would appear vast and insurmountable.

The suspense imposed upon him by his Lady was too unwelcome to the Marchese to be unnecessarily prolonged; and at the expiration of a few weeks, during which Varàno had given as few symptoms of tranquillity as on the day of his arrival, he ventured to impart to him his wishes concerning Olivia, representing the severe loss himself and his family would sustain, should he obstinately refuse to marry, and the distressing uncertainty into which they would be thrown, should he determine to defer it; observing that having once given his assent to a marriage which, though he might permit, he could never reasonably approve, he might now, presuming on the dutiful affection of his son, expect some indulgence in return.

"In regard to myself," continued the Marchese, "independent of the many advantages which will accrue to you from such an alliance, herself the sole heiress of the ancient house of Montelina, I have seldom seen a young woman I have thought so pleasing, so lovely as my niece. The vivacity of her conversation, and the sweetness of her disposition, render her beloved by all who know her, and doubly so to those who have the honour to be connected with her. I do not expect—I do not even wish," continued he, "for a hasty and immediate decision; it is a subject which may require—which may appear, at least, to *you* to require some thought. Invested with the legal privileges of a father, I once presumed to command; I now only intercede, only entreat your compliance."

Varàno listened to these arguments without any apparent surprise or emotion. A more favourable moment than the present one could scarcely have occurred. Wounded by ingratitude, or what he mistook for such, his mind had acquired a total indifference as to every possible event; or if it could be said to have a wish, it was that of promoting, by its acquiescence, the happiness of his parents.

"Should you accede to my request," continued the Marchese, observing something in the expressive countenance of Varàno not altogether repulsive, "I will make an application to the Count, and the affair shall be determined. You are not strangers; —months of courtship are therefore unnecessary."

The Marchesa was silent, but her looks testified the deep interest she took in the conversation; and having long trembled for its consequences, her astonishment was at least equal to her joy when Varàno, with a sort of desperate resolution, promised obedience to the proposal—premising only that, should Olivia be disinclined to it, no arbitrary procedure should enforce her compliance.

The Marchese, overjoyed at his success, transmitted without

delay an account of it to Naples, artfully suppressing the mention of Varàno's former engagement to Cecilia, and the effects which the dissolution of it had produced upon his son. He then consulted privately with the Marchesa on the subject of their removal, ordered the Palace to be repaired for the reception of the new bride, and agreed for the purchase of a splendid villa near St. Casciano, with which he intended to surprise her on the day of her marriage.

The Marchesa perceiving, in the preparations already commenced at the Palace, new subject for regret, persuaded Varàno to accompany her in an expedition to Pisa, hoping on their return that all arrangements would be completed, and depending upon her own influence over his feelings that he would be disposed to receive Olivia with due respect and affection.

Here, however, every object that met his view operated not less forcibly on his imagination that those he had quitted. On the evening after his arrival, as he was sitting alone in an apartment overlooking the quay, wrapped in one of those melancholy reveries which were now become habitual, he was told that a lady, who had accidentally seen him from the window as she was passing hastily through the city, and who appeared to be in great affliction, requested an audience. Varàno, without enquiry, desired her to be admitted; and while he was busying himself with conjectures who this unknown might be, Signora di Rosalvo, to his utter amazement and confusion, appeared before him. He arose, and tremulously, and with an awkwardly assumed animation, attempted to greet her. As she spoke, he remarked with anguish an expression of distress, almost despair pictured on her features. Delicacy forbade his enquiries into the cause of her sorrow; alas! it was, he believed, but too well known to him; and while a thousand agonizing reflections pressed tumultuously upon his mind, his tongue unconsciously pronounced the name of Cecilia.

"She is in safety," cried the Signora; "Cecilia lives—lives for your love! Unjustly has she been suspected—cruelly injured!"

"Great Heaven!" exclaimed Varàno, "what is it I hear?"

"Read here," added the Signora, presenting him with two papers, one a letter from Rosalvo, the other from Cecilia, "a confirmation of her innocence, and of my misfortune."

Varàno took the papers; but hardly could his trembling fin-
gers unfold them, his astonished eyes connect the words, or his
perturbed brain conceive their import. Enough, however, was
understood to rack and torture him to madness!—Cecilia was
innocent, and, the horrid mystery unfolded, his imagined rival
her brother!—To know that she was true, and at the same time
that he had lost her, was agonizing—was distracting! How was
he now to support a marriage which it was impossible to avoid?
The preparations had already begun—the overtures, as he could
not doubt, accepted. To recede was impossible—it would even
be dishonourable. To add to these misfortunes, Rosalvo, the man
whom he had so deeply wronged by his suspicions, was a prisoner
—was confined on a charge of murder in the carcere[1] at Naples.
He was accused, and might be convicted of a crime, of which
death must be the consequence. Could he not—ought he not to
endeavour to rescue the brother of his Cecilia? Might he not, by
using his influence with the Count di Montelina, whose interest
in the Court of Naples was powerful and extensive, obtain his
enlargement?—Somewhat cheered by this hope, he again examined the papers; and having written a hasty letter to the Count as
explicitly and as coherently as his present feelings would allow
of, he committed it to the Signora, who was then on her way to
Naples, with orders that she should deliver it immediately on her
arrival.

Varàno, when the Signora was departed, flew directly to the
Marchesa;—his looks were wild, his countenance pale, and his
eyes swimming in tears. The instant he saw her, he threw himself
into a chair; and putting the papers into her hand, which in the
hurry and confusion of the moment he had neglected to return,
anticipated her enquiries by relating all that had happened.

The Marchesa found the grief she pitied, too reasonable to
attempt its alleviation. She knew that premature endeavours at
consolation were seldom successful; and, mingling her tears with
his, deplored with him the cruel and unhappy mistake which had
plunged two beings so dear to her in irremediable misery. To
retract his new engagement was difficult—it was indeed imprac-

1 Gaol.

ticable. The Marchese would oppose violently such a measure. Olivia would be indignant—the Count justly offended. Such a conduct, the overtures coming from them, would effectually destroy all intercourse between the families. Nor was it likely that Cecilia, with so nice a sense of honour, would be inclined, under such circumstances, to accept him. Entreating him, therefore, to conceal, as much as possible, this new cause of grief from the Marchese, she renewed her former promises concerning Cecilia, whom she assured him she should consider from henceforth as her child, and whom she would reward with independence, and even with affluence.

Day after day passed on without allowing even a short respite to the sufferings of the now repentant Varàno. Bitterly did he bewail that strong, that culpable propensity to jealousy which had always been his torment, and was now his destruction; and often would the soul-harrowing recollection of that moment when, amid the terrors of his horrible and unmerited accusations, Cecilia, the innocent Cecilia, unable alike to satisfy him or to resist, had fallen senseless at his feet! How—Oh how was he to obtain pardon for an offence so great?—how ever make restitution for mischiefs so complicated?—how but, by avenging himself on a wretch who, by an act of almost unprecedented malignity, had made her subservient to his power, and dependant upon his mercy? Soon, however, was he recalled from this visionary scheme of revenge, and hope once more returned to illumine his before darkened prospects. The sweet countenance of the Marchesa, as she pressed him fondly to her bosom, was again arrayed in smiles; but, apprehensive of the sudden effects of joy, hardly dared she impart to him the joyful tidings her sympathizing heart yet throbbed to utter. The Conte di Montelina, having relinquished every hope of an alliance with the house of Varàno, had already engaged his daughter. This intelligence had been conveyed to the Marchesa by a letter from her Lord.

Varàno's transports on this occasion may easily be conceived. All impediments to his marriage with Cecilia, would she deign to accept him, were now removed. From her letter it appeared that she was in a Convent in some part of Switzerland; but in which of the Cantons it was situated, or where resided the friends in whose party she left Italy, were circumstances of which no mention was made. This neglect, however, might be remedied by an application to Le Chatre, then at Venice; who, by prosecuting an enquiry concerning them at Padua, would easily gain the information so necessary to his future plans. To him, therefore, Varàno wrote, acquainting him with every event which had taken place since the day of their separation; and having desired him to direct for him at Milan, he took a tender adieu of the Marchesa, and set forward for Switzerland.

CHAPTER IX

> Black'ning the night a funeral train
> On a cold bier a coffin brings;
> Their slow pace measur'd to a strain,
> Sad as the saddest night bird sings.
>   SPENSER'S LEONORA.

AN interval of about four days brought Varàno to Placentia, and three more to Milan. A letter from Le Chatre awaited his arrival.

––––––––

"I cannot," said he, "enough congratulate you on this happy change in your affairs, or forbear smiling at the idea of your setting out for Switzerland in quest of people whom you know only by name, and to whom you depend solely on my enquiries, the success of which must be doubtful, to procure the necessary direction. Were you not a lover, without alluding to the analogy subsisting between the two characters, I might mistake you for a lunatic. But to be serious:—I have fortunately seen a person known to, though not intimately acquainted with, this Raymond, who so generously interposed his services in behalf of our sweet friend. M. St. Aubin, his father, is, I am told, a man of very considerable property; and though somewhat inclined to eccentricity, of great benevolence. He resides sometimes in France, but more generally in Switzerland. Besides an elegant house at Berne, he has a seat, where he usually spends the summer, near the Lake of Lucerne. These hints will be sufficient. A man of his character must be well known;—your reception cannot be otherwise than favourable.

"Were you not in danger of fresh assaults from that hydra-headed monster, Jealousy, I should be inclined to enlarge a little upon the portrait given to me of this Raymond; but I will not afflict you again with pangs you have felt so severely. His virtues, allowing the representation not to be overdrawn, and the signal service he has rendered you, entitle him to an admission amongst the number of your friends. Friendship, however, no less than love, inclines us to jealousy. I shall expect, therefore, to retain my former place in your heart."

———————

Varàno was overjoyed at this intelligence; and, attended only by Benedetto, and a young valet named Latour, he instantly renewed his course. Latour was a Swiss, a native of Appenzel; having expatriated at an early age, he knew little of his country, but nevertheless professed for it a romantic attachment.

Having traversed the winding shores of the *Tesino*, they embarked upon the *Lago Maggiore* at the little town of Siesto, situated near the spot where that river discharges itself into the lake. They emerged rapidly from its shores, studded over with villas and splendid Palaces, among which, on the Piedmontese side, were exhibited those of Casa, Visconti, and Case Otolino, with the noble Castle of Angiera; while far over the wide expanse appeared the beautiful Boromean Islands—the whole crowned with a distant view of the Alps.

They disembarked at Locarno; and quitting the fertile territories of the Milanese, proceeded, conducted by a guide, through a wild and stupendous tract of country, the road through which, often winding round the edges of rocks and fearful precipices, was rendered yet more dangerous by their frequent rencontres with Milanese and other Italian merchants, who, with their mules and projecting baggage, had been conveying spices, coffee, and other articles of commerce, in exchange for the muslins of Gall and Zuric.

The slow motion of the mules—the frequent ascent and descent of the mountains, grandly irregular, and where the summit of one formed only the base of another, presenting an extensive outline of dark and barren ridges, seemed to mock the impatience of Varàno, whose attention was nevertheless sometimes engrossed by the sublime and occasionally beautiful scenes which burst abruptly upon his view from the various breaks in the rocks, and the richly covered vallies, from which he looked down from almost inaccessible cliffs, often listening to the rush of waters that rolled in thunder at his feet, or to the shrill cry of the eagle or the vulture, sailing high amongst the clouds. The wild strains, too, of the Swiss peasant would sometimes fascinate his regard.

"Truly, Latour," said he one day, as he was attending to a little rural air proceeding from a small cabin amid the cliffs, "that musician, whoever he is, has some skill. You are a performer yourself, Latour—did you mark that cadence?"

"Aye, Signor, this is music," said Latour, with a characteristic shrug; "the Swiss strains are rude, but they touch the heart. They are not like the artful warblings of Italy, which mean nothing because they do not come from here," laying his hand upon his breast.

"Thou art a true Swiss," said Varàno.

"Ah, Signor, and he cannot be a true Swiss, who does not love his country."

Varàno smiled at this enthusiasm, and was often tempted to listen to Latour's remarks as they rode along, and the resemblance he sometimes imagined between the scenes they passed through, and those of his own province.

"Except," said he, as they arrived within about a league of Mount St. Gotardo, "that the nearer prospect is not so bold, nor the cataracts neither so frequent nor so graceful, this spot might be said to be little inferior to Innerooden. But though the woods and the lakes which fill up the knolls of the mountains might be thought something of in Italy, they are nothing, absolutely nothing, Signor, to the woods and lakes of Innerooden."

They had traversed the gigantic steeps of Mount St. Gotardo, and had just descended into one of those deep vallies formed by the mountains it overtops, and fertilized by the united waters of the Reuss and the Tesino, which there rise, when they were surprised by the low tinkling of bells, intermingled with the lowing of herds, and the murmur of approaching voices.

"Oh maestro, maestro!" exclaimed Latour, and instantly he leaped from his mule, and began to caper and dance as if seized with the sudden frenzy of madness.

"What is the matter, Latour?" said Varàno; "hast thou lost thy senses?—or has the wonderful insect of Apulia pursued thee to thine own country?"

While he spoke, he perceived a *senn*, or cow-keeper, clad in the accustomed manner, with his yellow trowsers and embroidered braces, his leathern cap and curiously carved bowl, slung, not ungracefully, across his shoulders, descending, attended by a numerous herd, the opposite mountain. He was followed by four goats, from whose necks were suspended bells, harmoniously tuned, chiming in with the lively measure of the *ranz des Vaches*. The bells—the voice of the *senn* in concert with this animating melody, attracted various groups of villagers from the adjacent hamlets; some following with oboes, others with flagelets.

Latour was almost frantic with delight. He danced, sung, and was often so noisy in his mirth, that Varàno could with difficulty recal him to any sense of decorum, or prevent his accompanying them to the mountains they had so lately descended, and where the cattle were to be stationed for the summer quarter.

A wide and magnificent extent of country conducted our travellers to Altorfo; having passed which, and arrived within a few miles of Lucerne, the lake began to expand itself, stretching away on the left to the Canton of Zug, and on the right to that of Underwalden; whilst far above its neighbouring rocks appeared Mount Pilate, exalting its vast unsheltered head, in defiance of the storm that rolled above, and of the lofty, but more humble Rigi, which was seen pouring down its numerous torrents.

Various and uneasy surmises agitated the busy mind of Varàno as he passed the borders of the Lake. The abrupt manner in which he had torn himself from Cecilia at the Castello di Montani—the little dependance that he had placed upon her word when she solemnly assured him of her innocence, and the strong expressions conveyed in the cruel, the insulting letter she had since received from him, conspired together to excite doubts as to her forgiveness. He dreaded lest his arbitrary, and now, he considered, injurious treatment of her might have alienated her affections, and that Raymond, the more happy Raymond, might succeed to her love; or, should this not be the case, that she had ere this determined absolutely upon a life which would render all remonstrance and entreaty ineffectual. Such were his reflections as they pursued their way to a little cottage within view of the lake, where they purposed to remain for the night.

When they alighted at the cottage, Varàno commanded Benedetto to make enquiries against morning concerning the residence of M. St. Aubin; and then, invited by the novelty and grotesque beauty of the scene, he took a stroll among the rocks. The sun, which till the evening had tipped with refulgent splendour every surrounding object, now shed only a stunted lustre through the thick shades of beech and alder which clothed the edge of the lake. Varàno watched its last parting gleam till it faded slowly from his view; and the stealing advance of twilight began to blend every colour of the landscape in one soft hue.

He remained for some moments with his eyes fixed upon the lake, when he was startled by the sound of a bell; and turning to a little solitary spot amongst the rocks, descried the turrets of a Convent. He partly descended the rock on which he stood; and looking earnestly into the dell, perceived four Monks bearing a coffin on their shoulders, while a fifth walked before them, carrying a crucifix. The habit of their order was grey; they were barefooted, and their venerable figures seemed well suited to their pious occupation. They were attended by four Friars, holding torches in their hands. A train of Nuns, conducted by their Superior, followed at some distance, bearing also lights, crosses, and Madonas. They moved with a slow and solemn step, their eyes fixed intently upon the ground, and their thoughts apparently engrossed by the awful business they were engaged in. He watched them till he saw them enter a *cimetiere*, when, warned by the approach of night, he repaired hastily to the cottage, and soon afterwards to his chamber.

As soon as day began to dawn, he arose. The morning was fine, and he again wandered from the cottage. He followed the track among the rocks, which gradually receded, till he descended at length into a thick grove, whose deep shades formed a retreat so tranquil, so solemn, yet so beautiful, that every sense was fascinated. He passed on with unequal steps, often pausing to survey the wild grandeur of the landscape which broke in upon him from the opening vistas, till the shades suddenly retired; and proceeding by a narrow path beneath the rocks, he discovered the very spot which he had visited on the preceding night. The gate of the *cimetiere* was open. He recollected the funeral of the Nun, and the solemnity of the scene around, and the soft and not unpleasing melancholy it inspired, invited him to enter. He advanced with cautious steps, as if fearful of intruding upon the awful repose of the dead, and then stopped to contemplate it. The simple graves of the Nuns, bound over with willow, and bordered with groves of gloomy cypress, without a cross or a stone to tell who slept beneath, turned his mind to correspondent sorrow. He pictured to himself a young and beautiful woman, consigned by avarice, or adverse accidents, to a life of melancholy and seclusion, gradually sinking into premature decay, and at last finding an asylum from misfortune in the gloomy caverns of the grave. Imagination pursued her through all the gradations of ideal wretchedness. He saw the bitter tear, he heard the agonizing sigh with which she bade an eternal adieu to the yet untasted pleasures of the world, while life was new, and the yet hurrying pulse beat high with expectation. He saw her kneeling at the shrine, raising her clasped hands and streaming eyes in silent supplication—he saw her cheek now flushed and now pale, as actuated by the various impulses of a mind torn by its own conflicting energies—he heard her call down blessings upon him whom no penance, no effort of her own could teach her to forget—the youth of her fondest affections; now hanging over his beloved idea with enthusiastic fondness—now recalling his looks, his words, his parting anguish, till the holy Sisterhood draw nigh, and with slow and solemn step, "answering in awful pauses to the sounding organ," recal her from temporal to heavenly musings. His imagination still pursued her. He saw her in her cell: her lovely form, pale and emaciated, stretched upon a scanty supply of straw—the cruci-

fix and the scull the only ornaments of her wretched chamber!
No parent's hand to close her eyes—no friendly voice to sooth
the keen agonies of dissolution!—He shuddered at the picture
which his fancy had drawn; and looking round, beheld at some
distance a newly covered grave, which he believed to be that of
the poor Nun whose remains he had seen borne to their last silent
receptacle. He approached, and in a few minutes perceived two
females, whom he discovered to be lay-sisters belonging to the
Convent, bearing each a basket filled with flowers. They stopped
at the foot of the grave; and setting down their baskets, entered
upon their occupation. They wore the habit of the order, and
their long white veils flowing loosely over their garments, gave a
tragic solemnity to their figures.

"Save you, Sisters!" said Varàno; "your's is a pious task, and
well accords with your devout and holy characters. These
flowers, emblematic of your innocence, are a sweet and suitable
offering at the shrine of departed excellence. May the beautiful
spirit of her who reposes there, hover over and protect you!"

"Her path," cried one of the Sisters, partially raising her veil,
"has been thorny. The flowers that would not diversify it in life,
we have culled to decorate her grave, and never shall a weed disgrace it."

"Attachment such as your's," said Varàno, "must receive a
more than adequate reward in its own delightful feelings. What
you have lost in the world, is supplied to you by the sweets of
reciprocal affection; and, immured as you are, you have enjoyments transcending the impure and fickle gratifications which
life affords to us. Dead to the world, you are dead also to its cares;
and as you rise above us in devotion, so are your enjoyments
superior to our's."

"On which side happiness preponderates," said the Nun pensively, "can be resolved only by those to whom both situations
are alike known, and who have viewed both with an impartial
eye. Life teems with misfortunes from which we are exempt, and
from which no thought, no foresight of their own can defend
those who are still in the world. Yet that world has its allurements
to which all are attached, though not in equal degrees, and which
nothing but experience can convince us are fallacious. The vestal,

born in some solitary nook of her own native mountains, and consigned, while yet too young to decide from the impulse of the understanding, to a monastic life, fancies the world a scene of unexplored wonders, where happiness reigns without alloy, and youth revels in scenes of perpetual enchantment. Impressed with these ideas, she regards the lessons of wisdom as the fabrications of disgust, and turns from the general monotony of her avocations with its consequent uneasiness. To such the calm pleasures of a conventual life can afford no real satisfaction. Those only can be happy who, having tried life under its least seductive form, have voluntarily resigned it—not from weariness and disgust, but from a firm persuasion that a moderate degree of happiness is all that can be expected here; and that this may be enjoyed with less danger of interruption within the walls of a cloister, than whilst at large in the world.

"Those who enter with minds worn with disappointment, or harrowed with remorse—and those who are hurried into retirement without the consent of the understanding, are alike subject to those intellectual maladies for which there is no cure. In the former case, the sick heart, brooding over its own real or imaginary calamities, is incapable of exertion; the springs of life are corroded, and the unhappy victim to despair sinks to an untimely grave. Of this class was the dear companion whose death we have so lately witnessed. Her wrongs have been great, but she sleeps in peace; and, her probation at an end, will awake to an eternity of blessedness!"

"The tender sympathy which you have discovered for this poor Nun," returned Varàno, "does credit to the benevolence of your order, and to her worth."

"She was not a Nun," interrupted the Sister, "but a pensioner; though, had she lived, she would probably have taken the veil in our Convent. Of her story we know little: all that we could learn was, that she was a native of France; and that, previous to her arrival here, she had been confined in a gloomy chateau in Languedoc, by a Nobleman of whom she frequently accused as the author of all her miseries and misfortunes. Whether or not he was her husband, we had no means of ascertaining; since she mentioned him only in the last period of her illness, and in the intervals of reason, which were indeed not frequent, invariably declined the subject."

Varàno seemed scarcely to breathe while the Nun was speaking; an expression of the deepest horror was painted on his features. He enquired with an unsteady voice if she knew the name of the pensioner, or could recollect that of the person whom she had mentioned. Her reserve as to her own story—her French origin—her confinement in a gloomy chateau in Languedoc, and her alluding to the persecutions of some relentless tyrant, formed a combination of circumstances sufficient to authorize the supposition that it might be Cecilia.

"She often spoke," continued the Nun, purposely evading the question, "of some one whom she loved, and said she had been basely and most cruelly slandered. This was the arrow which transfixed her heart—the poison that drank up its vital current."

Varàno's terror was now excessive; he feared to repeat the question—he almost wished it not to be resolved. To remain thus dreadfully perplexed was, however, to realize all the horrors of conviction, and he again demanded its answer.

"Speak," said he falteringly, and with an agitation that alarmed them, "her name."

"I never knew it," said the Nun, "nor are the rest of the community better informed than myself. The name of him whom she termed her persecutor," resumed she, looking earnestly upon him as she spoke, "was Morsino."

The colour forsook the cheek of Varàno—he reeled; and casting a look of agony toward heaven—"Oh Cecilia," cried he, "thou art sufficiently revenged!" and fainted.

The consternation this occasioned to the Nun, who had been the involuntary cause of this emotion, can scarcely be conceived; and not till at the reiterated entreaties of her companion, could she sufficiently command herself, to afford him the least assistance.

Fortunately at this moment Varàno's servants, who had been in pursuit of him, entered the *cimetiere*. He revived as they approached; but his senses again forsook him, nor did he recover his perception till he found himself in a small, but elegant apartment, encompassed with faces he had never before seen. This event, however surprising, was scarcely noticed by Varàno. No word, no exclamation of astonishment escaped his lips; sighs and heavy groans were the only signs he gave of existence.

This horrible convulsion of his mind was succeeded toward evening with some strong symptoms of fever; and at the expiration of two days, notwithstanding the utmost care and assiduity on the part of his attendants, profuse bleedings, and every possible precaution, it arose to such a height, that his situation was now as hazardous as it had been before alarming. He raved continually of Cecilia, called himself her slanderer—her murderer; declared that he had seen her spectre—that it had undrawn his curtains at the dead of night; and so strongly did the idea of this phantom fasten upon his mind, that he was restrained only by force from attempting to pursue it.

Exhausted at length with these ravings, he became gradually more composed. Sleep stole upon his senses; and after an interval of some hours, starting from his slumbers, and snatching aside the curtains, he beheld a lady sitting alone by his bed-side. An enquiry where he was, indicated the return of reason.

"You are with friends," said the lady, mildly, and with a look the most soothing.

"Friends!" repeated he emphatically, "alas! I have no friends! —I deserve none!—I have killed, I have destroyed an angel!"

"Of whom is it you are speaking?" said the lady.

"Ah, you knew her not," cried he despondingly, "or you would abhor, you would spurn me! Oh Madam!"—(and he melted into tears)—"you know not how I have been deceived."

"And are you sure," returned she, hesitatingly, "that the lady is dead?—Is it not possible——"

"Ah, do not mock me!" said Varàno; "she is gone—I have seen her grave!—and, Oh! if you have pity, let mine be made near it!"

"Be calm," cried she, "and hope—happiness may yet be your's."

"Never, never," said Varàno; "I cannot—dare not hope!"

"But suppose I could prove," pursued the lady, "that you have no grounds for this despair—that, misled by the impetuosity of your own nature, and the coalition of some strong circumstances, you have suffered yourself to be again deceived, and that even now——"

"Gracious Heaven!" interrupted Varàno, "what mean you?—Oh torture me not with suspense!"

"When you are more composed," said the lady, rising, "I may venture to be more explicit."

She then withdrew to recal his servants and to give orders respecting his treatment; commanding, at the same time, that no enquiries he might make should be answered.

CHAPTER X

————Non opimas
Sardiniæ segetes feracis:
Non æstuosæ grata Calabriæ
Armenta: * * * * *

———— Me pascunt oliviæ
Me chichorea, levesque malvæ
Frui paratis & valido mihi,
Latoe, dones, & precor, integra
Cum mente: nec turpem senectam
Degere, nec cithara carentem.

HORACE.

I demand not the abundant harvests of the fertile Sardinia, nor the oxen which enrich the burning Calabria; I am content with my olives, my endives, and my smooth mallows. I ask nothing, Oh son of Latona! but leave to enjoy my fortunes in health of body and mind, and to pass to an honourable old age, and always in the midst of the innocent pleasures of the Muses.

THE lady returned in about an hour, and found him stretched upon a couch pale and languid.

"Are you prepared," said she, smiling, "to hear tidings of joy?"

Varàno raised his head at these words, while his expressive eyes seemed to demand their import. She waited not his reply—she quitted the room, and in a few minutes, to his astonishment, his joy, which was now as ungovernable as his grief had been exquisite, ushered in Cecilia! To the meeting of these lovers, after their long and painful separation, no language can do justice. Imagination only can conceive—and to imagination we leave it.

The lady, as will be conjectured, was Madame St. Aubin. Benedetto, in pursuance of Varàno's orders, had made his enquiries in the village; and learning that the abode of M. St. Aubin was within the distance of half a mile, he hastened to give intelligence of it to his master. Not finding him at the cottage, he pursued the path which he had taken; and at last, assisted by Latour, traced him to the *cimetiere*. The vicinity of M. St. Aubin's villa to the Convent to which the *cimetiere* belonged, was the reason of his being conveyed thither.

M. St. Aubin and Raymond were then at Zuric. Cecilia, too, on his arrival, was fortunately absent with Mademoiselle St. Aubin, the daughter of her friend; and Madame, who had been prepared by Benedetto for the reception of her new guest, being informed of the nature and cause of his indisposition, and his motive in coming there, fearful of the consequences of a too hasty disclosure, resolved to keep him in ignorance of Cecilia's being then living beneath her roof, till the joyful news could be communicated without further danger to his health.

Cecilia's design of retiring to a Convent had been overruled by Madame St. Aubin and her husband, who insisted that she should remain with them till, without the risk of encountering fresh insults from the Count, she could be sent back to her friends.

Cecilia, when her first transports had subsided, which, in the ungoverned ecstacy of the moment, on finding herself restored at once to the esteem and affection of Varàno, were too violent to be controuled, enquired concerning Rosalvo. At the mention of his confinement in the *carcere* at Naples, her despair was unbounded; but the assurances of Varàno, who represented that, through the interest of the Count di Montelina, his innocence would, he hoped, be made clear, and his enlargement effected, restored her again to hope.

The next day M. St. Aubin and his son, after an absence of about a week, returned to the villa, attended by M. St. Louis, an old acquaintance of the former, who, being in a declining state of health, was come to spend the summer in Switzerland. Varàno,

though yet unable to leave his chamber, was immediately introduced to them.

A sort of dignified simplicity, indicative of benevolence, distinguished the manners of M. St. Aubin; whilst in Raymond he
perceived all the external graces and qualifications which he had
been authorized to expect; but he perceived, too, when addressing himself to Cecilia, an expression of deep sadness pictured on
his countenance, which, as it was scarcely possible to mistake the
cause, at once grieved and interested him.

Pity was perhaps the only avenue to love in the generous heart
of Raymond; and while, touched by her misfortunes, he indulged
this tender sentiment for Cecilia, his mind insensibly became
tinctured with a softer passion. That she was unhappy, was but
too apparent; but that love—unfortunate, ill-requited love,
formed any part of her distress, her delicacy had never suffered
him to imagine. To erase from her memory the recollection of
past sufferings—to place her, by his means, beyond the reach of
future ones, were the dearest hopes he had ever formed. Of the
acquiescence of his father in any scheme which might promote
his happiness, he had never suffered himself to doubt. What then
was his disappointment when he learned from Madame St. Aubin
her connection with Varàno, and the probability there appeared
that their marriage would now shortly take place!

If traits of melancholy were perceptible in the fine features
of Raymond, they were still more evidently portrayed in those
of St. Louis. He was several years younger than M. St. Aubin,
and seemed once to have been handsome. But though the brilliancy of his eyes had perhaps suffered from illness, they were yet
fraught with an expression which gave a most interesting turn
to his countenance. At the introduction of this stranger, Cecilia
changed colour. The MS at the chateau started to her recollection; the name of St. Louis was, nevertheless, too common in
France to authorise the supposition that the person she then saw,
and him to whom it was addressed, were the same. An idea, however, that this was possible prompted her enquiries; and having
acquired a knowledge, through Madame St. Aubin, of some of
the most interesting, as well as most melancholy events of his
life, she discovered him to be indeed that St. Louis for whom the

MS was written. She therefore requested that he might be made acquainted with her strange discovery of it at the chateau, and, happy by this providential rencontre (for as such she considered it), to be empowered to fulfil the wishes of the writer, of her intention of sending the MS for his inspection immediately on her arrival in Italy; leaving it to the discretion of Madame St. Aubin whether or not to inform him of the recent death of the Countess, who, from the conversation lately held between Varàno and the Nun, had doubtless breathed her last in the adjacent Convent.

That the grave he had visited was that of the unhappy Countess, appeared so evident to Varàno, that, having formerly received from Cecilia some account of the MS, and also of the sudden removal of the Countess from her confinement in the turret, he wondered it had never before occurred to him that the person there interred might be the wife of the Count.

When a disclosure of these circumstances was made to St. Louis, he repaired to the Convent; and having gained an audience of the Superior, he obtained all the information she could afford, and all that was indeed necessary concerning her late pensioner. Of her family and name she knew nothing; but the time of her arrival—her own assertion that she had been immured in a chateau in Languedoc, the description of her person, and that of her conductor, whose name, he was told, was Pandolfo, all accorded so exactly with Cecilia's information and his own too faithful recollection, that, persuaded it could be no other than the Countess, he flew to the *cimetiere*, knelt and wept upon her grave, and then returned to the villa, where a long and interesting conversation took place between him and Cecilia.

Varàno, when able to undertake the task, wrote to the Marchesa, acquainting her with his safe arrival in Switzerland—of his having found Cecilia, not, as he had expected, in a Convent, but in the family of M. St. Aubin; and the reception he had there met with from her truly hospitable protectors. The mention of his own illness, and the causeless alarm which had occasioned it, unwilling to create anxiety, he entirely suppressed.

Slowly recovering strength, he at length quitted his chamber;—the glow of returning health again faintly illumined his

features, and his friends, in the alteration which a few days had
produced, found all their apprehensions for his safety more than
adequately repaid. Eager to return to Italy, he proposed their
instant removal; but the express orders of the physician, who
insisted that such a step in the present debilitated state of his
frame, would be attended with great danger, obliged him to defer
it.

The villa of M. St. Aubin, though, from the extreme simplicity of its appearance, it might have been mistaken for a cottage,
evinced the taste of its owner. Surrounded by every object the
most smiling, beautiful, and romantic which Switzerland can
afford, it was a retreat for which the sweet poet of *Valclusa* might
have forsaken his own hallowed fountain.

> "A wilderness of sweets; for Nature here
> Wanton'd as in her prime, and play'd at will
> Her virgin fancies, pouring forth more sweets
> Wild above rule or art, enormous bliss!"

Nor did the Muses disdain to visit it. M. St. Aubin was himself a
poet; and Raymond, catching the hereditary spirit of enthusiasm,
would sometimes produce pieces which his father condescended
to approve.

The gardens, occupying a little dell on the back-ground of
the villa, harmonized in their simplicity with the scenery which
enclosed them. To the front extended the lake, expanding itself
into grandeur, and displaying, through its translucent waters, the
rocky inequalities of its shores. On the right arose the distant hills
of Uri; and to the west, half concealed by the blue mist arising
from their lake, the rocks of Underwalden; whilst farther still (to
the left) beneath the encircling and almost inaccessible crags of
the Rigi, appeared the little independent State of Gerouu.

Happy in his situation, in his family, and in himself, respected
by his superiors, beloved by his equals, and adored by the poor,
M. St. Aubin diffused liberally the blessings he enjoyed. Laura,
his only daughter, a lovely girl of sixteen, was the dispenser of
his charities; and perhaps, from the resemblance she bore to her
mother, the darling of his heart.

Near a fortnight had elapsed since Varàno wrote to the Marchesa, and he was now in daily expectation of hearing from her. A letter at length arrived, in the envelope of which was one also for Cecilia, abounding with many affectionate enquiries and tender appellations; and soliciting that she would attend Varàno immediately to Florence, where the Marchese and herself were then waiting, having deferred an intended visit to Venice, in order to be in readiness to witness the solemnization of their nuptials, which they had now the strongest reasons to request might no longer be delayed.

Cecilia, although gratified by the impatience expressed by this once proud family to receive her as a relative, saw, nevertheless, an impropriety in bestowing her hand till the fate of her brother should be ascertained; and Varàno, disappointed in the hope of receiving a satisfactory account concerning him by means of the Marchesa, yielding to her scruples, it was agreed they should proceed immediately to Naples.

"What say you, my little Laura," said M. St. Aubin to his daughter, as soon as he had been informed by his Lady of the purposed departure of his guests, "to an expedition to Italy?"

"I should say it would be charming," returned Laura timidly, "could I believe you were in earnest."

"I was never more so in my life," cried M. St. Aubin; "I am already resolved upon it; and if you are inclined to accompany me, Raymond, who I think has no inclination to revisit Naples, will remain with his mother till our return."

"I admire your plan," said Madame St. Aubin; "but our Laura," added she, smiling, "will have a thousand objections to it; she cannot leave her groves, her gardens, and her dairy-house."

"Oh yes—all, every thing," said Laura, blushing, "for such dear friends!"

Cecilia, delighted with the proposal, expressed, as did also Varàno, the utmost anxiety for its completion. It was therefore instantly concluded upon. Carlo, who was now admitted into Varàno's service, was to attend them; and their little arrangements being made, they bade adieu to the romantic wilds of Switzerland, and commenced their journey to Naples.

CHAPTER XI

Did I but purpose to embark with thee
On the smooth surface of a summer's sea,
While gentle zephyrs play in prosp'rous gales,
And Fortune's favour fills the swelling sails,
But would forsake the ship, and make the shore,
When the winds whistle, and the tempests roar?

PRIOR.

THE Signora di Rosalvo arrived in the meantime at Naples. Alighting at the Palazzo di Montelina, she sent up her name, and was soon ushered into the presence of the Count. He received her with the politeness due to her appearance, and promised to exert his interest in behalf of her husband; but, understanding that the supposed delinquent was confined on a charge of murder, and that his persecutor was no less a person than Count Morsino, a courtier, whose influence in the State of Naples was not less powerful than his own, he betrayed much uneasiness and perplexity.

The Signora had been informed at Casal of Rosalvo's arrest; and supposing it to be in consequence of his late quarrel with Morsino, who she knew had been wounded, though not dangerously, she pursued him to Genoa; and having with difficulty obtained admission into the interior of his prison, acquired, amidst many struggles between shame and affection, an elucidation of the mystery which had so long and greatly disturbed her. She remained with him at Genoa till Rosalvo, by an order from Count Morsino, was sent under a guard to Naples; when, determined that death only should divide them, she prepared to follow him.

The Count attended her to the *carcere*. At the sight of this gloomy and immense fabric, the sensations of the now afflicted Signora were inconceivably agonizing. They entered a long extent of passage, at the end of which they were met by two men bearing keys belonging to the chambers and dungeons of the prison. The Count enquired for Rosalvo. The men looked at each other in silence.

"You know his room," said the *carceriere*[1]; "it is the Genoese prisoner who arrived last, and who is to be tried for a murder!"

The Signora shuddered.

"Lead the way," cried the Count sternly; "we have business, and must be admitted immediately."

The men obeyed without speaking; and opening a small iron door, conducted them into a cell.

"My wife!—my Giuliana!" said Rosalvo, attempting to spring forward, "and do we meet once more!"

"Yes," hastily articulated the Signora, as she rushed almost fainting into his arms, "and never will we part again!"

A silence more eloquent than words succeeded. Rosalvo could only sigh—he could only weep upon her bosom. The Count, unable to suppress his feelings, hastily withdrew.

"Be calm, my love," said Rosalvo; "these tears—these precious tears—for whom is it that they are shed?—Oh, look up—look up!—I am not, nor whilst you are with me, can I be completely wretched!—Forgive—say but you forgive all the anguish I have cost you—all the wrongs you have endured; and then, although malevolence and despotism should unite their powers, and triumph over me, I shall die in peace!"

"Die! die!" exclaimed she wildly; "Oh no! Live, live, Rosalvo, and we may yet be happy!"

"It would be cruel to deceive you, my love," said Rosalvo—"I must die!"

"Gracious Heaven!" interrupted the Signora, clasping her hands together with a look of unutterable anguish, "what mean these words?—Are you not innocent?"

"As to an actual intention of murder, the horrid charge on which I was committed," said Rosalvo, "*most innocent*. But am I not in the power of wretches whom oaths cannot restrain—am I not inleagued with devils?"

The Signora trembled.

1 Gaoler.

"Will my single evidence prevail against villains bribed to perjury, and who will swear they saw me in the very act of which I am accused? What can innocence avail against the arts of a wretch bent on my destruction?"

"There is a God above," cried the Signora, "and I think he dare not."

"Ah, Giuliana! little do you know of those who, having forgotten what is due from man to man, have forgotten also what is due to their Creator."

"Hope for the best," said the Count, re-entering, "and let not the pangs of anticipation heighten the sense of present misery; you have a friend who will strain every nerve for your deliverance; and if there is villany, by Heaven it shall be brought to light!"

Rosalvo shook his head. The ardour, however, with which the Count had espoused his cause, touched him sensibly; and learning that he had already suggested a plan, which he omitted to explain, but which was to present a petition to his Sicilian Majesty to solicit his release without the intervention of a Court of Justice, his gratitude was excessive; but there was a cast of despair in his countenance when the Count spoke of his acquittal, which shewed what little confidence he placed even in his exertions. When he looked at the Signora, a faint smile brightened his languid features; but it was a smile so nearly akin to sorrow—so expressive of the anguish that laboured at his heart, that its observation was new agony.

The night being now advanced, the Count proposed their departure. The Signora, still clinging to Rosalvo, could with difficulty be torn from him; but on the Count's assuring her that her stay would not be permitted—the doors being about to be closed for the night, and promising at the same time to accompany her thither in the morning, she consented to return with him.

The next day was spent entirely by the Signora in the dungeon of Rosalvo. A low, dismal kind of chamber, without any furniture except a mattress, and whose grated windows only rendered the gloom more impressive, as it contained the only idol of her affections, was in her estimation superior to the most gorgeous Palace. All the ills that surrounded her, every idea of self vanished before the fond solicitude which filled her bosom for the safety of a beloved husband; and although his situation was replete with horrors, even these she thought were not insupportable while *she* was allowed to share them.

The rattling of chains—the hollow sound of doors creaking slowly on their sullen hinges—the frequent oath—the laugh of intoxication resounding from different parts of the *carcere*—the savage aspect of the keepers, and all the horrid accompaniments of guilt, were unheard and unnoticed in the nearer interest that engrossed her heart. Often would Rosalvo, fearful of the damp air of his prison, urge the necessity of her departure, and as often would she persist that no place, whilst he was there, was so dear to her as that cell; and that having united her fate with his, in the sweet hope of sharing with him those joys which love and fortune seemed once to promise them, nothing should now prevent her from participating his sorrows.

CHAPTER XII

It must not be—there is no power in Venice
Can alter a decree established.
'Twill be recorded for a precedent;
And many an error, by the same example,
Will rush into the State. It cannot be!
                                    SHAKESPEARE.

THE Count di Montelina repaired, as usual, to the *Palazzo del Re*, and attending in the council-chamber till the rest of the courtiers were retired, presented his petition. The King received it with a gracious smile; but when informed, during the eloquent entreaty which the Count offered for the culprit, of the name of the prosecutor and of the prisoner, and of the grounds on which the latter had been committed, he declared it to be his opinion that he was guilty of the charge; adding that, if his opponent was Count Morsino, who he believed was generally considered throughout Naples as a man of character and honour, he had doubtless sufficient testimonies of his guilt, and would therefore confirm and substantiate, by fuller details, his present accusation.

If D'Arnaud could be proved to be the wilful murderer of

Conte di Minotti, it was right, he said, and, in justice to the laws of his country, he ought to suffer for it. In this case the punishment, to be proportioned to the offence, must be death. The law could not be wrested to different purposes. Clauses admitting of alleviation would sometimes present themselves in matters of less moment, and due allowances were often made where the offence was not capital; but in the present instance the prisoner, after submitting to an examination, must be condemned, or acquitted, according as the proper Court should decide.

To the Count's proposition whether a boon of mercy might not be granted, and the matter hushed up, the King's answer was as follows:—

"If the prisoner is conscious of his innocence, why should he shrink from an investigation, in which that innocence will be rendered clear?—or how can he accept a pardon for an offence in which *he*, in your person, declares himself guiltless—and which, if he really is so, will involve his prosecutor, not him, in its consequent disgrace? The fear of an examination contains a presumptive proof of his guilt."

The Count reminded his Majesty that it was the friends of the prisoner, and not the prisoner himself, who had solicited his intercessions, and, he believed, without his knowledge. The daughter of Conte di Minotti was, he informed him, the wife of the prisoner; and as she was the only remaining relative, she of course was the chief person interested in the bringing her father's murderer, whoever he might be, to justice. She was then, he added, at Naples; and from the conversation which he had lately held with her at his Palace, it was plain she considered the whole of her husband's prosecution as an artful manœuvre, intended for the gratification of some malicious purpose.

The King expressed surprise that the Count should speak of an assassination, providing it could be proved to be such, as a mere private injury. An infringement on the laws of the realm could not, he added, be considered as an individual, but a general concern. The State, the country at large were interested in detecting those by whom those laws, the safeguard of their property and lives, were violated. Assassinations were already too frequent; and the authors of them, owing to the security afforded them by the Churches, were seldom brought to judgment. Examples rarely occurred; it was therefore proper that such examples should be held forth to public notice whenever they did occur. As a Sovereign, it was a duty he owed to his people—and, as a man, to himself, to prevent every possible invasion of the laws in his own peculiar provinces.—In reply to what had been urged respecting the friends of the accused, he observed that, if every petition offered by the fathers, mothers, wives, and nearest relations of the offender was to be allowed to influence those who were called upon by their situations to administer justice to the people, all order would be destroyed, and addresses of this kind would become so frequent, that an execution would rarely, if ever, take place; the just and equitable laws of the kingdom would be considered as mere bugbears to frighten children—right and wrong would be confounded, and the State become a chaos of discord and confusion.

"If it can be proved," added he, "that the accused armed only on the defensive, his enlargement will of course be certain, and his acquittal honourable; but if, on the contrary, he is ascertained to have been the challenger—or, what is worse, the wilful murderer of Conte di Minotti, he must submit to the atonement which the law in either case imposes."

Thus ended an interview of which such sanguine expectations had been formed. The Count repaired to the Palace, and the Signora read in his desponding looks the ill success of his application. She forbore to ask of him any confirmation of her husband's wretchedness, and gave a loose to all the terrors of her new hopeless situation.

Several weeks of anguish, of suspense, which became every day more torturing, had performed their course, and not one ray of hope had as yet pierced through the dark and portentous clouds which appeared to overhang her future prospects, when one night, as she was attending Rosalvo in his cell, supporting his aching head upon her arm, her eyes filled with tears, and her heart throbbing with agony, a voice, eloquently sweet, uttered his name; and before her agitation suffered her to recollect that the accents of it were familiar to her, Cecilia, accompanied by Varàno, the Contessa, and Olivia, entered the prison.

She flew to the Signora—she would have spoke; but as her eye caught the form of Rosalvo loaded with heavy irons, under whose pressure many victims had before languished—his countenance, in which the image of death was already stamped, she hid her face upon the bosom of her beloved friend, and heaving a profound sigh, remained motionless, till the eager exclamations of Rosalvo, whose despair, on beholding Cecilia conducted thither by Varàno, was converted into the wildest expressions of joy, recalled her from her stupor, and she sprang to his embrace.

Various and agonizing were their emotions whilst Rosalvo, with all the ardour of fraternal affection, strained her to his beating breast; nor were those of Varàno, on beholding the greatly injured Rosalvo, less exquisite and insurmountable. The gross, the contemptuous epithets with which, in the unguarded moment of indignation, he had formerly insulted him, aggravated his present feelings to a degree of distraction. The warmth of his salutations—the look, at once tender and confiding, which beamed from his again animated eyes as he commended Cecilia to his protection, while they convinced him of his forgiveness, and unlimited reliance on his honour, heightened his remorse. The generous manner in which Rosalvo forbade the expression of those self-reproaches which he could not listen to without pain, and for which he was ever ready to make excuses, gave new dignity to his character, changing pity into admiration. But when in the most pathetic language imaginable, amidst stifled groans, and with an expression of smothered anguish which found its way to the heart, and augmented its feelings into agony, addressing himself alternately to Cecilia and Varàno, he consigned Giuliana to their friendship, tears flowed in torrents from the eyes of his surrounding friends.

"Receive," said he, "as a beloved sister, the best, the noblest of women; shield her with your tenderness from the assaults of new sorrows, and let the pang of that awful hour which gives her a widowed heart, be the last she shall experience, till that mortal one which shall precede the union of her pure spirit with mine in those regions of eternal blessedness, to which a sweet confidence within tells me I am hastening. Support her with your counsels, console her with your endearments, and let her never feel the loss of him whose only wish for life arises from the hope of being enabled to discharge a portion of that great debt—Oh how vast, how impossible to be repaid!"

The feeling eloquence of his voice—his look—his gestures, as he confided this precious charge to their affection, were so affecting both to Cecilia and Varàno, and so distressing to the Signora, who was with difficulty kept from fainting, that the Contessa and Olivia, after a number of assurances, expostulations, and entreaties, were obliged to insist upon their separation, promising them, however, another interview in the morning.

In the evening, when the Signora had retired, Rosalvo being then alone in his cell, the keeper who conveyed his food entered with the allotted portion. This man was more humane than his companions; and when not otherwise engaged, he would often stop, and speak mildly to his prisoner.

Rosalvo perceived, as he set down the scanty meal, that he eyed him with great concern. As he was retiring—"You have been kind," cried he, recalling him, "and I would thank you for your attention."

The keeper turned, and observing him, as before, with a look of sorrowful commiseration—"I am unwilling," said he, "to be the harbinger of unwelcome tidings;—your situation, whilst here, will not be so tolerable as formerly; you are to be removed, I am told, into another cell, appropriated to the worst of criminals; and what will, I fear, be a severer trial, no one will be allowed to visit you!"

Rosalvo demanded the reason of his removal.

"Of this," returned the keeper, "I am as ignorant as yourself: such orders have been issued, but by whom, or for what purpose, I have not been able to learn. You must prepare, therefore, to leave this place. If it be in my power to attend upon you, I will; if not, I can only pity you!"

He withdrew; and Rosalvo, relapsing into his former attitude of despondency, sat with his eyes fastened upon the door at which he had departed, when it was slowly unclosed, and a figure, of which the expiring taper it held gave him but the faint outline, threw something upon the floor, and retired.

Rosalvo arose, and endeavoured to grope his way to the door, when he perceived something rustle beneath his feet like paper; and instantly seizing it, discovered it to be a letter. He hastened to open it; but the cell was now in gloom, and he awaited with impatience for the returning light of the morning to display the contents of an epistle so mysteriously conveyed to him.

As soon as it began to dawn, he turned to the grate, and read the following lines:—

"When you are summoned to take your trial, demand that Lancellotto della Pucini be called into the Court. He is your friend, and will deliver you."

CHAPTER XIII

———Quid tam dextro pede concipis, ut te
Conatus non pœniteat votique peracti?

JUV.

"What in the conduct of our life appears
So well designed, so luckily begun,
But, when we have our wish, we wish undone?"

MORSINO, though in the ardour and vexation of his resentment, he had dispatched emissaries to the Court of Genoa for the removal of Rosalvo to Naples, and had even issued fresh orders for his confinement in the lower dungeons of the *carcere*, no sooner arrived at Naples, than he began bitterly to repent the measure; and consulting with the *Giudice prócessante*,[1] made a number of unsuccessful attempts to evade, if it were possible, the progress of the prosecution. He then sent through various parts of the city in search of Signor Pandolfo, who he had heard was then at Naples, and whose presence was now necessary to his future proceedings. But of him, or of Lancellotto, of whom he also enquired, and after whom he had already sent messengers into most of the Italian States, he could learn nothing. It was evident they had both abandoned him, and the consequences of such a desertion were but too apparent.

1 The prosecuting Judge.

Perplexed, bewildered, almost maddened with his surmises, days and weeks passed away in uncertainty and suspense; and he was deliberating upon an escape, when his *Avvocato*[1] and a *Notaro* waited upon him for his deposition, informing him that the trial was now immediately to take place.

The hour for the criminal examination arrived, Rosalvo was conveyed from his dungeon to the Court of Justice. His fine figure—his undaunted step—the interesting dejection that overspread his features as he placed himself at the bar, arrested universal attention; and while the commiseration which common humanity inspires, threw a veil over his supposed crime, a latent hope that he would obtain mercy filled every breast. Morsino at length approached. He seated himself by the Judge; and the eyes of the spectators were now withdrawn from the prisoner, and fixed, with a gaze of eager curiosity, on the countenance of his accuser.

The trial commenced according to the usual forms; and the Count's deposition being read aloud, the prisoner, by the *Avvocato* for the prosecutor, was called upon for his defence.

Rosalvo made none.

"Have you no evidences," enquired the Judge, "to appeal to? —If not, the consequences of such an accusation are obvious as tremendous!"

"I demand," said Rosalvo, "that Lancellotto della Pucini be summoned to appear in this Court; if his evidence be insufficient, I have no other!"

Morsino trembled, but was silent. Lancellotto della Pucini was now ordered to come forth.—"Make way—make way!" was reechoed throughout the Court, and in a moment Lancellotto della Pucini mounted the bench.

The Judge demanded if he knew the prisoner. On his answering that he did not—"You are ignorant then," resumed he, "whether he is guilty or not of the charge of which he is here accused?"

"I swear," said Lancellotto, "that the prosecutor, and not the prisoner, is the murderer of Conte di Minotti."

1 Advocate.

Rosalvo started, and looked wildly at the witness.

The Count shuddered; the flush of surprise which had coloured his cheek suddenly faded, and his countenance exhibited the livid paleness of guilt.

A pause of wonder ensued.

After the usual enquiries who he was, and what testimonies he could adduce in support of his declaration, Lancellotto deposed that, on the evening of the 16th of September, 1763, as he was returning to Naples from the Island of *San Lucia*, he was startled by a deep groan; and turning round, discovered, at a little distance, the body of a wounded man stretched upon the ground. The groan was not like that of a person dying, but seemed to be occasioned by great bodily anguish. He was proceeding to his assistance, but on perceiving Count Morsino—or, as he was then called, Signor Guidotto, he concealed himself behind some trees, where he heard the deceased tell the prosecutor that he had met D'Arnaud—that he had drawn his sword upon him, and was wounded, though not mortally; adding—"If he is innocent, may God forgive *me* and *you*; if not, I may yet live to revenge myself."

He then desired him to bind up his wounds; instead of which, the prosecutor drew his dagger, and with a look of savage desperation plunged it into his heart. He (the witness) then advanced; and the Count, finding himself observed, gave him money to keep the secret, alledging in his defence that the deceased was his friend, and being wounded past recovery, he had been tempted to put a final period to his sufferings by dispatching him immediately. He then enquired into his occupations; and learning that his office was to assist the snow-merchants in carrying snow about the streets of Naples, offered to receive him into his family. To this, after various promises and incitements, he finally consented; but on discovering that an innocent person was to be made answerable for this late horrible transaction, he had resolved to confess the fact.

Hope, fear, astonishment, and expectation usurped by turns their empire in the yet incredulous mind of Rosalvo as he listened to this disclosure—a disclosure fraught with such strong and atrocious instances of guilt, falsehood, and malignity as are scarcely to be paralleled.

The Count, who, while Lancellotto was speaking, had had time to recollect himself, protested that the witness was an impostor. He acknowledged that a person of the name of Lancellotto della Pucini had once been one of his household, but insisted that there was not even the smallest personal resemblance between him and the witness. It was evident, therefore, that he had been hired to criminate him; but whether employed by the prisoner, or by some more secret enemy, the mystery was too intricate for him to develop. With the flagitious stratagems devised by those whose situations were become desperate, the Court, he observed, was sufficiently well acquainted—they were frequent and notorious; and the success of them, owing to the excellent construction of the laws and unbiased equity of the Judges, too rare to allow him to fear any thing from its decisions.

The *Avvocato* for the prosecutor then demanded of the prisoner how long he had known the witness, and whether he had any means of proving that it was the same Lancellotto della Pucini who had formerly resided with the Count.

Rosalvo replied that he had never before, to his knowledge, seen the witness, and was entirely ignorant that a person of that name had ever lived with the prosecutor.

"How," demanded the opposing counsel, "came you to summon here in your behalf a person whom you have never before seen, and with whom, as your declaration would prove, you are in every respect unacquainted?"

"By a letter," resumed Rosalvo, presenting the mysterious billet to be examined by the *Avvocato*, "was I informed of his name and intentions. Whether or not he is an impostor, the Court must ascertain."

The *Avvocato* read it; and then delivering it to the witness, demanded if he was the author of it, or could declare by whom it had been written.

Lancellotto protested that he was not the author of it, nor could he, he said, swear to the hand-writing; but he believed it to be that of Signor Giuseppe Pandolfo, an acquaintance of the Count, who was then in the Court, and who would corroborate his allegation concerning his late residence with the Count.

Signor Giuseppe Pandolfo was then commanded to appear.

The confusion of the Count, as this new evidence advanced, was apparent to the whole Court. All hopes of his any longer evading justice seemed to vanish at the appearance of this more formidable accuser; his limbs trembled, and a deep and deathly hue alternately varied his features.

The enquiries made by the *Giudice prócessante* of the witness, whether he was the writer of that billet, and whether the person calling himself Lancellotto della Pucini had been in the service of the prosecutor, were both answered with an affirmative. On being asked whether he knew any thing of the murder committed in the evening of the 16th of September, 1763, on the body of Conte di Minotti, he deposed that, in the afternoon of the same day, he had been told by Count Morsino (then Signor Guidotto) that an affair of honour was about to be decided between the deceased and the prisoner, and that the appointed place was *San Lucia*. He therefore requested that he (Signor Pandolfo) would attend him thither immediately, to which he consented.

Having arrived near the Island, the Count proposed that he should continue behind with his people, whilst he proceeded alone toward the spot where the combatants were to meet. On his return he was informed that Conte di Minotti had fallen, and was already dead—that the survivor had escaped, and that he must assist the Count and his servants in conveying the body to a vessel, and from thence to Naples. They accordingly disembarked, and near the entrance to *San Lucia* found the bleeding corse of the deceased. A dagger, the blade of which was bloody, lay at some distance. Supposing it to be the prisoner's, he instantly secured it; but on his return from *San Lucia*, discovered it to be the property of Conte Morsino.

The dagger, which the witness had conveyed with him, was then produced, and examined. The haft was of gold, curiously inlaid with some gems of onyx; the letters F.G. the initials of the Count's former name, were inserted in it. The blade was spotted over, and rusted with blood. Being questioned whether he knew of any quarrel between the prosecutor and the prisoner prior to the murder of Conte di Minotti, the evidence deposed that an intrigue had been long and secretly carried on between Conte Morsino and the Contessa, the wife of Conte di Minotti; and apprehensive lest a discovery should be made of it through the prisoner, who had in some way become acquainted with it, they had designed a plot for his destruction. Of this he was informed by a conversation which he had accidentally overheard between Conte Morsino and the Contessa a few days after the late bloody transaction in the Island of *San Lucia*.

This account was so perfectly consistent with Rosalvo's deposition, in which the whole affair had been explained, that the stronger testimony of the dagger was scarcely necessary to the elucidation of this unexampled piece of treachery. That the murder, on the suspicion of which Rosalvo had been committed, was perpetrated by the prosecutor, was sufficiently obvious. The Judge, therefore, rising in a serious and collected manner, addressed himself to the Count, whilst the whole assembly arose with an air of awful respect.

"Filippo, Conte Morsino, you stand charged by the corresponding evidences of Lancellotto della Pucini and Signor Giuseppe Pandolfo, with the wilful murder of Conte di Minotti, and are now, by their confessions, amenable to our laws."

Rosalvo, by an order from the Court, was then released from his fetters. The Count was committed for further examination. To remedy as much as possible the infamy sustained in the prosecution, it was decreed that one half of the delinquent's property should be secured to Rosalvo, who, amidst all the transport he experienced on finding himself dismissed without the slightest imputation of guilt—on discovering that he was not even the unintentional destroyer of the father of his amiable Giuliana, indulged the tenderest sentiments of commiseration for his fallen enemy.

No qualms of conscience, or scruples of honour, had impelled Pandolfo to these exertions in the cause of Rosalvo. To avenge himself upon the Count, upon whose now shattered fortune his demands had of late been so frequent and so exorbitant as to render a refusal of them indispensable, was the sole motive of his interference. The acquaintance between the Count and Pandolfo had commenced at Venice. Meeting accidentally at the *Busina*, a disagreement of a political nature took place between the Signor and a young merchant of the city, who, in order to gratify his resentment, threw an accusation of disaffection into the *Bocchi parlanti*. Orders were soon issued by the Inquisidor General through the city for the seizure of the offender, who, after a confinement of some days beneath the lead-roofs at St. Mark's, through the intercessions of the Count and some of the Nobles of his acquaintance, was released, on condition of his leaving Venice, which he altogether abandoned; and repairing with the Count to Naples, became from that moment the confidant and auxiliary of his numerous villanies. To raise his own fortune upon the fears of his employer, which he imagined would compel him to grant every thing he should think proper to demand, was the only object of his agency.

Baffled in this hope, and irritated by the scornful and impetuous behaviour of the Count, on the requisition of a large sum, which he had at last absolutely refused to afford, no sentiment but that of hatred remained on his mind; and while he fought to hurl vengeance upon his colleague without criminating himself, Fortune, by throwing Lancellotto in his way, seemed to have pointed out the means at once.

Rosalvo was conveyed in triumph from the hall of justice to the Palazzo di Montelina. The rapturous emotions of the Signora, of Cecilia, and Varàno, on his honourable and unexpected acquittal, were almost insupportable. The Count, happy to find him in no way implicated in this late diabolical prosecution, yielded to him his unreserved friendship and esteem; and, warmly participating in the general joy, he commanded that a splendid banquet should be prepared in compliment to his guest, to which a number of the Nobility of Naples and its environs were invited. This was succeeded in a few days by another equally magnificent, in honour of the marriage of the Lady Olivia di Montelina with Signor Vincentio Giustiniano, eldest son of the Marchese di Velasco.

The festivities on this happy occasion continued near a week. At the conclusion of them, Cecilia and Varàno, attended by Rosalvo and the Signora, M. St. Aubin and his daughter, departed for Tuscany.

CHAPTER XIV

—————L'etat du marriage
Est des humains le plus cher avantage
Quand le rapport des espirits et des cœurs
Des sentiments, des tastes, et des humeurs
Serre ce nœud tissus par la nature
Que l'amour forme, et que l'honneur epure.

VOLTAIRE.

THE reception of Cecilia, Rosalvo, the Signora, and their friends in the noble family at the Palazzo di Varàno was flattering to the whole party. The Marchesa mingled tears with embraces in her maternal salutations of Cecilia, and then conducted her to the Marchese, who, seated upon a sofa in one of the grand saloons in the Palace, was awaiting her introduction.

He was observing a picture by Tiziano, representing the royal nuptials of Giovanni de Medici and the beautiful Camilla Martello, a noble lady of his house, when Cecilia, accompanied on one side by the Marchesa, and on the other by Varàno, entered the room. The Marchese arose, and with an air of solemnity which the occasion seemed to require, and which he generally chose to assume, united her hand with Varàno's, bidding them each be mindful of the duties which their exalted stations imposed, whilst they emulated in their conduct the illustrious virtues of his ancestors.

A tear of transport fell from Varàno's eye, as he was speaking, upon the hands his father had joined. The Marchesa was silent—her looks alone expressed the rapturous feelings of her heart. Varàno then introduced his friends, who were courteously received.

The Marchese, who had delayed his purposed journey to Venice considerably longer than he had intended, having obtained the consent of Varàno and his guests to accompany him, insisted that his son's marriage should now immediately take place. Accordingly, on the appointed day, Varàno, in the

Church of the *Santa san Virgine dell Carmine*, and amidst all the pageantry of priestly decoration, received his charming bride from the hand of the Marchese. The rites of the Church were afterwards privately performed between Rosalvo and his lovely Giuliana, to whom, by the name of D'Arnaud, he again plighted his vows. A month passed away in constant routine of amusements. Various and magnificent entertainments were given at the Palace, which was ornamented on this occasion in the highest degree of splendour. From Florence, after a residence of some weeks, they proceeded to Venice.

The Lady Bianca di Bellanio, who, preparatory to their arrival, had arranged every thing in her Palace in such a manner as she thought would be most agreeable to the Marchese, received him and his friends with many demonstrations of joy. When alone with Cecilia, she lamented the strange unhappy mistake which had occasioned them so much confusion and distress at their first interview.

"Your life, my love," said she with great sweetness, "has presented hitherto a continued series of unhappy events; may your future one be more fortunate and happy!"

Anxious to shew every possible respect to her nephew, to whom she was always fondly attached, the Lady Bianca had been long engaged in purchasing jewels and other ornaments of dress as presents for her niece, when her attention was recalled by the indisposition of her daughter, the Lady Fioretta di Bellanio, who had been finishing her education at the school of *San Ursula*, and who, attended by her tutoress, a Nun of the order of Misericordia, was now conveyed to the Palace.

The terrors of the Lady Bianca at the idea of her daughter's danger, were every moment increasing; but after a confinement of about a week, all the alarming symptoms disappeared, and she gradually recovered. Sister Vittoria, the Nun, was her almost constant attendant; it was seldom indeed that the fair invalid would permit her to leave her chamber. One night, as she was retiring, the Lady Bianca, who had frequently spoken of her to her guests in terms of the highest commendation, led her into the banquet-room, where the whole company, except the Marchese and D'Arnaud, were assembled.

The Nun raised her veil as she approached, and discovered a face which appeared once to have been eminently beautiful; but time and affliction had left only a small remains. The angelic meekness of devotion characterized her countenance, and gave a milder expression to features which, although clouded as they were with sorrow, were still pleasing. Her manners were such as ought to accompany such a countenance; and there was a sweetness in her voice—a melancholy and correspondent softness which at once charmed and interested the beholders.

As soon as she had left the room, M. St. Aubin lamented that so charming a woman as Sister Vittoria should be concealed in a cloister.

"What pity," said he, "that the loveliest part of the sex should be consigned to a situation which must eventually exclude them from the pleasure as well as from some of the most important duties of life!"

"The Nuns of this order," said the Marchesa, "are not excluded from either, unless, which I am sure you will not allow, there is no pleasure in performing acts of benevolence. The lives of the Nuns of Misericordia are at once simple and useful. They are not devoted, as in other institutions, to solitary penance and austere devotion. Subject to no severe laws, they are permitted personally to administer to the necessities of their fellow-creatures; to visit the sick, to comfort the distressed, and to relieve, as much as is in their power, the wants of the indigent, form their principal occupations."

"The order of Misericordia is perhaps the only one," pursued M. St. Aubin, "to which uselessness and abstracted devotion may not be indiscriminately applied. Yet might not the members even of this community render themselves more eminently serviceable, were their sphere of action enlarged? Might they not, as wives and mothers, diffuse felicity around them in larger proportions than in their present situations? They are not, as you observe, absolutely immured; but they are undoubtedly restrained within certain limits."

"Every city," rejoined the Marchesa, "Venice not excepted, presents a continual succession of objects to engage their attention; and though I am no advocate for celibacy, I think women thus situated may render themselves as essentially, if not as generally, useful as under the circumstances you mention."

"I never see a female recluse," said Laura," but I feel a strange inclination to know something of her story: if they are not always the *best*, they are certainly the most interesting people upon earth."

"I have seldom seen a countenance," said Cecilia, "more affectingly so than that of Sister Vittoria; how mild, how sweet, how dignified is its expression!"

"And the tones of her voice too!" resumed Laura; "but I'm sure she is unhappy."

"You are very penetrating, my little Laura," said M. St. Aubin; "how long is it since you have taught yourself to read countenances, and to decide from the tones of the voice?"

"Oh, but her's," cried Laura, "is so eloquent!—and though I would see all happy, yet I love those most who are not so."

They were startled at this instant by a loud scream upon the stairs, and in a moment Carlo darted in, pale and trembling.

"I have seen her!" exclaimed he in a voice of terror and distraction; "it was herself—her very look!"

"Who—who?" demanded the whole party at once.

"My Lady—my revered——"

"Verezio," cried the Nun, re-entering, "is it you, or do my eyes deceive me? Is it possible?—Yes, it is—it is my faithful Verezio! —How——and when came you here?"

"With—with your daughter, Madam!" returned Verezio, still more agitated.

"With my daughter!" repeated the Nun, "*my* daughter!"

Cecilia shrieked, and rushed into her arms. Trembling and faint, the astonished mother could only clasp her long-lost child to her bosom, which throbbed with transport amounting to a degree of agony.

"And have I found," said she, recovering, "my daughter, my Cecilia, whom I have so long mourned as dead?"

Cecilia's emotions on beholding a mother from whom she was, as she imagined, for ever separated by death, deprived her for some moments of speech; she could only answer with her tears.

The Lady Bianca, though greatly astonished, was collected; and having obtained from Verezio some explanation of this mystery, she united her congratulations with the rest of the party; and after they had recovered from their joy and surprise, introduced Varàno to the fair Nun—or, as we shall now call her, Madame D'Arnaud.

"Permit me," said she, in a low voice, "to present to you my nephew and your son."

Madame D'Arnaud fixed her eyes upon the Lady Bianca as if to demand a confirmation of what she had said; and then turned them upon Cecilia with an expression of such tender solicitude, that her cheek was suddenly suffused with blushes.

"Little did I think," said Cecilia tremulously, "that I had a parent's consent to ask."

She stopped, and a deeper hue took possession of her features.

"Deign, Madam," said Varàno, throwing himself at her feet, "to receive me as your son. Allow me, too, to express my happiness on having found a mother who will not be less dear to me than my own; and let the affection which Cecilia and I have long cherished, receive the sanction of your approbation and pious benediction!"

Madame D'Arnaud gazed alternately on her daughter and Varàno.

"Bless you, my children!" said she, laying her hand upon the forehead of each with a touching solemnity; "and may that Power, which has in his mercy spared me to witness this hour, render you worthy of each other!"

D'Arnaud, who had been absent with the Marchese, now returned to the room. Having been met by M. St. Aubin, the joyful intelligence of this discovery was already imparted. But who can describe this astonishment when in the supposed unknown features of Madame D'Arnaud, he beheld those of his deliverer, the beautiful Nun of Misericordia, who had so wonderfully preserved his life. Madame instantly recollected him; but while she embraced him as the son of her beloved, her lost Chevalier, she suppressed, from motives of delicacy, all mention of the circumstance which had introduced them to each other.

In the course of another hour (Madame D'Arnaud and Verezio

only being present), Cecilia grew composed enough to enter upon a satisfactory account of her little history; including the extraordinary manner in which her relationship with D'Arnaud had been discovered, his misfortunes and subsequent imprisonment, and the miseries she had undergone from her retention of the fatal secret with which he had entrusted her.

Verezio, struck by Madame's words—"My child, whom I have so long mourned as dead!" demanded by whom she had been deceived into the supposition of Cecilia's death, nothing having occurred during his former correspondence with her when in Spain, that could authorize such a surmise.

"You may probably recollect," said Madame D'Arnaud, "that when I last spoke to you at the grate, I was attended by a Novice called Sister Francesca, who I told you was in my confidence.'"

"I remember it perfectly," returned Verezio.

"She alone," resumed Madame D'Arnaud, "was entrusted with my story, and it was from her I received the tidings of my daughter's demise. Francesca was an Italian, the daughter of a Venetian Nobleman. On her refusal to resign a lover, whom her friends once allowed her to receive openly as her future husband, but who, owing to some heavy losses which he had sustained at sea, had been since cruelly discarded, it was deemed expedient to remove her from Italy. She was accordingly conveyed to Madrid, and from thence to Fontcarrel; her friends imagining, from the distance in which they were now thrown, that all connection between the parties would be soon at an end. In this, however, they were mistaken. Signor Valini (for so he was called) soon followed her thither; and, concealed under the disguise of a Religieux, obtained frequent, though secret interviews with his mistress. I alone was entrusted with the knowledge of them. I pitied the unhappy Francesca; and, knowing it was her intention to quit her Convent before her novitiate year expired, resolved to aid her escape. She would have persuaded me to accompany her, but all her solicitations were for some time in vain. It was not because I was contented with my situation; for this, since the death of the Lady Almeria, the former Abbess, who expired about two years after my return to Fontcarrel, was painful in the extreme. The certainty that I should be excluded, by my departure, from all future opportunities of seeing you, and of hearing from you of my child, was my only objection to quitting it.

"One night Francesca entered my cell, and began to converse with me as usual on her intended expedition. The approaching vigil of San Stefano was the time agreed upon between the lovers for the execution of their project. No opportunity could have offered more favourable to their purpose:—the pilgrims, on their way to Mountserrat, are then entertained in the Convent, and music and feasting supply the place of devotion. I congratulated her on the prospect of her approaching release, which I doubted not would be accomplished with the utmost ease and celerity. She wept as I talked of parting—hung round me, and renewed her former entreaties for me to escape with her with so much earnestness, and with such an expression of tender sorrow at the thoughts of leaving me, that my resolution was staggered. My vows, as constrained, I had never considered as binding. I had no friend except Francesca; but the idea of my child again darted to my thoughts, and cruel as was my situation, I resolved to continue in it.

"Francesca looked earnestly in my face.

"'I have news to tell you,' said she. 'Have you fortitude?'

"I started. I demanded if she had seen Verezio.

"'*I have*,' repeated she solemnly, '*and your daughter——*'

"She stopped—her countenance declared the rest. I sunk lifeless into her arms. Francesca trembled at my emotions; she clasped me to her heart—our tears flowed together. The night was spent in sighs and lamentations. Francesca continued with me till midnight. I excused myself from attending chapel. Francesca left me, but returned as soon as service was concluded.

"Several days elapsed. I grew composed, but was still wretched; and yielding at length to the pressing and repeated importunities of Francesca, promised to escape with her. Disguises were procured; and mingling in the throng as pilgrims at the ensuing festival of San Stefano, our flight was not only unobserved, but unsuspected.

"Our journey was long and fatiguing. We embarked at the Bay of Roses, and landed at Genoa. Here Valini received the hand of the amiable Francesca.

"But, alas! hardly had the adoring husband conveyed her with him to Venice, when he was doomed to attend her to the grave! I accompanied her in her last moments, but was seldom alone with her. Once she seemed struggling to unfold something, but her speech failed her; and with her hand fast locked in mine, she expired without a sigh or a groan.

"Her motive for this deception concerning the death of my child, was doubtless to draw me from my Convent; and she had evidently no intention of continuing it beyond the bounds of our journey. On her decease I removed immediately to the School of San Ursula. Near fifteen years have elapsed since I entered into this Order. Nothing material has occurred to me during this space. The exalted pleasures of religion have long occupied by thoughts; and though my mind sometimes recurred with anguish to the recollection of past sorrows, I have long acquired a serenity which the sublime precepts of a religion pure and holy like our's can alone bestow.

"The report of my death may be easily accounted for. When a Nun quits her Convent, she is always said to be dead; her grave is made, nor is the solemn farce of a funeral always omitted."

Carlo thanked his beloved Lady for her hasty recital, whilst Cecilia, tears of tenderness and delight trembling in her eyes, uttered mentally her thanks to Heaven for the preservation of her angelic mother.

M. St. Aubin and Laura, having continued for some time in the enjoyment of the happy society of their friends, turned their course toward Switzerland. The week following was appointed by the Marchese for the return of his family to Florence. Bitterly did Madame D'Arnaud regret that, by an act which it was now impossible to recal, she was withheld from accompanying her beloved daughter into Tuscany. Cecilia equally lamented the necessity which prevented her attendance upon her mother; she felt, although the wife of Varàno, that her happiness would be incomplete since her amiable and revered parent was not permitted to share it; nor could she, when the moment of separation arrived, tear herself from her embrace till assured by Varàno that he would regularly spend several months in the year at Venice.

Louisette, who had been left by the Signora at the Castello

di Montani, repaired shortly to Florence. Claudia also quitted her service in the family of the Lady Viola to attend upon the fair bride; and on Louisette's marriage with Benedetto, which happened a few months after her arrival, she had the honour of succeeding as chief woman and occasional companion to her Lady. The faithful Carlo was invested with the important office of *Intendente*, and Lancellotto rewarded amply for his integrity in the cause of D'Arnaud.

Morsino, after a long and painful confinement in the lower dungeons of the *carcere*, was reconducted to the Court of Justice; and no documents appearing in his favour, received sentence of condemnation, and was led, amid the shouts of a deriding people, and with all the gloomy forms of preparation, to the scaffold. No eye wept at his sufferings—no heart, except of those whom he had most injured, sympathized in his disgrace. The half of his once splendid fortune, according to the decree of the former Court, was confirmed to D'Arnaud; but on his refusal to accept it, it was divided amongst the nearest relatives of the delinquent—the rest was forfeited to the crown. His body was taken from the scaffold, and interred, without distinction, in the usual manner of criminals. No tomb is erected on the spot; the cross of the murderer alone marks it out to the gaze of the passenger.

Pandolfo did not long survive his infamous associate. Finding himself, as he thought, near his end, compunction for his misdeeds operated so powerfully upon his conscience, that he could not die without disclosing the numerous villanies he had committed. He accordingly sent for a Priest, to whom, amongst various other offences, he confessed that he had been employed by Morsino to assassinate Varàno (whom he had long regarded with an eye of jealous ferocity) at the last Carnival at Venice; an attempt which, owing to his never finding him alone, or in situations at all favourable to his intentions, was fortunately unsuccessful.

His death was succeeded in about a year by that of Signor di Boraccio, who acknowledged in his last moments, and with equal signs of contrition, his having defrauded and betrayed Cecilia, commanding, as a recompence, that the sum of 4000 *Louis d'ors*, in addition to that of 300 to be divided at discretion amongst the old domestics at St. Foix, should be immediately paid.

The Lady Viola di Boraccio, deprived, in the ruined fortunes of her husband, of her once magnificent establishment, repaired to Florence. She was not attended there, as formerly, by her favourite escort, Signor Girolamo. On the death of Boraccio he had withdrawn his attendance, and now acted in his old capacity of *cicisbeo* to another lady of distinction at Genoa.

To the Marchese and Marchesa ever happy was the return of that day which bestowed upon the illustrious heir of their house the then humble Cecilia, whose virtues were as eminently conspicuous in prosperity as they had been in adversity.

M. Langlois, whose paternal regard for Cecilia had in every instance been manifested, delayed not to visit Italy. D'Arnaud fixed his residence in Florence, where, restored to the world's esteem and to his own, and to the confidence of his noble-minded Giuliana, he experienced happiness unalloyed.

The lives of these celebrated personages present, throughout the whole of them, a striking instance of the goodness as well as justice of Providence—that Power which overlooks and directs all human events.

The moral of our tale cannot need a comment. Happiness, we are assured, either here or hereafter, will be the reward of rectitude; and although innocence may occasionally suffer under the stroke of persecution, yet let it not despair; the triumphs of wickedness are short, whilst the complacent delight which results from a well-regulated mind, and the recollection of days and years usefully employed, shall exist for ever.

FINIS.